Praise for

THE LAST MRS. PARRISH

Reese Witherspoon's Hello Sunshine
Book Club Pick
USA Today Bestseller
Wall Street Journal Bestseller
Library Reads Pick • Skimm Reads Pick
One of BookBub's Biggest Psychological Thrillers
of the Year

⁂

"*The Last Mrs. Parrish* by Liv Constantine
will keep you up. In a 'can't put it down' way.
It's *The Talented Mr. Ripley* with XX chromosomes."
—The Skimm

"If you like your thrillers with an unexpected twist,
this one's for you."
—*New York Post*

"A bravura performance."
—*Sunday Times* (UK)

"[A] haunting psychological thriller. . . .
Engrossing."
—*Real Simple*

"*The Last Mrs. Parrish* should be the very
next book you read."
—Huffington Post

Also by Liv Constantine

THE STRANGER IN THE MIRROR
THE WIFE STALKER
THE LAST TIME I SAW YOU

THE
LAST MRS.
PARRISH

LIV CONSTANTINE

A NOVEL

HARPER

An Imprint of HarperCollins*Publishers*

Excerpt from *The Stranger in the Mirror* copyright © 2021 by Lynne Constantine and Valerie Constantine.

THE LAST MRS. PARRISH. Copyright © 2017 by Lynne Constantine and Valerie Constantine. All rights reserved. Printed in the United States of America. No part of this book may be used or reproduced in any manner whatsoever without written permission except in the case of brief quotations embodied in critical articles and reviews. For information, address HarperCollins Publishers, 195 Broadway, New York, NY 10007.

First Harper mass market printing: June 2021
First Harper paperback printing: July 2018
First Harper hardcover printing: October 2017

Print Edition ISBN: 978-0-06-311130-1
Digital Edition ISBN: 978-0-06-266759-5

Designed by Bonni Leon-Berman
Cover design by James Iacobelli
Cover photograph © NinaMalyna/iStock/Getty Images

Harper and HarperCollins are registered trademarks of HarperCollins Publishers in the United States of America and other countries.

21 22 23 24 25 CPI 10 9 8 7 6 5 4 3 2 1

THE
LAST MRS.
PARRISH

[PART I]

AMBER

ONE

Amber Patterson was tired of being invisible. She'd been coming to this gym every day for three months—three long months of watching these women of leisure working at the only thing they cared about. They were so self-absorbed; she would have bet her last dollar that not one of them would recognize her on the street even though she was five feet away from them every single day. She was a fixture to them—unimportant, not worthy of being noticed. But she didn't care—not about any of them. There was one reason and one reason alone that she dragged herself here every day, to this machine, at the precise stroke of eight.

She was sick to death of the routine—day after day, working her ass off, waiting for the moment to make her move. From the corner of her eye, she saw the signature gold Nikes step onto the machine next to her. Amber straightened her shoulders and pretended to be immersed in the magazine strategically placed on the rack of her own machine. She turned and gave the exquisite blond woman a shy smile, which garnered a polite nod in her direction. Amber reached for her water bottle, deliberately moving her foot to the edge of the machine, and slipped, knocking the magazine to the floor, where it landed beneath the pedal of her neighbor's equipment.

"Oh my gosh, I'm so sorry," she said, reddening.

Before she could step off, the woman stopped her

pedaling and retrieved it for her. Amber watched the woman's brow knit together.

"You're reading *is* magazine?" the woman said, handing it back to her.

"Yes, it's the Cystic Fibrosis Trust's magazine. Comes out twice a year. Do you know it?"

"I do, yes. Are you in the medical field?" the woman asked.

Amber cast her eyes to the floor, then back at the woman. "No, I'm not. My younger sister had CF." She let the words sit in the space between them.

"I'm sorry. That was rude of me. It's none of my business," the woman said, and stepped back onto the elliptical.

Amber shook her head. "No, it's okay. Do you know someone with cystic fibrosis?"

There was pain in the woman's eyes as she stared back at Amber. "My sister. I lost her twenty years ago."

"I'm so sorry. How old was she?"

"Only sixteen. We were two years apart."

"Charlene was just fourteen." Slowing her pace, Amber wiped her eyes with the back of her hand. It took a lot of acting skills to cry about a sister who never existed. The three sisters she did have were alive and well, although she hadn't spoken to them for two years.

The woman's machine ground to a halt. "Are you okay?" she asked.

Amber sniffed and shrugged. "It's still so hard, even after all these years."

The woman gave her a long look, as if trying to make a decision, then extended her hand.

"I'm Daphne Parrish. What do you say we get out of here and have a nice chat over a cup of coffee?"

"Are you sure? I don't want to interrupt your workout."

Daphne nodded. "Yes, I'd really like to talk with you."

Amber gave her what she hoped looked like a grateful smile and stepped down. "That sounds great." Taking her hand, she said, "I'm Amber Patterson. Pleasure to meet you."

⁂

Later that evening Amber lay in a bubble bath, sipping a glass of merlot and staring at the photo in *Entrepreneur* magazine. Smiling, she put it down, closed her eyes, and rested her head on the edge of the tub. She was feeling very satisfied about how well things had gone that day. She'd been prepared for it to drag out even longer, but Daphne made it easy for her. After they dispensed with the small talk over coffee, they'd gotten down to the real reason she'd elicited Daphne's interest.

"It's impossible for someone who hasn't experienced CF to understand," Daphne said, her blue eyes alive with passion. "Julie was never a burden to me, but in high school my friends were always pushing me to leave her behind, not let her tag along. They didn't understand that I never knew when she'd be hospitalized or if she'd even make it out again. Every moment was precious."

Amber leaned forward and did her best to look interested while she calculated the total worth of the diamonds on Daphne's ears, the tennis bracelet on her wrist, and the huge diamond on her tanned and perfectly manicured finger. She must have had at least a hundred grand walking around on her size-four body, and all she

could do was whine about her sad childhood. Amber
suppressed a yawn and gave Daphne a tight smile.

"I know. I used to stay home from school to be with
my sister so that my mom could go to work. She almost
lost her job from taking so much time off, and the last
thing we could afford was for her to lose our health insurance." She was pleased with how easily the lie came
to her lips.

"Oh, that's terrible," Daphne clucked. "That's another
reason my foundation is so important to me. We provide
financial assistance to families who aren't able to afford
the care they need. It's been a big part of the mission of
Julie's Smile for as long as I can remember."

Amber feigned shock. "Julie's Smile is *your* foundation? It's the same Julie? I know all about Julie's Smile,
been reading about all you do for years. I'm so in awe."

Daphne nodded. "I started it right after grad school.
In fact, my husband was my first benefactor." Here she'd
smiled, perhaps a bit embarrassed. "That's how we met."

"Aren't you preparing for a big fund-raiser right now?"

"As a matter of fact we are. It's a few months away,
but still lots to do. Say . . . oh, never mind."

"No, what?" Amber pressed.

"Well, I was just going to see if maybe you'd
like to help. It would be nice to have someone who
understands—"

"I'd love to help in any way," Amber interrupted. "I
don't make a lot of money, but I definitely have time
to donate. What you're doing is so important. When I
think of the difference it makes—" She bit her lip and
blinked back tears.

Daphne smiled. "Wonderful." She pulled out a card
engraved with her name and address. "Here you are.

Committee is meeting at my house Thursday morning at ten. Can you make it?"

Amber had given her a wide smile, still trying to look as though the disease was first in her mind. "I wouldn't miss it."

TWO

The rocking rhythm of the Saturday train from Bishops Harbor to New York lulled Amber into a soothing reverie far removed from the rigid discipline of her workday week. She sat by the window, resting her head against the seat back, occasionally opening her eyes to glance at the passing scenery. She thought back to the first time she'd ridden on a train, when she was seven years old. It was July in Missouri—the hottest, muggiest month of the summer—and the train's air-conditioning had been on the blink. She could still picture her mother sitting across from her in a long-sleeved black dress, unsmiling, back erect, her knees squeezed together primly. Her light brown hair had been pulled back in its customary bun, but she had worn a pair of earrings—small pearl studs that she saved for special occasions. And Amber supposed the funeral of her mother's mother counted as a special occasion.

When they'd gotten off the train at the grubby station in Warrensburg, the air outside was even more suffocating than the inside of the train had been. Uncle Frank, her mother's brother, had been there to meet them, and they piled uncomfortably into his battered blue pickup truck. The smell is what she remembered most—a mixture of sweat and dirt and damp—and the cracked leather of the seat digging into her skin. They rode past endless fields of corn and small farmsteads with tired-looking wooden houses and yards filled with rusted machinery, old cars on cinder blocks, tires with no rims, and broken metal crates. It was even more depressing than where they lived, and Amber wished she'd been left at home, like her sisters. Her mother said they were too young for a funeral, but Amber was old enough to pay her respects. She'd blocked out most of that horrendous weekend, but the one thing she would never forget was the appalling shabbiness surrounding her—the drab living room of her grandparents' home, all browns and rusty yellows; her grandfather's stubby growth of beard as he sat in his overstuffed recliner, stern and dour in a worn undershirt and stained khaki pants. She saw the origin of her mother's cheerless demeanor and poverty of imagination. It was then, at that tender age, that the dream of something different and better was born in Amber.

Opening her eyes now as the man opposite her rose, jostling her with his briefcase, she realized they'd arrived at Grand Central Terminal. She quickly gathered her handbag and jacket and stepped into the streaming mass of disembarking passengers. She never tired of the walk from the tracks into the magnificent main concourse—what a contrast to the dingy train depot of all those years ago. She took her time strolling past the shiny storefronts of the station, a perfect precursor to the sights and sounds of the city waiting outside, then exited the building and walked the few short blocks along Forty-Second Street to Fifth Avenue. This monthly pilgrimage had become so familiar that she could have done it blindfolded.

Her first stop was always the main reading room of the New York Public Library. She would sit at one of the long reading tables as the sun poured in through the tall windows and drink in the beauty of the ceiling frescoes. Today she felt especially comforted by the books that climbed the walls. They were a reminder that any knowledge she desired was hers for the asking. Here, she would sit and read and discover all the things that would give shape to her plans. She sat, still and silent, for twenty minutes, until she was ready to return to the street and begin the walk up Fifth Avenue.

She walked slowly but with purpose past the luxury stores that lined the street. Past Versace, Fendi, Armani, Louis Vuitton, Harry Winston, Tiffany & Co., Gucci, Prada, and Cartier—they went on and on, one after another of the world's most prestigious and expensive boutiques. She had been in each of them, inhaled the aroma of supple leather and the scent of exotic perfumes, rubbed into her skin the velvety balms and costly ointments that sat tantalizingly in ornate testers.

She continued past Dior and Chanel and stopped to admire a slender gown of silver and black that clung to the mannequin in the window. She stared at the dress, picturing herself in it, her hair piled high on her head, her makeup perfect, entering a ballroom on her husband's arm, the envy of every woman she passed. She continued north until she came to Bergdorf Goodman and the timeless Plaza Hotel. She was tempted to climb the red-carpeted steps to the grand lobby, but it was well past one o'clock, and she was feeling hungry. She'd carried a small lunch from home, since there was no way she could afford to spend her hard-earned money on both the museum and lunch in Manhattan. She crossed Fifty-Eighth Street to Central Park, sat on a bench facing the busy street, and unpacked a small apple and a baggie filled with raisins and nuts from her sack. She ate slowly as she watched people hurrying about and thought for the hundredth time how grateful she was to have escaped the dreary existence of her parents, the mundane conversations, the predictability of it all. Her mother had never understood Amber's ambitions. She said she was trying to get too far above herself, that her kind of thinking would only land her in trouble. And then Amber had shown her and finally left it all— though maybe not the way she'd planned.

She finished her lunch and walked through the park to the Metropolitan Museum of Art, where she would spend the afternoon before catching an early-evening train back to Connecticut. Over the past two years she had walked every inch of the Met, studying the art and sitting in on lectures and films about the works and their creators. At first her vast lack of knowledge had been daunting, but in her methodical way, she took it step-by-step, reading from borrowed books all she could about art, its history, and its masters. Armed with new information each month, she would visit the museum again and see in person what she had read about. She knew now that she could engage in a respectably intelligent conversation with all but the most informed art critic. Since the day she'd left that crowded house in Missouri, she'd been creating a new and improved Amber, one who would move at ease among the very wealthy. And so far, her plan was right on schedule.

After some time, she strolled to the gallery that was usually her last stop. There, she stood for a long time in front of a small study by Tintoretto. She wasn't sure how many times she had stared at this sketch, but the credit line was engraved on her brain—"A gift from the collection of Jackson and Daphne Parrish." She reluctantly turned away and headed to the new Aelbert Cuyp exhibition. She'd read through the only book about Cuyp that the Bishops Harbor library had on its shelves. Cuyp was an artist she'd never heard of and she'd been surprised to learn how prolific and famous he was. She strolled through the exhibit and came upon the painting she'd so admired in the book and had hoped would be a part of the exhibit, *The Maas at Dordrecht in a Storm*. It was even more magnificent than she'd thought it would be.

An older couple stood near her, mesmerized by it as well.

"It's amazing, isn't it?" the woman said to Amber.

"More than I'd even imagined," she answered.

"This one is very different from his landscapes," the man offered.

Amber continued to stare at the painting as she said, "It is, but he painted many majestic views of Dutch harbors. Did you know that he also painted biblical scenes and portraits?"

"Really? I had no idea."

Perhaps you should read before you come to see an exhibit, Amber thought, but simply smiled at them and moved on. She loved it when she could display her superior knowledge. And she believed that a man like Jackson Parrish, a man who prided himself on his cultural aesthetic, would love it too.

THREE

A bilious envy stuck in Amber's throat as the graceful house on Long Island Sound came into view. The open white gates at the entrance to the multimillion-dollar estate gave way to lush greenery and rosebushes that spilled extravagantly over discreet fencing, while the mansion itself was a rambling two-story structure of white and gray. It reminded her of pictures she'd seen of the wealthy summer homes in Nantucket and Martha's Vineyard. The house meandered majestically along the shoreline, superbly at home on the water's edge.

This was the kind of home that was safely hidden from the eyes of those who could not afford to live this way. That's what wealth does for you, she thought. It gives you the means and the power to remain concealed from the world if you choose to—or if you need to.

Amber parked her ten-year-old blue Toyota Corolla, which would look ridiculously out of place among the late-model Mercedes and BMWs that she was sure would soon dot the courtyard. She closed her eyes and sat for a moment, taking slow, deep breaths and going over in her head the information she'd memorized over the last few weeks. She'd dressed carefully this morning, her straight brown hair held back from her face with a tortoiseshell headband and her makeup minimal—just the tiniest hint of blush on her cheeks and slightly tinted balm on her lips. She wore a neatly pressed beige twill skirt with a long-sleeved white cotton T-shirt, both of which she'd ordered from an L.L.Bean catalog. Her sandals were sturdy and plain, good no-nonsense walking shoes without any touch of femininity. The ugly large-framed glasses she'd found at the last minute completed the look she was after. When she took one last glimpse in the mirror before leaving her apartment, she'd been pleased. She looked plain, even mousy. Someone who would never in a million years be a threat to anyone—especially not someone like Daphne Parrish.

Though she knew she ran a slight risk of appearing rude, Amber had shown up just a little early. She'd be able to have some time alone with Daphne and would also be there before any of the other women arrived, always an edge when introductions were made. They would see her as young and nondescript, simply a worker bee Daphne had deigned to reach down and anoint as a helper in her charity efforts.

She opened the car door and stepped onto the crushed stone driveway. It looked as if each piece of gravel cushioning her steps had been measured for uniformity and purity, and perfectly raked and polished. As she neared the house, she took her time studying the grounds and dwelling. She realized she would be entering through the back—the front would, of course, face the water—but it was, nevertheless, a most gracious facade. To her left stood a white arbor bedecked with the summer's last wisteria, and two long benches sat just beyond it. Amber had read about this kind of wealth, had seen countless pictures in magazines and online tours of the homes of movie stars and the superrich. But this was the first time she'd actually seen it up close.

She climbed the wide stone steps to the landing and rang the bell. The door was oversize, with large panes of beveled glass, allowing Amber a view down the long corridor that ran to the front of the house. She could see the dazzling blue of the water from where she stood, and then, suddenly, Daphne was there, holding the door open and smiling at her.

"How lovely to see you. I'm so glad you could come," she said, taking Amber's hand in hers and leading her inside.

Amber gave her the timid smile she'd practiced in front of her bathroom mirror. "Thank you for inviting me, Daphne. I'm really excited to help."

"Well, I'm thrilled you'll be working with us. Come this way. We'll be meeting in the conservatory," Daphne said as they came into a large octagonal room with floor-to-ceiling windows and summery chintzes that exploded with vibrant color. The French doors stood open, and Amber breathed in the intoxicating smell of salty sea air.

"Please, have a seat. We have a few minutes before the others arrive," Daphne said.

Amber sank into the plush sofa, and Daphne sat down across from her in one of the yellow armchairs that perfectly complemented the other furnishings in this room of nonchalant elegance. It irked her, this ease with wealth and privilege that Daphne exuded, as though it were her birthright. She could have stepped out of *Town & Country* in her perfectly tailored gray slacks and silk blouse, her only jewelry the large pearl studs she wore in her ears. Her lustrous blond hair fell in loose waves that framed her aristocratic face. Amber guessed the clothes and earrings alone were worth over three grand, forget the rock on her finger or the Cartier Tank. She probably had a dozen more in a jewelry box upstairs. Amber checked the time on her own watch—an inexpensive department-store model—and saw that they still had about ten minutes alone.

"Thanks again for letting me help, Daphne."

"I'm the one who's grateful. There are never too many hands. I mean, all of the women are terrific and they work hard, but you understand because you've been there." Daphne shifted in her chair. "We talked a lot about our sisters the other morning, but not much about ourselves. I know you're not from around here, but do I remember you telling me you were born in Nebraska?"

Amber had rehearsed her story carefully. "Yes, that's right. I'm originally from Nebraska, but I left after my sister died. My good high school friend went to college here. When she came home for my sister's funeral, she said maybe it would be good for me to have a change, make a fresh start, and we'd have each other, of course. She was right. It's helped me so much. I've been in Bishops Harbor for almost a year, but I think about Charlene every day."

Daphne was looking at her intently. "I'm sorry for your loss. No one who hasn't experienced it can know how painful it is to lose a sibling. I think about Julie every day. Sometimes it's overwhelming. That's why my work with cystic fibrosis is so important to me. I'm blessed to have two healthy daughters, but there are still so many families afflicted by this terrible disease."

Amber picked up a silver frame with a photograph of two little girls. Both blond and tanned, they wore matching bathing suits and sat cross-legged on a pier, their arms around each other. "Are these your daughters?"

Daphne glanced at the picture and smiled with delight, pointing. "Yes, that's Tallulah and this is Bella. That was taken last summer, at the lake."

"They're adorable. How old are they?"

"Tallulah's ten, and Bella's seven. I'm glad they have each other," Daphne said, her eyes growing misty. "I pray they always will."

Amber remembered reading that actors think of the saddest thing they can to help them cry on cue. She was trying to summon a memory to make her cry, but the saddest thing she could come up with was that she wasn't the one sitting in Daphne's chair, the mistress of this incredible house. Still, she did her best to look downcast as she put the photograph back on the table.

Just then, the doorbell rang, and Daphne rose to answer it. As she left the room, she said, "Help yourself to coffee or tea. And there are some goodies too. Everything's on the sideboard."

Amber got up but put her handbag on the chair next to Daphne's, marking it as hers. As she was pouring a cup of coffee, the others began filing in amid excited hellos and hugs. She hated the clucking sounds groups of women made, like a bunch of cackling hens.

"Hey, everyone." Daphne's voice rose above the chatter, and they quieted down. She went to Amber and put her arm around her. "I want to introduce a new committee member, Amber Patterson. Amber will be a wonderful addition to our group. Sadly, she's a bit of an expert—her sister died of cystic fibrosis."

Amber cast her eyes to the floor, and there was a collective murmur of sympathy from the women.

"Why don't we all have a seat, and we'll go around the room so that you can introduce yourselves to Amber," Daphne said. Cup and saucer in hand, she sat down, looked at the photo of her daughters, and, Amber noticed, moved it just slightly. Amber looked around the circle as, one after another, each woman smiled and said her name—Lois, Bunny, Faith, Meredith, Irene, and Neve. All of them were shined and polished, but two in particular caught Amber's attention. No more than a size two, Bunny had long, straight blond hair and large green eyes made up to show their maximum gorgeousness. She was perfect in every way, and she knew it. Amber had seen her at the gym in her tiny shorts and sports bra, working out like mad, but Bunny looked at her blankly, as if she'd never laid eyes on her before. Amber wanted to remind her, *Oh, yes. I know you. You're the one who brags about screwing around on your husband to your girl posse.*

And then there was Meredith, who didn't at all fit in with the rest of them. Her clothing was expensive but subdued, not like the flashy garb of the other women. She wore small gold earrings and a single strand of yellowed pearls against her brown sweater. The length of her tweed skirt was awkward, neither long nor short enough to be fashionable. As the meeting progressed, it became apparent that she was different in more ways than appearance. She sat erect in her chair, shoulders back and head held high, with an imposing bearing of wealth and breeding. And when she spoke, there was just the hint of a boarding-school accent, enough to make her words sound so much more insightful than the others' as they discussed the silent auction and the prizes secured so far. Exotic vacations, diamond jewelry, vintage wines—the list went on and on, each item more expensive than the last.

As the meeting came to a close, Meredith walked over and sat beside Amber. "Welcome to Julie's Smile, Amber. I'm very sorry about your sister."

"Thank you," Amber said simply.

"Have you and Daphne known each other a long time?"

"Oh, no. We just met, actually. At the gym."

"How serendipitous," Meredith said, her tone hard to read. She was staring at Amber, and it felt as if she could see right through her.

"It was a lucky day for both of us."

"Yes, I should say." Meredith paused and looked Amber up and down. Her lips spread into a thin smile, and she rose from the chair. "It was lovely to meet you. I look forward to getting to know you better."

Amber sensed danger, not in the words Meredith had spoken but from something in her manner. Maybe she was just imagining it. She put her empty coffee cup back on the sideboard and walked through the French doors that seemed to invite her onto the deck. Outside she stood looking at the vast expanse of Long Island Sound. In the distance she spotted a sailboat, its sails billowing in the wind, a magnificent spectacle. She walked to the other end of the deck, where she had a better view of the sandy beach below. When she turned to go back inside, she heard Meredith's unmistakable voice coming from the conservatory.

"Honestly, Daphne, how well do you know this girl? You met her at the gym? Do you know anything about her background?"

Amber stood silently at the edge of the door.

"Meredith, really. All I needed to know was that her sister died of CF. What more do you want? She has a vested interest in raising money for the foundation."

"Have you checked her out?" Meredith asked, her tone still skeptical. "You know, her family, education, all those things?"

"This is volunteer work, not a Supreme Court nomination. I want her on the committee. You'll see. She'll be a wonderful asset."

Amber could hear the irritation in Daphne's voice.

"All right, it's your committee. I won't bring it up again."

Amber could hear footsteps on the tile floor as they left the room, and she stepped in and quickly pushed her portfolio under a pillow on the sofa, so it would look like she'd forgotten it. In it were her notes from the meeting and a photograph, tucked into one of the pockets. The lack of any other identifying information would ensure that Daphne would have to root around to find the photo. Amber was thirteen in the picture. That had been a good day, one of the few her mother had been able to leave the cleaner's and take them to the park. She was pushing her little sister on the swings. On the back, Amber had written "Amber and Charlene," even though it was a picture of her with her sister Trudy.

Meredith was going to be tricky. She'd said she was looking forward to getting to know Amber better. Well, Amber was going to make sure she knew as little as possible. She wasn't going to let some society snob screw with her. She'd made sure that the last person who tried that got what was coming to her.

FOUR

Amber opened the bottle of Josh she'd been saving. It was pathetic that she had to ration a twelve-dollar cabernet, but her measly salary at the real estate office barely covered the rent here. Before moving to Connecticut, she'd done her research and chosen her target, Jackson Parrish, and that's how she ended up in Bishops Harbor. Sure, she could have rented in a neighboring town for much less, but living here meant she had many opportunities to accidentally run into Daphne Parrish, plus access to all the fabulous town amenities. And she loved being so close to New York.

A smile spread across Amber's face. She thought back to the time she'd researched Jackson Parrish, googling his name for hours after she read an article on the international development company he'd founded. Her breath had caught when his picture filled the screen. With thick black hair, full lips, and cobalt-blue eyes, he could have easily been on the big screen. She'd clicked on an interview in *Forbes* magazine that featured him and how he built his Fortune 500 company. The next link—an article in *Vanity Fair*—wrote about his marriage to the beautiful Daphne, ten years younger than he. Amber had gazed at the picture of their two adorable children, taken on the beach in front of a gray-and-white clapboard mansion. She'd looked up everything she could about the Parrishes, and when she read about Julie's Smile, the foundation founded by Daphne and dedicated to raising money for cystic fibrosis, the idea came to her. The first step in the plan that developed in her mind was to move to Bishops Harbor.

When she thought back to the small-time marriage she'd tried to engineer back in Missouri, it made her want to laugh. That had ended very badly, but she wouldn't make the same mistakes this time.

Now she picked up her wineglass and lifted it in salute to her reflection in the microwave oven. "To Amber." Taking a long sip, she rested the glass on the counter.

Opening her laptop, she typed "Meredith Stanton Connecticut" into the search bar and the page filled up with link after link about Meredith's personal and philanthropic efforts. Meredith Bell Stanton was a daughter of the Bell family, who raised Thoroughbred racehorses. According to the articles, riding was her passion. She rode horses, showed horses, hunted, jumped, and did anything else you could do with horses. Amber wasn't surprised. Meredith had "horsewoman" written all over her.

Amber stared at a photograph of Meredith and her husband, Randolph H. Stanton III, at a charity event in New York. She decided old Randolph looked like he had a yardstick up his ass. But she guessed banking was a pretty dry business. The only good thing about it was the money, and it looked like the Stantons had piles of it.

Next, she searched for Bunny Nichols, but didn't find as much. The fourth wife of March Nichols, a prominent New York attorney with a reputation for ruthlessness, Bunny looked eerily similar to the second and third wives. Amber guessed that blond party girls were interchangeable to him. One article described Bunny as a "former model." That was a laugh. She looked more like a former stripper.

She took a last sip from her glass, corked the bottle, and logged onto Facebook under one of her fake profiles. She pulled up the one profile that she checked every night, scanning for new photos and any status updates. Her eyes narrowed at a picture of a little boy holding a lunch box in one hand and that rich bitch's hand in the other—"First day at St. Andrew's Academy" and the insipid comment "Mommy's not ready," with a sad-face emoji. St. Andrew's, the school back home she had yearned to attend. She wanted to type her own comment: *Mommy and Daddy are lying skanks.* But instead she slammed the laptop shut.

FIVE

Amber looked at the ringing phone and smiled. See-ing "private" on the caller ID, she figured it was Daphne. She let it go to voice mail. Daphne left a mes-sage. The next day, Daphne called again, and again Amber ignored it. Obviously, Daphne had found the portfolio. When the phone rang again that night, Amber finally answered.

"Hello?" she whispered.

"Amber?"

A sigh, and then a quiet "Yes?"

"It's Daphne. Are you okay? I've been trying to reach you."

She made a choking sound, then spoke, louder this time. "Hi, Daphne. Yeah, sorry. It's been a rough day."

"What is it? Has something happened?" Amber could hear the concern in Daphne's voice.

"It's the anniversary."

"Oh, sweetie. I'm sorry. Would you like to come over? Jackson's out of town. We could open a bottle of wine."

"Really?"

"Absolutely. The children are sleeping, and I've got one of the nannies if they should need anything."

Of course one of the nannies is there. God forbid she should have to do anything for herself. "Oh, Daphne, that would be so great. Can I bring anything?"

"No, just yourself. See you soon."

When Amber pulled up to the house, she got out her phone and texted Daphne: **I'm here. Didn't want to ring and wake the girls.**

The door opened, and Daphne motioned her in. "How thoughtful of you to text first."

"Thanks for having me over." Amber handed her a bottle of red wine.

Daphne hugged her. "Thank you, but you shouldn't have."

Amber shrugged. It was a cheap merlot, eight bucks at the liquor store. She knew Daphne would never drink it.

"Come on." Daphne led her into the sunroom, where there was already a bottle of wine open and two half-filled glasses on the coffee table.

"Have you had dinner?"

Amber shook her head. "No, but I'm not really hungry." She sat, picked up a wineglass, and took a small sip. "This is very nice."

Daphne sat down, picked up her own glass, and held it up.

"Here's to our sisters who live on in our hearts."

Amber touched her glass to Daphne's and took another swallow. She brushed a nonexistent tear from her eye.

"I'm so sorry. You must think I'm a basket case."

Daphne shook her head. "Of course not. It's okay. You can talk about it to me. Tell me about her."

Amber paused. "Charlene was my best friend. We shared a room, and we'd talk late into the night about what we were going to do when we grew up and got out of that house." She frowned and took another long sip of her wine. "Our mother used to throw a shoe at the door if she thought we were up too late. We'd whisper so she wouldn't hear us. We'd tell each other everything. All our dreams, our hopes . . ."

Daphne kept quiet while Amber continued, but her beautiful blue eyes filled with compassion.

"She was golden. Everybody loved her, but it didn't go to her head, you know? Some kids, they would have become bratty, but not Char. She was beautiful, on the inside and out. People would just stare at her when we were out, that's how gorgeous she was." Amber hesitated and cocked her head. "Sort of like you."

A nervous laugh escaped from Daphne's lips. "I would hardly say that about myself."

Yeah, right, Amber thought. "Beautiful women take it for granted. They can't see what everyone else does. My parents used to joke that she got the beauty, and I got the brains."

"How cruel. That's terrible, Amber. You are a beautiful person—inside and out."

It was almost too easy, Amber thought—get a bad haircut, leave off the makeup, don a pair of eyeglasses, slouch your shoulders, and voilà! Poor homely girl was born. Daphne needed to save someone, and Amber was happy to oblige. She smiled at Daphne.

"You're just saying that. It's okay. Not everyone has to be beautiful." She picked up a photo of Tallulah and Bella, this one in a cloth frame. "Your daughters are gorgeous too."

Daphne's face lit up. "They're great kids. I'm extremely blessed."

Amber continued to study the photograph. Tallulah looked like a little adult with her serious expression and hideous glasses, while Bella, with her blond curls and blue eyes, looked like a little princess. There was going to be a lot of rivalry in their future, Amber thought. She wondered how many boyfriends Bella would steal from her plain older sister when they were teenagers.

"Do you have a picture of Julie?"

"Of course." Daphne got up and retrieved a photograph from the console table. "Here she is," she said, handing the frame to Amber.

Amber stared at the young woman, who must have been around fifteen when the picture was taken. She was beautiful in an almost otherworldly way, her big brown eyes bright and shining.

"She's lovely," Amber said, looking up at Daphne. "It doesn't get any easier, does it?"

"No, not really. Some days it's even harder."

They finished the bottle of wine and opened another while Amber listened to more stories of Daphne's tragic fairy-tale relationship with her perfect dead sister. Amber threw a full glass down the sink when she went to the bathroom. As she returned to the living room, she added a little wobble to her walk, and said to Daphne, "I should get going."

Daphne shook her head. "You shouldn't drive. You should stay here tonight."

"No, no. I don't want to put you out."

"No arguments. Come on. I'll take you to a guest room."

Daphne put an arm around Amber's waist and led her through the obscenely large house and up the long staircase to the second floor.

"I think I'm going to need the bathroom." Amber made the words sound urgent.

"Of course." Daphne helped her in, and Amber shut the door and sat down on the toilet. The bathroom was enormous and elaborate, with a Jacuzzi tub and shower big enough to accommodate the entire royal family. Her studio apartment would have practically fit inside it. When she opened the door, Daphne was waiting.

"Are you feeling any better?" Daphne's voice was filled with concern.

"Still a bit dizzy. Would it be all right if I did lie down for a minute?"

"Of course," Daphne said, guiding her down the long hallway to a guest room.

Amber's keen eye took it all in—the fresh white tulips that looked beautiful against the mint-green walls. Who had fresh flowers in a guest room when they weren't even expecting guests? The shiny wood floor was partially covered with a thick white flokati rug that added another touch of elegance and luxury. Billowy gauze curtains seemed to float down from the tall windows.

Daphne helped her to the bed, where Amber sat and ran her hand over the embroidered duvet cover. She could get used to this. Her eyes fluttered shut, and she didn't need to pretend that she felt the dizzying sensation of impending slumber. She saw movement and opened her eyes to see Daphne standing over her.

"You're going to sleep here. I insist," Daphne said, and, walking to the closet, opened the door and took out a nightgown and robe. "Here, take your things off and put on this nightgown. I'll wait out in the hallway while you change."

Amber peeled off her sweater and threw it on the bed, and stepped out of her jeans. She slipped into the silky white nightgown and crawled under the covers. "All set," she called out.

Daphne came back in and put a hand on her forehead. "You poor dear. Rest."

Amber felt a cover being tucked around her.

"I'll be in my room, just down the hall."

Amber opened her eyes and reached out to grab Daphne's arm. "Please don't go. Can you stay with me like my sister used to?"

She saw the briefest hesitation in Daphne's eyes before she went over to the other side of the bed and lay next to Amber.

"Sure, sweetie. I'll stay until you fall asleep. Just rest. I'm right here if you need anything."

Amber smiled. All she needed from Daphne was everything.

SIX

Amber flipped through the pages of *Vogue* as she sat listening to the whiny client on the other end of the phone continuing to bitch about the $5 million house that had been sold out from under her. She hated Mondays, the day she was asked to sit in for the receptionist at lunchtime. Her boss had promised her she'd be free of it as soon as the new hire began in another month.

She'd started as a secretary in the residential division of Rollins Realty when she first moved to Bishops Harbor, and she'd hated every minute of it. Almost all of the clients were spoiled women and arrogant men, all with a hugely elevated sense of entitlement. The kind of people who never slowed their expensive cars at a four-way stop because they believed they always had the right-of-way. She'd set appointments, call them with updates, set up appraisal and inspection appointments, and still they barely acknowledged her. She did notice that they were only a little more courteous to the agents, but their lack of manners still infuriated her.

She used that first year to take evening classes in commercial real estate. She checked books out of the library on the subject and read voraciously on weekends, sometimes forgetting to eat lunch or dinner. When she felt ready, she went to the head of the commercial side of Rollins, Mark Jansen, to discuss her thoughts on a potential opportunity regarding a zoning change vote she'd read about in the paper and what a successful vote could mean for one of their clients. He was blown away by her knowledge and understanding of the market, and started stopping by her desk occasionally to chat about his side of the business. Within a few months she was sitting right outside his office, working closely with him. Between her reading and his tutelage, her knowledge and expertise increased. And to Amber's good fortune, Mark was a great boss, a devoted family man who treated her with respect and kindness. She was right where she had planned to be from the start. It had just taken time and determination, but determination was one thing Amber had in spades.

She looked up as Jenna, the receptionist, walked in with a crumpled McDonald's bag and a soda in her hands. No wonder she was so fat, Amber thought in disgust. How could people have so little self-control?

"Hey, girlie, thanks so much for covering. Did everything go okay?" Jenna's smile made her face even more moonlike than normal.

Amber bristled. *Girlie?* "Just some moron who's upset because someone else bought her house."

"Oh, that was probably Mrs. Worth. She's so disappointed. I feel bad for her."

"Don't waste your tears. Now she can cry on her husband's shoulder and get the eight-million-dollar house instead."

"Oh, Amber. You're so funny."

Amber shook her head in puzzlement at Jenna and walked away.

Later that night, as she sat soaking in the tub, she thought about the last two years. She'd been ready to leave it all far behind—the dry-cleaning chemicals that burned her eyes and nose, the filth from soiled clothing that clung to her hands, and the big plan that had gone awry. Just when she thought she'd finally grabbed the brass ring, everything had come crashing down. There was no question of her hanging around. When she left Missouri, she'd made sure that anyone looking for her wouldn't find even a trace to follow.

The water was turning cooler now. Amber rose and wrapped herself in a thin terry-cloth robe as she stepped out of the bath. There'd been no old school friend to invite her to Connecticut. She'd rented the tiny furnished apartment just days after she arrived in Bishops Harbor. The dingy white walls were bare, and the floor was covered with an old-fashioned pea-green shag that had probably been there since the 1980s. The only seating was an upholstered love seat with worn arms and sagging pillows. A plastic table sat at the end of the small sofa. There was nothing on the table, not even a lamp, the single lightbulb with its fringed shade hanging from the low ceiling being the only illumination in the room. It was hardly more than a place to sleep and hang her hat, but it was only a placeholder until her plan was complete. In the end, it would all be worth it.

She quickly dried off, threw on pajama bottoms and a sweatshirt, and then sat at the small desk in front of the only window in the apartment. She pulled out her file on Nebraska and read over it once again. Daphne hadn't asked her any more questions about her childhood, but still, it never hurt to refresh. Nebraska had been her first stop after leaving her hometown in Missouri, and it was where her luck had begun to change. She bet she knew more about Eustis, Nebraska, and its Wurst Tag sausage festival than even the oldest living resident. She scanned the pages, then put the folder back and picked up the book on international real estate she'd gotten from the library on her way home that night. It was heavy enough to make a good doorstop, and she knew it was going to take some very long nights and lots of concentration to get through it.

She smiled. Even if her place was small and cramped, she had spent so many nights longing for a room of her own when she and her three sisters were packed in the attic her father had turned into a bunkhouse of sorts. No matter how hard she'd tried, the room was always a mess, with her sisters' clothes, shoes, and books strewn all over. It made her crazy. Amber needed order—disciplined, structured order. And now, finally, she was the master of her world. And of her fate.

SEVEN

Amber dressed carefully that Monday morning. She had quite accidentally run into Daphne and her daughters at the town library late yesterday afternoon. They'd stopped to chat, and Daphne had introduced her to Tallulah and Bella. She had been struck by their differences. Tallulah, tall and thin with glasses and a plain face, appeared quiet and withdrawn. Bella, on the other hand, was an adorable little sprite, her golden curls bouncing as she cavorted around the shelves. Both girls had been polite but uninterested, and had leafed through their books as the two women spoke. Amber had noticed that Daphne didn't seem her usual cheery self. "Is everything all right?" she said, putting her hand gently on Daphne's arm. Daphne's eyes had filled. "Just some memories I can't shake today. That's all."

Amber had gone on full alert. "Memories?"

"Tomorrow is Julie's birthday. I can't stop thinking about her." She ran her fingers through Bella's curly hair, and the child looked up at her and smiled.

"Tomorrow? The twenty-first?" Amber said.

"Yes, tomorrow."

"I can't believe it. It's Charlene's birthday, too!" Amber silently berated herself, hoping she hadn't overplayed her hand, but as soon as she saw the look on Daphne's face, she knew she'd struck just the right chord.

"Oh my gosh, Amber. That's unbelievable. I'm beginning to feel like the heavens have brought us together."

"It *does* seem like it's meant to be," Amber had said, then paused for a few seconds. "We should do something tomorrow to celebrate our sisters, to remember the good things and not dwell on the sadness. How about if I pack us some sandwiches, and we can have lunch at my office? There's a small picnic bench on the side of the building near the stream."

"What a good idea," Daphne had said, more animated then. "But why should you go to the trouble of packing a lunch? I'll pick you up at your office, and we'll go to the country club. Would you like that?"

That was precisely what Amber had been hoping Daphne would suggest, but she hadn't wanted to seem too eager. "Are you sure? It really isn't any trouble. I pack lunch every day."

"Of course I'm sure. What time shall I pick you up?"

"I can usually duck out around twelve thirty."

"Perfect. I'll see you then," Daphne had said, and shifted the pile of books in her arms. "We'll make it a happy celebration."

Now Amber studied herself in the mirror one last time—white boat-neck T-shirt and her one nice pair of navy slacks. She'd tried on the sturdy sandals but exchanged them for white ones. She wore faux pearl studs in her ears and, on her right hand, a ring with a small sapphire set in gold. Her hair was pulled back with the usual headband, and her only makeup was a very light pink lip balm. Satisfied that she looked subdued but not too frumpy, she grabbed her keys and left for work.

By ten, Amber had checked the clock at least fifty times. The minutes dragged unbearably as she tried to concentrate on the new shopping center contract in front of her. She reread the final four pages, making notes as she went along. Ever since she'd found an error that could have cost the company a bundle, her boss, Mark, didn't sign anything until Amber had reviewed it.

Today was Amber's day to cover the phones for Jenna, but Jenna had agreed to stay so that Amber could go out for lunch.

"Who are you having lunch with?" Jenna asked.

"You don't know her. Daphne Parrish," she answered, feeling important.

"Oh, Mrs. Parrish. I've met her. A couple years ago, with her mother. They came in together 'cause her mom was going to move here to be closer to the family. She looked at tons of places, but she ended up staying in New Hampshire. She was a real nice lady."

Amber's ears perked up. "Really? What was her name? Do you remember?"

Jenna looked up at the ceiling. "Lemme see." She was quiet a moment and then nodded her head and looked back at Amber. "I remember. Her name was Ruth Bennett. She's a widow."

"She lives alone?" Amber said.

"Well, sort of, I guess. She owns a B&B in New Hampshire, so she's not really alone. Right? But on the other hand, they're all pretty much strangers, so she kind of does live alone. Maybe you could say she lives semi-alone, or only alone at night when she goes to bed," Jenna prattled on. "Before she left, she brought a real nice basket of goodies to the office to thank me for being so nice. It was really sweet. But kinda sad too. It seemed like she really wanted to move here."

"Why didn't she?"

"I don't know. Maybe Mrs. Parrish didn't want her that close."

"Did she say that?" Amber probed.

"Not really. It just seemed like she wasn't too excited about her mom being so close by. I guess she didn't really need her around. You know, she had her nannies and stuff. One of my friends was her nanny when her first daughter was a baby."

Amber felt like she'd struck gold. "Really? How long did she work there?"

"A couple years, I think."

"Is she a good friend of yours?"

"Sally? Yeah, me and her go way back."

"I bet she has some stories to tell," Amber said.

"What do you mean?"

Is this girl for real? "You know, things about the family, what they're like, what they do at home—that kind of thing."

"Yeah, I guess. But I wasn't really interested. We had other stuff to talk about."

"Maybe the three of us could have dinner next week."

"Hey, that would be great."

"Why don't you call her tomorrow and set it up? What's her name again?" Amber asked.

"Sally. Sally MacAteer."

"And she lives here in Bishops Harbor?"

"She lives right next door to me, so I see her all the time. We grew up together. I'll ask her about dinner. This'll be really fun. Like the three musketeers." Jenna skipped back to her desk, and Amber went back to work.

She picked up the contract and put it on the desk in Mark's empty office so they could discuss it that afternoon when he got back from his appointment in Norwalk. She looked at her watch and saw that she had twenty minutes to finish and freshen up before Daphne's arrival. She returned two phone calls, filed a few loose papers, and then went to the bathroom to check her hair. Satisfied, she went to the front lobby to watch for Daphne's Range Rover.

It pulled up at exactly twelve thirty, Amber noticed, appreciating Daphne's promptness. As Amber pushed open the glass door of the building, Daphne rolled the car window down and called out a cheerful hello. Amber walked to the passenger side, opened the door, and hoisted herself into the cool interior.

"It's great to see you," Amber said with what she hoped sounded like enthusiasm.

Daphne looked over at her and smiled before putting the car into gear. "I've been looking forward to this all morning. I couldn't wait for my garden club meeting to be over. I know it's going to make the day so much easier to get through."

"I hope so," Amber said, her voice subdued.

They were both quiet for the next few blocks, and Amber leaned back against the soft leather seat. She turned her head slightly in Daphne's direction and took in her white linen pants and sleeveless white linen top, which had a wide navy stripe at the bottom. She wore small gold hoops and a simple gold bangle bracelet next to her watch. And her ring, of course, the rock that could have sunk the *Titanic*. Her slender arms were nicely tanned. She looked fit, healthy, and rich.

As they pulled into the driveway of the Tidewater Country Club, Amber drank it all in—the gently winding road with precision-cut grass on either side, not a weed in sight; tennis courts with players in sparkling whites; the swimming pools in the distance; and the impressive building looming before them. It was even grander than she had imagined. They drove around the circle to the main entrance, and were met by a young guy in a casual uniform of dark khakis and a green polo shirt. On his head was a white visor with the Tidewater logo embroidered in green.

"Good afternoon, Mrs. Parrish," he said as he opened her door.

"Hello, Danny," Daphne said and handed him the keys. "We're just here for lunch."

He walked around to open Amber's door, but she had already stepped out.

"Well, enjoy," he said, and got into the car.

"He's such a nice young man," Daphne said as she and Amber walked up the wide stairs into the building. "His mother used to work for Jackson, but she's been very ill the last few years. Danny takes care of her and is also working to put himself through college."

Amber wondered what he thought about all the money he saw thrown around at this club while he nursed a sick mother and worked to make ends meet, but she bit her tongue.

Daphne suggested they eat on the deck, and so the maître d' led them outside, where Amber breathed in the bracing sea air she loved so much. They were seated at a table overlooking the marina, its three long piers filled with boats of all shapes and sizes bobbing up and down in the choppy waters.

"Wow, this is just beautiful," Amber said.

"Yes, it is. A nice setting to remember all the wonderful things about Charlene and Julie."

"My sister would have loved it here," Amber said, and meant it. None of her perfectly healthy sisters would have even been able to imagine a place like this. She tore her gaze away from the water and turned to Daphne. "You must come here a lot with your family."

"We do. Jackson, of course, heads right for the golf

course whenever he can. Tallulah and Bella take all kinds of lessons—sailing, swimming, tennis. They're quite the little athletes."

Amber wondered what it would be like to grow up in this kind of world, where you were groomed from infancy to have and enjoy all the good things in life. Where you made friends almost from birth with the right people and were educated in the best schools, and the blinds were tightly drawn against outsiders. She was suddenly overwhelmed with sadness and envy.

The waiter brought two tall glasses of iced tea and took their lunch order—a small salad for Daphne and ahi tuna for Amber.

"Now," Daphne said, as they waited. "Tell me a good memory about your sister."

"Hmm. Well, I remember when she was just a few months old, my mom and I took her for a walk. I would have been six. It was a beautiful, sunny day and Mom let me push the carriage. Of course she was right next to me, just in case." Amber warmed to her subject, embellishing the story as she continued. "But I remember feeling so grown-up and so happy to have this new little sister. She was so pretty, with her blue eyes and yellow curls. Just like a picture. And I think from that day on, I sort of felt like she was my little girl too."

"That's really lovely, Amber."

"What about you? What do you remember?"

"Julie and I were only two years apart, so I don't remember much about when she was a baby. But later, she was so brave. She always had a smile on her beautiful face. Never complained. She always said if someone had to have cystic fibrosis, she was glad it was her because she wouldn't have wanted another child to suffer." Daphne stopped and looked out at the water. "There was not one ounce of unkindness in her. She was the best person I've ever known."

Amber shifted in her chair and felt a discomfort she didn't quite understand.

Daphne went on. "The part that's hard to think about is all she went through. Every day. All the medications she had to take." She shook her head. "We used to get up early together, and I would talk to her while she had her vest on."

"Yes, the vibrating contraption." Amber remembered reading about the vest that helped dislodge mucus from the lungs.

"It became routine—the vest, the nebulizer, the inhaler. She spent more than two hours a day trying to stave off the effects of the disease. She truly believed she would go to college, marry, have children. She said she worked so hard at all her therapies and exercised because that's what would give her a future. She believed to the very end," Daphne said, as a single tear ran down her cheek. "I would give anything to have her back."

"I know," Amber whispered. "Maybe our sisters' spirits have somehow brought us together. It sort of makes it like they're here with us."

Daphne blinked back more tears. "I like that idea."

Daphne's memories and Amber's stories continued through the lunch, and as the waiter took their plates away, Amber felt a flash of brilliance and turned to him. "We're celebrating two birthdays today. Would you bring us a piece of chocolate cake to share?"

The smile that Daphne bestowed on Amber was filled with warmth and gratitude.

He brought them the cake with two lighted candles, and with a flourish said, "A very happy birthday to you."

Their lunch lasted a little over an hour, but Amber

didn't have to hurry back since Mark wasn't due back in the office until at least three o'clock, and she had told Jenna she might be a little late.

"Well," Daphne said when they'd finished their coffee. "I suppose I should get you back to the office. Don't want to get you in trouble with your boss."

Amber looked around for their waiter. "Shouldn't we wait for the check?"

"Oh, don't worry," Daphne said, waving her hand. "They'll just put it on our account."

But of course, Amber thought. It seemed the more money you had, the less you had to actually come into contact with the filthy stuff.

When they pulled up to the realty office, Daphne put the car in park and looked at Amber. "I really enjoyed today. I've forgotten how good it is to talk to someone who really understands."

"I enjoyed it too, Daphne. It helped a lot."

"I was wondering if you might be free on Friday night to have dinner with us. What do you say?"

"Gosh, I'd love to." She was thrilled at how quickly Daphne was opening up to her.

"Good," Daphne said. "See you on Friday. Around six o'clock?"

"Perfect. See you then. And thank you." As Amber watched her drive away, she felt like she had just won the lottery.

EIGHT

The day after her lunch with Daphne, Amber stood behind Bunny in the Zumba class at the gym. She laughed to herself, watching Bunny trip over her feet trying to keep up with the instructor. What a klutz, she thought. After class, Amber took her time dressing behind the row of lockers next to Bunny's in the locker room, listening to the trophy wife and her sycophants discuss her plans.

"When are you meeting him?" one asked.

"Happy hour at the Blue Pheasant. But remember, I'm with you girls tonight, if your husbands ask."

"The Blue Pheasant? Everyone goes there. What if someone sees you?"

"I'll say he's a client. I do have my real estate license, after all."

Amber heard snickering.

"What, Lydia?" Bunny snapped.

"Well, it's not exactly like you've been doing much with it since you married March."

March Nichols's net worth of $100 million stuck in Amber's head—that and the fact that he resembled Methuselah. Amber could understand why Bunny looked elsewhere for sex.

"We won't be there long, anyway. I reserved a room at the Piedmont across the street."

"Naughty, naughty. Did you book it under Mrs. Robinson?"

They were all laughing now.

Old husband, young lover—there was a certain poetry to it. Amber had what she needed, so she jumped into the shower, then rushed back to the office, excuse at the ready to explain her long absence.

Later that day, she got to the bar early and sat with her book and a glass of wine at a table near the back. As it began to fill up, she tried to guess which one he was. She'd settled on the cute blond in jeans when McDreamy walked in. With jet-black hair and bright blue eyes, he was a dead ringer for Patrick Dempsey. His camel-colored cashmere jacket and black silk scarf were meticulously sloppy. He ordered a beer and took a swig from the bottle. Bunny came in, eyes laser-focused on him, and, rushing to the bar, she flung her arms around him. Standing so close a matchbook wouldn't have fit between them, they were obviously besotted with each other. They finished their drinks and ordered another round. McDreamy put his arm around Bunny's waist, pulling her even closer. Bunny turned up that adorable little face to him and locked her lips against his. At that precise moment, Amber turned her iPhone to silent, raised it, and snapped several photos of their enraptured display. They finally pulled apart long enough to gulp down the second drink they'd ordered and then leave the bar arm in arm. No doubt they were not going to waste any more time at the bar when the hotel across the street beckoned.

Amber finished her drink and scrolled through the pictures. She was still laughing as she walked to her car. Poor old March would be getting some very enlightening photographs tomorrow. And Bunny—well, Bunny would be too distraught to continue with her duties as Daphne's cochair.

NINE

Amber had been counting the days until Friday. She would finally get to meet Jackson at dinner, and she was giddy with anticipation. By the time she rang the doorbell, she felt ready to burst.

Daphne greeted her with a dazzling smile, taking her by the hand. "Welcome, Amber. So good to see you. Please, come in."

"Thanks, Daphne. I've been looking forward to this all week," Amber said as she entered the large hallway.

"I thought we might have a drink in the conservatory before dinner," Daphne said, and Amber followed her into the room. "What will you have?"

"Um, I think I'd like a glass of red wine," Amber said. She looked around the room, but Jackson was nowhere in sight.

"Pinot noir okay?"

"Perfect," Amber said, wondering where the hell Jackson was.

Daphne handed her the glass and, as if reading her mind, said, "Jackson had to work late, so it'll just be us girls tonight—you, me, Tallulah, and Bella."

Amber's exhilaration evaporated. Now she'd have to sit and listen to the mind-numbing chatter of those kids all evening.

Just then Bella came tearing into the room.

"Mommy, Mommy," she wailed, thrusting herself

forward onto Daphne's lap. "Tallulah won't read to me from my *Angelina Ballerina* book."

Tallulah was right behind her. "Mom, I'm trying to help her read it by herself, but she won't listen," she said, sounding like a miniature adult. "I was reading way harder books at her age."

"Girls. No quarreling tonight," Daphne said, ruffling Bella's curls. "Tallulah was just trying to help you, Bella."

"But she knows I can't do it," Bella said, her face still in Daphne's lap and her voice muffled.

Daphne stroked her daughter's head. "It's all right, darling. Don't worry, you will soon."

"Come on, ladies," Daphne addressed them all. "Let's go out to the deck and have a nice dinner. Margarita made some delicious guacamole we can start with."

Summer would be coming to an end soon, and there was a slight breeze that held just a hint of cooler days to come. Even a casual dinner on Daphne's deck took on an air of style and sophistication, Amber thought. Triangular dishes of bright red sat on navy blue place mats, and napkin rings decorated with silver sailboats held blue-and-white-checked napkins. Amber noticed that each place setting was identically placed. It reminded her of the British films about aristocracy, where the waitstaff actually measured every item placed on the dining table. Couldn't this woman ever relax?

"Amber, why don't you sit there," Daphne said, pointing to a chair directly facing the water.

The view, of course, was stunning, with a velvety lawn gently sloping to a sandy beach and the water beyond. She counted five Adirondack chairs clustered on the sand, a few yards back from the water's edge. How picturesque and inviting it looked.

Bella was eyeing Amber from across the table. "Are you married?"

Amber shook her head. "No, I'm not."

"How come?" Bella asked.

"Darling, that's a rather personal question." Daphne looked at Amber and laughed. "Sorry about that."

"No, it's okay." Amber turned her attention to Bella. "I suppose I haven't met Mr. Right."

Bella narrowed her eyes. "Who's Mr. Right?"

"It's just an expression, silly. She means she hasn't met the right one for her," Tallulah explained.

"Hmph. Maybe it's 'cause she's kind of ugly."

"Bella! You apologize this minute." Daphne's face had turned bright pink.

"Why? It's true, isn't it?" Bella insisted.

"Even if it's true, it's still rude," Tallulah offered.

Amber cast her eyes downward, trying to appear hurt, and said nothing.

Daphne stood up. "That's it. The two of you can eat by yourselves in the kitchen. Sit there and think about the proper way to speak to others." She rang for Margarita and sent the girls off, amid protests. She came over to Amber and put an arm around her shoulder. "I am so, so sorry. I'm beyond embarrassed and appalled by their behavior."

Amber gave her a small smile. "You don't need to apologize. They're kids. They don't mean anything by it." She smiled again, buoyed by the thought that now they could spend the rest of the evening unfettered by the little brats.

"Thank you for being so gracious."

They chatted about this and that and enjoyed a delicious dinner of shrimp scampi over quinoa and a spinach salad. Amber noticed, though, that Daphne had barely taken two bites of the scampi and not much more of her salad. Amber finished every bit of hers, not about to waste this expensive food.

It was beginning to get cool, and she was relieved when Daphne suggested they go back in the sunroom for coffee.

She followed Daphne until they reached a cheerful room decorated in yellows and blues. White bookcases lined the walls, and Amber lingered in front of one set, curious to see what Daphne liked to read. The shelves were lined with all the classics, in alphabetical order by author. Starting with Albee all the way to Woolf. She would bet there was no way Daphne had read them all.

"Do you like to read, Amber?"

"Very much. I'm afraid I haven't read most of these, though. I'm more into contemporary authors. Have you read all of these?"

"Yes, many of them. Jackson likes to discuss great books. We're only to the *H*'s. We're tackling Homer's *The Odyssey*. Not quite light reading." She laughed.

A lovely porcelain turtle, as blue as the Caribbean, caught Amber's attention and she reached out to touch it. She'd seen a few others throughout the house, each one unique and more exquisite than the last. She could tell they were all expensive, and she wanted to smash them to the floor. Here she was, struggling to make rent every month, and Daphne could throw money away collecting stupid turtles. It was so unfair. She turned away and took a seat on the silk love seat next to Daphne.

"This has been so much fun. Thanks again for having me."

"It's been wonderful. I enjoyed having another adult to talk to."

"Does your husband work late a lot?" Amber asked.

Daphne shrugged. "It depends. He's usually home for dinner. He likes the family to eat together. But he's working on a new land deal in California, and with the time difference sometimes it can't be helped."

Amber went to pick up the coffee cup from the table in front of her, and her grip slipped. The cup went crashing to the floor.

"I'm so sorry—" The horrified look on Daphne's face stopped Amber midsentence.

Daphne flew from her chair and out of the room, returning a few minutes later with a white towel and a bowl with some sort of mixture in it. She started blotting the stain with the towel, and then rubbing it with whatever concoction she had mixed up.

"Can I help?" Amber asked.

Daphne didn't look up. "No, no. I have it. Just wanted to make sure I got to it before the stain set."

Amber felt helpless, watching Daphne attack the stain as if her life depended on it. Wasn't that what the help was for? She sat there, feeling like an idiot, while Daphne scrubbed furiously. Amber began to feel less bad and more annoyed. So she'd spilled something. Big deal. At least she hadn't called anyone ugly.

Daphne stood, took a last look at the now-clean rug, and gave Amber a sheepish shrug. "Goodness. Well, can I get you a new cup?"

Was she for real? "No, that's okay. I really should be going anyway. It's getting late."

"Are you sure? You don't have to go so soon."

Normally Amber would have stayed, played things out a little longer, but she didn't trust herself not to give her annoyance away. Besides, she could see that Daphne was still on edge. What a clean freak she was. She'd probably examine the rug with a magnifying glass once Amber left.

"Absolutely. This has been such a great evening. I've really enjoyed hanging out with you. I'll see you next week at the committee meeting."

"Drive safely," Daphne said as she closed the door.

Amber glanced at the time on her phone. If she hurried, she could get to the library before it closed and check out a copy of *The Odyssey*.

TEN

By the third committee meeting, Amber was ready to execute the final stage of Operation Bye-Bye Bunny. Today she was wearing a thin wraparound sweater from the Loft over her best pair of black slacks. She dreaded seeing the other women and enduring their condescending glances and too-polite conversation. She knew she wasn't one of them, and it infuriated her that she let it get to her. Taking a cleansing breath, she reminded herself that the only one she needed to worry about was Daphne.

Forcing a smile, she rang the bell and waited to be escorted inside.

The housekeeper opened the door in uniform.

"Missus will be down shortly. She left a paper in the conservatory for you to look at while you wait."

Amber smiled at her. "Thanks, Margarita. By the way, I've been meaning to ask you. The guacamole you made the other evening was divine—never had any as good. What's your secret ingredient?"

Margarita looked pleased. "Thank you, Miss Amber. You promise not to tell?"

Amber nodded.

She leaned in and whispered, "Cumin."

Amber hadn't actually tasted the green goo—she hated avocados—but every woman thinks her own recipes are so special, and it was an easy way to get on someone's good side.

The room was set up with a breakfast buffet: muffins, fruit, coffee, and tea. Grabbing a mug, Amber filled it to the brim with coffee. She had already reviewed the agenda when Daphne walked into the room, perfectly turned out as usual. Amber rose and gave her a hug. Holding up the piece of paper, she frowned and pointed at the first item. "New cochair needed? What happened to Bunny?"

Daphne sighed and shook her head. "She called me a few days ago and said she had a family emergency to deal with. Something about having to leave town to care for a sick uncle."

Amber affected a perplexed expression. "That's a shame. Wasn't she supposed to have finished organizing the silent auction by today?" It was a huge job, requiring good organizational skills and attention to detail. All of the items had been secured, but Amber was quite sure that Bunny had left plenty of work that still needed to be completed, given that her world had collapsed a week ago.

"Yes, she was. Unfortunately, she just let me know yesterday that she hadn't finished organizing all of it. Now we're really behind the eight ball. I feel so bad asking someone to step in and take over. They'll have to work nonstop to have everything ready in time."

"I know I'm the newbie here, but I've done this sort of thing before. I would love to do it." Amber looked down at her fingernails, then back up at Daphne. "But the other women probably wouldn't like it."

Daphne's eyebrows shot up. "It doesn't matter that you're new. I know you're here because your heart's truly in it. But it's an awful lot of work," she said. "All the item write-ups still need to be done, the bid forms have to be matched, and the bid numbers need to be set up."

Amber tried to keep her voice casual. "I managed one for my old boss. The best thing is to have the bid form in triplicate, three different colors, and to leave the bottom copy with the item after the auction closes and take the other two to the cashier. It eliminates confusion."

She'd hit her mark from her Google research from the night before. Daphne looked duly impressed.

"It would make me feel like I was doing something for Charlene," Amber continued. "I mean, I don't have the money to make big donations, but I can offer my time." She gave Daphne what she hoped was a pitiful look.

"Of course. Absolutely. I would be honored to have you as my cochair."

"What about the other women? Will they be okay with it? I wouldn't want to ruffle any feathers."

"You let me worry about them," Daphne said and lifted her coffee mug in salute to Amber. "Partners. For Julie and Charlene."

Amber picked up her mug and touched it to Daphne's.

A half hour later, after eating Daphne's food and catching each other up on their scintillating lives, the women all finally got down to the business of the meeting. It must be nice to have all morning to fritter away like this. Once again, Amber'd had to take a vacation day to be there.

Amber held her breath as Daphne cleared her throat and addressed the room. "Unfortunately, Bunny had to resign from the committee. She's been called out of town to care for an ailing uncle."

"Oh, what a shame. I hope it's not too serious," Meredith said.

"I don't have any other details," Daphne said, then paused. "I was going to ask one of you to step in as co-chair, but Amber has graciously offered to do it."

Meredith looked at her, then at Daphne. "Um, that's very generous, but do you think that's really wise? No offense intended, but Amber just joined us. It's a lot to get up to speed on. I'd be happy to do it."

"The main thing left is to handle the silent auction, and Amber has experience with it," Daphne replied in a nonchalant tone. "Plus, Amber has a very personal stake; she wants to honor her sister as well. I'm sure she would welcome your help and that of everyone on the committee."

Amber turned her gaze from Daphne to Meredith. "I would be so appreciative of any advice you're willing to give. Once I've assessed where we are, I can divvy up some assignments." The thought of having that rich bitch reporting to her made her flush with pleasure. She didn't miss the look of irritation on Meredith's face and struggled to hide a smirk.

Meredith cocked an eyebrow. "Of course. We're all happy to do our part. Bunny had planned on laying out all the items in her house and having a few of us come and help with the bid sheets and descriptions. Should we plan on coming to your house, Amber?"

Before Amber could respond, Daphne dove in to rescue her. "The items are already here. I sent for them yesterday afternoon. No sense in moving them again."

Amber fixed her eyes on Meredith as she spoke. "I'm planning on automating the forms anyhow. It will be much more efficient for me to e-mail them to each of you with a picture of the item, and you can fill out the descriptions and send them back. Then I can have them printed and set them with the items. I'll send everyone an e-mail tonight with the groupings, and you can let me know which you'll write up. No need to waste time all sitting around together."

"That's a great idea, Amber. See, ladies? Nice to have some new blood."

Amber leaned back into her armchair and smiled. She felt Meredith's appraising eyes on her, and noticed once again how everything about her screamed old money, from her double strand of pearls to the slightly worn camel jacket. Minimal makeup, no particular style to her hair, quiet wristwatch and earrings. Her wedding ring, a band of sapphires and diamonds, looked like a family heirloom. Nothing ostentatious about this woman except the distinct aura of *Mayflower* lineage and trust funds. Her arrogance reminded Amber of Mrs. Lockwood, the richest woman in the town where she grew up, who would bring her cashmere sweaters, wool suits, and formal gowns into the dry cleaner's every Monday morning, putting them gingerly on the counter as if she couldn't bear for her sacred garments to touch the clothes of the underclass. She never greeted Amber and never responded to a hello with anything but a forced, sour smile that looked as if she'd smelled something rotten.

The Lockwood family lived in a huge home at the top of a hill overlooking the town. Amber had met Frances, their only daughter, at a county fair, and the two had become fast friends. The first time Frances took Amber to her home, Amber had been awestruck at its size and magnificent furnishings. Frances's bedroom was a young girl's dream, all pink and white and frilly. Her dolls—so many!—were lined up neatly on built-in shelves, and on one long wall stood a case filled with books and trophies. Amber remembered feeling like she never wanted to leave that bedroom. But the friendship had been short-lived. After all, Amber was not the sort Mrs. Lockwood wanted as a friend for her precious daughter. As quickly as the two girls had connected, the cord was severed by Frances's imperious mother. It had stuck in Amber's craw ever since, but she'd found a way to get even when she met Matthew, Frances's handsome older brother. Mrs. Lockwood hadn't known what hit her.

And now, here she was, confronting the same condescension from Meredith Stanton. So far, though, it was Amber one, Meredith nothing.

"Amber." Daphne's voice startled her from her reverie. "I'd like to get a picture for a little advance publicity. Let's have you and the rest of the auction committee with some of the items. I'm sure the *Harbor Times* will publish it with a blurb about the fundraiser."

Amber couldn't move. *A picture? For the newspaper?* She couldn't let that happen. She had to think quickly. "Um." She paused a moment. "Gee, Daphne, I'm so new to the group. I don't think it's fair for me to be in the photo. It should include members who have worked on this longer than I have."

"That's very gracious of you, but you are the cochair now," Daphne said.

"I'd really feel more comfortable if other people's accomplishments were highlighted." Looking around, Amber realized she'd scored points for humility. It was a win-win. She could maintain the rank of poor but sweet and unassuming little waif to these privileged snobs. And most importantly, no ghosts from the past would come sniffing around. She just needed to keep a low profile for now.

ELEVEN

The next morning Jenna came dancing into Amber's office, her smile so wide that her cheeks practically obscured her squinty little eyes. "Guess what?" she demanded breathlessly.

"No clue," Amber said flatly, not even bothering to look up from the commission reports she was working on.

"I talked to Sally last night."

Amber's head shot up, and she put her pen down.

"She said she'd like to come to dinner with us. Tonight."

"That's great, Jenna." For the first time, Amber was thankful for Jenna's doggedness. She had pestered Amber from her first day on the job, and every time Amber refused her invitations, she had bounced back up like a Punchinello toy and asked her again, until finally Amber relented. Jenna had gotten what she wanted, and now it was all about to pay off for Amber too.

"What time, and do we have a place in mind?"

"Well, we could do Friendly's. Or Red Lobster. Tonight they're having all the shrimp you can eat."

Amber pictured Jenna sitting across from her, cocktail sauce dripping down her chin as she devoured all those little pink shrimp. She didn't think she could stomach that. "Let's go to the Main Street Grille," she said. "I'm free right after work."

"Okay. I'll tell Sally to meet us around five thirty.

This is going to be so much fun," Jenna squealed, clapping her hands together and prancing out of the office.

When Amber and Jenna arrived at the Grille, they were seated in a booth near the back of the restaurant, with Jenna facing the door so she would see Sally when she arrived. Jenna began yammering away about a new client who had come in today looking for properties in the $5 million range and how nice and friendly she was, then suddenly stopped and waved her hand. "Here's Sally," she said and stood up.

As Sally approached the table, Amber knew her surprise registered on her face. This woman was not at all what she'd expected.

"Hi, Jenna." The newcomer gave Jenna a hug and then turned to Amber. "You must be Amber, the one Jenna is always talking about." She smiled, reached a slender arm across the table, and shook Amber's hand. Sally wore fitted jeans and a long-sleeved white T-shirt that showed off her trim figure, tanned skin, and luxuriant brown hair. As she took the seat next to Jenna, Amber was struck by her eyes, so dark they were almost black, with thick, long eyelashes.

"It's nice to meet you, Sally," Amber said. "I'm glad you could make it tonight."

"Jenna and I have been promising to get together for ages, but we've been so busy with work that we haven't had time. I'm glad we finally made it happen." Amber wondered what these two could possibly have in common besides living on the same street.

"I'm starving. Do you two know what you want?" Jenna said.

Sally picked up her menu and quickly scanned it.

"The grilled salmon with spinach sounds good," Amber said, and Jenna wrinkled her nose.

"Yes, I think I'll have the same." Sally put down the menu.

"Yuck. How can you choose salmon instead of a hot turkey sandwich with mashed potatoes and gravy? That's what I'm getting. And no spinach."

The waitress took their orders, and Amber ordered a bottle of the house red. She wanted everyone relaxed and loose-tongued tonight.

"Here," she said, and poured the wine into their glasses. "Let's sit back and enjoy. So tell me, Sally, where do you work?"

"I'm a special education teacher at a private school, St. Gregory's in Greenwich."

"That's great. Jenna told me that you had been a nanny. You must love kids."

"Oh, I do."

"How many years did you nanny?"

"Six years. I only worked for two families. The last one was here in town."

"Who was that?" Amber asked.

"Geez, Amber, did you forget? The day you had lunch with Mrs. Parrish, I told you Sally used to work for her," Jenna said.

Amber gave her a hate-filled look. "Yes, I did forget." She turned back to Sally. "What was it like—working there, I mean?"

"I loved it. And Mr. and Mrs. Parrish were great to work for."

Amber wasn't interested in a fairy tale of how perfect the Parrish family was. She decided to take another tack. "Nannying must be a tough job at times. What were the hardest parts, do you think?"

"Hmm. When Tallulah was born, it was sort of tiring. She was small—only weighed five pounds at birth—so she had to eat every two hours. Of course the nurse took the night feedings, but I would get there at seven in the morning and stay till she came back at night."

"So the nurse fed her through the night? Mrs. Parrish didn't nurse the baby?"

"No, it was sad, really. Mr. Parrish told me she tried at first, but her milk wouldn't come in. He asked me not to say anything because it made her cry, so we never talked about it." Sally took a forkful of salmon. "I sometimes wondered about it."

"What do you mean?"

Amber detected discomfort in Sally, who seemed to be trying for nonchalance. "Oh, nothing, really."

"It doesn't sound like nothing," Amber pressed.

"Well, I guess I'm not telling you something everybody doesn't already know."

Amber leaned in closer and waited.

"A while after Tallulah was born, Mrs. Parrish went away. To a sort of hospital where you rest and get help."

"You mean a sanitarium?"

"Something like that."

"Did she have postpartum depression?"

"I'm really not sure. There was a lot of gossip at the time, but I tried not to listen to it. I don't know. There were police involved somehow. I remember that. There were rumors that she was a danger to the baby, that she shouldn't be alone with her."

Amber tried to hide her fascination. "Was she? A danger?"

Sally shook her head. "I had a hard time believing that. But I never really saw her again. Mr. Parrish let me go right before she came home. He said they wanted someone to speak French to Tallulah, and I had been thinking about going back to school full-time anyhow.

Later, they did end up hiring my friend Surrey for the weekends. She never mentioned anything strange."

Amber was wondering what had happened to make Daphne require hospitalization. Her mind was miles away when she realized Sally was still talking.

"I'm sorry. What were you saying?" Amber asked her.

"It was Mrs. Parrish who encouraged me to continue and get my master's degree. She said the most important thing was for a woman to be independent and know what she wanted. Especially before she considers marriage." Sally took a sip of her wine. "Good advice, I think."

"I suppose. But she was pretty young when she married Mr. Parrish, wasn't she?"

Sally smiled. "In her twenties. It seems like they have a perfect marriage, so I guess it was a good decision."

What a load of crap, Amber thought as she divided the last of the wine between their glasses. "Jenna told me that Mrs. Parrish's mother was thinking about moving here at one time. Did you ever meet her?"

"I met her a few times. She didn't visit that often. She mentioned that she ran a B&B up north, but it still seemed odd that she wasn't there more, you know, to see the baby and all."

"Do you know why she decided not to move to Bishops Harbor?"

"I'm not sure exactly, but she seemed put off by all the help the Parrishes had. Maybe she thought she'd be in the way," Sally said, then sipped her wine. "You know, Mrs. Parrish has an extremely well ordered and tightly scheduled life. Precision is a hallmark in her house—nothing out of place, every room spotless, and every item perfectly placed. Maybe it was a little too regimented for Mrs. Bennett."

"Wow, it sure sounds like it." Amber had not failed to notice the very same thing every time she visited Daphne, which was more and more often lately. The house looked as if no one lived in it. The moment you finished drinking from a glass or emptied your plate, it was whisked away and disappeared. There was never a misplaced thing, which was hard to achieve with two young kids around. Even the girls' bedrooms were immaculate. Amber had looked into the rooms the morning after she'd spent the night and was astounded at the meticulous placement of books and toys. Nothing was out of order.

As she drank more wine, Sally seemed to be warming to her subject. "I heard from Surrey that Tallulah and Bella never get to watch cartoons or kid shows. They have to watch documentaries or educational DVDs." She waved her hand. "I mean, not that that's bad, but it is sad that they can't watch anything just for fun or entertainment."

"I guess Mrs. Parrish values education," Amber said.

Sally looked at her watch. "Speaking of which, I really should get going. School in the morning." She turned to Jenna. "If you're ready to go, I can give you a ride home."

"That'd be good." Jenna clapped her hands together. "What a fun night it's been. We should do this again."

They settled the check, and Jenna and Sally left. Amber finished her wine and sat back in her seat, reviewing the nuggets of information she'd gathered.

When she got home, the first thing she did was look up Daphne's mother. After a bit of searching, she found that Ruth Bennett owned and ran a B&B in New Hampshire. It was a quaint inn with lovely grounds. Nothing extravagant, but very nice nonetheless. The picture of her on the website showed her to be an older, not quite as beautiful version of her daughter. Amber wondered what it was between them, why Daphne'd been reluctant to have her mother move near her.

She bookmarked the page and then logged onto Facebook. There he was, looking older and fatter. Guess the last few years hadn't been so good for him. She laughed and shut the lid of her laptop.

TWELVE

Waiting on the platform, Amber sipped the hot coffee in her gloved hand, trying to stay warm. White vapor escaped from her mouth every time she opened it, and she marched in place to generate some heat. She was meeting Daphne, Tallulah, and Bella for a day of shopping and sightseeing in New York, the primary attraction being the Christmas tree at Rockefeller Center. She had purposely dressed like a tourist: sensible shoes, warm down jacket, and a tote bag to hold her treasures. Just what a gal from Nebraska would wear. The only makeup she had on was a cheap frosted lipstick she'd picked up at Walgreens.

"Amber, hi," Daphne called as she came running toward her, a little girl attached to each hand. "Sorry we're late. This one couldn't decide what to wear." She tilted her head toward Bella with a smile.

Amber smiled. "Hi, girls. Nice to see you again."

Bella eyed her suspiciously. "That's an ugly coat."

"Bella!" Daphne and Tallulah exclaimed in unison. Daphne looked mortified. "That's a terrible thing to say."

"Well, it's true."

"I'm so sorry, Amber," Daphne said.

"It's okay." Amber squatted down until she was eye level with Bella. "You're right. It *is* an ugly coat. I've had it forever. Maybe you can help me pick a new one out today." She wanted to smack the little brat. She was all of six or seven, and she was wearing a pair of silver sneakers that Amber recognized from a package that had been sitting open on the kitchen table when she'd dropped off gift certificates for the auction at the house the other day. She'd gone home and looked up the shoes to discover that they cost almost $300. The spoiled kid was already a fashion snob.

Bella turned to her mother and whined, "When is the train coming? I'm cold."

Daphne wrapped her arms around her and kissed the top of her head. "Soon, darling."

After another five minutes of Bella's complaints, the train pulled in and they scrambled aboard, luckily finding a vacant spot in the front of the car—two rows facing each other. Amber sat down, and Bella stood in front of her, little arms crossed over her chest.

"You took my seat. I can't sit backward."

"No problem." Amber moved to the other side and Tallulah took the seat next to Bella.

"I want Mommy to sit next to me."

Were they really going to let this little monster bark orders all day?

Daphne gave her a stern look. "Bella, I'm right across from you. Stop this nonsense now. I'm going to sit next to Amber."

Bella gave her a dark look and kicked her little foot against the seat across from her. "Why'd *she* have to come, anyway? This is supposed to be a family trip."

Daphne stood up. "Excuse us for a moment." She grabbed Bella by the hand and walked her to the end of the aisle. Amber could see her gesturing with her hands as she talked. After a few minutes, Bella nodded and the two returned.

Bella took her seat and looked up at Amber. "I'm sorry, Amber."

She didn't look one bit sorry, but Amber gave her what she hoped was a kind look.

"Thank you, Bella. I accept your apology." She turned her attention to Tallulah. "Your mom tells me that you're a Nancy Drew fan."

Tallulah's eyes lit up, and she unzipped the small backpack she carried and brought out *The Secret of the Wooden Lady*. "I have all my mom's old books. I love them."

"So do I. I wanted to be just like Nancy Drew," Amber said.

Tallulah started to soften. "She's so brave and smart and always on an adventure."

"Boooooring," the little furby next to her called out.

"How would you know? You can't even read," Tallulah responded.

"Mom! She's not supposed to say that to me," Bella said, her voice rising.

"All right, girls, that's enough," Daphne said mildly.

Now Amber felt like slapping Daphne. Couldn't she see that kid needed to be put in her place? A good spank across the rump would probably do wonders.

They finally pulled into Grand Central and poured out of the train into the crowded station. Amber stayed behind Daphne as she and the girls walked up the steps and into the main terminal. Her spirits lifted as she looked around at the magnificent architecture and thought again how much she loved New York.

Daphne stopped and gathered them together. "Okay, here's what's on our agenda. We're going to start by looking at all the holiday window displays, then lunch at Alice's Teacup, then American Girl Store, and finally ice-skating at Rockefeller Center."

Kill me now, Amber thought.

❋

Amber had to admit that the window displays were fabulous, each one more elaborate than the last. Even the little princess was bewitched and stopped her whining. When they arrived at Alice's Teacup, Amber groaned inwardly at the long line, but apparently Daphne was well known there, and they were whisked right in. Lunch was fine, no major incidents, and Amber and Daphne actually got to have a conversation longer than five minutes.

While the girls took their time eating their French toast, Amber finished her ham and cheese croissant and sipped her tea.

"Thanks again for including me, Daphne. It's so nice to be a part of a family day this time of year."

"Thank *you*. You're making the day so much more fun for me. When Jackson bailed out, I almost canceled." She leaned in and whispered, "As you've seen, Bella can be a little bit of a handful. It's great to have some help."

Amber felt her back go up. Was that what she was? Help?

"Wasn't the nanny available today?" she couldn't resist asking.

Daphne didn't seem to notice the jab. She shook her head absently. "I'd already given her the day off since we had planned this." She smiled brightly at Amber and squeezed her hand. "I'm so glad you came with us. This is the kind of thing I'd be doing with my sister if she were alive. Now I have a special friend to enjoy it with."

"That's funny. When we were looking at the beautiful animations in the store windows, I imagined how much Charlene would have loved it. Christmas was her favorite time of year." In fact, Amber's childhood Christmases had been mean and disappointing. But if Charlene *had* existed, she might have liked Christmas.

"Julie loved Christmas too. I've never told this to anyone, but very late on Christmas Eve each year, I write a letter to Julie."

"What do you tell her?" Amber asked.

"All that's happened in the last year, you know, like those Christmas letters that people send out. But these letters are different. I tell her what's in my heart and all about her nieces—how much she would have loved them and they her. It keeps me connected to her in a way I can't explain."

Amber felt a brief stab of sympathy that quickly turned to envy. She had never felt that kind of love and affection for anyone in her family. She wondered what that would be like. She didn't know quite what to say.

"Can we go to American Girl now?" Bella was standing, pulling on her coat, and Amber was grateful for the intrusion.

They left the restaurant and grabbed a cab. Amber sat in front with the driver. The inside of the car smelled of old cheese, and she wanted to gag, but as soon as she rolled the window down, Queen Bella piped up from the backseat.

"I'm cold."

Amber gritted her teeth and put it back up.

When they arrived at Forty-Ninth and Fifth, the line going into the store went all the way around the block.

"The line is so long," Tallulah said. "Do we really have to wait?"

Bella stomped her foot. "I need a new dress for my

Bella doll. Can't you get us in ahead of them, Mommy? Like you did at the restaurant?"

Daphne shook her head. "Afraid not, sweetie." She gave Tallulah a beseeching look. "I *did* promise her."

Tallulah looked like she wanted to cry.

Amber had an inspiration. "Say, I noticed we passed a Barnes & Noble just a few blocks back. Why don't I take Tallulah there, and you and Bella can meet us when you finish?"

Tallulah's eyes lit up. "Can we, Mom? Please?"

"Are you sure, Amber?" Daphne asked.

Was she ever. "Of course. This way, they're both happy."

"Super. Thanks, Amber."

As she and Tallulah began to walk away, Daphne called out. "Amber, please stay with her in the store."

She bit back a sarcastic retort. Like she'd really let the kid wander in Manhattan on her own. "I won't take my eyes off her."

As they headed south on Fifth Avenue, Amber seized the opportunity to get to know Tallulah better.

"You're not into American Girl dolls?"

"Not enough to stand in line for hours. I'd much rather look at books."

"What kinds of things *do* you like?"

She shrugged. "Well, books. And I like to take pictures, but with old cameras and film."

"Really? Why not digital?"

"The resolution is better, and I've found that . . ."

Amber tuned out the rest of her explanation. She didn't care. All she needed to know was what she liked, not the three paragraphs of science behind it. Tallulah was like a little professor masquerading as a kid. Amber wondered if she had any friends at all.

"Here we are."

She followed Tallulah around the enormous store until they reached the mystery section, and she pulled out an armful of books. They found a cozy place to sit, and Amber grabbed a few books off the shelves as well. She noticed Tallulah holding a collection of Edgar Allan Poe stories.

"Did you know Edgar Allan Poe was an orphan?" Amber asked.

Tallulah looked up. "What?"

Amber nodded. "Yes, his parents died when he was four. He was raised by a wealthy merchant."

Tallulah's eyes widened.

"Sadly, his new parents cut him out of their will, and he ended up very poor. Maybe he wasn't as nice to them as he was to his real parents." Amber smiled inwardly at Tallulah's shocked expression. It was a good lesson for the kid to keep in mind.

They spent the next two hours reading, Tallulah lost in her Poe book, ignoring Amber, Amber looking through a book on Formula One racing. She'd read that Jackson was an avid fan. When she'd had enough of that, she opened the Facebook app on her phone. Rage overcame her when she read the update. So, the bitch was pregnant. How could that have happened? The three of them smiling like idiots. Who was stupid enough to announce a pregnancy at only eight weeks? Amber consoled herself with the thought that maybe she'd miscarry. She heard someone approach and looked up to see Daphne, laden with shopping bags, rushing toward them.

"There you are!" Daphne was out of breath, and Bella's hand was in hers as she ran to keep up with her mother. "Jackson just called. He's going to meet us after all. We'll grab a cab and meet him at SixtyFive. We'll have dinner and then see the tree." She smiled.

"Wait," Amber said, grabbing the arm of Daphne's coat. "I don't want to intrude on your family time." In truth, she was surprised at how nervous she was at the prospect of meeting Jackson. The suddenness threw her off balance. She wanted advance warning, time to ready herself to meet the man she knew so much about.

"Don't be silly," Daphne gushed. "You won't be intruding. Now come on. He's waiting for us."

Tallulah got up immediately, putting all the books into a pile and picking them up.

Daphne waved her hand. "Leave them, sweetie. We need to get going."

THIRTEEN

He was waiting at the best table in the place. Its view was even more stunning than Amber had imagined. So was he, for that matter. The sex appeal practically oozed out of him. Drop-dead gorgeous. There was no other way to say it. And the impeccably tailored custom suit made him look like he'd just stepped off the set of a Bond movie. He stood as they approached, and when his dazzling blue eyes rested on Daphne, his smile widened, and he greeted her with a warm kiss on the lips. He was crazy about her, Amber realized with frustration. He crouched down, opening his arms, and the girls ran into them.

"Daddy!" Bella grinned, looking happy for the first time all day.

"My girls. Did you have a great day with Mommy?"

They both started chattering at once, and Daphne ushered them into their seats while she took the one next to Jackson. Amber sat in the remaining seat, across from him, next to Bella.

"Jackson, this is Amber. I told you about her; she's come to my rescue on the gala committee."

"Very nice to meet you, Amber. I understand you've been a great help."

Her eyes were drawn to the delectable dimple that appeared when he smiled. If he wondered what she was doing having dinner with them, he at least had the good grace not to show it.

They ordered cocktails for themselves and appetizers for the kids, and after a little while Amber blended into the background and sat observing them.

"So tell me about your day," Jackson said. "What was the highlight?"

"Well, I got two new dresses for my Bella doll, a stable set, and a tutu to match mine, so she can come to ballet with me."

"How about you, Lu?"

"I liked Alice's Teacup. It was cool. Then Amber took me to Barnes & Noble."

He shook his head. "My little bibliophile. You come to the city, and that's where you go? We have one right around the corner," he said, not unkindly.

"Yeah, but's it not huge, like here. Besides, we come here all the time. No big deal."

Amber swallowed her anger at Tallulah's sense of entitlement. No big deal, indeed. She'd like to ship her off to some rural location for a few years and let her see how the rest of America lived.

Jackson turned to Daphne, resting his hand briefly on her cheek. "And you, my darling? What was your highlight?"

"Getting the call from you."

Amber wanted to vomit. Were they for real? She took a long swallow from her wineglass. No need to pace herself; he could afford to keep it coming.

When he finally tore his eyes off his gorgeous wife, Jackson glanced at Amber. "Are you from Connecticut, Amber?"

"No, Nebraska."

He looked surprised. "What brought you east?"

"I wanted to expand my horizons. A friend of mine moved to Connecticut and invited me to room with her," she said, then took another sip of wine. "I fell in love with the coastline right away—and being so close to New York."

"How long have you been here?"

Was he really interested or just being polite? She couldn't tell.

Daphne answered before she could. "About a year, right?" She smiled at her. "She's in real estate too, works in the commercial division of Rollins Realty."

"How did you meet again?"

"I told you, it was quite by accident," Daphne said.

He was still looking at Amber, and she suddenly felt as though she was being interrogated.

"Helloooooooo? This is boring," Bella sang out. Amber was grateful to the little wretch for distracting him.

Jackson turned his attention to her. "Bella, we don't interrupt adults when they're talking." His voice was firm. Thank God one of them has a backbone, Amber thought.

Bella stuck her tongue out at him.

Tallulah gasped and looked at Jackson, as did Daphne. It felt like time had stopped as everyone waited to see his reaction.

He burst out laughing. "I think someone's had too long a day."

Everyone at the table seemed to exhale.

Bella pushed her chair back and ran over to him, burying her head in his chest. "I'm sorry."

He stroked her blond curls. "Thank you. Now you're going to behave like a lady, right?"

She nodded and skipped back to her seat.

Score another point for the little hooligan, Amber

thought. Who knew that the biggest thorn in her side was going to be this little pint-sized gremlin?

"How about another surprise?" he said.

"What?" the girls asked in unison.

"How about we go see the Christmas show at Radio City and then spend the night here?"

The girls' voices rose in excitement, but Daphne put her arm on Jackson's and said, "Sweetheart, I hadn't planned to stay the night. And I'm sure Amber wants to get home."

In fact, Amber was thrilled to stay. Her curiosity about the Parrishes' apartment outweighed any desire to get back home.

Jackson glanced at Amber as if she were a pesky problem to be solved. "Tomorrow's Sunday. What's the big deal? She can borrow a change of clothes." He looked right at Amber. "Is that a problem for you?"

Amber was dancing on the inside, but she gave him a sober and appreciative look. "That would be fine with me. I'd hate to disappoint Bella and Tallulah. They seem really excited to stay."

He smiled and squeezed Daphne's arm. "See? It's fine. We'll have a great time."

Daphne shrugged, resigned to the change in plans. They went into the theater and watched Santa and the Rockettes for the next hour and a half. Amber thought the show was moronic, but the girls loved every minute.

When they came out, it was snowing, and the city looked like a winter wonderland, with white lights twinkling on the bare tree branches now covered in the magic powder. Amber looked around in awe. She'd never seen New York this late at night. It was a sight to behold, the lights making everything shimmer and glow.

Jackson took the phone from his pocket, pulled off his leather glove, and, hitting a key, brought it to his ear and said, "Send the driver to the front entrance of Radio City."

When the black limousine with dark windows pulled up, Amber craned her neck to see what celebrity might step out, but as a tall, uniformed chauffeur got out and opened the back door, she realized that the limo was empty and that it was there for them. Now *she* felt like the celebrity. She'd never been in a limousine. She noticed that Daphne and the girls didn't look the least bit fazed. Jackson took Daphne's hand and guided her in first. Then he gave Bella and Tallulah a playful shove, and they followed after their mother. He gestured to indicate that Amber should enter next, but he barely looked at her. The car was large enough for the two women and two children to sit four across. Jackson spread out on the seat opposite them, his arm draped across the back of the seat and his legs spread wide. Amber tried with difficulty to keep her eyes off him. He was positively brimming with power and masculinity.

Bella was leaning against her mother, almost asleep, when Tallulah said, "Are we going right to the apartment, Daddy?"

"Yes, I—"

But before he got another word out, Bella shot up, now wide awake. "No, no, no. Not the apartment. I want to go where Eloise is. I want to sleep at the Plaza."

"We can't do that, sweetheart," Daphne had said. "We don't have a reservation. We'll do that another time."

Bella wasn't having it. "Daddy, please. I'll be the first one in my class to stay where Eloise lives. Everyone will be so jealous. Please, please, please?"

At first Amber had wanted to grab the little whiner

and wring her selfish little neck, but there was something in her that Amber recognized, something that made her see how she could turn her into an ally instead of an enemy. And anyway, who cared whether they stayed at the apartment or the Plaza? Either one was a treat for Amber.

※

The next morning Amber rolled over, pulling the duvet closer around her until it touched her chin. She sighed and wriggled her body against the silky sheet, feeling its softness caress her. She'd never slept in such a sumptuously comfortable bed. In the one next to hers, Tallulah stirred. The suite had only two bedrooms—Bella had bunked with her parents, and though Tallulah hadn't looked too happy about sharing a room with Amber, she'd obliged. Amber threw off the covers, rose, and went to the window. The Grand Penthouse Suite looked out over Central Park, and New York lay before her as if for the taking. She scanned the beautiful room, with its tall ceilings and elegant furnishings. The suite was fit for royalty, larger than the average house. Jackson had succumbed to Bella's request, of course, had even sent his chauffeur to get clothes for everyone from the apartment. Unbelievable, how easy it was for the rich—how unfairly easy.

She slipped off the pajamas Daphne had lent her, then showered and dressed in the clothes she'd also been given last night: a pair of blue wool slacks and a white cashmere sweater. The material felt divine against her clean skin. She looked in the mirror, admiring the perfect cut and clean lines. When she glanced at the bed, she saw that Tallulah still slept, so she tiptoed quietly out of the room. Bella was already up, sitting on the green tufted sofa with a book in her hands. She looked up briefly as Amber entered, said nothing, and gave her attention back to the book. Amber sat on a chair opposite the sofa and picked up a magazine from the coffee table, not saying a word and pretending to read. They stayed that way for the next ten minutes, silent, uncommunicative.

Finally, Bella closed her book and stared at Amber. "Why didn't you go home last night? This was supposed to be a family night."

Amber thought for a moment. "Well, Bella, to tell you the truth, I knew everyone at my office would be envious if they knew I got to stay at the Plaza and have breakfast with Eloise." She paused for effect. "I guess I wasn't thinking about the family thing. You're right about that. I should have gone home. I'm really sorry."

Bella tilted her head and gave Amber a suspicious look. "Your friends know about Eloise? But you're a grown-up. Why do you care about Eloise?"

"My mother read all the Eloise books to me when I was little." This was total bullshit. Her mother had never read anything to her. If Amber hadn't spent all her spare time in the library, she'd be illiterate now.

"Why didn't your mom take you to the Plaza when you were little?"

"We lived far away from New York. Have you ever heard of Nebraska?"

Bella rolled her eyes. "Of course I've heard of Nebraska. I know all fifty states."

This brat was going to take more than camaraderie and kid gloves.

"Well, that's where I grew up. And we didn't have enough money to come to New York. So, there you have it. But I do want to thank you for making one of my dreams come true. I'm going to let everyone at the office know that it was all because of you."

Bella's face was inscrutable, and before she answered, Jackson and Daphne came into the room.

"Good morning." Daphne's voice was cheery. "Where's Tallulah? It's time for breakfast. Is she up yet?"

"I'll go see," Amber said.

Tallulah was up and almost finished dressing when Amber knocked and went in. "Good morning," she said to her. "Your mom asked me to check on you. I think they're ready to go down to breakfast."

Tallulah turned to look at her. "Okay, I'm ready." And they walked together to the living room where the others waited.

"Did you girls sleep well?" Jackson's voice boomed as they headed to the elevator. They all spoke at once, and as the elevator descended, he looked at Bella and said, "We're going to have breakfast with Eloise in the Palm Court."

Bella smiled and looked at Amber. "We've been wanting to do that for a long time," she said.

Maybe she finally had this little hellion in her pocket, Amber thought. Now it was time to work on Jackson.

FOURTEEN

Amber and Daphne sat beside each other at the Parrish dining room table, which was covered in paper, including the list of attendees and a ballroom diagram of the table arrangements. Since almost all of these people were unknown to Amber, Daphne was dictating the seating for each table while Amber dutifully entered all the information into an Excel file. There was a lull as Daphne studied the names before her, and Amber took the opportunity to gaze around the room and out the long bank of floor-to-ceiling windows that looked out to the sea. The room could comfortably seat sixteen for dinner, but it still had a feeling of intimacy. The walls were a muted gold, a perfect backdrop for the magnificent oils of sailboats and seascapes in gilded frames. She could imagine the formal dinner parties they must have here, with elegant place settings of china, crystal, fine silver, and table linens of the highest quality. She was pretty certain that there was not a paper napkin to be found anywhere in the house.

"Sorry to take so long, Amber. I think I finally have table nine figured out," Daphne said.

"No problem. I've been admiring this beautiful room."

"It's lovely, isn't it? Jackson owned the house before we were married, so I haven't done very much to change things. Just the sunroom, really." She looked around and shrugged. "Everything was already perfect."

"Gosh, how wonderful."

Daphne gave her an odd look that passed quickly—too quickly for Amber to identify it.

"Well, I think we're finished with the seating. I'll send the list to the printer to make up the table cards," Daphne said, rising from her chair. "I can't thank you enough. This would have taken forever without your help."

"Oh, you're welcome. I'm happy to do it."

Daphne looked at her watch and then back at Amber. "I don't have to pick the girls up from tennis for another hour. How about a cup of tea and a bite to eat? Do you have time?"

"That would be great." She followed Daphne out of the dining room. "Could I use the restroom?"

"Of course." They walked a bit farther, and Daphne indicated a door on the left. "When you come out, turn right and keep walking to the kitchen. I'll put the tea on."

Amber entered the first-floor powder room and was stunned. Every room in the house offered a staggering reminder of Jackson Parrish's great wealth. With its polished black walls and silver picture-frame wainscoting, it was the epitome of quiet opulence. A waterfall slab of marble was the focus of the room, and on top of it sat a marble vessel sink. Amber looked around in wonder once again. Everything original, custom-made. What would it be like to have a custom-made life, she wondered?

She washed her hands and took one last look in the mirror, a tall, beveled piece of glass set in a frame that looked like rippled silver leaves. As she walked the length of the corridor to the kitchen, she slowed to look at the art on the walls. Some she recognized from her exhaustive reading and Met courses—a Sisley and a stunning Boudin. If these were the real thing, and they probably were, the paintings alone were worth a small fortune. And here they were, hanging in a little-trafficked hallway.

As she entered the kitchen, she saw that tea and a plate of fruit sat waiting on the island.

"Mug or cup?" Daphne asked, standing in front of an open cabinet door.

The shelves of the cabinet looked as if they could have been a display for a luxury kitchen showroom. Amber imagined someone using a ruler to measure an exact distance between each cup and glass. Everything lined up perfectly, and everything matched. It was disconcerting in some strange way, and she found herself mutely staring, mesmerized by the symmetry.

"Amber?" Daphne said.

"Oh. Mug, please." She sat on one of the cushioned stools.

"Do you take milk?"

"Yes, please," Amber said.

Daphne swung the refrigerator door open, and Amber stared again. The contents were lined up with military precision, the tallest at the rear and all labels facing front. The absolute precision of Daphne's home was off-putting. It felt to Amber like more than a desire for a neat home and more like an obsession, a compulsion. She remembered Sally's account of Daphne's time in a sanitarium after Tallulah's birth. Perhaps there had been more going on than just postpartum depression, she thought.

Daphne sat opposite Amber and poured their tea. "So, we have just two weeks before the big night. You've been amazing. I've felt such a wonderful synergy with you. We both have so much of our hearts invested in this."

"I've loved every minute of it. I can't wait until the fund-raiser. It's going to be a huge success."

Daphne took a sip of tea and placed the mug on the counter between her hands. Looking at Amber, she said, "I'd like to do something to show my appreciation for all your hard work."

Amber tilted her head and gave Daphne a questioning look.

"I hope you'll let me buy you a dress for the fund-raiser," Daphne said.

Amber had hoped this was going to happen, but she had to play it carefully. "Oh no," she said. "I couldn't let you do that."

"Please. I'd really love to. It's my way of saying thank you."

"I don't know. It feels like you're paying me, and I didn't work on this to get paid. I wanted to do it." Amber smiled inwardly at her brilliant show of humility.

"You mustn't think of it as payment. Think of it as gratitude for your immense help and support," Daphne said as she pushed back a blond wave, her diamond ring flashing brightly.

"I don't know. I feel sort of funny having you spend money on me."

"Well," Daphne said and paused. "How would you feel about borrowing something of mine, then?"

Amber could have kicked herself for protesting too much, but she guessed borrowing a dress was the next best thing. "Gee, I hadn't thought of that. I *would* feel better if you weren't spending your money." As if this woman didn't have millions to burn.

"Great." Daphne stood up from the stool. "Come upstairs with me, and we'll look through my closet."

They climbed the stairs together, and Amber admired the Dutch masters on the wall.

"You have magnificent artwork. I could spend hours looking at it."

"You're more than welcome to. Are you interested in art? Jackson is absolutely passionate about it," Daphne said as they reached the landing.

"Well, I'm no art expert, but I do love museums," Amber replied.

"Jackson too. He's a board member of the Bishops Harbor Art Center. Here we are," Daphne said, leading her into a large room—given its size, it could hardly be called a walk-in closet—filled with racks of clothing lined up in perfect, parallel rows. Every piece of clothing was in a transparent garment bag, and two walls were lined with shelves that held shoes of all styles, arranged by color. Built-in drawers on a third wall held sweaters, one each, with a small see-through panel to identify them. At one end of the room stood a three-way mirror and a pedestal. The lighting was bright but flattering, without the harshness of department-store fitting rooms.

"Wow," Amber couldn't help herself from remarking. "This is something."

Daphne waved her hand dismissively. "We attend a lot of functions. I used to go shopping for each one, and Jackson said I was wasting too much time. He started having things sent to the house for me to look at." She was leading Amber to a rack near the back when suddenly a young woman came walking into the room.

"Madame," she said. "*Les filles*. It is time to pick them up, *non*?"

"Oh my gosh, you're right, Sabine," she exclaimed, looking at her watch again. "I've got to go. I promised the girls I would get them today. Why don't you just look through these dresses till I get back? I won't be long." She patted Amber's arm. "Oh, and, Amber, this is Sabine, our nanny." She rushed out of the room.

"Nice to meet you, Sabine," Amber said.

Sabine, reserved, gave a small nod of her head and in thickly accented English responded, "My pleasure, miss."

"Mrs. Parrish told me you'd been hired to teach French to the girls. Do you enjoying working here?"

Sabine's eyes softened a moment before she regained her austere composure. "Very much. Now you will please excuse me?"

Amber watched as she walked away. So she was French—big deal. She was still just a nanny. But, Amber thought, Daphne's friends would all think it was so grand, not the usual Spanish-speaking nanny, but one who would teach her daughters French.

Amber looked around the room in wonder. Daphne's closet, indeed. This was more like having an exclusive department store at your disposal. She sauntered, slowly examining the rack upon rack of clothes, all meticulously sorted by color and type. The shoes were lined up with the same fastidiousness as the china in the kitchen cabinets. Even the spacing between garments was uniform. When she got to the three-way mirror, she noticed two comfortable club chairs on either side—apparently meant for Jackson or whoever was nodding approval as Daphne modeled her choices. On the rack Daphne had indicated, she began to look through the dresses. Dior, Chanel, Wu, McQueen—the names went on and on. This wasn't some chain department store sending clothes for Daphne to look at; these were couture houses making their designs available to a moneyed client. It boggled her mind.

And Daphne was so casual about all of it–the luxury, the fine art, the "closet" full of designer suits, dresses, and shoes. Amber unzipped one of the bags and brought out a turquoise Versace evening dress. She carried it to the three-way mirror and stepped onto the pedestal, holding the beautiful dress against her body and staring at her reflection. Even Mrs. Lockwood had never brought anything remotely like this to be dry-cleaned.

Amber hung the dress up and, when she turned away, suddenly noticed a door at the far end of the room. She moved toward it and paused with her hand on the knob only a moment before opening it. Before her was a sumptuous space that was a dazzling mix of luxury and comfort. She walked around slowly, her fingers brushing the yellow silk wallpaper. A white velvet chaise longue sat in a corner of the room, and the light from the Palladian window threw dazzling prisms of color on the walls as it pierced the crystals that hung from the large chandelier. She reclined onto the chaise, looking at the picture on the opposite wall, the only piece of art in the room, and felt herself drawn into the peaceful scene of trees and sky. Her shoulders relaxed, and she surrendered to the stillness and calm of this special place.

She closed her eyes and, imagining this was her room, stayed that way for a while. When she finally rose, she examined the space more closely, the delicate table with photographs of a young Daphne and her sister, Julie. She recognized the slight girl with long, dark hair and beautiful almond-shaped eyes from photographs she'd seen throughout the house. She moved to the front of an antique armoire with an abundance of small drawers. Reaching over, she opened one of them. Some lacy underwear. Another with exotic soaps. More of the same in the other drawers, all meticulously folded and placed. She opened the cabinet and found mounds of plush bath towels. She was about to close the door when she noticed a rosewood box toward the back. Amber took it in her hand, undid the catch, and opened it. Inside, nestled on rich green velvet, sat a small pearl-handled pistol. She gently lifted it from the box and saw etched on the barrel the initials YMB. What was this gun doing here? And who was YMB?

Amber wasn't sure how long she had been standing there when she heard the sound of voices and doors opening and closing. She quickly replaced the gun, took one more glance around the room to make sure she hadn't disturbed anything, and left. As she reentered the clothing room, the children came bounding in, Daphne close behind them.

"Hi, we're back. Sorry we were so long. Bella forgot her painting, so we went back to get it," Daphne said.

"It's fine," Amber said. "The dresses are all so beautiful, I can't decide."

Bella frowned and whispered to her mother, "What's she doing here?"

"Sorry," Daphne said to Amber and then took Bella's hand. "We're finding a dress for Amber to borrow for the fund-raiser. Why don't you and Tallulah help her? Wouldn't that be fun?"

"All right," Tallulah said with a smile, but Bella looked at Amber with undisguised hostility, turned on her heel, and stalked out of the room.

"Don't let her upset you. She just doesn't know you well enough yet. It takes Bella a while to warm up."

Amber nodded. She better get used to me, she thought. I'm going to be around a long, long time.

FIFTEEN

Amber was pissed. It was December 24, and Rollins was staying open until two o'clock. What kind of idiots looked at houses on Christmas Eve? Why weren't they at home, wrapping their big-ticket presents and decorating their twelve-foot trees? But they probably didn't do all those things themselves, she reflected. That's what people like Amber were for.

Around noon Jenna stood in the doorway of Amber's office. "Hey, Amber, can I come in?"

"What is it?" Just what I need now, she thought peevishly.

Jenna walked in with a large wrapped package in her hand and placed it on Amber's desk. "Merry Christmas."

Amber glanced at the gift and then at Jenna. She hadn't even thought to buy a present for Jenna, and was discomfited by her gesture.

"Open it!" Jenna said.

Amber picked it up and tore off the paper, then took the lid off the box. Inside was a glorious assortment of Christmas cookies, each one more delicate and delicious-looking than the last. "Did you make these?"

Jenna clapped her hands together. "Yes, me and my mom do it every year. She's a spectacular baker. Do you like them?"

"I do. Thank you so much, Jenna. It was really nice of you." Amber paused a moment. "I'm so sorry, but I didn't get you anything."

"It's okay, Amber. I didn't make them so you'd get me a gift. It's just something my mom and I love doing. I give them to everyone in the office. I hope you enjoy them. Merry Christmas."

"Merry Christmas to you too."

※

Amber slept late on Christmas morning. When she awoke, the sky was blue, the sun was shining, and only an inch of snow had fallen. She took a long, hot shower and, after wrapping her terry-cloth robe around her, made a strong pot of coffee. She took her mug back into the bathroom and began to blow-dry her wet hair into soft waves—plain but classic. She applied a little blush, a dab of very discreet eye shadow, and some mascara. She stepped back from the mirror to examine the finished product. She looked youthful and fresh but without a trace of sexiness.

Daphne had asked her to come over around two o'clock, so after she finished a cup of yogurt, she sat down to read *The Odyssey*, which she'd borrowed from the library last week. Before she knew it, it was time to dress and gather everything up. Hanging on the closet door was the outfit she'd chosen—gray wool slacks and a white-and-gray turtleneck sweater. Small pearl studs in her ears—not real, of course, but who cared—a simple gold-colored bangle on her left wrist, and only her sapphire ring on her finger. She wanted to look pure and virginal. She took one last look in the full-length mirror, nodded approval at her image, and swept the presents into a large shopping bag.

Fifteen minutes later, she pulled into the open gates and parked her car in the circular driveway. Grabbing the bag of presents, she strode to the door and rang the bell. She saw Daphne coming down the hall, Bella right behind her.

"Welcome! Merry Christmas. I'm so glad you could come," Daphne said, flinging open the door and embracing her.

"Merry Christmas to you. Thank you so much for letting me share this day with you and your family," Amber said.

"Oh, it's our pleasure," Daphne said as she shut the door.

Bella was dancing around next to Daphne like a jumping bean.

"Hi, Bella. Merry Christmas." Amber gave her a big fake smile.

"Do you have a present for me?" Bella asked.

"Oh, Bella, you didn't even say hello. That was very rude," Daphne scolded.

"Of course I brought you a present. How could I not give one of my favorite girls a present?"

"Goody. Can I have it now?"

"Bella! Amber hasn't even taken her coat off." She gave her daughter a little shove. "Let me have your coat, Amber, and let's all go into the living room."

Bella looked as if she was going to protest but did as she was told.

Jackson and Tallulah looked up from the dollhouse they were furnishing as Amber, Daphne, and Bella entered the room. "Merry Christmas, Amber. Welcome," Jackson said with a warmth that indeed made her feel welcome.

"Thank you for inviting me. My whole family is back in Nebraska, and I would have been alone today. You don't know how much I appreciate it."

"No one should be alone on Christmas. We're glad you're here."

Amber thanked him again and then turned to Tallulah. "Hi, Tallulah. Merry Christmas. What a cool dollhouse."

"Would you like to come see it?" she asked.

These kids were like night and day. She didn't like children, but at least Tallulah had manners, not like the little animal who thought the sun and the moon revolved around her. Amber went and sat down next to Tallulah in front of the dollhouse. She had never seen anything like it, even in photographs. What she and her sisters would have given for a toy like this, with all the fabulous furnishings and dolls to go with it! It was enormous, with three stories, real wood floors, tile bathrooms, electric chandeliers that actually worked, and beautiful paintings on the walls. As she looked closer, she realized it was a replica of the actual house they lived in. It had to have been custom-made. What must that have cost?

"How about a glass of eggnog, Amber?" Daphne asked.

"I'd love one, thank you." She continued to watch as Tallulah carefully placed sofas, tables, and chairs in the house. Bella was on the other side of the room, busy with her iPad.

As she sat there, Amber took in all of the presents sitting open under the tree. They were piled high upon one another, tissue and ribbon mingled in the mix and spilled far into the room. She thought back to the miserly Christmases of her youth and felt keenly sad. She and her sisters had always gotten presents that were utilitarian, like underwear or socks, never a gift that was a luxury or even just a fun toy to play with. Even their stockings had been filled with useful or edible things, like the huge orange at the bottom to take up room, pencils and erasers for school, and sometimes a little puzzle that would become tiresome after one day.

The display in the Parrishes' living room left her speechless. She saw what looked like silk lingerie peeking out from one of the boxes and several smaller boxes that must have contained more jewelry for Daphne. Tallulah's presents were stacked in a neat pile. Bella's, on the other hand, were haphazardly spread out over a large part of the room, and once she put down the iPad, she went from one to another in quick order.

The one thing missing from this scene, Amber thought to herself, was Daphne's mother. Why wouldn't the girls' grandmother, a widow living only a car ride away, not be invited to spend Christmas with her only daughter and granddaughters? It seemed to her that the value placed on lavish presents was way above that of family.

Daphne came back into the living room with three glasses of eggnog and put them on the mahogany butler's table between the two large sofas.

"Amber, come sit with me," she said, and patted the cushion next to her. "Will you have some time off before the new year?"

"I do, actually. That's the advantage of working on the commercial side of real estate." She took a sip of eggnog. "Are you and Jackson going away over the holiday?"

"As a matter of fact, we leave on the twenty-eighth for St. Bart's. We usually leave the day after Christmas, but Meredith is having a surprise fiftieth birthday party for Rand the day after tomorrow, so we pushed the date."

"How nice," Amber said, seething inside. She would

be spending the rest of the holidays in her cheerless apartment trying to stay warm while they basked in the sun.

She rose from the sofa, hoping her expression hadn't betrayed her jealousy. "I've brought some presents. Let me get them," she said.

Bella jumped up from the floor and ran over. "Can I see my present? Can I, can I?"

Amber noticed Jackson smiling as he watched Bella jump around with anticipation.

"Here you go, Bella." Amber handed her the wrapped book set. Luckily, she had also gotten her a sparkly necklace and bracelet to match. Bella loved shiny things.

She ripped greedily into the paper, looked briefly at the books, and then opened the smaller box. "Ooh, pretty."

"How lovely. Let me help you put on the necklace," Daphne said.

"Here, Tallulah, this one is for you."

She slowly unwrapped the package. "Thank you, Amber. I love this book."

Bella, finished with the necklace and bracelet, began looking through the books Amber had given her and stomped her foot. "No fair. I already have this book in the series!"

Jackson swept her up in his arms and tried to console her. "It's okay, baby. We'll take it back to the store and get one you don't have, okay?"

"Okay," she whined and put her head on his shoulder.

Daphne retrieved a wrapped package from under the Christmas tree and handed it to Amber. "This is for you. I hope you like it."

Amber untied the red velvet ribbon and gently tore

off the black-and-gold paper. The small box held an elegant gold chain with a single pearl. It was beautiful. For a moment Amber was overwhelmed. She'd never owned something so lovely. "Oh, Daphne, thank you. I love it. Thank you so much."

"You're so welcome."

"I have something for you too."

Daphne unwrapped the box and then held up the bracelet. When she read Julie's name on the charm, her eyes filled with tears. She slipped the bangle onto her wrist. "What a wonderful gift. I'll wear it always. Thank you!"

Amber held her arm out in front of her. "I have one too. We'll have our sisters with us all the time."

"Yes." Daphne choked up as she pulled Amber to her, hugging her tightly.

"Let me see, Mommy." Bella ran to the sofa and flopped onto her mother's lap.

"You see, a pretty bracelet with Aunt Julie's name engraved on it. Isn't it lovely?"

"Uh-huh. Can I wear it?"

"Maybe later, okay?"

"No, now."

"Well, just for a few minutes, and then Mommy wants it back." Daphne took the bracelet off and handed it to her. Bella pushed her fist through it, but the bracelet was too big to stay on her tiny wrist, and she passed it back to Daphne. "Here, Mommy. I don't like it. You have it."

Amber was furious that this unpleasant child had interrupted what should have been a serious bonding moment, but she picked up the other gift and held it out to Daphne, "One more that I thought you might like."

"Amber. Really, this is too much. You've gone overboard."

No, Amber thought, overboard is what is surrounding us in this room full of lavish presents amid discarded ribbons and wrappings. "It's nothing, Daph. Just a little thing."

Daphne opened the box and pulled out the turtle wrapped in tissue paper. As she unwound the paper and the crystal turtle came into view, she lost her grip and dropped it onto the floor.

Amber reached down to pick it up, glad to see that it hadn't broken. "Good"—she placed it on the coffee table—"still intact."

Jackson strode over to them, scooped up the turtle to examine it, and turned it over in his hands. "Look, Daphne. You don't have one like this. What a nice addition to your collection." Jackson set the turtle down. "Great gift, Amber. Now how about we go to the dining room for some Christmas dinner?"

"Oh, wait," Amber said. "I have a gift for you too, Jackson."

"You really needn't have done this," he said as he took the package she handed to him. She watched as he removed the decorative paper and stared at the book in his hands. He looked up at Amber in surprise, and for the first time she felt he was really looking at her. "This is amazing. Where did you find it?"

"I've always been interested in the cave paintings. It's apparent that you and Daphne are discerning art lovers, so when I came across it on an antiquarian book site, I thought you might be interested in them too." She'd searched the antiquarian bookstores online and had finally found one she thought he'd appreciate—*The Lascaux Cave Paintings* by F. Windels. She'd gulped when she'd seen the $75 price, but decided to go ahead and make this her one splurge. The paintings were over

17,000 years old, and the French caves had been named a UNESCO World Heritage Site. She had hoped he would be impressed.

Amber smiled to herself. She had definitely scored with this one.

Daphne rose from the sofa. "Okay, everyone, time for dinner."

"Just a second. One more thing." Amber handed her the box of cookies.

"Goodness, Amber. These look delicious. Look, girls, don't they look yummy?"

"I want one." Bella stood on tiptoe and looked in the box.

"After dinner, sweetheart. Amber, this is so sweet of you."

"Well, Rollins closed early yesterday, so I enjoyed baking them last evening."

"What? You made these?"

"It's not a big deal. It was fun, really."

They walked into the dining room together, and suddenly Bella was by Amber's side. She took hold of Amber's hand and smiled up at her. "You're a really good cookie maker. I'm glad you came today."

Amber looked down at the little brat and smiled back. "Me too, Bella."

She felt a swell of satisfaction rise inside her.

SIXTEEN

Amber had a New Year plan that she hoped would ramp things up. Her panicked phone call had done the trick, and now Daphne waited for her as she walked to the door.

A worried look crossed Daphne's face as she ushered Amber in. They went directly to the sunroom.

"What's happened?" Daphne asked with concern.

"I've been trying to work this out on my own, but I just can't take it anymore. I have to talk to someone about it."

"Come, sit." Daphne took Amber by the hand and led her to the sofa. "Now, what is it?" She leaned forward, her eyes focused on Amber's face.

Amber took a deep breath. "I was fired today. But it's not my fault, and I can't do anything about it." She began to cry.

"What do you mean? Back up and tell me everything."

"It started a few months ago. It seemed whenever I went into his office, Mark—my boss, Mark Jansen—would find some reason to touch me. Brushing something off my shoulder or putting his hand on mine. At first I thought it was nothing. But then, last week, he asked if I would go with him on a client dinner."

Daphne was staring at her intently, and Amber wondered if she thought she was too homely to be hit on.

"Is it usual for you to attend client dinners?" Daphne asked.

Amber shrugged. "Not really. But at the time I was flattered. I figured he valued my opinion and wanted my input. And maybe, you know, there might be a promotion in the future. I drove myself and met him at Gilly's. He was already there, but he was alone. He told me the client had called and was running late. We had a couple of beers, and I started to feel funny." She stopped again, taking a deep breath. "The next thing I knew, his hand was on my knee and then moving up my thigh."

"What?" Daphne's voice exploded in anger.

Amber wrapped her arms around herself and rocked back and forth. "It was horrible, Daph. He slid closer to me in the booth and stuck his tongue in my mouth and started fondling my breast. I pushed him away and ran."

"That pig! He won't get away with this." Her eyes were blazing. "You have to report him."

Amber shook her head. "I can't."

"What do you mean, you can't?"

"The next day, he claimed *I* had hit on *him*. Told me no one would believe me."

"That's ridiculous. We're going to march right over there and talk to Human Resources."

"I'm so ashamed to tell you this, but at the office holiday party a few weeks ago, I had too many drinks and ended up kissing one of the agents. Everyone saw. They're going to believe him, believe that I'm loose."

"Still, that's not the same thing as your boss taking advantage of you."

"I can't make trouble. He offered me two months' pay if I leave quietly. My mother is still paying off Charlene's medical bills, and I send her money every month.

I can't afford not to take it. I'll find something else. I'm just so humiliated."

"He's paying you off to shut you up. I can help you with money until you find another job. I think you should fight it."

Now she was talking, but Amber had to up the ante and see the act through.

"And have every real estate firm in Connecticut afraid to hire me? No, I have to keep my mouth shut. Besides, maybe I *did* give him the wrong idea."

Daphne stood up, pacing. "Don't you dare blame yourself. Of course you didn't do anything wrong. That piece of garbage—he'll probably do it to someone else too."

"Believe me, I've thought about that too. But, Daphne, I have too many people depending on me. I can't report him and take the chance of not being able to get a job."

"Damn him. He knows he has you in a corner."

"He gave me a good reference. I just need to hit the pavement now." She smiled at Daphne. "And the upside is that my days are free, so I'm free to work full-time on the fund-raiser."

"You find the good in everything, don't you? I'll respect your wishes, even though I'd love to go over and let him have it. It's so noble of you, helping your mom." Amber watched Daphne's face as she grew quiet, seemingly contemplating something. Amber wondered if Daphne was thinking of her own mother and feeling guilty. "You know what? I'm going to talk to Jackson. There might be something for you at his company."

Amber made herself look surprised. "You really think so? That would be amazing. I'd be willing to do anything. Even starting as an administrative assistant or something like that would be great." This time her smile was genuine.

"Of course. They must have something for you. I'll speak to him tonight. In the meantime, let's do something to cheer you up. How about a little shopping?"

She must have noticed the look on Amber's face and realized that shopping was the last thing she could afford now that she was out of work. Honestly, how long had it been since this woman had lived in the real world?

"Sorry, you must think me terribly insensitive. What I meant was, I'd love to take you shopping—my treat. And before you argue, remember, I didn't grow up with all this." She swept her arm across the room. "I'm from a little town in New Hampshire. Probably not that different from where you were raised. When I first met Jackson and saw this house, I thought it was ridiculous, all the excess. Over time, you get used to it—maybe too used to it. And spending time with the women here, I must admit, I've lost myself a little."

Amber kept silent, curious to see where Daphne's little confession was going.

"You've helped me remember what's really important, why I came here to begin with—to help other families and to ease the suffering of those with this terrible disease. Jackson's made a lot of money, but I don't want that to build a wall between you and me. For the first time since I lost my sister, I actually feel close to someone. Please, let me do this."

Amber liked the sound of that. The best part was that she could make Daphne feel like Amber was the one being generous. She wondered if she could get her to spring for a whole new work wardrobe.

She widened her eyes. "Are you sure?"

"Very."

"Well, I suppose I could use a few things for my job search. Can you help me pick out a new interview outfit?"

"I would love to."

Amber suppressed a laugh. Daphne was so nice, she almost felt guilty. She had figured it would take some subtle hinting and footwork to nudge Daphne into suggesting a job at Parrish International, but Daphne had bitten before she'd even tasted the bait. And poor, happily married Mark Jansen, whose reputation she had besmirched, had never made anything resembling an advance toward her. She would call Mark this afternoon and resign. The engine was humming. It was now just a matter of driving the car.

SEVENTEEN

The big evening had finally arrived and, despite herself, Amber was as nervous as an actress on opening night. The fund-raiser began at eight, but Jackson and Daphne were picking her up at six so they could be there early and make sure everything was in order. Daphne had spared her the worry of how she would come up with the $250 for the ticket by purchasing the whole table and inviting her.

Amber poured herself a glass of chardonnay. The wine and music would relax her as she dressed. This was not her night to shine, but on the other hand, she didn't want to show up looking like some small-town hick. She went to the bed, where she'd laid out her clothes for the evening, picking up the black lace thong and slipping it over her slender hips. Nobody would see her underwear, but she would know how sexy she looked underneath that dress, and it would make a difference in the way she felt. Then the dress, the gorgeous Valentino she'd chosen from Daphne's closet. It was a simple, floor-length black number with a high neck, long sleeves, and draped back. Subtly sexy, but not in the least obvious. She pulled her hair back into a sleek chignon and applied minimal makeup. The only jewelry she wore was the pearl necklace Daphne had given her for Christmas and her small pearl earrings. She took one last look in the mirror and smiled at her reflection. Satisfied, she grabbed her handbag, a small silver clutch she'd picked up cheap at DSW. She caught a whiff of Daphne's perfume as she draped the silver silk shawl Daphne had lent her around her shoulders.

She stood at the door and, before turning out the light, looked back at the room she lived in. She tried to ignore her surroundings, but it was becoming more and more difficult as she was exposed to the way Daphne and her friends lived. She had graduated from the dreary home of her youth to this monklike existence. She sighed, banished the memories from her mind, and closed the door behind her.

At ten to six, she walked down the short path from the building to the street. At precisely six o'clock, the black Town Car pulled up. She wondered what her neighbors on her modest street were thinking as the chauffeur got out of the car and opened the door for her. She slid into the backseat across from Jackson and Daphne.

"Hello, Daphne, Jackson. Thanks so much for picking me up."

"Of course," Daphne said. "You look lovely. The dress looks like it was made for you. You should keep it."

Jackson looked at her a long moment and then turned away. He seemed slightly annoyed, Amber thought. Great, she'd been hoping to make a lasting impression on him, and she was, but for the completely wrong reason. She never should have agreed to borrow a dress from Daphne. What had she been thinking?

"I went to the hotel a little earlier to see the auction setup," Daphne said, smoothing over the awkwardness. "It looks beautiful. I think we'll do well."

"I think so too," Amber said. "The silent auction items are fabulous. Can't wait to see how much the villa in Santorini goes for."

The small talk continued as they drove to the hotel.

She noticed that Jackson held his wife's hand for the entire drive, and when they arrived, he gently and lovingly helped her out of the car, leaving the chauffeur to lend Amber a hand. He was nuts about Daphne, Amber thought, and felt her determination wilt a bit.

They were not the first to arrive. The decorating committee was already there, putting the finishing touches on the auction table and placing the floral centerpieces on the fifty tables covered in pink tablecloths and black napkins. The band was setting up at the far end of the room, and the bartenders were arranging their stock; they'd be busy tonight.

"Wow, Daphne, it looks amazing," Amber said.

Jackson put his arm around Daphne's waist and, pulling her to him, nuzzled her ear. "Great job, my darling. You've outdone yourself."

Amber looked at them, Jackson resembling a movie star in his black dinner jacket, and Daphne absolutely gorgeous in a strapless chiffon gown of emerald green that hugged every curve of her body.

"Thank you, sweetheart. That means so much to me." She looked at Jackson and then pulled away. "I really need to check on my volunteers and see if anyone needs anything. You'll excuse me, yes?" Daphne turned to Amber. "Stay here and keep Jackson company while I see if Meredith has everything she needs."

"Sure," Amber said.

Jackson continued to watch Daphne as she walked across the ballroom, seemingly unaware that Amber was even there.

"You must be very proud of your wife tonight," Amber said.

"What?" He tore his eyes away from Daphne.

"I said, you must be very proud of your wife tonight."

"She's the most beautiful and accomplished woman in this room," he said with pride.

"Daphne's been wonderful to me. My best friend, really."

Jackson frowned. "Your best friend?"

Amber sensed immediately that she'd made a mistake. "Well, not best friend exactly. More like a mentor. She's taught me so much."

She saw him relax a little. This was proving to be an exercise in futility. Obviously, nothing in her plan was going to move forward tonight.

"I think I'll go see if I can be of any help," she said to Jackson.

He gestured absently. "Right-o, good idea."

The evening was a smashing success. The bidding was frenzied, and the crowd drank and danced until midnight. Amber walked around the room, taking it all in—the designer dresses and opulent jewels, the snippets of gossip and laughter from clustered groups of women, the men in black tie loudly discussing the latest S&P 500 losing streak. The world of the rich and mighty, mingling and toasting each other, smug and confident in their little one-percent corner of the world.

Despite being seated at Daphne's table, though, Amber felt as out of place here as she had at the dry cleaner's. She wanted to belong somewhere, to have people look up to her, fawn over her the way they did Daphne. She was tired of being the girl no one noticed or cared about.

But tonight was not turning out the way she'd hoped. Jackson never took his eyes off Daphne. He was always reaching for her hand or running his hand up and down her back. For the first time, Amber was discouraged, wondering if her plan was unworkable, if the prize was out of reach.

She watched the dancers from her seat, some of the May-December couples looking comically unsuited to one another. Something flashed in the corner of her eye, making Amber turn to see a photographer. She turned her head quickly as the flashing continued, praying her image had not been caught on camera.

Jackson and Daphne had been on the dance floor a good portion of the evening, and now they came walking back to the table. She saw Daphne give Jackson a discreet push, and he stood in front of Amber. "Would you care to dance?" he asked.

Amber looked at Daphne, who smiled and nodded at her. "I'd love to." She rose and took Jackson's hand as he led her to the dance floor.

She relaxed into Jackson's strong arms, inhaling the clean, masculine smell of him, enjoying the feel of his arms around her and his body against hers. She closed her eyes and pretended he belonged to her, that she was the envy of every woman in the room. The high lasted even though the dance ended. He didn't ask her again, but that one dance was enough to get her through the rest of the evening. At twelve thirty, Amber strode to the long table where volunteers sat waiting to help winning bidders check out. She sat down at the credit card machine next to Meredith.

"We did well tonight," Meredith said.

"Yes, it was a great success. Of course, you were a big part of that." Amber was laying it on thick, but Meredith wasn't biting.

"Oh please, it was a group effort. Everyone worked equally," she said stiffly.

Amber had nothing to say in response. This bitch would never accept her, so why should she even try? They continued to work side by side in silence as people checked out. As they were finishing up, Meredith turned to Amber. "Daphne tells me you're from Nebraska."

"I am."

"I've never been there. What's it like?" she said, with not one iota of curiosity in her voice.

Amber thought for a moment. "I come from a small town. They're pretty much all the same."

"Mm. I suppose they are. What town exactly?"

"Eustis. You've probably never heard of it."

Before Meredith could continue her interrogation, Daphne appeared in front of them.

"You're all amazing," she said to the volunteers at the table. "Thank you so much for this phenomenal night. Now go home and get some much-needed rest. I love all of you." She looked at Amber. "Are you ready to go?"

"Yes, we're all finished. I'll just get my things."

On the drive home, Jackson and Daphne looked like lovebirds, his hand firmly on her thigh.

"Your speech was good." Jackson squeezed her leg.

Daphne looked surprised. "Thank you."

"I wish you had let me look it over."

"You were so busy. I didn't want to bother you."

He stroked her leg. "I'm never too busy to help you, darling."

Daphne leaned her head against his shoulder and closed her eyes.

Amber grew disheartened as she watched their interaction. It was obvious to her that Jackson took a loving interest in every aspect of Daphne's life. Daphne had been easy pickings, but Jackson was going to be a different matter entirely. He was going to require all of Amber's cunning and ingenuity.

EIGHTEEN

It had been a month since the fund-raiser, but Amber was still feeling off balance after seeing Jackson's devotion to Daphne that night. Her connection to Daphne was just getting stronger, though. She was on her way to Tallulah's eleventh birthday party, having become fully ensconced in Daphne's life and invited to almost all family events. Daphne was so trusting of her that it almost made her feel bad . . . almost. Amber had gotten Tallulah a book on the life of Edgar Allan Poe and had thought it wise to also pick up a little something for Bella. She was beginning to understand the workings of the little brat's mind and figured watching Tallulah open a ton of gifts would not be at the top of Bella's list of fun things to do.

When she entered the playroom, the children were seated in a big circle as two women unloaded cages with exotic birds and small zoo animals. Amber walked to where Daphne and an older woman stood watching the fun.

"Amber, welcome. Come meet my mother." Daphne clasped Amber's hand in hers. "Mom, this is my friend Amber."

The woman stretched her arm out for a handshake. "I'm pleased to meet you, Amber. I'm Ruth."

"Nice to meet you," Amber replied, juggling the presents she'd brought so that she could shake Ruth's hand.

"My goodness," Daphne said. "What have you got there?"

"Oh, just a few presents."

"Why don't you put them in with the others in the conservatory? The zoo show will start soon. You don't want to miss that," Daphne said.

When Amber entered the conservatory, she was startled once again by the excess. Not that she wouldn't have wanted the same kind of party as a kid, but she hadn't even known anything like this existed when she was little. The presents were piled high, and a large table had been moved into the room for the children's lunch. Each place was carefully set with colorful plates and napkins, and beautifully wrapped goodie bags were perched at each spot. It was completely kid-friendly and sublimely elegant at the same time. She put her gifts down and left the room. As she walked back to the party room, she saw Jackson coming down the hall. He gave her a charming smile.

"Hi there. So glad you could join us today," he said with enthusiasm.

"Um, thank you. I'm glad to be here," she stuttered.

He gave her another wide smile and held the playroom door for her.

They stood together and watched as the handlers brought out one animal after another and explained a little about them, Jackson with a drink in hand. Amber had difficulty keeping her eyes from straying to him. She wondered how long it would take to get him into bed. The thought that she could have this man of power and wealth under her spell exhilarated her. She knew how to please a man and suspected that after over a decade of marriage, the sex between him and Daphne had to be pretty boring and stale. Amber could picture the things she could do to make him want her if given half the chance. She resolved to take her time and carefully stick to her plan. No sense in rushing and messing things up like before.

When the show ended, the adults tried to calm the children as they tromped into the conservatory for lunch. It was noisy and riotous, with raucous laughter and high-pitched voices. Amber felt like she was going to scream, and she noticed that Jackson wasn't in the room where everyone was eating.

Finally, Margarita brought out the huge birthday cake covered in chocolate icing and topped with eleven white candles in the shape of ballerinas. Amber noticed a small chunk missing from one side of the cake.

"Okay," Daphne said in a loud voice. "Time to sing 'Happy Birthday,' and then Tallulah can open her presents."

Amber could see the storm clouds gathering behind Bella's eyes as the children and adults sang to her sister. Her mouth was set in a straight line, and her arms were crossed in front of her. She was having none of it.

The minute the singing stopped and Tallulah had blown out the candles, Daphne began handing her the presents. At the table, the children were happy and occupied eating cake as Tallulah unwrapped one after another and thanked the giver. After the seventh one, Bella's voice rang out. "It's not fair. Tallulah's getting all the presents. Where's mine?"

This was the moment Amber had been waiting for. "Hey, Bella. I brought a present for Tallulah, but I brought one for you too. I'll give Tallulah hers, and here's the one for you. I hope you like it."

Daphne smiled at her, and Ruth looked at her with an expression Amber couldn't quite read. Amber noticed that Jackson had just come back into the room, and she hoped he had seen the exchange. Bella ripped off the wrapping paper and opened the box. She held up the pink sweater with a white faux-fur collar and the small pink handbag with its shiny handle and smiled. She ran to Amber and flung her arms around her waist. "I love you, Amber. You're my best friend ever."

Everyone laughed at this show of affection, but Amber noticed that Ruth didn't seem as amused as the rest of the guests. Tallulah was nearing the end of the presents, the last one a small box from Sabine. "Ooh, Sabine, *je suis très heureuse. Merci.*" Tallulah held up a gold chain with a slender cross.

"*De rien,*" Sabine said.

The local glitterati soon began arriving to pick up their little rich kids, who had once again been treated to splendiferous entertainment, yummy food, and expensive swag bags. No wonder they all grew up with a sense of entitlement. They knew nothing else.

After all the guests had gone, Surrey, the other nanny, gathered up the presents.

"Would you take the gifts upstairs with the girls? If you bathe them and get them into pajamas, we'll have a light dinner around six," Daphne instructed her.

Jackson poured himself another scotch. "Can I get anyone a drink?"

"I'll have a glass of wine, sweetheart," Daphne said. "Mom, would you like anything?"

"I'll have a club soda."

Jackson looked at Amber. "And you?"

"May I have a glass of wine too?"

Jackson laughed. "You may have anything you want."

That's what I'm hoping, Amber thought, but she simply smiled back at him.

"Daphne, have you showed Amber the photos from the fund-raiser?" Ruth said, then looked at Amber. "There were some very good ones in the *Bishops Harbor Times*. You look very pretty in one of them."

Amber's heart stopped. Photos? In a newspaper? She'd been so careful to avoid the photographer that night. When had he gotten a picture of her? Daphne brought the newspaper in and handed it to her. She picked it up with trembling hands and scanned the pictures. There she was, large as life, completely recognizable. Her name wasn't there, not that it would have mattered—her face was the problem. She just had to assume that this small-town newspaper with its limited range would not be seen farther afield.

"Would you excuse me?" She needed to get out of that room and calm her nerves. She closed the bathroom door, put the lid down on the toilet seat, and sat with her head in her hands. How could she have been so careless? After a while, her breathing settled and she promised herself she would be more vigilant in the future. She splashed some water on her face, stood up straight, and slowly opened the door. She could hear Ruth and Daphne as she walked back to the conservatory.

"Mom, you don't understand. I have my hands full here."

"You're right, Daphne, I don't understand. You used to love singing in the church choir. It seems to me you don't do any of the things you used to love. You've let all this money go to your head. If you know what's good for you, you'll remember your roots and come down off your high horse."

"That's completely unfair. You don't know what you're talking about."

"I know what I see—two nannies, for heaven's sake. And one that just speaks French. Really! A daughter who's spoiled rotten that you can't control. The club, all your lessons. For goodness sake, I practically have to make an appointment to see my granddaughters. What's happened to you?"

"That's enough, Mother."

For the first time, Amber heard real fury in Daphne's voice. And then the sound of the nanny and the girls coming down the stairs. They all entered the conservatory at the same time, and the conversation between mother and daughter abruptly ended.

Bella ran to Daphne, putting her head on her mother's lap. Her cries were muted, and then she looked up and said, "Tallulah got so many presents, and I only got two. It's not fair."

Ruth leaned over and stroked Bella's face. "Bella, darling, it's Tallulah's birthday. When it's your birthday, you'll get all the presents. Right?"

Bella jerked away from her grandmother's hand. "No. You're ugly."

"Bella!" Daphne seemed horrified.

Jackson suddenly appeared, strode over to the sofa, and picked Bella up. She wiggled and squirmed, but he held her tightly and she finally was still. He put her down on the other side of the room and, kneeling so they were eye level, spoke quietly to her. After a few minutes, they came back together, and Bella stood before her grandmother.

"I'm very sorry, Grandmamma," she said, and bowed her head.

Ruth gave Daphne a triumphant look and took Bella's

hand. "I forgive you, Bella. But you mustn't say things like that in the future."

Bella looked at her father and got only a stern look in return. "Yes, Grandmamma."

Margarita peered into the room and announced that dinner was ready. Jackson took Ruth's arm, and the two of them marched into the dining room together, Bella and Tallulah right behind them. As Daphne rose, Amber gave her a pat on the shoulder.

"It's been a long day. Bella's just overtired. Don't let them all get to you," she said to her.

"Sometimes that's really hard," Daphne said.

"You're a wonderful mom. Don't let anyone tell you that you're not."

"Thanks, Amber. You're such a good friend."

In a way, Daphne was a wonderful mother. She gave her kids everything, especially love and affection. She was certainly a better mother than Amber's, who'd made it clear every day of her life that her kids were a loathsome burden.

"Don't leave yet. Stay and have dinner with us," Daphne said.

Amber wasn't sure that dinner with an exhausted, exasperated Bella and a disapproving grandmother was going to further her plans in any way. "I'd love to, Daph, but I have tons of laundry and cleaning to do. Thanks for asking, though."

"Oh, all right," Daphne said, linking her arm in Amber's. "At least come to the dining room and say good night to everyone."

She obediently followed Daphne into the room where the family was all seated and being served by Margarita.

"Good night, all," Amber said, waving her hand. "It was a wonderful party."

A chorus of farewells came from the group, and then Jackson's smooth voice rang out. "Good night, Amber. See you tomorrow at the office."

NINETEEN

Amber dressed carefully for her first day at Parrish International. Her hair was pulled back into a ponytail, and she wore plain gold-colored hoop earrings and minimal makeup. Getting up at four o'clock to catch the 5:30 train was murder, but she had to make a good impression. How anyone could stand doing this on a long-term basis was beyond her. Hopefully, it would only be temporary.

The glass tower that housed Jackson's company was enormous, and she marveled that he owned it. It must have cost a fortune to own a building like this in Manhattan. The lobby was empty except for security, and she nodded as she scanned her identity badge and was green-lighted through the turnstile. When she reached the thirtieth floor, she was surprised to see a few people already in their offices. She'd have to get an even earlier train tomorrow. Her tiny cubicle was outside her boss's office. She would be reporting to his first assistant, Mrs. Battley, or Mrs. Battle-Ax as Amber thought of her after their meeting last week at orientation. The Battle-Ax was somewhere between sixty-five and seventy-five with steel-wool-gray hair, thick glasses, and thin lips. She was the very definition of no-nonsense, and Amber hated her on sight. She had made it clear that she wasn't pleased that Amber had been thrust upon her. It was going to be a challenge getting the old bird to like her.

"Good morning, Mrs. Battley. I'm going to get some coffee. Would you like some?"

She didn't look up from her laptop. "No. I've already had my one cup. I have some filing for you, so please see me when you've gotten yours." Amber cast a discreet glance in the direction of Jackson's corner office. His door was closed, but she could see movement through the slatted blinds covering one glass wall.

"Do you need something?" Battley's gravelly voice interrupted her thoughts.

"Sorry, no. My coffee can wait. I'll take the filing now."

"Here you are," she said, handing Amber a pile of papers. "And here's a list of new clients to add to the database. I've left instructions on your desk on how to do so. You'll also need to add their websites and all social media channels to their profiles."

Amber took the folder and returned to her tiny cube. She'd traded in her office with a window view for this claustrophobic cube, but at least now her plan was progressing. The hours passed as she immersed herself in her work, determined to be the most efficient assistant Old Battle-Ax had ever had. She'd brought a bag lunch and ate at her desk, working without a break. At six o'clock, Battley was standing at her cube with her coat on.

"I didn't realize you were still here, Amber. You can leave at five, you know."

She stood up and gathered her things. "I wanted to finish up. I like to come in to a clean desk in the morning."

This actually elicited a smile from the older woman. "Quite right. I've always felt the same way."

She turned to leave, but Amber called out, "I'll walk down with you."

They walked in silence to the elevator bank, and when they got on, Amber gave her a shy smile.

"I want to thank you for giving me this chance. You don't know how much it means to me."

Battley raised her eyebrows. "Don't thank me. I had nothing to do with it."

"Mrs. Parrish told me how valuable your opinion is to Mr. Parrish," Amber said. "She made it quite clear that I was here on a probationary basis. If you don't find me up to snuff, then I'll have to look elsewhere."

Amber could tell that the woman's pride made her believe this bullshit. Battley stood a little straighter. "We shall see, then."

Yes, we shall, Amber thought.

After a month, she'd still had no direct contact with Jackson, but Old Battle-Ax had begun to rely on her more and more. Amber would arrive at least fifteen minutes before her, so that she could bring Battley her morning coffee with a little something extra in it. Amber had a three-month supply of Elavil from her internist. She had told him that she was having panic attacks, and he'd recommended it. He did mention some possible side effects: short-term memory loss and confusion. She'd started dosing low, and hoped that Battley's predilection for flavored creamer obscured any trace of the pills in her coffee.

Battley arrived that morning, seemingly more confused than normal. Amber noticed that her pace had become slower and that she paused often, looking around her desk as if unsure of what to do next.

When Battley got up to go to the bathroom, Amber

quickly went into her office and took the woman's keys from her purse and moved them. She then refiled a folder that was sitting on her desk. Battley came back to her office and searched for the missing file, panic in her eyes. At the end of the day, Battley opened her purse and looked inside. Amber watched as she moved the contents around and finally poured everything out on her desk. No keys. She looked stricken. "Amber," she called. "Have you seen my keys?"

Amber hurried into Battley's office. "No, I haven't. Aren't they in your handbag?"

"No," she said, almost in tears.

"Here," Amber said, taking the purse from the desk. "Let me look." She pretended to root around. "Hmm. You're right. Not here." She stood a moment as if thinking. "Have you looked in your drawers?"

"Of course not. I never take them from my pocketbook. I would never put them in my desk," she insisted.

"Why don't we look, just in case."

"Ridiculous," Battley huffed, but opened the drawer. "See, they're not there."

Amber leaned over to look and then glanced past them, at the wastebasket next to the file cabinet. She pulled it toward her.

"They're in the trash can." Amber reached in and pulled them out, handing them to Battley.

Battley stood still, staring at the ring of keys in her hand as she swallowed hard. It was apparent that the woman was distraught, but all she said was good night before turning and leaving without another word. Amber smiled as she watched her walk away.

A few days later Amber rearranged the cards in Battley's Rolodex—she must have been the last person on earth to still have one. As the weeks wore on, the stress was having the intended effect—a haunted look of constant worry was in the older woman's eyes. Amber felt a little bad about what she was doing, but the woman really needed to retire. Her time would have been much better spent with her grandkids. She'd told Amber she had five and complained that she didn't get to see them enough. Now she'd get to be with them more, and Jackson would probably give her a good retirement package—especially if he believed she had dementia. Amber was doing her a favor, really.

And didn't Jackson deserve someone more hip and this-century helping him out? He was probably keeping her on out of loyalty. Amber was doing them both a favor, when she thought about it. This morning, she'd printed off a paper with gibberish and slipped it in between the pages of a report Battley had just finished. She knew the woman would think she'd really lost it when she saw it, and of course, she'd never mention it to anyone. Amber figured it would only take another few weeks. Between her eroding self-confidence and the mistakes she was soon to make, arousing Jackson's suspicions, Amber would be sitting pretty in Battley's office in no time.

TWENTY

It took much longer than Amber anticipated, but after three months, it had all become too much for Battley, and she handed in her resignation. Amber was now filling in while Jackson began the search for a new head assistant. She was still in her tiny cubicle, while Battley's office remained vacant, and while it bothered Amber that he hadn't yet considered letting her step in permanently, she was confident he would soon find her indispensable. She had already spent the past seven nights learning everything she could about his newest clients from Tokyo—it was amazing what people put on their social media profiles. Even if they did have the smarts to set up their privacy settings properly, what they didn't realize was that every photo they were tagged in linked to someone else's page, and not everyone was as diligent. Between using her background-check software and trolling all the social sites, she had a comprehensive picture of each of them, including their disgusting predilections. She had also conducted a thorough search of their recent business deals to get an idea of their negotiating skills and any tricks they might have up their sleeves.

Jackson summoned her to his office, and she gathered the report on the client. He was leaning back in his black leather chair, reading something on his iPhone. His jacket was off and his shirtsleeves rolled up, showing off his tanned forearms. The Parrishes had just returned from Antibes. She figured they were able to practice the French language they seemed to worship. He didn't look up as she entered the office.

"I'm slammed today, but I forgot Bella's play at camp is this afternoon. I have to duck out after lunch. Move my appointments."

What must it be like to have a powerful father who cared enough about you to take time from his busy schedule to come to your play? And the little brat appreciated nothing. "Of course."

"Did you make reservations at Catch for Tanaka and his team tomorrow?"

"Actually, no."

His head snapped up. She had his full attention. "What?"

"I made them at Del Posto. Tanaka loves Italian, and he's allergic to shellfish."

He looked at her with interest. "Really? How do you know that?"

She handed him her report. "I took the liberty of doing some research. On my own time, of course," she added quickly. "I thought it would be helpful. With social media it's not that hard to find things out."

He smiled widely, giving her a glimpse of his perfect teeth, and reached out for the report. After thumbing through it, he looked up again. "Amber, I'm very impressed. Great initiative. This is fantastic."

She beamed. She bet Battley didn't even know how to use Facebook.

She stood up. "If there's nothing else, I'll go take care of sorting your appointments."

"Thanks," he mumbled, immersed in the report again.

She was making progress with him, although she was a little disappointed that he didn't seem to notice how good her legs looked in the short skirt and high heels she'd worn that day. He was that rare commodity—a man who only had eyes for his wife. Daphne, on the other hand, seemed complacent, like she took it for granted that he worshipped her. It irritated Amber. It was obvious to her that Daphne wasn't as passionate about Jackson as he was about her, and that she really didn't deserve him.

She opened up Jackson's calendar on her computer and began contacting his afternoon appointments to reschedule. As she was about to make another call, he appeared.

"Amber, why don't you sit in Mrs. Battley's office until we find her replacement? It'll be more convenient to have you right outside. Give Facilities a call; they can move your things."

"Thank you, I will."

She watched him as he strode away, his Brioni suit looking as though it had been hand-crafted by the gods. She wondered what it would be like to wear a garment that cost more than some people made in a year.

She picked up her phone and texted Daphne.

Are you free tomorrow? Would love to meet for a drink.

Her text tone sounded. **Sure. I'll have Tommy pick you up and we can go to Sparta's. Seven thirty good?**

Great! See you tomorrow.

If Daphne was having Tommy drive them, it meant she was in the mood to drink, which was perfect because Amber was ready to get her to spill her guts. She had discovered that after one martini Daphne became much more relaxed, making it easy to pour a few more down her throat.

TWENTY-ONE

The Parrish Town Car was waiting outside her apartment right on time. She was about to call out a hello to Daphne when she realized the backseat was empty.

"Where's Mrs. Parrish?" she asked Tommy as he opened the door for her.

"Mr. Parrish came home unexpectedly. She asked me to collect you and drop you at Sparta's, then swing around for her."

She felt annoyance choke out her good mood. Why hadn't Daphne just called and asked if they could move the time back? She felt like an appointment being handled. And why should it matter that Jackson came home? Why didn't Daphne just tell him she already had plans? Where was her backbone?

When she got to the bar, she chose a cozy table in the corner and ordered the 2007 Sassicaia. It was $210, but Daphne would be picking up the bill, and it served her right for making Amber wait. She took a sip of the red delight and savored the opulent flavor. It was amazing.

She looked around as the lounge began to fill and wondered if any of Daphne's so-called friends would be coming in tonight. She hoped not—she wanted Daphne all to herself.

Daphne finally arrived, looking harried and, frankly, a little unkempt. Her hair was a bit frizzy and her makeup splotchy.

"I'm sorry, Amber. Just as I was leaving, Jackson

came in, and . . ." She threw her hands up. "Not even worth getting into. I need a drink." She glanced at the bottle, and a little frown furrowed her brow.

"I hope you don't mind that I ordered a bottle. I forgot my reading glasses and couldn't really see that well, so I asked the waiter for a recommendation."

Daphne started to say something and then seemed to think better of it. "It's fine."

A glass appeared, and she poured herself a generous serving. "Mmm. Delish." She took a deep breath. "So, how are things going at Parrish International? Jackson tells me you're proving to be quite valuable."

Amber studied her for any traces of suspicion or jealousy but saw none. Daphne looked genuinely happy for her, but there was also a touch of concern in her face.

"Is everyone treating you well? No problems, right?"

Amber was surprised by the question. "No, none at all. I'm loving it. Thank you so much for recommending me. It's so different from Rollins. And everyone is really nice. So, what was the big emergency?"

"What?"

"Jackson coming home—what did he need that disrupted your plans?"

"Nothing. He just wanted a few minutes with me before I went out."

Amber arched an eyebrow. "A few minutes for what?"

Daphne turned red.

"Oh, *that*. He can't seem to get enough of you. That's pretty amazing. You've been married, what, nine years?"

"Twelve."

Amber could tell she was making Daphne uncomfortable, so she switched tactics. She leaned in and lowered her voice. "Consider yourself lucky. One of the reasons I left home was because of my boyfriend, Marco."

"What do you mean?"

"I was crazy about him. We'd been dating since high school. He was the only one I'd ever been with, so I didn't know."

Now Daphne was bending closer. "Didn't know what?"

She squirmed and made herself look embarrassed. "That it wasn't normal. You know. That guys should sort of be . . . ready. I had to do things just to help him be able to make love to me. He told me I wasn't pretty enough to get him excited without some help." She was laying it on pretty thick, but it seemed like Daphne believed it.

"The last straw was when he asked me to bring another man into the bedroom."

"What?" Daphne's mouth fell open.

"Yeah. Turned out he was gay. Didn't want to admit it or something. You know how those small towns can be."

"Have you dated anyone since?"

"A few guys here and there, but no one serious. Truthfully, I'm a little nervous about sleeping with someone again. What if I find out that it really was me?"

Daphne shook her head. "That's crazy, Amber. His sexual orientation had nothing to do with you. And you're lovely. When you find the right man, you'll know it."

"Is that how you felt when you found Jackson?"

Daphne paused a moment, taking a sip of her wine. "Well . . . I guess Jackson swept me off my feet. My father became ill after we began dating, and Jackson was my rock. After that, things moved really quickly, and before I knew it, we were married. I never expected it. He dated sophisticated and accomplished women. I wasn't quite sure what he saw in me."

"Come on, Daph, you're gorgeous."

"That's sweet, but so were they. And they were wealthy and worldly. I was just a girl from a small town. I didn't know anything about his world."

"So what do you think it was that made you special?"

Daphne refilled her wineglass and took a long swallow. "I think he liked having a blank canvas. I was young, only twenty-six, and he was ten years older. I was so focused on building Julie's Smile, I wasn't taken in by him. He told me later that he never knew whether the women he went out with wanted him or his money."

Amber found that hard to believe. Even if he'd been dead broke, he was still gorgeous, brilliant, and charming. "How did he know you didn't care about his money?"

"I actually tried to cool things off. He didn't really turn my head. But then, he was so wonderful to my family, and they all encouraged me not to let him get away."

"See, you *are* lucky. Look how wonderful it turned out. You have such a great life."

Daphne smiled. "Nobody's life is perfect, Amber."

"It sure seems it. It looks as close to perfect as you can pretty well get."

"I'm very fortunate. I have two healthy children. That's something I never take for granted."

Amber wanted to keep things focused on marriage. "Yes, of course. But your relationship seems like a fairy tale from the outside. Jackson looks at you like he worships you."

"He's very attentive. I suppose sometimes I just need a little breathing room. It can feel confining, having to fit into the mold of the CEO's wife. He has high expectations. Sometimes I'd like to just sit around and watch *House of Cards* instead of going to another charity function or business event."

Oh, boohoo, Amber thought. It must be so hard to have to dress up in designer gowns and drink expensive wine and munch on caviar. She mustered a sympathetic look. "I can see that. I would feel so out of place having to do all that. But you make it look so easy. Did it take you long to fit in?"

"The first couple of years were rough. But Meredith came to my rescue. She helped me navigate the treacherous social circles here in Bishops Harbor." She laughed. "Once you have Meredith on your side, everyone falls into line. She's been the foundation's staunchest supporter—until you, that is."

"You must have felt very lucky. Sort of like I feel having you."

"Exactly."

The bottle was empty, and Amber was about to suggest they order another when Daphne's phone lit up with a text.

She scanned it, then looked at Amber apologetically.

"It's Bella. She's had a nightmare. I need to go home."

That little brat. Even when she wasn't present, she was messing up Amber's plans.

"Oh, poor darling. Does that happen often?"

Daphne shook her head. "Not too often. Sorry to have to cut our evening short. If you don't mind, I'll have Tommy take me right away, then drop you home."

"Of course. Give her a kiss from Aunt Amber," Amber said, throwing it out there. Why not elevate her status?

Daphne squeezed her hand as they walked out to the waiting car. "I like that. I will."

Although she was disappointed that she wouldn't get another glass of that divine wine, she'd gotten some of what she'd wanted: the beginning of a profile of Jackson's perfect woman. She would build it, tidbit by tidbit, until she was an exact replica of what he found irresistible.

Only she would be a newer, younger version.

TWENTY-TWO

Amber inhaled the intoxicating smell of the ocean. It was a perfectly gorgeous Sunday morning, and she and Daphne had already been out on the water for the last hour. Jackson was in Brussels on business, and Daphne had invited Amber to spend the weekend. She had been slightly dubious when Daphne suggested they go kayaking, as she'd never done it before and wasn't sure she wanted her first foray to be on the deep waters of Long Island Sound. But she'd had nothing to worry about. The water was still as glass when they started out, and within a half hour, Amber was feeling sure and confident. They stayed close to the shore at first, and Amber marveled at the peacefulness of the early-morning quiet, the only sounds birdsong and the lapping of water against their paddles. Everything was still, so wonderfully devoid of the bustle and noise of everyday life. They glided along beside each other, both silent and content.

"Shall we go out a little farther?" Daphne broke the silence.

"I guess so. Is it safe?"

"Perfectly."

Amber worked to keep up with Daphne's sure strokes, breathing hard as she exerted herself. She was impressed with Daphne's stamina. As they moved farther from shore, the water took on an entirely different aura. The first time a boat passed them, she thought she would be swamped by its wake, but the second time it happened, she got an adrenaline rush riding the small swells.

"I love this, Daph. I'm so glad you made me come."

"I knew you'd like it. I'm glad. Now I'll have a partner. Jackson doesn't really enjoy kayaking. He'd rather be on the boat."

Well, Amber thought, the boat would be good too. She hadn't been on his Hatteras yet, but she knew it wouldn't be long before she got an invitation.

"Don't you like the boat?" Amber asked.

"Oh sure, I like it, but it's a completely different experience. It needed some work before going back into the water. Should be sometime in late June. We'll all go out together. Then you can make your own judgment."

"What's the name of it?"

"*Bellatada*," Daphne answered, her smile holding a touch of embarrassment.

Amber thought for a minute. "Oh, I get it. The beginning of each of your names. Jackson's three girls."

"A little silly, I guess."

"Not at all. I think it's sweet." Inwardly she was choking on her words.

"Shall we head back? It's almost ten." Daphne looked at her watch and adjusted her visor.

It didn't take long to reach the beach in front of the house and deposit the kayaks. As they walked up the path to the house, the sounds of laughter and girlish squeals reached them. Bella and Tallulah were splashing around in the swimming pool with their father.

Amber turned to Daphne. "I thought Jackson was coming back tonight."

"Me too," Daphne said and picked up her pace.

He looked up and ran a hand through his wet hair. "Hello, you two. Been out kayaking?"

"We have. When did you get home? I'm sorry I wasn't here, but I thought you were coming in tonight," Daphne said, sounding strained.

"We finished up last night, so I decided to fly home this morning." Bella was holding on to his back and splashing with her feet. He turned to grab her, and she squealed with delight as he tossed her back into the water. She pushed up through the water and swam to him. "More, Daddy."

But he began walking to the shallow end of the pool, wiping the water from his face. "That's all, sweetie. Time to take a break."

For once there was no obnoxious complaining from Bella. It had to have been a first.

Jackson handed towels to the girls and started drying himself with his own. It was impossible not to look at his body, wet and glistening, as he stepped closer to Daphne and kissed her. "It's good to be home," he said.

Daphne had asked Amber to spend the day, but now that Jackson was home, Amber knew she had to deliver the obligatory I-don't-want-to-be-in-the-way speech. "I had a great time kayaking, Daph. Thanks a bunch. I'm going to let you have your family time now."

"What do you mean? You can't leave yet."

"I really should. I'm sure Jackson would like to be alone with you and the girls."

"Nonsense. You know how he feels about you. You're like family. Come on. We'll have fun."

"Absolutely," Jackson said. "You're more than welcome to stay."

"Are you sure?"

"Of course," Daphne said. "Let's go inside and make lunch. Margarita is off this weekend, so we're the cooks."

They worked together in the kitchen, but when they finished loading the tortillas with refried beans, veggies, and cheese, they didn't end up with neat and beautiful burritos like Margarita's.

"They look pretty sad, don't they?" Daphne said with a laugh.

"What the heck. They'll taste good, anyway." Amber washed her hands and tore off a section of paper toweling while Daphne reached into a cabinet and pulled out two trays. "Here we go. I think everything will fit. We'll eat outside by the pool."

"Oooh, yummy," Bella called as they carried the food out.

They sat, the five of them, under the large umbrella, the reflection of the sun on the turquoise pool water making shimmery diamonds and triangles. A slight breeze sliced through the warmth—a perfect late-spring day. Amber closed her eyes a moment, pretending this all belonged to her. If anything, the last few weeks had shown her that Daphne now considered Amber her closest friend and confidante. Last night, after the girls had gone to bed, she and Daphne had sat at the kitchen table and talked late into the night. Daphne had told her all about her childhood, how much her parents had tried to make their lives seem completely normal despite the illness that crouched in the background, ready to pounce without warning at any moment.

"Mom and Dad encouraged Julie to do everything healthy kids can. They gave her the freedom to live her life the way she wanted, to try all the things she wanted to," Daphne had said.

At first, when Daphne talked about all the hospital stays, the hacking coughs that brought up gloppy mucus, the runny bowels and trouble digesting food, Amber had begun to feel sympathy. But when she compared her own childhood to Daphne's, and even Julie's, her resentment returned. At least Julie had grown up in a nice house with money and parents who cared about her. Okay, she was sick and then she died. So what? A lot of people were sick. A lot of people died. Was that a reason to make them saints? How about Amber and what she'd gone through? Didn't she deserve a little sympathy too?

She looked around the table at all of them. Bella, lazing back in her chair and swinging her legs back and forth, taking distracted bites out of her burrito without a care in the world, the pampered and indulged child of wealth. Tallulah, sitting up straight and concentrating on the lunch before her. Daphne, sun-kissed and casually beautiful, making sure her brood had refills and napkins and anything else they needed. And Jackson, the master of it all, sitting like a knighted lord watching over his vast domain and faultless family. Suddenly the terrible emptiness inside Amber was a physical gnawing, as if the very life were being squeezed from her. This was no time to go soft. She would win this time.

TWENTY-THREE

Things were so busy at work that Amber hadn't seen Daphne in two weeks, since their kayaking day. But Jackson was out of town again, so she'd called Daphne to see if she'd like to see a movie, and Daphne had invited her to the house instead.

She had started fantasizing about the day the house would belong to her. She wanted to leave her mark on it everywhere. On one occasion, when Daphne left her at the house alone to go pick up the girls, she'd tried on every pair of Daphne's underwear. Sometimes she'd go upstairs and use Daphne's bathroom, brush her hair with Daphne's brush, apply a little of her lipstick. They almost looked the same, she would think as she looked in the mirror at herself.

She arrived right at seven. Bella opened the door a crack and peeked out.

"What are you doing here?"

"Hi, sweetie. Mommy invited me over."

Bella rolled her eyes. "We're watching *The Wizard of Oz* tonight. Don't try and change it to some boring adult movie." She opened the door, then turned her back on Amber.

Now Amber rolled *her* eyes. *The Wizard of Oz*. If she had to listen to Dorothy keep saying "There's no place like home," she might kill herself.

"There you are. Bella said you were here. Come on

in the kitchen." Daphne appeared, looking perfect in a romper that looked very much like a Stella McCartney Amber had seen in a recent *Vogue*.

Amber sat down at the enormous marble island.

"Can I get you a drink?"

"Sure, whatever you're having."

Daphne poured her a glass of chardonnay from the open bottle.

"Cheers." Daphne raised her glass.

Amber took a small sip. "I understand we've got *The Wizard of Oz* on tap for tonight."

Daphne gave her an apologetic look. "Yes, sorry. I forgot I'd promised the girls." She lowered her voice so Bella wouldn't hear. "Once we're half an hour in, we can sneak into the other room and chat. They won't notice."

Whatever, Amber thought.

The doorbell rang. "Is someone else coming?" Amber asked.

Daphne shook her head. "I'm not expecting anyone. Be right back."

A minute later, Amber heard voices, and then Meredith was there, following Daphne back into the kitchen. She looked determined.

"Hi, Meredith," Amber greeted her, feeling uneasy.

Daphne had a look of concern on her face and put a hand on Amber's arm. "Meredith says she needs to talk to us in private."

Amber's thoughts raced. Could she have discovered the truth? Maybe the photo from the fund-raiser had been her undoing after all. She took a deep breath to stop the hammering in her chest. No need to get upset until she heard what Meredith had to say. She rose from her stool.

"Margarita, could you please feed the girls now? We'll be back in a little while." Daphne turned to Amber and Meredith. "Let's go into the study."

Amber's heart was still pounding as she followed them down the hallway and into the wood-paneled study. She stared straight ahead at the wall of books, willing herself to be calm.

"Let's all have a seat." Daphne pulled out a chair and sat at the mahogany card table in the corner of the room. Amber and Meredith followed suit.

Meredith looked at Amber as she spoke. "As you know, I run all our committee applications through a background check."

"Didn't you do that months ago?" Daphne interrupted.

Meredith put a hand up. "Yes, I thought I had. Apparently the agency misfiled Amber's. They ran it last week and called me today."

"And?" Daphne prodded.

"And when they ran the social, they discovered that Amber Patterson has been missing for four years." She held up a copy of a missing person flyer, with a photo of a young woman with dark hair and a round face, who looked nothing like Amber.

"What? That must be some sort of mistake," Daphne said.

Amber kept quiet, but her heartbeat slowed. So that was all. She could work with this.

Meredith sat up straighter. "No mistake. I called the Eustis, Nebraska, records department. Same social security number." She pulled out a photocopy of an article from the *Clipper-Herald* with the headline "Amber Patterson Still Missing" and handed it to Daphne. "Want to tell us about it, Amber, or whatever your name is?"

Amber put her hands up to her face and cried real tears of panic. "It's not what you think." She choked back a sob.

"What is it, then?" Meredith's tone was steely.

Amber sniffled and wiped her nose. "I can explain. But not to *her*." She spat out the last word.

"Give it up, girl." Meredith's voice rose. "Who are you, and what do you want?"

"Meredith, please. This isn't helping," Daphne said. "Amber, calm down. I'm sure there's a good explanation. Tell me what this is all about."

Amber sank back into the chair, hoping she looked as distraught as she felt. "I know it looks bad. I didn't want to have to tell anyone. But I had to get away."

"Away from what?" Meredith insisted, and Amber shrank back more.

"Meredith, please let me ask the questions," Daphne said and put her hand gently on Amber's knee. "What were you running away from, sweetie?"

Amber closed her eyes and sighed. "My father."

Daphne looked like she'd been struck. "Your father? Did he hurt you?"

Amber hung her head as she spoke. "I'm so ashamed to tell you this. He . . . he raped me."

Daphne gasped.

"I've never told another soul."

"Oh my God," Daphne said. "I'm so sorry."

"It went on for years, from the time I was ten. He left Charlene alone as long as I was around and didn't tell. That's why I had to stay. I couldn't let him hurt her."

"That's horrible . . . couldn't you tell your mother?"

She sniffled. "I tried. But she didn't believe me, said I was just trying to get attention, and she'd whip my butt if I ever told anyone else such a 'vile lie.'" A quick glance out of the corner of her eye assured her that Daphne believed her, but Meredith looked unconvinced.

"So what happened exactly?" Meredith's voice sounded almost mocking, and Amber saw Daphne give her a look.

"I stayed until Charlene died. He told me if I left, he'd hunt me down and kill me. So I had to change my name. I hitchhiked to Nebraska and met a guy in a bar. He found me a roommate. I worked waitressing and saved my money until I had enough to come here and start over. He worked at the hall of records and got me the information on the missing girl, introduced me to someone who made me an ID in Amber's name."

Amber waited a beat for the women to respond.

To her great relief, Daphne rose and took her in her arms. "I'm so sorry," she said again.

Meredith wasn't letting it go, though. "What? Daphne, do you mean to tell me you're just going to take her word for it and not investigate? I can't believe this."

Daphne's eyes were cold. "Please go, Meredith. I'll call you later."

"You have a blind spot where she's concerned." Meredith walked to the door in a huff and turned around before she left. "Mark my words, Daphne—this will not end well."

Daphne took Amber's hand. "Don't you worry. No one will ever hurt you again."

"What about Meredith? What if she tells people?"

"You let me worry about Meredith. I'll make sure she doesn't breathe a word."

"Please don't tell anyone, Daphne. I have to keep pretending I'm Amber. You don't know how he is. He'll find me, wherever I am."

Daphne nodded. "I won't tell another soul, not even Jackson."

Amber felt a little guilty for painting her father in such a bad light. After all, he'd worked nonstop at the cleaner's to support her mother and her three sisters, and he would never have touched any of his daughters. Of course, he'd also made all of them work at that damn store for free, which she was pretty sure was child slave labor, close enough to child abuse. So what if he never touched her? He still took advantage of her.

Suddenly she didn't feel so guilty anymore. She raised her head from Daphne's shoulder and looked her in the eye. "I don't know what I did to deserve a friend like you. Thank you for always being there for me."

Daphne smiled and smoothed Amber's hair. "You'd do the same for me."

Amber gave her a forlorn smile and nodded.

Daphne started to walk from the room, then turned back. "I'll tell Bella that *The Wizard of Oz* will have to wait. I think you deserve to pick tonight."

Amber smiled a genuine smile—she couldn't wait to see the look of disappointment on the little princess's face. "That would really help me get my mind off things."

TWENTY-FOUR

Growing up, Amber had always hated the Fourth of July. The only good thing about that day was that her father closed the dry cleaner's. She and her three sisters would watch the parade—the high school marching band that was always screechingly off-key, at least one majorette who would drop her batons, and some plump-faced farm girl who would wave with glee from a hay-filled wagon. It was all so hokey and embarrassing, Amber cringed every time.

But this year was different. Quite different. Amber sat with Daphne on the back deck of the Parrishes' sixty-five-foot Hatteras as it sped across the Sound. They were spending the entire weekend on the boat, and Amber was over the moon. She'd gone shopping with Daphne and spent more than she had planned, but she wanted to look her absolute best every moment since she'd be near Jackson twenty-four/seven. She bought a new white bikini and then splurged on a one-piece black suit with a long, low V in the front and cutouts on the sides. It was one of the sexiest suits she'd ever seen, and Daphne had nodded her approval when Amber walked out from the dressing room. Her cover-up was sheer, so her body would never be hidden from him. For when they went ashore, she'd gotten white shorts that barely covered her buttocks and tank tops that clung just a bit. She'd brought skinny white pants for evening, a few T-shirts, and a casual navy sweater to throw over her shoulders. She'd even gotten a spray tan. This was her time to shine.

Jackson stood at the controls, his legs tanned and muscular, in a pair of khaki shorts and white golf shirt. He moved with utter confidence and mastery. He turned to where Daphne and Amber sat and called to them over the noise, "Hey, sweetheart, can you get me a beer?"

Daphne reached into the cooler and brought out a can of Gordon Ale, dripping with cold water. She had to admit, Daphne's black bikini showed off her perfect body to its best advantage. She had hoped Daphne would be wearing something more matronly, but no such luck. Daphne handed it to Amber. "Here, why don't you give it to him? You can get a lesson on how to handle a boat."

Amber took the can from Daphne and jumped up. "Sure. . . . Hey." She tapped Jackson on the shoulder. "Here's your beer."

"Thanks." He opened it, took a sip, and Amber noticed his long fingers and fine hands, immediately imagining them on her body.

"Daphne said you'd give me a boat-driving lesson," she said coyly.

"Boat driving. Is that what she called it?" He laughed.

"Well, maybe not. I can't remember."

"Here," he said, moving slightly to the right. "Take the wheel."

"What? No. What if we crash?"

"You're cute. What are we going to crash into? You really don't have to move it much. Just point the end of the bow in the direction you want to go and don't make any sudden jerking moves."

She put her hands on the wheel and concentrated on the water, her nerves subsiding a bit as she got the feel of it.

"Good," he said. "Steady as you go."

"This is fun," she said, throwing her head back and laughing. "I could do this all day."

Jackson patted her on the back. "Great. It's good to have a partner up here. Daphne isn't crazy about the boat. Prefers the kayak."

Amber widened her eyes. "Really? I can't imagine that. This is way better than kayaking."

"Maybe you can convince my wife of that." He took another sip of ale and looked back to where Daphne sat, quietly reading *The Portrait of a Lady*.

Amber followed his gaze and put a reassuring hand on his arm. "I'm sure she likes it more than you think. I know I would."

She stayed at the wheel for the next hour, asking questions and praising Jackson for his depth of navigation knowledge. She made him promise to show her the charts later, so she could study them and learn about the waters around Connecticut. And every now and then, she'd move close enough that her body would barely touch his. When she thought it might be too obvious, she turned the wheel back over to Jackson and went back to sit with Daphne. They were approaching Mystic, and the sun was beginning to set.

Daphne looked up from her book. "Well, you seemed to be enjoying yourself. Did you learn a lot?"

Amber searched Daphne's face for any sign of annoyance, but she seemed genuinely delighted that Amber was having a good time. "I liked it," she said. "Jackson knows so much."

"This boat is his favorite thing. He'd be on it every weekend if I let him."

"You don't love it, do you?"

"I like it. I just don't like spending all my time on it.

We have a beautiful home, the beach, and a pool. I like being there. On the boat there's just endless water, and it takes so much time to get anywhere. I start to get bored. And the girls begin to get antsy too. It's a small space, and it's hard to keep everything in order."

Amber wondered again at Daphne's obsession with neatness. Did she ever lighten up and relax?

"Well, you have to admit it's pretty exciting. The wind rushing through your hair and ripping through the water," Amber said.

"I especially don't enjoy speeding. To tell you the truth, I prefer sailing. It's quiet. I feel much more connected to nature when I'm on a sailboat."

"Does Jackson like it?" Amber asked.

"Not much. Don't get me wrong—he's a good sailor. Knows his stuff. But he can fly at top speed on this, and he likes fishing too." She pushed her hair back from her face. "My boyfriend in college grew up sailing, so we spent a lot of time on his family's sailboat. That's where I learned."

"I guess I can understand why you'd like that better," Amber said.

"It's fine, really. I make sure to bring a good book, and the girls bring games. And of course it's always fun to have a friend like you aboard."

"Thanks for asking me, Daph. It's a real treat for me."

"You're welcome," Daphne said, yawning and rising from her chair. "I'm going below to check on the girls. You don't mind if I lie down for a few minutes before dinner, do you?"

"Of course not. Go ahead and rest." Amber watched her go down the stairs and immediately took up her position next to Jackson again. "Daphne's taking a nap. I think she was getting bored."

She watched his face for a reaction, but if he had any irritation, he certainly didn't show it.

"She's a good sport about it."

"She is. She was telling me about all the fun she had in college when she and her old boyfriend would go sailing together." Amber noticed a slight twitch in Jackson's cheek. "I don't know. That seems so tame compared to this."

"Why don't you have another go? I'll grab us a couple of drinks."

She gripped the wheel and felt like she might finally, slowly, be taking control of the helm.

※

Later that night, after a leisurely dinner in Mystic, the five of them walked back to the marina under a warm, star-studded sky.

"Daddy," Tallulah said as they ambled. "Are we going to anchor out and watch the fireworks tomorrow night?"

"Absolutely. Just like we always do."

"Goody," Bella said. "I want to sit way up on the fly bridge all by myself. I'm old enough now."

"Not so fast, little one." Jackson took one of her hands and Daphne grabbed the other, and they swung her between them. "You can't go alone yet."

"I want to lie down on the forward deck like I did last year and watch from there," Tallulah piped up.

"Daddy will sit on the bridge with you, Bella, and I'll be on deck with Tallulah." She turned to Amber. "And you should go up with Jackson and Bella. It's a great place to watch from, especially since this is your first time."

That's fine with me, Amber thought.

It was a little past ten when they got back to the boat, and once again, Amber found herself alone with Jackson as Daphne took the children below to get them ready for bed. He had gotten some wine from the galley and was back with three glasses in one hand and the bottle of muscat in the other.

"Too early to finish the night. What do you say we have a glass before turning in?"

"Sounds great," Amber said.

They sat in the warm night air, sipping wine and chatting about Parrish International's latest acquisition and how the financing would work. When Daphne appeared, Jackson poured another glass and handed it to her. "Here, sweetheart."

"No, thank you, darling. I'm feeling rather sleepy. Probably shouldn't have had such a big meal. I think I'll hit the sack."

Actually, Amber thought, Daphne really did look tired. But big meal? She'd hardly touched her food.

"Well, good night, you two." She smiled at Jackson. "I'll keep the night-light on for you."

"I'll be down soon. You get some rest."

After she disappeared, Amber poured herself another glass of wine. "I remember how tired my mother used to get, and how she stopped staying up late. My father would joke and say things had really changed from their hot dating days."

Jackson looked into his glass as he twirled the stem. "Are your parents alive?"

"Yes. They're back in Nebraska. Daphne reminds me a lot of my mom."

A faint hint of surprise registered on his face and was

quickly replaced by his usual inscrutability. Amber was beginning to realize that he was particularly skilled at keeping his thoughts and feelings hidden.

"How are they alike?"

"Well, they're both homebodies. My mom liked nothing better than watching a sentimental movie with us kids. A lot of times, when you're away, Daph invites me over for movie night with Tallulah and Bella. It's fun, reminds me of home. And I think she gets sort of tired of all these charity events and art openings and all those things. At least, that's what she tells me."

"That's interesting," Jackson said. "What else?"

"Well, she likes quiet things, my mom, like Daphne. My mom would have hated how fast this boat goes and all the wind in her face. Not that we had boats, but my dad did have a motorcycle. She hated it—the noise and the speed. She preferred her bicycle, slow and quiet." More crap, but she was making her point.

He was quiet.

"I thought it was thrilling, being at the helm and speeding across the water. But maybe tomorrow we should take it a little slower, so that Daphne enjoys it too."

"Yes, good idea," he said idly and finished the wine in his glass.

Things were humming along now. And she hoped that tomorrow night, there would be more fireworks than the ones in the sky.

TWENTY-FIVE

Right after the Fourth of July, Amber finally secured the coveted position of Jackson's first assistant. The résumés had dwindled, and anything that looked too good, Amber had tossed. She had made herself indispensable to Jackson since Mrs. Battley's departure, so when he called her into his office, she felt sure it was to tell her she was officially his new assistant. She took a pad and pen with her and sat in a leather armchair across from his desk, careful to cross her black-stockinged legs to their best advantage. She looked at him through thick lashes she had gotten plumped at the aesthetician's and slightly parted glossy lips. She knew her teeth, recently whitened at the dentist's, looked perfect against her lips.

Jackson stared at her a moment and then began. "I think you know how helpful you've been these last months. I've decided to suspend the search for a new assistant and am offering the position to you if you're interested."

She wanted to jump up and shout but didn't betray her glee. "I'm overwhelmed. I'm definitely interested. Thank you."

"Good. I'll talk to Human Resources." He looked down at a document in front of him, clearly dismissing her, and Amber rose. "Oh," he said, and she stopped and turned around. "Of course, there will be a substantial raise."

To get close to him, she would have worked there for nothing, but in truth, she had been working damn hard and felt she deserved her now-six-figure salary. It didn't take long for her to anticipate his needs in her new role, and in a very short time, they were working together with the precision of a fine Swiss watch. Amber loved the importance the job gave her, her proximity to the big boss. The admins looked at her with envy, and the executives treated her with respect. No one wanted to be on the wrong side of the person who had the ear of Jackson Parrish. It was a heady experience. She thought of that Lockwood son of a bitch back home and how he'd treated her—as if she were some piece of trash he could throw away.

She jumped when her buzzer sounded late Friday and got up and went to his office. When she approached his desk, she saw what looked like a stack of bills and a large checkbook. "I'm sorry to burden you with this. Battley used to take care of it, and I just don't have time to look this all over."

"Did you really just use that word with me? You should know by now that nothing you give me to do is a burden."

Jackson smiled at her. "Touché. You do it all with pleasure. I should put PA after your name on your business cards. Perfect Assistant."

"Hmm. Perfect Boss. I guess we're a team made in heaven."

"Here's the test," he said, with a wry smile.

"What is it?" she asked.

"Bills. They're all on auto pay, but I want you to go over them, match them to the receipts, and be sure they're accurate. And of course there are some bills that need to be paid by check. I've indicated which those are, so you'll write a monthly check for those—Sabine and Surrey, school expenses, those kinds of things."

"Of course. No problem." She picked up the pile and the checkbook but hesitated before leaving his office. "You know, I'm feeling like Telemachos."

Jackson's eyebrows went up in surprise. "What?"

"You know, from *The Odyssey*."

"I know who Telamachos is. You've read *The Odyssey*?"

Amber nodded. "A few times. I love it. I love the way he takes on more and more responsibility. So . . . don't ever feel like you're giving me too much."

The way he looked at her felt to Amber as if he was appraising her, and it seemed to her that she had definitely scored a lot of points. She smiled sweetly and left him still studying her as she walked out the door.

She dropped everything onto her desk and began going through the folders. It turned out to be a very interesting exercise. Amber was astounded at the enormous sums of money Daphne spent each month. There were charges at Barney's, Bergdorf Goodman, Neiman Marcus, Henri Bendel, and independent boutiques, not to mention the couture houses and jewelers. In one month alone she'd bought over $200,000 worth of merchandise. Then came the nanny salaries, and the housekeeper and the driver. Daphne's gym membership and private yoga and Pilates classes. The girls' riding and tennis lessons. The country-club dues. The yacht-club fees. The shows and dinners. The trips. It went on and on, like a freaking fairy tale.

Amber's new salary was a pittance compared to the money Daphne could access. One bill in particular stopped her in her tracks—it was for a red crocodile Hermès Birkin. She did a double take when she saw the price: $69,000. For a purse! That was more than half her annual salary. And Daphne would probably use it a couple of times, then throw it in her closet. Amber's outrage was so palpable, she thought she would choke. It was obscene. If Daphne really wanted to help families living with CF, why didn't she donate more of her own money to them and be satisfied with the dozen designer purses she already had? What a little hypocrite. At least Amber was honest with herself about her motives. When she was married to Jackson, she wouldn't waste her time pretending to care about charity work.

Daphne didn't have to lift a finger at home, could buy anything she wanted, and had a husband who loved her, and she couldn't even pay her own bills? How spoiled could you get? Amber would never be lazy enough to give someone else an inside view into her lifestyle. Now that she had seen even more deeply into the pampered life Daphne led, she realized how limitless Jackson's wealth was and became even more determined to carry out her plan.

It took her over an hour and a half to wade through all the bills and receipts, and by the time she was finished, she was positively steaming. She got up from her desk and went to the coffee bar down the hall. On the way back, she stopped in the ladies' room and looked at herself in the mirror. She liked what she saw, but it was time to up the ante, make herself just a bit sexier, but in a subtle way—have him wonder what was different about her. When she got back to her desk, she saw that Jackson had already left for the day. She put the bills and checkbook in her drawer, locked it, and drank her coffee. When she finally closed her office door and walked out of the building, plans were forming in her mind. She had the whole weekend to perfect them.

TWENTY-SIX

On Saturday she met Daphne at Barnes & Noble, and then they went to lunch at the small café across the street. They sat at a small booth near the back of the restaurant, and Amber ordered a green salad with chicken. She was surprised when Daphne ordered a cheeseburger and fries, but said nothing.

"So, Jackson tells me you're doing an amazing job. Do you like it?"

"I do. It *is* a lot of work, but I really love it. I can't thank you enough for recommending me."

"I'm so glad. I knew you'd be great."

Amber looked at the package on the seat next to Daphne, which she'd been carrying all morning. "What's in the bag, Daph?"

"Oh, that. It's a bottle of perfume I have to return. It's the one I used to wear when Jackson and I met, and he loved it. I haven't worn it in a long time, so I decided to try it again, but I must be allergic now. Broke out in hives."

"That's terrible. What's it called?"

"Incomparable. Ha. That's how I felt when I wore it."

Their food arrived, and Daphne dug into the cheeseburger as if she hadn't eaten in days. "Mm. Delicious," she said.

"What was it like? You know, when you and Jackson were dating?"

"I was so young and inexperienced, but in some crazy

way, I think that appealed to him. He'd been with so many glamour girls who knew their way around, I think he liked that he could take me to places I'd never been and show me things I'd never seen." She paused and had a faraway look in her eyes. "I hung on his every word." She looked back at Amber. "He likes to be adored, you know." She laughed. "And it's pretty easy to adore him. He's one of a kind."

"Yes, he is," Amber agreed.

"Anyway, I guess nothing stays the same. Of course, now things are different."

"What do you mean?"

"Oh, you know. Children come along. Things become routine. Lovemaking isn't as passionate. Sometimes you're just too tired, and sometimes you just don't feel like it."

"Must be especially hard when you have a new baby. It must be so exhausting. You read all the time about new moms having postpartum depression."

Daphne was quiet and looked down for a moment. With her eyes still fixed on the floor, she said, "I'm sure it's a terrible thing."

After a few awkward minutes, Amber tried again. "Well, anyway. Having children didn't seem to put the damper on your romance. Every time I'm with you guys, it's obvious that he's crazy about you."

Daphne smiled. "We've been through a lot together."

"I hope I have such a great marriage one day. Like you and Jackson. The perfect couple."

Daphne took a sip of her coffee and looked at Amber a long moment. "Marriage is hard work. If you love someone, you don't let anything destroy it."

This is getting interesting, Amber thought. "Like what?"

"There was a bump in the road. Right after Bella was born." She paused again, tilting her head. "There was an indiscretion."

"He cheated on you?"

Daphne nodded. "It was just once. I was exhausted. Busy with the baby. We hadn't made love in months." She shrugged. "Men have their needs. Plus, it took me a long time to get back in shape."

Was Daphne seriously justifying what he did? She was even more gullible than Amber thought.

"I'm not saying what he did was right. But he was sorry after and swore it would never happen again." She gave Amber what looked like a forced smile. "And he never has."

"Wow. That must have been so hard for you. But at least you bounced back. The two of you seem very happy," Amber said. She looked at her watch. "Well," she said. "I guess we should be going. I have a salon appointment to get to."

After their lunch, Amber went home and ordered a bottle of Incomparable online. She looked up from the computer and smiled to herself, relishing her new piece of intel. He'd cheated before! If he could do it once, he could surely do it again.

※

Monday brought with it drowning rain and cold winds, which soaked Amber as she waited for the train. The only thing Amber disliked about her job was the long commute into the city. It was fine to come in for a leisurely day of checking out museums, but rush-hour travel was its own special torture. As she sat, still windblown and wet, wedged between a large man who smelled of cigars and a young boy with a dirty back-pack, she read the advertisements above the windows across from her. She could practically recite them by heart now. She wondered what it was like to see your picture on the walls of trains or the side of buses. Did the models get a kick out of it? She fantasized about being the object of desire for thousands of men. Her body was certainly good enough, and with the right hair and makeup, she bet she'd look every bit as good as those stuck-up models, even though she was just five-seven, a few inches shorter than Daphne. They probably thought they were so special, sticking their fingers down their throats just to stay skinny. She would never do that—but then again, she was lucky to be naturally thin.

By the time she arrived at Fifty-Seventh Street, the hems of her pants were almost dry. The rain had stopped, but the wind was still whipping furiously. She nodded at the doorman and said good morning to the guard at the front desk.

"Good morning, Miss Patterson. Filthy weather out there. You still manage to look perfect though. New hairstyle?"

She loved that they all knew who she was. "Yes, thanks." She swiped her ID badge and walked to the elevator. Her first stop when she got upstairs was the ladies' room. She pulled out her cordless flat iron and smoothed her hair, now shoulder length and a light-champagne blond. After she dabbed a drop of Incomparable on her wrists, the tennis shoes came off, and on went the nude Louboutins. She wore a black turtleneck sweater dress and a black lace push-up bra that beautifully enhanced her ample assets. On her wrist was a wide silver cuff bracelet. The only other jewelry was her earrings, hammered silver and stylishly simple. She smiled in the mirror, confident that she looked like she had just completed a Ralph Lauren photo shoot.

When she entered her office, she saw that Jackson's door was closed and the windows still dark. She made it her business to be there early every day, but Jackson still managed to beat her. Today was a rare exception. She started answering e-mails, and the next time she looked up, it was eight thirty. Jackson sauntered in after ten.

"Good morning, Jackson. Everything okay?"

"Morning. Yeah, fine. Had a conference at Bella's school." He unlocked his office door and then stopped. "By the way, we have a show tonight. Would you make a six o'clock dinner reservation for two at Gabriel's?"

"Certainly."

He started to go inside but stopped again. "You look very nice today."

Amber felt the heat rise on her neck. "Thank you. That's very kind of you."

"Nothing kind about it. Just the truth." He walked into his office and closed the door.

The thought of Daphne and Jackson having a romantic dinner and then sitting side by side in a Broadway theater pissed her off. She wanted to be the one sitting next to him in those primo seats, everyone looking at her with envy. But she knew that she had to keep her head about her. It wouldn't serve her to lose her cool and do something stupid.

Later that afternoon, she and Jackson were going over his itinerary for next week's trip to China when Daphne called his cell. Amber heard only his side of the conversation, but it was apparent he wasn't pleased. He clicked off and threw the phone onto the desk. "Shit. Totally screws up the plans for tonight."

"Is Daphne all right?"

He closed his eyes and rubbed the bridge of his nose. "She's fine. So to speak. Says Bella's not well. Doesn't want to come in for the play."

"I'm sorry," Amber said. "Shall I cancel the reservation?"

Jackson thought about this a few seconds and then gave Amber an appraising look. "Any chance you'd be interested in dinner and a show?"

Amber felt her stomach drop. This was too easy, falling into her lap like a gift from the heavens. "I'd love to. I've never been to a Broadway show." She hadn't forgotten that he liked innocence and first-timers.

"Good. These tickets for *Hamlet* are a hot item, limited run, and I don't want to miss it. Let's finish up by five thirty or so and we'll grab a cab to the restaurant. Reservation's at six?"

"Yes."

"Good. Let's get back to work."

Amber went back to her desk and phoned Daphne, who answered after one ring.

"Daphne, it's Amber. Jackson told me Bella's not well. I hope it's nothing serious."

"No, I don't think so. Just some sniffles and a low-grade fever. You know, she just wants Mommy. I didn't want to leave her."

"Yes, I can understand why you wouldn't." She paused. "Jackson asked me to fill in for you tonight. I just wanted to let you know. You don't mind, do you?"

"Of course I don't mind. I think it's a great idea. Enjoy yourself."

"Okay. Thanks, Daphne. I hope Bella's feeling better soon."

For once, Amber was filled with gratitude for the little nuisance.

They left the office at five thirty on the dot. She felt a rush sitting next to him in the taxi. It was better than the best high she'd ever experienced. When they walked into the restaurant, she was pleased by the admiring glances of those around her. Amber knew she looked good, and the man with his hand on her back was one of the richest men in the room. They were seated at a table in a quiet corner of the posh restaurant, bathed in candlelight.

"Wow, I've never been in a restaurant like this."

"This was one of the first places I brought Daphne when we started dating."

Daphne was the last thing Amber wanted to talk about, but if he insisted, maybe she could spin it to her advantage. "Daphne's talked a lot about your dating days, how different it was then."

He sat back in his chair and smiled. "Different? Yes, it was different then. There's nothing like the rush that comes with falling in love. And I fell hard, that's for sure. I'd never met anyone like her." He took a sip of wine, and once again, Amber admired his fine hands.

"Sounds like you were made for each other." She practically had to choke the words out.

He put the glass down and nodded. "Daphne has grown into such an amazing woman over the years. I look at all she's accomplished and am so proud of her. I have the perfect wife."

Amber almost gagged on her salad. Just when she thought he might be noticing the changes in her, the new, stylish, and attractive Amber, he was going on about his golden wife.

They talked mostly about business after that, and he treated her as any colleague he might have been dining with. When they got to the theater and took their seats—in a box—she let herself imagine again what it would be like to be married to him. If only he were interested in her as a woman and not just an assistant, the night would have been perfect.

When the curtain fell at eleven, Amber was not ready to end the evening. There were still plenty of bustling crowds on the street, and it looked as if all the restaurants and cafés were filled with patrons.

As they strolled toward Times Square, Jackson looked at his watch. "It's getting late, and we have an early day tomorrow—the meeting with Whitcomb Properties."

"I'm wide awake. Not tired at all," she said.

"You might feel different when your alarm—" He stopped midsentence. "You're going to be exhausted in the morning. Daphne and I were going to stay at the apartment tonight, and when she couldn't make it, I told her I was going to go ahead and stay by myself. You could stay in the guest room. It seems foolish for you to take a train at this late hour, and you've stayed with us in the city before. I suppose the only problem is clothing."

"I'm sure Daphne wouldn't mind if I borrow something. After all, she lent me a designer gown for the fund-raiser. I'm only one size smaller than she is." Amber hoped he didn't miss the comparison.

"Okay, then." Jackson hailed a cab, and Amber sank back into the seat, happy with this turn of events.

The taxi let them off in front of an uptown building, and they walked under the long canopy to the entrance. "Good evening, Mr. Parrish." The doorman's face showed no reaction to Amber, whether because of discretion or lack of interest, she didn't know.

The private elevator opened directly into the foyer of the large space. It was unlike their house, a more modern and minimalist design, all in shades of white and gray. The focal points were the paintings on the walls, abstract art with bursts of color that fused it all together. She took it all in, overwhelmed.

"I'm going to grab a nightcap," Jackson said. "The guest bedroom is the third door on the right. Fresh towels and toothbrushes, everything you might need. But before that, why don't you take a look in Daphne's closet and pick something out for the morning?" He went to the glass cart that held bottles and decanters and poured himself a scotch.

"Okay. I won't be long." She walked into the sumptuous bedroom, wanting nothing more than for Jackson to swoop in and throw her onto the king-size bed. Instead, she searched the bureau for Daphne's lingerie. She pondered again the evidence of an uptight Daphne whose drawers were in such order as to be almost laughable. Pulling out black lace panties, she held them up and nodded. They would do. Next, she went to the closet, where each garment was evenly spaced, just as it was at home. She took out a delicious red Armani suit and white camisole. *Perfect. Now the stockings.* She opened several drawers before finding them and chose a pair of sheer and silky thigh-highs in beige. She'd look like a million bucks tomorrow.

Amber grabbed her items and reluctantly left the bedroom.

Jackson looked up from his drink. "All set?"

"Yes. Thank you, Jackson. It's been a wonderful evening."

"Glad you enjoyed it. Good night," he said and gave a little nod as he headed toward his bedroom.

The guest room was supplied to fulfill every possible need, just as Jackson had said. Amber stripped out of the day's clothes, showered, brushed her teeth, and got into bed. She relaxed into the soft feather mattress that seemed to hug her and pulled the down comforter up to her chin. It felt like she was resting on a cloud, but she was having a difficult time falling asleep, knowing that Jackson was lying in bed just a few rooms away. She hoped he would feel how much she lusted for him, and find his way into her bed, where he'd forget all about his perfect wife. After what seemed like an eternity, she realized it wasn't going to happen and fell into a fitful sleep.

The next morning, after she'd showered and dressed, she phoned Daphne to let her know she'd spent the night. She didn't want to give Daphne any reason to distrust her. Everything aboveboard—as far as Daphne was concerned, anyway. And Daphne, in her usual sweet manner, assured Amber that it was perfectly fine.

TWENTY-SEVEN

N ow that Amber had a front-row seat to the finances underpinning Daphne's world, she understood why Daphne always looked fantastic—who wouldn't, with that kind of money? From the top of her head to the bottom of her loofahed feet, people ministered to her on a daily basis. Amber got a taste of it when Daphne invited her to a small dinner party at the Parrish home. That's where Amber met Gregg, the perfect antidote to her paltry wallet.

They were seated next to each other at the dinner for fourteen. Gregg was young, and although he was good-looking, Amber thought his chin weak and the reddish tint to his hair not to her liking. But the more she examined him, the more she saw that other women would probably find him very attractive. It was just next to Jackson that he didn't measure up.

With so many individual conversations going on around the table, it was easy for Gregg to monopolize her for almost the entire evening. Amber found the conversation banal and Gregg boring beyond belief. He talked on and on about his work at the family's hugely successful accounting firm.

"It's so fascinating to see how it all balances out, how perfectly it comes out in the end." He was talking about the profit-and-loss statements, and Amber thought she'd rather have been having a root canal than listening to him talk about these stupid numbers.

"I'm sure it's incredible. But tell me, what do you do outside of work? You know, what kinds of hobbies do you have?" Amber had asked, hoping he might get the message.

"Ah, hobbies. Well, let's see. I golf, of course, and I home-brew my own beer. I play bridge. Really enjoy that."

Was he for real? Amber examined his face to see if he was putting her on, but no, he'd been perfectly serious.

"How about you?" Gregg asked.

"I love art, so I visit museums whenever I can. I love to swim, and I've come to enjoy kayaking. I read a lot."

"I don't read much. I feel like, why read about someone else's life when you should be out living your own?"

Amber kept herself from spitting out her food in astonishment and simply nodded. "That's an interesting take on books. Never heard that one before."

Gregg smiled as if she'd handed him a blue ribbon or something.

She'd decided he would be useful, if tough to endure. He'd serve her purposes for the time being. He'd be her temporary ticket to dinners out, plays, and posh events. She figured she could easily get him to buy her expensive presents. She'd keep him by her side and hope that Jackson would look at him as a rival. She'd already seen his watchful eye on them tonight at dinner. And she'd seen too that Daphne looked pleased at Amber's apparent attentiveness to Gregg. But Amber wasn't interested in someone with a rich daddy. She wanted the rich daddy himself.

In the meantime, she strung Gregg along, letting him take her out to nice restaurants and buy her presents. He'd already sent her flowers to the office twice since the dinner, and she was delighted that Jackson looked none too pleased when he picked up the card and read it. She supposed Gregg was nice enough and good-looking in his way, but he was such a dolt. Boring as an old shoe. He was a good cover, though, and as she moved her plan into overdrive, he would serve her well in making sure Daphne didn't get suspicious or suddenly jealous of her.

⁂

A month had gone by since she and Gregg met at Daphne's dinner party, and tonight they were all having dinner at the country club. She'd manipulated Daphne into it the other night on the phone.

"I really want the four of us to get together," she said on the phone. "But I don't think Jackson wants to socialize with me, since I work for him."

Daphne hadn't answered right away. "What do you mean?" she finally asked.

"Well, you and I are so close. Best friends. And I want Gregg to get to know you, since I always tell him how we're like sisters. He's tried to arrange it with Jackson, but he always makes an excuse. Can you get him to do it?"

Of course Daphne had. She would pretty much do anything Amber wanted; Amber'd play the little-sister card, and Daphne would fold.

She suspected that Jackson was a snob at heart and didn't consider her worthy of him socially. She didn't hold it against him; she'd feel the same in his position. But she also noticed the way his body stayed a little closer to her when they were reviewing a document, the way his eyes held hers just a moment longer than necessary. And when he saw her with Gregg, she hoped the seeds of jealousy would take root and hasten the seduction.

She took her time getting dressed and dabbed on the perfume that Daphne was now allergic to. Maybe it would make her eyes water, Amber thought spitefully. The dress was just low-cut enough to show off her cleavage, but not so low as to be slutty. She wore five-inch heels, wanting to be taller than Daphne for a change since Daphne had hurt her ankle playing tennis and was stuck in sensible shoes until it healed.

Gregg picked her up right on time, and she ran down the stairs to his waiting Mercedes convertible. She loved slipping into the luxurious car and being seen in it as they drove around. Sometimes he let Amber drive it, and she loved the feel of this singularly superior vehicle. Gregg loved pampering her, and she milked it for all it was worth.

She got in, admiring the saddle leather, and leaned in close to kiss him. He was a good kisser at least, and when she closed her eyes, she could pretend it was Jackson's tongue in her mouth.

"Mmm, you're delicious," she said, sliding back over. "But we'd better get going. Don't want to keep Daphne and Jackson waiting."

Gregg took a deep breath and nodded. "I'd much rather sit here kissing you."

Even his lines were dull. She feigned desire. "Me too, but you promised you'd take it slow. I told you how hurt I was in my last relationship. I'm not ready yet." She gave him a pretty pout.

He took off, and they made small talk on the way to the club. They pulled through the gates right behind Jackson's Porsche Spyder.

"Park next to them, and we can walk in together."

She wanted Jackson to see her walking next to Daphne.

Daphne and she got out of their cars at the same time, and Amber walked over to give her a kiss, noticing that Daphne was carrying the new Hermès purse.

"Good timing!" Daphne smiled and gave her arm a squeeze.

"Love your bag," Amber said, trying to make herself sound sincere.

"Oh, thanks." She shrugged. "Just a little gift from Jackson." She looked over at him and smiled. "He's so good to me."

"Lucky lady," Amber said, wanting to spit.

The four of them walked in together, and Amber had to struggle to keep her eyes off Jackson and on Gregg.

After they'd been seated and gotten their drinks, Gregg lifted his glass. "Cheers. So glad we were finally able to get together." He put his arm around Amber. "I can't thank you enough for introducing me to this gem."

Amber leaned over next to Gregg and kissed him. When she sat back up, she tried to gauge Jackson's reaction, but his expression was unchanged.

"We're glad it worked out. I had a feeling you two would be perfect for each other," Daphne answered.

Amber snuck a glance at Jackson. He was frowning. Good. Licking her lips, she raised her glass of wine and took a long swallow, then looked at Gregg.

"You were right; this is a better choice than the house cabernet. I wish I knew as much about wines as you."

"I'll teach you," he answered with a smile.

"Actually," Jackson said, "the 1987 vintage was better." He gave Gregg an apologetic look. "Sorry, old

chap, but I'm something of a sommelier. I'll order a bottle, and you'll taste the difference."

"No worries. That's the year I was born, so it was a
good year," Gregg answered, perfectly seriously.

Amber had to struggle to keep from laughing. Gregg
had put Jackson in his place even though he was too
thick to realize it. But of course Jackson picked up on it
right away. No matter how much more money or smarts
Jackson had, he couldn't make himself fifteen years
younger.

"Obviously age is what makes a wine so much more
desirable. The older the better," Amber said, slowly
moving her tongue along her lips and looking at Jackson.

TWENTY-EIGHT

Amber was about to get a new glimpse into the Parrishes' life. When she did the bills, she had seen that they rented a house on Lake Winnipesaukee from Memorial Day to Labor Day, although they probably used it less than an accumulated four weeks. Amber was curious to see what kind of place warranted such an exorbitant rental fee, and today she would. She was waiting for Daphne to pick her up for a weekend at the lake house in New Hampshire. Jackson was on another of his many business trips abroad.

At 8:30 sharp, the white Range Rover pulled up. Daphne jumped out of the car and opened the back hatch for Amber's luggage.

"Good morning." Daphne hugged her and then took the bag from her. "So glad you're coming with us."

"Me too."

It was a four-and-a-half-hour drive to Wolfeboro, but it seemed to go quickly with the girls sleepy and quiet in the back as Amber and Daphne chatted up front.

"How are things at the office? Are you still liking it now with all the responsibilities?"

"I really love it. Jackson's a great boss." She looked at Daphne. "But you must know that."

"I'm glad. By the way, I never thanked you for pinch-hitting for me the time you went to see *Hamlet* with him. Did you enjoy it?"

"I did. It was so different to see it onstage. I'm sorry you had to miss it."

"I'm not a huge Shakespeare fan." Daphne chuckled. "I know that's an awful thing to admit, but I'm more suited to Broadway musicals. Jackson, on the other hand, adores Shakespeare." She took her eyes from the road and glanced briefly at Amber. "He has tickets to *The Tempest*. I think it's the week after next. Since you enjoyed *Hamlet*, if you don't mind, I'll ask him to take you instead."

"I'm sure he would want you to go." Amber didn't want to seem overly anxious.

"He'll love the idea of introducing you to more Shakespeare. And besides, you'd be doing me a big favor. I'd much rather be at home with the girls than listening to language I don't understand half of."

This was too delicious. Daphne was practically handing Jackson to her on the proverbial silver platter. "Well, when you put it that way, I guess it would be okay."

"Good. That's settled, then."

"Will your mom be coming to stay at all? I imagine she's not too far from here."

She noticed Daphne's hand tighten on the wheel. "New Hampshire's bigger than you think. She's actually a couple of hours away."

Amber waited for her to go on, but there was an awkward silence. She decided not to press it. A few minutes later, Daphne looked in the rearview mirror and spoke to the girls.

"We've got about an hour left. Everyone okay, or do we need a bathroom break?"

The girls said they were fine, and Amber and Daphne chatted about their plans for the rest of the day once they got to the house.

They arrived at the charming little town of Wolfe-boro around lunchtime and continued to the lake house, passing mile after mile of sparkling water and verdant hillsides. The homes along the banks were an exciting combination of old and new, some imposingly important and others small and eclectic. Amber was enchanted by the clear call of summer pleasures that seemed to hover over everything. Daphne pulled into the driveway, and the moment they opened the doors, the smell of honey-suckle and pine filled the car. Amber stepped onto the gravel, which was covered in pine needles, and breathed in the fresh air. This was paradise.

"If everyone grabs something, we can do this in one trip," Daphne called from the back of the Rover.

Bags in hand, with even Bella helping out, they walked down the dirt path leading to the house. Amber stopped and stared, openmouthed, at the structure in front of her, an immense three-story cedar house abounding with porches, balconies, and white railings. Beyond it stood a large octagonal gazebo and a small boathouse that overlooked the pristine waters.

The inside of the house was homey and comfortable, with old pine floors and cushioned furniture that invited relaxation. The front porch spanned the entire front of the house and looked over the lake.

"Mom, Mom, Mom." Bella had already gone upstairs and changed into her bathing suit. "Can we go swim-ming now?"

"In a bit, sweetheart. Wait till we all get into our swimsuits."

Bella plopped herself onto one of the sofas to wait.

The lake water was cold and clean. It took a while for them all to get used to it, but soon they were squealing and splashing and laughing. Amber and Daphne took a break and sat on the edge of the pier, legs dangling in the water as they watched the girls swim. The afternoon sun warmed their shoulders as the cold lake water dripped from their hair.

Daphne kicked up a splash of water and turned to Amber. "You know," she said, "I feel closer to you than anyone I know. It's almost as if I have my sister back." She looked out over the lake. "This is exactly what Julie and I would be doing now if she were alive—sitting here watching the girls, just enjoying being together."

Amber tried to think of a sympathetic response and then said, "It's very sad. I understand."

"I know you do. It hurts me to think of all the things I would love to be sharing with her. But now, with you, I can do that. It's not the same, of course, and I know you understand what I mean. But it makes me a little happier that we can make it hurt less."

"Just think, when Bella and Tallulah are grown, they'll sit together like this. It's nice that they'll have each other."

"You're right. But I've always felt it was a shame we didn't have more."

"Did Jackson want to stop at two?"

Daphne leaned back and looked up at the sky. "Quite the opposite. He was desperate for a son." She squinted and put her hand up to shield her eyes from the light. Turning to Amber, she said, "It never happened though. We tried and tried, but I never got pregnant after Bella."

"I'm sorry," Amber said. "Did you think of trying fertility treatments?"

Daphne shook her head. "I didn't want to be greedy. I felt like we'd been blessed with two healthy children, and I should be grateful for that. It was really only because Jackson had always wanted a boy." She shrugged. "He talked about having a little Jackson Junior."

"It could still happen. Right?"

"I guess anything is possible. But I've given up hoping for it."

Amber nodded solemnly, though she was dancing inside. So he wanted a boy, and Daphne couldn't deliver. This was the best news yet.

They were both quiet, and then Daphne spoke again. "I've been thinking; you shouldn't have to do that commute every day while the apartment is just sitting there, empty. You're more than welcome to stay at the apartment the nights Jackson isn't there."

Amber was genuinely floored. "I don't know what to say."

Daphne put her hand on top of Amber's. "Say nothing. That's what friends are for."

TWENTY-NINE

Amber was looking forward to sleeping in Daphne's bed tonight. She was going to take Daphne up on her offer to use the apartment for the weekend. Since it was the last week in August, and Jackson had been telecommuting from the lake, the apartment was available. Amber had no big plans for the weekend, so she'd spend Saturday roaming around Manhattan. She texted Daphne to let her know and to thank her.

She hadn't been there in a while and was taken aback again at the sheer elegance and luxury. She imagined that bastard back home and his snotty mother—if they could see her in this palatial apartment! She flung off her heels and stepped barefoot onto the fluffy carpet. Then, sinking into the white, half-moon sofa, she surveyed her surroundings with pleasure. It almost felt as if it were hers. She put her head back and closed her eyes, feeling incredibly indulged. After a few minutes, she went into the master bedroom to search for a robe.

Amber chose a gorgeous Fleur number in silk and lace. It felt like a warm, sultry breeze gliding over her skin. Next, she opened Daphne's drawers and picked a white pair of Fox & Rose lace panties that made her feel like a seductress—not that she had anyone to seduce, but it felt good nonetheless. She went into the bathroom and brushed out her long hair, now even blonder from her frequent trips to the salon. It fell loosely around her shoulders, thick and shiny. *Maybe not as beautiful as Daphne, but certainly younger.*

She looked over at the bed, which was covered in a downy pale-green comforter. She would sleep here tonight and pretend it was all hers, see how it felt to be Daphne. She sat on the bed and bounced a few times, and then she lay down and spread out. It was like being hugged by a thousand clouds. How lovely it would be to wake up whatever time she chose in this heavenly room and then explore the city. What could be a more perfect Friday and Saturday?

Amber nestled a little longer. The rumbling in her stomach reminded her that she hadn't eaten since breakfast. She reluctantly rose and padded into the kitchen. She'd picked up a salad from the market, and she scraped it out of its container and onto one of Daphne's china plates. She'd opened a bottle of malbec earlier and now poured herself a glass. After her dinner, she put a few jazz CDs in the player and sat with her second glass of wine, thinking about what she would do tomorrow. Maybe the Guggenheim or the Whitney. The third disc was playing when Amber heard a noise outside the apartment. She bolted to a standing position and listened. Yes. Definitely. It was the elevator. Suddenly, the doors opened and Jackson walked in.

He looked surprised. "Amber. What are you doing here?"

She pulled the robe tighter around herself. "I, uh, I . . . Daphne gave me a key and said I could use it if I was too tired to get the train. She said she told you. I figured with all of you at the lake, it would be empty. I'm sorry. I had no idea you were coming." She blushed.

He dropped his briefcase and shook his head. "It's fine. I should have let you know."

"I thought you were staying at the lake until Sunday night."

"It's a long story. Let's just say I've had better weeks."

"Well, I'll go and get my things and get out of your way." She hated to go, but figured he'd expect her to offer.

He shook his head and moved past her toward the bedroom. "It's late, you should feel free to stay till morning. I'm going to go change."

She heard him on the phone, but couldn't make out what he was saying. He stayed in the bedroom for close to an hour, and Amber wondered if he was ever going to come out. She debated changing from the robe into some clothes, but decided against it. She had a good feeling about tonight. She sat back down with her glass of wine and a magazine, waiting for him.

He finally came out, got a drink, and sat down on the other end of the sofa. He seemed to register what she was wearing for the first time. "That robe looks nice on you. A little tight for Daphne lately."

"She's gained a little weight. It happens to the best of us," Amber said, choosing her words carefully.

"She's not been herself lately."

"I've noticed that too. Whenever we're together, she seems distracted, like something's on her mind."

"Has she said anything to you? About being unhappy or anything?"

"I really wouldn't want to repeat anything she's said to me, Jackson."

He sat up straight. "So she *has* said something to you."

"Please, if she's not happy, that's something you and Daphne need to discuss."

"She told you she's not happy?"

"Well, not in so many words. I don't know. I don't want to betray a confidence."

He took a long swallow from his glass. "Amber, if there's something I should know, something that can help, then tell me. Please."

"I don't think you want to hear what I have to say."

"Tell me."

She let out a sigh and allowed the robe to fall open just enough to show a teasing bit of cleavage. "Daphne told me the sex is boring and routine. And that she's thrilled every month when she gets her period and knows she's not pregnant." She pretended to look nervous. "But please don't tell her I told you. She told me how much you want a boy, and she might not want you to know she doesn't feel the same way."

He was speechless.

"I'm sorry, Jackson. I didn't want to tell you, but you're right: you have a right to know how she feels. Just . . . please . . . don't say anything to Daphne."

He remained silent, his face red and set with a grim expression that Amber saw only rarely. He was furious.

She rose from the sofa and walked toward him. She made sure her robe opened slightly against her leg as she approached him. She stood in front of him and put her hand on his cheek. "Whatever is going on, I'm sure it will pass. How could anyone be unhappy with you, Jackson?"

He took her hand from his face and held it. Amber ran her other hand through his hair and he moaned, but then slowly pushed her away. "Forgive me, Amber. I'm not myself."

She sat next to him. "I understand. It's hard when you discover someone you love doesn't want the same thing you do."

He gazed steadily at her. "Did she really say those things? That she was happy every time she knew she wasn't pregnant?"

"She did. I'm sorry."

"I can't believe it. We've talked about how wonderful it would be. I just can't believe it." He put his head in his hands, his elbows resting on his knees.

Amber caressed his back. "Please don't tell Daphne I told you. She made me promise to keep her secret." She thought for a moment and then decided to go all the way. "You know," she said sadly, "she was kind of laughing about it, about how she fooled you and you never even realized." She prayed the lie wouldn't blow up in her face, but she needed to move this game forward.

When Jackson looked up at her, his eyes were filled with confusion and pain. "She laughed about it? How could she?"

She put her arms around his neck and pulled him close to her. "I don't understand it either. Let me help you," she said, kissing his cheek.

He pushed her away again. "Amber, no. This is wrong."

"Wrong? And what she's done is right? Betraying you? Laughing at you?" Amber rose and stood before him once again. "Let me make you feel good. It doesn't have to change anything."

He shook his head. "I can't think right now."

"I'm here for you. That's all you have to think about." She slowly untied the sash of her robe and let it fall from her shoulders, standing before him in only the lace panties. He looked up at her, and she pulled his head toward her until it was buried against her belly. She pushed him back so she could straddle his lap, and once she had, she put her mouth against his ear and whispered how much she wanted him as she moved her hips and ground against him.

She found his lips and thrust her tongue deep inside his mouth. She felt his resistance weaken as he pulled her closer to him and returned her kiss.

Their lovemaking was fierce and powerful. They barely let go of each other when they moved into the bedroom in the middle of the night. Finally, at dawn, they fell into a deep and satisfying slumber.

Amber awoke first. She turned on her side and looked at Jackson, sleeping next to her. He had been an expert lover, an added bonus and one she hadn't expected. She was so used to planning every move that it now seemed impossible that their being alone together in the apartment had happened so serendipitously. She closed her eyes and lay back against the pillow. Jackson stirred beside her, and then she felt his hand gliding up her thigh.

They stayed in bed until after twelve, dozing off and on. Amber was still half asleep when Jackson got up to shower and dress. He was in the kitchen making coffee when she came out, now in a long white T-shirt of Daphne's.

"Good morning, Superman." She moved toward him, but he backed away.

"Listen, Amber. This can't happen again. I'm sorry. I love Daphne. I would never want to hurt her. You understand, don't you?"

Amber felt as if she'd been struck. She took a moment to think things through, to alter her game plan. There was no way she was going to let him cast her aside. "Of course I understand, Jackson. Daphne's my best friend, and the last thing I would ever want is for her to be hurt. But don't beat yourself up. You're a man, and you have needs. There's no reason for you to be ashamed of that.

I'm here for you whenever you want. Just between us. Daphne doesn't need to know."

Jackson looked at her. "That's hardly fair to you."

"I would do anything for you, so hear me again: Whenever you want. No questions asked, no strings attached, and no spilling secrets." She put her arms around his neck and felt his close around her.

"You're making it impossible for me to resist you," he whispered, his lips against her ear.

She pulled slightly away and looked up into his eyes as her hand moved below his waist to caress him.

"Ah." He put his head back and closed his eyes in pleasure.

"Why would you try to resist me?" Her voice was silky. "I told you. I'm here for you. Come to me for whatever you need. Our little secret."

THIRTY

Amber clutched a silky pillow to her, closing her eyes to get a few more minutes of sleep. She and Jackson had been sleeping together for over two months now, and they had stayed up all night making love. She was drifting off again when she felt him shaking her arm.

"You've got to get up. I forgot! Matilda's here to clean."

Her eyes flew open. "What should I do?"

"Get dressed! Go in the guest room and make it look like you stayed there last night. We'll have to make something up for Daphne."

Annoyed, she threw on the robe at the foot of the bed and ran down the hallway to the guest room. Would it be so terrible if Daphne found out? Yes, it was too soon. She had to make sure he was firmly in her grasp before anything happened to jeopardize her position. Outside of his office she was the consummate professional, but inside, with the door shut, she used every trick at her disposal to make sure he couldn't get enough of her. It got a little tiresome—especially his affinity for blow jobs—but she could retire her services after she had a ring on her finger. And afterward, she demanded nothing and went about the day as if they had nothing more than a professional relationship. They usually stayed together at the apartment a few nights a week. She loved that the best. Waking up next to him, in that fabulous apartment, as if it was all hers. Now she made sure to schedule late appointments and dinners for him so he'd be more inclined to spend the night, and she always had an overnight bag at the ready.

※

It was becoming harder and harder to play the part of Daphne's best friend. She hated having to pretend that she was nothing more than Jackson's assistant; that she didn't know every inch of his body probably better than his own wife did. For now, though, she had to play it cool. But when Daphne phoned to send her on an errand, she was livid.

"Amber, dear. Can you do me a big favor?" Daphne had asked.

"What is it, Daphne?"

"Bella has a party to go to and needs an accessory for one of her American Girl dolls. I just can't get into the city in time. Would you mind picking it up for me and bringing it to the house?"

She damn well did mind. She wasn't Daphne's servant. Amber had planned to stay overnight at the apartment, but now she had to change her plans.

"Certainly, Daphne, what is it?" she said with a distinct lack of enthusiasm.

"She wants the Pretty City Carriage. They're going to pretend they're in Central Park. I've called and charged it already. They're holding it in your name."

Amber was still fuming when her train got in to Bishops Harbor just before six. She took a cab right to their house and wondered if Jackson had returned from his business trip yet.

When she arrived, Daphne was in the kitchen with the girls, and Jackson was nowhere in sight.

"Ah, you're a doll. Thank you!" Daphne gushed. Tilting her head toward Bella, she went on, "I would have had a major meltdown on my hands if you hadn't come through."

Amber forced a smile. "Can't have that."

"Drink?" Daphne held up a bottle of red wine, half empty. It was a little early for her, Amber thought.

"Just one. I have a date with Gregg tonight," she lied. She didn't want to get stuck here all night. "I see you've gotten a head start."

Daphne shrugged and poured a glass for Amber. "TGIF."

Amber accepted the glass and took a sip. "Thanks. Where's Jackson?"

Daphne rolled her eyes. "In his office, where else?" She lowered her voice so the girls wouldn't hear and stood closer to Amber. "Honestly, he's been gone all week, and the first thing he does when he gets home is complain that Bella left her shoes in the hall." She shook her head. "Sometimes it's easier when he's away."

Don't worry, honey, Amber wanted to tell her. *You won't have to put up with it for long.* She put on her concerned face instead. "You're ruining my fantasy of marriage." She laughed.

"It's okay. After he cooled down, he and I had a little afternoon delight. It was the first time in a while." She put her hand up to her mouth. "I can't believe I just told you that! Enough about me, tell me more about what's going on with Gregg." She linked her arm in Amber's, and they went into the sunroom, Daphne calling over her shoulder, "Sabine, please give the girls their baths when they've finished eating."

"I need to use the restroom," Amber said as she hurried past her. She went in and slammed the door, her back against it. Was he getting tired of her already? Daphne's smug expression infuriated her. It began as a tingling in her fingers, and then she was digging her fingernails into her hands to stop from screaming. She was a furnace, ready to explode, adrenaline pumping through her so fast that she couldn't catch her breath. She wanted to break something. Her eyes went to the delicate green glass turtle on the shelf in front of her. She picked it up and threw it on the floor and stomped on it with both feet, grinding the pieces into the carpet. She hoped Daphne cut her feet on them. She flung the door open and headed back to the sunroom. This is what happened when he got out of her sight for too long. She would have to do something about it, and fast.

Daphne patted the seat next to her when Amber walked in. "So, spill. How's it going with Gregg?"

As far as Gregg was concerned, she saw him just enough to keep Daphne's suspicions at bay. She'd go to dinner with him, usually on a Friday or Saturday night, or she'd play the occasional tennis game at the club with him. He believed her story that she needed more time to get over the abusive ex-boyfriend she'd invented—the one that no one else but he "knew" about.

"He's very sweet and attentive. I don't see him as much as I'd like because of work." She put her hand up. "Not that I'm complaining. I appreciate my job, believe me."

Daphne smiled. "I know that. Don't worry. The boss's wife won't say anything."

Amber was inwardly seething. "I don't think of you as the boss's wife."

Daphne raised an eyebrow.

Amber reached out and squeezed her hand. "What I mean is, I think of you as my best friend. If I do ever get married, I'd want you to be my matron of honor."

"Aw. You're sweet. I'm probably a little old for that, though?"

Amber shook her head. "Of course not. Forty isn't old."

"Excuse me! I'm thirty-eight. Don't push me over the hill yet."

She knew exactly how old Daphne was. But really, thirty-eight, forty—what did it matter? Amber was twenty-six. There was no competing with that. "Sorry, Daph. I'm awful with ages. You look young, anyway."

"Oh, before I forget, I've got some clothes I'm getting rid of but thought I'd see if you want any of them first," Daphne said.

Amber didn't need her castoffs. She had a whole new wardrobe of her own, thanks to Jackson. But she couldn't show her hand—not yet.

"That's so nice. I'd love to look at them. Why don't you want them anymore? Do they not fit?" She couldn't resist.

The color rose in Daphne's cheeks. "Excuse me?"

Amber looked at the floor. How was she going to get out of this one? Before she could say anything else, Daphne spoke again.

"I *have* gained weight. I can't seem to stop snacking. I eat when I'm stressed, and I'm worried about Jackson. He's acting strange, and I don't understand it." She sighed loudly.

"Oh, Daph. I wasn't sure if I should tell you, but he *has* been spending lots of time with one of his vice presidents. She's a new hire, and her name is Bree. I don't know if anything's going on, but they've been taking some awfully long lunches . . ." Bree was a knockout who had started there a few weeks ago. Amber had actually been wary of her and ready to do some sabotage until she found out Bree was a lesbian. But Daphne didn't know that. Bree and Jackson had been working a lot together, but it was perfectly innocent—and now Daphne would start nagging him about her and drive him right back into Amber's arms.

Daphne's hand flew to her mouth. "I know who you mean. She's gorgeous."

Amber bit her lip. "I know. She's a real snake too. I've seen the way she looks at him. She's always putting a hand on his arm or crossing her legs and wearing short skirts. She's rude to me too, suddenly going straight to Jackson to make an appointment like she has special access or something."

"What should I do?"

Amber raised her brows. "I know what I'd do if it were me."

"What?"

"I'd tell him to get rid of her."

Daphne shook her head. "I can't do that. It's his business. He'll think I'm crazy."

Amber pretended to think. "I know. Go talk to her."

"I can't do that!"

"Sure you can. You come to the office and very quietly tell her that you're on to her, and if she values her job she'd better leave your husband alone."

"You really think so?"

"Do you want to lose him?"

"Of course not."

"Then, yes, get your tail in there and show her who's

really boss. I'll make sure to keep him occupied while you do, so he doesn't find out."

Daphne took a deep breath. "Maybe you're right."

Amber smiled. It was perfect—Daphne would embarrass him at his office, which would make him livid. "I'll be behind you all the way."

THIRTY-ONE

It was becoming more difficult to keep Gregg out of her bed. Not that she would have minded taking him for a spin—he was a decent enough kisser, and she could tell he was more than willing to please her. But she couldn't risk it. When she got pregnant, it would be with Jackson's kid, not Gregg's. Besides, as soon as her position with Jackson was assured, she'd be kicking Gregg to the curb. All she had to do until then was what she'd learned best in high school. Pushing herself up off her knees, she brushed his stomach with her lips, then kissed him on the lips before going into the bathroom to wash her mouth out. He was still standing there, a dazed look on his face, pants around his ankles.

He gave her a sheepish look and pulled his trousers up. "Sorry. You're really out of this world, baby." He pulled her to him, and she had to resist the urge to squirm out of his arms. "When are you going to be ready to make love? I don't know how much longer I can take this."

"I know, me too. My doctor said I need to wait another six weeks. Then everything will be healed up. It's killing me too." He was getting impatient, and she'd had to make up a new excuse. She told a lame story about having some cysts removed that necessitated holding off on intercourse. When she'd started to get graphic, he'd put his hands up and told her to stop, that he didn't need to know the details.

"Better get dressed, we'll be late for the play if we

don't start dinner soon," she said sweetly. *Snap out of it*, she wanted to say. They had come into New York to see *Fiddler on the Roof* and were spending the night at his parents' apartment across from Central Park. Amber had wanted to see *Book of Mormon*, but when she'd mentioned it, Gregg had said he wasn't interested in seeing a religious play.

She'd stupidly agreed to prepare dinner for them before the show—packaged grilled chicken over minute rice and a green salad. Now she was rummaging through cabinets for pots, bowls, and utensils when she felt Gregg bump into her from behind. She turned around and stared at him.

"Oh, sorry," he said. "I was trying to help you find things."

"I've found everything I need," she answered curtly.

As Amber turned on the faucet to fill the pot, Gregg's arm reached out in front of her.

"What are you doing?" she asked.

"I'm trying to help you. I was going to take the pot from you and put it on the stove."

"I think I can handle that," she said, walking to the stove, but Gregg ran ahead of her to turn the burner on, and they collided. The pot bobbled in Amber's hand, and water flew everywhere, soaking the front of Amber's dress.

"Oh my gosh. Are you okay?" Gregg said, grabbing a tea towel and pressing it against Amber's dress.

Are you a flipping moron? she almost yelled, but instead smiled thinly and said, "I'm fine. How about you go sit down, and I'll finish in here?"

They arrived at the Broadway Theatre in plenty of time, and he went to the bar to get them each a drink. Amber looked around at the magnificent theater while she waited, admiring the grand chandelier in the opulent lobby of red and gold. Gregg returned with their drinks, two glasses of white wine, even though she'd repeatedly told him she preferred red. Did the moron ever listen?

"I think you'll be pleased with the seats. Front-row orchestra," he said, brandishing the tickets with a flourish.

"Great. A front-row seat to all that singing." Amber had seen the movie, and she didn't really get what all the fuss was about. *Fiddler* was old news as far as she was concerned. These were his parents' tickets, and apparently even they weren't interested in going.

"Have you seen it before?" she asked.

He nodded. "Seven times. It's my favorite play. I just love the music."

"Wow, seven times. That must be a record," Amber said, looking distractedly around the lobby.

Gregg stood up straighter and said with pride, "My family are quite the theater aficionados. Dad buys tickets to all the best shows."

"How nice for you."

"Yes, it is. He's a great man."

"And what about you?" Amber asked without much interest.

"What do you mean?"

"Are you a great man?" she said, playing with him.

Gregg chuckled. "I will be one day, Amber. I am being groomed right now to be a great man," he said, looking at her in earnest. "And I hope you will be by my side."

Amber controlled the urge to laugh in his face and instead said, "We'll see, Gregg, we'll see. Shall we go take our seats now?"

Amber found she was enjoying the play despite her earlier reservations. Just when she'd begun to think the evening wasn't such a waste after all, Gregg started tapping his foot in time to the music. Next he was humming along, and the people around them began to look over.

"Gregg!" she hissed under her breath.

"Huh?"

"You're humming."

"Sorry! It's just so catchy."

He quieted down, but then began to bob his head back and forth in time to the music. She wanted to slug him.

Three hours later, they left the theater. Amber came away with a headache.

"Feel like a drink?" Gregg asked.

"I guess." Anything was better than going straight back to his parents' apartment and being pawed.

"How about Cipriani's?"

"That sounds fine. Can we grab a cab, though? I don't want to walk in the rain."

"Of course."

"I still don't get what the big deal was when the young daughter married the Russian," Gregg said as they were seated in the taxi. "I mean, geez, weren't the Jews complaining about being judged because of their religion, and then Tevye goes and does the same thing."

Amber looked at him in astonishment. "You do realize that the Russians were the ones making them leave, right? Also she was marrying outside of her religion." *He had seen this seven times and was still confused?*

"Yeah, yeah. I know. But I'm just saying. It's not very politically correct. But, whatever, the music sure is great."

"Do you mind if we skip drinks? My head is pounding; I really need to just go to sleep." If she had to spend any more time talking to him tonight, she might have to choke him.

"Of course, babe." He gave her a concerned look. "So sorry you don't feel well."

She smiled tightly. "Thanks."

When they got back to the apartment, she crawled under the covers and curled into a tight ball. She felt the mattress shift as he lay next to her, pressing his body close.

"Want me to massage your temples?" he whispered.

I want you to get lost, she thought. "No. Just let me try and fall asleep."

He draped an arm around her waist. "I'm right here if you change your mind."

Not for long, Amber thought.

THIRTY-TWO

A bright beam of light peeked through the heavy bed-room curtains of Amber's room at the Dorchester Hotel, rousing her. She jumped out of bed and pushed back the green drapery to let the full radiance of the sun warm her body. Despite the early hour, there was lots of activity in Hyde Park; joggers, dog walkers, people on their way to work. They'd been in London three glorious days, and Amber was lapping up every minute of it. She was here as Jackson's assistant, as he had brought along the whole family, and she had her own room just down the hall from the family suite. Jackson and Amber worked during the day while Daphne and the girls went sightseeing.

On their second night, they all went to St Martin's Theatre to see *The Mousetrap*, but last night Daphne had decided to take Tallulah and Bella to the Royal Ballet to see *Sleeping Beauty* while Jackson and Amber went to a business dinner. The truth was, there was no business dinner. Amber and Jackson had spent those four hours in her room. He was frenzied after not being able to be alone with her for the last three days. He wasn't used to such long dry spells; she'd made sure of that, and when she had her period she pleased him in other ways. Jackson now stayed at the New York apartment at least three nights a week, and Amber stayed with him. Daphne could reach either one of them by cell phone, so there was no way for her to figure out they were together. On the weekends, Amber was usually hanging at the Parrish house with her good friend Daphne, and on at least two occasions, she and Jackson had had sex in the downstairs bathroom while Daphne was putting the girls to bed. The danger of it had been absolutely thrilling. And they had snuck out of the house late one night after Daphne fell asleep on the couch and gone skinny-dipping in the heated pool, then did it in the gazebo. He couldn't get enough of her. She had him lassoed, and as soon as she was pregnant, she would tighten the rope.

Amber draped her leg over Jackson's body and nestled against his shoulder. "Mmm. I could stay like this forever," she mumbled sleepily.

Jackson pulled her closer and stroked her thigh. "They'll be back soon. We need to put on our dinner duds and wait for them in the suite." He rolled over on top of her. "But first . . ."

※

Amber was meeting Daphne and the girls for breakfast in the hotel, and when she walked in, the striking mix of copper, marble, and butterscotch-colored leather filled her senses once again. Daphne and the children were seated with Sabine at a round table near the middle of the restaurant.

"Good morning," Amber said as she took a seat. "How was the ballet last night?"

Before Daphne could say anything, Bella piped up. "Oh, Auntie Amber, you would have loved it. Sleeping Beauty was so beautiful."

"I guess that's why they call her Sleeping Beauty," Amber said.

"No, no. They call her that because she fell asleep and no one could wake her up until the prince kissed her." Bella's face was flushed with excitement.

"Aunt Amber was kidding. That was a joke, stupid," Tallulah said.

Bella hit the cereal bowl with her spoon. "Mom!"

"Tallulah, apologize to your sister at once," Daphne said.

Tallulah gave her mother a look. "Sorry," she muttered to Bella.

"That's better," Daphne said. "Sabine, will you take Tallulah and Bella for a walk in the park? The barge down the Thames to Greenwich doesn't leave until eleven."

"*Oui.*" She pushed her chair out and looked at Bella and Tallulah. "*Allez les filles.*"

Daphne was on her second cup of coffee when Amber's full English breakfast arrived, and she dug into it with gusto.

"You have quite an appetite this morning," Daphne commented.

Amber looked up from her plate. She realized that she and Jackson had never eaten last night. It had been the last thing on their minds.

"I'm absolutely famished. I hate dinner business meetings. Your food gets cold while you talk, and then it's completely unappetizing."

"I'm sorry you had to work and miss the ballet. It was superb."

"Me too. I would much rather have done that."

Daphne absently stirred her coffee for a moment before speaking.

"Amber." Her voice was low and serious. "I need to talk to you about something that's been bothering me."

Amber put down her knife and fork. "What is it, Daph?"

"It's about Jackson."

Amber pushed down the panic threatening to rise. "What about Jackson?" she said, her face a mask.

"I really do think he's seeing someone."

"Did you talk to Bree?"

"I know it has nothing to do with Bree. She's gay—I met her partner at a party we attended recently. I'm so glad I never went to the office and accused her. But he's been very distant lately. He's spending most of the week at the apartment in New York. He never used to do that. Maybe a night here and there, but it was the exception. Now it seems to be the rule. And even when he's home, he's not really there. His mind is always somewhere else." She put her hand on Amber's arm. "And we haven't made love in weeks and weeks."

Nothing could have pleased Amber more. So he wasn't sleeping with Daphne any longer. It didn't surprise her. She made sure she left him satisfied in every way possible.

"I'm sure you're wrong," she said, putting her hand on Daphne's. "He's closing on that huge project in Hong Kong, and it's been brutal. Plus, the time difference between here and there has him on calls at all hours. He's totally exhausted and consumed by it. You have nothing to worry about. As soon as this deal closes, he'll be back to normal. Trust me."

"You really think so?"

"I do." Amber smiled. "But if it makes you feel better, I'll keep my eyes and ears open and let you know if anything looks suspicious."

"I'd appreciate that. I knew I could count on you."

※

Amber joined them later on the boat ride down the Thames to Greenwich, and together they wended their way up the big hill to the Royal Observatory. They ate lunch in the town and strolled around most of the afternoon, also visiting the National Maritime Museum. By the time they got back to the hotel, Bella and Tallulah were fading and ready for naps. Amber was feeling like she could use a quick nap too, and they all went to their rooms to rest. Amber was out in seconds, and when she awoke, it was six o'clock. She called the suite to see what the plan was for dinner.

"Did you get some rest?" Daphne asked when she picked up.

"I did. How about you?"

"Yes, we all slept. I've been up for a while, but Tallulah and Bella just got up. The girls are eating in tonight." Daphne's voice got a little softer. "I think you must be right. Jackson wants a romantic dinner, just the two of us. He apologized for all the nights away and his preoccupation with work. I should have known you were right. Thank you for setting me straight."

"You're welcome." Amber's voice was strangled. What the hell was he playing at? A romantic dinner with Daphne? After he had made love to Amber that morning?

Daphne's voice startled her. "Thanks again. See you tomorrow."

Amber put the phone down and sat on the bed, stewing. She was furious. Did he think he could just use her and then run back to Daphne? She heard her mother's words, repeated so often that Amber remembered wanting to stuff a rag in her mouth. *Don't be someone's trash can.* What a vile admonition, Amber had always thought when she heard her mother say it. But that's precisely what she felt like now.

She was putting the finishing touches on her makeup when she heard knocking at her door.

She opened it, and Jackson slid in. He looked at her, a puzzled expression forming.

"Are you going out?"

She smiled, put one leg on the bed, pulled up a sheer stocking, and clipped it to her garter.

"Daphne told me that you had plans, so I called an old friend, and we're meeting for drinks."

"What old friend?"

She shrugged. "Just an old boyfriend. I called my mom earlier today, and she told me he'd moved here a few years ago with his wife," she lied.

Jackson sat on the bed, still looking at her.

"Poor thing, he just got divorced. I thought he could use some cheering up."

"I don't want you to go."

"Don't be silly. He's ancient history."

He grabbed both her hands in his and pushed her backward until she was against the wall. Kissing her hungrily, he moved his body against hers and lifted her skirt above her thighs. Standing up and half undressed, they made love with urgency, and when they were finished, Jackson pulled her to the bed to sit beside him.

"Cancel on him," he said.

"You can't expect me to sit alone in this hotel room while you're out with Daphne. Besides, don't you trust me?"

He stood from the bed, his face red, his hands balled

into fists, and glared at her. "I don't want you going out with another man." He pulled a box from his pocket. "This is for you."

He handed it to her, and when she opened it, there sat a magnificent diamond bracelet.

"Wow," she breathed. "I've never seen anything more beautiful. Thank you! Will you put it on me?" She gave him a long kiss. "I suppose I could cancel if it bothers you that much. How long will your dinner take?"

"I'll make it quick. Meet you back here in two hours."

The bracelet was the most amazing piece of jewelry she'd ever seen. And it was hers. All hers. She turned slowly and, never taking her eyes from Jackson, began to undress. When she was finally wearing nothing but the bracelet, she walked over to him and purred, "Hurry back, and then I'll show you how very grateful your girl is."

After he left, she pulled out her phone and took a selfie—a very erotic selfie. She waited an hour, knowing he'd be in the middle of dinner, then texted it to him. That ought to have him calling for the check.

THIRTY-THREE

A mber delighted in soaking in Daphne's bathtub, more often than not with Jackson. She luxuriated in the soft-as-silk sheets as she lay next to Daphne's husband and drove him mad with lust. And how liberating it was to know that no matter how many towels she used, no matter how mussed the sheets became, no matter how many glasses of wine or dishes of food she consumed, she could walk out the door in the morning and know the maid would have everything spick-and-span when she and Jackson returned in the evening. The doorman nodded politely to her on arrival and departure, a model of discretion, just like the new maid. Matilda, the old one, had been fired. Apparently she'd stolen some of Daphne's jewelry. The same jewelry that Amber had hocked for a little extra cash.

The night before, they'd gone to an art opening at a small gallery on Twenty-Fifth Street. The artist, Eric Fury, was one Jackson had discovered a few years ago and had introduced to his collector friends. The moment they'd entered the gallery, they had been surrounded. It'd been clear not only that Jackson was well known but also that people wanted to be in the orbit of his power and charm. Amber had been careful not to put her arm in his or appear too intimate.

As soon as Eric Fury saw Jackson, he'd rushed over to shake his hand.

"Jackson. Wonderful to see you." He swept his arm around to indicate the crowded room. "Isn't it great?"

"It is, Eric, and you deserve every bit of it," Jackson said.

"It's all thanks to you. I can never tell you how grateful I am."

"Nonsense. I just made the introductions. Your art speaks for itself. You wouldn't be here if you didn't have the talent."

Fury turned to Amber. "You must be Daphne."

"Actually, this is my assistant, Amber Patterson. Unfortunately, my wife was unable to be here, but she loves your work as much as I do."

Amber extended her hand. "It's a pleasure to meet you, Mr. Fury. I read recently that you're moving away from canvas and instead painting on wood you collect from old buildings."

Jackson had looked at her in surprise, and Fury said, "You are absolutely right, Miss Patterson. It's a statement about what we lose when we let historical edifices be torn down."

Suddenly a man appeared with a camera. "Hey, Mr. Fury. How about a photo for tomorrow's edition?"

Eric smiled and stood next to Jackson as Amber quickly moved away from the twosome. The last thing she needed was another picture of her in the newspaper.

"Okay, kid. Get back to your fans and sell some art," Jackson said when the photographer finished. When the artist walked away, Jackson walked over to where Amber stood admiring one of the works.

"I didn't realize you knew anything about Eric Fury," he said.

"I don't really. But when you asked if I wanted to go

to the exhibit, I read up on him. I always like to know something beforehand. It makes the experience much more rewarding."

He nodded his head in approval. "Impressive."

Amber smiled.

"That was discreet of you. Moving out of the picture. I hope you didn't feel uncomfortable," he said.

That was funny. He thought she was protecting him. "Not at all. You know I'll always have your back." She smiled and moved a little closer to him. "And your front too," she whispered.

"I think it's time to split," he said.

"You're the boss."

As they circled the room, bidding everyone good night, Amber experienced just what it would feel like to be Jackson's wife, to be at the center of the universe with him—and it felt sublime. She only needed to bide her time.

They grabbed a taxi back to the apartment and were practically tearing each other's clothes off as the private elevator ascended. They never got to the bedroom, but made furious love on the living room floor. That was one of the things Amber especially loved—she made sure that they'd had sex in every room, even both of the girls' bedrooms. That one had been a challenge, but she wanted her scent everywhere, like an alley cat.

⁂

She heard the shower going and turned lazily to look at the clock on the night stand. Seven thirty! Jackson came out of the bathroom with a towel around his waist, his chest still shiny with dampness. He sat on the edge of the bed and ruffled her hair. "Good morning, sleepyhead."

"I didn't even hear the alarm. I'll get up."

"You put on quite a show last night. No wonder you're exhausted." He leaned down and gave her a long, sensuous kiss.

"Ooh, come back to bed," she cooed.

He ran his hand down the front of her body. "Nothing I'd like more, but remember? I have a ten o'clock with Harding and Harding."

"Oh, that's right. Sorry I kept you up so late."

"Don't ever apologize for that." He rose, dropped the towel, and began dressing. Amber snuggled against the pillow and admired the toned and muscular body that she now knew so intimately. He finished dressing as she slowly got out of bed. "I'm off," he said as he pulled her naked body to him. "Give me a kiss and hustle. We need to prepare for that meeting."

Amber hurriedly poured a glass of juice and then got into the shower. She chose the red Oscar de la Renta suit Jackson had bought for her last week and was out the door close to eight. She made it to the office by eight forty-five and strolled into Jackson's office. She knew he was watching her as she strutted in the fitted jacket and short skirt that hugged her bottom.

At twelve o'clock, the meeting in Jackson's office was still going on when Amber looked up to see Daphne approaching her desk. She looked like she had gained more weight and was not her usual, impeccable self. Her lipstick was mussed, her blouse so tight that the buttons were straining. Amber noticed, too, that she wore no jewelry other than her ring.

Amber rose from her desk. "Daphne, what a surprise. Is everything all right?" What was *she* doing here?

"Yes, everything's fine. I was in town and just wondered if Jackson might be available for lunch."

"Was he expecting you?"

"Well, no. I just took a chance. I tried calling you to get his schedule, but they said you weren't in yet. Is he here?"

Amber stood up straighter. "He's in a meeting with a group of investors. I'm not sure when they'll be finished."

Daphne looked disappointed. "Oh. Did the meeting just start?"

Amber shuffled some papers on her desk. "I don't know. I had car trouble this morning, so I missed my train. That's why I was late." She stared at Daphne.

"Well, maybe I'll wait a little bit. Do you mind if I sit in here with you? I won't bother you if you have work to do."

"Of course not. Please have a seat."

"By the way, that's a beautiful suit you're wearing."

"Thank you. I got it at a consignment shop here in the city. Amazing what you can find for cheap." She wanted to add, *and guess whose red bra and panties I'm wearing.*

Daphne sat, and Amber went back to the pile of work on her desk while fielding phone calls.

"You've really taken to this job, haven't you? Jackson says he wouldn't know what to do without you. I knew you'd be perfect for him."

Amber bristled. She was sick and tired of Daphne patronizing her. She was so out of tune with her own husband's needs and desires it was laughable.

Just then, the door to Jackson's office opened and the four-member Harding and Harding team stood there shaking hands and saying their good-byes. Amber could tell from the look on Jackson's face that the meeting had gone well. She was glad. This would mean a financial leap into a whole new stratosphere. Jackson, now standing alone, looked surprised to see Daphne.

"Hi, darling," she said, rising from her chair and embracing him.

"Daphne, how nice. What are you doing in New York?"

"Can we go into your office?" she asked in a sweet voice.

Jackson followed her in and closed the door behind them. After twenty minutes, Amber was fuming. What could possibly be going on in there? Suddenly, Jackson was at the door and said, "Amber, can you come in and bring my schedule with you? I seem to have erased it somehow."

Daphne looked up as Amber entered. "You see, Amber? What on earth would he do without you? Jackson's just been telling me what an innovator you are."

"How's my afternoon looking, Amber? My wife wants to take me to lunch."

Amber pulled up the calendar on her iPhone. "It looks like you have a lunch appointment at twelve forty-five with Margot Samuelson from Atkins Insurance." He didn't, but Amber wasn't about to let Jackson and Daphne have a meal together. She turned to Daphne. "I'm so sorry you came in for nothing."

Daphne got up from her seat. "Don't worry. I had to come in for a foundation meeting this morning. It's no problem." She walked behind the desk and gave Jackson a kiss. "I'll see you tonight?"

"Absolutely. I'll be home for dinner."

"Good. We've missed you."

Amber walked her out, and Daphne gave her a hug. "I'm glad he's coming home tonight. The girls miss him. He never used to stay overnight in the city this often. Are you sure you're not noticing anything suspicious? No one calling here for him or anything?"

"Believe me, Daphne—no one is calling or coming around. I even stayed at the apartment one night when you and Jackson were at the lake, and there's no sign that anyone but Jackson has been there. It's just a super-busy season here. I'm sure there've been times like this before."

"Yes, I suppose you're right. There have been. It feels different this time, though."

"I think you're imagining things."

"Thanks for keeping me on an even keel."

"Anytime."

Once Daphne was gone, Amber went straight to Jackson's office. "What did she want?"

"She wanted to have lunch, just like she said."

"You were alone a long time. What was that all about?"

"Whoa. She's my wife, remember?"

Amber did her best to backpedal. "I know. Sorry. It's just . . ." She choked back fake tears. "It's just that I care about you so much, I can't stand the thought of your being with anyone else."

Jackson got up from his desk chair and opened his arms. "Come here, you little worrier." He hugged her, and she held on to him tightly. "Stop fretting. It will all work out, I promise you."

Amber knew better than to challenge him by asking him *how* and *when* it was all going to work out. "You're going back to Connecticut tonight?"

He moved her back, his hands on her shoulders, and looked into her eyes. "I have to. Besides, I want to check things at home. Daphne looks like she's having problems."

"Yes, I noticed that too. She's gained more weight, hasn't she?" Amber said.

"She looked sloppy, and that's not like her. I want to check on the girls too, make sure everything's okay."

Amber wiggled back into his arms. "I'll miss you so much."

He dropped his arms and walked to the office door. Amber was already unzipping her skirt as she heard the lock click.

THIRTY-FOUR

Jackson told Amber he had a surprise for her. The chauffeur picked them up from the apartment and drove them to Teterboro Airport, where a private jet waited for them. When Amber saw the airfield, she turned to Jackson. "What are we doing?" she asked.

Jackson pulled her closer to him. "We're taking a little trip."

"A trip? Where? I don't have any clothes with me."

"Of course you don't. But you won't be in them much anyway," he said with a laugh.

"Jackson!" Amber feigned outrage. "But really. I didn't pack anything."

"Don't worry—there are stores in Paris."

"Paris?" she cried. "Oh, Jackson. We're going to Paris?"

"The most romantic city in the world."

Amber unbuckled her seat belt, slid onto Jackson's lap, and kissed him. They almost undressed right there in the car, but they had pulled to a stop near the jet stairs. Jackson was the first to pull away. "Here we are," he said, and opened his door.

They boarded the plane, and Amber looked around while Jackson talked to the pilot. The only planes she'd been on were commercial airliners crowded with rows and rows of seats, and naturally, Amber had never sat anywhere but in economy. Even that time she'd met Jackson and the family in London, she had flown commercially. She knew that private jets existed, but she'd never imagined they looked like this. Supple leather sofas in a beautiful cream color sat on both sides of the plane, facing each other. There was a large-screen TV, and a dining table for four had a round crystal vase filled with fresh flowers. A door opened onto a bedroom with a king-size bed, and the bathroom was almost as luxurious as the one in the New York apartment. In fact, Amber thought, it was like being in a smaller but just as sumptuous home.

Jackson came up behind her and put his arms around her waist. "You like?"

"What's not to like?"

"Follow me," he said.

He led her into the bedroom, where he opened the closet doors. Indicating a mass of clothing hanging there, he said, "Look through them and decide what you want to keep. Keep all of them if you like."

"When did you have time to do this?"

"I took care of it last week," he said.

Amber went to the closet and went through the hangers one by one, examining the dresses, tops, pants, jackets, and sweaters, every one still with a tag on it. Obviously, he'd bought them just for her. She excitedly began pulling them out to try on, kicking off her shoes and removing her dress. Jackson sat on the bed. "You don't mind if I watch this little show, do you?"

"Not one little bit."

She tried on every last piece, modeling them for Jackson, who approved of it all. Of course, he had chosen everything, so it stood to reason that he would.

"There are shoes in there too. Up top, on the shelf," he said.

"You think of everything, don't you?"

"I do."

Amber looked up and counted fifteen shoe boxes with names she had only dreamed about. Each pair cost about the same as her monthly rent, some of them even more. When she got to the Jimmy Choos with white suede, crystals, and ostrich feathers, she put them on and took off everything else, then wiggled into the delicious red and black lace corset he'd bought for her. She felt like a movie star, with her stupendously expensive duds, a private jet to travel in, and a gorgeous man dying to make love to her. She walked over to Jackson, still seated on the bed, and, running her fingers through his hair, pulled his face against her chest. She pushed him down and began to work her magic. In a matter of seconds, she would do her best to take him to another world.

Later they had dinner by candlelight, Amber still in her high heels, but now with a silk robe over her naked body.

"I'm famished," she said as she cut into her filet mignon.

"No wonder. You must have burned up five thousand calories."

"If I could stay in bed with you and never have to come up for air or food, I would be the happiest girl alive." She made sure to stroke his ego every chance she got.

Jackson raised his wineglass. "That would be a perfect world, my hungry little sexaholic."

When they landed at Le Bourget Airport in Paris, they were whisked by chauffeur to the Hotel Plaza Athénée. Amber loved the hotel, with its red awnings and crimson bouquets everywhere you looked. She toured its 35,000-bottle wine cellar and was pampered at the Dior Institut spa. It was the most glorious week of her life, strolling along the Champs-Élysées and dining in intimate cafés with soft lighting and delectable food. The Eiffel Tower thrilled her. She was overwhelmed by the vastness of the Louvre and its masterpieces, moved by the grand edifice of Notre-Dame, and charmed by the city's amber hue as lights glowed in the twilight. And in between this eye-opening journey, she never let Jackson forget how virile and exciting she found him.

The visit had seemed to fly by, Amber thought as they boarded the private plane for their return. She sat without speaking for the next hour, while Jackson gathered papers from his briefcase and began making notes. When he finished, she went over and sat next to him.

"This has been the most wonderful week of my life. You've really opened up my world."

Jackson smiled but said nothing.

"It's been heaven having you all to myself. I hate the thought of sharing you with Daphne."

Jackson frowned, and Amber knew immediately that she'd made a mistake. She never should have mentioned her. Now he was probably thinking about Daphne and the girls. Damn. She usually didn't make that kind of slipup. She'd have to try to recover.

"I've been thinking," he finally said. "How would you feel about having your own apartment in New York?"

She was nonplussed. "Why would I want that? I like living in Connecticut. Besides, when I want to stay in New York with you, we have your place."

"But it's getting complicated. If you had your own apartment, you could have all your own things there. You wouldn't have to hide your clothes or make sure they're out of my apartment in case Daphne comes into the city."

She didn't want her own place. She wanted Daphne's place.

When she didn't answer, Jackson went on. "I'd buy it for you, of course. We'd furnish it together, buy all the art and books you love. It would be our own hideaway. Just ours."

Their hideaway. She didn't want to be hidden. She wanted to be very much out in the open, to be Mrs. Jackson Parrish.

"I don't know, Jackson. It might be too soon for something like that. Besides, wouldn't Daphne wonder how I got the money for a New York apartment? And what about Gregg? I've been able to hold him off, but if he thinks I'm a New York sophisticate, I won't be able to play the innocent little girl. And we have to keep up that little charade for Daphne's sake—although I'm having more and more trouble keeping Gregg's hands off me. I've stopped him a couple of times before he could finish what I think was going to be a proposal."

Jackson's face grew red, just as Amber had hoped. "Have you slept with him?"

"Really? Are you serious?" She took the napkin from her lap and threw it on the table. "I'm finished." She rose from her chair and strode into the bedroom. She wasn't going to be cast aside again. It felt like her plans were all going awry. Oh, Jackson was under her spell at the moment, and he was buying her expensive things and taking her on fabulous trips, but she wanted more— much more. And she'd be damned if she was going to let anything stand in her way, especially now that she'd missed two periods.

THIRTY-FIVE

Tonight was the night. Amber was now ten weeks pregnant and couldn't hide it much longer. Jackson thought she was on the pill, and she'd even made sure to get a prescription and take a pill out of the dispenser each day so he wouldn't be suspicious. Then she'd flush it. The only medication she was taking was Clomid, for fertility. She probably didn't need it, but she wasn't taking any chances. She needed to get pregnant before he tired of her. She had been a little worried about twins, but then she figured, if one was good, two would be even better.

She'd hoped to find out the sex at the last appointment, but it was apparently still too soon. With the computer skills she'd honed in months of night classes, she'd been able to doctor the image from the ultrasound, so she'd tell him it was a boy. By the time they were married, if she ended up having a girl, it would be too late for him to do anything about it anyway.

She'd gone to Babesta earlier in the day and bought a bib—"Daddy's little boy"—that she planned to give him tonight after they made love. Then he'd finally leave Daphne, and she could drop the facade and stop pretending to be her friend. She couldn't wait to see the look on Daphne's face when she found out that Amber was pregnant. It would be almost as delicious as telling Bella she wouldn't be the youngest anymore. *Move over, baby, you're old news now.*

Once she was Mrs. Parrish, those two brats were on borrowed time. They could go to community college as far as she was concerned. But she was getting ahead of herself; first, she had to convince Jackson to leave them.

※

When Jackson arrived at the apartment, Amber was wearing a black leather corset and collar. Daphne had complained to her on a recent night out that Jackson's tastes were becoming more unconventional. When she'd pressed for more details, the prude had turned red and mentioned something about restraints. Amber had decided to test the waters, and what she'd found was that Jackson was craving more adventure in the sack. She'd gladly given it to him, and together they'd scoured a few online stores and ordered all sorts of interesting sex toys. She encouraged him to push the limits, was ready to do whatever she had to, to make him compare Daphne unfavorably to her. She kept all their toys in a drawer in the guest room, half hoping Daphne might snoop when she was there and Amber could have a nice laugh at her expense. But Daphne never mentioned anything to her.

"That was amazing." She nuzzled closer to him. "If I were Daphne, I'd never let you out of my bed." She bit his earlobe.

"I don't want to talk about Daphne," he whispered.

She giggled. "She likes to talk about you."

He sat up, his brow furrowed. "What do you mean?"

"Oh, nothing. Just little wifely complaints. No big deal."

"I want to know. What did she say?" There was a hard edge to his voice.

She slid back so she could see his face, her finger

tracing a pattern on his chest as she spoke. "Just stuff about how she's at a point in her life when she wants to chill out, and you're always pushing her to socialize. Said she'd rather stay home and watch old *Law & Order* reruns. I told her she was lucky to go places with you, but she just shook her head and said she was getting too old for all these dinners and galas keeping her out late." It was a total lie, but so what. He'd never know.

She watched his face to see how he reacted, pleased to see his jaw clench.

"I don't appreciate the two of you discussing me." He slid from the bed and threw on his silk robe.

Amber went to him, still naked, and pressed herself against him. "We don't talk about you, I promise. She just complains and I defend you, then change the subject. I adore you, you know that." She hoped he believed that.

His eyes narrowed. He didn't look convinced.

She changed her approach. "I think Daphne's out of her element. You're so brilliant and accomplished. You know all about art and culture, and she . . . well, she's just kind of a simple girl. It's hard to keep up the pretense."

"I suppose," he said.

"Come back to bed. I have a surprise."

He shook his head. "I'm not in the mood."

"Okay, then. Let's go to the living room. I have a present for you." She grabbed his hand.

He yanked it back from her. "Stop telling me what to do. You're starting to sound like a nagging wife."

She felt tears of rage spring to her eyes. How dare he talk to her like that? She swallowed her anger and made her voice sweet. It wouldn't do to let him see how pissed she was. "I'm sorry, sweetie. Would you like a drink?"

"I'll get it myself."

She didn't follow him, but sat down and forced herself to read a magazine, then another to give him some time to cool off. After about an hour, she retrieved the small gold bag with the bib from inside the closet and carried it into the living room. He was sitting in one of the dining room chairs, still brooding.

"Here you go."

"What is it?"

"Open it, silly."

He moved aside the tissue paper and pulled out the bib. He looked up at her, puzzled.

She took his hand and put it on her belly. "Your baby is in here."

His mouth dropped open. "You're pregnant? With a boy?"

She nodded. "Yes. I couldn't believe it myself. I didn't want to say anything until I was sure. There's something else in there."

He rooted around and found the sonogram picture.

"That's our son." Her smile was victorious.

"A boy? Are you sure?"

"One hundred percent."

He stood up, grinning from ear to ear, and picked her up. "This is wonderful news. I'd given up on ever having a son. Now you have to let me get you a place here."

Was he serious? "A place here?"

"Well, yes. You can't very well stay where you are now."

The blood was pounding in her ears. "You're right, Jackson. I can't. And I don't want my son to grow up wondering why his father has him hidden in some back alley. He needs to be with family. Once he's born, we'll go back to Nebraska."

She turned and stomped from the room.

"Amber, wait!"

She threw on a pair of jeans and a sweatshirt and began packing a bag. Did he really expect her to go on being his secret now that she was giving him an heir? He was crazy if he thought she'd let Daphne continue to reap the benefits of being Mrs. Parrish while she worked in his office like a slave and he snuck in visits to his son. The hell with that.

"What are you doing?"

"Leaving! I thought you loved me. What a fool I've been. I don't see Daphne giving you a son, although she looks more pregnant than I do."

He grabbed her hands. "Stop. I was insensitive. Let's talk."

"What's there to talk about? Either we're going to be a family, or we're not."

He sat down on the bed and ran his hand through his hair. "I need to think. We'll figure this out. Don't even think about moving away."

"She doesn't appreciate you, Jackson. She told me she cringes when you touch her. But I love you so much. All I want to do is take care of you, be the wife you deserve. I'll always put you first—even before this child. You're everything to me." She got down on her knees, the way he liked, and showed him just how much she adored him. When she finished, he pulled her to him.

"How was that, Daddy?"

He gave her an inscrutable smile and stood up, picking up the sonogram picture again. His fingers traced it.

"My son." He looked up at Amber. "Does anyone else know? Your mother, your friends?"

She shook her head. "Of course not. I wanted you to be the first."

"Good. Don't tell anyone yet. I have to figure out a way to get out of this marriage without Daphne taking me to the cleaners. If she finds out you're pregnant, it could cost me a lot of money."

Amber nodded. "I understand. I won't breathe a word to anyone."

He continued to sit, a look of such deep concentration on his face that she was afraid to speak.

Finally he stood and began to pace back and forth. "Okay. This is how we're going to play it. You'll get everything out of this apartment, and we'll move you into a rental for now. If Daphne gets suspicious, the last thing we need is for her to find your things here."

"But Jackson," she whined, "I don't want to move to some awful rental. I'll be all alone."

He stopped pacing and stared at her. "What do you mean, 'Some awful rental'? What kind of cheapskate do you think I am? If you don't want an apartment, we'll get a large suite at the Plaza. You'll have people to wait on your every need."

"But what about you? When will I see you?"

"We have to be careful, Amber. I'm going to have to spend a little more time at home. You know, to allay any suspicion. You'll have to stop working once you're showing. Stay out of the way, so no talk gets back to Daphne."

"And what am I supposed to tell Daphne? She'll get suspicious if I stop hanging out with her."

He chewed his lip and then nodded. "You'll say someone in your family is sick. You're taking some time off to go help."

This was beginning to sound like a bad plan to Amber. She'd be stuck away in some hotel, completely dependent on his being true to his word. It felt like she was being put out on a boat without a life jacket or a paddle and could be swept away at Jackson's whim.

"I don't want to be in some impersonal hotel. It won't be good for me to be in some strange place that doesn't feel like home. It won't be good for the baby either."

He sighed. "Fine. We'll rent an apartment. A nice one that will feel like home. You can buy whatever you'd like for it."

She thought about that a few minutes. It was probably the best offer she was going to get at this point. "How long?"

"I don't know. Maybe a few months? We should settle it all by then."

She was angry and scared now, which made it easy to cry. "I hate this, Jackson. I love you so much, and now we're going to have to be separated. I'll be alone in some apartment that isn't even ours. It makes me feel so afraid, the way I used to feel when I was little and we moved all the time because we couldn't pay the rent." She sniffled and wiped the tears from her cheeks, hoping this tale of woe might move him.

He gave her a long look. "Do you want me to lose everything? You're just going to have to trust me."

He wasn't biting. She'd have to go along with the plan and hope he meant what he said until she could come up with something else. But what if he proved to be untrustworthy? Then what? She'd be shit out of luck, just like she was when she fled from Missouri. She wasn't going to let him get away with throwing her and this kid she was carrying aside, even if she had to take more drastic action this time. No more screwing Amber. Those days were over.

PART II

DAPHNE

THIRTY-SIX

I didn't use to be afraid of my husband. I thought I loved him, back when he was kind—or pretended to be. Before I knew what a monster looks like up close.

I met Jackson when I was twenty-six. I'd finished my graduate studies in social work and was in the planning stages of the foundation I was starting in honor of Julie. I'd gotten a job in operations at Save the Children and had been there for six months. It was a great organization, where I could work at something I loved while learning everything I'd need to run my own foundation one day.

A coworker recommended I get in touch with Parrish International, an international real estate firm with a reputation for giving back. She had an in—her father was a business associate. I had expected to be pawned off on some junior executive. Instead, I was granted an audience with Mr. Parrish himself. Jackson was nothing like the captain of industry I had read about. With me, he was amiable and funny, and he put me at ease from the start. When I told him my plans for the foundation and why I was starting it, he shocked me by offering to fund Julie's Smile. Three months later I'd quit my job and was the head of my own foundation. Jackson had assembled a board, which he joined, provided the funding, and found me office space. Things had remained professional between us—I hadn't wanted to jeopardize his support of the foundation, and to be honest, I was also a little scared. But over time, when the lunches turned into dinners, it seemed natural—inevitable even—that our relationship would turn more personal. His wholehearted embrace of my charity turned my head, I'll admit. So I agreed to go to his house for a dinner to celebrate.

The first time I saw his thirty-room estate, the vastness of his wealth hit me. He lived in Bishops Harbor, a picturesque town on the coast of Long Island Sound with a population of about thirty thousand. The town's shopping area could rival Rodeo Drive, with stores far too expensive for my budget, and the only domestic cars on its pristine roads belonged to household staff. The houses dotting the shoreline in the area were magnificent, set far back from the road, shielded by gates, and on grass so lustrous and green it didn't look real. When Jackson's driver pulled the car into the long driveway, it took a minute for the house to come into view. My breath caught in my throat when we approached the tremendous gray estate.

When we walked into the grand foyer, with a chandelier that would have been at home in Buckingham Palace, I gave him a strained smile. Did people really live this way? I remember thinking that the excesses surrounding me could pay so many medical bills for the CF families struggling to keep their heads above water.

"It's very nice."

"Glad you approve." He'd looked at me with a puzzled expression, called for the housekeeper to take our coats, and whisked me off to the deck, where a roaring fire awaited in an outdoor fireplace and we could take in the spectacular view of Long Island Sound.

I was attracted to him—how could I not be? Jackson Parrish was undeniably handsome, his dark hair the perfect frame for eyes bluer than the Caribbean. He was the stuff fantasies were made of—thirty-five-year-old CEO of the company he'd built from the ground up, generous and philanthropic, beloved in the community, charming, boyishly handsome—not the sort of man someone like me dated. I'd read all about his reputation as a playboy. The women he went out with were models and socialites, women whose sophistication and allure far outweighed my own. Maybe that was why his interest took me so by surprise.

I was relaxed, enjoying the soothing view of the Sound and the salty smell of the sea air, when he handed me a glass of something pink.

"A Bellini. It will make you feel like it's summer." An explosion of fruit filled my mouth, and the combination of tart and sweet was delectable.

"It's delicious." I looked out at the sun setting over the water, the sky painted gorgeous shades of pink and purple. "So beautiful. You must never tire of this view."

He sat back, his thigh next to mine making me more lightheaded than the drink.

"Never. I grew up in the mountains and didn't realize what an enchantress the sea is until I moved east."

"You're from Colorado, right?"

He smiled. "Doing some research on me?"

I took another sip, emboldened by the alcohol. "You're not exactly a private figure." It seemed like I couldn't open a newspaper without reading about wonder boy Jackson Parrish.

"Actually I'm a very private person. When you reach the level of success that I have, it's hard to know who your real friends are. I have to be careful who I let get close to me." He took my glass and refilled it. "But enough about me. I want to know more about you."

"I'm not very interesting, I'm afraid. Just a girl from a small town. Nothing special."

He gave me a wry smile. "If you call getting published at fourteen nothing special. I loved the piece you did for *is* magazine about your sister and her brave fight."

"Wow. You did your research too. How did you even find that?"

He winked at me. "I have my ways. It was very touching. So, you and Julie had both planned on going to Brown?"

"Yes, from the time we were little. After she died, I felt like I had to go. For both of us."

"That's rough. How old were you when you lost her?"

"Eighteen."

He put his hand on mine. "I'm sure she's very proud of you. Especially what you're doing, your dedication. The foundation is going to help so many people."

"I'm so grateful to you. Without your help it would have taken me years to get a space and a staff."

"I'm happy to do it. You were lucky to have her. I've always wondered what it would have been like to grow up with brothers and sisters."

"It must have been lonely being an only child," I said.

He had a faraway look. "My father worked all the time, and my mother had her charity duties. I always wished I had a brother to go outside and throw a football with, to go shoot some hoops." He shrugged. "Oh, well, plenty of people had it much worse."

"What does your father do?"

"He was the CEO of Boulder Insurance. Pretty big job. He's retired now. My mother was a stay-at-home mom."

I didn't want to pry, but he seemed like he wanted to talk. "Was?"

He suddenly stood up. "She died in a car crash. It's a bit chilly. Why don't we go inside?"

I stood, feeling woozy, and put a hand on the chair to steady myself. He turned toward me then, his eyes intense, caressed my cheek, and whispered, "When you're with me, I don't feel lonely at all." I said nothing as he scooped me into his arms and carried me into the house and up to his bed.

Parts of that first night we spent together are still a blur. I hadn't planned on making love to him—I had felt it was too soon. But before I knew it, we were naked and tangled up in the sheets. He held my eyes the entire time. It was unnerving, like he was staring into my very soul, but I couldn't look away. When it was over, he was tender and sweet, and he fell asleep wrapped in my arms. I watched his face in the moonlight and traced the outline of his jaw. I wanted to erase all his sad memories and make him feel the love and nurturing he'd missed as a child. This gorgeous, strong, and successful man that everyone looked up to had shared his vulnerabilities with me. He needed me. There is nothing more enticing to me than being needed.

When morning came, I had a pounding headache. I wondered if I'd been simply another conquest, if now that he'd had me, we'd go back to being business associates. Would I join the ranks of his ex-lovers, or was this the start of a new relationship? I worried that he was comparing me to the glamour girls he was used to sleeping with, and that I came up short. He seemed to read my mind. Propping himself up on one elbow, he traced my breast with his right hand.

"I like having you here."

I didn't know what to say, so I simply smiled. "I bet you say that to all the girls."

His face darkened, and he pulled his hand back. "No, I don't."

"I'm sorry." I took a deep breath. "I'm a little nervous."

He kissed me then, his tongue insistent, his mouth pressed to mine. Then he pulled away and caressed my cheek with the back of his hand. "You don't have to be nervous with me. I'll take good care of you."

A mixture of feelings washed over me. I untangled myself from his arms and gave him a sincere smile. "I need to go. I'll be late."

He pulled me back to him. "You're the boss, remember? You don't answer to anyone but the board." He was on top of me then, his eyes holding mine again in that hypnotizing stare. "And the board doesn't mind if you're late. Please stay. I just want to hold you a little longer."

Everything had begun with such promise. And then, like a windshield chipped by a tiny pebble, the chip turned into deep cracks that spread until there was nothing left to repair.

THIRTY-SEVEN

Dating as a means to getting to know someone is highly overrated. When your hormones are raging and the attraction is magnetic, your brain takes a vacation. He was everything I never knew I needed.

At work, I was back in my comfort zone, though I kept flashing back to our night together with a smile. Hours later, a commotion outside my small office made me look up. A young man was pushing a cart with vase after vase of red roses. Fiona, my secretary, was behind him, her face flushed and hands waving.

"Someone sent you flowers. Lots of flowers."

I stood up and signed for them. I counted a dozen vases. I put one bunch on my desk and looked around, wondering what to do with the rest. We placed them along the floor of my small office, since we had nowhere else to set them.

Fiona shut the door when the deliveryman left and plopped down in the chair across from me. "Okay, spill."

I hadn't wanted to discuss Jackson with anyone yet. I didn't even know what we were. I reached over and pulled out the card.

Your skin is softer than these petals. Missing you already.

J

They were everywhere. It was too much. The cloying smell of the flowers overwhelmed me and made my stomach roil.

Fiona was staring at me with an exasperated expression. "Well?"

"Jackson Parrish."

"I knew it!" She gave me a triumphant look. "The way he was looking at you when he stopped by to see the offices the other day, I knew it was just a matter of time." She leaned forward, her chin in her hands. "Is it serious?"

"I don't know." I shook my head. "I like him—but I don't know." I gestured toward the flowers. "He comes on awfully strong."

"Yeah, what a jerk, sending you all these beautiful roses." She got up and opened door.

"Fiona?"

"Yes?"

"Take a couple for your desk. I don't know what to do with the rest."

She shook her head. "Sure thing, Boss. But I gotta tell you, he's not going to be so easy to cast off."

I needed to get back to work. I'd figure out Jackson later. I was about to make a phone call when Fiona opened the door again. Her face was ashen.

"It's your mother."

I grabbed the phone and held it to my ear. "Mom?"

"Daphne, you need to come home. Your father's had a heart attack."

"How bad is it?" I choked out.

"Just come. As soon as you can."

THIRTY-EIGHT

The next phone call I made was to Jackson. As soon as I managed to get the words out, he took over.

"Daphne, it's going to be okay. Deep breaths. Stay where you are. I'm on my way."

"But I have to get to the airport. I need to find a flight. I—"

"I'll take you. Don't worry."

I'd forgotten he owned a plane. "Can you do that?"

"Listen to me. Stay there. I'm leaving now to get you. We'll go by your place and get some clothes and be in the air in about an hour. Just breathe."

The rest was a blur. I did what he told me, threw things in a suitcase, followed directions until I was seated on his plane, grasping his hand tightly while I looked out the window and prayed. My father was only fifty-nine—surely he couldn't die.

When we landed in New Hampshire at a private airport, Marvin, a waiter at the inn, was waiting for us. I guess I made the introductions, or maybe Jackson just took over. I don't remember. All I remember is the feeling in the pit of my stomach that I might never get to talk to my father again.

As soon as we arrived at the hospital, Jackson took charge. He found out who Dad's doctor was, assessed the facility, and immediately had him moved to St. Gregory's, the large hospital an hour from our small town. There is no doubt in my mind that he would have died had Jackson not seen the ineptitude of his treating doctor at County General and the lack of sophisticated equipment. Jackson arranged for a top cardio doctor from New York to meet us at the hospital. The doctor arrived shortly after we did, and upon examining my dad, declared that he hadn't had a heart attack after all, but an aortic dissection. He explained that the lining of his heart had torn, and if he didn't operate immediately, my father would die. Apparently his high blood pressure had been the cause. He warned us that the delay in the diagnosis had diminished his chance of survival to fifty percent.

Jackson canceled all his meetings and never left my side. After a week, I was prepared for him to go back to Connecticut, but he had something else in mind.

"You girls go on ahead," he told me and my mom. "I've talked to your dad about it already. I'm going back to the B&B to make sure everything runs smoothly."

"What about your company? Don't you need to get back?"

"I can handle things from here for now. I've rearranged things a bit. A few weeks away isn't going to kill me."

"Are you sure? There's staff that can fill in for now."

He shook his head. "I can conduct my business from anywhere, but the B&B is a hands-on operation, and when the boss isn't around, things slide. I intend to protect your dad's interests until he's moved back to the inn and your mother can keep an eye on things."

My mother gave me one of those looks then that said, *Don't let go of this one.* She put her hand on Jackson's shoulder. "Thank you, dear. I know Ezra will breathe easier knowing that you're there."

With typical Jackson efficiency and flair, he threw

himself into making sure everything ran smoothly—
even better than when my father was at the helm. The
kitchen was stocked, he oversaw the staff, he even made
sure the bird feeders were never empty. One evening
when we were short-staffed, I came back to the inn to
see him waiting tables. I think that's when I really fell
for him. It was a huge load off my mother, and when
she saw how easily he stepped in, she was free to spend
all her time at the hospital without worrying what was
going on back at the B&B.

By the end of the month, my mother was as bewitched
as I was.

"I think you've found the one, sweetheart," my
mother whispered one night after Jackson had left the
room.

How had he managed to do that? I wondered. It was
as though he'd been around forever, already a part of
the family. All my earlier reservations about him evaporated. He wasn't some self-indulgent playboy. He was
a man of substance and character. In the space of a few
short weeks, he had become indispensable to all of us.

THIRTY-NINE

Dad was home from the hospital, still weak, but doing better, and Jackson and I were flying to New Hampshire to spend Christmas with my family. My cousin, Barry, and his wife, Erin, were coming with their daughter, and we were all excited about spending Christmas together.

We arrived Christmas Eve to falling snow and the perfect New England setting. The inn was decked out in holiday cheer. Standing in the small church where I'd gone every Sunday from the time I was a little girl, I felt at peace, my heart overflowing. My father had survived, and I was in love. It was like a fairy tale—I'd won the prince I never even knew existed in real life. He caught me looking at him and smiled that dazzling smile at me, his cobalt-blue eyes shining with adoration, and I could hardly believe that he was mine.

When we got back to the inn, my father opened a bottle of champagne and poured a glass for each of us. He put his arm around my mother. "I want you all to know how much it means to have you here. A few months ago, I wasn't so sure I'd live to see another Christmas." He brushed a tear from his cheek and lifted his glass. "To family. Those of us here, and to our darling Julie, in heaven. Merry Christmas."

I took a sip, closed my eyes, and said my own silent Merry Christmas to my sister. I still missed her so much.

We sat down on the sofas by the tree to exchange gifts. My parents had started a family tradition of giving us three gifts, symbolic of the ones the wise men gave to Jesus. Jackson had a pile of three to open as well, and I was grateful that my mother had thought to include him. The gifts were modest but special—a sweater she'd knitted him, a Beethoven CD, and a hand-painted sailboat ornament for his Christmas tree. Jackson held the fisherman's sweater up to his chest.

"I love it. This will keep me nice and warm." He stood up and walked over to the tree. "My turn." He took great delight in handing out the gifts he had selected for everyone. I had no idea what he had bought; he wanted to keep it all a surprise. I had mentioned to him that the gifts would be modest, and asked him not to go overboard. He started with my little niece, who was eight at the time. He had gotten her a lovely silver charm bracelet with Disney characters, and she was thrilled. For Barry and Erin, a Bose Bluetooth speaker, top-of-the-line. I was starting to get a little nervous thinking of the book on classic cars they had given to him and how they must feel. He took no apparent notice, but I could see from the expression on Barry's face that he was uncomfortable.

Jackson took something from his pocket and, kneeling in front of me, handed me a small foil-wrapped box.

My heart began to pound. Was this really happening? My hands shook as I tore the paper. I removed the black velvet box and popped the top open.

It *was* a ring. I didn't realize how much I'd hoped it would be until just then. "Oh, Jackson. It's beautiful."

"Daphne, would you do me the honor of becoming my wife?"

My mother gasped and clapped her hands together.

I threw my arms around him. "Yes! Yes!"

He slipped the ring on my finger.

"It's gorgeous, Jackson. And so big."

"Nothing but the best for you. It's a six-carat round cut. Flawless. Like you."

It fit perfectly. I held my hand out and turned it this way and that. My mother and Erin rushed to my side, oohing and aahing.

My father stood apart, strangely quiet, an inscrutable expression on his face. "It's a little fast, isn't it?"

The room went silent. An angry look passed quickly over Jackson's face. Then he smiled and walked over to my father.

"Sir, I understand your reservations. But I have loved your daughter from the moment I set eyes on her. I promise you, I will treat her like a queen. I hope you'll give us your blessing." He held his hand out to my father.

Everyone was watching them. My father reached out and clasped Jackson's hand in his.

"Welcome to the family, son," he said, and smiled, but I think I was the only one who noticed that the smile didn't quite reach his eyes.

Jackson pumped his hand and looked him straight in the eye. "Thank you." Then, with a cat-that-swallowed-the-canary look, he pulled something from his pant pocket. "I wanted to save this until last." He handed an envelope to my father.

My father opened it, a frown pulling at his mouth. There was a look of confusion in his eyes as he gave it back to Jackson. He shook his head. "This is too extravagant."

My mother walked over. "What is it, Ezra?"

Jackson answered. "A new roof. I know you've been

having problems with leaks with this old one. They'll do it in the spring."

"Well, that's so thoughtful, but Ezra's right, Jackson, it's way too much."

He put his arm around me and smiled at them both. "Nonsense. I'm a part of the family now. And family takes care of each other. I absolutely won't take no for an answer."

I didn't know why they were being so stubborn. I thought it was a wonderful gesture and knew it wouldn't put a dent in Jackson's finances.

"Mom, Dad, let go of that Yankee pride of yours," I tried to tease. "It's a wonderful gift."

My father looked directly at Jackson. "I appreciate it, son, but it's not the way I do things. It's my business, and I'll put a new roof on when I'm good and ready. Now I don't want to hear any more about it."

Jackson's jaw clenched, and he dropped the hand from my shoulder. He deflated before my eyes, put the envelope back in his pocket, and spoke again, this time barely a whisper.

"Now I've offended you when I just wanted to do something nice. Please forgive me." His head was bent, and he raised his eyes to look at my mother, like a boy in trouble looking for reprieve. "I wanted to be a part of your family. It's been so hard since my mother died."

My mother swooped over and put her arms around him. "Jackson, of course you're part of the family." She gave my father a disapproving look. "Family does help family. We'll be happy to accept your gift."

That was the first time I saw it—that little smile that played at his lips, and the look in his eyes that read *Victory*.

FORTY

Though he'd recovered from the surgery, Dad wasn't doing well, and I didn't know how long he really had. Part of the reason we rushed to get married was so that I could be sure he would be around to walk me down the aisle. The wedding was a small affair. My father insisted on paying for it, and despite entreaties, would not be persuaded to allow Jackson to contribute. Jackson had wanted to have a huge wedding back in Bishops Harbor and invite all his business associates. I promised Jackson that when we returned from our honeymoon, we could have a party to celebrate, and that appeased him.

We got married in February at my family's Presbyterian church and held the reception at the B&B. Jackson's father flew in for the wedding, and I was a nervous wreck before meeting him. His father was bringing a date, and Jackson wasn't happy about it. Jackson had sent his private plane for them and had a driver waiting at the airport to bring them to the inn.

"I can't believe he's bringing that simpering idiot. He shouldn't even be dating yet."

"Jackson, that's a bit harsh, isn't it?"

"She's a nothing. It's an insult to my mother. She's a *waitress*."

I thought of the lovely women who worked at the restaurant at the inn and felt my defenses go up. "What's wrong with being a waitress?"

He sighed. "Nothing, if you're in college. She's in her

sixties. And my father has a lot of money. She's probably latching on to him as her next meal ticket."

I felt a nagging feeling in the pit of my stomach. "How well do you know her?

He shrugged. "I've only met her once. A couple of months ago when I flew to Chicago on business, we had dinner together. She was loud and not particularly bright. But she hung on his every word. My mother had a mind of her own."

"Are you sure you're not just having a hard time seeing him with someone other than your mother? You've told me how close you were to her. I'm sure it's not easy seeing her replaced."

His face turned red. "My mother is irreplaceable. That woman will never be able to hold a candle to her."

"I'm sorry. I didn't mean it that way." He hadn't shared much about his parents, beyond that his father was a workaholic who never had time for him when he was growing up. I suppose, being an only child, he had an even closer relationship with his mother. Her death the year before had hit him hard, and from what I could see, his grief was still raw. I didn't want to dwell on the unwelcome thought racing through my head—that he was a snob. I chalked it up to angst over his mother and pushed it to the back of my mind.

When I met Flora, I thought she was nice enough, and his father seemed happy. They were cordial to my parents, and everyone got along fine. The next day, when my father walked me down the aisle, all I could think about was how lucky I was to have found the love of my life and to be starting a new life with Jackson.

※

"Don't you think it's time you let me in on the big secret?" I asked as we boarded his plane for our honeymoon. "I don't even know if I packed the right clothes."

He leaned in and kissed me. "Silly girl. There are suitcases upon suitcases full of clothes I've bought for you already on board. Just leave everything to me."

He'd bought new clothes for me? "When did you have time to do that?"

"Don't you worry about it, my darling. You'll find that I'm very good at planning ahead."

Once we got settled in our seats and I took a sip of my champagne, I tried again. "So when do I find out?"

He pulled the shade to my window down. "When we land. Now lie back and relax. Maybe even get some sleep. And when you wake up, we'll have a little fun in the clouds." His hand moved up and down my inner thigh as he spoke, and desire spread through me like hot liquid.

"Why don't we have that fun right now?" I whispered as I pressed my lips against his ear.

Jackson smiled, and when I looked into his eyes, I saw the same craving I felt. He rose and took me into his muscular arms, carrying me to the bedroom where we fell to the bed, bodies entwined. We slept afterward—I'm not sure how long, but soon after we awakened and made love again, the captain phoned Jackson to let him know we would be making our descent in a few minutes. He was careful not to name a destination, but when I peered out the window, I saw miles and miles of blue water beneath us. Wherever we were, it looked like paradise. Jackson threw off the bedcovers and came to my side by the window, putting his arm around my naked waist. "See that?" He pointed to a glorious mountain that seemed to emerge like a noble monolith out of the sea. "That's Mount Otemanu, one of the most beautiful sights in the world. And soon I'll show you the magnificence of Bora Bora."

Polynesia, I thought. I turned to look at him. "You've been here before?"

He kissed my cheek. "I have, my darling girl. But never with you."

I was somehow disappointed but didn't quite know how to put it into words. I made a clumsy attempt. "I just assumed we would go someplace neither of us had ever been, so that, you know, we could experience everything together. For the first time."

Jackson pulled me down onto the bed and tousled my hair. "I've traveled a lot. Any place worth going to is a place I've been. Would you have preferred Davenport, Iowa? That's a place I haven't seen. You know, I did have a life before we met."

"Of course," I said. "I just wanted this time to be new for both of us, something only the two of us shared." I wanted to ask him if he'd been here alone or with another woman, but I was afraid to ruin the mood even more. "Bora Bora," I said. "It's a place I never thought I'd go to."

"I've booked an over-water bungalow. You're going to love it, my sweet." And he pulled me into his arms once again.

We were back in our seats as the wheels went down, and we landed at the airport on the tiny islet of Motu Mute. The door opened, and we walked down the jet stairs to be greeted by smiling islanders who draped leis around our necks. I reached out to touch his.

"I like your lei better. Blue's my favorite color."

He took it from his neck and put it around mine. "Looks better on you anyway. By the way, in Bora Bora, they're called *hei*s."

The warm, fragrant air was intoxicating. I was already in love with the place. We were whisked by boat to our bungalow, which looked more like a lavish floating villa, with glass floors that offered a vision of the lagoon life below.

Our luggage arrived, and I changed into a casual sundress, Jackson into navy pants and a white linen shirt. His tanned skin against the white shirt made him look even more handsome, if that was possible. We had just settled on our private deck when an outrigger canoe pulled up to our bungalow to serve us champagne and caviar. I looked at Jackson in surprise. "Did you order this?" I asked.

He looked at me as if I were a naive little country girl. "This is part of the service, my dear. They'll bring us anything we want. If we choose to stay in for dinner, they'll bring it to us; in for lunch, we get lunch— whatever our whims dictate." He spooned a dollop of caviar onto a round cracker and held it to my mouth. "Only the best for my girl. Get used to it."

To tell the truth, caviar and champagne were two of my least favorite things, but I supposed I needed to develop a taste for them.

He took a long sip of champagne, and we sat there feeling the fresh air waft across our faces, mesmerized by the turquoise water before us. I leaned back and closed my eyes, listening to the sound of the water lapping against the pilings.

"We have a dinner reservation at eight at La Villa Mahana," he said.

I opened my eyes and looked at him. "Oh?"

"It's a little gem with just a few tables. You'll love it."

Once again I had that initial feeling of disappointment. Obviously he'd been to the restaurant before. "I suppose you can tell me precisely what to order and what the best things on the menu are," I said, somewhat flippantly.

He gave me a cold look. "If you'd rather not go, I'll cancel the reservation. I'm sure there are throngs of couples on the waiting list who would love to dine there."

I felt like an ungrateful fool. "I'm sorry. I don't know what got into me. Of course we'll go."

Jackson had already unpacked and carefully hung everything he'd bought for me. The clothing was lined up not only by type of outfit but also by color. Shoes sat on a top shelf over the rod and were separated into flat sandals and heels, every color, every type. He held up a long, white dress with slender straps and fitted bodice. There were more clothes than days we would be there: evening shoes, sandals, bathing suits, cover-ups, jewelry, casual daytime outfits, and floaty slip dresses for evening. "Here," he said. "This will be perfect for tonight, my beautiful girl."

It felt so odd, someone choosing my clothes for me, but I had to admit the dress was lovely. It fit perfectly, and the turquoise drop earrings he'd picked were set off beautifully by the pure white material.

We stayed in the second night and had dinner brought to us. We sat on our deck and savored the food as well as the setting sun that made pink and blue ribbons across the sky. It was magical.

This was our pattern—alone in our bungalow one night, the next night at a restaurant like Bloody Mary's or Mai Kai or St. James. They each had their own delightful ambience, and I especially loved the casual island feel of Bloody Mary's, with its sand floor and delicious rum cake. Even the bathrooms had sand floors. When we had dinner out, we'd walk along the beach holding hands and make love after getting home. On the nights we ate in, our lovemaking began earlier and lasted longer. My skin was turning a warm brown, and it felt clean and taut, after days in the sun and water. I'd never been so aware of my body, the touch of someone's hand on me, the thrill of coming together and feeling as one.

Every moment had been planned by him, from swimming and snorkeling to private tours and romantic dinners. We made love on the sands of a private beach, in a boat on the lagoon, and, of course, in the private haven that was the bungalow. He had thought of everything, down to the smallest detail. And even though there were times I had a small, nagging feeling in my stomach, I never consciously understood how much his need for order and control would overpower my life.

FORTY-ONE

I was packed and ready when he came home, excited at the prospect of four uninterrupted days at the Green-brier with my new husband. We had been married a little over three months. My suitcase was sitting on the bed, and after kissing me hello, he went over to it and opened it.

"What are you doing? Your suitcase is right there." I pointed to the matching one by his dresser.

He gave me an amused smile. "I'm aware." He pulled out what I had packed, a frown appearing on his face as he looked through all my clothes.

I stood there, wanting to tell him to take his hands off my things, but the words wouldn't come. I watched, fro-zen, as he rifled through everything and looked at me.

"You do realize this is not some hick bed-and-breakfast like your parents run?"

I recoiled as though I'd been struck.

He noticed my expression and laughed. "Oh, come on. I didn't mean it that way. It's just that this is the Greenbrier. They have a dress code. You need a few cocktail dresses."

My face was hot with embarrassment and anger. "I know what the Greenbrier is. I've actually been there before." I hadn't, but I had looked at it online.

He raised his eyebrows and studied me for a long mo-ment. "Really? When was that?"

"That's not the point. What I'm getting at is that you

don't have to go through my things as though I'm a child. What I've packed is fine."

He threw his hands up in surrender. "Fine. Have it your way. But don't come crying to me when you realize you're wildly underdressed compared to the other women."

I strode past him, zipped my case, and flung it to the floor. "See you downstairs." I went to pick it up when he stopped me.

"Daphne."

I turned around. "What?"

"Leave it. We have help for that." Then he shook his head and muttered something under his breath.

I picked it up. I still hadn't gotten used to all these people underfoot, waiting to do for me what I could easily do for myself. "I'm perfectly capable of carrying my own suitcase." I stormed into the study and poured myself a glass of whiskey. Throwing it back in one swig, I closed my eyes and breathed deeply. It burned going down, but then I felt a calmness pervade me and thought, *So this is how people become alcoholics.* Walking to the window, I drank in the water view, and it settled what was left of my jangling nerves.

I was learning that emotional intimidation could be just as unsettling as physical. Little things had begun to grate on his nerves, and despite my best efforts to please him, nothing was ever good enough. I'd chosen the wrong wineglass or left a damp towel on the wood table. Maybe it would be that I'd forgotten my hair dryer on the counter. What made it even more difficult to live with was the uncertainty. Which Jackson was I talking to now? The one with the easy laugh and charming smile that put everyone at ease? Or the one with the scowl and critical tone who let me know with just one look that I had done something else to disappoint him? He was a chameleon, his transitions so quick and seamless they left me breathless at times. And now he didn't even think I had the ability to pack my own suitcase.

A hand on my shoulder startled me.

"I'm sorry."

I didn't turn around or answer him.

He began to massage my shoulders, moving closer until his mouth was on my neck, and his lips sent quivers down my spine. I didn't want to respond, but my body had other ideas.

"You can't talk to me like that. I'm not one of your minions." I pulled away.

"I know. You're right. I'm sorry. This is all a little new for me."

"Me as well. Still . . ." I shook my head.

He stroked my cheek. "You know that I adore you. I'm used to being in charge. Give me some time to adjust. Let's not have this fight spoil our trip." He kissed me again, and I felt myself respond. "I'm really more interested in what you're *not* wearing this weekend."

So I let it go, and off we went.

We were both in good moods by the time we arrived, and when we entered the sumptuous suite, with deep-red carpets and walls, thick gray draperies, and ornate mirrors and paintings, I felt like I'd stepped back in time. It was enormous and formal and a bit intimidating. There was a dining room table that could seat ten, a formal living room, and three bedrooms. Suddenly I wondered if I *had* packed the right clothes.

"It's beautiful, but why do we need such a large suite? It's just us."

"Only the best for you. I wasn't going to have us cramped in a little room. Is that what you did when you came here?"

I tried to picture the rooms I'd seen on the website and waved my hand dismissively. "I stayed in a regular room."

"Really? And when was that again?"

He was looking at me with an amused expression, but his eyes—his eyes were angry.

"What difference does it make?"

"You know, I had a best friend. We used to do everything together from the time we were kids. When we were in college, we were supposed to go on a camping trip with his family. He called me the night before and canceled—said he was sick. I found out on Monday that he'd been at a local bar with his girlfriend." He was pacing now. "Do you know what I did?"

"What?"

"I seduced his girlfriend, had her break up with him for me, then I dumped them both."

My blood ran cold. "That's horrible. What did the poor girl ever do to you?"

He smiled. "I'm joking about the girl. But I did end the friendship."

I didn't know what to believe. "Why are you telling me this?"

"Because I think you're lying. And if there's one thing I cannot abide, it's a liar. Don't take me for a fool. You've never been here before. Admit it now, before it's too late."

"Too late for what?" I asked in a voice braver than I felt.

"Too late for me to trust you."

I burst into tears, and he walked over and put his arms around me.

"I didn't want you to think I'd never been anywhere nice or been exposed to things you take for granted."

He lifted my chin and kissed my tears away. "My darling, you don't ever have to pretend with me. I love being the one to show you new things. You don't have to try and impress me. I love that everything is new to you."

"I'm sorry for lying."

"Promise me it will be the last time."

"I promise."

"All right, then. It's all good. Let's unpack, and then I'll show you around."

As I hung my meager ensembles next to his custom suits and ties, I turned to him with a sinking feeling. "How would you like to do a little shopping after that tour?" I asked.

"Already in the plans," he answered.

The next two days were wonderful. We went horseback riding, spent hours in the spa, and couldn't get enough of each other in bed. It was our last day, and just as we were on our way to breakfast, my phone rang. It was my mother.

"Mom?" I could hear in her voice that something was wrong.

"Daphne. I have some bad news. Your fa—" The sound of her crying came over the line.

"Mom! What is it? You're scaring me."

"He died, Daphne. Your dad. He's gone."

I started to cry. "No, no, no."

Jackson rushed over and took the phone from me, pulling me to him with the other arm. I couldn't believe it. How could he be dead? I'd just talked to him last week. I remembered his cardiologist's warning that his full recovery was far from complete. Jackson held me as I sobbed, and gently led me to the sofa while he packed us up.

We flew straight to the inn and stayed there for the next week. As I watched my father's casket being lowered into the ground, all I could think about was the day we'd done the same thing for Julie. Despite Jackson's strong arm around my shoulder and my mother standing next to me, I felt utterly and completely alone.

FORTY-TWO

Jackson wanted kids right away. We'd only been married for six months when he talked me into putting away my diaphragm. I was twenty-seven, he reminded me; it could take a while. I got pregnant the first month. He was delighted, but it took me longer to warm up to the idea. Of course, we had already been tested to make sure he didn't carry the CF gene. I had the recessive gene, and if he had it as well, we wouldn't have been able to have a child without the risk of passing on the disease. Even after the doctor's assurances that we had the all-clear, I still found it hard to get rid of my anxiety. There were plenty of other diseases or birth defects that might await our child, and if I'd learned anything growing up, it was that the worst can and often does happen. I shared my concerns with Jackson over dinner one night.

"What if something's wrong?"

"We'll know. They'll do the testing, and if it isn't healthy, we'll terminate."

He spoke with such detachment that my blood ran cold. "You say it like it's no big deal."

He shrugged. "It isn't. That's why they do the tests, right? So we have a plan. Nothing to worry about."

I wasn't finished discussing it. "What if I don't want to have an abortion? Or what if they say the baby's fine and it isn't, or they say it isn't and it is?"

"What are you talking about? They know what they're doing," he said, an impatient edge in his voice.

"When my cousin's wife, Erin, was pregnant, they told her that her baby was going to have major birth defects, but she didn't end the pregnancy. That was Simone. She was perfect."

An exasperated sigh. "That was years ago. Things are more precise now."

"Still . . ."

"Damn it, Daphne, what do you want me to say? Whatever I tell you, you come up with an illogical retort. Are you trying to be miserable?"

"Of course not."

"Then stop it. We're going to have a baby. I certainly hope this nervous Nellie act goes away before the birth. I can't abide those anxious mothers who worry about every little thing." He took a swig from his tumbler of Hennessy.

"I don't believe in abortion," I blurted out.

"Do you believe in allowing children to suffer? Are you telling me that if you found out that our baby was going to have some horrible disease, you'd have it anyway?"

"It's not so black-and-white. Who are we to say who deserves life and who doesn't? I don't want to make decisions that only God can make."

He raised his eyebrows. "God? You believe in a God who would allow your sister to live a life of suffering and then die when she was still a child? I think we've seen where God's position on these things takes us. I'll make my own choices, thank you very much."

"It's not the same thing at all, Jackson. I can't explain why bad things happen. I'm just saying that I'm carrying a life inside me, and I don't know if I could terminate, no matter what. I don't think I'm capable of that."

He got very quiet, pursed his lips, then spoke deliberately. "Let me help you out then. I cannot raise a disabled child. I know that that is something that I am not capable of."

"The baby is probably fine, but how can you say you can't raise a child with a disability or an illness? It's your child. You don't throw a life away because it's not what you consider perfect. How can you not see that?"

He looked at me a long time before answering. "What I see is that you have no idea what it's like to grow up normally. We shouldn't even be having this conversation yet. If—and that's a big if—it turns out we have something to worry about, we'll discuss it then."

"But—"

He put a hand up to stop me. "The baby will be perfect. You need help, Daphne. It's obvious that you're incapable of letting go of the past. I want you to see a therapist."

"What? You're not serious?"

"I've never been more serious. I won't have you raising our son with all your phobias and paranoia."

"What are you talking about?"

"Everything is colored by your sister's illness. You can't separate that and what it did to you from your present life. You've got to move past it. Put it to bed, for God's sake. Therapy will close the issue once and for all."

I didn't want to dredge up my childhood and live through it again. "Jackson, please, I *have* let go of the past. Haven't we been happy? I'll be fine, I promise you. I was just thrown a little. That's all. I'll be fine. Really."

He arched a perfect brow. "I want to believe you, but I have to be sure."

I gave him a wooden smile. "We're going to have a perfect baby and all live happily ever after."

His lips curled upward. "That's my girl."

Then something he'd said a moment ago registered. "How do you know it's going to be a boy?"

"I don't. But I'm hoping it will. I've always wanted a son—someone I could do all the things with that my father never had time to do with me."

I felt a nervous stirring in my gut. "What if it's a girl?"

He shrugged. "Then we'll try again."

FORTY-THREE

Of course, we had a girl—Tallulah, and she was perfect. She was an easy baby, and I reveled in being a mother. I loved nursing her at night when the house was quiet, staring into her eyes and feeling a connection that I'd never felt before. I followed my mother's advice and slept when she slept, but I was still more exhausted than I'd anticipated. At four months, she still wasn't sleeping through the night, and because I was nursing, I'd refused Jackson's offer of a night nurse. I didn't want to pump and have her fed from a bottle. I wanted to do it all. But that meant I had less time for Jackson.

That's when things began to unravel. By the time he fully revealed himself to me, it was too late. He had used my vulnerability to his advantage, like a general armed for battle. His weapons were kindness, attention, and compassion—and when victory was assured, he discarded them like spent casings, and his true nature emerged.

Jackson faded to the background, and all my time and energy was focused on Tallulah. That morning, I'd pulled the scale out from under the vanity, thrown my robe off, and stepped on—139. I stared at the number in shock. I heard the door open, and he was standing there, looking at me with a strange expression on his face. I went to step off, but he put a hand up, walked toward me, and peered over my shoulder. A look of disgust crossed his face so quickly that I almost missed it. He reached out and patted my stomach, raising his eyebrows.

"Shouldn't this be flat by now?"

I felt the color rush to my face as shame filled me. Stepping off the scale, I grabbed my robe from the floor and threw it on. "Why don't you try having a baby and see how your stomach looks?"

He shook his head. "It's been four months, Daph. Can't use that excuse anymore. I see lots of your friends at the club in their tight jeans. They've all had kids too."

"They probably all had tummy tucks after their C-sections too," I shot back.

He took my face in his hands. "Don't get defensive. You don't need a tummy tuck. You just need some discipline. I married a size four, and I expect you to get back into all those expensive clothes I've bought you. Come on." He took my hand and led me to the love seat in the corner of our bedroom suite. "Sit down and listen."

He put an arm around my shoulder and took a place next to me on the love seat.

"I'm going to help you. You need accountability." Then he pulled out a journal.

"What's that?" I asked.

"I picked it up for you a few weeks ago." Flashing a smile, he continued. "I want you to weigh yourself every day and write it here. Then write down what you've eaten in the food journal part here." He pointed to the page. "I'll check it every night when I get home."

I couldn't believe it. He'd been holding on to this for weeks now? I wanted to curl up and die. Yes, I still wasn't back to my pre-baby weight, but I wasn't fat.

I looked at him, afraid to ask but needing to know. "Do you find me unattractive?"

"Can you blame me? You haven't worked out in months."

I held back the tears and bit my lip. "I'm tired, Jackson. I'm up with the baby in the middle of the night, I'm tired in the morning."

He covered my hand with his. "That's why I keep telling you to let me hire a full-time baby nurse."

"I cherish that time with her. I don't want a stranger here at night."

He stood up, anger in his eyes. "You've done it for months, and look where it's gotten you. At this rate, you'll be as big as a house. I want my wife back. I'm calling the service today and getting a nurse here. You will sleep through the nights again and have your mornings back. I insist."

"But I'm nursing."

He sighed. "Yeah, that's another thing. It's disgusting. Your breasts are like two overblown balloons. I don't want your tits hanging to the floor. Enough is enough."

I stood on shaky legs, nausea overtaking me, and ran to the bathroom. How could he be so cruel? I took my robe off again and examined myself in the full-length mirror. Why hadn't I noticed all that cellulite before? I took a hand and swiped at it on one of my thighs. Like jelly. Pushing both hands on my stomach was like kneading dough. He was right. I turned around and looked over my shoulder, my eyes drawn to the dimpling in my buttocks. I had to fix this. It *was* time to return to the gym. My eyes rested on the breasts my husband found disgusting. I swallowed the lump in my throat, got dressed, and went downstairs. Picking up the grocery list sitting on the counter, I added another item: formula.

Margarita had prepared a breakfast buffet that morning to rival the Ritz. When Jackson came in, he filled his plate to overflowing with pancakes, bacon, strawberries, and a homemade muffin. I thought about the journal he'd just given me and felt the heat spread to my face. He was crazy if he thought I'd have him dictating what I ate. I'd start my diet tomorrow and on my own terms. I grabbed a plate and picked up the fork on the pancake platter, ready to take one, when he cleared his throat. I looked over at him. He inclined his head ever so slightly toward the fruit platter. I took a deep breath, stabbed three pancakes with my fork, and dropped them onto my plate. Ignoring him, I grabbed the syrup and poured until they were swimming in it. As I lifted the fork, I held his gaze as I stuffed a fluffy slice of pancake slathered in syrup into my mouth.

FORTY-FOUR

I paid for my little act of rebellion. Not right away, because that wasn't his style. By the time he executed his plan three weeks later, I had nearly forgotten about it. But he hadn't. My mother was coming for a visit. After my father died, she came often—every few months—and I encouraged her visits. The night before she was due to arrive, he exacted his revenge. He waited until Tallulah had been put down and came into the kitchen, where I was talking to Margarita about the menu for dinner the next night. He was standing in the archway, leaning against the doorframe, arms crossed, with an amused expression on his face. When she left, he walked over to me, pushed a lock of hair from my forehead, then leaned down to whisper in my ear.

"She's not coming."

"What?" My stomach turned to jelly.

He nodded. "I just got off the phone with her, let her know you're not feeling well."

I pushed him away from me. "What are you talking about? I feel fine."

"Oh, but you don't. You have a terrible stomachache from stuffing yourself with pancakes."

Was he really still holding a grudge from weeks ago? "You're joking, right?" I said, hoping he was.

His eyes were cold. "I've never been more serious."

"I'm calling her right now." He grabbed my arm before I could move.

"And tell her what? That your husband lied? What would she think of that? Besides, I told her that you had food poisoning and asked me to call her. I assured her you would be better in a few days." Then he laughed. "I also mentioned that you'd been a bit stressed and that having her visit so often was putting a strain on you, that maybe she should let a little more time elapse between visits."

"You can't do this. I won't let you make my mother think I don't want her here."

He squeezed my arm harder. "It's done. You should have heard how sad she sounded. Poor, dumb hick." He laughed.

I wrenched my arm away and slapped him. He laughed again.

"Too bad she didn't die when your father did. I really hate having in-laws."

I exploded. I raked my nails down his face, wanting to tear it to shreds. I felt wetness on my hands and realized I'd drawn blood. Horrified, I backed away, my hand to my mouth.

He shook his head slowly. "Now look what you've done." Pulling his phone from his pocket, he held it in front of his face. It took me a minute to realize what he was doing. "Thanks, Daph. Now I have proof that you have an explosive temper."

"You intentionally provoked me?"

A cold smile. "Here's a little tip: I will always be ten steps ahead of you. Keep that in mind when you decide you know better than I do what's good for you." He moved toward me, and I stood rooted to the floor, too shocked to move. He touched my cheek, and the look in his eyes grew tender. "I love you. Why can't you see that? I don't want to punish you—but what am I to do when you insist on doing things that are bad for you?"

He's crazy. How did it take me this long to see that he's crazy? I swallowed hard and flinched when his fingers traced the tears running down my cheeks. I ran from the room, grabbed a few things from the bedroom, and went into one of the guest rooms. I caught a glimpse of myself in the mirror—white as a ghost, whole body shaking. Moving into the guest bathroom, I washed my hands, cleaning his blood from under my nails, and tried to come to grips with how I had let myself lose control. I'd never done something like that before. His cavalier comment about my mother dying made me realize there was no going back after tonight. I had to leave. Tomorrow I would pack up the baby and go to my mother's.

After a few minutes, I went in to check on Tallulah and found him standing over her crib. I hesitated at the doorway, something about the picture not striking me as quite right. His stance was menacing; his face in shadow, ominous. My heart beat faster as I approached.

He didn't turn toward me or acknowledge my presence. In his hands he held the enormous teddy bear he had bought for her when she was born.

"What are you doing?" I whispered.

As he spoke, he continued to stare at her. "Did you know that over two thousand babies die of SIDS each year?"

I tried to answer, but no words would come.

"That's why you put nothing in the crib." Then he turned to face me. "I keep telling you not to put her stuffed animals in with her. But you are so forgetful."

I found my voice. "You wouldn't dare. She's your child, how could you—"

He threw the bear onto the rocking chair, and his expression was neutral once again. "I was just joking around. You take everything so seriously." He grabbed both of my hands in his. "Nothing will ever happen to her as long as she has two parents looking out for her."

I turned from him to watch my baby breathing in and out, and was crushed by her vulnerability.

"I'm going to sit here for a while," I whispered.

"Good idea. Do some thinking while you're at it. I'll be waiting for you in bed. Make sure you don't take too long."

I glared at him. "You can't be serious. I'm not getting near you."

A thin smile played on his lips. "You might want to rethink that. Tire me out, or I may sleepwalk and find myself back in the nursery." He stretched his hand out to me. "On second thought, I want you now."

Silent and dying inside, I took his hand, and he led me to our room and to the bed. "Take your clothes off," he commanded.

I sat on the bed and began to pull off my slacks.

"No. Stand up. Do a strip-tease for me."

"Jackson, please."

I gasped as he yanked me by my hair toward him. He pinched my breast hard. "Don't piss me off. Do it. Now."

My legs were so jellylike, I don't know how I remained standing. I made my mind go blank, shut my eyes, and pretended I was anywhere but there. I unbuttoned my blouse one button at a time, opening my eyes and looking at him to see if I was doing it right. He nodded, and as I stripped, he began to stroke himself. I didn't know who this man was, sitting on my bed, looking like my husband. All I could think to ask myself was how he had done it. How had he played the part for over a year? What kind of a person can keep up a charade for that long? And why was he showing me the truth now? Did he think that I'd stay with him just because we had a child together? Tomorrow, I would go, but tonight, I'd do what he said, do whatever it took to make him think he'd won.

I continued the performance until I was naked. He reached out for me and threw me onto the bed. Then he was on top of me, his touch maddeningly tender and attentive. I would have preferred for him to take me roughly, and for the sake of my daughter, I forced my body to betray me and respond—for he was nothing if not perceptive, and I knew he would never abide my holding back.

FORTY-FIVE

The next morning after he'd left for work, I raced through the house, packed up as much as I could, put the baby in the car, and began the long drive to New Hampshire. I knew my mother was going to be shocked when she found out the truth, but I would be able to count on her support. It would take us around five hours to reach the inn. My thoughts raced as I tried to sort out how this would all shake out. I knew he'd be furious, of course, but there was nothing he could do once we were gone. I would tell the police about his threats to the baby. Surely they could protect us.

He called my cell phone when we reached Massachusetts. I let it go to voice mail. My text tones kept sounding: ping, ping, ping—rapid-fire like a machine gun. I didn't look at the texts until I stopped at a rest stop for gas.

What are you doing in Massachusetts? Daphne, where is the baby?
You haven't hurt her, have you? Please answer me.
I didn't think you were serious last night. Don't listen to the voices.
Daphne, please answer! I'm worried about you.
Call me. Please. I'll get you help. Just don't hurt Tallulah.

What was he doing? And how did he know where I was? I hadn't given him any indication that I was leaving. I had made sure that none of the staff had seen me. Did he have a tracker on my car somehow?

I picked up the phone and dialed him. He answered on the first ring.

"You bitch! What the hell do you think you're doing?" I could feel his fury over the phone.

"I'm going to see my mother."

"Without telling me? You turn that car around and get back here now. Do you hear me?"

"Or what? You can't tell me what to do. I've had enough, Jackson." My voice shook, and I glanced at the backseat to make sure Tallulah was still asleep. "You threatened to hurt our baby. Did you really think I'd let you do that? You're not getting near her again."

He started to laugh. "You're such a little fool."

"Go ahead and insult me. I don't care. I'm going to tell my mother everything."

"This is your last chance to come back, or you'll regret it."

"Good-bye, Jackson." I pressed end and put the car back in gear.

My text tone started pinging again. I turned the phone off.

With every passing mile, my resolve strengthened, and my hope blossomed. I knew I was doing the right thing, and no amount of threatening on his part would sway me. I was still in Massachusetts when a flash of lights in my rearview mirror gave me pause. As the police car closed the gap between us, I realized he wanted *me* to pull over. I was only going a few miles over the speed limit. I pulled the car to the side of the road, and the state trooper approached.

"License and registration, please."

I retrieved them from the glove box and handed them over.

The officer returned to his car with them, and after a few minutes he came back. "Please step out of the car."

"Why?" I asked.

"Please, ma'am. Out of the car."

"Have I done something wrong?"

"An emergency confinement order is in effect. It claims you're a danger to your child. The baby will have to stay with us until your husband arrives."

"She's *my* child!" That bastard had actually called the police on me.

"Please don't make me cuff you. I need you to come with me."

I got out of the car, and the officer took hold of my arm. Tallulah had woken up and started crying. Her little face was beet red, her cries turning to screams. "Please, she's frightened. I can't leave my baby!"

"We'll take care of her, ma'am."

I pulled my arm away and tried to get to the car, to take her from her seat and comfort her. "Tallulah!"

"Please stop. I really don't want to have to restrain you." He pulled me away and into the waiting cruiser, and I had to leave her there with the police while they drove me to a local hospital.

I didn't find out until the next day that Jackson had put a contingency plan into effect weeks before. He'd convinced a judge that I was suffering from depression and had threatened to harm the baby. He even had two signed statements from physicians—doctors I'd never even met. I could only imagine that his money had bought them. My claims that I'd been set up fell on deaf ears. Crazy people have no credibility, and I was now considered crazy. During my hold at the hospital, I was evaluated by a number of doctors who agreed that I needed treatment. No one believed me when I told them what he had done, how he'd manipulated the situation. They looked at me like I was a lunatic. The only thing they would tell me was that Jackson had picked Tallulah up right away from the police station and taken her home. I'd been informed that I was being transferred to Meadow Lakes Hospital, which was in Fair Haven, the town neighboring Bishops Harbor. After seventy-two hours of screaming, begging, and crying, I was no closer to being released than when I'd first arrived, and by then I was doped up with who knew what. My only hope rested in convincing Jackson to get me out.

Once they moved me to Meadow Lakes, he left me there for seven days before he finally came to see me. I had no idea what he'd told my mother or the staff about why I was gone. When he showed up in the common room, I wanted to kill him.

"How could you do this to me?" I hissed under my breath, not wanting to make a scene.

He sat next to me and took my hand in his, smiling at a woman across from me who didn't bother to hide her curious stare as she observed us.

"Daphne, I'm only looking out for you and our child." He made sure to speak loudly enough for everyone to hear.

"What do you want from me?"

He squeezed my hand hard. "I want you to come home, where you belong. But only when you're ready."

I bit my tongue to keep myself from screaming. Taking deep breaths until I could speak without my voice shaking, I said, "I'm ready."

"Well, that's for your therapist to decide."

I stood. "Why don't we take a walk on the grounds?"

Once we were outside and no one could hear us, I let my anger show. "Cut the crap, Jackson. You know I don't belong here. I want my baby. What did you tell everyone?"

He looked straight ahead as we walked. "That you're sick and will be home as soon as you're better."

"What about my mother?"

He stopped and turned to look at me. "I told her that you had been increasingly depressed about Julie and your dad, and had tried to kill yourself."

"What?" I shouted.

"She wants you to stay as long as necessary—make sure you get better."

"You're hateful. Why are you doing this?"

"Why do you think?"

I started to cry. "I loved you. We were so happy. I don't understand what happened. Why did you change? How can you expect me to stay with you when you threaten our child and are so horrible to me?"

He started to walk again, maddeningly calm. "I don't know what you're talking about. I didn't threaten any-one. And I treat you like a queen. You're the envy of everyone you meet. If I have to keep you in line oc-casionally, well, that's part of being married. I'm not whipped like your father was. This is how a strong man handles his wife. Get used to it."

"Get used to what? Being abused? I'll never get used to that." My face was burning.

"Abused? I've never laid a hand on you."

"There are other kinds of abuse," I said. I searched his face for any sign of the man I had first believed him to be. Deciding to try a different tactic, I softened my voice. "Jackson?"

"Hmm?"

I took a deep breath. "I'm not happy, and I don't think you are either."

"Of course I'm not happy. My wife tried to steal my child out from under me with no warning."

"Why do you want me to come home? You don't love me."

He stopped walking and looked at me, his mouth agape. "What? Are you serious? Daphne, I've spent the past two years teaching, coaching, grooming you to be a wife I can be proud of. We have a beautiful family. Everyone looks up to us. How can you ask me why I'd fight to keep my family?"

"You've mistreated me since Tallulah was born, and it gets worse every day."

"Accuse me again, and you'll stay here forever and never see her again." He started walking again, fast this time.

I struggled to catch up, dropping the conciliatory tone. "You can't do that!"

"Just watch me. The law's on my side. And did I mention that I just donated ten million dollars for a new wing at this hospital? I'm sure they'll be happy to have you stay for as long as I like."

"You're insane."

He swung around, grabbed me, and pulled me close. With his mouth inches from mine, he spoke. "This is the last time we're having this conversation. You are mine. You'll always be mine, and you'll listen to what I say from now on. If you are a good little wife and obey, everything will be fine." He leaned closer, put his lips on mine, then bit down hard. I yelled and sprang back, but his hand on my head prevented my pulling away. "If you don't, then trust me: you'll spend the rest of your life wishing you did, and your child will have a new mother."

I knew he had me. It didn't matter that he was the one who was crazy. He had the money and the influence, and he'd played his hand brilliantly.

How had this happened? I struggled to get a deep breath, to come up with something, anything, that would help me to believe there was a way out. Looking at my husband, this stranger who held my future in his hands, I could come up with nothing. Filled with despair, I whispered, "I'll do whatever you say. Just get me out of here."

He smiled. "That's my girl. You'll have to stay for a month or so. It wouldn't look right if you came right out. Your therapist and I go back a long way. We've been friends since college. He had a little trouble a few years back." He shrugged. "Anyhow, I helped him out, and he owes me. I'll tell him to release you in thirty days. He'll claim it was a hormonal imbalance or something easily fixed."

Thirty-five days later, I was released. We had to go to family court to prove I was a fit mother. We met with his attorney, and I played along. He made me corroborate his lie that I was hearing voices telling me to hurt my baby. I had to agree to keep seeing Dr. Finn, Jackson's friend, which was a total joke. He was always solicitous, asking how I was adapting to being home again, but we both knew the sessions were a charade. Now Jackson had something else to hold over my head, to make sure I never left again, and I knew Dr. Finn's notes would say whatever Jackson wanted them to. When I was finally allowed to go home, the only thing I cared about was being back with Tallulah. I told myself that eventually I'd find a way to escape him. In the meantime, I did what any good mother would do: I sacrificed my happiness to protect my child.

FORTY-SIX

I'd only been at Meadow Lakes for a little over a month, but it felt like years. Jackson came to fetch me himself, and I sat in the passenger seat of his Mercedes roadster, looking out the window, afraid to say the wrong thing. He was in a good mood, humming as if this were any ordinary day and we were simply out for a drive. When he pulled up to the house, I felt strangely outside myself, like I was watching someone else's life. Someone who lived in a beautiful estate on the water who had lots of money and everything she could want. Suddenly I longed for the haven of my room at the hospital, far from the prying eyes of my husband.

The first thing I did when I got inside was race up the stairs to Tallulah's nursery. I flung open the door, eager to gather her in my arms. Sitting in the chair rocking Tallulah was a beautiful dark-haired young woman I'd never seen before.

"Who are you?"

"Sabine. Who are you?" She had a thick French accent.

"I'm Mrs. Parrish." I held out my arms. "Please give my daughter to me."

She stood, turned her back on me, and moved away. "I'm sorry, madame. I need to hear from Mr. Parrish that it is okay."

I saw red. "Give her to me," I screamed.

"What's going on?" Jackson strode into the room.

"This woman won't give me my child!"

Jackson sighed and took the baby from Sabine and handed her to me. "Please excuse us, Sabine."

She threw a look at me and left.

"Where's Sally? Did you hire that, that . . . creature? She completely disrespected me."

"Sally's gone. Don't blame Sabine, she didn't know who you were. She was looking out for Tallulah. Sabine will teach her to speak French. You have to think of our child's well-being. Things are running smoothly now. Don't try and come back here and upset the apple cart."

"'Upset the apple cart'? She's *my* child."

He sat down on the bed. "Daphne, I know you grew up poor, but there are certain things that will be expected of our children."

"What do you mean, I grew up poor? I'm from a middle-class family. We had everything we needed. We weren't poor."

He sighed and threw his hands up in the air. "Excuse me. Okay, you weren't poor. But you certainly weren't rich."

I felt my stomach tighten. "Our definitions of rich and poor are vastly different."

His voice rose. "You know damn well what I'm trying to say. You're not used to how people with money do things. Doesn't matter. The point is, leave it to me. Sabine will be a big asset to our family. Now that's enough. I have a special dinner planned. Don't spoil it."

All I wanted was to be with the baby, but I knew better than to complain. I couldn't risk being sent back to Meadow Lake. Another month there, and I would have truly lost my mind.

All during dinner, he was in an unusually good mood. We shared a bottle of wine, and he'd had Margarita prepare my favorite seafood dish—crab imperial. There was even cherries jubilee for dessert—all very festive, as though my exile hadn't been by his design and had instead been a relaxing vacation. My mind was racing the entire evening as I tried to keep up with his uncharacteristic nonstop chatter and be engaging. By the time we went upstairs to bed, I was exhausted.

"I bought you something special for tonight." He handed me a black box.

I opened it with trepidation. "What is this?" I pulled the black leather straps out, studied it, not sure exactly what it was supposed to be. There was a thick collar too, with a round metal ring attached to it.

He walked around behind me and slid a hand down to my hip. "It's just a little role-playing fun." He took the collar from my hand and put it up to my neck.

I shoved his hand away. "Forget it! I'm not wearing that . . . thing." I threw it on the bed along with the corset of straps. "I'm bushed. I'm going to sleep." I left him standing there and went into the bathroom to brush my teeth. When I came out, he was in bed, his light out, eyes closed.

I should have known it was too easy.

I tossed and turned until I heard the soft sound of his snoring and relaxed enough to drift off. I don't know what time it was when I was awakened by the feeling of something hard and cold on my lips. My eyes flew open, and I was trying to swat it away when I felt his hand grip my wrist.

"Open your mouth." His voice was low, guttural.

"What are you doing? Get off of me."

His grip tightened, and with the other hand, he yanked my hair until my chin was pointing to the ceiling. "I'm not asking again."

I opened my mouth and tensed as he shoved a cylinder into it until I started to gag. He laughed. Then he was straddling me, reaching for the lamp by my side of the bed. When the light came on, I realized what was in my mouth—the barrel of a gun.

He's going to kill me. Panic swallowed me, and I laid perfectly still, terrified to move. I watched in horror as his index finger moved to the trigger.

"What will I tell Tallulah when she grows up?" he sneered. "How will I explain that her mother didn't even love her enough to live?"

I wanted to yell out but was afraid to move. I felt tears rolling down the side of my face into my ears.

"I guess I could lie and say suicide runs in your family. She'd never know. Maybe one day I'll even tell her that Aunt Julie killed herself." He laughed. Leaning forward, he kissed my forehead, and then his eyes grew cold. "Or you could start doing what you're told."

He pulled the gun from my mouth, traced my neck, my breasts, and my stomach with it, like a lover's caress. I squeezed my eyes shut, and all I could hear was the blood pounding in my ears. *I'm never going to see my child grow up.* My body tensed in anticipation.

"Open your eyes."

He moved away, the gun still pointed at me.

I exhaled, and a sigh of relief escaped.

"Put on the outfit."

"Whatever you want, just, please, put the gun away," I managed in a whisper.

"Don't make me say it again."

I slid from the bed and retrieved the bag from the chair where I'd thrown it. My hands were shaking so hard that I kept dropping the bustier. Finally, I figured out how to get it on.

"Don't forget the collar."

I fastened the leather collar around my neck.

"Make it tighter," he commanded.

I reached back and moved the collar one more notch. My heart was pounding, and I struggled to steady my breathing. Maybe if I just did what he said, he'd put the gun away.

A lazy smile appeared, and he walked toward me, grabbed the metal ring on the collar, and pulled hard. I jerked forward. He pulled harder until I fell to the floor.

"Get on your knees."

I did as I was told.

"That's a good little slave." Walking over to his closet, he snatched a necktie and brought it over. "Put your hands behind your back." He wrapped the tie around my wrists and knotted it tight, then stood back and held his hands as if pretending to frame a picture. "Not quite right." He walked back to the closet and came out carrying a ball.

"Open wide." He stuffed the soft plastic gag in my mouth.

"That's nice." He put the gun on his nightstand and, grabbing his cell phone, started snapping pictures. "This will make a delightful scrapbook." He undressed and walked toward me. "Let me replace that ball with something else." He pushed himself inside my mouth and snapped more pictures. He pulled away and looked at me with derision. "You don't deserve me. Do you know how many women would love to put their lips on me, and you act like it's a chore?"

"I'm sorry."

"You should be. You stay there and think about what it means to be a good wife, how to prove to me that you find me desirable. Maybe I'll let you pleasure me in the morning." He got in bed. "And don't even think of moving until I give you permission—or the next time, I'll pull the trigger." He slid the gun under his pillow.

The room went black as he turned out the light, and suddenly, I almost wished he had.

FORTY-SEVEN

lived in constant fear of losing Tallulah. The social worker, the attorneys, the bureaucrats, they all looked at me the same way—with a mixture of suspicion and disgust. I knew they were thinking, *How could she threaten to hurt her child?* In town, I heard the whispers—it's impossible to keep something like this quiet. I confided in no one, couldn't tell any of my friends the truth, not even Meredith. I had to live the hateful lie that he had thrust upon me, and after a while, even I almost believed it.

From then on, I did whatever he said. I smiled at him, laughed at his jokes, bit my tongue when I was tempted to argue or talk back. It was a tightrope walk, because if I acted too compliant, he'd get angry and accuse me of being a robot. He wanted some spunk, but I never knew how much. I was always off balance, one leg dangling over the abyss. I watched him with Tallulah, terrified he'd hurt her, but as time went on I realized his twisted games were focused only on me. Anyone looking at us from the outside would have believed we were the perfect family. He took great pains to ensure that I was the only one who saw the mask drop. When we were around anyone else, I had to act like the adoring wife to a wonderful husband.

The days turned to weeks and months, and I learned how to be exactly what he wanted. I became an expert at reading his face, hearing the strain in his voice, doing everything I could to avoid some imagined slight or insult. Months would go by when nothing horrible would happen. He'd even be nice, and we'd go through the days acting as though we were a normal couple. Until I got too complacent and forgot to complete an errand he'd asked me to do, or ordered the wrong caviar from the caterer. Then the gun would make an appearance again, and I always wondered if that would be the night he'd kill me. The next day a gift would arrive. A piece of jewelry, a designer purse, some expensive perfume. And every time I had to wear any of it, I'd be reminded of what I'd endured to receive it.

When Tallulah turned two, he decided it was time for another baby. One night, I was in the bathroom looking in the drawer for my diaphragm—I put it in nightly, never knowing when he'd want to have sex. I wished I could take the pill, but I'd had an adverse reaction to it and my doctor insisted I use something else. When Jackson came into the room, I turned to him.

"Have you seen my diaphragm?"

"I threw it out."

"Why?"

He walked over and pushed himself against me. "We should make another baby. A boy this time."

I felt my stomach turn and tried to swallow. "So soon? Tallulah's only two."

He led me over to the bed and untied the belt holding my robe shut. "It's perfect timing."

I stalled. "What if it's another girl?"

His eyes narrowed. "Then we'll keep going until you give me what I want. What's the big deal?"

The telltale vein in his temple started pulsating, and I rushed to smooth things over before he lost his temper. "You're right, darling. It's just that I've enjoyed being able to focus my attention on you. I wasn't thinking about another baby. But if that's what you want, then I want it too."

He tilted his head and leveled a long stare at me. "Are you patronizing me?"

I inhaled. "No, Jackson. Of course not."

Without another word he pulled my robe off and fell on top of me. When he finished, he grabbed two pillows and put them under my hips.

"Stay that way for half an hour. I've been tracking your cycles. You should be ovulating."

I started to protest, but stopped myself. I could feel the frustration and anger welling up until it was a physical force that wanted to erupt, but I breathed deeply and smiled at him instead. "Here's hoping."

It took nearly nine months this time, and when it finally happened, he was so happy that he forgot to be cruel. And then we went for the twenty-week visit—the one that would reveal the sex of the baby. He'd cleared his schedule so he could go with me that day. I was on eggshells all morning, dreading his reaction if it didn't go his way, but he was confident, even whistling in the car on the way over.

"I've got a good feeling about this, Daphne. Jackson Junior. That's what we'll call him."

I looked at him from the corner of my eye. "Jackson, what if—"

He cut me off. "No negativity. Why do you always have to be such a downer?"

As the ultrasound wand moved around my belly and we looked at the heartbeat and the torso, I was making such a tight fist that I realized my nails were digging into my palm.

"Are you ready to know what you're having?" the doctor asked in her cheery, singsong voice.

I looked at Jackson's face.

"It's a girl!" she said.

His eyes went cold, and he turned and left the room without a word. The doctor looked at me, surprised, and I came up with something on the fly.

"He just lost his mother. She always wanted a girl. He was embarrassed for you to see him cry."

She gave me a strained smile and spoke stiffly. "Well, let's get you cleaned up, and you can go home."

He didn't speak to me the entire ride home. I knew better than to try and say anything to make it better. I had screwed up again, and even though I knew that of course it wasn't my fault, I felt my anger turn inward. Why couldn't I just have given him a son?

He stayed in the New York apartment for the next three nights, and I was grateful for the reprieve. When he came home the next night, he almost seemed back to normal—or whatever normal was for him. He'd texted me to let me know he'd be home at seven, and I'd made sure to have stuffed pheasant ready for dinner, one of his favorites. When we sat down to eat, he poured himself a glass of wine, took a sip, then cleared his throat.

"I've come up with a solution."

"What?"

He sighed loudly. "A solution to your ineptitude. It's too late to do anything about this one." He gestured at my stomach. "Everyone already knows you're pregnant. But the next time, we're getting an earlier test. CVS. I looked it up. It can tell us the sex, and we can do it well before your third month."

"What will that accomplish?" I asked, even as I knew what the answer would be.

He raised his eyebrows. "If the next one's a girl, you can abort it, and we'll keep trying until you get it right."

He picked up his fork and took a bite. "By the way, can I trust you to remember to send in Tallulah's application to St. Patrick's preschool? I want to make sure she gets into the threes program next year."

I nodded mutely as the asparagus in my mouth turned to mush. I discreetly spit it into my napkin and took a swallow from the glass of water in front of me. *Abortion?* I had to do something. Could I get my tubes tied without him finding out? I'd have to figure something out after this baby was born. Some way to make sure it was the last pregnancy I ever had.

FORTY-EIGHT

The children were what helped me to keep my sanity. As the saying goes, the days were long but the years were short. I learned to put up with his demands and his moods, only occasionally messing up and daring to talk back or refuse him something. On those occasions, he made sure to remind me of what was at stake if I screwed up. He showed me an updated letter from two doctors certifying my mental illness, which he kept locked in a safe-deposit box. I didn't bother asking what he had on them to get them to go along with his lies. If I tried to leave again, he said, this time he'd lock me up in the loony bin forever. I wasn't about to test him.

I became his pet project. By the time Bella was in first grade, both girls were in school all day, and he decided my education should continue as well. I had a master's degree, but that wasn't enough. He came home one night and handed me a catalog.

"I've signed you up for French lessons three days a week. The class starts at 2:45. That way you can still get to the foundation on your two days there and the gym beforehand."

The girls were doing their homework at the kitchen island, and Tallulah looked up, pencil poised in the air, waiting for me to answer.

"Jackson, what are you talking about?"

He looked at Tallulah. "Mommy's going back to school. Isn't that great?"

Bella clapped her hands. "Yay. Will she come to my school?"

"No, darling. She'll go to the local university."

Tallulah pursed her lips. "Didn't Mommy already go to college?"

Jackson walked over to her. "Yes, my sweet, but she doesn't know how to speak French like you two do. You don't want a stupid mommy, do you?"

Tallulah's eyebrows furrowed. "Mommy's not stupid."

He laughed. "You're right, sweetie. She's not stupid. But she's not polished. She came from a poor family where they don't know how to behave in polite society. We need to help her learn. Right, Mommy?"

"Right," I answered through clenched teeth.

The class was right in the middle of the day, and I hated it. The professor was a snobby Frenchwoman who wore fake eyelashes and too-red lipstick and talked about how crass Americans were. She took special delight in pointing out the flaws in my accent. I'd only been to one class and was already sick of it.

I was nonetheless getting ready to go back the next week when I got an emergency call from Fiona at the foundation. One of our clients needed to get his son to the hospital, and his car wouldn't start. I offered to take him, even though it meant missing a class. Of course, I never mentioned a thing to Jackson.

The following Monday, I received a frantic call from the girls' school just as I got back to the house after a long massage and facial.

"Mrs. Parrish?"

"Yes."

"We've been trying to reach you for three hours."

"Is everything okay? Are the children all right?"

"Yes. But they are quite upset. You were supposed to pick them up at noon."

Noon? What was she talking about? "They don't get dismissed until three."

An exasperated sigh on the other end. "It's a teacher planning afternoon. It's been on the calendar for a month, and we sent a note home. You should also have received an e-mail and a text."

"I'm so sorry. I'll be right there. I didn't receive any calls on my cell," I said apologetically.

"Well, we've been dialing it for hours. We couldn't reach your husband either. He's apparently out of town."

Jackson wasn't on a business trip, and I had no idea why his assistant hadn't put her through.

I hung up and ran to the car. What could have happened? I pulled out my phone and looked at it. No missed calls. I checked my texts. Nothing.

At the red light, I searched through my e-mails and didn't see any from the school. A sick feeling wound its way from my belly up to my chest. Jackson had to be responsible, but how? Had he deleted the e-mails and texts from my phone? Could he have blocked the school phone number? And why would he do this to the girls?

I skulked up to the main office, dying of embarrassment, and took my little girls from the office of the *disapproving* headmistress.

"Mrs. Parrish, this isn't the first time. This behavior cannot continue. It's not fair to your daughters, and frankly, it's not fair to us either."

I felt my cheeks go warm, and I wished the floor would swallow me up right then and there. Only a couple of weeks before, I'd been over an hour late for pickup, and Jackson had been called to retrieve the children. Earlier that day, he'd come home for lunch, and after he'd left, I was suddenly exhausted and lay down for a quick nap. I didn't wake up until the three of them came in the door at four o'clock. I had slept right through the phone alarm.

"I'm sorry, Mrs. Sinclair. I don't know what happened. I don't have any of the e-mails or texts, and for some reason my phone never rang."

Her expression made it clear she didn't believe a word I was saying. "Yes, well. Please see to it that it doesn't happen again."

I went to take their hands, and Bella pulled hers away, stomping ahead of me toward the car. She didn't speak to me the entire ride home. When we got to the house, Sabine was waiting, fixing a snack for them.

"Sabine, were you here this afternoon? The school was trying to reach me."

"No, madam. I was at the grocer's."

I picked up the house phone and dialed my cell. It rang in my ear, but the cell phone in my hand didn't buzz. What was going on? With a sinking feeling, I unlocked my phone and went to Settings, tapped Phone, and looked at My Number. My mouth dropped open as it revealed a number I didn't recognize. I took a closer look. It was a new phone. My old one had a tiny crack in the plastic by the home key. Jackson must have replaced it. Now I wondered about the other time I'd been late for pickup. Had he drugged me?

"Daddy's home!" Bella squealed.

As she ran into his arms, he leveled a look at me over her head. "How's my girl?"

She stuck her lip out. "Mommy forgot us at school again. We had to sit in the office all day. It was terrible."

A look passed between Jackson and Sabine.

He hugged her tighter and kissed the top of her head.

"My poor darling. Mommy has been very forgetful lately. She missed her French class too."

Tallulah looked over at me. "What happened, Mom?"

Jackson answered for me. "Mommy has a drinking problem, sweetie. Sometimes she just gets too drunk to do what she needs. But we'll help her, won't we?"

"Jackson! That's not—"

I heard Sabine gasp.

"Don't lie anymore, Daphne. I know you missed your French class last week," he interrupted. He took my hand in his, squeezing hard. "If you just admit you have a problem, I can help you. Otherwise, you may need to go back to the hospital."

Tallulah jumped up, tears springing to her eyes. "No, Mommy! Don't leave us." She threw her arms around my waist.

I struggled to find my voice. "Of course not, sweetheart. I'm not going anywhere."

"Sabine will pick you up from now on. That way, the school won't get the wrong idea if Mommy forgets again. Right, Mommy?"

I took a deep breath, trying to slow the pounding in my chest. "Right."

He reached out and touched the sleeve of my shirt. "And that's a really ugly outfit you have on. Why don't you go change? Bella, go help Mommy find a nice dress for dinner."

"Come on, Mommy. I know what would look pretty on you."

FORTY-NINE

All of a sudden, everywhere I looked, there were turtles. They hid behind photographs, peered out from
bookshelves, perched menacingly on dresser tops.

In the early days, before I learned not to share my
soul, I'd told Jackson why I hated them. When Julie and
I were young, my father bought a turtle for us. We'd always wanted a dog or a cat, but unrelated to her CF, Julie
was allergic to both. My mom had asked him to get a box
turtle, but he brought home a snapping turtle instead. It
had been returned to the store after a year because its
previous owner couldn't care for it anymore. That very
first day, I was feeding him a carrot, and he snapped and
bit my finger. His jaw was so strong I couldn't free it,
and I screamed while Julie ran to find my mother. I can
still remember the pain and my panicked feeling that he
would bite it off. My mother's quick thinking of offering him another carrot worked, and his mouth opened
again. I pulled my bleeding finger out of its mouth, and
we went to the emergency room. Of course, we returned
the turtle, and I was left with a permanent fear of anything with a hard shell.

Jackson had listened, murmuring comfort, and it
had felt good to unburden myself of another childhood
trauma. When Bella was a baby, I put her down for her
nap one day, and as I was leaving her nursery, something
leaning over the shelf caught my eye. It was positioned
among her stuffed animals. I called Jackson at work.

"Where did the turtle in Bella's room come from?"

"What?"

"The turtle. It was in with her stuffed animals."

"Are you serious? I'm in the middle of a killer day, and you're asking me about a stuffed animal. I have no idea. Is there anything else?"

I suddenly felt foolish. "No. Sorry to bother you."

I took the damn thing and threw it in the trash.

The next day, Meredith stopped by for a visit, and I invited her to have coffee in the conservatory. She walked over to the floor-to-ceiling bookcases and picked something up.

"This is lovely, Daphne. I've never noticed it before." She was holding a white-and-gold porcelain turtle.

I dropped my cup, spilling hot coffee all over myself.

"Oh my gosh, what a klutz," I sputtered and rang for Margarita to clean up. "Jackson must have picked that up. I hadn't noticed." I clasped my hands together to stop them shaking.

"Well, it's quite beautiful. Limoges."

"Take it."

She shook her head. "Don't be silly. I was only admiring it." She gave me a strange look. "It's time I was going. I'm meeting Rand at the club for lunch." Then she put her hand on my arm. "Are you okay?"

"Yes, just tired. I'm still adjusting to the baby's schedule."

She smiled. "Of course. Try and get some rest. I'll call you later."

After she left, I searched online to find the turtle. Over $900!

That night, I placed it on the table in front of his plate. When he sat down to dinner, he glanced at it, then back at me.

"What's this doing here?"

"That's exactly what I'd like to know."

He shrugged. "It belongs in the conservatory."

"Jackson, why are you doing this? You know how I feel about turtles."

"Do you hear how crazy you sound? It's just a little figure. Can't hurt you." He was looking at me with that smug expression, challenging me with his eyes.

"I don't like them. Please stop."

"Stop what? You're being awfully paranoid. Maybe that postpartum depression has returned. Should we talk to the doctor?"

I threw my napkin on my plate and stood up. "I'm not crazy. First the stuffed animal, and now this."

He shook his head and made a circular motion with his finger by his ear—like kids do in school to indicate someone is cuckoo.

I flew up the stairs and slammed the bedroom door. Flinging myself on the bed, I screamed into my pillow. When I lifted my head, two marble eyes were staring at me from my nightstand. I picked up the glass turtle and threw it as hard as I could against the bedroom wall. It didn't shatter, but merely landed on the floor with a soft thud. It sat there, appraising me with its reptilian eyes, perched as though it was preparing to crawl toward me and punish me for what I had done.

FIFTY

When you discover you are married to a sociopath, you have to become resourceful. There's no point in trying to change him—once the pot is in the kiln, it's too late. The best I could do was study him—the real him, the one hiding behind his well-polished veneer of humanity and normalcy. Now that I knew the truth, it was easy to spot. Things like the small smile playing at his lips when he was pretending to be sad. He was a brilliant mimic and knew just what to say and do to ingratiate himself into the affections of others. Now that he'd dropped the facade with me, I had to figure out how to beat him at his own game.

I took him up on his suggestion to take more courses at the university. But I didn't study art. I bought the text-books for the art class and figured I would read up on my own in case he quizzed me. Instead, I signed up for psychology courses, paying cash for them and register-ing under a different name with a post office box. The campus was large enough that there was little chance of my French professor seeing me while I was pretending to be someone else, but just in case, I wore a baseball cap and sweats to those classes. It's worth noting that by this point in my marriage, these measures didn't seem extreme to me. I had adjusted to a life where subterfuge and deceit were as natural as breathing.

In my abnormal psychology class, I began to put the pieces together. My professor was a fascinating woman who had a private practice. Hearing her describe some of her patients was like listening to a description of Jackson. I took another abnormal psych course with her as well as her class on personality. Then I spent hours at the university library reading everything I could get my hands on about the antisocial personality.

Interviews with sociopaths have revealed that they're able to identify a potential victim merely by the way the person walks. Our bodies apparently telegraph our vulnerabilities and sensitivities. Spouses of sociopaths are said to have an overabundance of empathy. I found that bit of information hard to understand. Is there really such a thing as too much empathy? It had a certain poetic irony, though. If sociopaths are said to lack empathy and their victims to have too much, they would seem to make a perfect match. But of course, empathy can't be divvied up. *Here, you take some of mine; I have extra.* And sociopaths can't acquire it anyway—the lack of it is what defines them in the first place. I think they're wrong, though. It's not too much empathy. It's misplaced empathy, a misguided attempt to save someone that can't be saved. All these years later, I know what he saw in me. The question I still wrestle with is, what did I see in him?

When Bella turned two, he'd begun badgering me to get pregnant again—he was dying for a son. There was no way I would willingly bring another child of his into this world. Unbeknownst to him, I went to a free clinic in another town, used a fake name, and got fitted for an IUD. Every month he charted my cycles, knew exactly when I was ovulating, and made sure that we had even more sex during that window. We had a big blowout one day when I got my period.

"What the hell is wrong with you? It's been three years."

"We could see a fertility doctor. Maybe your sperm count is low."

He scowled. "There's nothing wrong with me. You're the dried-up old prune."

But I had sown a doubt; I could see it in his eyes. I was counting on the fact that his ego could never handle any threat to his virility.

"I'm sorry, Jackson. I want it as much as you do."

"Well, you're not getting any younger. If you don't get pregnant soon, it's never going to happen. Maybe you should get on some fertility drugs."

I shook my head. "The doctor will never do that. They have to do a complete workup on both of us. I'll call Monday and make an appointment."

A look of indecision crossed his face. "This week's bad for me. I'll let you know when I have some time."

It was the last time he brought it up.

FIFTY-ONE

I needed Jackson to be in a good mood. I'd been looking forward to having my mother here for Tallulah's birthday party, and I had to work even harder to please him the entire month leading up to it so he wouldn't cancel her visit at the last minute. That meant initiating sex at least three times a week, instead of waiting for him to, wearing all his favorite outfits, praising him to my friends in front of him, and keeping up with the growing piles of books on my nightstand that arrived weekly from his online orders. My books by contemporary authors such as Stephen King, Rosamund Lupton, and Barbara Kingsolver were replaced with books by Steinbeck, Proust, Nabokov, Melville—books he believed would make me a more interesting dinner companion. These were in addition to the classics that we were reading together.

It had been six months since Mom's last visit, and I was desperate to see her. Over the years, she'd come to accept that we were no longer close, believing that I'd changed, that the money had gone to my head, that I had little time for her. It's all what he made her believe.

It had taken everything I had not to tell her the truth, but if I had, there was no knowing what he would have done to us, or even just to her. So I went along and only invited her twice a year, for the girls' birthdays. The inn kept her occupied for the holidays, which eliminated my having to tell her she wasn't welcome. Jackson refused to allow us to travel to see her, claiming it was important for children to be in their own home during the holidays.

This year, Tallulah was turning eleven. We were having a big celebration. All of her friends from school were coming. I'd arranged for a clown, bouncy house, ponies—the works. None of our adult friends were invited, except Amber. We'd been friends for a few months by then, and I was starting to feel like she was family. I'd arranged for plenty of help to keep watch over the children. We'd have both nannies there. Sabine only worked during the week, so Jackson had hired a young college student, Surrey, to spend the weekend with us and help with whatever needed doing. However, Sabine wanted to be there for the party. I was telling Amber about the planning. She'd stopped by to return a movie she'd borrowed.

"I'd really love to meet your mother, Daphne," she gushed.

"You will. I'll have you over while she's here, but are you sure you really want to come to the party? It's going to be twenty screaming children. I'm not sure I even want to go." I was joking, of course.

"I can help you. I mean, I know you have hired help and all, but it's nice to have a friend too."

Jackson hadn't been happy when I'd told him she was coming.

"What the hell, Daphne? This is a family affair. She's not your sister, you know. She's always around."

"She has no one here. And she's my best friend." I realized my mistake as soon as the words left my lips. Was she? I hadn't had one for years. It's impossible to be close to someone when you're living a lie. All my relationships, except for the ones with my children, were superficial by necessity. But with Amber, I felt a bond that no one else could understand. As much as I loved Meredith, she couldn't relate to how I felt losing my sister.

"Your best friend? You may as well say Margarita's your best friend. She's a nothing."

I corrected myself. "Of course, you're right. That's not what I meant. I meant she's the one person who understands what I've been through. I feel like I owe her something. Besides, she always says how welcome you make her feel and how much she admires you."

That mollified him. For a man so smart, you'd think he would have seen through it. But that was the thing with Jackson: he always wanted to believe that everyone adored him.

So she'd come, and it *was* nice to have a friend. To watch Jackson interact with her, you would never know how he truly felt. When she arrived, he gave her a big smile and embrace.

"Welcome. So glad you could come."

She smiled shyly and murmured a thank-you.

"Let me get you a drink. What'll you have?"

"Oh, I'm fine."

"Come on, Amber. You're going to need it to get through the day." He gave her a dazzling smile. "You like Cabs, right?"

She nodded.

"Be right back."

"Where can I put my gift?" she asked me.

"You shouldn't have."

"It's just a little something I thought she would like."

Later, when Tallulah was opening her gifts, I watched with interest as she came to Amber's present. It was a book on the life of Edgar Allan Poe.

Tallulah looked over and gave her a subdued thank-you.

"I remembered you were reading his stories that day in New York," Amber called over to her.

"Isn't she a bit young for Poe?" my mother asked within Amber's earshot, never one to hold back.

"Tallulah's very advanced for her age. She's reading at an eighth-grade level," I said.

"There's a difference between intellectual development and emotional development," my mother pointed out.

Amber said nothing, merely looked at the ground, and I felt torn between defending her and validating my mother's concerns.

"I'll look it over, and if you're right, I'll put it aside until she's older." I smiled at my mother.

I looked up to see Surrey running to retrieve some presents that were scattered on the floor.

"Good heavens, what is going on?" my mother asked.

"Bella threw them from the pile," Amber said.

"What?" I ran over to see what had happened.

Bella was standing in front of the table, hands on her hips, her bottom lip stuck out as far as it would go.

"Bella, what's wrong?"

"It's not fair. She gets all these presents, and no one brought me anything."

"It's not your birthday. You had your birthday six months ago."

She stomped her foot. "I don't care. I didn't get this many presents. And I didn't have ponies." She raised her little fist and smashed it down on the corner of the cake.

I didn't need this today. "Surrey, would you please take Bella inside until she calms down?" I pointed at the cake. "See if you can fix that."

Surrey tried to get Bella to go with her, but Bella refused, running in the other direction. I was glad that none of the other children's mothers were around to witness it. I didn't have the energy to go after her. At least she wasn't bothering anyone now.

When I walked back to Amber and my mother, I was fixed with a disapproving look from the latter.

"That child is spoiled rotten."

The blood pounded in my ears. "Mother, she just has a hard time managing her emotions."

"She's overindulged. Maybe if you didn't leave the parenting to the nannies, she'd be better behaved."

Amber gave me a sympathetic look, and I took a deep breath, afraid of saying something I'd regret.

"I would appreciate it if you kept your parenting opinions to yourself. Bella is my daughter, not yours."

"No kidding. If she were mine, she wouldn't act like that."

I jumped up and ran into the house. Who was she to judge me? She had no idea what my life was like. *And whose fault is that?* a little voice asked. I wished she was a bigger part of my life, that she understood my reasons for the way I parented. But right now her disapproval and critical comments were just one more voice in a sea of accusations that I lived with daily.

I grabbed a Valium from my purse and downed it dry. Amber walked into the kitchen, came over, and put a hand on my shoulder.

"Mothers," she said.

I blinked back the tears and said nothing.

"Don't let her get to you. She means well. You're a terrific mother."

"I try to be. I know Bella's a handful, but she has a good heart. Do you think I'm too easy on her?"

She shook her head. "Of course not. She's a darling. Just impetuous, but she'll grow out of it. What she needs is understanding and nurturing."

"I don't know."

I couldn't blame my mother. It *did* look like I turned a blind eye to Bella's misbehavior. What my mother didn't know was that Bella cried herself to sleep more nights than not. Jackson may have been the doting father in public, but in private, he knew just the right things to say to pit the girls against each other and to make Bella feel inferior to her older sister. Bella struggled with her reading and was behind her schoolmates. First grade was almost over, and she was not even close to reading. When Tallulah finished first grade, she was reading at a fifth-grade level. Jackson was quick to remind Bella of that. Poor Bella was lucky if she could get through the primers. Her teacher strongly recommended testing, but Jackson refused. We'd had an argument about it in the car on the way home from the conference.

"She may have a learning disability. It's not so uncommon."

He kept his eyes straight ahead and answered me through clenched teeth. "She's just lazy. That child does what she wants to when she wants to."

I felt frustration well up. "That's not true. She tries so hard. She's in tears every night trying to get through a page or two. I really think she needs help."

He slammed his hand on the steering wheel. "Damn it, we're not having her labeled as dyslexic or whatever. That will follow her forever, and she'll never get into Charterhouse. We'll hire a private tutor, and I don't care if she has to work five hours a day, she *will* learn to read."

I'd closed my eyes in resignation. There was no use in

arguing with him. When the girls reached high school, he planned to send them away to Charterhouse, an exclusive boarding school in England. But I knew in my heart that before that day ever came, I would find a way for us to escape. In the meantime, I pretended to go along.

I'd hired a tutor with a background in special education. Without Jackson or Bella realizing it, she had evaluated her and suspected dyslexia. How was Bella going to get through school without any accommodations, without anyone knowing the way she learned? I knew she was in the wrong place. St. Luke's didn't have the resources to provide her with what she needed, but Jackson refused to discuss moving her anywhere else.

The poor child went to school all day and then came home to more lessons with the tutor just to keep up. They worked together for hours, Bella's progress torturously slow and further impeded by her resistance to more desk time. She wanted to go play, and she should have been able to. But every night at dinner, Jackson would insist she read to us. When she stumbled over a word or took too long to sound something out, he'd drum his fingers on the table until she began to stutter even more. The ironic thing was, he didn't understand how his impatience was having the opposite of its intended effect. He actually thought he was doing the right thing, being on top of her schooling—or at least that's what he claimed. We all began to dread family dinners. And Bella, poor thing, was exhausted all the time, overwrought and beset with self-doubt.

One particular night haunts me. Bella had had a horrible day at school and a meltdown with the tutor. By the time we sat down to dinner, she was like a volcano ready to erupt. After we'd finished eating, Margarita brought out the dessert.

"None for Bella until she reads," Jackson commanded.

"I don't want to read. I'm too tired." She reached for the plate with the brownies.

"Margarita." His voice had been so sharp that we'd all turned to look at him. "I said no."

"Mister, I will bring them back for everyone after."

"No, Tallulah can have hers. *She's* a smart girl."

"That's okay, Daddy. I can wait." Tallulah had looked down at her plate.

Margarita had reluctantly put the plate on the table and made a hasty retreat.

Jackson had gotten up from his seat and handed Bella the book he had brought home. She'd thrown it on the floor, and his face had turned bright red.

"You've been getting help for six months now. You're in first grade. It should be easy for you. Read the first page." He'd bent to retrieve it from the floor.

I'd looked at the book. *Charlotte's Web*. There was no way she could do it.

"Jackson, this isn't accomplishing anything."

Ignoring me, he'd slammed the book down on the table, making Bella jump.

My eyes were drawn to the throbbing vein in his forehead. "Either she reads this damn book, or I'm firing her worthless tutor. Let's see what you've learned. Now!"

Bella picked up the book with shaking hands, opened it, and in a trembling voice, began to read. "Wwwww hhheerrr s Pap a ggggoinn g wiith thaat ax?"

"Oh, for crying out loud. You sound like a moron! Spit it out."

"Jackson!"

He'd given me a dark look and then turned to Bella. "You look ugly when you read like that."

Bella had burst into tears and ran from the table. I'd hesitated only a moment, then rushed after her.

After I calmed her down and tucked her in, she'd looked at me with those big blue eyes and asked, "Am I stupid, Mommy?"

I'd been pierced to the core.

"Of course not, sweetie. You're very smart. Lots of people have trouble learning to read."

"Tallulah doesn't. She was born with a book in her hand. I'm the one that's thick as a brick."

"Who told you that?"

"Daddy."

I wanted to kill him. "You listen to me. Do you know who Einstein is?"

She looked up at the ceiling. "The funny-looking man with the crazy hair?"

I forced a laugh. "Yes. He was one of the smartest men ever, and he didn't learn to read until he was nine. You are very smart."

"Daddy doesn't think so."

How could I make this better? "Daddy doesn't mean those things. He just doesn't understand the way different brains work. He thinks if he says those things, you'll work harder." It sounded lame even to my ears, but it was all I could offer.

She yawned and her eyes fluttered shut. "I'm tired, Mommy."

I'd kissed her on the forehead. "Good night, angel."

So she misbehaved sometimes—who wouldn't with that kind of pressure? But how do you explain to people around you that you're cutting your child some slack because her father has reduced her to rubble?

FIFTY-TWO

When Jackson was bored, he liked to hide my things, putting things in places where I'd never find them. My brush often turned up in the guest bathroom, my contact lens solution in the kitchen. Today I was running late for an important meeting with a potential donor at Julie's Smile, and my keys were nowhere to be found. Our driver, Tommy, was off for a family emergency, and Sabine had taken the girls to the Bronx Zoo, as school was closed for another teacher planning day.

Jackson was aware that I had been preparing for the meeting all week, and I knew it was no coincidence that my keys had gone missing. I needed to be there in fifteen minutes. I called a cab and got to my meeting with one minute to spare. I was so frazzled that I was off my game. When the meeting was over, I picked up the phone and dialed Jackson.

"You might have cost the foundation hundreds of thousands." I didn't bother with any preamble.

"Excuse me?"

"My keys are missing."

"I have no idea what you're talking about. Don't blame me because you're disorganized." His tone was maddeningly patronizing.

"I always put them in the drawer in the hall table. Both sets were gone, and Tommy is conveniently off today. I had to call a cab."

"I'm sure there's someone who would find the quotidian details of your day interesting, but it doesn't happen to be me." He ended the call.

I slammed the phone down.

⁕

He worked late and didn't get home until after nine. When he arrived, I was in the kitchen, icing cupcakes for Bella's class bake sale. He opened the refrigerator and started cursing.

"What's the matter?"

"Come here."

I braced myself for whatever this latest tirade was going to be and came up behind him. He pointed.

"Can you tell me what's wrong?"

I followed the line of his finger. "What?" Everything had to be perfect; he had started using a measuring tape to ensure the glasses were exactly an eighth of an inch apart. He would have surprise inspections of drawers and cabinets to make sure everything was in its place.

He shook his head and looked at me with loathing. "Do you not see that the Naked juices are not lined up alphabetically? You've got the cranberry behind the strawberry."

The absurdity of my life struck me, and I began to giggle uncontrollably. He was looking at me with increasing animosity, and all I could do was laugh. I tried to stop, felt the terror rise from my stomach. *Stop laughing!* I didn't know what was wrong with me, even when I saw his eyes get dark with anger, I couldn't stop—in fact, it made me laugh even harder. I was becoming hysterical.

He grabbed the bottle, twisted the top off, and poured it on my head.

"What are you doing?" I jumped back.

"Still think it's funny? You stupid cow!" In a rage, he started pulling everything out and throwing things to the floor. I stood, transfixed, as I watched. When he got to the eggs, he began throwing them at me. I tried to shield my face but felt the sting on my cheeks as he whipped them at me as hard as he could. Within minutes, I was covered in fluids and food. He shut the refrigerator door and stared at me for a long moment.

"Why aren't you laughing now, slob?"

I stood rooted to the spot, too afraid to speak. My lip trembled as I muttered an apology.

He nodded. "You should be sorry. Clean this shit up, and don't even think of asking any of the staff for help. It's your mess." He walked over to the plate of cupcakes I'd been frosting and threw it on the floor. He unzipped his pants and urinated all over them. I started to cry out, but caught myself in time.

"You'll have to tell Bella you were too lazy to make her cupcakes." He wagged his finger at me. "Bad Mommy."

Then he turned around and opened the drawer where I kept my keys and jangled them in his hands before throwing them at me. "And your keys were here the whole time, dummy. Next time, look harder. I'm so tired of having such a lazy, stupid wife." He stormed from the kitchen and left me there, huddled in the corner, shaking.

It took me over an hour to clean everything up. In a numb haze, I threw away all the ruined food, mopped, wiped, and cleaned until all the surfaces shone again. I couldn't let the staff see a mess when they arrived early tomorrow morning. I would have to stop at the bakery tomorrow and pick up cupcakes to replace the ones he'd ruined. I dreaded going upstairs, hoping he'd be asleep by the time I showered and got in bed—but I knew that it excited him to humiliate me. The lights were out when I finished drying my hair and walked over to my side of the bed. His breathing was even, and I heaved a sigh of relief that he was asleep. I pulled the covers up to my chin and was just about to drift off when I felt his hand on my thigh. I froze. *Not tonight.*

"Say it," he commanded.

"Jackson—"

He squeezed harder. "Say it."

I closed my eyes and forced the words out. "I want you. Make love to me."

"Beg me."

"I want you now. Please." I knew he wanted me to say more, but that was all I could force out.

"You don't sound very convincing. Show me."

I pushed the covers back and lifted my nightgown off. Straddling him the way he liked, I positioned myself so that my breasts were in his face.

"You're such a whore." He thrust into me with no regard to my readiness. I gripped the sheets and made my mind blank until he finished.

FIFTY-THREE

The next day, as usual, there was a gift. This time it was a watch—a Vacheron Constantin worth upward of fifty grand. I didn't need it, but of course I'd wear it, especially around his business associates and at the club, so everyone could see how generous my husband was. I knew how it would go. He would be charming for the next few weeks: compliment me, take me out to dinner, act solicitous. In truth, it was almost worse than his derision. At least when he was debasing me, I could feel justified in my hatred. But when he went for days on end masquerading as the compassionate man I fell in love with, it was confusing, even when I knew it was all an act.

He checked in with me every morning to go over what I had planned for the day. That morning I had decided to skip my Pilates class and get a massage and facial instead. He called me at ten, like he did every day.

"Good morning, Daphne. I've e-mailed you an article on the new exhibit at the Guggenheim. Make sure you take a look. I'd like to discuss it tonight."

"Okay."

"On your way to the gym?"

"Yes, see you later," I lied. I wasn't in a mood for a lecture on the importance of exercise.

Later that night, I was having a glass of wine in the sunroom and reading the damn Guggenheim article while the girls were being bathed. As soon as I saw his face, I knew something was wrong.

"Hello." I made my voice bright.

He was holding a drink. "What are you doing?"

I lifted my iPad. "Reading the article you sent."

"How was Pilates?"

"Fine. How was your day?"

He sat down across from me on the sofa and shook his head. "Not great. One of my managers lied to me."

I looked up from the screen. "Oh?"

"Yeah. And about something really stupid. I asked him if he'd made a phone call, and he said yes." He took a long swallow from his glass of bourbon. "Thing is, he hadn't. All he had to do was tell me, say he'd planned to later." He shrugged. "It would have been no big deal. But he lied."

My heart fluttered, and I picked up my wineglass, taking a sip. "Maybe he was afraid you'd be angry."

"Well, that's the thing. Now I am. Really pissed, actually. Insulted too. He must think I'm an idiot. I *hate* being lied to. I'll put up with a lot of things, but lying, I can't abide it."

Unless he was the one doing the lying, of course. I gave him a neutral look. "I get it. You don't like liars." Now who was treating someone like an idiot? I knew there was no manager, that it was his passive-aggressive way of confronting me. But I wouldn't give him the satisfaction. I did wonder how he knew I'd skipped my class. "So what did you do?"

He walked over to me, sat down, put his hand on my knee. "What do you think I should do?"

I slid away from him. He inched closer.

"I don't know, Jackson. Do whatever you think is right."

He pursed his lips, started to say something else, then sprang up from the sofa.

"Enough of this bullshit. Why did you lie to me today?"

"About what?"

"Going to the gym. You were at the spa from eleven to two."

I frowned at him. "How do you know that? Are you having me followed?"

"No."

"Then how?"

He gave me a vicious smile. "Maybe people are following you. Maybe cameras are watching you. You just never know."

My throat started to close up. I couldn't catch my breath, and I gripped the side of the sofa as I tried to stop the room from spinning. He said nothing, merely watched with an amused expression. When I finally found my voice, the only word that came out was "Why?"

"Isn't it obvious?"

When I didn't answer, he went on.

"Because I can't trust you. And I was justified. You lied to me. I won't be made a fool of."

"I should have told you, I was just tired today. I'm sorry. You can trust me."

"I'll bestow trust on you when you deserve it. When you stop lying."

"Someone must have really hurt you in the past, made a fool out of you," I said in a sympathetic tone, knowing it would get under his skin.

Anger flashed in his eyes. "No one made a fool out of me, and no one ever will." He grabbed my glass of wine, walked over to the wet bar, and poured the remains in the sink. "I think you've consumed enough calories—especially considering you were too lazy to exercise today. Why don't you go and change for dinner? I'll see you then."

After he left, I poured myself a new glass and thought about this latest revelation. I bet he was spying on me in other ways too. I couldn't let my guard down at all. Maybe he'd bugged the phone or put cameras in the house. It was time for action on my part, and I needed a plan. He controlled all of the money. I was given a cash allowance for incidentals but had to give him receipts for everything I spent. All the rest of the bills went to his office. He gave me no discretionary spending—just one more way he tried to keep me under his thumb. He didn't know that I'd accumulated my own secret stash.

I'd set up an e-mail account and cloud credentials under a fake name on one of the laptops in the office and hid the computer in a closet underneath brochures and flyers—somewhere he'd never think to look. I sold some of my designer purses and clothing on eBay and had the money wired into an account he knew nothing about. I had everything go to a post office box I'd set up in Milton, New York, a thirty-minute ride from the house. It was slow going, but over the past five years, I'd put together a decent enough emergency fund. To date, I'd saved close to $30,000. I also bought a pack of burner cells that I kept at the office. I didn't know yet what I was going to do with all of it, only that I'd need it one day. Jackson thought he had every angle covered, but, unlike him, I was unfettered by delusions of grandeur. I had to believe that somehow they would be his undoing.

FIFTY-FOUR

Christmas used to be my favorite holiday. I sang in our church choir every Christmas Eve, and Julie was always front and center, cheering me on. Then we'd go back to the inn and have dinner, happy to be the ones waited on for a change. We could give one gift early and save the rest for Christmas Day. The last Christmas that I spent with Julie, she'd been fidgety all through dinner, as though she was bursting with some secret she couldn't wait to share. I gave her my gift—a pair of gold ball earrings that I'd scrimped and saved for with my tips at the inn. When it was her turn, she handed me a small box, her eyes bright with excitement.

I tore open the paper and lifted the lid. I gasped. "No, Julie. This is your favorite."

She smiled and took the heart pendant from the box, holding it toward me to put on. "I want you to have it."

She'd been so much weaker lately. I think she knew, or at least accepted, before we did that her time was running out.

I held back tears and grasped the thin chain in my hand. "I'll never take it off." And I didn't. Until after I married him, and I knew that if I didn't hide it away, he'd take it from me too. It was safely nestled under the cardboard bottom of one of the many velvet jewelry boxes that contained his gifts to me.

For the past ten years, Christmas had been nothing more than an obscene display of consumption. We didn't go to church. Jackson was an atheist and refused to expose our children to what he called "a fairy tale." But he had no problem perpetuating the Santa myth. I had stopped trying to reason with him.

I did take pleasure in the girls' enjoyment. They loved the decorating, baking, and sights and sounds of the season. This year, I had another reason to be excited. I had Amber. I had to hold myself back from showering her with too many presents. I didn't want to embarrass her. There was something about her that made me want to take care of her, to give her all the things she never had. It was almost like I was giving Julie all the things she'd never lived to enjoy.

We got up before the girls and went down to have our coffee. It wasn't long before they swept in, little tornados attacking the mountains of gifts with glee, and yet again I worried at the message we were sending them.

"Mommy, aren't you going to open any presents?" Tallulah asked.

"Yeah, Mommy. Open a present," Bella chimed in. Mine were stacked in a tall pile—beautifully decorated in gold foil and elaborate red velvet ribbons. I knew what the boxes would contain—more designer outfits that he'd chosen, jewelry to show off how good he was to me, expensive perfume that he liked, none of the things I would have picked for myself. Nothing at all that I wanted.

We had both agreed that the children's presents to us would be handmade, though, and I was looking forward to that.

"Open mine first, Mommy," Bella said. She dropped the half-unwrapped package she had been opening and ran over to me.

"Which is yours, sweetie?" I asked.

She pointed to the only package covered in Santa paper. "We wrapped it special so it'd be easy to spot," she said proudly.

I tousled her curls as she handed it to me, smiling as she perched on tiptoes, watching me wide-eyed. "Can I open it for you?"

I laughed. "Of course."

She ripped the paper and threw it on the floor, then pulled the lid off the box and gave it back to me.

It was a painting—a family portrait. It was quite good. I hadn't realized what a sharp eye she had.

"Bella! It's amazing. When did you do this?"

"In school. My teacher said I have talent. Mine was the best one. You couldn't even tell what most of the others were. She's going to talk to you about art classes for me."

The picture was twelve by twelve, and it was painted in watercolors. We were all standing on the beach, the ocean behind us, Jackson in the middle with me on one side and Tallulah on the other. Bella stood across from the three of us, noticeably larger than we were. Jackson, Tallulah, and I were dressed in drab grays and whites, Bella in bright oranges, pinks, and reds. Jackson and Tallulah were both turned, looking at me, Tallulah looking glum, Jackson smug, and I was staring at Bella with a wide smile. The picture unsettled me. It didn't take a psychologist to figure out that the family dynamics were off-kilter. I shook off the troubling thoughts and pulled her to me for a hug.

"It's beautiful, and I love it. I'm going to hang it in my office so I can look at it all day."

Tallulah looked over. "Why are you so much bigger than the rest of us?"

Bella stuck her tongue out at her sister. "It's called pesperective," she said, stumbling on the word.

Jackson laughed. "I think you mean perspective, my dear."

Tallulah rolled her eyes and brought me her present. "Open mine now."

It was a clay sculpture that she'd made of two hearts united with a ribbon, on which she'd painted the word *love*.

"It's you and Aunt Julie," she said.

My eyes filled with tears. "I love this, darling. It's perfect."

She smiled and embraced me. "I know sometimes you get sad. But your hearts will always be together."

I was so grateful for this thoughtful child.

"Open one of mine," Jackson said as he handed me a small box wrapped in red foil.

"Thank you." I took the package from him and began tearing the paper to reveal a plain white box, then lifted the lid to find a gold chain with a gold circle charm attached. I pulled it from the box and gasped.

Tallulah took the necklace from my hand and looked at it and then at me. "Who's YMB, Mommy?"

Before I could find my voice, Jackson spoke, the lie coming smoothly off his lips. "They're the initials of your mom's grandmother, who she loved very much. Let me put it on for you." He fastened it around my neck. "I hope you'll wear it all the time."

I gave him a big smile that he would know was fake. "Just another reminder of how you feel about me."

He pressed his lips to mine.

"Eeew!" Tallulah said, and both girls giggled.

Bella had gone back to her pile of presents and was

tearing through the rest of the packages when the doorbell rang.

Jackson had agreed to let Amber come over and
have dinner with us, since she was going to be alone for
Christmas. It hadn't been easy, but I staged the conversation in front of some of our friends, and he wanted to
look like the Good Samaritan by including her.

He greeted her like she was family, got her a drink,
and we all sat around very agreeably for the next few
hours, while the children played with their things and
we made small talk.

Amber gave us all lovely gifts—a book for Jackson
that he actually seemed to appreciate; books for the
girls plus some shiny jewelry for Bella, which she loved.
When she handed me my gift, I was a little nervous,
hoping she hadn't spent too much. Nothing could have
prepared me for the thin silver bangle, with two round
charms engraved with the names Julie and Charlene.

"Amber, this is so thoughtful and beautiful."

She held her arm up, and I saw that she wore the
same bracelet. "I have one too. Now our sisters will be
with us all the time."

Jackson was watching the exchange, and I could see
the anger in his eyes. He was always telling me I thought
about Julie too much as it was. But even Jackson couldn't
take my joy away. Two gifts that honored my sister and
the love I felt for her. I felt heard and understood for the
first time in so long.

"Oh, and one other little thing." She handed me a
small gift bag.

"Another present? The bracelet was enough."

I pushed aside the tissue paper and felt something
hard. My breath caught in my throat as I lifted it from
the bag. A glass turtle.

"I know how much you love them," she said.

Jackson's lips curled into a smile, and delight shone in his eyes.

And just like that, my feeling of being known and understood evaporated.

FIFTY-FIVE

Meredith was throwing her husband a surprise fifti-eth birthday party at Benjamin Steakhouse. Truth-fully, it was the last thing I was in the mood for. I was still tired from all the Christmas preparations and we were leaving for St. Bart's in two days, but I didn't want to let Meredith down. She was insistent that the party be on the twenty-seventh, Rand's actual birthday, since over the years it had always been underplayed due to its proximity to Christmas.

I'd just arrived in the city; Jackson had asked me to meet him at the Oyster Bar at Grand Central. That way, we'd be right down the street from the restaurant, and it would only take us a few minutes to walk there.

Even as I put on the Dior dress, I knew I was making a mistake. It was a favorite of mine, but Jackson didn't like the color. It was a pale gold silk, and he claimed it made my skin sallow. But it was a party for *my* friend, and I wanted to make a decision for a change. The mo-ment I saw his face, the barely perceptible furrow of the brow, the small wrinkle worrying between his eyes, I knew he was angry. He stood to kiss me, and I took a seat on the stool next to him. He picked up the crystal tumbler and, with one flick of his wrist, downed the re-maining amber liquid and flagged the bartender over.

"I'll have another Bowmore, and a Campari and soda for my wife."

I was about to protest—I'd never even tasted Campari—but I choked back the words before they escaped. It would be best to let whatever plan he had concocted play itself out.

"Meredith asked that we get to the restaurant by seven so we don't run into Rand. She wants him to be surprised."

Jackson arched a brow. "I'm sure the bill will be surprise enough."

I laughed dutifully, then looked at my watch. "We've got about half an hour, and then we'd better get going."

The bartender placed the drink in front of me.

Jackson lifted his glass. "Cheers, darling." He toasted me with such force that my drink ended up all over the front of my champagne-colored dress, now splashed with red.

"Oh dear, look what you've done." He didn't even try to hide his smirk.

Heat spread to my cheeks, and I took a deep breath, willing myself not to cry. Meredith was going to be so disappointed. I looked at him with no change in expression. "What now?"

He threw his hands up. "Well, obviously you can't turn up to the restaurant like that." He shook his head. "If only your dress were darker, or if you weren't such a klutz."

If only you were dead, I wanted to answer.

He called for the check. "We'll have to go to the apartment and get you changed. Of course, by the time we do that, it'll be too late to make it in time for the surprise."

I forced my mind to go blank and followed him numbly from the bar. We got into the limo, and he ig-

nored me while reading e-mails on his phone. I pulled
my phone out and texted my apologies to Meredith.

Because of traffic, it took over forty-five minutes for
us to get there. I smiled at the doorman, and we rode
the elevator in silence. I went to the bedroom, threw the
dress on the floor, and stood looking at the closet. I felt
him before I heard him—his breath on my neck, then
his lips on my back.

I suppressed the urge to scream. "Sweetheart, we
don't have time."

His mouth traveled down my back, to the top of my
panties. He slid them off and cupped my buttocks with
his hands. He moved closer, and I realized he'd taken
off his pants. I could feel him hard against me.

"There's always time for this."

His hands moved to cup my breasts, then he grabbed
my hands and placed them flat against the wall, his
pressed on top of them. I braced myself as he took me,
hard and rough, moving into a frenzied crescendo. It
was over within minutes.

I went into the bathroom to clean myself up, and
when I emerged, my black Versace was hanging on the
bedroom door. I grabbed it and laid it on the bed.

"Hold on," he said, walking toward me. "Wear this
underneath."

It was a black Jean Yu thong with a matching strapless bra. He'd had it made to order for me, and it felt
amazing—like a silk caress—but the sight of it only reminded me of what he'd done before he gave it to me. I
took it from him though, and gave him my best imita-
tion of a smile.

"Thank you."

He insisted upon dressing me, pulling the stockings

up my legs, stopping every few moments to brush his lips against my skin as he did so.

"Are you sure you wouldn't rather stay home and let me ravish you again?" He gave me a rakish smile.

Did he really believe I had any desire for him? I licked my lips. "As tempting as that sounds, we did promise. And Randolph is an old friend."

He sighed. "Yes, of course, you're right." He zipped my dress and tapped me on the behind. "Let's go, then."

When I turned around, he looked me up and down. "It's lucky you spilled your drink—that one's much better on you anyway."

By the time we arrived, an hour and a half later, everyone was just nibbling on the passed appetizers. I gave Meredith an apologetic look as we rushed over to greet her.

"I'm so sorry we're late—"

"Yes," Jackson cut in, "I tried to tell her we were running behind, but she insisted on squeezing in a massage. It put us behind about an hour." He shrugged.

Meredith's face registered shock, and she turned to me, hurt obvious in her eyes. "Why did you text me that you spilled something on your dress and had to go home and change?"

I stood there, paralyzed by indecision. If I told her the truth, I'd have to contradict Jackson. Public humiliation would bring a heavy price. But now my good friend thought I'd lied to her just so I could indulge in some pampering.

"I'm sorry, Mer. It was both. I had a pulled muscle, I spilled . . ." I stumbled on my words. Jackson watched me, an amused smile on his face. "What I mean, is that, yes, I did get a massage—my back was really bothering me—but we still would have made it in time if I hadn't spilled my drink all over myself like an idiot. I'm really sorry."

Jackson shook his head and smiled at Meredith. "You know how clumsy our little Daphne can be. I'm always telling her to be more careful."

FIFTY-SIX

When I first met Amber, I could never have imagined that she would become someone I depended on. I'll admit, my first impression was of a somewhat homely and meek young woman with little to interest me except for the fact that she'd experienced a similar heartache. Her grief seemed so raw and fresh that it helped me put my own pain on the back burner to help her. I wanted to make it all better, to give her a reason to wake up in the morning.

Looking back, I suppose I should have seen the signs. But I was eager for a friend, a true friend. No, that's not quite right. I was desperate for a sister—for *my* sister, which was of course, impossible. The next best thing was a friend who'd suffered the same loss I had. It's bad enough to lose a sibling, but to watch one die a little each day—there's no explaining that to someone who hasn't experienced it. So when Amber appeared so unexpectedly in my life, she felt like a gift. I had no one in my life that I could trust. Jackson had done his job well, isolating me from everyone in my past and erecting impenetrable walls around my life. None of my friends knew the reality of my marriage or my life. But with Amber, I could share genuine emotion. Even Jackson couldn't do anything about that.

The flowering friendship made him nervous—he didn't like for me to see any of my friends more than once every few weeks unless, of course, he was there.

When I'd asked him to find a job for her at Parrish, he'd been indignant at first.

"Come on, Daphne. Isn't this little charity act wearing thin yet? What could you possibly have in common with that frumpy mouse?"

"You know what we have in common."

He rolled his eyes. "Give it a rest, will you? It's been twenty years. Haven't you mourned enough? So her sister died too. That doesn't mean I want her working in my company. She's around our family too much as it is."

"Jackson, please. I care about her. I do everything you want, don't I?" I forced myself to walk over to him and put my arms around his neck. "She isn't a threat to you. She really needs a job. Her family back home depends on her. I can brag to everyone about how you rescued her." I knew he'd like playing the hero.

"Hilda does need an assistant. I suppose we could give her a chance. I'll call Human Resources and have her set up for an interview."

I didn't want to take any chances. "Couldn't you try her out without an interview on my word? She's smart as a whip; she's done a better job as my cochair than anyone before her. And working at Rollins, she knows a lot about your business. She worked on the commercial side."

"Rollins! That's not saying much. If she's so good, why'd they let her go?"

I had hoped to avoid telling him, but I saw no out. "Her boss was sexually harassing her."

He started laughing. "Is he blind?"

"Jackson! That's cruel."

"Seriously, that dirty-dishwater hair, the ugly glasses, and don't get me started on her lack of fashion sense," he said, shaking his head.

I was glad that he didn't find her attractive. Not because I cared if he strayed, but because I didn't want anything to cause me to lose her as a friend. And working for Hilda Battley, she'd be cocooned from any funny business from the men there. I felt good about helping her and knowing that no one would traumatize her again.

"Please, Jackson. It would make me very happy, and you'd be doing a good thing."

"I'll arrange it. She can start Monday. But you have to do something for me."

"What?"

"Cancel your mother's visit for next month."

My heart sank. "She's been looking forward to it. I've already bought tickets to *The Lion King*. The girls are really excited."

"It's up to you. If you want me to hire your friend, then I'll need some peace and quiet. When your mother's here, I can't relax. Besides, she was just here for Tallulah's birthday."

"All right. I'll call her."

He gave me a cold smile. "Oh, and tell her that you're canceling because the girls want to take Sabine instead of her to the show."

"There's no need to be cruel."

"Okay. No job."

I picked up the phone and dialed. When I hung up, heartsick at the hurt in my mother's voice, he gave me an approving nod.

"Well done. See? You don't need anyone but me, anyhow. I'm your family."

FIFTY-SEVEN

I loved having a best friend again. I hadn't realized how lonely I was until Amber came along. Her manipulation was so subtle and gradual that I never had a twinge of suspicion.

It wasn't long until we were always in touch with each other: texting when something funny happened, phone calls, lunches. I wanted her at the house all the time. I was ready to leave to meet her when I heard his car in the driveway. Stomach lurching, I contemplated sneaking out the back, but when I looked out the window, he was out of the car and talking to Tommy, our driver. *Shit.*

He slammed the front door and stalked over to me. "Why do you need Tommy tonight? He said he's picking up Amber too. Are you planning on drinking yourselves into oblivion like some sluts?"

I shook my head. "Of course not. Just a glass or two, but I don't want to drive. She's been so busy with work, we wanted an evening to catch up. I thought you were taking clients out tonight—"

"The dinner was canceled." He studied me for a long moment. "You know, she's the help now. It's actually rather unseemly for you to be friends with her. What if someone sees you together?"

The heat spread from my neck to my face. "She's become like a sister to me. Please don't ask me to stop being friends with her."

"Upstairs," he commanded.

The girls were getting their baths; I had already said my good nights. "I don't want the girls to hear me. I'll have to go through the routine all over again."

He grabbed my hand and pulled me into his office, slammed me against the wall, and locked the door. He unzipped his pants and pushed me down to my knees.

"The quicker you get to it, the faster you can leave."

Hot tears of humiliation ran down my face, ruining my makeup. I wanted to refuse him, to tell him how much he repulsed me, but I was terrified. The slightest resistance to anything he wanted could result in the gun coming out again.

"Stop crying! You make me sick."

"I'm sorry."

"Shut up and get to it."

After I finished, he tucked his shirt back in and zipped up his pants.

"Was it as good for you as it was for me?" He laughed. "By the way, you look like shit. Your makeup's all smeared."

He unlocked the door and left without another word.

I stumbled to the bathroom and ran some water under my eyes. I texted Tommy and told him to get Amber and come back for me. I couldn't let anyone see me this way.

When I finally got to the bar and saw Amber waiting, I wanted nothing more than to pour out my heart, tell her what he was really like. Her friendship had lulled me into such a strong sense of security that I almost told her the truth about why I was late. But the words wouldn't come. And what could she do anyway?

As she looked at me with stars in her eyes, asking about my perfect marriage, I wanted to lay it all bare. But she couldn't help me, and there was nothing to be gained by being truthful. So I did what I had learned to do best: I pushed the reality to the back of my mind and pretended that my charmed life was all that it seemed.

FIFTY-EIGHT

The night that Meredith came to tell me that she'd discovered that Amber wasn't her real name, at first I believed Amber's explanation, that she'd been abused and had to run from her crazy father. After all, I understood what it was like to be a captive. If I thought I could survive and Jackson wouldn't find us, I'd have gladly assumed a false identity. But something in her story was familiar. Then it hit me: she'd used the same phrase—*I'm so ashamed to tell you this*—when she told me about her boss making a pass at her. The more I thought about it, the more her story sounded suspicious. I decided to listen to my gut and investigate, but I pretended to believe her. I had my own reasons, but Meredith thought I was crazy. She'd come over the day after the confrontation.

"I don't care what she says, Daphne. You can't trust her. She's an impostor. I wonder if she even has a sister."

That was impossible, though. Even if she'd lied about everything else, she had to have a sister. I couldn't bear to believe that someone could be so cruel as to pretend she had suffered as I had, to make up stories about a sister struggling with this dreadful disease. That would make her a monster. And my best friend couldn't be a monster.

"I believe her. Not everyone has the resources that we do. Sometimes lying is the only option."

She shook her head. "There's something very off with her."

"Look, Mer. I know you're only trying to protect me. But I know Amber. Her grief over her sister is genuine. She's had a rough life, and I understand that. Please, have a little faith in my judgment."

"I think you're making a mistake, but it's your call. For your sake, I hope she's telling the truth."

After she'd gone, I ran up to my bedroom, opened my nightstand drawer, and pulled out the glass turtle Amber had given me. Holding it by the edges, I placed it in a plastic bag. I threw my hair into a ponytail, pulled a baseball cap low on my face, and changed into jeans and a T-shirt. I left the house with only my wallet and the burner phone I'd bought a few months earlier and walked the two miles into town. The cab I'd called was waiting in front of the bank on Main Street, and I jumped in the back.

"I need to go to Oxford. This address please."

I handed him the slip of paper and slid back in the seat, looking around to make sure no one I knew had seen me. My thoughts were racing as I considered the implications of Meredith's findings, and I felt sick. Was it possible that our entire relationship was built on pretense? Was she using me for my money, or was she after my husband? Slow down, I thought. Wait and see.

Forty minutes later, the cab came to a stop in front of the brick building.

"Can you wait for me?" I gave him a hundred-dollar bill. "I won't be long."

"Sure, ma'am."

I went up to the fourth floor and found the door marked "Hanson Investigations." I'd found the agency online, using a computer at the library. I went inside to a small, empty reception area. No one sat behind the desk, but a door behind it opened, and a man walked out. He was younger than I'd expected, clean-cut and kind of cute. He smiled and walked toward me, his hand outstretched.

"Jerry Hanson."

I shook his hand. "Daphne Bennett," I said. The chances that he knew Jackson or anyone in our world were slim, but I wasn't taking any chances.

I followed him into a pleasant room with bright colors. Instead of sitting behind his desk, he took one of the armchairs and indicated I should take the one across from him.

"How can I help you? You sounded pretty shaken up on the phone."

"I need to find out if someone who's gotten close to me is who she says she is. I have her fingerprints." I handed him the bag. "Can you find who they belong to?"

"I can try. I'll start with a criminal check. If her prints aren't there, I'll see if I can reach out to some folks who might be able to tap into private databases where she might have been printed for a job."

I handed him the newspaper article with her picture. I had circled her face. "I don't know if this will help. She claims to be from Nebraska, but I don't know if she made that up. How long will it take before you find anything out?"

He shrugged. "Shouldn't take more than a few days. If we find a hit, I can put together a full report for you. To be safe, let's say next Wednesday."

I stood. "Thanks so much. Text me if there's any delay; otherwise, I'll see you on Wednesday. Is noon good?"

He nodded. "Yeah, that works. Listen, Mrs. Bennett, be careful, you hear?"

"Don't worry. I will."

I took the stairs, feeling as though I would jump out of my skin if I didn't keep moving. I thought about all the intimate conversations, the parts of me I had shared with her. Julie. My darling Julie. If she did anything to make a mockery of my sister's memory, I didn't know what I would do. Maybe it would just be a misunderstanding.

I got back into the cab to head home. Now all I had to do was wait.

FIFTY-NINE

It's not good, Mrs. Bennett," Jerry Hanson said as he slid the manila folder across the desk toward me. "There's quite a bit to look through. I'm gonna take a walk, get some coffee. I'll be back to discuss everything with you in about half an hour."

I nodded, already immersed in the file. The first thing I saw was a newspaper article with Amber's photo. Her eyes were heavily lined with black, and her hair was bleached platinum blond. She looked sexy, but hard. Only her name wasn't Amber. It was Lana. Lana Crump. I read the article, then looked through the rest of the document. My hands shook as I put down the last piece of paper. I broke out in a sweat, reeling from the betrayal. It was far worse than I'd imagined. She had made everything up. There had been no sick sister, no abusive father. I had let her into my life, my children's lives, let her get close to me and told her things I'd never shared with another human being. She had played me, and brilliantly. What a fool I'd been. I'd been so blinded by my grief over Julie that I'd actually invited that jackal into my life.

My heart actually ached. She was a criminal, a fugitive. And what she had done—it showed such a clear lack of conscience, no remorse. How could I not have seen it?

Her entire life was here in these pages. A new picture began to form. A poor girl from a small town consumed by jealousy and want: covetous, predatory. She'd mapped out a plan, and when it had failed, she'd exacted her revenge. She had fooled everyone there too, had turned another family's life upside down, irrevocably damaged them, then run away. Then she'd taken on a different identity. A chill passed through me as I thought of the real Amber Patterson's disappearance. Had Lana had a hand in it? Now I understood why she always hid from cameras. She was afraid of someone she'd known in her other life seeing her photo.

The door opened, and the detective returned. "How did someone like you get mixed up with someone like her?"

I exhaled. "Doesn't matter. Tell me, according to this, there's an open warrant out for her. What would happen if I called the police?"

He leaned back in his chair and tented his hands. "They'd pick her up, call the Missouri police, and have her taken back there to stand trial."

"What kind of sentence does perjury and jury tampering carry?"

"Varies by state, but it's a felony and usually carries a prison sentence of at least a year. The fact that she skipped out on bail is going to add some time as well."

"What about what happened to that poor boy? Will that factor in?"

He shrugged. "There's not a punitive component to the criminal charges, so not technically. But I'm sure the despicable intent will sway a sentencing judge, even if he or she doesn't admit it."

"This is all confidential, right?"

He raised his eyebrows. "Are you asking me if I'm obligated to turn her in?"

I nodded.

"I'm not an officer of the court. This is your report; you do what you want with it."

"Thank you. Um, this has nothing to do with Amber, but I need you to look into one more thing for me." I filled him in, handed him a folder, and left.

I hailed a cab and had it take me to the bank—the one twenty miles from home, where Jackson didn't know I had an account or a safe-deposit box. I looked through the file one more time before putting it away. A picture caught my eye: a woman who must have been Amber's mother. That's when I realized the other thing she had done—and that is what convinced me beyond a shadow of a doubt that Amber, aka Lana, was as devoid of a conscience as Jackson. That revelation was liberating. It meant that I could proceed with the plan that I had begun to formulate in my mind.

I wasn't going to turn her in. No, she wasn't going back to Missouri to serve a measly couple of years in prison. She was going to get a life sentence right here in Connecticut.

SIXTY

If there's one thing living with an abusive psychopath has taught me, it's how to make the best of a bad situation. Once I recovered from the betrayal, I realized Amber could be the answer to everything. It was now obvious that she'd only used me to get close to Jackson. She had manipulated me into getting her a job so she'd be right there every day. But the problem was, Jackson wouldn't be as easily fooled as I was. And as cunning as Amber was, she had only half the picture, no real idea what made him tick, what turned him on. That's where I'd come in. I would feed her the information she needed to succeed in turning his obsessive focus from me to her. Little by little, I would play her, just as she'd played me.

I had to make him want her more than he wanted me. His money, power, and meticulous planning ensured that my only way out was for him to let me go. Up until then, he'd had no reason to do so. That was all about to change. I decided that I needed to pretend that he had once cheated on me. I wanted her to believe there was a crack in my marriage, that Jackson was capable of being tempted.

We met at Barnes & Noble that Saturday, and when she approached, I almost didn't recognize her.

"Wow. You look fantastic." Her hair was no longer dishwater brown, but a beautiful ash blond, her brows shaped into perfect arches over thick, luscious lashes and perfectly applied eyeliner. Contoured cheekbones, just the right amount of blush, and glossed lips completed the picture. She looked like a different woman. She hadn't wasted any time transforming herself.

"Thanks. I went to one of those makeup places at Saks and they helped me. I couldn't go to work in a fancy New York office looking like a country mouse."

Please, that was a Red Door makeover if I ever saw one. I wondered where she'd gotten the money. "Well, you look wonderful."

After browsing a bit, we went across the street to a café for lunch.

"So how are things going? Still loving the job?" I asked.

"Yes. I'm learning so much. And I really appreciate Jackson giving me the chance to fill Battley's shoes. I know it wasn't easy for him, after working with her for so many years."

I had to hand it to her, she gave nothing away. I don't know how she did it, but when Jackson came home a few short months after Amber had started and told me that Battley had resigned, I'd suspected she'd had a hand in it. "She was a gem. So loyal. Jackson didn't really tell me why she decided to retire early. Do you have any idea?"

She raised her eyebrows. "Well, she was up there in age, Daph. I think she was really more tired and taxed than she let on. I had to cover for her more than once." She leaned in toward me conspiratorially. "I probably saved her getting fired on a few occasions when she deleted an important meeting from Jackson's calendar. Luckily I caught it in time and fixed it."

"How lucky for her."

"Well, I guess she realized it was time. I think she was ready to have more time for her grandkids too."

"I'm sure—but enough about work. What's going on with your personal life? Any cute guys at the office?"

She shook her head. "Not really. I'm starting to wonder if I'll ever meet someone."

"Have you considered a dating service?"

"No. I'm not really one for those kinds of things. I'm a big believer in fate."

Sure she was. "I get it. You want the old-fashioned boy-meets-girl story."

She smiled. "Yes. Like you and Jackson. The perfect couple."

I gave a small laugh. "Nothing's perfect."

"The two of you sure make marriage seem easy. He looks at you like you're still on your honeymoon."

I had my opening to make her think there was trouble in paradise. "Not lately. We haven't had sex in two weeks." I cast my eyes downward. "Sorry—I hope you don't mind my talking about this."

"Of course not, that's what friends are for." She twirled the straw in her iced tea. "I'm sure he's just tired, Daph. It's been crazy at work."

I sighed. "If I tell you something, do you promise not to tell a soul?"

She leaned in closer. "Of course."

"He cheated on me before."

I saw the delight in her eyes before she was able to disguise it.

"You're kidding? When?"

"Right after Bella was born. I still had some extra weight, and I was tired all the time. There was this client—she was young and pretty and hung on his every word. I had met her at a social function, and from the way she looked at him, I knew she was trouble."

She licked her lips. "How did you find out?"

Now I was just making it up as I went along. "I found her panties in the apartment."

"Are you kidding? He took her to your place in New York?"

"Yes. I think she left them deliberately. When I confronted him, he fell apart. Begged my forgiveness. Told me that he'd just felt so ignored with all the time I spent with the new baby, and she'd flattered him so much. He admitted that her adoration was just too hard to resist."

"Wow. That must have been so hard for you. But at least you bounced back. The two of you seem very happy. And you have to give it to him for not lying."

I could see the wheels turning in her mind. "I think he did feel bad. He swore it would never happen again. But now I'm seeing some of the same signs I did back then. He's working late all the time, not initiating sex, seems distracted. I think there must be someone else."

"I haven't seen anything suspicious at the office."

"There's no one there that seems to be hanging around him more than usual?"

She shook her head. "Not that I can think of. I'll keep an eye on him for you, though, and let you know if I think there's anything you have to worry about."

I knew she'd keep an eye on him—and maybe more than that. "Thanks, Amber. I feel so much better knowing you're there looking out for me."

She put her hand on mine and gave me a steady look. "I would do anything for you. We have to stick together. Soul sisters, right?"

I squeezed her hand back and smiled. "Right."

SIXTY-ONE

It was easy to arrange. He had been looking forward to seeing *Hamlet*, and I knew he wouldn't want to waste the valuable second ticket. Bella wasn't really sick, but I purposely bowed out of the show, hoping he'd invite Amber. He was furious that I'd missed it. My phone rang that night at midnight.

"Don't you ever do that again; you hear me?"

"Jackson, what's wrong?"

"I wanted you with me tonight. I had plans for you after the play."

"Bella needed me."

"*I* needed you. The next time you break plans with me, there'll be serious consequences. You got it?"

Apparently Amber had no idea about his bad mood. She called me the next morning with just the right things to say.

"Hello?"

"Hi, Daph, it's me."

"Hey. How was the play?"

Rustling papers on her end. "Amazing. My first Broadway play. I was in awe the whole time."

Her Pollyanna act was getting old.

"I'm glad. So what's up?"

"Oh, well, I just wanted to let you know that by the time we got out, it was late, and so we stayed at the apartment."

"Oh?" I made my voice sound appropriately on guard.

"Jackson insisted that it was silly for me to go all the way home when I had to be back so early in the morning. I took the sheets off the guest room bed and put them in the laundry room so the housekeeper would know they needed to be changed."

Clever of her. She couldn't come out and state that she'd stayed in the guest room, or she'd be implying that there was a chance she'd slept with my husband, but she was letting me know that nothing had happened.

"That was thoughtful. Thanks."

"And I borrowed your red Armani suit, the one with the gold buttons. I hope you don't mind. I obviously hadn't brought a change of clothes."

I tried to figure out how I would feel if I still thought she was my friend. Would I have minded?

"Of course not. I bet it looks great on you. You should keep it." Let her see that it meant nothing to me, that Jackson's wife had so much, I could afford to give her my castoffs as if they were no more significant than a pair of gloves. A sharp intake of breath came over the line.

"I couldn't. It's a two-thousand-dollar suit."

Did I detect just the slightest bit of reproach in her voice? I forced a laugh. "Did you google it?"

A long moment of silence. "Um, no. Daphne, are you angry? I think I've upset you. I knew I shouldn't have gone. I just—"

"Come on, I'm just teasing. I'm glad you went. Got me off the hook. Don't tell Jackson, but I find Shakespeare a bore." That wasn't true, but I knew she'd use that bit of misinformation to her advantage. "I mean it about the suit. Please, I want you to have it. I have more than I can wear. What are friends for?"

"I guess, if you're sure. Listen, I've got to run. Jackson needs me."

"Sure. Before you go, are you free this Saturday? We're having a few friends over for a dinner party, and I would love it if you'd come. There's someone I'd like you to meet."

"Oh, who?"

"A guy from the club who happens to be newly single and perfect, I think, for you." I had invited Gregg Higgins, a trust-fund baby. He was in his late twenties and extremely good-looking, which was fortunate for him, since he didn't have much going on upstairs. His father had given up hoping that Gregg would take over in the family business, but had given him a big office and title and let him spend his days having long lunches entertaining clients. He would be putty in Amber's hands and falling all over her, which is just what I wanted Jackson to witness. He wasn't in the same league as Jackson by any stretch, so I didn't worry about him actually distracting her, but he would be irresistible to her for the time being—her ticket to the club, glamorous events, and someone to pamper her until she achieved her ultimate goal. I figured she was also smart enough to realize a little competition would be good for arousing Jackson's interest.

Her voice was warm now. "That sounds interesting. What time should I be there?"

"Starts at six, but you're welcome to come a little early. Why don't you come at noon, and we can hang at the pool for a while and then get ready around two? Bring your clothes, and you can shower and dress here. In fact, why don't you plan to spend the night?"

"Fantastic, thanks."

I wanted Jackson to see Amber in her bikini, and

given how she'd stepped up her game lately, I knew she'd come over looking like something from the pages of the Victoria's Secret catalog.

I ended the call, grabbed my tennis racket, and left. I was meeting Meredith for a doubles game. Things were still a little strained between us since her confrontation with Amber. I knew Meredith was angry that I had bought Amber's story about being on the run from an abusive father, but once she saw I was immovable, she'd finally let it go. I hated for our friendship to become a casualty of my plan, but for the first time in ten years, I felt a flicker of hope. I wasn't going to let anything get in my way.

⁕

I ate a ton of carbs all the next week. Cookies, crackers, chips. Jackson had just left on a business trip, so he wasn't there to stop me. The girls were thrilled to have some junk food in the house. Normally, he inspected the refrigerator and cabinets daily and threw out anything remotely resembling snack food. I had to swear the girls to secrecy and even hide it from Sabine, who'd already gone running to Jackson when I kept Tallulah up late one night watching a movie. But yesterday I'd insisted she take a couple of days off, and her delight outweighed her sense of duty.

I wanted to make sure to pack on a few pounds before Saturday, so Jackson would notice how much better Amber looked in her bathing suit than I did in mine. It's amazing how quickly the weight comes back when you're used to eating fewer than twelve hundred calories a day. I was on my fourteenth food journal—Jackson inspected it every day when he got home and kept all

the completed ones lined up in his closet, his little keep-
sakes proving his control over me. Occasionally I would
write down a food that wasn't on the approved list—he
was too smart to believe I never cheated on my diet. On
those days, he'd sit and watch while he made me run five
miles on the treadmill in our home gym to make up for
it. I hadn't decided yet whether or not I would include
some extras on the journal this week or just pretend that
perimenopause was to blame for the extra weight. The
idea that my fertility was declining would make Amber
that much more appealing in comparison.

I'd forgotten how good sugar tasted. By Friday my
stomach had a nice little pooch to it, and my whole body
was a bit puffy. I put all the wrappers and cartons in
a trash bag and drove them to the dump. When he returned Friday night, the kitchen was in tip-top shape
again. It was just past nine when I heard his car in the
garage. I grabbed the remote and clicked off the television. I pulled roast duck out of the oven and set a place
for him at the island.

He walked in the kitchen as I was pouring myself a
glass of pinot noir.

"Hello, Daphne." He nodded toward the plate. "I ate
on the plane. You can put that away."

"How was your flight?"

He picked up the glass of wine and took a swallow.
"Fine, uneventful." His brow creased. "Before I forget, I
looked through the Netflix queue. I see that you watched
some low-rate drama. I thought we talked about this."

I'd forgotten to wipe the queue clean. Damn it. "I
think it came on automatically after the biography of
Lincoln I'd been watching with the girls. I must have
left the Netflix on."

He leveled a look at me and cleared his throat. "Be more responsible next time. Don't make me cancel the subscription."

"Of course."

He scrutinized my face, put a hand on my cheek, and pressed. "Are your allergies acting up?"

I shook my head. "I don't think so, why?"

"You look puffy. You haven't been eating sugar, have you?" He opened the cabinet containing the trash and looked through it.

"No, of course not."

"Get me your diary."

I ran upstairs and retrieved it. When I came back to the kitchen, he was looking through all the cabinets.

"Here."

He snatched it from my hands, sat down, and went through it, tracing each item with his finger. "Aha! What's this?" He pointed to an entry from yesterday.

"A baked potato."

"That turns right into sugar. You know that. If you have to be a pig and eat a potato, make sure it's a sweet potato. At least that has some nutritional value." He looked me up and down. "You make me sick. Fat pig."

"Daddy?"

Tallulah was standing in the doorway. She looked at me, worry in her eyes.

"Come give Daddy a hug. I was just telling your mommy she has to stop stuffing her face. You don't want a fat mommy, do you?"

"Mommy's not fat," she said, her voice cracking.

He looked at me and scowled. "You stupid sow. Tell your daughter that you need to watch what you eat."

"Daddy, stop!" Tallulah was crying now.

He threw his hands up in the air. "The two of you! I'm going to my study. Put the crybaby to bed, and then I want to see you in my office." Then he leaned in and whispered in my ear. "If you're so hungry all the time, I'll give you something to suck on."

SIXTY-TWO

A mber reached for the bottle of tanning lotion and squirted some in her hand. After she applied it to her arms and face, she handed it to me. "Would you do my back?"

I took it from her and caught a whiff of coconut as I rubbed my hands together.

"Want to go sit on the bench in the pool?" It was sweltering, and I wanted to cool off.

"Sure."

Amber's bikini was practically pornographic—all she had to do was sit the wrong way and all the goods would be on display. I was glad Tallulah and Bella were out for the day with Surrey. It was obvious that she hadn't missed any time at the gym, although with the hours she was putting in working for Jackson, I didn't know how she fit it in. I had purposely worn a one-piece that hugged my body and revealed the little pooch my belly was sporting. Jackson would notice it as soon as he looked at me.

We sat side by side on the built-in seat in the shallow end. The water was a perfect eighty-five degrees and felt wonderful. I looked out at the vast stretch of blue and the beach beyond, relaxing as I took a deep breath of salt air.

Jackson came outside for his daily swim.

"Hi, girls, I hope you put some sunscreen on. Hottest time of the day."

I smiled. "I have, but Amber here is covered in tanning oil."

She sat up straighter, sticking out her chest for full effect. "I like to tan."

"That's because you're too young to know the sun gives you wrinkles," I said.

Jackson walked to the diving board and surprised me by turning around and executing a perfect back dive into the pool. Was he showing off? When he broke the water's surface, Amber clapped.

"Bravo! Well done."

He swam to the side of the pool, pushed himself up and out and gave a little bow.

"It was nothing."

"Come join us for a minute," I said.

He grabbed a towel from the outdoor armoire behind the bar and sat on one of the cushioned seats across from us.

"I've got a little work to do before the party."

"Anything I can help with?" Amber asked.

Jackson smiled. "No, no. It's your day off. Don't be silly. Besides, Daphne would kill me if I put you to work."

"That's right. You're a guest today."

"I'm really hot, just going to get all the way wet." She pushed off the bench and slipped underwater. My eyes were on Jackson, who was watching Amber as she swam to the steps and climbed out, giving him a front-row seat to her wet body and see-through suit.

"That felt great," she said, looking straight at him. She was getting quite brazen.

"Well, I've got to get to it," Jackson said as he walked back to the house.

Amber came back to where I was and took a seat once

again. "Thanks again for inviting me over today. This is such a treat." Did she think I was an idiot? "What time is everyone coming again?"

"Around six. We can relax for a couple of hours and then go shower and change. I've asked Angela to come by at three to do our hair." I had more planned for the afternoon, intending to let her see every little benefit Jackson's money provided.

"How wonderful. Does she always do your hair?"

"Only when we entertain or I'm going somewhere special. We have her on retainer, so she pretty much drops whatever else she has if I need her." What I now recognized as a look of resentment flashed in her eyes, but she quickly recovered.

"Wow."

"Of course, I try to give her notice. Don't want to intentionally mess up someone else's plans."

"Is it fancy tonight?"

I stretched my legs out in front of me. "Not really. Three other couples from the club and Gregg, the guy I want you to meet."

"Tell me more about him."

"He's in his late twenties, reddish-blond hair, blue eyes. Your typical good-looking preppy." I laughed.

"What does he do?"

"His father owns Carvington Accounting. He works in the family business. They have gobs of money."

Now I had her attention. "I'm not sure he'll be interested in me. He's probably used to debutantes and girls from important families."

This pitiful act was beginning to tire me. I looked up to see the two masseuses walk out to the tile patio. "I have a surprise for you."

"What?"

"We're each getting a nice, long massage."

"Don't tell me they're on retainer too?" Amber asked.

"No. They're part-time. Jackson and I couldn't survive without at least two massages a week." It wasn't true, but I wanted her green with envy.

The afternoon passed in a pleasant haze. After the hour-long massage, I soaked in the tub while Amber's hair was done; then she sat and talked to me while Angela did mine. By three thirty, we had drinks in hand and sat in the sunroom overlooking the Sound. In a few hours, phase two of my plan would begin.

By six o'clock, we were having drinks on the veranda, and Gregg, as I had anticipated, was falling all over Amber. I couldn't help but compare the girl who had come to that first committee meeting with the poised and self-assured young woman standing there. No one meeting her for the first time would have a clue that she was out of place. Everything about her telegraphed money and refinement. Even her dress, a Marc Jacobs shift, was worlds away from the L.L.Bean separates she used to wear.

I walked over to her and Gregg. "I see you've met our Amber."

He gave me a broad smile. "Where've you been hiding her? I haven't seen her at the club." He gave her a knowing look. "I would have remembered."

"I don't belong," she said.

"Then you'll just have to come as my guest." He looked at her empty glass. "Can I get you a refill?"

She put a hand on his arm. "Thank you, Gregg. You're such a gentleman. I'll walk over with you."

Gregg's hand rested on the small of her back as they made their way to the bar, and I looked up to see that Jackson was watching them. There was a proprietary look in his eyes, one that said, *You're pissing on my lawn.* It was working.

I walked over to him.

"Looks like Amber and Gregg are clicking." I could see that she was playing him, but all Jackson could see were the pheromones jumping off Gregg.

"She can do better than that idiot."

"He's not an idiot. He's a nice young man. He hasn't taken his eyes off her all night."

Jackson drank the rest of his bourbon in one swallow. "He's as dull as a stone."

By the time we were seated for dinner, Gregg was thoroughly infatuated. Amber already had him wrapped around her finger. All she had to do was look thirsty, and he was waving the server over to get her another drink. The other women didn't miss it either.

Jenka, a brunette beauty married to one of Jackson's golf buddies, leaned over to me and whispered, "Doesn't it make you nervous? A girl like that right outside his office every day? I know he loves you, but he is a man, after all."

I laughed. "I trust Jackson implicitly, and Amber's a good friend."

She looked dubious. "If you say so. There's no way I'd let Warren hire somebody who looked like that to be his assistant."

"You're too suspicious, darling. I've nothing to worry about."

Gregg was the last to leave. He gave Amber a chaste kiss on her cheek. "See you Sunday. Pick you up at noon."

When he'd gone, I turned to her. "Sunday?"

"He's invited me to have lunch with him at the club and then see *Cat on a Hot Tin Roof* at the Playhouse."

"How lovely. Well, I'm exhausted. Shall we go to bed?"

She nodded.

I gave her the guest room across the hall from us. I wanted Jackson to know she was close by.

He was in bed when I came into the bedroom.

"Nice evening, right?" I said.

"Except for that moron, Gregg. I don't know why you invited him in the first place," Jackson grumbled.

"It would have been awkward for Amber not to have a companion. He's nice enough. Just drinks a little too much."

"A little too much? The guy's a drunk. I detest people who can't control themselves."

I slid under the covers. "Amber has a date with him on Sunday."

"She's too smart for him."

"Well, she seems to like him." Good. He was jealous.

"If he didn't have a rich father, he'd be living in a studio apartment over someone's garage."

"Jackson, I need to ask you something."

He sat up and turned the light back on. "What?"

"You know how much I miss Julie. Amber's the closest thing to a sister I'll ever have. Your interest in her seems more than just professional."

His voice rose. "Now just a minute. Since when have I ever given you a reason to be jealous?"

I put a gentle hand on his arm. "Don't be mad. I'm not accusing you of anything. But I see how she looks at you. She adores you. And who can blame her?" Did I sound convincing? "I just don't want anything to happen between you. Anyone can slip. Amber is my only true friend. If you should find yourself attracted to her, please don't give in to it. That's all I'm saying."

"Don't be ridiculous. I'm not interested in other women."

But I knew that look. The determination in his eyes. No one told Jackson Parrish what he could and couldn't have.

SIXTY-THREE

Duplicity suited me. All the years of living with Jackson had taught me a thing or two. It was hard at times, knowing that Amber believed herself so clever and me so stupid, but it would be worth it in the end. It had been tortuous that weekend she was at the lake house with the girls and me. I hated going to that house, period. My mother was really only an hour away, and he wouldn't let me invite her. He chose it specifically for that purpose—to make my mother believe that I was so self-absorbed that I didn't think to include her. She had too much pride to ever ask to come. But inviting Amber to the lake had been necessary for moving my plan along. That was the weekend I gave her the vital tidbit that I hoped she would pounce upon—the fact that Jackson desperately wanted a son, and I couldn't give him one. I also gave her a key to the New York apartment, knowing it wouldn't be long before she found an excuse to use it.

When I got her text Friday morning asking if it was okay to use the New York apartment for the weekend, I came up with a plan. Jackson had been working from the lake house all week, making life miserable for the girls and me. He didn't believe in letting schedules slide, even on vacation. When he wasn't there, we'd lounge by the lake all day, eat when we wanted, stay up late and watch movies. But when he was around, it was lunch at noon, dinner at seven, girls in bed by eight. No junk food, only organic and healthy. I'd have to hide the books on my nightstand and replace them with his selection of the week.

That week, though, I did little things to irritate him. I came in from swimming with smeared makeup under my eyes, left my hair a mess, left crumbs on the counter. By Friday, I could tell he was reaching the breaking point. We'd just finished lunch, and I'd made sure that a piece of spinach was lodged between my front teeth.

He looked at me with disgust. "You're a pig. You have a big green thing in your teeth."

I pulled my lips back and leaned close to him. "Where?"

"Ugh. Go look in a mirror." He shook his head.

As I got up, I purposely bumped my hip into the table, and my plate went clanging to the floor.

"Look where you're going!" His eyes traveled up and down my body. "Have you put on weight?"

I had actually—ten pounds. I shrugged. "I don't know. There's no scale here."

"I'll bring one next week. For the love of . . . What the hell do you do when I'm not here? Stuff yourself with junk?"

I picked up the plate and walked to the sink, deliberately leaving a piece of cucumber on the floor.

"Daphne!" He pointed.

"Oops, sorry."

I ran the dish under the water and put it in the dishwasher—facing the wrong way.

"Oh, Jackson. The Lanes are coming over for dinner tonight." I knew that would be the final straw. Our neighbors at the lake lived in Woodstock the rest of the year, and their politics were to the left of Marx. Jackson couldn't bear to be in the same room as them.

"Are you serious?" He came up behind me, grabbed my shoulders, and turned me around. His face was inches from mine. "I've been very patient with you this week, put up with your slovenly appearance, your ineptitude around the house. This is too much."

I looked at the floor. "Stupid me! I thought this was a week you'd be away. I got the dates confused. I'm so sorry."

He sighed loudly. "In that case, it will be. I'm heading home today."

"I've arranged to have all the carpets cleaned over the weekend. You really shouldn't be there, with all the chemicals."

"Shit. I'll go to the apartment then. I should go into the office anyhow. Thanks for screwing everything up once again."

He stormed off to the bedroom to pack.

I would text Amber in the morning with the text I'd "meant" to send today—informing her that Jackson was coming to the apartment, and she couldn't use it after all. I'd tell her that I'd forgotten to hit send, and hoped that she hadn't been startled when Jackson showed up.

Walking into the bedroom, I tossed *Ulysses* to the floor and replaced it with the latest Jack Reacher. I stretched out on the bed and took a deep breath. We'd have pizza for dinner. The Lanes were enjoying the concert they were attending; they'd told me about it when they were over for dinner the week before.

※

Hours later, my phone rang.

"What the hell are you up to?" Jackson said.

"What do you mean?"

"Amber's here. What kind of game are you playing, Daphne?"

I feigned surprise. "I texted her and told her you were using the apartment. Wait. Let me look at my phone." I waited a few seconds. "I'm such an idiot. I never hit send. I'm so sorry."

He cursed. "You are intent on ruining my weekend. I just want some peace and quiet. I don't feel like making small talk with the help."

"Tell her to leave, then. Do you want me to call her?"

He sighed. "No, I'll handle it. Thanks for nothing!"

I hit send and typed another message to Amber. **Sorry. Meant to let you know Jackson was headed to the apartment. May want to stay out of his way. He's not in the best mood, thanks to me.**

That should be enough to have her lending him a sympathetic ear. After that, it would just be a hop, skip, and a jump before they were in bed together.

SIXTY-FOUR

He's got it bad. Amber must be really good. Most nights he claimed to be working too late to come all the way home, so he decided to stay at the apartment. Just to test my theory after the third night in a row, I offered to come in and keep him company, but he demurred, saying he would be at the office until all hours. It was also apparent in Amber's demeanor. She thought she was so clever and that I couldn't tell, but I noticed the looks that passed between the two of them when she was at the house, and the way she was beginning to finish his sentences.

During our trip to London, her perfume lingered on his clothes and in his hair every time he came back from a meeting. Apparently the infidelity turned him on, because he wanted sex even more than usual. I never knew when he would grab me. The sex was different too—faster and rougher, like a dog staking his claim. I pretended to Amber that he hadn't touched me in weeks. I needed her to believe he had eyes only for her—except for the one time I let my pride get the better of me and told her that we'd just slept together. The look of shock and anger on her face was delicious. I was worried, though, that it might be only a matter of time before he would tire of her and return to me, more obsessed than ever. My only hope was for Amber to elicit in him the same feelings I had evoked when we first met. He had to become focused on possessing her. She was already doing her part—trying to make herself into a younger version of me. I'd noticed her copying my perfume, wearing her hair the same as mine; she'd even copied my lipstick color. And I continued to feed her the ammunition. But would it be enough? What was taking her so long to get pregnant? Of course, unless it was a boy, it would do no good. We'd been down that road before. He had no use for another daughter.

I made myself look even more pitiful to him. I wanted him to see Amber as my perfect replacement. I wore long underwear under my clothes so I would sweat and blamed it on hot flashes. I started dropping hints that I was going through early menopause, so he would know that if he stayed with me, his dream of a son would go unfulfilled. I was placing all my hope on her getting pregnant with a boy. But if that didn't work, I was hoping she was clever enough to find another way to hook him.

The night he came back from Paris, he was in a good mood. She had told me she was taking a few days off to go visit a friend so I wouldn't be suspicious. But I'd known she was with him, had seen the lingerie he tucked into his suitcase at the last minute.

I was almost asleep when he walked into the bedroom and turned on a bedside lamp.

"You weren't sleeping, were you?" He came around to my side of the bed and stood looking down at me.

"I was."

"I'm hurt. I thought you'd be waiting up for me. You know how I miss you when I'm gone."

My eye started twitching. I gave him a tight smile. "Of course I missed you. But I thought you'd be tired anyway."

A slow smile spread across his face. "Never too tired for you. I brought you a present."

I sat up and waited.

It was the red and black corset I'd seen in his suit-case. I took it from him, and the smell of Incomparable wafted over me. The sick bastard wanted me to wear this after she had.

"Here are the stockings that go with it. Get up and put them on."

"Why don't you let me pick something out and sur-prise you?" I didn't want them touching my skin after they'd been on her body.

He threw the corset at me. "Now!" He grabbed my hand and pulled me from the bed. "Arms."

I lifted my arms, and he pulled off my nightgown so that I was standing there in only my panties.

"You're getting fat." He pinched the flesh on my waist and made a face. "I'm going to have to buy you a girdle soon. Don't make any plans for the rest of the week. You'll be spending it with the trainer every day. We have dinner at the club on Thursday, and I've bought you a new dress. It had better fit." He shook his head. "Lazy bitch. Now put on the outfit your nice husband went to all the trouble of buying for you."

I pulled the stiff fabric up over my hips and stomach. It was tight, but I managed to make it fit. My face was hot with shame, and I had to look up at the ceiling to keep from crying. When I had fastened the stockings, he made me do a pirouette for him.

He shook his head. "Looks like shit on you." He pushed me down. "All fours."

I fell to the floor, the hard wood sending waves of pain through my knees. Before I could brace myself, I heard his pants unzip and felt him behind me. He was rough, and I felt like I was being torn in two. When he finally finished, he stood up and looked down at me. "Still the best around, Daph."

I felt my body go weak as I slumped to the floor in anguish. Had all of this been for nothing? Was he already tired of Amber? Now that I had allowed myself to envision a life away from him, there was no way I was giving up. One way or another, I would be free.

SIXTY-FIVE

She must have given him an ultimatum. I heard him whispering on the phone in the bathroom last night, telling her he needed more time. She'd better play her cards right, I thought, or it could all blow up. Jackson was not a man to be threatened. I'd seen her the day before when I stopped by the office, and I could tell. She was definitely pregnant, at least three months along. I wondered if it was a boy or girl. I don't think I've ever prayed so hard for anything in my life since Julie died.

All of us walked on eggshells all through dinner. I could hear his phone pinging with texts from the dining room. At one point he got up, threw his napkin on the chair, and stormed from the room. Minutes later he was back, and I didn't hear any more texts coming in.

After I put the girls to bed, we watched a documentary on penguins. Finally, around ten, he looked at me.

"Let's turn in."

To my relief, he washed up, got into bed, and fell asleep. I lay there in the dark, wondering what was going on between them. I had started my period last night and had just gotten up to take something for my dull headache, then got back into bed and fell asleep.

I thought I was dreaming. Something bright was hurting my eyes, and I tried to turn but found myself immobilized. My eyes flew open. He was straddling me, shining a flashlight at them.

"Jackson, what are you doing?"

"Are you sad, Daphne?"

I shielded my eyes from the light and turned my head to the side. "What?"

He pushed my cheek so that I was looking into the light again. "Are you sad that you got your period? Another month and no baby."

What was he talking about? Could he have somehow found out about the IUD? "Jackson, please, that hurts."

He turned the light off, and I felt the cold steel of the gun against my neck.

He clicked the flashlight on again. Then off. On and off while the hand holding the gun pressed against my neck. "Are you laughing behind my back every month? Knowing how much I want a son?"

"Of course not. I would never laugh at you." The words came out in a whisper.

He slid the gun from my neck up to my face and positioned it over one eye. "It would be hard to cry without an eye."

He's going to kill me this time.

Then he moved it to my mouth and ran it around my lips. "It would be hard to talk about me without a mouth."

"Jackson, please. Think of the children."

"I am thinking of the children. The ones I don't have. The son I don't have because you're a withered-up old prune. But don't worry. I have a solution."

He moved the gun to my stomach and drew a figure eight. "It's okay, Daphne, if you're too used up to carry a baby in here. I've decided we can adopt."

"What are you talking about?" I was too afraid to move, worried the gun would go off.

"I know someone who's going to have a baby, and she doesn't want it. We could take it."

My whole body tensed. "Why would we want to adopt someone else's baby?"

I heard him cock the gun. He leaned over and turned the lamp on so that I could see.

He smiled at me. "There's only one bullet. Let's see what happens. If I pull the trigger and you live, we'll adopt. If you die, we won't. Sound fair?"

"Please . . ."

I watched in terror as his finger moved back and held my breath until I heard the click. The breath whooshed out of me, and a cry escaped my lips.

"Good news. We're going to have a son."

[P A R T   I I I]

SIXTY-SIX

Amber left the apartment on East Sixty-Second Street carrying a small suitcase, her credit card, and a wad of money. Jackson had called earlier to let her know he'd be there by nine in the evening, and she was going to make sure he walked into an empty apartment. She was tired of this waiting game. One day he was going to tell Daphne, and the next day he had an excuse for why he couldn't. She wasn't going to take it any longer. This was showdown time.

She'd booked a room at a small hotel under a different name. The note she left said simply:

> *I'm afraid you don't love me or our son. I don't think you have any intention of leaving Daphne to marry me. If you don't want this child, I will see that he doesn't come into this world.*
>
> *With great sorrow,*
Amber

At ten past nine her cell phone began ringing. She ignored it. In a few minutes it rang again, and once more she refused to answer. This continued for twenty minutes, and then he left a message. *Amber, please. Don't do anything foolish. I love you. Please call me.*

Amber heard the pleading and panic in his voice, smiled, and turned off her ringer. Let him call all night and wonder where she was and what she'd done. She turned on the TV and laid down on the bed. This would be a long, boring night, but the time had come for a drastic move on her part. I'm not going to be the patsy again, she thought, and fell into a fitful sleep.

She'd gotten up several times through the night to go to the bathroom, and each time she checked her phone. Call after call from Jackson, and messages and texts that alternated between begging and fury. The last time she got up was four in the morning, and finally she slept uninterrupted until eight o'clock. She got up and called room service. Decaffeinated tea and yogurt were delivered twenty minutes later, along with the morning paper. She scanned the pages with little interest, and then she waited. And waited. And waited.

At two in the afternoon she punched in Jackson's number. He answered before the first ring was complete. "Amber! Where are you? I've been trying to reach you since last night."

She whispered into the phone with a quivery voice. "I'm sorry, Jackson. I love you, but you forced me." She let out a quiet sob to emphasize her pitifulness.

"What are you talking about? What have you done?"

"I have an appointment in an hour, Jackson. I'm sorry. I love you." And she hung up.

Let him stew with that for a while, she thought. Her phone rang again, and this time she picked it up on the fifth ring.

"What?" she said.

"Amber, listen to me. Don't do this. I love you. I love our son. I want to marry you. I will marry you. I'll tell Daphne tonight. Please. Believe me."

"I don't know what to believe anymore, Jackson." She made her voice sound weak and tired.

"Amber, you can't go through with this. You're carrying my son. I won't lose my son." He sounded furious.

"You've forced me to do it, Jackson. It's your fault." She heard him sigh, and then his tone changed.

"No, no. I know I've been dragging my feet, but it's all for us. I was waiting for the right time."

"That's just it. It seems like the right time is never going to come. I can't wait forever, Jackson. And neither can this appointment."

"You would actually kill our child? I can't believe that. Our beautiful little boy?"

"I can't have this baby by myself and unmarried. Maybe you think it's all right, but I wasn't raised that way."

"I promise you we'll be married before he's born. I promise. But come back to me, Amber. Where are you? I'll come get you now."

"I don't know—"

Jackson cut her off. "We'll go back to my apartment. You can stay there. Forever. Please."

Her lips curled into a catlike smile.

※

Jackson was there within the hour. She got into the back of the limo and gave him what she hoped was a pitiful look. His lips were white, and his face was set in a scowl.

"Don't you ever do that to me again."

"Jackson, I—"

He grabbed her hand and squeezed it tight. "How could you threaten to kill our child? To hold him hostage."

"You're hurting me."

He dropped her hand. "I don't know what I would do if something happened to my son. Or to you."

There was something in his manner and voice that unnerved her, but she shrugged it off. Of course he was angry. Worried. He wasn't acting like himself.

"I won't, Jackson. I promise."

"Good."

They went back to the apartment, and she coaxed him into bed. They stayed there until dark, Amber begging him for forgiveness while trying to ensure that their plans were still on track.

"Are you hungry?" she asked him.

"Starving. How about an omelet?" Jackson said, throwing the covers back and bouncing out of bed. Amber followed him to the kitchen, and he began to crack eggs into a bowl. Now is the time to get down to it, she thought. Before he changes his mind.

"I've been thinking, Jackson. You're not going to move out of the house, are you? It was yours before you married her."

Amber had wanted that house from the first day she saw it. She wanted to be the mistress of the house, have Bella and Tallulah have to listen to *her*. They would be guests in *her* house now, and Bella would feel the sting of her hand if she continued with her shenanigans. The first thing she was going to do would be to have a portrait of herself done—one of those full nudes while she was pregnant. She'd hang it in a place where they'd have to see it every time they came to visit. She'd make it so miserable for them that they wouldn't want to come for weekends, and she'd make sure that Jackson didn't care either. In time, she would make him see that they were little bloodsuckers, just like their mother.

"I can't very well kick her out when I'm the one leaving the marriage," he said, flipping the eggs over.

"I suppose you're right. But . . . she hates that house. She's told me how pretentious she thinks it is. I really don't think she deserves it. She'll probably move her mother in with them. Do you really want that beautiful house to belong to her? Will she even keep it up?"

She could see his wheels turning.

"Well, I did have it long before I met her. Let me see what I can do. Maybe I can persuade her to let me have it."

"Oh, Jackson! That would be wonderful. I love that house. We're going to be so happy there."

The only thing that would make her happier than moving in and staking her claim would be if Daphne had to move in to Amber's one-room hovel. She knew she was being a bitch, but she didn't care. Daphne had been spoiled for far too long. It would do her good to see how it felt to have the designer shoe on the other foot. She might have pretended to be Amber's friend, but Amber knew that, deep down, Daphne still considered her the help. Reaching down like Lady Bountiful to help poor, pathetic Amber. It infuriated her to realize that Daphne had never considered her a threat. Daphne thought she was so much more beautiful than Amber, was so secure in Jackson's love for her. *Well, guess what, Daphne. He loves me now. He belongs to me now. And I'm giving him a brand-new family. You and your brats are obsolete.*

SIXTY-SEVEN

It was finally happening! Jackson had called her that morning and asked her to come to the New York apartment to discuss something "serious." Daphne didn't need to wonder what it was about because, thanks to a lesson with private eye Jerry Hanson, she'd learned how to clone a cell phone. She'd been privy to texts between Amber and Jackson for the past month. She had to give it to Amber, that disappearing stunt of hers was a stroke of genius. Jackson would do just about anything to ensure he didn't lose the son he'd been waiting to have for so long.

She arrived at five o'clock, and when she walked into the apartment, she could smell Amber's perfume. The two of them were sitting on the sofa.

She pretended to be shocked. "What's going on?"

"Sit down, Daphne," Jackson answered. Amber said nothing, merely sat there with a tight smile and a malicious look in her eyes. "We need to talk to you."

Daphne continued to stand and looked at Amber. "We?"

Amber looked down at her hands, but her lips were still curled in a smile.

"Whatever is going on, just tell me."

Jackson leaned back and stared at her a long moment. "I think it's pretty clear that we've been unhappy lately."

Unhappy lately? Daphne wanted to say. *When have we ever been happy?* "What are you talking about?"

He stood up and started pacing and then turned to

look at her. "I'm divorcing you, Daphne. Amber is pregnant with my son."

For their benefit, Daphne feigned shock and sank into the chair. "Pregnant? You're sleeping with her?"

"What did you expect?" His eyes traveled up and down her body. "You've let yourself go. Fat, slovenly, and lazy. No wonder you couldn't produce a son for me. You treat your body like shit."

It took everything she had not to tell them how stupid they both were. Instead, she pasted on a sad expression and looked at Amber. "How long have you been sleeping with my husband?"

"I didn't mean for it to happen. We fell in love." At this, she looked at Jackson, and he took her hand in his.

"Really?" Daphne's voice rose. "Then how long have you been in love?"

"I'm sorry, Daphne. I never meant to hurt you." Her eyes told a different story. It was obvious that she was relishing every moment.

"I trusted you, treated you like a sister, and this is how you repay me?"

She sighed. "We couldn't help ourselves. We're soul mates."

Daphne almost started laughing, and a sound escaped that she hoped they mistook for a sob.

"I'm really sorry, Daphne," she repeated. "Sometimes these things just happen." She put a hand on her belly and rubbed. "Our children will be related, so I hope in time you'll come to forgive me."

Daphne's mouth dropped open. "Seriously? Are you cra—"

"Enough," Jackson interrupted. "We want to get married, and I want to do it before my son is born. I'll make it worth your while to give me a quick divorce."

Daphne stood. "I have a lot to think about. When I'm ready to discuss it, I'll let you know. And I don't want *her* there."

As soon as she walked out of the apartment and out of their line of sight, she broke into a smile of her own. It was already worth her while, but she wouldn't tell him that. How can you put a price on your freedom? But she'd take the money for her children's sake. Why should Amber have it all? No, she'd make sure that the settlement was generous, and then she'd grant him his quick divorce.

SIXTY-EIGHT

A mber closed her eyes as the manicurist massaged her hands with creamy lotion. She'd told the girl that she was getting married, and immediately she'd gushingly suggested a French manicure. How completely tacky. She opened her eyes and looked at her left hand. It was the first time she'd taken the Graff diamond—one carat larger than Daphne's—off her finger. She smiled and watched as the polish went on and then suddenly pulled her hand away.

"I don't like that color. Take it off and let me see what else you have," she demanded.

The young woman obediently gathered more bottles and set them before Amber. She took her time looking them over and finally chose a champagne nude. "This one." She pointed to the bottle and sat back in the leather chair. She'd had the works today—massage, facial, pedicure. Tomorrow she would look beautiful, and all her dreams would become a reality as she stood before a clerk of the court and became Mrs. Jackson Parrish. Jackson's divorce had become final just in time. The baby was due any day, and she wanted to be Jackson's wife when he was born. Jackson had been in a state of ecstasy about the coming birth of his son, and he wanted a huge wedding to introduce his pregnant new wife to all of his friends.

"We'll have it at the house and invite everyone. It'll be huge, at least three hundred people. I want them all

to meet my gorgeous wife. We'll announce the impending arrival of our amazing son," he'd said.

"Jackson, really. Everyone knows about the baby. The
divorce, the pregnancy, our engagement—it's all been
the choicest gossip for the last six months. Besides, I
want something small and intimate. Just the two of us."
There was no way she was going to have all the snobs in
Bishops Harbor looking at her fat and pregnant, talking
behind her back at her wedding and reporting back to
Daphne. "We can have a big party later, after the baby's
born." She laughed and gave him a peck on the cheek.
"Besides, then I won't have this enormous belly and can
wear something beautiful. Please?" She wanted to make
sure that the first time she appeared in print as Jackson's
wife, she looked the part. She wasn't worried any longer
about being recognized. No one from her Podunk town
would make the connection. They would never in a million years imagine that Lana Crump had become the
fabulous Amber Parrish. And besides, if anyone came
nosing around, she'd have plenty of money to make any
pesky problem disappear.

He had pursed his lips and nodded. "Okay. We'll do
it later. But what about Tallulah and Bella? They should
be there."

She wasn't about to let an angry and morose Tallulah
and a spoiled Bella take center stage at her wedding.
They would ruin everything. Better that they hear about
it after the fact, when it was too late for any tears and
tantrums that might discourage their father.

"Yes, you're right. I wonder, though, do you think it
will upset them to see me pregnant? I don't want them to
be sad that it's not their mother who's having the baby.
I would hate for them to be hurt or feel they're being
replaced. Maybe it'll be easier once he's born. He'll be

their brother, and it won't really matter who the mother is. Let them wait for the big celebration afterward. I think that will be much easier for them."

"I don't know. It might not look right if they're not there," he'd said.

"They'll have much more fun at the party we throw later."

"I guess you're right."

"I just want them to like me. Accept me as their step-mother. I've even discussed it with the pediatrician. She thought it might be too much for them, but said to run it by you." Amber had made up the pediatrician part, but her eyes were wide with a look of innocence.

"You have a point. I suppose it's not really necessary. After all, none of our other family will be there."

Amber had smiled at him and taken his hand. "We'll be one big, happy family. You'll see. I'm sure they'll love their little brother."

"I can't wait to meet this little guy."

"Soon," she'd said. "But in the meantime, how would my handsome husband-to-be like a little gratification?" Amber reached over and unbuckled his belt.

"You turn me on like no one else," he said and slumped back in his chair. As she got on her knees, she reminded herself that once she was Mrs. Parrish, she wouldn't have to pretend to enjoy this anymore.

⁂

Amber rose early the next morning. She had told Jackson that it was bad luck for the bride and groom to see each other the night before they got married, so he'd taken a hotel room at the Plaza while she stayed at the apart-ment. She didn't give a crap about those silly superstitions, but she wanted the morning to herself. There were calls she wanted to make, and she didn't want Jackson around to hear them. She had a light breakfast of yogurt and fruit and checked her e-mails. There were three from Jackson's new administrative assistant. Amber had taken her time and chosen very carefully from a slew of applicants. She thought her selection perfect—young, attractive, smart, technologically up-to-date, outside-the-box thinker, and, best of all, male. Of course the checkbook would be coming home, too. Only Amber would see what was spent in their household. She would never make the stupid mistakes that Daphne had.

After a luxurious bath, she dried herself off, spread some exorbitantly expensive body cream all over, and turned sideways to see her belly in the mirror. The huge ball disgusted her. She couldn't wait for this kid to be born and to get her figure back. She shook her head and, looking away, grabbed one of the terry-cloth robes. She'd gotten one for each of them, monogrammed and plush and expensive. She laughed to herself. Whenever she bought something, she went to the Internet and typed in "most expensive" whatever it was. She was a quick learner.

Amber and Jackson were meeting at city hall at one o'clock, so she still had plenty of time to get dressed and call for the limo. She reclined on the velvet chaise longue in the bedroom and punched in the telephone number on her mobile.

"Hello?" It was Daphne.

"I want to speak to the girls."

"I'm not sure they wish to speak with you." Daphne's words were clipped and chilly.

"Listen, you can stand in my way all you want, but it behooves you to cooperate with me, or your little brats will be out of the picture faster than you can say 'divorce agreement.'"

Amber heard nothing for a moment, and then the sound of Tallulah's voice came on. "Hullo?"

"Tallulah, sweetheart, where's your sister? Can you put her on the extension?"

"Hold on, Amber."

Tallulah yelled for Bella to pick up the phone and waited a few minutes. "Bella, are you on the phone?"

"Yes."

"Tallulah, are you still there?" Amber asked.

"Yes, Amber."

"I want to tell you both that I'm very sad you won't be at the wedding today. I told your father I wanted it to be only family and not a big party. I just wanted the two of you and no one else, but your father thought you were too young to be there." Amber made a sniffling sound, as if she were crying. "You have to understand that your father is very excited to be having a baby boy, so sometimes he forgets about you two. I want us to be very good friends, and I will make sure that you're part of our new family. Do you understand?"

"Yes," Tallulah said flatly.

"Bella, what about you?" Amber pressed.

"My daddy loves me. He won't forget me."

Amber could picture Bella stamping her imperious little foot.

"Of course you're right, Bella. I wouldn't worry if I were you. By the way, did I tell you that the new baby will have your father's name? Jackson Marc Parrish Junior?"

"I hate you," Bella said and clicked off.

"I'm sorry, Amber. You know how Bella gets," Tallulah said.

"I know, Tallulah. But I'm sure you'll be able to talk some sense into her, right?"

"I'll try," she said. "Talk to you later."

"Bye, sweetheart. The next time we talk, I'll be your stepmother."

Amber hung up, satisfied that she had gotten her message across. Tallulah was a peacekeeper and would present no problems. Some sparkly jewelry and new toys would be enough to eventually bring Bella around. Not that Amber intended for them to be at the house often enough for it to matter.

She pulled her computer next to her and answered the e-mails that needed attention, then rose to dress. There wasn't much she could do to look sexy and desirable for Jackson, but apparently the baby belly was enough to induce his euphoria anyway. She squeezed herself into a cream-colored dress and put on the new Ella Gafter pearls Jackson had bought her as a wedding present. She wore no other jewelry except her emerald-cut diamond ring.

※

When she arrived, Jackson and Douglas, his new assistant, stood waiting for her in front of the building. "You look absolutely beautiful," Jackson said, taking her hand.

"I look like a beached whale."

"You are an image of loveliness. I don't want to hear another word."

Amber shook her head and turned to Douglas. "Thank you for agreeing to be our witness today."

"My pleasure."

Jackson put his arm around her, and the three of them climbed the stairs to the entrance.

They waited their turn, and when it was time, they stood in front of an officiant. Before they knew it, he was telling Jackson he could kiss his bride. *His bride.* Amber tasted the word in her mouth. She savored how delicious it was.

"Well, I guess I'll get back to the office. Congratulations," Douglas said, reaching out and shaking Jackson's hand.

As Douglas walked away, Amber leaned against her new husband and felt a thrill of electricity go through her body. A thin platinum band now complemented the diamond on her ring finger. They were finally married. *Anytime now* was the silent message she sent their unborn son. As they got in the limousine and she sat back against the fine leather, she envisioned the life ahead of her—expensive homes around the world, fantasy trips, nannies and maids at her command, designer clothes and jewelry.

The stuck-up women in Bishops Harbor would soon enough be bowing before her—that much she was sure of. It only took lots and lots of money and a powerful husband. They'd be falling over themselves to be her friend. Ha. She loved it. Everyone in the club would be clamoring to sit at her table at the annual regatta dinner. She'd had to do a little damage control to make sure that Gregg's family didn't do anything to mess that up for her. Once she and Jackson had broken the news to Daphne, Amber had invited Gregg out to meet her for a drink. She figured he'd have an easier time keeping a stiff upper lip if they were out in public. They'd met at the White Whale in Bishops Harbor, a little tavern on the water. She was already seated at a table when he arrived. He walked over and leaned down to kiss her. She turned her face so that he got her cheek. Off balance, he took the seat across from her.

"Is everything okay?"

She'd blinked back tears and pointed at the glass of whiskey in front of him. "Take a sip. I ordered it for you."

A look of confusion had passed over his face, and he'd taken a long swallow. "You're scaring me."

"There's no easy way to say it, so I'm going to just come out with it. I've fallen in love with someone else."

His mouth had dropped open. "What? Who?"

She'd put a hand over his. "I didn't mean for it to happen. It's just—" She'd stopped and brushed a tear from her cheek. "It's just that we were together every day. Working together day in and day out, and we discovered we're soul mates."

He'd frowned and looked even more puzzled.

Is he that stupid? She'd suppressed a sigh. "It's Jackson."

"Jackson? Jackson Parrish? But he's married. And so much older than you. I thought you were in love with me." His lower lip trembled.

"I know he's married. But he wasn't happy. Sometimes these things happen. You know how it is to work closely with someone and how feelings can develop. I've seen the way your assistant looks at you at the office."

He'd narrowed his eyes then. "Becky?"

She'd nodded. "Yes. And she's quite lovely too. You must have noticed how enamored she is of you."

She'd had to stay for another two drinks before she could leave, and he'd told her he understood. She'd begged him not to take his friendship from her, made him believe that she needed him to be there for her in this time of uncertainty and public judgment. And the idiot fell for it. There would be no trouble from him at the club. And Becky should thank Amber. She was about to be promoted from assistant to fiancée.

Jackson and Amber Parrish would be the new golden couple of Bishops Harbor. And as soon as this baby was born, she'd be sure it would be the last. She was going to have her body back. The glow of happiness and satisfaction surrounding her at that moment could have lit up Manhattan.

SIXTY-NINE

Daphne knew it would only take one visit to the house that used to be theirs to make the girls never want to go back. Up to now, the visits had taken place in neutral territory. But Amber and Jackson wanted to have them over for the weekend, and she'd finally relented.

Amber had moved into his social circles seamlessly, and if Daphne had cared more about the women she'd spent the last ten years with, she might have been hurt that they embraced her husband's new wife so easily. But then again, no one in this town would dare to snub the new Mrs. Jackson Parrish. The one friend who didn't desert Daphne was Meredith. She had remained a true friend. Daphne wished she could tell Meredith the full truth, but she couldn't risk it. So she let her think that she was foolish and naive.

They pulled up to the house and got out of the car.

"Let me ring the bell," Bella shouted as the two of them ran up to the front door.

"Whatever," Tallulah answered.

A uniformed man appeared. *So they have a butler.* She didn't know why she was surprised.

He opened the door. "You must be Bella and Tallulah. Mrs. Parrish is expecting you."

Hearing Amber called Mrs. Parrish was jarring, but Daphne walked in behind them, nodding at him.

"Please wait here, and I'll get madam."

Moments later, Amber breezed in, holding her new son.

Bella looked up at her and asked, "Where's my daddy?"

"Bella, don't you want to meet your little brother, Jackson Junior?" Amber asked as she brought the baby closer.

Bella stared at the child, a pout on her face. "He's ugly. He's all wrinkled."

A look of hatred flashed across Amber's face, and she turned to Daphne. "Why don't you teach your children some manners?"

For once, Daphne was grateful for Bella's bluntness. She gave Amber a cool look and put a hand on Bella's shoulder. "Darling, don't be rude."

"Maybe your father forgot you were coming," Amber said. "He's buying toys for baby Jackson. He loves him so much. Do you want me to call and remind him?"

Tallulah looked up at Daphne in horror. Daphne wanted to kill Amber right then and there.

"Maybe we should reschedule the visit—" Daphne started, but Bella stomped her foot and interrupted her.

"No! We haven't seen Daddy in weeks."

"Of course you should stay," Amber said. She turned to her butler. "Edgar, would you take Bella and Tallulah to the drawing room where they can wait for Mr. Parrish? I have things to do."

"Please stay until Daddy comes," Tallulah whispered to her mother.

Daphne squeezed Tallulah's hand and whispered, "Of course I will."

"Amber."

"Yes?"

"I'll wait with the girls. How long do you think he'll be?"

She rolled her eyes. "You're so overprotective. Suit yourself. I'm sure he'll be home soon."

Daphne took both of the girls' hands in hers, and they followed Edgar to the "drawing room," where an enormous portrait of Amber, pregnant and naked, was perched on the wall above the marble fireplace. One hand covered her breasts, and the other rested on her pregnant belly. The entire room showcased photos from their wedding, and Daphne realized that Amber wanted them to see it. She'd orchestrated Jackson's being gone, knowing that Daphne wouldn't leave the girls until he returned.

"I hate her," Tallulah announced.

"Come here." She pulled Tallulah into her arms and whispered, "I know she's horrible. Try to ignore her and just enjoy your father."

"Girls!" They looked up to see Jackson come in, and they both ran into his arms.

"I guess that's my cue." Daphne stood. "I'll be back on Sunday to pick them up."

Jackson wouldn't even look in her direction, and she watched as the three of them left the room.

She went back to the foyer, and as her hand reached for the doorknob, Amber's voice rang out.

"Bye, Daph. Don't worry. I'll take good care of your little brats."

Daphne swung around, glaring at her. "You harm one hair on their heads, and I'll kill you."

She laughed. "You're so dramatic. They'll be fine. Just don't be late picking them up. I have naughty plans for *my* husband. He can't get enough of me."

"Enjoy it while you can."

Her face darkened. "What's that supposed to mean?"

Daphne smiled. "You'll find out soon enough."

SEVENTY

Daphne was about to play her trump card. They had been divorced for two months now, and Daphne had already put the millions she walked away with to good use. She had gotten custody of the girls, and Jackson had weekend visitation rights. She was here to change that.

She walked up to Jackson's assistant's desk.

"Good morning, Douglas. Is he alone?"

"Yes, but is he expecting you?"

"No, but I'll only take a moment. Promise."

"Okay."

She walked into Jackson's office.

He looked up, surprised. "What are you doing here?"

"Good morning to you too. I have a bit of news that you'll find most interesting," she told him as she shut the door and handed him a file.

"What the hell is this?" His face turned white as he scanned the contents. "This can't be right. I've seen her passport."

"Amber is a missing person. Your wife, Lana, is using her identity. How does it feel to be the one on the other side? She's nothing but a common con artist." She laughed. "Makes you wonder if she really wants you or just your money."

The vein in his temple was pulsating so hard she thought it might break through the skin.

"I don't understand," he sputtered, continuing to look the article over.

"It's quite simple. Amber—I mean Lana—targeted you. She insinuated herself into my life with the express purpose of landing a rich husband. Of course, once I was onto her, she became my golden ticket out."

"What are you talking about? You knew she and I were together?"

"I orchestrated it. I practically gift-wrapped her for you. The weekend at the lake, I drove you right into her arms. And the reason I couldn't get pregnant? Well, let's just say it's hard to get pregnant when you're using an IUD."

His eyes opened wide in surprise. "You played me?"

"I learned from the best."

"You fuc—"

"Now, now, Jackson. It won't do to lose your cool."

His breath was coming faster. "Are you planning on exposing her?"

"That depends on you."

"What do you want?"

"For you to terminate your parental rights."

"Are you crazy? I'm not signing away my rights to my children."

"If you don't, I'll go to the police and tell them who she is. They'll arrest her. Is that the legacy you want for your son? A convict for a mother? He'll never get into Charterhouse with that kind of background."

He slammed his fist on the desk. "You bitch!"

Daphne arched an eyebrow, feeling calm in his presence for the first time in years. "If you're going to start name-calling, I'll just go ahead and phone the police. Maybe the newspapers too, so they can see your new wife leave the house in handcuffs."

He took several loud, deep breaths, clenching and un-clenching his fists. "How do I know once I sign away my rights you won't turn her in anyway?"

"You don't. But you know I'm not like you. I just want to get away from you once and for all. As long as you're with Amber, I know you'll leave me alone. That's all I want. So you'll sign?"

"What will people think? I can't have them thinking I've abandoned my children," he said.

She shook her head. "You tell them I wouldn't grant you the divorce unless you agreed to let me go to California; that I've been cheating on you, whatever you want. You're good at making things up. Paint me as the horrible parent and pretend you come out to see them every chance you get. No one will know."

"You don't care how you look?"

"No. That's your game." All she cared about was getting her children and herself as far away from him as possible. "You'll have everything you want. And before you even think of doing anything to stop me, please know that if anything happens to me, all the evidence will be forwarded to Meredith. And I've made other contingency plans as well."

He had no idea what private detective she had used or how many fail-safes she had set up. The detective had all the information, for one, and if anything were to happen to Daphne, he'd go to the police. She'd also told her mother everything and given her copies of Amber's file.

"Do you have the papers with you?"

She opened her purse and took out the envelope. "Have your attorney review them. There's a place for his signature. They need to be notarized. There's also a statement from you that you made up all the charges against me with the Department of Children and Families."

"Why would I sign that?"

"Because if you don't, I'll call the police. I'm not letting you have any more leverage over my life. Sign it, and no one will ever see it unless you try and come after the kids."

He sighed. "Fine. You can have your life back, Daphne. I was tired of you anyway. You're old and used up." His eyes traveled up and down her body. "At least I got your youth."

She shook her head, unaffected by his words. "I almost feel sorry for you. I don't know if you were born this way or if your parents screwed you up, but you're a miserable son of a bitch. You're never going to be happy. But the truth is, I can't even regret being with you. Because if I hadn't, I wouldn't have the two most amazing gifts in my life. So I'll trade those horrible years with you for my children. And I have plenty of love and life left in me."

He yawned. "Are you finished?"

"I was finished years ago." She stood. "And by the way, you're a terrible lover."

He exploded with fury and flew from his chair toward her.

She opened the door and retreated.

"I'll expect those papers tomorrow," she said as she left.

SEVENTY-ONE

Amber's happiness was short-lived. After the baby was born, Amber and Jackson had gone on a belated honeymoon to Bora Bora. He'd been everything she could have hoped for in a husband. All she had to do was ask for whatever she wanted, and it was hers. Round-the-clock nurse care for their son, unlimited shopping allowance, and all the pampering she desired. She loved the way everyone in the stores and the spas kowtowed to her, and she enjoyed being able to be as rude as she wanted with no repercussions. No one would dare insult Mrs. Jackson Parrish, especially with the kind of money she threw around.

Amber didn't have to worry about having those little monsters around since Daphne had moved with them to California. Jackson told her he would visit them there.

So when she woke that morning to Jackson standing over the bed, staring at her, she had no idea what was to come. She rubbed her eyes and sat up.

"What are you doing?"

He was scowling. "Wondering if you're ever going to get your lazy ass out of bed."

She thought at first he was joking.

Laughing, she answered. "You love this ass."

"It's getting a little fat for my taste. When's the last time you went to the gym?"

She was pissed now. Throwing off the covers, she

jumped up. "You may have been able to talk to Daphne that way. But not me."

He pushed her, and she fell back on the bed.

"What the hell—"

"Shut up. I know all about your past."

Her eyes widened. "What are you talking about?"

He threw a file folder on the bed. "That's what I'm talking about."

The first thing she saw was a copy of a newspaper article with an old picture of her. She picked it up and quickly scanned it. "Where did you get this?"

"Doesn't matter."

"Jackson, I can explain. Please, you don't understand."

"Save it. No one makes a fool of me. I should turn you in, let you go to jail."

"I'm the mother of your child. And I love you."

"Do you, now? Like you loved him?"

"I . . . it wasn't like that . . ."

"Don't worry. I'm not going to tell anyone. It wouldn't be good for my son to have a mother in jail." He leaned closer to her, his face inches away. "But I own you now. So I will talk to you however I want. And you'll take it, do you understand?"

She'd nodded, frantically calculating her next move. She thought he was just angry—that once she could come up with a believable story, he'd calm down and things would go back to the way they were.

But instead, things began to escalate. He put her on a strict allowance, making her account for every dime she spent. She was still trying to figure out how to fix that. Then he wanted to choose her clothes, her books, and her leisure activities. She had to go to the gym every day. He expected her to volunteer for that stuck-up garden club Daphne had been so involved in. She could tell that the women didn't want her there, and she couldn't give a crap about it. Why did she need to learn about gardening? Isn't that what gardeners were for? And the journal—the damn food journal that he insisted she keep, along with her daily weight. It was humiliating. That was what put her over the edge and made her call his bluff. It was just last week.

"Are you crazy? I'm not reporting to you on what I eat every day. You can take that journal and stick it up your ass." She'd thrown it on the floor.

His face had turned red, and he stood looking at her like he wanted to kill her. "Pick it up," he'd said through clenched teeth.

"I will not."

"I'm warning you, Amber."

"Or what? You already said you weren't going to turn me in. Stop threatening me. I'm not weak and malleable, like your first wife."

At this he'd exploded. "You can't hold a candle to Daphne, you low-class whore. You can read all you want, study all you want, and you'll never be anything but poor white trash."

Before she had time to think, her hand was around the crystal clock on the table next to her, and she'd thrown it at him. It crashed to the floor, missing him completely. She watched as he advanced toward her, a murderous look in his eyes.

"You crazy bitch. Don't you ever try and hurt me." He'd grabbed her wrists and squeezed until she yelled out in pain.

"Don't threaten me, Jackson. I'll take you down." Inside she was trembling, but she knew she had to put on a brave face if she had any hope of keeping the upper hand.

He'd abruptly let go, turned, and left, and she thought she'd won.

※

When he came home that night, neither of them said a word about the fight. Amber had asked Margarita to prepare something French for dinner—coq au vin. She'd googled it, along with the right wine and dessert to serve. She'd show him who had class. He arrived home at seven and went straight to his study, where he stayed until she called him for dinner at eight.

"How do you like it?" she asked after he took a bite.

He gave her a droll look. "Why do you ask? It's not as though you made it."

She threw her napkin on the table. "I chose it. Look, Jackson, I'm trying to make peace here. I don't want to fight. Don't you want things to go back to the way they were between us?"

He took a sip of his wine and looked at her. "You tricked me into leaving Daphne. You made me think you were something you're not. So, no, Amber. I don't think things can go back to the way they were before. If it weren't for our son, you'd be in prison."

She was sick of hearing about the sainted Daphne. "Daphne couldn't stand you. She used to complain all the time that you made her skin crawl." Daphne had never said any such thing to Amber, but it shut him up.

"What makes you think I believe a word that comes out of your mouth?"

She was making things worse. "It's true. But I love you. I *will* win your trust back."

They finished their dinner in silence. Afterward, Jackson went to his office, and Amber stopped by the nursery to look in on Jackson Junior. Mrs. Wright, the nanny, was sitting in the rocking chair, reading a book. Amber had talked Jackson into hiring a live-in nanny to help with the baby. Sabine was gone. Amber didn't need that stuck-up French slut around. Surrey still helped out on the weekends. Bunny had referred Mrs. Wright, and she'd come with excellent credentials. She was also a respectable age, and no one that Jackson would ever look at twice.

"Any problem putting him down?" Amber asked.

"No, ma'am. Drank his bottle and went right to sleep. He's a sweet one, that one."

Amber leaned over and planted a soft kiss on his head. He was a beautiful child, and she looked forward to the day when he'd become interesting. When he could carry on a conversation and play games instead of just lying around like a lump.

Amber got in bed and pulled out the detective novel she'd hidden in her nightstand. Close to an hour later, Jackson finally came up, and she put it away before he could see it. It had been two weeks since they'd had sex, and she was getting worried. When he slipped under the covers, she reached over and began to stroke him. He pushed her hand away.

"Not in the mood."

She tossed and turned and finally fell asleep, still wondering how she was going to restore harmony between them.

Suddenly she couldn't breathe. She woke up in a panic and realized he was straddling her, his hand over her nose. She pried his fingers from her face, and gasping, cried out.

"What are you doing?"

"Ah, good. You're awake."

He flipped the lamp on. Her eyes flew open when she saw that he was holding a gun; the same gun she'd found in Daphne's closet all those months ago.

"Jackson! What are you doing?"

He pointed the gun at her head. "If you ever throw anything at me again, you won't wake up the next time."

She went to push his hand away, certain he was just playing around. "Ha, ha."

He grabbed her wrist with his other hand. "I'm serious."

Her mouth fell open. "What do you want?"

"Bye, Amber."

She screamed as his finger depressed the trigger. *Click.* Nothing happened.

She felt something wet and realized her bladder had emptied. A look of disgust filled his face.

"You're weak. Pissing the bed like a child."

He jumped off, still pointing the gun at her.

"This time you get a pass. Next time you might not be so lucky."

"I'll call the cops."

He laughed. "No, you won't. They'd end up arresting you. You're a fugitive, remember?" He pointed to the bed. "Get up and change the sheets."

"Can I take a shower first?"

"No."

She got up and began to strip the bed, sobbing as she did so. He stood, watching the entire time, not saying a word. After she'd finished, he spoke again.

"Go take a shower, and then we'll have a little talk." She began to walk away, and he called her back.

"One more thing." He threw the gun at her, and it fell to the floor before she could catch it. "Don't worry, it's not loaded. Take a look at the initials."

She picked it up and saw the letters she'd first read months before: YMB. "What does it stand for?"

He smiled. "You're mine, bitch."

※

So now she listened to everything he said, like an obedient child. When he told her to lose five pounds, she didn't argue, even though she was back to her pre-baby weight already. When he called her "stupid" and "white trash," she didn't argue with him, but apologized for whatever perceived infraction she'd committed. He showered her with expensive clothes and jewelry, but now she understood that it was all for show. And in public they were the golden couple, she the adored and adoring wife, he the handsome indulgent husband.

The sex became more demeaning and debasing—he'd demand oral pleasure from her when she was on her way out the door, or after she'd just gotten dressed, so he could make sure to leave his mark and humiliate her further. What had she ever done to deserve this? Life was so unfair. She'd worked so hard to escape her life in that wretched town where everyone looked at her like she was trash. Now she was Mrs. Jackson Parrish, one of the richest women in town, surrounded by the best of everything. And yet she was still being looked down on, still being treated like garbage. All she'd wanted was the life she deserved. It didn't occur to her that she had gotten it.

SEVENTY-TWO

Eight Months Later

Daphne gripped the phone tightly in her hand while looking out the window of the New York cab. She'd been too nervous to eat anything on the plane, and her stomach was growling insistently now. Rooting through her bag, she found a mint and put it in her mouth. She took a deep breath and braced herself when they pulled up to the front of Jackson's office building. After today, she could leave Connecticut behind her for good and get on with the new life she was forging.

Once the divorce was final, Daphne had taken the girls and gone to see her mother at the inn. She hadn't called ahead—she didn't really know how to begin. After they'd settled in and the girls had gone to sleep, she and Ruth sat together and she told her everything from beginning to end.

Her mother had been heartbroken. "My poor girl. Why didn't you ever tell me? You should have come to me."

Daphne had sighed. "I tried. When Tallulah was a baby, I left. But that's when he had me committed and put together all that evidence against me. There was nothing I could do." Daphne reached out and grabbed her mother's hand. "And there was nothing you could do."

Ruth was crying. "I should have known. You're my daughter. I should have seen through him. Realized you hadn't really changed into the person he made you out to be."

"No, Mom. You couldn't have known. Please don't blame yourself. What matters is that I'm free now. We can be together now."

"Your father never liked him," Ruth had said quietly.

"What?"

"I thought he was being overprotective. You know, just a dad not wanting his little girl to grow up. He thought he was too slick, too practiced. I wish I'd listened."

"I wouldn't have listened. It would have only pushed us further apart than we already were." She put her head on her mother's shoulder. "I miss him so much. He was a wonderful father."

They'd stayed up all night, catching up and reconnecting. Her mother surprised her the next day with her decision.

"How would you feel if I sold the inn to Barry and moved with you to California?"

"I'd be thrilled! Are you serious?"

She'd nodded. "I've missed enough. I don't want to miss any more."

The girls had been ecstatic to learn that their grandmother would be living with them.

California had been good for all of them. The constant sunshine and happy dispositions of everyone around them had done wonders. The girls still missed their father, of course, but every day it got a little easier. They blamed Amber for the estrangement, and Daphne was happy to let them. When they were old enough, she would tell them the truth. In the meantime, the girls were healing, with the help of a gifted therapist, a neighborhood full of kids, and a yellow lab they called Mr. Bandit—renamed for his tendency to steal their toys.

They'd found a lovely four-bedroom home in Santa Cruz a mile and a half from the beach. At first she was worried that the girls would find it hard to go from living in their estate on the water to this charming but cozy two-thousand-square-foot house. She had more than enough money from the settlement to buy something bigger, but she was finished living that kind of life. Her mother had sold the B&B to Barry and insisted on contributing to the purchase of the house. Daphne had put the money from the settlement in a trust for the girls, which provided enough interest for them to live on. Douglas would be taking the reins at Julie's Smile, and Daphne would be on his board. She'd go back to working, of course, but not yet. Now was a time for healing.

When she brought the girls to look at the house, she had held her breath, waiting for their reaction. They had immediately run up the stairs to see where their rooms would be.

"Oh, can this be mine, Mommy? I love the pink walls!" Bella had asked after checking them all out.

Daphne had looked at Tallulah. "Fine with me. I like the one with the built-in bookcases," Tallulah said.

"It's settled, then." She'd smiled. "You like it?" They'd both nodded.

"Mommy, will this be your room?" Bella had taken her hand and pulled her to the master bedroom.

"Yes, this will be mine, and Grandmom will have the third floor to herself."

"Yay! You'll be so close to me."

"That makes you happy?" she'd asked.

Bella had nodded. "I used to get scared in that big

house, with you and Daddy so far from me. This is so nice."

Daphne had hugged her. "Yes, it is." And she'd said a silent thanks that she would never have to lock her bedroom door again.

The refrigerator was filled with their favorite foods; there was ice cream in the freezer and candy in the pantry. Daphne had left her scale in Connecticut and felt healthier and more beautiful than she ever had. Sometimes she would still reach for her food journal, and she'd have to remind herself that she didn't have to write things down anymore. She'd brought it with her as a reminder never to let anyone control her again. She was delighted to keep those extra ten pounds she'd put on, which gave her a feminine and shapely form. Walking into the family room and hearing SpongeBob's braying laughter, watching her daughters revel in the silliness, overjoyed her. She relished the freedom to make her own choices without fear of reprisal. It was like letting out a sigh of relief that had been pent up for years.

School would let out in another three weeks, and they were all looking forward to a lazy summer collecting seashells and learning how to surf. She loved the simplicity of their life here. No more packed schedules and regimented days. When she drove them to school on their first day, Bella had looked at her with surprise.

"Aren't we going to have a nanny that will drive us?"

"No, darling. I'm happy to take you."

"But don't you need to get to the gym?"

"Why do I need the gym? I can ride my bike to the beach and take a walk. Lots of things to do. It's too beautiful here to be stuck inside."

"But what if you get fat?"

It had been like a knife to the heart. Clearly Jackson's

imprint wasn't going to be as easy to wash away as she'd hoped.

"We're not going to worry about fat or thin anymore—only healthy. God made our bodies very smart, and if we put good things in them and do fun things for exercise, it will all be okay."

Both girls had looked at her a bit dubiously, but she'd work on it over time.

Daphne's mother had arrived last week, and had been as enchanted with the house and the area as Daphne. It felt so good to have her mother back in her life for real.

Now the cab was pulling to a stop, and Daphne paid the driver. When she walked into the office building, the familiar feeling of dread engulfed her. She squared her shoulders, took a long breath, and reminded herself that now she had nothing to fear. She didn't belong to him anymore. She sent a text and waited. Five minutes later, Douglas, Jackson's assistant, came down on the elevator and walked over. He gave Daphne a hug.

"I'm glad you made it. I just got the call. They'll be here any minute."

"Does he have any idea?"

Douglas shook his head.

"How bad is it?"

"Bad. I've been giving them the spreadsheets for months now. I was finally able to get some of the account numbers two weeks ago. Pretty sure that's what clinched it."

"Shall we go up?" Daphne asked.

"Yes, let me sign you in." He turned around and looked behind her. "They're here," he whispered.

There were four men clad in shiny blue raid jackets, the gold letters "FBI" embossed across the left breast, entering the building. They approached the security desk, flashing their credentials.

"Come on, let's get upstairs before they do," Douglas said.

As the elevator ascended, she felt a throbbing pulse in her wrists and a tingling all the way to her fingertips. Her face was hot, and she felt a sudden wave of nausea overwhelm her.

"Are you okay?" Douglas asked.

She swallowed, put her hand on her stomach, and nodded. "I'll be fine. Just felt a little woozy there for a minute." She tried to smile. "Don't worry. I'm all right."

"You sure? You don't have to be here, you know."

"Are you kidding? I wouldn't miss this for the world."

The elevator doors opened, and Daphne followed Douglas into the suite of offices and went with him to his, directly outside Jackson's.

She had a thought and quickly turned to Douglas. "I'll be right back."

"Where are you going?"

"I have something to say to him before they go in."

"You'd better hurry."

She flung open the door without bothering to knock, and after a confused second, Jackson looked at her in surprise. He rose from his chair, looking impeccable in his custom suit, an angry scowl on his face.

"What are *you* doing here?"

"I've come to give you a little going-away present," Daphne answered sweetly, pulling a small package out of her handbag.

"What the hell are you talking about? Get out of my building before I have you thrown out." Jackson picked up the phone on his desk.

"Don't you want to see what I have, Jackson? The gift I've brought for you."

"I don't know what your little game is, Daphne, but I'm not interested. You're boring me. You always bored me. Get the hell out of here."

"Well, guess what. Your life is about to get really interesting. No more boredom." She tossed the package onto his desk. "Here you go. Enjoy your time away."

She opened the door and held her breath when she saw the men from the lobby advance toward the offices. Their faces were unsmiling and ominous.

Jackson and Daphne turned to look as Douglas escorted the suited quartet into Jackson's office.

Daphne stepped aside as one of the men held out his credentials. "Jackson Parrish?"

Jackson nodded. "Yes."

"FBI," the older agent said, as the others fanned out around Jackson.

"What is this all about?" Jackson's voice cracked as he raised it. The office was now deathly quiet. Chairs pivoted toward the commotion, all eyes on Jackson.

"Sir, I have a warrant for your arrest."

"This is bullshit. For what?" Jackson said, his voice having returned.

"For thirty-six counts of wire fraud, money laundering, and tax evasion. And I assure you it is not bullshit."

"Get the hell out of here! I haven't done anything. Do you know who I am?"

"I most definitely do. Now if you would kindly turn around and put your hands behind your back."

"I'll sue your asses. You'll be lucky to be writing parking tickets when I'm through with you."

"Sir, I am going to ask you one more time to turn

around and put your hands behind your back," the agent said as he firmly pivoted Jackson, leaning him against the wall.

With his cheek against the wall, he sputtered, "You! This is your doing, isn't it?"

Daphne smiled. "I wanted to see the justice system in action. You know, it's educational. You taught me that I should always be improving my mind."

He lunged for her, but the men stopped him and cuffed him. "You bitch! No matter how long it takes, I'll get even with you." He struggled against the agent holding him. "You'll be sorry you did this."

A rather large agent standing behind Jackson pushed the chain of the cuffs that were in his hand gently toward the ground. Having no choice, Jackson dropped to his knees, wincing in pain.

Daphne shook her head. "I'm not sorry. And you can't hurt me anymore. You have no one to blame but yourself. If you hadn't gotten greedy and set up those offshore accounts, and if you'd paid taxes on that money like you should have, none of this would be happening. All I did was make sure your new assistant was someone with the integrity to turn you in."

"What are you talking about?"

Douglas came and stood next to Daphne. "My sister has CF. Daphne's foundation saved her life." He looked at one of the men and nodded.

"Excuse me, ma'am . . . sir, I need the two of you to step back, please." The agent sneaked in a wink and a wry smile. "Let's go, Mr. Parrish," he said, lifting him off his knees and in the direction of the elevator.

"Wait," she said. "Don't forget your present, Jackson."

She grabbed the package from the desk and slipped it into his pocket.

"Sorry, ma'am. I need to see that." The tallest of the men put his hand out.

She took the package from him and unwrapped it, holding up a cheap plastic turtle from the dollar store. "Here you are, sweetie," she said as she dangled it in front of him. "Something to remember me by. Like you, it has no power over me anymore."

SEVENTY-THREE

Daphne had one more stop to make. She got out of the cab and told the driver to wait for her. It still felt strange, having to ring the bell to her former home. Margarita opened the door and threw her hands up in surprise. "Missus! It's so good to see you."

She gave her a hug. "You too, Margarita." She lowered her voice. "I hope she's treating you okay."

Margarita's face became a mask, and she looked around nervously. "Did you come to see Mister?"

She shook her head. "No, I'm here to see Amber."

Her eyebrows rose. "I be right back."

"What are *you* doing here?" Amber appeared, looking rail-thin and pale.

"We need to talk."

She looked at Daphne suspiciously. "About what?"

"Let's go inside. I don't think you want your staff overhearing."

"This is *my* house now. I'll do the inviting." She pursed her lips and then looked around nervously. "Fine, follow me."

Daphne followed her into the living room and took a seat in front of the fireplace. An enormous portrait of Amber and Jackson on their wedding day had replaced the family portrait. Even though Amber had been pregnant and showing at the time, she'd had the artist paint her sylphlike, without the bulging belly.

Looking at Daphne warily, she spoke. "What gives?"

"Don't ever bother my children again."

She rolled her eyes. "All I did was send them an invitation to their brother's baptism. Did you fly all the way from California just to complain about that?"

Ignoring Amber's taunting, Daphne leaned toward her. "You listen to me, you little bitch. If you ever send them so much as a postcard, I'll have your head. Is that clear, Lana?"

She leaped out of the chair and came close. "What did you call me?"

"You heard me . . . Lana. Lana Crump." Daphne wrinkled her nose. "Such an unfortunate last name. It's no wonder you don't use it."

Amber's face was red, and her breath came fast. "How did you know?"

"I hired a detective after Meredith confronted you. I found out everything then."

"But you were still my friend. You believed me. I don't understand."

"Did you really think I was that stupid? That I didn't know exactly what you were up to? Please." She shook her head. *"Oh, Amber, I'm so worried about Jackson cheating. I could never give him a son.* You ate it all up, did everything just the way I'd hoped you would, even ordered the perfume I was 'allergic' to." She put air quotes around *allergic.* "And once you were carrying his son, I knew you had him. The reason I never got pregnant was because I had an IUD."

Her mouth dropped open. "You planned all of this?"

Daphne smiled. "You thought you were getting the perfect life, the perfect man. How do you like him now, Lana? Has he shown you his true colors yet?"

Amber glared at Daphne. "I thought it was just me. That it was because of what he found out. He told me

I was nothing better than white trash." She looked at Daphne with hatred. "You're the one who gave him the file?"

She nodded. "I read all about how you framed that poor boy Matthew Lockwood for rape when he wouldn't marry you. How you let him sit in prison for two years for a crime he didn't commit."

"That son of a bitch deserved it. He kept me his dirty secret, slept with me all summer while his rich girlfriend was away. And his mother—you'd think she'd have wanted her grandchild. But she said I should have it aborted, that any child of mine would be nothing but trash. I laughed while they put her precious son away. I loved seeing the Lockwood name tainted with scandal and dirt. They thought they were so wonderful, so high-and-mighty."

"You still feel no remorse? Even though because of you, he was beaten in prison and is in a wheelchair for the rest of his life?"

Amber stood up and began to pace. "So what? If he was too much of a weakling to take care of himself in prison, that's not my fault. He's nothing more than a coddled mama's boy." She shrugged. "Besides, he has money; he's well taken care of. And his simpering girl-friend married him."

"And what about your son?"

"What *about* Jackson Junior?"

"No, your *other* son. How could you just aban-don him?"

"What should I have done? My mother found my diary and went to the police. They found that juror I convinced to fight for the conviction, and he agreed to testify against me. They arrested me. What kind of mother turns in her own daughter? She said she felt sorry for Matthew—like that spoiled brat deserved any sympathy. Once I got out on bail, I had to run. No way was I going to prison just for giving Matthew what he deserved." She took a deep breath. "But I would like to get my son back, punish Matthew and his fat cow wife. She's raising him like she's his mother. He's my kid, not hers. It's not fair."

"Fair?" Daphne laughed. "He's so much better off without you. Tell me something, who is Amber Patterson? Did you have anything to do with her going missing?"

She rolled her eyes again. "Of course not. I hitched a ride out of town with a trucker from Missouri to Nebraska. I got a job waitressing there, and one of my regulars was a guy who worked in the records department. He got me the credentials."

"How did you get her passport?"

She smiled then. "Oh, well, you know how small towns are. After a while, I finagled a way to meet her poor mom. She worked at the grocery store in town. Took a few months, but I guess I reminded her of her lost daughter. It helped that I wore my hair the way she had and talked to some of her friends and pretended I liked the same things. Her mom would make me dinner once a week—what a shitty cook. I found out Amber was supposed to have gone to France with her senior class—that's the only reason the stupid hick had a passport. So I stole it." She shrugged. "She also had a nice sapphire ring. I took that too. She didn't need it anymore."

Daphne shook her head. "There really is nothing beneath you."

"You could never understand. Growing up dirt-poor, with everyone looking down on me, I learned early on that if you want something, you have to get it for yourself. No one's going to just hand it over."

"And do you have what you want now?"

"I did at first. Until he found out about my past." Her earlier bravado was waning. She straightened and looked at Daphne. "If you hadn't given him that file, I could leave him, get child support and alimony. But if I do, he'll turn me in." Her demeanor changed suddenly, and Daphne could almost see the transformation taking place. "Daphne, you know what he's like. We're both victims now. You have to help me. You figured out a way to escape. There must be something I could use on him. Is there?" She was the old Amber now; the one Daphne had believed was her friend. She was narcissistic enough to believe that she could still manipulate her.

Daphne looked at her. "Tell me something, honestly: did you ever consider me a friend?"

Amber took Daphne's hand in hers. "Of course I was your friend. I loved you, Daph. It was just too tempting. I had nothing, and you had everything. Please forgive me. I know what I did was wrong, and I'm sorry. Our children are related. It's like we *are* sisters now. You're a good person. Please, help me."

"So if I help you, then what? You'll leave him, and we can go back to being friends again?"

"Yes. Friends again. For Julie and Charlene." As soon as the words left her mouth, Amber realized her mistake.

"Yeah. For Charlene. Who never existed." Daphne stood up. "Enjoy your bed, Amber. You'll be spending lots of time in it. Jackson's a man of strong appetites."

Amber scowled at Daphne. "You want to know the truth? I was never your friend. You had all the money, all the power, and you gave me your crumbs. You didn't even appreciate what you had. All that money he spent on you and your bratty kids. It was obscene. All the while, I was working in his office like a dog." Her eyes were cold. "I did what I had to do. It was so boring, listening to all your depressing stories. *She's dead!* I wanted to scream. *No one cares about Julie. She's been rotting in the ground for twenty years. Let it go.*"

Daphne grabbed her wrist and held it tight. "Don't you ever speak my sister's name again—do you hear me? You deserve everything you're getting." She let go of her. "Take a look around. Try and commit to memory what it was like living the good life, because it's over now."

"What are you talking about?"

"I've come from Jackson's office. The FBI just took him out of his office in handcuffs. Seems they got access to his offshore accounts. Pity. He never paid taxes on that money. I'm pretty sure when all is said and done, you'll be lucky if the two of you can afford to live in your old apartment. That is, if they don't give him jail time, but knowing Jackson, he'll figure a way out of that. He'll have to deplete all his resources, of course. Maybe you can help him start a new business."

"You're lying." Her voice was shrill.

Daphne shook her head. "You know that male assistant you made sure he hired so there'd be no funny business at the office? Douglas? Well, he's an old friend of mine. See, his sister *does* have CF. Julie's Smile has been a tremendous help to his family. He's been spying on Jackson, and he finally got the account numbers he needed to go to the feds. Take a good look around. You may not have all this for long." She started to walk away, then stopped and turned back. "But at least you still have Jackson."

Daphne walked out of the house for the last time. As the driver pulled away, she watched as the house receded from sight. How different it looked to her now from when she'd first seen it. Settling back against the seat, she took in, for the last time, the magnificence of each house they passed, and wondered what secrets each of them held. She grew lighter with each passing mile, and when they drove out of the pristine borders of Bishops Harbor, she left the pain and shame she'd lived with while she was still its prisoner behind her. A new life awaited—one where no one terrorized her in the middle of the night or made her pretend to be something she was not. A life where her children would grow up secure and loved, free to be whomever and whatever they desired to be.

She looked up at the sky and imagined her beloved Julie watching from above. She pulled out a pen and the small notepad she kept in her purse and began to write.

My darling Julie,

I often wonder if I'd have made different choices if you were still here. A sister can keep you from making those big mistakes. You wouldn't have allowed my need to save everyone blur my vision. If only I could have saved you, maybe I would have tried harder to save myself.

How I miss confiding in you, in having that one person that I always knew was in my corner no matter what, sharing my life. And how foolish I was to think that I could ever find that same solace from anyone else.

I suppose I have been looking for you everywhere since I lost you. But I know now, I didn't lose you. You're still here. In the twinkle in Bella's eyes and the kindness in Tallulah's heart. You live on in them and in me, and I'll hold tight to the precious memories of the time we had together until, one day, we are reunited. I feel you watching over me: you are the warmth of the sun as I romp with your nieces on the beach, the cool breeze that caresses my cheek in the evenings, the feeling of peace that now resides in the place of turmoil. And despite my desperate wish to have you back, I must believe that you, too, are finally at peace, forever free from the disease that bound you.

Remember when we saw our first Shakespeare play? You were just fourteen and I was sixteen, and we both thought Helena was a fool for wanting a man who didn't want her. It occurs to me that I've become Helena in reverse.

And so, my dear Julie, a chapter has closed and a new one begun.

I love you

Daphne put the notebook in her purse and leaned back. Smiling and looking up, she whispered the Bard's famous words from that play she and Julie had seen so long ago:

"The king's a beggar, now the play is done:
All is well ended . . ."

ACKNOWLEDGMENTS

Long before a book is born, there is a group comprised of friends, family, and professionals that make its eventual existence possible. We are deeply grateful to them for their indispensable roles in that process.

To our wonderful agent, Bernadette Baker-Baughman of Victoria Sanders & Associates, thank you for being our biggest champion and advocate and for making the journey so enjoyable with your graciousness, wit, and dedication. You are an answer to a prayer, and it is a joy to work with you.

To our fabulous editor, Emily Griffin, your infectious excitement and dedication to excellence took the story to the next level and made it so much better than we ever could have done without you.

To the stellar team at Harper, thank you for your excitement about the book and all you did to make it happen. Jonathan Burnham, thank you for your electrifying enthusiasm and most inspiring note, making us certain we'd found the right publishing home. Jimmy Iacobelli, who designed our brilliant cover, and the creative team who designed the interior pages—we fell in love with your vision the minute we laid eyes on it. Thanks to Nikki Baldauf for her expert steering through copyediting and production. Heather Drucker and the PR team, thank you for your incredible passion and talent. Katie O'Callaghan and the marketing team, we know we are in the very best of hands. Huge thanks to Virginia Stanley and the amazing Library Sales team for a fantastic job getting the early word out. Deepest appreciation to Carolyn Bodkin, who worked so diligently in managing the foreign rights. To Amber Oliver (aka the Other Amber), and to all the incredibly hard working people at HarperCollins, our deepest gratitude for all you do.

Appreciation and love to our sisters-in-law and sisters in heart, Honey Constantine and Lynn Constantine, for reading, rereading, reading again, and cheering and encouraging us every step of the way.

To Christopher Ackers, wonderful son and nephew, for listening in and offering advice on our numerous plot conversations and always infusing them with your customary humor.

Thank you to our beta readers: Amy Bike, Dee Campbell, Carmen Marcano-Davis, Tricia Farnworth, Lia Gordon, and Teresa Loverde, your enthusiasm was a great motivator.

To the wonderful authors and friends who make up the Thrillerfest community, an incredible well of camaraderie, understanding, and mutual support, many thanks.

To David Morrell for your thoughtful advice. Thank you for always being available to talk.

To Jaime Levine for your continual support and encouragement and being there from the beginning.

To Gretchen Stelter, our first editor. You brought clarity and insights that ratcheted up the tension and made the manuscript more compelling.

Thanks to Carmen Marcano-Davis for your psychological expertise that helped us to shape Jackson, and to Chris Munger for authenticating the FBI scenes in the book.

To Patrick McCord and Tish Fried of Write Yourself Free for sharing your talent and skill. Your workshops made us better writers.

Lynne thanks her husband, Rick, and her children,

Nick and Theo, for their unwavering support and forbearance while she spent hours locked in her office Skyping with Valerie on plot lines or working late into the night to meet deadlines. And to Tucker, for always being by her side while she works. All my love to all of you always.

Valerie thanks her husband, Colin, for his constant encouragement and support, and her children, her greatest cheerleaders. I love you all.

Read on for a sneak peek at Liv Constantine's
next psychological thriller

THE
STRANGER
IN THE
MIRROR

Coming soon in hardcover from Harper

One

ADDISON

I'd like to think I'm a good person, but I have no way of knowing for sure. I don't remember my real name, where I'm from, or if I have any family. I must have friends somewhere, but the only ones I recognize are the ones I've made in the two years since the new me was born—every memory before that has been wiped away. I don't remember how I got the crescent-shaped scar on my knee or why the smell of roses turns my stomach. The only thing I have is here and now, and even that feels tenuous. There are some things I do know. I like chocolate ice cream better than vanilla, and I love to watch the sunset paint the sky in vibrant orange and pink at dusk. And I love taking pictures. I think it's because I feel more comfortable behind the camera and looking out. Looking inward is too painful when there's nothing much to see.

We're celebrating my engagement on this beautiful September day, and I'm surrounded by people who say they love me, but who is it really that they love? How can you truly know someone when their entire past is a mystery? Gabriel, my fiancé, is sitting next to me, looking at me in an adoring way that makes me feel warm all over. He's one of those people whose eyes smile, and you can't help but feel good when he's around. He is the one who is helping me discover the parts of myself that feel authentic. I take pictures. Gabriel tells me that I'm an amazing talent. I don't know if I'd go that far, but I love doing it. When I'm behind the camera, I'm me again. I know instinctively that this is something I've done and loved doing for a long time. It's the thing that has saved me, given me a living, and led me to Gabriel. He's actually giving me my first break—a show at his family's gallery—in October. Soon, they'll be my family too.

The clinking of a glass gets my attention. It's Patrick, Gabriel's best man.

"As you all know, this clown and I have been friends since we were six. I could stand here all day and tell you stories. But since both our sets of parents are present, I'll spare you the gory details and just say that we've had our share of good times and laughs, and our share of trouble. I never thought he'd settle down, but the minute I saw him with Addison, I knew he was a goner." Patrick lifts his glass toward us both. "To Addy and Gabriel. Long life!"

My eyes scan the restaurant and land on Darcy. Her glass is lifted, but her smile seems forced, and her eyes are sad.

We all raise our glasses and sip. Gabriel's sister, Hailey, is my maid of honor, but she cannot regale the crowd with stories of our shared past because, like Gabriel, she's only known me for six months. Despite the festive mood around me, darkness descends again, and I feel hollow. Gabriel seems to sense my mood shift and squeezes my hand under the table, then leans over and whispers, "You all right?"

I squeeze back and force a smile, nodding, willing the tears not to fall.

Then Gigi gets up and takes the microphone from Patrick.

"I may have only known Addison for a couple of years, but I couldn't love her any more. When she came into our lives, it was the biggest blessing we could have asked for." She looks at me. "You're like a daughter to us, and Ed and I are so happy for you. To new beginnings."

I know she's trying to make it right for me, but it's hard to toast to new beginnings when they're all I have. I do it anyway, because I love her too, and because she and Ed try to be the parents that I don't have. Ed will give me away at the wedding, and while I'm grateful to have him, I can't help but worry that I have a father somewhere wondering what happened to me. That's what makes it so impossible for me to fully embrace anyone with my whole heart. What if my parents are out there somewhere mourning for me, agonizing over what's happened to me or thinking I'm dead? Or even worse, what if there is no one looking?

The doctors have told me that I have to be patient. That memory is a tricky thing. The more I try to force it, the more elusive it becomes. I have no real clues to my identity, no identification, no cell phone containing pictures or contacts. My body, on the other hand, shares some clues—the jagged scars that tell their own story—just not to me.

K. Mc

W9-BMR-790

Praise for *The Breaker*

"Erotically charged . . . Fans who have followed Walters's
growing mastery over the course of her five other novels
won't be disappointed by this one, which stakes her claim
as a worthy rival to sisters-in-crime P. D. James and Ruth
Rendell. With her insightful psychology and intriguing
contemporary characters . . . Walters gives the English vil-
lage mystery a fine new spin . . . tantalizing psychological
thriller."

—*People* (starred review)

"Walters is a master of the macabre who imbues her novels
with an intensely eerie atmosphere. Long after a reader fin-
ishes one of her books, that atmosphere lingers, infecting the
mundane world for days to come . . . Walters . . . knows
exactly what to do to keep her readers engaged and anxious."

—*The Washington Post Book World*

"Walters has managed to balance tawdriness with hope and
romance to produce gripping, pleasing stories . . . *The
Breaker* . . . is yet another gem."

—*New York Post*

"A brilliant new example of psychological suspense at its
best . . . This knockout whodunit is possibly on its way to
nomination as the best British crime story of the year."

—*The Buffalo News*

continued . . .

"Walters's dark edginess conflicts with the image of gentle English mysteries . . . If you haven't yet discovered Minette Walters, do so with haste. Her books are some of the best mysteries being written on either side of the Atlantic, so well-plotted and beautifully crafted that it takes effort to read slowly enough to appreciate her multifaceted talent."
—*The Kansas City Star*

"[An] intelligent, honed mystery . . . Walters makes nice work of confounding readers while developing an enjoyable subset of characters."
—*New York Daily News Online*

"British novelist Walters . . . just keeps getting better . . . a wonderfully convoluted whodunit that will perplex even expert villain spotters . . . a sordid tale of sexual deviance, obsession, and desperation . . . Her characters are carefully constructed: they're real people, not crime-novel stock figures . . . Not only Walters's fans but anyone who likes a smart, well-constructed mystery will be spellbound until the final scenes have been played out."
—*Booklist* (starred review)

"[A] nightmarish suspense novel."
—*Mary Higgins Clark Mystery Magazine*

"A dark, complex, and somehow intimate mystery . . . The plot is so strong that it carried me along with it, making *The Breaker* an engrossing read."
—*The Mystery Reader*

continued . . .

Minette Walters . . .

"flirts with gothic menace and intricacy."
—*The Washington Post Book World*

"makes an art of uncertainty."
—*The New York Times Book Review*

"is a virtuoso of psychological suspense."
—*The San Diego Union-Tribune*

"knows the cruel kinkiness that can lurk behind the most sedate of façades."
—*Los Angeles Times Book Review*

THE
BREAKER

Minette Walters

JOVE BOOKS, NEW YORK

Map on pp. xiv © British Crown Copyright/MOD.
Reproduced with the permission of the Controller of
Her Britannic Majesty's Stationery Office.

THE BREAKER

A Jove Book / published by arrangement with
the author

PRINTING HISTORY
G. P. Putnam's Sons edition / May 1999
Jove edition / August 2000

The Penguin Putnam Inc. World Wide Web site address is
http://www.penguinputnam.com

ISBN: 0-515-12882-1

A JOVE BOOK®
Jove Books are published by The Berkley Publishing Group,
a division of Penguin Putnam Inc.,
375 Hudson Street, New York, New York 10014.
JOVE and the "J" design
are trademarks belonging to Penguin Putnam Inc.

PRINTED IN THE UNITED STATES OF AMERICA
10 9 8 7 6 5 4 3 2 1

With particular thanks to
Sally and John Priestley of *XII Bar Blues*
and Encombe House Estate

For Marigold and Anthony

Chapman's Pool   Emmetts Hill   Quarry Valley   St. Alban's Head

Eastern Perspective

Egmont Bight   Houns-tout Cliff   Chapman's Pool

Western Perspective

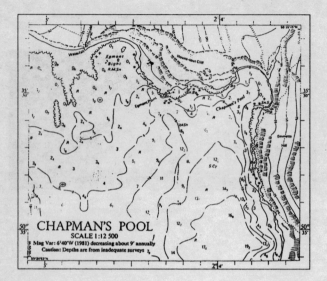

CHAPMAN'S POOL
SCALE 1:12 500
Mag Var: 6°40'W (1981) decreasing about 9' annually
Caution: Depths are from inadequate surveys

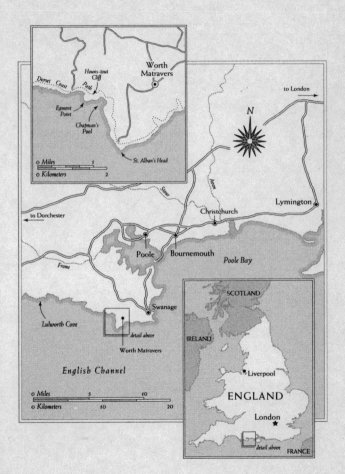

Worth
Matravers

Dorset Coast Path
Houns-tout
Cliff

Egmont
Point

Chapman's
Pool

St. Alban's Head

o Miles   1
o Kilometers   2

N

to London

Arun

Stour

Christchurch

Lymington

to Dorchester

Poole

Bournemouth

Poole Bay

Frame

Lulworth Cove

Swanage

detail above
Worth Matravers

English Channel

o Miles   5   10
o Kilometers   10   20

SCOTLAND

IRELAND

Liverpool

ENGLAND

London

detail above

FRANCE

Dorset: county of southwestern England, bordered to the south by the seas of the English Channel, to the east by the county of Hampshire, and to the west by the county of Devon. Some 100 miles southwest of London, Dorset's total area, mainly rural, is approximately 1,000 square miles. Urban development along the coastline is centered on the seaside resorts of Bournemouth and Poole, and farther to the west on Weymouth and Portland. West Dorset (main town—Dorchester) has been immortalized as Wessex in the writings of Thomas Hardy and was the scene of the Tolpuddle martyrs' historic stand for organized labor in the nineteenth century. The Isle of Purbeck, a small peninsula to the southwest of Poole (main town—Swanage) is an isolated area of great beauty, home to Purbeck marble and the magnificent medieval ruins of Corfe Castle.

While Scotland Yard still maintains links between British law-enforcement agencies and Interpol, its responsibilities are now limited to metropolitan London. In the forty-six counties of England, the responsibility for serious cases is borne by county constabulary headquarters, and it is these areas of excellence which take the lead in provincial murders. It should always be remembered that nowhere in England is very far from anywhere else—for example, Lymington, in Hampshire, is only thirty-odd miles from Poole, in Dorset—however, local knowledge is always invaluable, and in this story I have given a starring role to Police Constable Ingram, a uniformed constable in a tiny police station on the Isle of Purbeck, who may—*or may not?*— know what he's talking about. Dorset Constabulary HQ (familiarly known as Winfrith) is located equidistantly between Poole and Dorchester, and is home to my fictional heavyweights, Detective Superintendent Carpenter and Detective Inspector Galbraith.

Minette Walters

She drifted with the waves, falling off their rolling backs and waking to renewed agony every time salt water seared down her throat and into her stomach. During intermittent periods of lucidity when she revisited, always with astonishment, what had happened to her, it was the deliberate breaking of her fingers that remained indelibly printed on her memory, and not the brutality of her rape.

The child sat cross-legged on the floor like a miniature statue of Buddha, the gray dawn light leeching her flesh of color. He had no feelings for her, not even common humanity, but he couldn't bring himself to touch her. She watched him as solemnly as he watched her, and he was enthralled by her immobility. He could break her neck as easily as a chicken's, but he fancied he saw an ancient wisdom in her concentrated gaze, and the idea frightened him. Did she know what he'd done?

PROLOGUE

The most widely held view is that rape is an exercise in male domination, a pathological assertion of power, usually performed out of anger against the entire sex or frustration with a specific individual. By forcing a woman to accept penetration, the man is demonstrating not only his superior strength but his right to sow his seed wherever and whenever he chooses. This has elevated the rapist to a creature of legendary proportions—demoniacal, dangerous, predatory—and the fact that few rapists merit such labels is secondary to the fear the legend inspires.

In a high percentage of cases (including domestic, date and gang rape) the rapist is an inadequate individual who seeks to bolster poor self-image by attacking someone he perceives to be weaker than himself. He is a man of low intelligence, few social skills, and with a profound sense of his own inferiority in his dealings with the rest of society. A deepseated fear of women is more common to the rapist than a feeling of superiority, and this may well lie in early failure to make successful relationships.

Pornography becomes a means to an end for such a person because masturbation is as necessary to him as the regular fix is to a heroin addict. Without orgasm the sex-fixator experiences nothing. However, his obsessive nature, coupled with his lack of achievement, will make him an unattractive mate to the sort of woman his inferiority complex demands, namely a woman who attracts successful men. If he has a relationship at all, his partner will be someone who has been used and abused by other men, which only exacerbates his feelings of inadequacy and inferiority.

It could be argued that the rapist, a man of limited intelligence, limited sensation, and limited ability to function, is more to be pitied than feared, because his danger lies in the easy ascendancy society has given him over the so-called weaker sex. Every time judges and newspapers demonize and mythologize the rapist as a dangerous predator, they merely reinforce the idea that the penis is a symbol of power. . . .

Helen Barry, *The Mind of a Rapist*

CHAPTER

The woman lay on her back on the pebble foreshore at the foot of Houns-tout Cliff, staring at the cloudless sky above, her pale blond hair drying into a frizz of tight curls in the hot sun. A smear of sand across her abdomen gave the impression of wispy clothing, but the brown circles of her nipples and the hair sprouting at her crotch told anyone who cared to look that she was naked. One arm curved languidly around her head while the other rested palm-up on the sea-washed pebbles, the fingers curling in the tiny wavelets that bubbled over them as the tide rose; her legs, opened shamelessly in relaxation, seemed to invite the sun's warmth to penetrate directly into her body.

Above her loomed the grim shale escarpment of Houns-tout Cliff, irregularly striped with the hardy vegetation that clung to its ledges. So often shrouded in mist and rain during the autumn and winter, it looked benign in the brilliant summer sunlight. A mile away to the west, on the Dorset Coast Path that hugged the clifftops to Weymouth, a party of hikers approached at a leisurely pace, pausing every now and then to watch cormorants and shags plummet into the sea like tiny guided missiles. To the east, on the path to Swanage, a single male walker passed the Norman chapel on St. Alban's Head on his way to the rock-girt crucible of Chapman's Pool, whose clear blue waters made an attractive anchorage when the wind was light and offshore. Because of the steep hills that surround it, pedestrian visitors to its beaches were rare, but at lunchtime on a fine weekend upwards of ten boats rode at anchor there, bobbing in staggered formation as the gentle swells passed under each in turn.

A single boat, a thirty-two-foot Princess, had already nosed in through the entrance channel, and the rattle of its anchor chain over its idling engines carried clearly on the air. Not far behind, the bow of a Fairline Squadron carved through the race off St. Alban's Head, giving the yachts that wallowed lazily in the light winds a wide berth in its progress toward the bay. It was a quarter past ten on one of the hottest Sundays of the year, but out of sight around Egmont Point the naked sunbather appeared oblivious to both the shimmering heat and the increasing likelihood of company.

The Spender brothers, Paul and Daniel, had spotted the nudist as they rounded the Point with their fishing rods, and they were now perched precariously on an unstable ledge some hundred feet above her and to her right. They took turns looking at her through their father's expensive binoculars, which they had smuggled out of the rented holiday cottage in a bundle of T-shirts, rods, and tackle. It was the middle weekend of their two weeks' holiday, and as far as the elder brother was concerned, fishing had only ever been a pretext. This remote part of the Isle of Purbeck held little attraction for an awakening adolescent, having few inhabitants, fewer distractions, and no sandy beaches. His intention had always been to spy on bikini-clad women draped over the expensive motor cruisers in Chapman's Pool.

"Mum said we weren't to climb the cliffs because they're dangerous," whispered Danny, the virtuous ten-year-old, less interested than his brother in the sight of bare flesh.

"Shut up."

"She'd kill us if she knew we were looking at a nudie."

"You're just scared because you've never seen one before."

"Neither've you," muttered the younger boy indignantly. "Anyway, she's a dirty person. I bet loads of people can see her."

Paul, the elder by two years, treated this remark with the scorn it deserved—they hadn't passed a soul on their way around Chapman's Pool. Instead, he concentrated on the wonderfully accessible body below. He couldn't see much of the woman's face because she was lying with her feet pointing toward them, but the magnification of the lenses was so powerful that he could see every other detail of her. He was too ignorant of the naked female form to question the bruises that blotched her skin, but he knew afterward that he wouldn't have questioned them anyway, even if he'd known what they meant. He had fantasized about something like this happening—discovering a quiescent, unmoving woman who allowed him to explore her at his leisure, if only through binoculars. He found the soft flow of her breasts unbearably erotic and dwelled at length on her nipples, wondering what it would be like to touch them and what would happen if he did. Lovingly he traversed the length of her midriff, pausing on the dimple of her belly button, before returning to what interested him most, her opened legs and what lay between them. He crawled forward on his elbows, writhing his body.

"What are you doing?" demanded Danny suspiciously, crawling up beside him. "Are you being dirty?"

" 'Course not." He gave the boy a savage thump on the arm. "That's all you ever think about, isn't it? Being dirty. You'd better watch it, penis-brain, or I'll tell Dad on you."

In the inevitable fight that followed—a grunting, red-faced brawl of hooked arms and kicking feet—the Zeiss binoculars slipped from the elder brother's grasp and clattered down the slope, dislodging an avalanche of shale in the process. The boys, united in terror of what their father was going to say, abandoned the fight to wriggle back from the brink and stare in dismay after the binoculars.

"It's your fault if they're broken," hissed the ten-year-old. "You're the one who dropped them."

But for once his brother didn't rise to the bait. He was more interested in the body's continued immobility. With an awful sense of foreboding it dawned on him that he'd been masturbating over a dead woman.

CHAPTER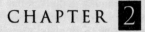

The clear waters of Chapman's Pool heaved in an undulating roll to break in rippling foam around the pebble shore of the bay. By now three boats were anchored there, two flying the red ensign—*Lady Rose,* the Princess, and *Gregory's Girl,* the Fairline Squadron; the third, *Mirage,* a French Beneteau, flew the tricolor. Only *Gregory's Girl* showed any sign of real activity, with a man and a woman struggling to release a dinghy whose winching wires had become jammed in the ratchet mechanism of the davits. On *Lady Rose,* a scantily clad couple lounged on the flying bridge, bodies glistening with oil, eyes closed against the sun, while on *Mirage,* a teenage girl held a video camera to her eye and panned idly up the steep grassy slope of West Hill, searching for anything worth filming.

No one noticed the Spender brothers' mad dash around the bay, although the French girl did zoom in on the lone male walker as he descended the hillside toward them. Seeing only with the tunnel vision of the camera, she was oblivious to anything but the handsome young man in her sight, and her smitten heart gave a tiny leap of excitement at the thought of another chance encounter with the beau-

tiful Englishman. She had met him two days before at the
Berthon Marina in Lymington, when with a gleaming
smile he'd told her the computer code for the lavatories,
and she couldn't believe her good luck that he was here . . .
today . . . in this shit-hole of boring isolation which her
parents described as one of England's gems.

To her starved imagination he looked like a longer-
haired version of Jean-Claude Van Damme in his sleeveless T-shirt and bottom-hugging shorts—tanned, muscled,
sleek dark hair swept back from his face, smiling brown
eyes, grittily stubbled jaw—and in the narrative tale of her
own life, romanticized, embellished, unbelievably innocent, she pictured herself swooning in his strong arms and
capturing his heart. Through the intimacy of magnification she watched his muscles ripple as he lowered his
rucksack to the ground, only for the lens to fill abruptly
with the frantic movements of the Spender brothers. With
an audible groan, she switched off the camera and stared
in disbelief at the prancing children, who, from a distance,
appeared to be showing enthusiastic delight.

Surely he was too young to be anybody's father?
But . . . A Gallic shrug . . .
Who knew with the English?

Behind the questing mongrel which zigzagged energeti-
cally in pursuit of a scent, the horse picked its way carefully down the track that led from Hill Bottom to the Pool.
Tarmac showed in places where the track had once been a
road, and one or two sketchy foundations among the overgrown vegetation beside it spoke of buildings long abandoned and demolished. Maggie Jenner had lived in this
area most of her life but had never known why the handful
of inhabitants in this corner of the Isle of Purbeck had
gone away and left their dwellings to the ravages of time.
Someone had told her once that "chapman" was an
archaic word for merchant or peddler, but what anyone
could have traded in this remote place she couldn't imag-

ine. Perhaps, more simply, a peddler had drowned in the bay and bequeathed his death to posterity. Every time she took this path she reminded herself to find out, but every time she made her way home again she forgot.

The cultivated gardens that had once bloomed here had left a lingering legacy of roses, hollyhocks, and hydrangeas amid the weeds and grasses, and she thought how pleasant it would be to have a house in this colorful wilderness, facing southwest toward the channel with only her dog and her horses for company. Because of the threat of the ever-sliding cliffs, access to Chapman's Pool was denied to motorized traffic by padlocked gates at Hill Bottom and Kingston, and the attraction of so much stillness was a powerful one. But then isolation and its attendant solitude was becoming something of an obsession with her, and occasionally it worried her.

Even as the thought was in her head, she heard the sound of an approaching vehicle, grinding in first gear over the bumps and hollows behind her, and gave a surprised whistle to bring Bertie to heel behind Sir Jasper. She turned in the saddle, assuming it was a tractor, and frowned at the approaching police Range Rover. It slowed as it drew level with her, and she recognized Nick Ingram at the wheel before, with a brief smile of acknowledgment, he drove on and left her to follow in his dusty wake.

The emergency services had rushed into action following a nine-nine-nine call to the police from a mobile telephone. It was timed at 10:43 A.M. The caller gave his name as Steven Harding and explained that he had come across two boys who claimed a body was lying on the beach at Egmont Bight. The details were confused because the boys omitted to mention that the woman was naked, and their obvious distress and garbled speech led Harding to give the impression that "the lady on the beach" was their mother and had fallen from the cliff while using a pair of binoculars. As a result the police and coastguards acted on the presumption that she was still alive.

Because of the difficulty of retrieving a badly injured person from the foreshore, the coastguards dispatched a Search and Rescue helicopter from Portland to winch her off. Meanwhile, PC Nick Ingram, diverted from a burglary investigation, approached via the track that skirted the inappropriately named West Hill on the eastern side of Chapman's Pool. He had had to use bolt cutters to slice through the chain on the gate at Hill Bottom, and as he abandoned his Range Rover on the hard standing beside the fishermen's boat sheds, he was hoping fervently that rubberneckers wouldn't grab the opportunity to follow him. He was in no mood to marshal petulant sightseers.

The only access from the boat sheds to the beach where the woman lay was by the same route the boys had taken—on foot around the bay, followed by a scramble over the rocks at Egmont Point. To a man in uniform, it was a hot and sweaty business, and Nick Ingram, who stood over six feet four inches and weighed upward of 240 pounds, was drenched by the time he reached the body. He bent forward, hands on knees, to recover his breath, listening to the deafening sound of the approaching SAR helicopter and feeling its wind on his damp shirt. He thought it a hideous intrusion into what was obviously a place of death. Despite the heat of the sun, the woman's skin was cold to the touch, and her widely staring eyes had begun to film. He was struck by how tiny she seemed, lying alone at the bottom of the cliff, and how sad her miniature hand looked waving in the spume.

Her nudity surprised him, the more so when it required only the briefest of glances about the beach to reveal a complete absence of towels, clothes, footwear, or possessions. He noticed bruising on her arms, neck, and chest, but it was more consistent with being tumbled over rocks on an incoming tide, he thought, than with a dive off a clifftop. He stooped again over the body, looking for anything that would indicate how it had got there, then retreated rapidly as the descending stretcher spiraled dangerously close to his head.

The noise of the helicopter and the amplified voice of the winch operator calling instructions to the man below had attracted sightseers. The party of hikers gathered on the clifftop to watch the excitement, while the yachtsmen in Chapman's Pool motored out of the bay in their dinghies to do the same. A spirit of revelry was abroad because everyone assumed the rescue wouldn't have happened unless the woman was still alive, and a small cheer went up as the stretcher rose in the air. Most thought she'd fallen from the cliff; a few thought she might have floated out of Chapman's Pool on an inflatable airbed and got into difficulties. No one guessed she'd been murdered.

Except, perhaps, Nick Ingram, who transferred the tiny, stiffening body to the stretcher and felt a dreadful anger burn inside him because Death had stolen a pretty woman's dignity. As always, the victory belonged to the thief and not to the victim.

As requested by the nine-nine-nine operator, Steven Harding shepherded the boys down the hill to the police car, which was parked beside the boat sheds, where they waited with varying degrees of patience until its occupant returned. The brothers, who had sunk into an exhausted silence after their mad dash around Chapman's Pool, wanted to be gone, but they were intimidated by their companion, a twenty-four-year-old actor, who took his responsibilities *in loco parentis* seriously.

He kept a watchful eye on his uncommunicative charges (too shocked to speak, he thought) while trying to cheer them up with a running commentary of what he could see of the rescue. He peppered his conversation with expressions like: *"You're a couple of heroes . . ." "Your mum's going to be really proud of you . . ." "She's a lucky lady to have two such sensible sons . . ."* But it wasn't until the helicopter flew toward Poole and he turned to them with a smile of encouragement, saying: "There you are, you can stop worrying now. Mum's in safe hands," that they realized his mistake. It hadn't occurred to either of them that what appeared to be general remarks about their own mother applied specifically to "the lady on the beach."

"She's not our mum," said Paul, dully.

"Our mum's going to be *really* angry," supplied Danny in his piping treble, emboldened by his brother's willingness to abandon the prolonged silence. "She said if we were late for lunch she'd make us eat bread and water for a week." (He was an inventive child.) "She's going to be even angrier when I tell her it's because Paul wanted to look at a nudie."

"Shut up," said his brother.

"*And* he made me climb the cliff so he could get a better look. Dad's going to kill him for ruining the binoculars."

"Shut *up.*"

"Yeah, well, it's all your fault. You shouldn't have dropped them. *Penis*-brain!" Danny added snidely, in the safe knowledge that their companion would protect him.

Harding watched tears of humiliation gather in the older boy's eyes. It didn't take much reading of the references to "nudie," "better look," "binoculars," and "penis-brain" to come up with a close approximation of the facts. "I hope she was worth it," he said matter-of-factly. "The first naked woman I ever saw was so old and ugly, it was three years before I wanted to look at another one. She lived in the house next to us, and she was as fat and wrinkled as an elephant."

"What was the next one like?" asked Danny with the sequential logic of a ten-year-old.

Harding exchanged a glance with the elder brother. "She had nice tits," he told Paul with a wink.

"So did this one," said Danny obligingly.

"Except she was dead," said his brother.

"She probably wasn't, you know. It's not always easy to tell when someone's dead."

"She was," said Paul despondently. "Me and Danny went down to get the binoculars back." He unraveled his bundled T-shirt to reveal the badly scratched casing of a pair of Zeiss binoculars. "I—well, I checked to make sure. I think she drowned and got left there by the tide." He fell into an unhappy silence again.

"He was going to give her mouth-to-mouth," said Danny, "but her eyes were nasty, so he didn't."

Harding cast another glance in the older brother's direction, this time sympathetic. "The police will need to identify her," he said matter-of-factly, "so they'll probably ask you to describe her." He ruffled Danny's hair. "It might be better not to mention nasty eyes or nice tits when you do it."

Danny pulled away. "I won't."

The man nodded. "Good boy." He took the binoculars from Paul and examined the lenses carefully before pointing them at the Beneteau in Chapman's Pool. "Did you recognize her?" he asked.

"No," said Paul uncomfortably.

"Was she an old lady?"

"No."

"Pretty?"

Paul wriggled his shoulders. "I guess so."

"Not fat then?"

"No. She was very little, and she had blond hair."

Harding brought the yacht into sharp focus. "They're built like tanks, these things," he murmured, traversing the sights across the bay. "Okay, the bodywork's a bit scratched, but there's nothing wrong with the lenses. Your dad won't be that angry."

Maggie Jenner would never have become involved if Bertie had responded to her whistle, but like all dogs he was deaf when he wanted to be. She had dismounted when the noise of the helicopter alarmed the horse, and natural curiosity had led her to walk him on down the hill while the rescue was under way. The three of them rounded the boat sheds together, and Bertie, overexcited by all the confusion, made a beeline for Paul Spender's crotch, shoving his nose against the boy's shorts and breathing in with hearty enthusiasm.

Maggie whistled, and was ignored. "Bertie!" she called. "Come here, boy!"

The dog was a huge, fearsome-looking brute, the result of a night on the tiles by an Irish wolfhound bitch, and saliva drooled in great white gobbets from his jaws. With a flick of his hairy head, he splattered spittle across Paul's shorts and the terrified child froze in alarm.

"Bertie!"

"It's all right," said Harding, grabbing the dog by the collar and pulling him off, "he's only being friendly." He rubbed the dog's head. "Aren't you, boy?"

Unconvinced, the brothers retreated rapidly to the other side of the police car.

"They've had a tough morning," explained Harding, clicking his tongue encouragingly and walking Bertie back to his mistress. "Will he stay put if I let him go?"

"Not in this mood," she said, pulling a lead from her back trouser pocket and clipping one end into the collar before attaching the other end to the nearest stirrup. "My brother's two boys adore him, and he doesn't understand that the rest of the world doesn't view him in quite the same way." She smiled. "You must have dogs yourself, either that or you're very brave. Most people run a mile."

"I grew up on a farm," he said, stroking Sir Jasper's nose and studying her with frank admiration.

She was a good ten years older than he was, tall and slim with shoulder-length dark hair and deep brown eyes that narrowed suspiciously under his assessing gaze. She knew exactly what type she was dealing with when he looked pointedly at her left hand for the wedding ring that wasn't there. "Well, thanks for your help," she said rather brusquely. "I can manage on my own now."

He stood back immediately. "Good luck then," he said. "It was nice meeting you."

She was all too aware that her distrust of men had now reached pathological proportions, and wondered guiltily if she'd jumped to the wrong conclusion. "I hope your boys weren't too frightened," she said rather more warmly.

He gave an easy laugh. "They're not mine," he told her. "I'm just looking after them till the police get back. They found a dead woman on the beach, so they're pretty shook up, poor kids. You'd be doing them a favor if you persuaded them Bertie's just an overgrown hearth rug. I'm not convinced that adding canophobia to necrophobia all in one morning is good psychology."

She looked undecidedly toward the police car. The boys did look frightened, she thought, and she didn't particularly want the responsibility of inspiring a lifelong fear of dogs in them.

"Why don't we invite them over," he suggested, sensing her hesitation, "and let them pat him while he's under control? It'll only take a minute or two."

"All right," she agreed halfheartedly, "if you think it would help." But it was against her better judgment. She had the feeling that once again she was being drawn into something she wouldn't be able to control.

It was after midday by the time PC Ingram returned to his car to find Maggie Jenner, Steven Harding, and the Spender brothers waiting beside it. Sir Jasper and Bertie stood at a distance, secure in the shade of a tree, and the aesthete in Nick Ingram could only admire the way the woman displayed herself. Sometimes he thought she had no idea how attractive she was; other times, like now, when she placed herself side by side with natural, equine, and human beauty, demanding comparison, he suspected the pose was deliberate. He mopped his forehead with a large white handkerchief, wondering irritably who the

Chippendale was and how both he and Maggie managed to look so cool in the intolerable heat of that Sunday morning. They were looking at him and laughing, and he assumed, in the eternal way of human nature, they were laughing at him.

"Good morning, Miss Jenner," he said with exaggerated politeness.

She gave a small nod in return. "Nick."

He turned inquiringly to Harding. "Can I help you, sir?"

"I don't think so," said the young man with an engaging smile. "I think we're supposed to be helping you."

Ingram was Dorsetshire born and bred and had no time for wankers in dinky shorts, sporting artificial tans. "In what way?" There was a hint of sarcasm in his voice that made Maggie Jenner frown at him.

"I was asked to bring these boys to the police car when I made the emergency call. They're the ones who found the dead woman." He clapped his hands across their shoulders. "They're a couple of heroes. Maggie and I have just been telling them they deserve medals."

The "Maggie" wasn't lost on Ingram, although he questioned her enthusiasm for being on Christian-name terms with such an obvious poser. She had better taste, he thought. Ponderously, he shifted his attention to Paul and Danny Spender. The message he had received couldn't have been clearer. Two boys had reported seeing their mother fall from a cliff while using a pair of binoculars. He knew as soon as he saw the body—not enough bruises—that it couldn't have fallen, and looking at the boys now—too relaxed—he doubted the rest of the information. "Did you know the woman?" he asked them.

They shook their heads.

He unlocked his car door and retrieved a notebook and pencil from the passenger seat. "What makes you think she was dead, sir?" he asked Harding.

"The boys told me."

"Is that right?" He examined the young man curiously, then deliberately licked the point of his pencil because he knew it would annoy Maggie. "May I have your name and address, please, plus the name of your employer if you have one?"

"Steven Harding. I'm an actor." He gave an address in London. "I live there during the week, but if you have trouble getting hold of me you can always go through my agent, Graham Barlow of the Barlow Agency." He gave another London address. "Graham keeps my diary," he said.

Bully for Graham, thought Ingram sourly, struggling to suppress rampant prejudices against pretty boys . . . Chippendales . . . Londoners . . . actors . . . Harding's address was Highbury, and Ingram would put money on the little poser claiming to be an Arsenal fan, not because he'd ever been to a match but because he'd read *Fever Pitch,* or seen the movie. "And what brings an actor to our neck of the woods, Mr. Harding?"

Harding explained that he was in Poole for a weekend break and had planned to walk to Lulworth Cove and back that day. He patted the mobile telephone that was attached via a clip to his waistband, and said it was a good thing he *had,* otherwise the boys would have had to hoof it to Worth Matravers for help.

"You travel light," said Ingram, glancing at the phone. "Aren't you worried about dehydrating? It's a long walk to Lulworth."

The young man shrugged. "I've changed my mind. I'm going back after this. I hadn't realized how far it was."

Ingram asked the boys for their names and addresses together with a brief description of what had happened. They told him they'd seen the woman on the beach when they rounded Egmont Point at ten o'clock. "And then what?" he asked. "You checked to see if she was dead and went for help?"

They nodded.

"You didn't hurry yourselves, did you?"

"They ran like the clappers," said Harding, leaping to their defense. "I saw them."

"As I recall, sir, your emergency call was timed at ten forty-three, and it doesn't take nearly three-quarters of an hour for two healthy lads to run around Chapman's Pool." He stared Harding down. "And while we're on the subject of misleading information, perhaps you'd care to explain why I received a message saying two boys had seen their mother fall from a cliff top after using a pair of binoculars?"

Maggie made a move as if she was about to say something in support of the boys, but Ingram's intimidating glance in her direction changed her mind.

"Okay, well, it was a misunderstanding," said Harding, flicking his thick dark hair out of his eyes with a toss of his head. "These two guys"—he put a friendly arm across Paul's shoulders—"came charging up the hill shouting and yelling about a woman on the beach beyond the Point and some binoculars falling, and I rather stupidly put two and two together and made five. The truth is, we were all a bit het-up. *They* were worried about the binoculars, and *I* thought they were talking about their mother." He took the Zeisses from Paul's hands and gave them to Ingram. "These belong to their father. The boys dropped them by accident when they saw the woman. They're very concerned about how their dad's going to react when he sees the damage, but Maggie and I have persuaded them he won't be angry, not when he hears what a good job they've done."

"Do you know the boys' father, sir?" asked Ingram, examining the binoculars.

"No, of course not. I've only just met them."

"Then you've only their word that these belong to him?"

"Well, yes, I suppose so." Harding looked uncertainly at Paul and saw the return of panic in the boy's eyes. "Oh, come on," he said abruptly. "Where else could they have got them?"

"Off the beach. You said you saw the woman when you rounded Egmont Point," he reminded Paul and Danny.

They nodded in petrified unison.

"Then why do these binoculars look as if they've fallen down a cliff? Did you find them beside the woman and decide to take them?"

The boys, growing red in the face with anxiety about their Peeping Tom act, looked guilty. Neither answered.

"Look, lighten up," said Harding unwarily. "It was a bit of fun, that's all. The woman was nude, so they climbed up for a better look. They didn't realize she was dead until they dropped the binoculars and went down to get them."

"You saw all this, did you, sir?"

"No," he admitted. "I've already told you I was coming from St. Alban's Head."

Ingram turned to his right to look at the distant promontory topped by its tiny Norman chapel, dedicated to St. Alban. "You get a very good view of Egmont Bight from up there," he said idly, "particularly on a fine day like this."

"Only through binoculars," said Harding.

Ingram smiled as he looked the young man up and down. "True," he agreed. "So where did you and the boys run into each other?"

Harding gestured toward the coastal path. "They started shouting at me when they were halfway up Emmetts Hill, so I went down to meet them."

"You seem to know the area well."

"I do."

"How come, when you live in London?"

"I spend a lot of time here. London can be pretty hellish in the summer."

Ingram glanced up the steep hillside. "This is called West Hill," he remarked. "Emmetts Hill is the next one along."

Harding gave an amiable shrug. "Okay, so I don't know it *that* well, but normally I come in by boat," he said, "and there's no mention of West Hill on the Admiralty charts. This whole escarpment is referred to as Emmetts Hill. The boys and I ran into each other approximately there." He pointed toward a spot on the green hillside above them.

Out of the corner of his eye, Ingram noticed Paul Spender's frown of disagreement, but he didn't remark on it.

"Where's your boat now, Mr. Harding?"

"Poole. I sailed her in late last night, but as the wind's almost nonexistent and I fancied some exercise"—he favored Nick Ingram with a boyish smile—"I took to my legs."

"What's the name of your boat, Mr. Harding?"

"*Crazy Daze.* It's a play on words. Daze is spelled D-A-Z-E, not D-A-Y-S."

The tall policeman's smile was anything but boyish. "Where's she normally berthed?"

"Lymington."

"Did you come from Lymington yesterday?"

"Yes."

"Alone?"

There was a tiny hesitation. "Yes."

Ingram held his gaze for a moment. "Are you sailing back tonight?"

"That's the plan, although I'll probably have to motor if the wind doesn't improve."

The constable nodded in apparent satisfaction. "Well, thank you very much, Mr. Harding. I don't think I need detain you any longer. I'll get these boys home and check on the binoculars."

Harding felt Paul and Danny sidle in behind him for protection. "You will point out what a good job they've done, won't you?" he urged. "I mean, but for these two, that poor little woman could have floated out on the next tide, and you'd never have known she was there. They deserve a medal, not aggro from their father."

"You're very well informed, sir."

"Trust me. I know this coast. There's a continuous south-southeasterly stream running toward St. Alban's Head, and if she'd been sucked into that, the chances of her resurfacing would have been nil. It's got one hell of a back eddy on it. My guess is she'd have been pounded to pieces on the bottom."

Ingram smiled. "I meant you were well informed about the woman, Mr. Harding. Anyone would think you'd seen her yourself."

CHAPTER 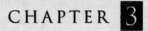 3

W*hy were you so hard on him?"* asked Maggie critically as the policeman shut the boys into the back of his Range Rover and stood with eyes narrowed against the sun watching Harding walk away up the hill. Ingram was so tall and so solidly built that he cast her literally and figuratively into the shade, and he would get under her skin less, she often thought, if just once in a while he recognized that fact. She only felt comfortable in his presence when she was looking down on him from the back of a horse, but those occasions were too rare for her self-esteem to benefit from them. When he didn't answer her, she glanced impatiently toward the brothers on the backseat. "You were pretty rough on the children, too. I bet they'll think twice before helping the police again."

Harding disappeared from sight around a bend, and Ingram turned to her with a lazy smile. "How was I hard on him, Miss Jenner?"

"Oh, come on! You all but accused him of lying."

"He *was* lying."

"What about?"

"I'm not sure yet. I'll know when I've made a few inquiries."

"Is this a male thing?" she asked in a voice made silky by long-pent-up grudges. He had been her community policeman for five years, and she had much to feel resentful for. At times of deep depression, she blamed him for everything. Other times, she was honest enough to admit that he had only been doing his job.

"Probably." He could smell the stables on her clothes, a musty scent of hay dust and horse manure that he half liked and half loathed.

"Then wouldn't it have been simpler just to whip out your willy and challenge him to a knob-measuring contest?" she asked sarcastically.

"I'd have lost."

"That's for sure," she agreed.

His smile widened. "You noticed then?"

"I could hardly avoid it. He wasn't wearing those shorts to disguise anything. Perhaps it was his wallet. There was precious little room for it anywhere else."

"No," he agreed. "Didn't you find that interesting?"

She looked at him suspiciously, wondering if he was making fun of her. "In what way?"

"Only an idiot sets out from Poole for Lulworth with no money and no water. That's twenty-five miles."

"Maybe he was planning to beg water off passersby or telephone a friend to come and rescue him. Why is it important? All he did was play the Good Samaritan to those kids."

"I think he was lying about what he was doing here. Did he give a different explanation before I got back?"

She thought about it. "We talked about dogs and horses. He was telling the boys about the farm he grew up on in Cornwall."

He reached for the handle on the driver's-side door. "Then perhaps I'm just suspicious of people who carry mobile telephones," he said.

"Everyone has them these days, including me."

He ran an amused eye over her slender figure in its tight cotton shirt and stretch jeans. "But you don't bring yours on country rambles, whereas that young man does. Apparently he leaves everything behind except his phone."

"You should be grateful," she said tartly. "But for him, you'd never have got to the woman so quickly."

"I agree," he said without rancor. "Mr. Harding was in the right place at the right time with the right equipment to report a body on a beach, and it would be churlish to ask why." He opened the door and squeezed his huge frame in behind the wheel. "Good day, Miss Jenner," he said politely. "My regards to your mother." He pulled the door closed and fired the engine.

The Spender brothers were of two minds whom to thank for their untroubled return home. The actor, because his pleas for tolerance worked? Or the policeman, because he was a decent bloke after all? He had said very little on the drive back to their rented cottage other than to warn them that the cliffs were dangerous and that it was foolish to climb them, however tempting the reason. To their parents he gave a brief, expurgated account of what had happened, ending with the suggestion that, as the boys' fishing had been interrupted by the events of the morning, he would be happy to take them out on his boat one evening. "It's not a motor cruiser," he warned them, "just a small fishing boat, but the sea bass run at this time of year, and if we're lucky we might catch one or two." He didn't put his arms around their shoulders or call them heroes, but he did give them something to look forward to.

Next on Ingram's agenda was an isolated farmhouse where the elderly occupants had reported the theft of three valuable paintings during the night. He had been on his way there when he was diverted to Chapman's Pool, and while he guessed he was wasting his time, community policing was what he was paid for.

"Oh God, Nick, I'm so sorry," said the couple's harassed daughter-in-law, who, herself, was on the wrong side of seventy. "Believe me, they did *know* the paintings were being auctioned. Peter's been talking them through it for the last twelve months, but they're so forgetful, he has to start again from scratch every time. He has power of attorney, so it's all quite legal, but, honestly, I nearly *died* when Winnie said she'd called you. And on a *Sunday,* too. I come over every morning to make sure they're all right, but *sometimes* . . ." She rolled her eyes to heaven, expressing without the need for words exactly what she thought of her ninety-five-year-old parents-in-law.

"It's what I'm here for, Jane," he said, giving her shoulder an encouraging pat.

"No it's not. You should be out catching criminals," she said, echoing the words of people across the nation who saw the police only as thief-takers. She heaved a huge sigh. "The trouble is their outgoings are way in excess of their income, and they're incapable of grasping the fact. The home help *alone* costs over ten thousand pounds a year. Peter's having to sell off the family silver to make ends meet. The silly old things seem to think they're living in the nineteen-twenties, when a housemaid cost five bob a week. It drives me mad, it really does. They ought to be in a home, but Peter's too soft-hearted to put them there. *Not* that they could afford it. I mean *we* can't afford it, so how could they? It would be different if Celia Jenner hadn't persuaded us to gamble everything on that beastly husband of Maggie's but . . ." She broke off on a shrug of despair. "I get so angry sometimes I could scream, and the only thing that stops me is that I'm afraid the scream would go on forever."

"Nothing lasts forever," he said.

"I know," she said mutinously, "but once in a while I think about giving eternity a hand. It's such a pity you can't buy arsenic anymore. It was so easy in the old days."

"Tell me about it."

She laughed. "You know what I mean."

"Should I order a postmortem when Peter's parents finally pop their clogs?"

"Chance'd be a fine thing. At this rate I'll be dead long before they are."

The tall policeman smiled and made his farewells. He didn't want to hear about death. *He could still feel the touch of the woman's flesh on his hands. . . .* He needed a shower, he thought, as he made his way back to his car.

The blond toddler marched steadfastly along the pavement in the Lilliput area of Poole, planting one chubby leg in front of the other. It was 10:30 on Sunday morning, so people were scarce, and no one took the trouble to find out why she was alone. When a handful of witnesses came forward later to admit to the police that they'd seen her, the excuses varied. *"She seemed to know where she was going." "There was a woman about twenty yards behind her and I thought she was the child's mother." "I assumed someone else would stop." "I was in a hurry." "I'm a bloke. I'd have been strung up for giving a lift to a little girl."*

In the end it was an elderly couple, Mr. and Mrs. Green, who had the sense, the time, and the courage to interfere. They were on their way back from church, and as they did every week, they made a nostalgic detour through Lilliput to look at the art deco buildings that had somehow survived the postwar craze for mass demolition of anything out of the ordinary in favor of constructing reinforced concrete blocks and red-brick boxes. Lilliput sprawled along the eastern curve of Poole Bay, and amid the architectural dross that could be found anywhere were elegant villas in manicured gardens and art deco houses with windows like portholes. The Greens adored it. It reminded them of their youth.

They were passing the turning to Salterns Marina when Mrs. Green noticed the little girl. "Look at that," she said disapprovingly. "What sort of mother would let a child of that age get so far ahead of her? It only takes a stumble and she'd be under a car."

Mr. Green slowed. "Where's the mother?" he asked.

His wife twisted in her seat. "Do you know, I'm not sure. I thought it was that woman behind her, but she's looking in a shop window."

Mr. Green was a retired sergeant major. "We should do something," he said firmly, drawing to a halt and putting the car into reverse. He shook his fist at a motorist who hooted ferociously after missing his back bumper by the skin of his teeth. "Bloody Sunday drivers," he said, "they shouldn't be allowed on the road."

"Quite right, dear," said Mrs. Green, opening her door.

She scooped the poor little mite into her arms and set her comfortably on her knee while her eighty-year-old husband drove to the Poole police station. It was a tortuous journey because his preferred speed was twenty miles an hour, and this caused mayhem in the one-way system around the civic center roundabout.

The child seemed completely at ease in the car, smiling happily out of the window, but once inside the police station, it proved impossible to prize her away from her rescuer. She locked her arms about the elderly woman's neck, hiding her face against her shoulder, and clung to kindness as tenaciously as a barnacle clings to a rock. Upon learning that no one had reported a toddler missing, Mr. and Mrs. Green set themselves down with commendable patience and prepared for a long wait.

"I can't understand why her mother hasn't noticed she's gone," said Mrs. Green. "I never allowed my own children out of sight for a minute."

"Maybe she's at work," said the woman police constable who had been detailed to make the inquiries.

"Well, she shouldn't be," said Mr. Green reprovingly. "A child of this age needs her mother with her." He pulled a knowing expression in WPC Griffiths's direction which resolved itself into a series of peculiar facial jerks. "You should get a doctor to examine her. Know what I'm saying? Odd people about these days. Men who should know better. Get my meaning?" He spelled it out. "P-E-do-*files*. S-E-X criminals. Know what I'm saying?"

"Yes, sir, I know exactly what you're saying, and don't worry"—the WPC tapped her pen on the paper in front of her—"the doctor's at the top of my list. But if you don't mind, we'll take it gently. We've had a lot of dealings with this kind of thing, and we've found the best method is not to rush at it." She turned to the woman with an encouraging smile. "Has she told you her name?"

Mrs. Green shook her head. "She hasn't said a word, dear. To be honest, I'm not sure she can."

"How old do you think she is?"

"Eighteen months, two at the most." She lifted the edge of the child's cotton dress to reveal a pair of disposable training pants. "She's still in nappies, poor little thing."

The WPC thought two years old was an underestimation, and added a year for the purposes of the paperwork. Women like Mrs. Green had reared their children on cloth diapers and, because of the washing involved, had had them potty-trained early. The idea that a three-year-old might still be in nappies was incomprehensible to them.

Not that it made any difference as far as this little girl was concerned. Whether she was eighteen months old, two years old or three, she clearly wasn't talking.

With nothing else to occupy her that Sunday afternoon, the French girl from the Beneteau, who had been an interested observer of Harding's conversations with the Spender brothers, Maggie Jenner, and PC Ingram through the video camera's zoom lens, rowed herself into shore and walked up the steep slope of West Hill to try to work out for herself what the mystery had been about. It wasn't hard to guess that the two boys had found the person who had been winched off the beach by helicopter, nor that the handsome Englishman had reported it to the police for them, but she was curious about why he had reemerged on the hillside half an hour after the police car's departure to retrieve the rucksack he'd abandoned there. She had watched him take out some binoculars and scan the bay and the cliffs before making his way down to the foreshore beyond the boat sheds. She had filmed him for several minutes, staring out to sea, but she was no wiser, having reached his vantage point above Chapman's Pool, than she'd been before, and thoroughly bored, she abandoned the puzzle.

It would be another five days before her father came across the tape and humiliated her in front of the English police. . . .

At six o'clock that evening the Fairline Squadron weighed anchor and motored gently out of Chapman's Pool in the direction of St. Alban's Head. Two languid girls sat on either side of their father on the flying bridge, while his latest companion sat, alone and excluded, on the seat behind them. Once clear of the shallow waters at the mouth of the bay, the boat roared to full power and made off at twenty-five knots on the return journey to Poole, carving a V-shaped wake out of the flat sea behind it.

Heat and alcohol had made them all soporific, particularly the father, who had overexerted himself in his efforts to please his daughters, and after setting the autopilot he appointed the elder one lookout before closing his eyes. He could feel the daggers of his girlfriend's fury carving away at his back, and with a stifled sigh, wished he'd had the sense to leave her behind. She was the latest in a string of what his daughters called his "bimbos," and as usual, they had set out to trample on the fragile shoots of his new relationship. Life, he thought resentfully, was bloody . . .

"Watch out, Dad!" his daughter screamed in sudden alarm. "We're heading straight for a rock."

The man's heart thudded against his chest as he wrenched the wheel violently, slewing the boat to starboard, and what his daughter had thought was a rock slid past on the port side to dance in the boisterous wake. "I'm too old for all of this," he said shakily, steering his three-hundred-thousand-pound boat back on to course and mentally checking the current state of his insurance. "What the hell was it? It can't have been a rock. There are no rocks out here."

The two youngsters, eyes watering, squinted into the burning sun to make out the black, bobbing shape behind them. "It looks like one of those big oil drums," said the elder.

"Jesus wept," growled her father. "Whoever let that wash overboard deserves to be shot. It could have ripped us open if we'd hit it."

His girlfriend, still twisted around, thought it looked more like an upturned dinghy but was reluctant to voice an opinion for fear of attracting any more of his beastly daughters' derision. She'd had a bucketful already that day and heartily wished she had never agreed to come out with them.

I bumped into Nick Ingram this morning," said Maggie as she made a pot of tea in her mother's kitchen at Broxton House.

It had been a beautiful room once, lined with old oak dressers, each one piled with copper pans and ornate crockery, and with an eight-foot-long, seventeenth-century refectory table down its middle. Now it was merely drab. Everything worth selling had been sold. Cheap white wall and floor units had replaced the wooden dressers, and a molded plastic excrescence from the garden stood where the monks' table had reigned resplendent. It wouldn't be so bad, Maggie often thought, if the room was cleaned occasionally, but her mother's arthritis and her own terminal exhaustion from trying to make money out of horses meant that cleanliness had long since gone the way of godliness. If God was in his heaven and all was right with the world, then he had a peculiar blind spot when it came to Broxton House. Maggie would have cut her losses and moved away long ago if only her mother had agreed to do the same. Guilt enslaved her. Now she lived in a flat over the stables on the other side of the garden and made only intermittent visits to the house. Its awful emptiness was too obvious a reminder that her mother's poverty was her fault.

"I took Jasper down to Chapman's Pool. A woman drowned in Egmont Bight, and Nick had to guide the helicopter in to pick up the body."

"A tourist, I suppose?"

"Presumably," said Maggie, handing her a cup. "Nick would have said if it was someone local."

"Typical!" snorted Celia crossly. "So Dorset will foot the bill for the helicopter because some inept creature from another county never learned to swim properly. I've a good mind to withhold my taxes."

"You usually do," said Maggie, thinking of the final reminders that littered the desk in the drawing room.

Her mother ignored the remark. "How was Nick?"

"Hot," said her daughter, remembering how red-faced he had been when he returned to the car, "and not in the best of moods." She stared into her tea, screwing up the courage to address the thorny issue of money, or more accurately lack of money, coming into the riding and livery business she ran from the Broxton House stableyard. "We need to talk about the stables," she said abruptly.

Celia refused to be drawn. "You wouldn't have been in a good mood either if you'd just seen a drowned body." Her tone became conversational as a prelude to a series of anecdotes. "I remember seeing one floating down the Ganges when I was staying with my parents in India. It was the summer holidays. I think I was about fifteen at the time. It was a horrible thing, gave me nightmares for weeks. My mother said . . ."

Maggie stopped listening and fixed instead on a long black hair growing out of her mother's chin which needed plucking. It bristled aggressively as she spoke, like one of Bertie's whiskers, but they'd never had the kind of relationship that meant Maggie could tell her about it. Celia, at sixty-three, was still a good-looking woman with the same dark brown hair as her daughter, touched up from time to time with Harmony color rinses, but the worry of their straitened circumstances had taken a heavy toll in the deep lines around her mouth and eyes.

When she finally drew breath, Maggie reverted immediately to the subject of the stables. "I've been totting up last month's receipts," she said, "and we're about two hundred quid short. Did you let Mary Spencer-Graham off paying again?"

Celia's mouth thinned. "If I did it's my affair."

"No it's not, Ma," said Maggie with a sigh. "We can't afford to be charitable. If Mary doesn't pay, then we can't look after her horse. It's as simple as that. I wouldn't mind so much if we weren't already charging her the absolute minimum, but the fees barely cover Moondust's fodder. You really must be a bit tougher with her."

"How can I? She's almost as badly off as we are, and it's our fault."

Maggie shook her head. "That's not true. She lost ten thousand pounds, peanuts compared with what we lost, but she knows she only has to turn on the waterworks for half a second and you fall for it every time." She gestured impatiently toward the hall and the drawing room beyond. "We can't pay the bills if we don't collect the money, which means we either decide to hand everything over now to Matthew and go and live in a council flat, or you go to him, cap in hand, and beg for some kind of allowance." She gave a helpless shrug at the thought of her brother. "If I believed there was any point in my trying, I would, but we both know he'd slam the door in my face."

Celia gave a mirthless laugh. "What makes you think it would be any different if I tried? That wife of his can't stand me. She'd never agree to keeping her mother-in-law and sister-in-law in what she chooses to call the lap of luxury when her real pleasure in life would be to see us destitute."

"I know," said Maggie guiltily, "and it serves us right. We should never have been rude about her wedding dress."

"It was difficult not to be," said Celia tartly. "The vicar nearly had a heart attack when he saw her."

Her daughter's eyes filled with humor. "It was the greenfly that did it. If there hadn't been a plague of the blasted things the year they got married, and if her wretched veil hadn't collected every single one in a twenty-mile radius while she walked from the church to the reception . . . What was it you called her? Something to do with camouflage."

"I didn't call her anything," said Celia with dignity. "I congratulated her for blending so well into her surroundings."

Maggie laughed. "That's right, I remember now. God, you were rude."

"You found it funny at the time," her mother pointed out, easing her bad hip on the chair. "I'll talk to Mary," she promised. "I can probably bear the humiliation of dunning my friends rather better than I can bear the humiliation of begging off Matthew and Ava."

CHAPTER 4

**Physical/psychological assessment of unidentified toddler:
"Baby Smith"**

Physical: The child's general health is excellent. She is well
nourished and well cared for, and is not suffering from any disease or ailment. Blood test indicates minute traces of benzodiazepine (possibly Mogadon) and stronger traces of
paracetamol in her system. There is no evidence of past or
recent abuse, sexual or physical, although there is some evidence (see below) that she has suffered past, continuing, or
recent psychological trauma. The physical evidence suggests
that she was separated from her parent/guardian within 3–4
hours of being found—most notably in terms of her overall
cleanliness and the fact that she hadn't soiled herself. In addition she showed no signs of dehydration, hypothermia, hunger,
or exhaustion, which would have been expected in a child who
had been abandoned for any length of time.

Psychological: The child's behavior and social skills are typical of a two-year-old; however, her size and weight suggest she

is older. She presents evidence of mild autism, although knowledge of her history is needed to confirm a diagnosis. She is uninterested in other people/children and reacts aggressively when approached by them. She is overly passive, preferring to sit and observe rather than explore her environment. She is unnaturally withdrawn and makes no attempt to communicate verbally, although will use sign language to achieve what she wants. Her hearing is unimpaired, and she listens to everything that's said to her; however, she is selective about which instructions she chooses to obey. As a simple example, she is happy to point to a blue cube when asked, but refuses to pick it up.

While she is unable or unwilling to use words to communicate, she resorts very quickly to screams and tantrums when her wishes are thwarted or when she feels herself stressed. This is particularly evident when strangers enter the room or when voices rise above a monotone. She invariably refuses any sort of physical contact on a first meeting but holds out her arms to be picked up on a second. This would indicate good recognition skills, yet she evinces a strong fear of men and screams in terror whenever they intrude into her space. In the absence of any indication of physical or sexual abuse, this fear may stem from: unfamiliarity with men as a result of being raised in a sheltered, all-female environment; witnessing male aggression against another—e.g. mother or sibling.

Conclusions: In view of the child's backward development and apparent stress-related disorders, she should not be returned to her family/guardians without exhaustive inquiries being made about the nature of the household. It is also imperative that she be placed on the "at risk" register to allow continuous monitoring of her future welfare. I am seriously concerned about the traces of benzodiazepine and paracetamol in her bloodstream. Benzodiazepine (a strong hypnotic) is not recommended for children, and certainly not in conjunction with paracetamol. I suspect the child was sedated but can think of no legitimate reason why this should have been necessary.

N.B. Without knowing more of the child's history, it is difficult to say whether her behavior is due to: (1) autism; (2) psychiatric trauma; (3) taught dependence, which, while leaving her ignorant of her own capabilities, has encouraged her to be consciously manipulative.

Dr. Janet Murray

CHAPTER

I t had been a long twenty-four hours, and WPC Sandra Griffiths was yawning as her telephone started to ring again at noon on Monday. She had done several local radio and television interviews to publicize the abandonment of Lily (named after Lilliput, where she was found), but although the response to the programs had been good, not one caller had been able to tell her who the child was. She blamed the weather. Too many people were out in the sunshine; too few watching their sets. She stifled the yawn as she picked up the receiver.

The man at the other end sounded worried. "I'm sorry to bother you," he told her, "but I've just had my mother on the phone. She's incredibly het-up about some toddler who looks like my daughter wandering the streets. I've told her it can't possibly be Hannah, but"—he paused— "well, the thing is we've both tried phoning my wife, and neither of us can get an answer."

Griffiths tucked the receiver under her chin and reached for a pen. This was the twenty-fifth father to phone since the toddler's photograph had been broadcast, and all were estranged from their wives and children. She had no higher hopes of this one than she'd had of the previous twenty-four, but she went through the motions willingly enough. "If you'll answer one or two questions for me, sir, we can establish very quickly whether the little girl is Hannah. May I have your name and address?"

"William Sumner, Langton Cottage, Rope Walk, Lymington, Hampshire."

"And do your wife and daughter still live with you, Mr. Sumner?"

"Yes."

Her interest sharpened immediately. "When did you last see them?"

"Four days ago. I'm at a pharmaceutical conference in Liverpool. I spoke to Kate—that's my wife—on Friday night and everything was fine, but my mother's positive this toddler's Hannah. It doesn't make sense though. Mum says she was found in Poole yesterday, but how could Hannah be wandering around Poole on her own when we live in Lymington?"

Griffiths listened to the rising alarm in his voice. "Are you phoning from Liverpool now?" she asked calmly.

"Yes. I'm staying in the Regal, room number two-two-three-five. What should I do? My mother's beside herself with worry. I need to reassure her that everything's all right."

And yourself, too, she thought. "Could you give me a description of Hannah?"

"She looks like her mother," he said rather helplessly. "Blond, blue eyes. She doesn't talk very much. We've been worrying about it, but the doctor says it's just shyness."

"How old is she?"

"She'll be three next month."

The policewoman winced in sympathy as she put the next question, guessing what his answer was going to be. "Does Hannah have a pink cotton dress with smocking on it and a pair of red sandals, Mr. Sumner?"

It took him a second or two to answer. "I don't know about the sandals," he said with difficulty, "but my mother bought her a smocked dress about three months ago. I think it was pink—no, it *was* pink. Oh God"—his voice broke—"where's Kate?"

She waited a moment. "Did you drive to Liverpool, Mr. Sumner?"

"Yes."

"Do you know roughly how long it will take you to get home?"

"Five hours maybe."

"And where does your mother live?"

"Chichester."

"Then I think you'd better give me her name and address, sir. If the little girl *is* Hannah, then she can identify her for us. Meantime I'll ask Lymington police to check your house while I make inquiries about your wife here in Poole."

"Mrs. Angela Sumner, Flat Two, The Old Convent, Osborne Crescent, Chichester." His breathing became labored—*with tears?*—and Griffiths wished herself a million miles away. How she hated the fact that, nine times out of ten, she was the harbinger of bad news. "But there's no way she can get to Poole. She's been in a wheelchair for the last three years and can't drive. If she could, she'd have gone to Lymington to check on Kate and Hannah herself. Can't I make the identification?"

"By all means, if that's what you prefer. The little girl's in the care of a foster family at the moment, and it won't harm her to stay there a few more hours."

"My mother's convinced Hannah's been abused by some man. Is that what's happened? I'd rather know now than later."

"Assuming the little girl is Hannah, then, no, there's no evidence of any sort of physical abuse. She's been thoroughly checked, and the police doctor's satisfied that she hasn't been harmed in any way." She glossed over Dr.

Murray's damning psychological assessment. If Lily were indeed Hannah Sumner, then that particular issue would have to be taken up later.

"What kind of inquiries can you make about my wife in Poole?" he asked in bewilderment, reverting to what she'd said previously. "I told you, we live in Lymington."

The hospital kind . . . "Routine ones, Mr. Sumner. It would help if you could give me her full name and a description of her. Also the type, color, and registration number of her car, and the names of any friends she has in the area."

"Kate Elizabeth Sumner. She's thirty-one, about five feet tall, and blond. The car's a blue Metro, registration F-five-two VXY, but I don't think she knows anyone in Poole. Could she have been taken to hospital? Could something have gone wrong with the pregnancy?"

"It's one of the things I'll be checking, Mr. Sumner." She was flicking through the accident reports on the computer while she was talking to him, but there was no mention of a blue Metro with that registration being involved in a road accident. "Are your wife's parents living? Would they know where she is?"

"No. Her mother died five years ago, and she never knew her father."

"Brothers? Sisters?"

"She hasn't got anyone except me and Hannah." His voice broke again. "What am I going to do? I won't be able to cope if something's happened to her."

"There's no reason to think anything's happened," said Griffiths firmly, while believing the exact opposite. "Do you have a mobile telephone in your car? If so I can keep you up to date as you drive down."

"No."

"Then I suggest you break your journey at the halfway mark to ring from a callbox. I should have news from the Lymington police by then, and with luck I'll be able to set your mind at rest about Kate. And try not to worry, Mr. Sumner," she finished kindly. "It's a long drive from Liverpool, and the important thing is to get yourself back in one piece."

She put through a call to the Lymington police, explaining the details of the case and asking for a check to be made of Sumner's address, then as a matter of routine dialed the Regal Hotel in Liverpool to inquire whether a Mr. William Sumner had been registered in room two-two-three-five since Thursday. "Yes, ma'am," said the receptionist, "but I can't put you through, I'm afraid. He left five minutes ago."

Reluctantly, she started on the list of hospitals.

For various reasons, Nick Ingram had no ambitions to move away from his rural police station, where life revolved around community policing and the hours were predictable. Major cases were handled thirty miles away at County HQ Winfrith, and this left him free to deal with the less glamorous side of policing, which for ninety-five percent of the population was the only side that mattered. People slept sounder in their beds knowing that PC Ingram had zero tolerance for lager louts, vandals, and petty thieves.

Real trouble usually came from outside, and the unidentified woman on the beach looked like being a case in point, he thought, when a call came through from Winfrith at 12:45 P.M. on Monday, 11 August. The coroner's office at Poole had ordered a murder inquiry following the postmortem, and he was told to expect a DI and a DS from headquarters within the hour. A scene-of-crime team had already been dispatched to search the beach at Egmont Bight, but Ingram was requested to stay where he was.

"I don't think they'll find anything," he said helpfully. "I had a bit of a scout around yesterday, but it was fairly obvious the sea had washed her up."

"I suggest you leave that to us," said the unemotional voice at the other end.

Ingram gave a shrug at his end. "What did she die of?"

"Drowning," came the blunt response. "She was thrown into the open sea after an attempt at manual strangulation which failed. The pathologist guesstimates she swam half a mile to try and save herself before she gave up from exhaustion. She was fourteen weeks pregnant, and her killer held her down and raped her before pitching her over the side."

Ingram was shocked. "What sort of man would do that?"

"An unpleasant one. We'll see you in an hour."

Griffiths drew a series of blanks with the name Kate Sumner—there was no record of her at any hospital in Dorset or Hampshire. It was only when she made a routine check through Winfrith to see if there was any information on the whereabouts of a small blond woman, aged thirty-one, who appeared to have gone missing from Lymington within the last forty-eight hours, that the scattered pieces of the jigsaw began to come together.

The two detectives arrived punctually for their meeting with PC Ingram. The sergeant, an arrogant, pushy type with ambitions to join the Met, who clearly believed that every conversation was an opportunity to impress, went down like a lead balloon with his rural colleague, and Ingram was never able afterward to remember his name. He talked in bullet points: "reference a major investigation" in which "speed was of the essence" before the murderer had a chance to get rid of evidence and/or strike again. Local marinas, yacht clubs, and harbors were being "targeted" for information on the victim and/or her killer. Victim identification was the "first priority." They had a possible lead on a missing female, but no one was counting chickens until her husband identified a photograph and/or the body. The second priority was to locate the boat she'd come off and give forensics a chance to strip it top-to-bottom in search of nonintimate samples that would connect it to the body. Give us a suspect, he suggested, and DNA testing would do the rest.

Ingram raised an eyebrow when the monologue came to an end but didn't say anything.

"Did you follow all that?" asked the sergeant impatiently.

"I think so, si-rr," he said in a broad Dorsetshire burr, resisting the temptation to tug his forelock. "If you find some of her hairs on a man's boat, that'll mean he's the rapist."

"Near enough."

"That's amazing, sir-rr," murmured Ingram.

"You don't sound convinced," said DI Galbraith, watching his performance with amusement.

He shrugged and reverted to his normal accent. "The only thing that nonintimate samples will prove is that she visited his boat at least once, and that's not proof of rape. The only useful DNA tests will have to be done on her."

"Well, don't hold your breath," the DI warned. "Water doesn't leave trace evidence. The pathologist's taken swabs, but he's not optimistic about getting a result. Either she was in the sea too long and anything useful was flushed away, or her attacker was wearing a condom." He was a pleasant-looking man with cropped ginger hair and a smiling, freckled face that made him look younger than his forty-two years. It also belied a sharp intelligence that caught people unawares if they were foolish enough to stereotype him by his appearance.

"How long was long?" asked Ingram with genuine curiosity. "Put it this way, how does the pathologist know she swam half a mile? It's a very precise estimate for an unpredictable stretch of water."

"He based it on the condition of the body, prevailing winds and currents, and the fact that she must have been alive when she reached the shelter of Egmont Point," said John Galbraith, opening his briefcase and extracting a sheet of paper. "Victim died of drowning at or around high tide, which was at one fifty-two A.M. British Summer Time on Sunday, ten August," he said, skip-reading the document. "Several indicators, such as evidence of hypothermia, the fact that a keeled boat couldn't have sailed too close to the cliffs, and the currents around St. Alban's Head suggest she entered the sea"—he tapped the page with his finger—"a *minimum* of half a mile west-southwest of where the body was found."

"Okay, well, assuming the minimum, that doesn't mean she swam half a mile. There are some strong currents along this part of the coast, so the sea would have caused her eastward drift. In real terms she would only have swum a couple of hundred yards."

"I presume that was taken into account."

Ingram frowned. "So why was she showing evidence of hypothermia? The winds have been light for the last week, and the sea's been calm. In those conditions, an average swimmer could cover two hundred yards in fifteen to twenty minutes. Also, the sea temperature would have been several degrees higher than the night air, so she'd be more likely to develop hypothermia on the beach than she would in the water, especially if she was naked."

"In which case she wouldn't have died from drowning."

"No."

"So what's the point you're making?" asked Galbraith.

Nick shook his head. "I don't know, except that I'm having trouble reconciling the body I saw with what the pathologist is saying. When the lifeboat crew at Swanage fished a corpse out of the sea last year, it was black with bruises and had swelled to twice its normal size."

The DI consulted the paper again. "Okay, well, there's a time constraint. He says the time of death must have coincided with high water to leave it stranded on the beach as the tide receded. He also makes the argument that if she hadn't reached the shelter of Egmont Point before she drowned, the body would have been pulled under by back eddies and towed out around St. Alban's Head. Put those two together and you have your answer, don't you? In simple terms she must have died within yards of the shore, and her body was stranded shortly afterward."

"That's very sad," said Ingram, thinking of the tiny hand waving in the spume.

"Yes," agreed Galbraith, who had seen the body in the mortuary and was as moved by the unnecessary death as Ingram was. He found the constable easy to like. But then he always preferred policemen who showed emotion. It was a sign of honesty.

"What evidence is there that she was raped if everything useful was flushed away?"

"Bruising to the inside of her thighs and back. Rope marks on her wrists. Bloodstream full of benzodiazepine . . . probably Rohypnol. Do you know what that is?"

"Mmm. The date-rape drug . . . I've read about it . . . haven't come across it, though."

Galbraith handed him the report. "It'll be better if you read it yourself. They're preliminary notes only, but Warner never commits anything to paper unless he's pretty damn sure he's right."

It wasn't a long document, and Ingram read it quickly. "So you're looking for a boat with bloodstains?" he said, laying the pages on the desk in front of him when he'd finished.

"Also skin tissue if she was raped on a wooden deck."

The tall policeman gave a doubtful shake of his head. "I wouldn't be too optimistic," he said. "He'll hose down the deck and the topsides the minute he gets into a marina, and what the sea hasn't already taken, fresh water will finish off."

"We know," said Galbraith, "which is why we need to get a move on. Our only lead is this tentative identification, which if it's true suggests the boat she was on might have come from Lymington." He took out his notebook. "A three-year-old kid was found abandoned near one of the marinas in Poole yesterday, and the description of the missing mother matches our victim. Her name's Kate Sumner, and she lives in Lymington. Her husband's been in Liverpool for the last four days, but he's on his way back now to make the identification."

Ingram picked up the incident report he'd typed that morning and squared it between his large hands. "It's probably just coincidence," he said thoughtfully, "but the guy who made the emergency call keeps a boat in Lymington. He sailed it into Poole late on Saturday night."

"What's his name?"

"Steven Harding. Claimed to be an actor from London."

"You think he was lying?"

Ingram shrugged. "Not about his name or his occupation, but I certainly think he was lying about what he was doing there. His story was that he'd left his boat in Poole because he fancied some exercise, but I've done a few calculations and by my reckoning there's no way he could have made it on foot in time to make the call at ten forty-three. If he was berthed in one of the marinas then he'd have to have taken the ferry to Studland, but as the first crossing isn't until seven that means he had to cover sixteen-odd miles of coastal path in just over three hours. If you take into account that a good percentage is sandy beach and the rest is a roller-coaster ride of hills, I'd say it was an impossibility. We're talking an average of over five miles an hour, and the only person I can think of who could sustain that sort of speed on that kind of terrain is a professional marathon runner." He pushed the report across. "It's all in there. Name, address, description, name of boat. Something else that's interesting is that he sails into Chapman's Pool regularly and knows everything there is to know about the back eddies. He's very well informed about the seas around here."

"Is he the one who found the body?"

"No, that was two young lads. They're on holiday with their parents. I doubt there's any more they can tell you, but I've included their names and the address of their rented cottage. A Miss Maggie Jenner of Broxton House talked to Harding for an hour or so after he made the call, but he doesn't appear to have told her much about himself except that he grew up on a farm in Cornwall." He laid a hand the size of a dinner plate on the report. "He was sporting an erection, if that's of any interest. Both Miss Jenner and I noticed it."

"Jesus!"

Ingram smiled. "Don't get too excited. Miss Jenner's a bit of a looker, so it may have been her that brought it on. She has that effect on men." He lifted his hand. "I've also included the names of the boats that were anchored in the bay when the body was found. One was registered in Poole, one in Southampton, and the third was French, although it shouldn't be too hard to find. I watched it leave yesterday evening, and it was heading for Weymouth, so I guess they're on holiday and working their way along the coast."

"Good work," said Galbraith warmly. "I'll be in touch." He tapped the pathologist's report as he turned to go. "I'll leave this with you. Maybe something will strike you that hasn't struck any of us."

Steven Harding woke to the sound of a dying outboard motor, followed by someone banging his fist on the stern of *Crazy Daze*. It was at its permanent mooring, a buoy in the Lymington River, and was well out of reach of casual visitors unless they had a dinghy of their own. The swell was sometimes unpleasant, particularly when the Lymington–Yarmouth ferry went past on its way to the Isle of Wight, but it was affordable, private, and suitably remote from prying eyes.

"Hey, Steve! Get up, you bastard!"

He groaned as he recognized the voice, then rolled over in his bunk, pulling the pillow over his head. His brain was splitting from a piledriver of a hangover, and the last person he wanted to see at the crack of dawn on Monday morning was Tony Bridges. "You're banned from coming aboard, arsehole," he roared angrily, "so bugger off and leave me alone!"

But *Crazy Daze* was sealed up as tight as a can of beans, and he knew his friend couldn't have heard him. The boat tilted as Tony climbed aboard after securing his dinghy next to Harding's on the aft cleat.

"Open up!" he said, hammering on the companionway hatch. "I know you're in there. Have you any idea what time it is, you stupid sod? I've been trying to get you on your mobile for the last three hours."

Harding squinted at his watch. Three ten, he read. He sat bolt upright and banged his already aching head on the planked ceiling. "Fucking Ada!" he muttered, crawling off his bunk and stumbling into the saloon to pull the bolt on the hatch. "I was supposed to be in London by midday," he told Tony.

"So your agent keeps telling me. He's been calling me nonstop since eleven thirty." Tony pulled back the main hatch and dropped down into the saloon, sniffing the ripe atmosphere with an expression of distaste. "Ever heard of fresh air?" he asked, pushing past his friend to open the forward hatch in the cabin and create a through draft. He looked at the rumpled sheets and wondered what the hell Steve had been doing. "You're a bloody fool," he said unsympathetically.

"Go away. I'm sick." Harding groaned again as he slumped onto the port settee in the saloon and dropped his forehead into his hands.

"I'm not surprised. It's like an oven in here." Tony handed him a bottle of mineral water from the galley. "Get some of this into you before you die of dehydration." He stood over him until he'd downed half the bottle, then lowered himself onto the facing settee. "What's going on? I talked to Bob and he said you were supposed to be crashing at his place last night and catching the early train to town this morning."

"I changed my mind."

"So I gather." Tony looked at the empty bottle of whisky on the table between them and the photographs scattered across its surface. "What the hell's up with you?"

"Nothing." He pushed the hair out of his eyes with a frown of irritation. "How did you know I was here?"

Tony jerked his head toward the stern. "I spotted your dinghy. Also I've tried everywhere else. Graham's after your blood, in case you're interested. He's pissed off that you missed the audition. It was in the bag, according to him."

"He's lying."

"Your big chance, he said."

"Fuck that!" said Harding dismissively. "It was a bit part in a kids' TV series. Three days' filming with spoiled brats to make something I wouldn't be seen dead in. Only idiots work with children."

Malice stirred briefly in Tony's eyes before he cloaked his anger behind a harmless smile. "Is that a dig at me?" he asked mildly.

Harding shrugged. "No one forced you to be a teacher, mate. It was your choice." He rocked his flattened palm. "Your funeral when the little bastards finally do your head in."

Tony held his gaze for a moment then picked up one of the photographs. "So how come you don't have a problem with this kind of crap?" he said, jabbing his finger at the image. "Doesn't this count as working with kids?"

No answer.

"You're being exploited by experts—*mate*—but you can't see it. You might as well sell your arse in Piccadilly Circus as let perverts drool over tacky porno pics of you in private."

"Shut it," growled Harding angrily, touching his fingertips to his eyelids to suppress the pain behind them. "I've had enough of your bloody lectures."

Tony ignored the note of warning. "What do you expect if you keep behaving like an idiot?"

An unfriendly smile thinned the other man's lips. "At

least I'm up-front about what I do"—his smile broadened—"in every respect." He stared Bridges down. "Unlike you, eh? How's Bibi these days? Still falling asleep on the job?"

"Don't tempt me, Steve."

"To do what?"

"Shop you." He stared at the photograph in a confusion of disgust and jealousy. "You're a fucking deviant. This kid's barely fifteen."

"Nearly sixteen . . . as you damn well know." Harding watched him tear the photograph to shreds. "Why are you getting so het-up about it?" he murmured dispassionately. "It's only acting. You do it in a movie and they call it art. You do it for a mag and they call it pornography."

"It's cheap filth."

"Wrong. It's *exciting* cheap filth. Be honest. You'd swap places with me any day. Hell, the pay's three times what you get as a teacher." He raised the bottle of mineral water to his mouth and tilted his head back, smiling cynically. "I'll talk to Graham," he said, wiping his wet lips with the back of his hand. "You never know. A little guy like you might go down a wow on the Internet. Pedophiles like 'em small."

"You're sick."

"No," said Harding, dropping his head into his hands, energy spent. "Just broke. It's the inadequate bastards who jerk off over my pictures who're sick."

CHAPTER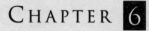

Forensic Pathology Report
<u>UF/DP/5136/Interim:</u> Ref: GFS/Dr. J. C. Warner

- **General description:** Natural blond—30 yrs. (approx.)—
  height 5′—weight: 102 lbs.—blue eyes—blood group
  O—excellent health—excellent teeth (2 fillings; RL wisdom removed)—no surgical scars—mother of at least
  one child—14 weeks pregnant (fetus male)—non-
  smoker—small traces of alcohol in blood—consumed last
  meal approx 3 hrs. before drowning—contents of stomach (other than sea water): cheese, apple—pronounced
  indentation 3rd finger L-hand indicates recent presence
  of ring (wedding or otherwise).

- **Cause of death:** Drowning. The evidence prevailing conditions—wind, tide, rocky shoreline; good condition of
  body—had she entered the sea on or near the shoreline
  she was obviously determined enough to save herself, and
  while there is some postmortem bruising, there is not
  enough to suggest that the corpse remained long in the
  water after death—points to her coming off a boat in the

open sea, alive, and swimming for some considerable time before exhaustion led to drowning within shelter of land.

- **Contributory factors in victim's death:** 0.5 liters of sea water in stomach—fingertip bruising either side of voice-box, indicative of attempted manual strangulation—residual benzodiazepine in bloodstream and tissues (Rohypnol?)—bruising and abrasions to back (pronounced on shoulder blades and buttocks) and inside of thighs, indicative of forced intercourse on a hard surface, such as a deck or an uncarpeted floor—some blood loss from abrasions in vagina (vaginal swabs negative, either due to prolonged immersion in sea water or assailant using a condom)—severe fingertip bruising on upper arms, indicative of manual restraint and/or manual lift (possibly inflicted during ejection from boat)—incipient hypothermia.

- **Condition of body:** Death had occurred within 14 hrs. of being examined—most likely time of death: at or around high water at 1:52 A.M. BST on Sunday, 10 August (see below)—general condition good, although hypothermal evidence, condition of skin, and vasocon-striction of the arterial vessels (indicative of prolonged stress) suggests victim spent considerable time in the sea before drowning—extensive abrasions to both wrists, suggesting she was bound with rope and made efforts to release herself (impossible to say whether she succeeded, or whether her killer released her prior to drowning her)—two fingers on L-hand broken; <u>all</u> fingers on R-hand broken (difficult at this stage to say what caused this—it may have been done deliberately or may have happened accidentally if the woman tried to save herself by catching her fingers on a railing?)—fingernails broken on both hands—postmortem bruising and grazing of back, breasts, buttocks, and knees indicate the body was dragged to and fro across rocks/pebbles prior to being stranded.

- **Ambient conditions where found:** Egmont Bight is a shallow bay, inaccessible to boats other than keelless vessels such as ribs/dinghies (lowest recorded depth = 0.5 m; variation between low and high water = 1.00–2.00 m). Kimmeridge Ledges to the west of Egmont Bight make sailing close to the cliffs hazardous, and sailors steer well clear of the shoreline (particularly at night, when that part of the coast is unlit). Due to a back eddy, a continuous SSE stream runs from Chapman's Pool toward St. Alban's Head, which suggests victim was inside the shelter of Egmont Point before she died and was stranded on the shoreline as the tide receded. Had she drowned farther out, her body would have been swept around the Head. SW winds and currents mean she must have entered the water WSW of Egmont Bight and was towed along the coast in an easterly direction as she swam toward the shore. In view of the above factors,* we estimate the victim entered the sea a minimum of 0.5 miles WSW of where the body was found.

- **Conclusions:** The woman was raped and subjected to a manual strangulation attempt before being left to drown in the open sea. She may also have had her fingers broken prior to immersion with the <u>possible</u> aim of hampering her efforts to swim toward the shore. She was certainly alive when she entered the water, so the failure to report her fall overboard suggests her killer expected her to die. The removal of distinguishing features (wedding ring, clothing) suggests a premeditated intent to hinder an investigation should the body surface or be washed ashore.

*These estimates are calculated on what an average swimmer could achieve in the conditions.

These conclusions are predicated on the rape taking place on board a boat, most probably on deck.

Difficult at this stage to say to what extent the benzodiazepine would have affected her ability to operate. Further tests required.

***NB:** In view of the fact that she came so close to saving herself, it is possible that she made the decision to jump while the boat was still in sight of land. However, both the failure to report her "missing overboard" and the evidence of premeditation leaves little room for doubt that her death was intended.

***Rohypnol** (manufactured by Roche) Much concern is being expressed about this drug. A soluble, intermediate-acting hypnotic compound—known on the street as the "date-rape drug," or more colloquially as a "roofie." It has already been cited in several rape cases, two being "gang-rape" cases. Very effective in the treatment of severe and disabling insomnia, it can induce sleep at unusual times. Used inappropriately—easily dissolved in alcohol—it can render a woman unconscious without her knowledge, thus making her vulnerable to sexual attack. Women report intermittent bouts of lucidity, coupled with an absolute inability to defend themselves. Its effects on rape victims have been well documented in the U.S., where the drug is now banned: temporary or permanent memory loss; inability to understand that a rape has taken place; feelings of "spaced-out" disconnection from the event; subsequent and deep psychological trauma because of the ease with which the victim was violated against her will (often by more than one rapist). There are enormous difficulties in bringing prosecutions because it is impossible to detect Rohypnol in the bloodstream after seventy-two hours, and few victims regain their memories quickly enough to present themselves at police stations in time to produce positive semen swabs or benzodiazepine traces in the blood.

***NB:** The U.K. police lag well behind their U.S. counterparts in both understanding and prosecution of these types of cases.

J. C. Woner

CHAPTER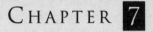

S alterns Marina lay at the end of a small cul-de-sac off the Bournemouth-to-Poole coastal road, some two hundred yards from where the Greens had rescued the blond toddler. Its approach from the sea in a pleasure craft was through the Swash Channel and then via the North Channel, which allowed a passage between the shore and the numerous moored boats that flew like streamers from the buoys in the center of the bay. It was a popular stopping-off place for foreign visitors or sailors setting out to cruise the south coast of England, and was often crowded in the summer months.

An inquiry at the marina office about traffic in and out over the previous two days, 9–10 August, produced the information that *Crazy Daze* had moored there for approximately eighteen hours on the Sunday. The boat had come in during the night and taken a vacant berth on "A" pontoon, and the nightwatchman had recorded the arrival at 2:15 A.M. Subsequently, when the office opened at 8:00 A.M., a man calling himself Steven Harding had paid for a twenty-four-hour stay, saying he was going for a hike but planned to be back by late afternoon. The harbormaster remembered him. "Good-looking chap. Dark hair."

"That's the one. How did he seem? Calm? Excited?"

"He was fine. I warned him we'd need the berth again by the evening and he said, no problem, because he'd be heading back to Lymington by late afternoon. As far as I recall he said he had an appointment in London on Monday—this morning in other words—and was planning to catch the last train up."

"Did he have a child with him?"

"No."

"How did he pay?"

"Credit card."

"Did he have a wallet?"

"No. He had the card tucked into a pocket inside his shorts. Said it was all you needed these days to go traveling."

"Was he carrying anything?"

"Not when he came into the office."

No one had made a note of *Crazy Daze*'s departure, but the berth was empty again by 7:00 P.M. on Sunday evening, when a yacht out of Portsmouth had been logged in. On this initial inquiry, there were no reports of an unaccompanied toddler leaving the marina or of a man taking a toddler away with him. However, several people pointed out that marinas were busy places—even at eight o'clock in the morning—and anyone could take anything off a boat if it was wrapped in something unexceptional like a sleeping bag and placed in a marina trolley to transport it away from the pontoons.

Within two hours of the Lymington police being asked to check William Sumner's cottage in Rope Walk, another request came through from Winfrith to locate a boat by the name of *Crazy Daze,* which was moored somewhere in the tiny Hampshire port's complex of marinas, river moorings, and commercial fishing quarter. It took a single telephone call to the Lymington harbormaster to establish its exact whereabouts.

"Sure I know Steve. He moors up to a buoy in the dog-leg, about five hundred yards beyond the yacht club. Thirty-foot sloop with a wooden deck and claret-colored sails. Nice boat. Nice lad."

"Is he on board?"

"Can't say. I don't even know if his boat's in. Is it important?"

"Could be."

"Try phoning the yacht club. They can pick him out with binoculars if he's there. Failing that, come back to me, and I'll send one of my lads up to check."

William Sumner was reunited with his daughter in the Poole police station at half past six that evening after a tiring two-hundred-and-fifty-mile drive from Liverpool, but if anyone expected the little girl to run to him with joyful smiles of recognition, they were to be disappointed. She chose to sit at a distance, playing with some toys on the floor, while making a cautious appraisal of the exhausted man who had slumped on a chair and buried his head in his hands. He apologized to WPC Griffiths. "I'm afraid she's always like this," he said. "Kate's the only one she responds to." He rubbed his red eyes. "Have you found her yet?"

Griffiths moved protectively in front of the little girl, worried about how much she understood. She exchanged a glance with John Galbraith, who had been waiting in the room with her. "My colleague from Dorset Constabulary Headquarters, DI Galbraith, knows more about that than I do, Mr. Sumner, so I think the best thing is that you talk it through with him while I take Hannah to the canteen." She reached out an inviting hand to the toddler. "Would you like an ice cream, sweetheart?" She was surprised by the child's reaction. With a trusting smile, Hannah scrambled to her feet and held up her arms. "Well, that's a change from yesterday," she said with a laugh, swinging her on to her hip. "Yesterday, you wouldn't even look at me." She cuddled the warm little body against her side and deliberately ignored the danger signals that shot like Cupid's arrows through her bloodstream, courtesy of her frustrated thirty-five-year-old hormones.

After they'd gone, Galbraith pulled forward a chair and sat facing Sumner. The man was older than he'd been expecting, with thinning dark hair and an angular, loose-limbed body that he seemed unable to keep still. When he wasn't plucking nervously at his lips, he was jiggling one heel in a constant rat-a-tat-tat against the floor, and it was with reluctance that Galbraith took some photographs from his breast pocket and held them loosely between his hands. When he spoke it was with deep and genuine sympathy. "There's no easy way to tell you this, sir," he said gently, "but a young woman, matching your wife's description, was found dead yesterday morning. We can't be sure it's Kate until you've identified her, but I think you need to prepare yourself for the fact that it might be."

A look of terror distorted the man's face. "It will be," he said with absolute certainty. "All the way back I've been thinking that something awful must have happened. Kate would never have left Hannah. She adored her."

Reluctantly, Galbraith turned the first close-up and held it for the other man to see.

Sumner gave an immediate nod of recognition. "Yes," he said with a catch in his voice, "that's Kate."

"I'm so sorry, sir."

Sumner took the photograph with trembling fingers and examined it closely. He spoke without emotion. "What happened?"

Galbraith explained as briefly as possible where and how Kate Sumner had been found, deeming it unnecessary at this early stage to mention rape or murder.

"Did she drown?"

"Yes."

Sumner shook his head in bewilderment. "What was she doing there?"

"We don't know, but we think she must have fallen from a boat."

"Then why was Hannah in Poole?"

"We don't know," said Galbraith again.

The man turned the photograph over and thrust it at Galbraith, as if by putting it out of sight he could deny its contents. "It doesn't make sense," he said harshly. "Kate wouldn't have gone anywhere without Hannah, and she hated sailing. I used to have a Contessa thirty-two when we lived in Chichester, but I could never persuade her to come out on it because she was terrified of turning turtle in the open sea and drowning." He lowered his head into his hands again as the meaning of what he'd said came home to him.

Galbraith gave him a moment to compose himself. "What did you do with it?"

"Sold it a couple of years ago and put the money toward buying Langton Cottage." He lapsed into another silence, which the policeman didn't interrupt. "I don't understand any of this," he burst out then in despair. "I spoke to her on Friday night, and she was fine. How could she possibly be dead forty-eight hours later?"

"It's always worse when death happens suddenly," said the DI sympathetically. "We don't have time to prepare for it."

"Except I don't believe it. I mean, why didn't someone try to save her? You don't just abandon people when they fall overboard." He looked shocked suddenly. "Oh, God, did other people drown as well? You're not going to tell me she was on a boat that capsized, are you? That was her worst nightmare."

"No, there's no evidence that anything like that happened." Galbraith leaned forward to bridge the gap between them. They were on hard-backed chairs in an empty office on the first floor, and he could have wished for friendlier surroundings for a conversation like this one. "We think Kate was murdered, sir. The Home Office pathologist who performed the postmortem believes she was raped before being deliberately thrown into the sea to die. I realize this must be a terrible shock to you, but you have my assurance that we're working around the clock to find her killer, and if there's anything we can do to make the situation easier for you, we will of course do it."

It was too much for Sumner to take in. He stared at the detective with a surprised smile carving ridges in his thin face. "No," he said, "there's been a mistake. It can't have been Kate. She wouldn't have gone anywhere with a stranger." He reached out a tentative hand for the photograph again, then burst into tears when Galbraith turned it over for him.

The wretched man was so tired that it was several minutes before he could stem his weeping, but Galbraith kept quiet because he knew from past experience that sympathy more often exacerbated pain than ameliorated it. He sat quietly looking out of the window, which faced toward the park and Poole Bay beyond, and stirred only when Sumner spoke again.

"I'm sorry," he said, striking the tears from his cheeks. "I keep thinking how frightened she must have been. She wasn't a very good swimmer, which is why she didn't want to go sailing."

Galbraith made a mental note of the fact. "If it's any comfort, she did everything in her power to save herself. It was exhaustion that beat her, not the sea."

"Did you know she was pregnant?" Tears gathered in his eyes again.

"Yes," said Galbraith gently, "and I'm sorry."

"Was it a boy?"

"Yes."

"We wanted a son." He took a handkerchief from his pocket and held it to his eyes for several moments before getting up abruptly and walking to the window to stand with his back to Galbraith. "How can I help you?" he said then in a voice stripped of feeling.

"You can tell me about her. We need as much background information as you can give us—the names of her friends, what she did during the day, where she shopped. The more we know the better." He waited for a response, which never came. "Perhaps you'd rather leave it until tomorrow? I realize you must be very tired."

"Actually, I think I'm going to be sick." Sumner turned an ashen face toward him, then, with a small sigh, slid to the floor in a dead faint.

The Spender boys were easy company. They demanded little from their host other than the odd can of Coke, occasional conversation, and help with threading their hooks with bait. Ingram's immaculate fifteen-foot dayboat, *Miss Creant,* sat prettily on the surface of a calm turquoise sea off Swanage, her white topsides turning pale pink in the slowly setting sun and a fine array of rods bristling along her rails like porcupine quills. The boys loved her.

"I'd rather have *Miss Creant* than a stupid cruiser any day," said Paul after helping the mighty policeman launch her down the Swanage slip. He had allowed the boy to operate the winch at the back of his ancient Jeep while he himself had waded into the sea to float her off the trailer and make her fast to a ring on the slip wall. Paul's eyes had gleamed with excitement because boating was suddenly more accessible than he'd realized. "Do you reckon Dad might buy one? Holidays would be great if we had a boat like this."

"You can always ask," had been Ingram's response.

Danny found the whole idea of sliding a long wriggling ragworm onto a barbed point until the steel was clothed in something resembling a wrinkled silk stocking deeply repugnant and insisted that Ingram do the business for him. "It's alive," he pointed out. "Doesn't the hook hurt it?"

"Not as much as it would hurt you."

"It's an invertebrate," said his brother, who was leaning over the side of the boat and watching his various floats bob on the water, "so it doesn't have a nervous system like us. Anyway, it's near the bottom of the food chain so it exists only to be eaten."

"Dead things are the bottom of the food chain," said Danny. "Like the lady on the beach. She'd've been food if we hadn't found her."

Ingram handed Danny his rod with the worm in place. "No fancy casting," he said, "just dangle it over the side and see what happens." He leaned back and tilted his baseball cap over his eyes, content to let the boys do the fishing. "Tell me about the bloke who made the phone call," he invited. "Did you like him?"

"He was all right," said Paul.

"He said he saw a lady with no clothes on, and she looked like an elephant," said Danny, joining his brother to lean over the side.

"It was a joke," said Paul. "He was trying to make us feel better."

"What else did he talk about?"

"He was chatting up the lady with the horse," said Danny, "but she didn't like him as much as he liked her."

Ingram smiled to himself. "What makes you think that?"

"She frowned a lot."

So what's new?

"Why do you want to know if we liked him?" asked Paul, his agile mind darting back to Ingram's original question. "Didn't *you* like him?"

"He was all right," said Ingram, echoing Paul's own answer. "A bit of a moron for setting out on a hike on a hot day without any suntan lotion or water, but otherwise okay."

"I expect they were in his rucksack," said Paul loyally,

who hadn't forgotten Harding's kindness even if his brother had. "He put it down to make the telephone call, then left it there because he said it was too heavy to lug down to the police car. He was going to pick it up again on his way back. It was probably water that was making it heavy." He looked earnestly toward their host. "Don't you think?"

Ingram closed his eyes under the brim of his cap. "Yes," he agreed, while wondering what had been in the rucksack that meant Harding hadn't wanted a policeman to see it. Binoculars? Had he seen the woman, after all? "Did you describe the lady on the beach to him?" he asked Paul.

"Yes," said the boy. "He wanted to know if she was pretty."

There were two hidden agendas behind the decision to send WPC Griffiths home with William and Hannah Sumner. The first derived entirely from the child's unfavorable psychiatric report and was intended to safeguard her welfare; the second was based on years of statistical evidence that showed a wife was always more likely to be murdered by her husband than by a stranger. However, because of the distances involved and the problems of jurisdiction—Poole being Dorsetshire Constabulary and Lymington being Hampshire Constabulary—Griffiths was advised that the hours would be long ones.

"Yes, but is he *really* a suspect?" Griffiths asked Galbraith.

"Husbands are always suspects."

"Come on, guv, he was definitely in Liverpool, because I phoned the hotel to check, and it's a hell of a long way from there to Dorset. If he's driven to and fro twice in five days, then he's done over a thousand miles. That's a hell of a lot of driving."

"Which may explain why he fainted," was Galbraith's dry response.

"Oh, great!" she said sarcastically. "I've always wanted to spend quality time with a rapist."

"There's no compulsion, Sandy. You don't have to do it if you don't want to, but the only other option is to leave Hannah in the care of foster parents until we're satisfied it's safe to return her to her father. How about you go back tonight and see how it goes? I've got a team searching the house at the moment, so I'll instruct one of the chaps to stay on and shadow you. Can you live with that?"

"What the hell!" she said cheerfully. "With any luck, it'll give me a chance to work babies out of my system."

As far as Sumner himself was concerned, Griffiths was the official "friend" who was supplied by any police force to a family in distress. "I can't possibly cope on my own," he kept telling Galbraith as if it was the fault of the police that he found himself a widower.

"We don't expect you to."

The man's color had improved after he had been given something to eat when he admitted he'd had nothing since a cup of tea at breakfast that morning. Renewed energy had set him chasing explanations again. "Were they kidnapped?" he asked suddenly.

"We don't think so. Lymington police checked the house inside and out, and there's no indication of any sort of disturbance. The neighbor let them in with a spare key, so the search was a thorough one. That doesn't mean we're ignoring the possibility of abduction, just that we're keeping an open mind. We're conducting a second search ourselves at the moment, but on the evidence so far it looks as if Kate and Hannah left of their own accord sometime after the post was delivered on Saturday morning. The letters had been opened and stacked on the kitchen table."

"What about her car? Could she have been taken from her car?"

Galbraith shook his head. "It's parked in your garage."

"Then I don't understand." Sumner appeared genuinely confused. "What happened?"

"Well, one explanation is that Kate met someone when she was out, a friend of the family perhaps, who persuaded her and Hannah to go for a sail in his boat." He was careful to avoid any idea of a prearranged meeting. "But whether she expected to be taken as far as Poole and the Isle of Purbeck we simply don't know."

Sumner shook his head. "She'd never have gone," he said with absolute certainty. "I keep telling you, she didn't like sailing. And, anyway, the only people we know with boats are couples." He stared at the floor. "You're not suggesting a couple could have done something like this, are you?" He sounded shocked.

"I'm not suggesting anything at the moment," said Galbraith patiently. "We need more information before we can do that." He paused. "Her wedding ring seems to be missing. We assume it was removed because it could identify her. Was it special in some way?"

Sumner held out a trembling hand and pointed to his own ring. "It was identical to this one. We had them engraved inside with our initials. 'K' entwined with 'W.' "

Interesting, thought Galbraith. "When you're ready, I'd like a list of your friends, particularly the ones who sail. But there's no immediate hurry." He watched Sumner crack his finger joints noisily, one after the other, and wondered what had attracted the pretty little woman in the mortuary to this gauche, hyperactive man.

Sumner clearly hadn't been listening. "When was Hannah abandoned?" he demanded.

"We don't know."

"My mother said she was found in Poole at lunchtime yesterday, but you said Kate died in the early hours of the morning. Doesn't that mean Hannah must have been on board when Kate was raped and was put ashore in Poole *after* Kate was dead? I mean, she couldn't possibly have been wandering around on her own for twenty-four hours before somebody saw her, could she?"

He was certainly no fool, thought Galbraith. "We don't think so."

"Then her mother was killed in front of her?" The man's voice rose. "Oh my God, I'm not sure I can bear this! She's only a baby, for Christ's sake."

Galbraith reached out a calming hand. "It's far more likely she was asleep."

"You can't know that."

No, thought Galbraith, I can't. As about everything else in policework, I can only guess. "The doctor who examined her after she was found thinks she was sedated," he explained. "But, yes, you're right. At the moment we can't be certain about anything." He rested his palm briefly on the man's taut shoulder, then withdrew tactfully into his own space. "But it really is better to stop tormenting yourself with what might have been. Nothing's ever as bleak as our imagination paints it."

"Isn't it?" Sumner straightened abruptly and let his head flop onto the chair back so that he was looking at the ceiling. A long sigh whispered from his chest. "My imagination tells me you're working on the theory that Kate was having an affair, and that the man she went with was her lover."

Galbraith saw no point in pretending. The idea of an affair that had turned sour was the first they'd considered, particularly as Hannah had apparently accompanied her mother on whatever journey she had made. "We can't ignore the possibility," he said honestly. "It would certainly explain why she agreed to go on board somebody's boat and take Hannah with her." He studied the man's profile. "Does the name Steven Harding mean anything to you?"

Sumner frowned. "What's he got to do with it?"

"Probably nothing, but he was one of the people on the spot when Kate's body was found, and we're questioning everyone connected with her death, however remotely." He waited a moment. "Do you know him?"

"The actor?"

"Yes."

"I've met him a couple of times." He steepled his hands in front of his mouth. "He carried Hannah's buggy over the cobbles at the bottom of the High Street one day when Kate was struggling with some heavy shopping, and she asked me to thank him when we bumped into him about a week later. After that he started popping up all over the place. You know what it's like. You meet someone, and then you see them wherever you go. He's got a sloop on the Lymington River, and we used to talk sailing from time to time. I invited him back to the house once, and he chewed my ear off for hours about some blasted play he was auditioning for. He didn't get the part, of course, but I wasn't surprised. He couldn't act his way out of a paper bag if his life depended on it." His eyes narrowed. "Do you think he did it?"

Galbraith gave a small shake of his head. "At the moment, we're just trying to eliminate him from the inquiry. Were he and Kate friends?"

Sumner's lips twisted. "Do you mean, were they having an affair?"

"If you like."

"No," he said adamantly. "He's a galloping poof. He poses for pornographic gay magazines. In any case she can't . . . couldn't stand him. She was furious when I took him back to the house that time . . . said I should have asked her first."

Galbraith watched him for a moment. The denial was overdone, he thought. "How do you know about the gay magazines? Did Harding tell you?"

Sumner nodded. "He even showed me one of them. He was proud of it. But then he loves all that. Loves being in the limelight."

"Okay. Tell me about Kate. How long have you and she been married?"

He had to think about it. "Getting on for four years. We met at work and married six months later."

"Where's work?"

"Pharmatec UK in Portsmouth. I'm a research chemist there, and Kate was one of the secretaries."

Galbraith lowered his eyes to cloak his sudden interest. "The drug company?"

"Yes."

"What sort of drugs do you research?"

"Me personally?" He gave an indifferent shrug. "Anything to do with the stomach."

Galbraith made a note. "Did Kate go on working after you married?"

"For a few months until she fell pregnant with Hannah."

"Was she happy about the pregnancy?"

"Oh, yes. Her one ambition was to have a family of her own."

"And she didn't mind giving up work?"

Sumner shook his head. "She wouldn't have it any other way. She didn't want her children to be brought up the way she was. She didn't have a father, and her mother was out all day, so she was left to fend on her own."

"Do you still work at Pharmatec?"

He nodded. "I'm their top scientist." He spoke the words matter-of-factly.

"So you live in Lymington and work in Portsmouth?"

"Yes."

"Do you drive to work?"

"Yes."

"That's a difficult journey," said Galbraith sympathetically, doing a rough calculation in his head. "It must take you—what?—an hour and a half of traveling each way. Have you ever thought of moving?"

"We didn't just think about it," said Sumner with a hint of irony. "We *did* it a year ago when we moved to Lymington. And, yes, you're right, it's an awful journey, particularly in the summer when the New Forest's packed with tourists." He sounded unhappy about it.

"Where did you move from?"

"Chichester."

Galbraith remembered the notes Griffiths had shown

him after Sumner's telephone call. "That's where your mother lives, isn't it?"

"Yes. She's been there all her life."

"You too? A born-and-bred Chichester man?"

Sumner nodded.

"Moving must have been a bit of a wrench, particularly if it meant adding an hour to your journey each way?"

He ignored the question to stare despondently out of the window. "You know what I keep thinking?" he said then. "If I'd stuck to my guns and refused to budge, Kate wouldn't be dead. We never had any trouble when we lived in Chichester." He seemed to realize immediately that his remarks could be interpreted in a number of ways and added what was presumably intended as an explanation: "I mean, Lymington's full of strangers. Half the people you meet don't even live there."

Galbraith had a quick word with Griffiths before she left to accompany William and Hannah Sumner home. She had been given time, while the scene-of-crime officers finished their search of Langton Cottage, to go home in order to change and pack a bag, and was dressed now in a baggy yellow sweater and black leggings. She looked very different from the severe young woman in the police uniform, and Galbraith wondered wryly if the father and daughter would feel more or less comfortable with the Sloppy Joe. Less, he fancied. Police uniforms inspired confidence.

"I'll be with you early tomorrow morning," he told her, "and I need you to prod him a bit before I get there. I want lists of their friends in Lymington, a second list of friends in Chichester, and a third list of work friends in Portsmouth." He ran a tired hand around his jaw, while he tried to organize his memory. "It would be helpful if he splits those with boats, or with access to boats, from those without, and even more helpful if he separates Kate's personal friends from their joint friends."

"Okey-doke," she said.

He smiled. "And try to get him to talk about Kate," he went on. "We need to know what her routine was, how she managed her day, which shops she used, that kind of thing."

"No problem."

"*And* his mother," he said. "I get the impression Kate forced him to move away from her, which may have caused some friction within the family."

Griffiths looked amused. "I don't blame her," she said. "He's ten years older than she was, and he'd been living at home with Mummy for thirty-seven years before they got married."

"How do you know?"

"I had a chat with him when I asked him for his previous address. His mother gave him the family home as a wedding present in return for him taking a small mortgage to help her buy a flat in some sheltered accommodation across the road."

"A bit too close for comfort, eh?"

She chuckled. "Bloody stifling, I should think."

"What about his father?"

"Died ten years ago. Up until then it was a ménage à trois. Afterward, a ménage à deux. William was the only child."

Galbraith shook his head. "How come you're so well informed? It can only have been a very little chat."

She tapped the side of her nose. "Sensible questions and a woman's intuition," she said. "He's been waited on all his life, which is why he's so convinced he won't be able to cope."

"Good luck then," he said, meaning it. "I can't say I envy you."

"Someone has to look after Hannah." She sighed. "Poor little kid. Do you ever wonder what would have happened to you if you'd been abandoned the way most of the kids we arrest are abandoned?"

"Sometimes," Galbraith admitted. "Other times I thank God my parents pushed me out of the nest and told me to get on with it. You can be loved too much as well as too little, you know, and I'd be hard-pushed to say which was the more dangerous."

CHAPTER 8

T*he decision to question Steven Harding was made at eight*
o'clock that Monday night when the Dorset police
received confirmation that he was on board his boat in the
Lymington River; although the interview itself did not
take place until after nine because the officer in charge,
Detective Superintendent Carpenter, had to drive from
Winfrith in order to lead it. DI John Galbraith, who was
still in Poole, was instructed to make his own way to
Lymington and meet his governor outside the harbormaster's office.

Attempts had been made to raise Harding on his radio
and his mobile telephone, but as both were switched off,
the investigating officers had no way of finding out
whether he would still be there on Tuesday morning. A
call to his agent, Graham Barlow, had elicited only a furious tirade against arrogant young actors "who are too big
for their boots to attend auditions" and who could "dream
on about future representation."

"Of course I don't know where he'll be tomorrow," he
had finished angrily. "I haven't heard a cheep out of him
since Friday morning, so I've sacked the bugger. I
wouldn't mind if he was making any money for me, but he

hasn't worked in months. From the way he talks, you'd think he was Tom Cruise. Ha! Pinocchio's nearer the mark . . . he's certainly wooden enough . . ."

Galbraith and Carpenter met up at nine o'clock. The superintendent was a tall rangy man with a shock of dark hair and a ferocious frown that made him look permanently angry. His colleagues had ceased to notice it, but suspects were often intimidated by it. Galbraith had already rung through a brief report of his conversation with Sumner, but he went through it again for the superintendent's benefit, particularly the reference to Harding being "a galloping poof."

"It doesn't square with what we've been told by his agent," said Carpenter bluntly. "He describes him as sex-mad, says he's got girls falling over themselves to get into bed with him. He's a cannabis smoker, a heavy-metal fanatic, collects adult movies, and when he's got nothing better to do, sits for hours in strip joints watching the girls shed their kit. He's got a thing about nudity, so when he's on his own, either on the boat or in his flat, he prances around bollock-naked. Chances are we'll find him with his dick hanging out when we go aboard."

"That's something to look forward to then," said Galbraith gloomily.

Carpenter chuckled. "He fancies himself—doesn't think he's doing the business unless he's got two birds on the go at one time. Currently there's a twenty-five-year-old in London called Marie, and another called Bibi or Didi, or something similar, down here. Barlow's given us the name of a friend of Harding's in Lymington, one Tony Bridges, who acts as his answering service when he's out at sea, so I've sent Campbell around to have a word with him. If he gets a line on anything he'll call through." He tugged at his earlobe. "On the plus side, the sailing lobby speak well of him. He's lived in Lymington all his life, grew up over a chip shop in the High Street, and he's been mucking around in boats since he was ten. He made it to the top of the waiting list for a river mooring just over

three years ago—they're like gold dust apparently—
whereupon he sank every last cent into buying *Crazy
Daze.* He spends his free weekends on her, and the number of man-hours he's put in to getting her shipshape
would leave lesser men weeping. That's a quote from
some fellow in the yacht club. The general consensus
seems to be that he's a bit of a lad, but his heart's in the
right place."

"He sounds like a ruddy chameleon," said Galbraith
cynically. "I mean that's three different versions of the
same guy. Arse-bandit, rampant stud, and all-around good
bloke. You pays your money and takes your choice, eh?"

"He's an actor, don't forget, so I doubt if any of them
are accurate. He probably plays to the gallery whenever
he's given a chance."

"A liar, more like. According to Ingram, he said he grew
up on a farm in Cornwall." Galbraith raised his collar as a
breeze blew down the river, reminding him that he had put
on light clothes that morning when the air temperature
had touched the low thirties. "Do you fancy him for it?"

Carpenter shook his head. "Not really. He's a bit too
visible. I think our man's more likely to be textbook material. A loner . . . poor work record . . . history of failed
relationships . . . probably lives at home with his mother . . .
resents her interference in his life." He raised his nose to
sniff the air. "At the moment, I'd say the husband sounds a
more likely candidate."

Tony Bridges lived in a small terraced house behind the
High Street and gave a nod of agreement when the gray-
haired detective sergeant at his door asked if he could talk
to him for a few minutes about Steven Harding. He had no
shirt or shoes on, just a pair of jeans, and he weaved
unsteadily down the corridor as he led the way to an
untidy sitting room. He was thin and sharp-featured, with
a peroxided crew-cut that didn't suit his sallow complex-
ion, but he smiled amiably enough as he gestured DS

Campbell through the door. Campbell, who thought he smelled cannabis in the air, had the distinct impression that visits from the police were not unusual and suspected the neighbors had much to put up with.

The house gave the impression of multiple occupancy, with a couple of bicycles leaning against the wall at the end of the corridor, and assorted clothes lying in heaps about the furniture and floor. Dozens of empty lager cans had been tossed into an old beer crate in a corner—left over, Campbell presumed, from a long-dead party—and overflowing ashtrays reeked into the atmosphere. Campbell wondered what the kitchen was like. If it was as rank as the sitting room, it probably had rats, he thought.

"If his car alarm's gone off again," said Bridges, "then it's the garage you want to talk to. *They* fitted the sodding thing, and I'm sick to death of people phoning you lot about it when he's not here. I don't even know why he bothered to have it put in. The car's a pile of crap, so I can't see anyone wanting to steal it." He picked up an opened Enigma can from the floor and used it to point to a chair. "Take a pew. Do you want a lager?"

"No thanks." Campbell sat down. "It's not about his alarm, sir. We're asking routine questions of everyone who knows him in order to eliminate him from an inquiry, and we were given your name by his agent."

"What inquiry?"

"A woman drowned on Saturday night and Mr. Harding reported finding the body."

"Is that right? Shit! Who was it?"

"A local woman by the name of Kate Sumner. She lived in Rope Walk with her husband and daughter."

"Fucking Nora! Are you serious?"

"Did you know her?"

Tony took a swill from the can. "I knew *of* her, but I never met her. She had this thing about Steve. He helped her out once with her kid, and she wouldn't leave him alone. It used to drive him mad."

"Who told you this?"

"Steve, of course. Who else?" He shook his head. "No wonder he drank himself stupid last night if he's the one who found her."

"He wasn't. Some boys found her. He made the phone call on their behalf."

Bridges pondered for several moments in silence, and it was clearly hard work. Whatever anesthetic he'd taken—cannabis, alcohol, or both—he was having trouble getting his mind into gear. "This doesn't make sense," he said with sudden belligerence, his eyes focusing on Campbell like two little spy cameras. "I know for a fact Steve wasn't in Lymington on Saturday night. I saw him Friday night, and he told me he was going to Poole for the weekend. His boat was out all Saturday and Sunday, which means there's no way he could have reported a drowning in Lymington."

"She didn't drown here, sir. She drowned off the coast about twenty miles from Poole."

"Ah, shit!" He emptied the lager can with one swallow, then crumpled it between his fist and threw it at the beer crate. "Look, it's pointless asking me any more questions. I don't know anything about anyone drowning. Okay? I'm a mate of Steve's, not his blasted keeper."

Campbell nodded. "Fair enough. So, as a mate, do you know if he has a girlfriend down here called Bibi or Didi, Mr. Bridges?"

Tony leveled an accusing finger. "What the hell *is* this?" he demanded. "Over my dead body are these routine questions. What's going on?"

The DS looked thoughtful. "Steve isn't answering his telephone, so his agent's the only person we've been able to talk to. He told us Steve had a girlfriend in Lymington called Bibi or Didi, and he suggested we contact you for her address. Is that a problem for you?"

"To-ony!" called a drunken female voice from upstairs. *"I'm wa-aiting!"*

"Too right it's a problem," said Bridges angrily. "That's Bibi, and she's *my* sodding girlfriend, not Steve's. I'll kill the bastard if he's been two-timing me."

There was the sound of a body slumping on the floor upstairs. *"I'm going to sle-ep again, Tony!"*

Carpenter and Galbraith traveled out to *Crazy Daze* in the harbormaster's rib—a souped-up dinghy with a fiberglass keel and a steering column—captained by one of his young assistants. The night air had become noticeably cold after the heat of the day, and both men wished they had had the sense to wear sweaters or fleeces under their jackets. A stiff breeze was funneling down the Solent, making rigging lines rattle noisily against the forest of masts in the Berthon and Yacht Haven marinas. Ahead of them the Isle of Wight crouched like a slumbering beast against the shadowy sky and the lights from the approaching Yarmouth–Lymington ferry danced in reflection across the waves.

The harbormaster had been amused by police suspicion over their fruitless attempts to raise Harding via radio or mobile telephone. "Do the man a favor! Why should he waste his batteries on the odd chance that you lot want to talk to him? There's no shore power to boats on the buoys. He lights the saloon with a butane gas lamp—claims it's romantic—which is why he prefers a buoy in the river to a pontoon in a marina. That, and the fact that once on board the girls are dependent on him and his dinghy to get them off again."

"Does he take many girls out there?" asked Galbraith.

"I wouldn't know. I've got better things to do than keep a tally of Steve's conquests. He prefers blonds, I know that. I've seen him with a right little stunner recently."

"Small, curly blond hair, blue eyes?"

"Far as I recall, she had straight hair, but don't quote me on it. I'm no good with faces."

"Any idea what time Steve's boat left on Saturday morning?" asked Carpenter.

The harbormaster shook his head. "I can't even see it from here. Ask at the yacht club."

"We already have. No luck."

"Wait till the weekenders come down on Saturday then. They'll be your best bet."

The rib slowed as it approached Harding's sloop. Yellow light glimmered in the midship portholes, and a rubber dinghy bobbed astern in the wash from the ferry. From inside came the faint sound of music.

"Hey, Steve," shouted the harbormaster's lad, rapping smartly on the port planking. "It's Gary. You've got visitors, mate."

Harding's voice came faintly. "Bog off, Gary! I'm sick."

"No can do. It's the police. They want to talk to you. Come on, open up, and give us a hand."

The music ceased abruptly, and Harding hoisted himself through the open companionway into the cockpit. "What's up?" he asked, surveying the two detectives with an ingenuous smile. "I guess this has something to do with that woman yesterday? Were the boys lying about the binoculars?"

"We've a few follow-up questions," said Detective Superintendent Carpenter with an equally ingenuous smile. "Can we come on board?"

"Sure." He hopped onto the deck and reached down to assist Carpenter before turning to help his companion.

"My shift ends at ten," the lad called to the police officers. "I'll be back in forty minutes to take you off. If you want to leave earlier call on your mobile. Steve knows the number. Otherwise get him to bring you back."

They watched him turn away in a wide circle, carving a gleaming wake out of the water as he headed upriver toward the town.

"You'd better come below," said Harding. "It's cold out here." He was dressed—much to Galbraith's relief—in the same sleeveless T-shirt and shorts he'd been wearing the day before, and he shivered as a wind blew across the salt flats at the entrance to the river. Barefoot himself, he looked critically at the policemen's shoes. "You'll have to take those off," he told them. "It's taken me two years to get the planking looking like this, and I don't want it marked."

Obligingly, the two men unlaced their boots before padding across to the companionway in search of welcome warmth. The atmosphere inside the saloon was still redolent of the previous night's heavy drinking session, and even without the evidence of the empty whisky bottle which stood on the table, neither officer had any difficulty guessing why Harding had described himself as "sick." The muted light of the single gas-operated lamp served only to accentuate the hollows in his cheeks and the dark stubble around his unshaven jaw, and the brief glimpse they had of the tumbled sheets in the forward cabin before he closed the door left neither of them in any doubt that he'd spent most of the day sleeping off a ferocious hangover.

"What kind of follow-up questions?" he asked, sliding onto a bench seat at the side of the table and gesturing them to take the other.

"Routine ones, Mr. Harding," said the superintendent.

"About what?"

"Yesterday's events."

He pressed the heels of his palms against his lids and rotated them fiercely as if to drive out demons. "I don't know any more than I told the other guy," he said, eyes watering as he lowered his hands. "And most of that was what the boys told me. They reckoned she drowned and got left on the beach. Were they right?"

"It certainly looks that way."

He hunched forward over the table. "I'm thinking about making a complaint against that copper. He was bloody rude, made out me and the kids had something to do with the body being there. I didn't mind for myself so much, but I was pretty pissed off for the boys. They were scared of him. I mean, let's face it, it can't be much fun finding a corpse—and then to have some idiot in hobnailed boots making the whole situation worse . . ." He broke off with a shake of his head. "Matter of fact I think he was jealous. I was chatting up this bird when he came back, and he looked bloody furious about it. I reckon he fancies her himself, but he's such a dozy pillock he hasn't done anything about it."

As neither Galbraith nor Carpenter rose in Ingram's defense, a silence fell during which the two policemen cast interested glances about the saloon. In other circumstances the light may well have been romantic, but to a couple of law officers intent on spotting anything that might connect its owner to a brutal rape and murder it was worse than useless. Too much of the interior was obscured by shadow, and if there was evidence that Kate and Hannah Sumner had been on board the previous Saturday then it wasn't obvious.

"What do you want to know?" asked Harding then. He was watching John Galbraith as he spoke, and there was something in his eye—*triumph? amusement?*—that made Galbraith think the silence had been deliberate. He had given them an opportunity to look, and they had only themselves to blame if they were disappointed.

"We understand you berthed in Salterns Marina on Saturday night and stayed there most of Sunday?" said Carpenter.

"Yes."

"What time did you tie up, Mr. Harding?"

"I've no idea." He frowned. "Pretty late. What's that got to do with anything?"

"Do you keep a log?"

He glanced toward his chart table. "When I remember."

"May I look at it?"

"Why not?" He leaned over and retrieved a battered exercise book from the clutter of paper on the lid of the chart table. "It's hardly great literature." He handed it across.

Carpenter read the last six entries.

09 August 97.	10:09	*Slipped mooring.*
" "	11:32	*Rounded Hurst Castle.*
10 August 97.	02:17	*Berthed, Salterns Marina.*
" "	18:50	*Slipped mooring.*
" "	19:28	*Exited Poole Harbor.*
11 August 97.	00:12	*Berthed, Lymington.*

"You certainly don't waste your words much, do you?" he murmured, flicking back through the pages to look at other entries. "Doesn't wind speed or course ever feature in your log?"

"Not often."

"Is there a reason for that?"

The young man shrugged. "I know the course to every-where on the south coast, so I don't need to keep remind-ing myself, and wind speed is wind speed. That's part of the beauty of it. Any journey takes as long as it takes. If you're the sort of impatient type who's only interested in arrivals, then sailing will drive you nuts. On a bad day it can take hours to go a few miles."

"It says here you tied up in Salterns Marina at two sev-enteen on Sunday morning," said Carpenter.

"Then I did."

"It also says you left Lymington at ten oh-nine on Sat-urday morning." He did a quick calculation. "Which means it took you fourteen hours to sail approximately thirty miles. That's got to be a record, hasn't it? It works out at about two knots an hour. Is that as fast as this thing can go?"

"It depends on the wind and the tide. On a good day I can do six knots, but the average is probably four. In fact I probably sailed sixty miles on Saturday because I was tacking most of the way." He yawned. "Like I said, it can take hours on a bad day, and Saturday was a bad day."

"Why didn't you use your motor?"

"I didn't want to. I wasn't in a hurry." His expression grew wary with suspicion. "What's this got to do with the woman on the beach?"

"Probably nothing," said Carpenter easily. "We're just tying up some loose ends for the report." He paused, assessing the young man thoughtfully. "I've done a little sailing myself in the past," he said then, "and I'll be honest with you, I don't believe it took you fourteen hours to sail to Poole. If nothing else, the offshore winds as the land cooled in the late afternoon would have boosted your speed well over two knots. I think you sailed on past the Isle of Purbeck, perhaps with the intention of going to Weymouth, and only turned back to Poole when you realized how late it was getting. Am I right?"

"No. I hove to off Christchurch for a few hours to do some fishing and have a nap. That's why it took so long."

Carpenter didn't believe him. "Two minutes ago you gave tacking as the explanation. Now you're claiming a fishing break. Which was it?"

"Both. Tacking and fishing."

"Why isn't it in your log?"

"It wasn't important."

Carpenter nodded. "Your approach to time seems a little"—he sought a suitable word—"individualistic, Mr. Harding. For example, you told the police officer yesterday that you were planning to walk to Lulworth Cove, but Lulworth's a good twenty-five miles from Salterns Marina, fifty in total if you intended to walk back again. That's an ambitious distance for a twelve-hour hike, isn't it, bearing in mind you told the harbormaster at Salterns Marina you'd be back by late afternoon?"

Harding's eyes gleamed with sudden amusement. "It doesn't look nearly as far by sea," he said.

"Did you make it to Lulworth?"

"Like hell I did!" he said with a laugh. "I was completely whacked by the time I reached Chapman's Pool."

"Could that be because you travel light?"

"I don't understand."

"You were carrying a mobile telephone, Mr. Harding, but nothing else. In other words you set out on a fifty-mile hike on one of the hottest days of the year with no fluids, no money, no sunscreen protection, no additional clothes if you started to burn, no hat. Are you usually so careless about your health?"

He pulled a wry face. "Look, all right it was stupid. I admit it. That's the reason I turned back after your bloke drove the kids away. If you're interested, the return journey took twice as long as the journey out because I was so damn knackered."

"About four hours then," suggested DI Galbraith.

"More like six. I started after they left, which was twelve thirty near enough, and got to the marina around six fifteen. I drank about a gallon of water, had something to eat, then set off for Lymington maybe half an hour later."

"So the hike out to Chapman's Pool took three hours?" said Galbraith.

"Something like that."

"Which means you must have left the marina shortly after seven thirty to be able to make the emergency call at ten forty-three."

"If you say so."

"I don't say so at all, Steve. Our information is that you were paying for your berth at eight o'clock, which means you couldn't have left the marina until several minutes later."

Harding linked his hands behind his head and stared across the table at the inspector. "Okay, I left at eight," he said. "What's the big deal?"

"The big deal is there's no way you could have hiked sixteen miles along a rough coastal path in two and a half hours"—he paused, holding Harding's gaze—"and that includes the time you must have lost waiting for the ferry."

There was no hesitation in his reply. "I didn't go along the coastal path, or not to start off with anyway," he said. "I hitched a lift with a couple on the ferry who were heading for the country park near Durlston Head. They dropped me off by the gates leading up to the lighthouse, and I got onto the path there."

"What time was that?"

He shifted his gaze to the ceiling. "Ten forty-three minus however long it takes to jog from Durlston Head to Chapman's Pool, I suppose. Look, the first time I remember checking my watch yesterday was just before I made the nine-nine-nine call. Up until then I couldn't have given a toss what time it was." He looked at Galbraith again, and there was irritation in his dark eyes. "I hate being ruled by the bloody clock. It's social terrorism to force people to conform to arbitrary evaluations of how long something should take. That's why I like sailing. Time's irrelevant, and there's bugger all you can do about it."

"What sort of car did the couple drive?" asked Carpenter, unmoved by the young man's flights of philosophical fancy.

"I don't know. A sedan of some sort. I don't notice cars."

"What color?"

"Blue, I think."

"What were the couple like?"

"We didn't talk much. They had a Manic Street Preachers album on tape. We listened to that."

"Can you describe them, Mr. Harding?"

"Not really. They were ordinary. I spent most of the time looking at the backs of their heads. She had blond hair, and he had dark hair." He reached for the whisky bottle and rolled it between his palms, beginning to lose his patience. "Why the hell are you asking me these questions anyway? What the fuck does it matter how long it took me to get from A to B, or who I met along the way? Does everyone who dials nine-nine-nine get the third degree?"

"Just tying loose ends, sir."

"So you said."

"Wouldn't it be truer to say that Chapman's Pool was your destination, and not Lulworth Cove?"

"No."

A silence developed. Carpenter stared fixedly at Harding while he continued to play with the whisky bottle. "Were there any passengers on board your boat on Saturday?" he asked then.

"No."

"Are you sure about that, sir?"

"Of course I'm bloody sure. Don't you think I'd have noticed them? It's hardly the *QE2*, is it?"

Carpenter leafed idly through the logbook. "Do you *ever* carry passengers?"

"That's none of your business."

"Maybe not, but we've been led to believe you're a bit of a lad." He lifted an amused eyebrow. "Legend has it that you regularly entertain ladies on board. I'm wondering if you ever take them sailing with you"—he jerked his head toward the cabin—"or does all the action take place in there when you're moored up to your buoy?"

Harding took time to consider his answer. "I take some of them out," he admitted at last.

"How often?"

Another long pause. "Once a month, maybe."

Carpenter slapped the exercise book onto the table and drummed his fingers on it. "Then why is there no mention of them in here? Surely you have a responsibility to record the names of everyone on board in case of an accident? Or perhaps you don't care that someone might drown because the coastguards assume you're the only person they're looking for?"

"That's ridiculous," said Harding dismissively. "The boat would have to turn turtle for a scenario like that, and the log'd be lost anyway."

"Have any of your passengers ever gone overboard?"

Harding shook his head but didn't say anything. His eyes flickered with open suspicion from one man to the other, tasting their mood in the way a snake flicks his tongue to taste scent on the air. There was something very studied about every movement he made, and Galbraith regarded him objectively, mindful that he was an actor. He had the impression that Harding was enjoying himself, but he couldn't think why this should be unless Harding had no idea the investigation involved rape and murder and was merely using the experience of an interrogation to practice "method-acting" techniques.

"Do you know a woman by the name of Kate Sumner?" asked Carpenter next.

Harding pushed the bottle aside and leaned forward aggressively. "What if I do?"

"That's not an answer to my question. Let me repeat it. Do you know a woman by the name of Kate Sumner?"

"Yes."

"Do you know her well?"

"Well enough."

"How well is well enough?"

"None of your bloody business."

"Wrong answer, Steve. It's very much our business. It was her body you saw being winched into the helicopter."

His reaction surprised them.

"I had a feeling it might be," he said.

CHAPTER  9

A head across the water, the lights of *Swanage* gleamed like brilliant jewels in the night. Behind, the dying sun dipped beneath the horizon. Danny Spender was yawning profusely, worn out by his long day and three hours' exposure to fresh sea air. He leaned against Ingram's comforting bulk while his older brother stood proudly at the wheel, steering *Miss Creant* home. "He was a dirty person," he confided suddenly.

"Who was?"

"That man yesterday."

Ingram glanced down at him. "What did he do?" he asked, careful to keep the curiosity out of his voice.

"He was rubbing his willy with his telephone," said Danny, "all the time the lady was being rescued."

Ingram looked at Paul to see if he was listening but the other boy was too enthralled by the wheel to pay them any attention. "Did Miss Jenner see him do it?"

Danny's eyelids drooped. "No. He stopped when she came around the corner. Paul reckons he was polishing it—you know, like bowlers do with cricket balls to make them turn in the air—but he wasn't, he was being dirty."

"Why does Paul like him so much?"

The child gave another huge yawn. "Because he wasn't cross with him for spying on a nudie. Dad would be. He was *furious* when Paul got hold of some porno mags. I said they were boring, but Paul said they were natural."

Detective Superintendent Carpenter's telephone rang. "Excuse me," he said, retrieving it from his jacket pocket and flipping open the mouthpiece. "Yes, Campbell," he said. "Right . . . go on . . ." He stared at a point above Steven Harding's head as he spoke, his inevitable frown lengthened and deepened by the shadows thrown by the gaslight as he listened to his DS's report on his interview with Tony Bridges. He clamped the receiver tight against his ear as the name "Bibi" was mentioned, and lowered his eyes curiously to the young man opposite.

Galbraith watched Steven Harding while the one-sided conversation proceeded. The man was listening acutely, straining to pick up what was being said at the other end, all too aware that the topic under discussion was probably himself. Most of the time he stared at the table, but once or twice he raised his eyes to look at Galbraith, and Galbraith felt a curious empathy with him as if he and Harding, by dint of their mutual ignorance of the conversation, were ranged against Carpenter. He had no sense that Harding was guilty, no intuition that he was sitting with a rapist; yet his training told him that that meant nothing. Sociopaths could be as charming and as unthreatening as the rest of humanity, and it was always a potential victim who thought otherwise.

Galbraith resumed his inspection of the interior, picking out shapes in the shadows beyond the gaslight. His eyes had become accustomed to the gloom, and he was able to make out a great deal more now than he had ten minutes ago. With the exception of the clutter on the chart table, everything else was neatly stowed away in lockers or on shelves, and there was nothing to indicate the presence of a woman. It was a masculine environment of wooden planking, black leather seats, and brass fittings, and no color intruded anywhere to adorn its austere simplicity. Monastic, he thought, with approval. His own house, a noisy toy-filled establishment created by a wife who was a power in the National Childbirth Trust, was too cluttered and . . . God forbid, *child-centered!* . . . for an endlessly weary policeman.

The galley, which was to starboard of the companionway, particularly interested him. It was built into an alcove beside the laddered steps and contained a small sink and Calor-gas hob set into a teak worktop with lockers below and shelves above. His attention had been caught by some articles pushed back into the shadows in the corner, and with the passage of time, he had been able to identify them as a half-eaten lump of cheese in a plastic wrapper with a Tesco's sticker and a bag of apples. He felt the shift of Harding's gaze as it followed his, and he wondered if the man had any idea that a forensic pathologist could detail what a victim had eaten before she died.

Carpenter disconnected and placed the telephone on the logbook. "You said you had a feeling the body was Kate Sumner's," he reminded Harding.

"That's right."

"Could you elaborate? Explain when and why you got this feeling?"

"I didn't mean I had a feeling it was going to be *her,* only that it was bound to be somebody I knew otherwise you wouldn't have come out to my boat." He shrugged. "Put it this way, if you do this kind of follow-up every time somebody makes an emergency call, then it's not bloody surprising the country's awash with unconvicted criminals."

Carpenter chuckled, although the frown didn't leave his face, and remained fixed on the young man opposite. "Never believe what you read in newspapers, Steve. Trust me, we always catch the criminals who matter." He examined the actor closely for several seconds. "Tell me about Kate Sumner," he invited. "How well did you know her?"

"Hardly at all," said Harding with airy unconcern. "I've met her maybe half a dozen times since she and her husband moved to Lymington. The first time was when she was having trouble pushing her little girl's buggy over the cobbles near the old Customs House. I gave her a hand with it, and we had a brief chat before she went on up the High Street to do her shopping. After that she always stopped to ask me how I was whenever she saw me."

"Did you like her?"

Harding's gaze strayed toward the telephone while he considered his answer. "She was all right. Nothing special."

"What about William Sumner?" asked Galbraith. "Do you like him?"

"I don't know him well enough to say. He seems okay."

"According to him, he sees you quite often. He's even invited you back to his house."

The young man shrugged. "So? Loads of people invite me to their houses. It doesn't mean I'm close mates with them. Lymington's a sociable place."

"He told me you showed him some photographs of yourself in a gay magazine. I'd have thought you'd need to be pretty friendly with a man to do that."

Harding grinned. "I don't see why. They're good photos. Admittedly he didn't think much of them, but that's his problem. He's pretty straight is old Will Sumner. Wouldn't show his tackle for anything, not even if he was starving, and certainly not in a gay mag."

"I thought you said you didn't know him well."

"I don't need to. You only have to look at him. He probably looked middle-aged when he was eighteen."

Galbraith agreed with him, which made Kate's choice of a husband even odder, he thought. "Still, it's an unusual thing to do, Steve, go around showing nude photos of

yourself to other guys. Do you make a habit of it? Have
you shown them around the yacht club, for example?"

"No."

"Why not?"

Harding didn't answer.

"Maybe you just show them to husbands, eh?" Galbraith lifted an inquiring eyebrow. "It's a great way to
convince a man you've no designs on his wife. I mean if
he thinks you're gay, he'll think you're safe, won't he? Is
that why you did it?"

"I can't remember now. I expect I was drunk, and he
was getting on my nerves."

"Were you sleeping with his wife, Steve?"

"Don't be stupid," said Harding crossly. "I've already
told you I hardly knew her."

"Then the information we've been given that she
wouldn't leave you alone and it was driving you mad is
completely wrong?" said Carpenter.

Harding's eyes widened slightly, but he didn't answer.

"Did she ever come on board this boat?"

"No."

"Are you sure?"

For the first time there was genuine nervousness in the
man's manner. He hunched his shoulders over the table
again and ran his tongue across dry lips. "Look, I don't
really get what all this is about. Okay, somebody drowned
and I knew her—not very well, but I *did* know her.
Okay—too—I can accept it looks like a bizarre coincidence that I was there when she was found—but, listen,
I'm always meeting up with people I know. That's what
sailing's about—bumping into guys that you had a drink
with maybe two years before."

"But that's the root of the problem," said Galbraith rea-
sonably. "According to our information, Kate Sumner
didn't sail. You've said yourself she was never on board
Crazy Daze."

"That doesn't mean she didn't accept a spur-of-the-

moment invitation. There was a French Beneteau called
Mirage anchored in Chapman's Pool yesterday. I saw her
through the boys' binoculars. She was moored up in
Berthon at the end of last week—I know that because they
have this cute kid on board who wanted to know the code
for the lavatories. Well—*Jesus!*—those French guys are
just as likely to have met Kate as I was. Berthon's in
Lymington, isn't it? Kate lives in Lymington. Maybe they
took her for a spin?"

"It's a possibility," agreed Carpenter. He watched Galbraith make a note. "Did you catch the 'cute kid's' name,
by any chance?"

Harding shook his head.

"Do you know of any other friends who might have
taken Kate out on Saturday?"

"No. Like I said, I hardly knew her. But she must have
had some. Everyone around here knows people who sail."

Galbraith jerked his head toward the galley. "Did you
go shopping on Saturday morning before you left for
Poole?" he asked.

"What's that got to do with anything?" Truculence was
back in his voice again.

"It's a simple question. Did you buy the cheese and
apples that are in your galley on Saturday morning?"

"Yes."

"Did you meet Kate Sumner while you were in town?"

Harding hesitated before he replied. "Yes," he admitted
then. "She was outside Tesco's with her little girl."

"What time was that?"

"Nine thirty, maybe." He seized the whisky bottle again
and laid it on its side, placing his forefinger against the
neck and turning it slowly. "I didn't hang around because
I wanted to get off, and she was looking for some sandals
for her child. We said hi and went our separate ways, and
that was it."

"Did you invite her to go sailing with you?" asked Carpenter.

"No." He lost interest in the bottle and abandoned it

with its open neck pointing directly at the superintendent's chest like the barrel of a rifle. "Look, I don't know
what you think I've done," he said, ratcheting up his irritation, "but I'm damn sure you're not allowed to ask me
questions like this. Shouldn't there be a tape recorder?"

"Not when people are merely helping us with our
inquiries, sir," said Carpenter mildly. "As a general rule,
the taping of interviews follows the cautioning of a suspect for an indictable offense. Such interviews can only be
conducted in a police station, where the proper equipment
allows an officer to insert a new blank tape into the
recorder in front of the suspect." He smiled without hostility. "However, if you prefer, you can accompany us to
Winfrith, where we will question you as a voluntary witness under taped conditions."

"No way. I'm not leaving the boat." He stretched his
arms along the back of the settee and gripped the teak
edging as if to emphasize the point. The movement
caused his right hand to brush against a piece of fabric
that was tucked onto the narrow shelf behind the edging
strip, and he glanced at it idly for a moment before crush-
ing it in his hand.

There was a short silence.

"Do you have a girlfriend in Lymington?" asked Carpenter.

"Maybe."

"May I ask what her name is?"

"No."

"Your agent suggested a name. He said she was called
Bibi or Didi."

"That's his problem."

Galbraith was more interested in what was crushed
inside Harding's fist because he had seen what it was. "Do
you have any children?" he asked him.

"No."

"Does your girlfriend have children?"

No answer.

"You're holding a bib in your fist," the DI pointed out,

"so presumably someone who's been on this boat has children."

Harding uncurled his fingers and let the object drop onto the settee. "It's been there for ages. I'm not much of a cleaner."

Carpenter slammed his palm onto the table, making the phone and the whisky bottle jump. "You're annoying me, Mr. Harding," he said severely. "This isn't a piece of theater put on for your benefit, it's a serious investigation into a young woman's drowning. Now you've admitted knowing Kate Sumner and you've admitted seeing her on the morning before she drowned, but if you've no knowledge of how she came to be lying on a shore in Dorset at a time when she and her daughter were assumed to be in Lymington, then I advise you to answer our questions as straightforwardly and honestly as you can. Let me rephrase the question." His eyes narrowed. "Have you recently entertained a girlfriend on board this boat who has a child or children?"

"Maybe," said Harding again.

"There's no maybe about it. Either you have or you haven't."

He abandoned his "crucifixion" pose to slump forward again. "I've several girlfriends with children," he said sulkily, "and I've entertained them all off and on. I'm trying to remember who was the most recent."

"I'd like the names of every one of them," said Carpenter grimly.

"Well you're not going to get them," said Harding with sudden decision, "and I'm not answering any more questions. Not without a solicitor and not without the conversation being recorded. I don't know what the hell I'm supposed to have done, but I'm buggered if you're going to stitch me up for it."

"We're trying to establish how Kate Sumner came to drown in Egmont Bight."

"No comment."

Carpenter righted the whisky bottle and placed a finger

on top of it. "Why did you get drunk last night, Mr. Harding?"

The man stared at the superintendent but didn't say anything.

"You're a compulsive liar, lad. You said yesterday that you grew up on a farm in Cornwall, when the truth is you grew up over a chip shop in Lymington. You told your agent your girlfriend's name was Bibi, when in fact Bibi's been your mate's steady girlfriend for the last four months. You told William Sumner you were a poof, while everyone else around here seems to think you're Casanova. What's your problem, eh? Is your life so boring that you have to play-act some interest into it?"

A faint flush reddened Harding's neck. "Jesus, you're a piece of shit!" he hissed furiously.

Carpenter steepled his hands over the telephone and stared him down. "Have you any objections to us taking a look around your boat, Mr. Harding?"

"Not if you've got a search warrant."

"We haven't."

Harding's eyes gleamed triumphantly. "Don't even think about it then."

The superintendent studied him for a moment. "Kate Sumner was brutally raped before being thrown into the sea to drown," he said slowly, "and all the evidence suggests that the rape took place on board a boat. Now let me explain the rules about searching premises, Mr. Harding. In the absence of the owner's consent, the police have various courses open to them, one of which—assuming they have reasonable cause to suspect that the owner has been guilty of an arrestable offense—is to arrest him and then search any premises he controls in order to prevent the disposal of evidence. Do you understand the implications of what I've just said, bearing in mind that rape and murder are serious arrestable offenses?"

Harding's face had gone very white.

"Answer me, please," snapped Carpenter. "Do you understand the implications of what I've just said?"

"You'll arrest me if I refuse."

Carpenter nodded.

Shock was giving way to anger. "I can't believe you're allowed to behave like this. You can't go around accusing people of rape just so you can search their boats without a warrant. That's abuse of police powers."

"You're forgetting reasonable cause." He enumerated points on his fingers. "*One,* you've admitted meeting Kate Sumner at nine thirty on Saturday morning shortly before you sailed; *two,* you've failed to give an adequate explanation of why it took you fourteen hours to sail between Lymington and Poole; *three,* you've offered conflicting stories about how you came to be on the coastal path above where Kate Sumner's body was found yesterday; *four,* your boat was berthed at a time and in the vicinity of where her daughter was discovered wandering alone and traumatized; *five,* you seem unwilling or unable to give satisfactory answers to straightforward questions . . ." He broke off. "Do you want me to go on?"

Whatever composure Harding had was gone. He looked what he was, badly frightened. "It's all just coincidence," he protested.

"Including little Hannah being found near Salterns Marina yesterday? Was that a coincidence?"

"I guess so . . ." He stopped abruptly, his expression alarmed. "I don't know what you're talking about," he said, the pitch of his voice rising. "Oh, shit! I need to think."

"Well, think on this," said Carpenter evenly. "If, when we search the interior of this boat, we discover a single fingerprint belonging to Kate Sumner—"

"Look, okay," he interrupted, breathing deeply through his nose and making damping gestures with his hands as if it was the detectives who needed calming and not himself. "She and her kid have been on board, but it wasn't on Saturday."

"When was it?"

"I can't remember."

"That's not good enough, Steve. Recently? A long time ago? Under what circumstances? Did you bring them out in your dinghy? Was Kate one of your conquests? Did you make love to her?"

"No, dammit!" he said angrily. "I hated the stupid bitch. She was always throwing herself at me, wanting me to fuck her and wanting me to be nice to that weird kid of hers. They used to hang around down by the fueling pontoon in case I came in for diesel. It used to bug me, it really did."

"So, let me get this straight," murmured Carpenter sarcastically. "To stop her pestering you, you invited her on board?"

"I thought if I was polite . . . Ah, what the hell! Go ahead, search the damn boat. You won't find anything."

Carpenter nodded to Galbraith. "I suggest you start in the cabin. Do you have another lamp, Steve?"

Harding shook his head.

Galbraith unhooked a flashlight from the aft bulkhead and flicked the switch to see if it was working. "This'll do." He propped open the cabin door and swung the beam around the interior, settling almost immediately on a small pile of clothes on the port shelf. He used the end of his pen to push a flimsy blouse, a bra, and a pair of panties to one side to reveal some tiny child's shoes nestling together on the shelf. He turned the beam of the flashlight full on them and stood back so they were visible to Carpenter and Harding.

"Who do the shoes belong to, Mr. Harding?"

No answer.

"Who do the women's clothes belong to?"

No answer.

"If you have an explanation for why these articles are on board your boat, Steve, then I advise you to give it to us now."

"They're my girlfriend's," he said in a strangled voice. "She has a son. The shoes belong to him."

"Who is she, Steve?"

"I can't tell you. She's married, and she's got nothing to do with this."

Galbraith emerged from the cabin with one of the shoes hooked on the end of his biro. "There's a name written on the strap, guv, H. Sumner. And there's staining on the floor in here." He pointed the flashlight beam toward some dark marks beside the bunk bed. "It looks fairly recent."

"I need to know what caused the stains, Steve."

In one lithe movement, the young man erupted out of his seat and grabbed the whisky bottle in both hands, swinging it violently to his left and forcing Galbraith to retreat into the cabin. "Enough, okay!" he growled, moving toward the chart table. "You're way off beam on this one. Now back off before I do something I'll regret. You've got to give me some space, for Christ's sake. I need to think."

He was unprepared for the ease with which Galbraith plucked the bottle from his grasp and spun him around to face the teak-clad wall while securing his wrists behind his back with handcuffs.

"You'll have plenty of time for thinking when we get you into a police cell," said the DI unemotionally as he pushed the young man facedown onto the settee. "I am arresting you on suspicion of murder. You do not have to say anything, but it may harm your defense if you do not mention, when questioned, something you later rely on in court. Anything you do say may be given in evidence."

Had William Sumner not had a key to his front door, Sandy Griffiths would have questioned whether he had ever lived in Langton Cottage, because his knowledge of the house was minimal. Indeed, the police constable who had stayed behind to act as her shadow was better informed than he was, having watched the scene-of-crime officers meticulously examine every room. Sumner looked at her blankly each time she asked him a question. Which cupboard was the tea in? He didn't know. Where did Kate keep Hannah's nappies? He didn't know. Which towel or flannel was hers? He didn't know. Could he at least show her to Hannah's room so that she could put the child to bed? He looked toward the stairs. "It's up there," he said, "you can't miss it."

He seemed fascinated by the invasion of his home by the search team. "What were they looking for?" he asked.

"Anything that will connect with Kate's disappearance," said Griffiths.

"Does that mean they think I did it?"

Griffiths eased Hannah on her hip and turned the child's head into her shoulder in a somewhat futile attempt to block her ears. "It's standard procedure, William, but I don't think it's something we should talk about in front of your daughter. I suggest you take it up with DI Galbraith tomorrow."

But he was either too insensitive or too careless of his daughter's welfare to take the hint. He stared at a photograph of his wife on the mantelpiece. "I couldn't have done it," he said. "I was in Liverpool."

At the request of Dorsetshire Constabulary, the Liverpool police had already begun preliminary inquiries at the Regal Hotel. It was early days, of course, but the account William Sumner had settled that morning made interesting reading. Despite being a heavy user of the telephone, coffee lounge, restaurant, and bar in the first two days, there was a period of twenty-four hours between lunchtime on Saturday and a noon drink in the bar on Sunday when he had failed to make use of a single hotel service.

CHAPTER 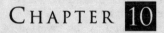 10

During the twenty minutes that he waited in the sitting room at Langton Cottage the following morning to speak to William Sumner, John Galbraith learned two things about the man's dead wife. The first was that Kate Sumner was vain. Every photograph on display was either of herself, or of herself and Hannah, and he searched without success for a likeness of William, or even of an elderly woman who might have been William's mother. In frustration he ended up counting the pictures that were there—thirteen—each of which showed the same prettily smiling face within its framework of golden curls. Was this the cult of the personality taken to its extreme, he wondered, or an indication of a deep-seated inferiority which needed constant reminders that to be photogenic was a talent like any other?

The second thing he learned was that he could never have lived with Kate. She delighted, it seemed, in applying frills to everything: lace curtains with frills, valances with frills, armchairs with frills—even the lampshades had tassels attached to them. Nothing, not even the walls, had escaped her taste for overembellishment. Langton

Cottage was of nineteenth-century origin with beamed ceilings and brick fireplaces, and instead of the plain white plaster that would have shown these features off to their best advantage, she had covered the walls of the sitting room—probably at considerable expense—with mock Regency wallpaper, adorned with gilt stripes, white bows, and baskets of unnaturally colored fruit. Galbraith shuddered at the desecration of what could have been a charming room and unconsciously contrasted it with the timbered simplicity of Steven Harding's sloop, which was currently being put under a microscope by scene-of-crime officers while Harding, exercising his right to remain silent, cooled his heels in a police cell.

Rope Walk was a quiet tree-lined avenue to the west of the Royal Lymington and Town yacht clubs, and Langton Cottage had clearly not been cheap. As he knocked on the door at eight o'clock on Tuesday morning after two hours' sleep, Galbraith wondered how big a mortgage William had had to raise to buy it and how much he earned as a pharmaceutical chemist. He could see no logic behind the move from Chichester, particularly as neither Kate nor William appeared to have any links with Lymington.

He was let in by WPC Griffiths, who pulled a face when he told her he needed to talk to Sumner. "You'll be lucky," she whispered. "Hannah's been bawling her head off most of the night, so I doubt you'll get any sense out of him. He's had almost as little sleep as I've had."

"Join the club."

"You, too, eh?"

Galbraith smiled. "How's he holding up?"

She shrugged. "Not too well. Keeps bursting into tears and saying it's not supposed to be like this." She lowered her voice even further. "I'm really concerned about Hannah. She's obviously scared of him. She works herself into a tantrum the minute he enters the room, then calms down rapidly as soon as he leaves. I ordered him to bed in the end to try and get her to sleep."

Galbraith looked interested. "How does he react?"

"That's the odd thing. He doesn't react at all. He just ignores it as if it's something he's grown used to."

"Has he said why she does it?"

"Only that, being out at work so much, he's never had a chance to bond with her. It could be true, you know. I get the impression Kate swaddled her in cotton wool. There are so many safety features in this house that I can't see how Hannah was ever expected to learn anything. Every door has a child lock on it—even the wardrobe in her own bedroom—which means she can't explore, can't choose her own clothes, or even make a mess if she wants to. She's almost three, but she's still sleeping in a crib. That's pretty weird, you know. More like prison bars than a nursery. It's a damned odd way to bring up a child and, frankly, I'm not surprised she's a withdrawn little thing."

"I suppose it's occurred to you that she might be scared of him because she watched him kill her mother," murmured Galbraith.

Sandy Griffiths spread her hand and made a rocking motion. "Except I don't see how he can have done it. He's made a list of some colleagues who can alibi him for Saturday night in Liverpool, and if that holds good then there's no way he could have been shoving his wife in the water at one A.M. in Dorset."

"No," agreed Galbraith. "Still . . ." He pursed his lips in thought. "Do you realize the SOCOs found no drugs in this house at all, not even paracetamol? Which is odd, considering William's a pharmaceutical chemist."

"Maybe that's why there aren't any. He knows what goes into them."

"Mmm. Or they were deliberately cleared out before we got here." He glanced toward the stairs. "Do you like him?" he asked her.

"Not much," she admitted, "but you don't want to go by what I say. I've always been a lousy judge of character where men are concerned. He could have done with a good smacking thirty years ago, in my opinion, just to teach him some manners but as things are, he seems to view women as serving wenches."

He laughed. "Are you going to be able to stick it out?"

She rubbed her tired eyes. "God knows! Your chap left about half an hour ago, and there's supposed to be some relief coming when William's taken away to identify the body and talk to the doctor who examined Hannah. The trouble is, I can't see Hannah letting me go that easily. She clings to me like a limpet. I'm using the spare room to grab kip when I can, and I thought I'd try to organize some temporary cover while she's asleep so I can stay on the premises. But I'll need to get hold of my governor to organize someone locally." She sighed. "I suppose you want me to wake William for you."

He patted her shoulder. "No. Just point me toward his room. I'm happy to do the business."

She was sorely tempted, but shook her head. "You'll disturb Hannah," she said, baring her teeth in a threatening grimace, "and I swear to God I'll kill you if she starts howling again before I've had a fag and some black coffee. I'm bushed. I can't take any more of her screaming without mega-fixes of caffeine and nicotine."

"Is it putting you off babies?"

"It's putting me off husbands," she said. "I'd have coped better if he hadn't kept hovering like a dark cloud over my shoulder." She eased open the sitting-room door. "You can wait in here till he comes. You'll love it. It has all the makings of a shrine."

Galbraith heard footsteps on the stairs and turned to face the door as it opened. Sumner was in his early forties, but he looked a great deal older than that today, and Galbraith suspected Harding would have been a lot harsher in his description if he could have seen Kate's husband like this. He was unshaven and disheveled, and his face was inexpressibly weary, but whether from grief or lack of sleep, it was impossible to say. Nevertheless, his eyes shone brightly enough, and Galbraith took note of the fact. Lack of sleep did not lead automatically to blunted intelligence.

"Good morning, sir," he said. "I'm sorry to bother you again so early but I've more questions to ask, and I'm afraid they won't wait."

"That's all right. Sit down. I feel I was less than helpful last night, but I was so whacked I couldn't think properly." He took an armchair and left Galbraith to the sofa. "I've made those lists you wanted. They're on the table in the kitchen."

"Thanks." He gave the man a searching look. "Did you get any sleep?"

"Not really. I couldn't stop thinking about it. It's all so illogical. I could understand if they'd both drowned, but it doesn't make sense that Kate's dead and Hannah's alive."

Galbraith agreed. He and Carpenter had been puzzling over that very fact most of the night. Why had Kate had to swim for her life while the toddler was allowed to live? The neat explanation—that the boat was *Crazy Daze,* that Hannah *had* been on board but had managed to release herself while Harding was walking to Chapman's Pool—failed to address the questions of why the child hadn't been pushed into the sea along with her mother, why Harding was so unconcerned about her wails being heard by other boat users in the marina that he'd left her on her own, and who had fed, watered, and changed her nappy in the hours before she was found.

"Have you had time to go through your wife's wardrobe, Mr. Sumner? Do you know if any of her clothes are missing?"

"Not that I can tell . . . but it doesn't mean much," he added as an afterthought. "I don't really notice what people wear, you see."

"Suitcases?"

"I don't think so."

"All right." He opened his briefcase on the sofa beside

him. "I've some articles of clothing to show you, Mr. Sumner. Please tell me if you recognize any of them." He removed a plastic bag containing the flimsy blouse found on board *Crazy Daze,* which he held out for the other man to look at.

Sumner shook his head, without taking it. "It's not Kate's," he said.

"Why so positive," Galbraith asked curiously, "if you didn't notice what she wore?"

"It's yellow. She hated yellow. She said it didn't suit people with fair hair." He gestured vaguely toward the door. "There's no yellow anywhere in the house."

"Fair enough." He took out the bags containing the bra and panties. "Do you recognize either of these as belonging to your wife?"

Sumner reached out a reluctant hand and took both bags, examining the contents closely through the clear plastic. "I'd be surprised if they were hers," he said, handing them back. "She liked lace and frills, and these are very plain. You can compare them with the other things in her drawers, if you like. You'll see what I mean."

Galbraith nodded. "I'll do that. Thank you." He took out the bag with the child's shoes and laid them on his right palm. "What about these?"

Sumner shook his head again. "I'm sorry. All children's shoes look alike to me."

"They have H. Sumner printed inside the strap."

He shrugged. "Then they must be Hannah's."

"Not necessarily," said Galbraith. "They're very small, more suited to a one-year-old than a three-year-old, and anyone can write a name into some shoes."

"Why would they want to do that?"

"Pretense, perhaps."

The other man frowned. "Where did you find them?"

But Galbraith shook his head. "I'm afraid I can't reveal that at this stage." He held the shoes up again. "Would Hannah recognize them, do you think? They may be a pair of cast-offs."

"She might if the policewoman showed them to her," said Sumner. "There's no point in my trying. She screams her head off every time she sees me." He swept imaginary dirt from the arm of the chair. "The trouble is I spend so much time at work that she's never had the chance to get to know me properly."

Galbraith gave him a sympathetic smile while wondering if there was any truth in the statement. Who could contradict him, after all? Kate was dead; Hannah was tongue-tied; and the various neighbors who'd already been interviewed claimed to know little about William. Or indeed, Kate herself.

"To be honest I've only met him a couple of times and he didn't exactly impress me. He works very hard, of course, but they were never ones for entertaining. She was quite sweet, but we were hardly what I'd call friends. You know how it is. You don't choose your neighbors; they get thrust upon you. . . ."

"He's not what you'd call sociable. Kate told me once that he spent his evenings and weekends working out formulas on his computer while she watched soaps on the telly. I feel awful about her dying like that. I wish I'd had more time to talk to her. I think she must have been quite lonely, you know. The rest of us all work, of course, so she was a bit of a rarity, staying at home and doing the housework. . . ."

"He's a bully. He took my wife to task about one of the fencing panels between our gardens, said it needed replacing, and when she told him it was his ivy that was pulling it down, he threatened her with court proceedings. No, that's the only contact we've had with him. It was enough. I don't like the man. . . ."

"I saw more of Kate than I saw of him. It was an odd marriage. They never did anything together. I sometimes wondered if they even liked each other very much. Kate was very sweet, but she hardly ever talked about William. To be honest, I don't think they had much in common. . . ."

"I understand Hannah cried most of the night. Does she usually do that?"

"No," Sumner answered without hesitation, "but then Kate always cuddled her when she was upset. She's crying for her mother, poor little thing."

"So you haven't noticed any difference in her behavior?"

"Not really."

"The doctor who examined her after she was taken to the Poole police station was very concerned about her, described her as unnaturally withdrawn, backward in her development, and possibly suffering from some sort of psychological trauma." Galbraith smiled slightly. "Yet you're saying that's quite normal for Hannah?"

Sumner colored slightly as if he'd been caught out in a lie. "She's always been a little bit"—he hesitated—"well, odd. I thought she was either autistic or deaf so we had her tested, but the GP said there was nothing wrong and just advised us to be patient. He said children were manipulative, and if Kate did less for her she'd be forced to ask for what she wanted and the problem would go away."

"When was this?"

"About six months ago."

"What's your GP's name?"

"Dr. Attwater."

"Did Kate take his advice?"

He shook his head. "Her heart wasn't in it. Hannah could always make her understand what she wanted, and she couldn't see the point of forcing her to talk before she was ready."

Galbraith made a note of the GP's name. "You're a clever man, Mr. Sumner," he said next, "so I'm sure you know why I'm asking you these questions."

A ghost of a smile flickered across the man's tired face. "I prefer William," he said, "and yes, of course I do. My daughter screams every time she sees me; my wife had ample opportunity to cheat on me because I'm hardly ever at home; I'm angry because I didn't want to move to Lymington; the mortgage on this place is way too high and I'd like to get shot of it; she was lonely because she hadn't made many friends; and wives are more usually murdered by their partners out of fury than by strangers out of lust." He gave a hollow laugh. "About the only thing in my favor is a cast-iron alibi, and believe me, I've spent most of the night thanking God for it."

Under the rules governing police detention, there is a limit to how long a person may be held without charge, and the pressure to find evidence against Steven Harding mounted as the hours ticked by. It was notable more for its absence. The stains on the floor of the cabin, which had looked so promising the night before, turned out to be whisky-induced vomit—blood group A, matching Harding's—and a microscopic examination of his boat failed to produce any evidence that an act of violence had occurred on board.

If the pathologist's findings were right—*"bruising and abrasions to back (pronounced on shoulder blades and buttocks) and inside of thighs, indicative of forced intercourse on a hard surface such as a deck or an uncarpeted floor—some blood loss from abrasions in vagina"*—the wooden planking of the deck and/or saloon and/or cabin should have had traces of blood, skin tissue, and even semen trapped between the grooved joints or under rogue splinters of wood. But no such traces were found. Dried salt was scraped in profusion from the deck planking, but while this might suggest he had scrubbed the topsides down with sea water to remove evidence, it was axiomatic that dried salt would be found on a sailing boat.

On the more likely probability that a blanket or rug had been spread on the hard surface before Kate Sumner had been forced onto it, every item of cloth on board was examined with similarly negative results, although it was all too obvious that any such item would have been thrown overboard along with Kate's clothes and anything else connecting her to the boat. Kate's body was re-examined inch by inch, in the hope that splinters of wood, linking her to *Crazy Daze,* had become embedded under her skin, but either the flaying action of the sea on open wounds had washed the evidence away or it had never been there in the first place. It was a similar story with her broken fingernails. If anything had ever been underneath them, it had long since vanished.

Only the sheets in the cabin showed evidence of semen staining, but as the bedclothes hadn't been washed for a very long time it was impossible to say whether the stains were the product of recent intercourse. Indeed, as only two alien hairs were discovered on the pillows and bed-clothes—neither of which was Kate's although both were blond—the conclusion was that, far from being the promiscuous stallion portrayed by the harbormaster, Steven Harding was in fact a lonely masturbator.

A small quantity of cannabis and a collection of unopened condoms were discovered in the bedside locker, together with three torn Mates wrappers minus their contents. No used condoms were found. Every container was examined for benzodiazepine, Rohypnol and/or *any* hypnotic. No indications were found. Despite a comprehensive search for pornographic photographs and magazines, none were found. Subsequent searches of Harding's car and flat in London were equally disappointing, although the flat contained thirty-five adult movies. All were on general release, however. A warrant was issued to search Tony Bridges' house in Lymington, but there was nothing to incriminate Steven Harding or to connect him or any-one else there with Kate Sumner. Despite extensive inquiries, police could come up with no other premises used or owned by Harding, and bar a single sighting of him talking to Kate outside Tesco's on Saturday morning, no one reported seeing them together.

There was fingerprint and palm evidence that Kate and Hannah Sumner had been on board *Crazy Daze,* but too many of the prints were overlaid with other prints, few of which were Steven Harding's, for the SOCOs to be confident that the visit had been a recent one. Considerable interest was raised by the fact that twenty-five different sets of fingerprints, excluding Carpenter's, Galbraith's, Kate's, Hannah's, and Steven's—at least five of the sets being small enough to be children's—were lifted from the saloon, some of which matched prints lifted from Bridges' house, but few of which were replicated in the cabin. Demonstrably, therefore, Harding had entertained people on board, although the nature of the entertainment remained a mystery. He explained it by saying he always invited fellow sailors into the saloon whenever he took a berth in a marina, and in the absence of proof to the contrary, the police accepted his explanation. Nevertheless, they remained curious about it.

In view of the cheese and apples in the galley, Kate Sumner's last meal looked like something the police could run with until the pathologist pointed out that it was impossible to link semidigested food with a particular purchase. A *Tesco's* Golden Delicious, minced with gastric acids, showed the same chemical printout as a *Sainsbury's* Golden Delicious. Even the child's bib proved inconclusive when the fingerprint evidence on the plastic surface demonstrated that, while Steven Harding and two unidentified others had certainly touched it, Kate Sumner had not.

Briefed by Nick Ingram, attention was paid to the only rucksack found on the boat, a triangular black one with a handful of sweet wrappers in the bottom. Neither Paul nor Danny Spender had been able to give an accurate description of it—Danny: *"It was a big black one . . .";* Paul: *"It was quite big . . . I think it might have been green . . ."*— but it told them nothing about what it might have contained on Sunday morning or indeed identified it as the one the boys had seen. Steven Harding, who seemed baffled by police interest in his rucksack, claimed it was certainly the one he had been using that day and explained he had left it on the hillside because it had a liter bottle of water in it, and he couldn't be bothered to lug it down to the boat sheds simply to lug it all the way up again. He further said that PC Ingram had never asked him about a rucksack, which is why he hadn't mentioned it at the time.

The nail in the coffin of police suspicion was supplied by a cashier at Tesco's in Lymington High Street who had been on duty the previous Saturday.

" 'Course I know Steve," she said, identifying his photograph. "He comes in every Saturday for provisions. Did I see him talking to a blond woman and child last week? Sure I did. He spotted them as he was about to leave and he said, 'Damn!' so I said, 'What's the problem?' and he said, 'I know that woman and she's going to talk to me because she always does,' so I said, *jealous*-like, 'She's very pretty,' and he said, 'Forget it, Dawn, she's married, and anyway I'm in a hurry.' And he was right. She did talk to him, but he didn't hang around, just tapped his watch and scarpered. You want my opinion? He had something good lined up, and he didn't want delaying. She looked mighty miffed when he left, but I didn't blame her for it. Steve's a bit of a hunk. I'd go for him myself if I wasn't a grandmother three times over."

William Sumner claimed to know little about the management of Langton Cottage or his wife's regular movements. "I'm away from the house for twelve hours a day, from seven in the morning till seven at night," he told Galbraith as if it were something to be proud of. "I was much more *au fait* with her routine in Chichester, probably because I knew the people and the shops she was talking about. Things register better when you recognize names. It's all so different here."

"Did Steven Harding feature in her conversation?" asked Galbraith.

"Is he the bastard who had Hannah's shoes?" demanded Sumner angrily.

Galbraith shook his head. "We'll get on a lot faster if you don't keep second-guessing me, William. Let me remind you that we still don't know if the shoes belonged to Hannah." He held the other man's gaze. "And, while I'm about it, let me *warn* you that if you start speculating on anything to do with this case, you could prejudice any prosecution we try to bring. And that could mean Kate's killer going free."

"I'm sorry." He raised his hands in apology. "Go on."

"Did Steven Harding feature in her conversation?" Galbraith asked again.

"No."

Galbraith referred to the lists of names he had produced. "Are any of the men on here ex-boyfriends? The ones in Portsmouth, for example. Did she go out with any of them before she went out with you?"

Another shake of the head. "They're all married."

Galbraith wondered about the naiveté of that statement, but didn't pursue the issue. Instead, he went on to try to build a picture of Kate's early life. It was about as easy as building houses out of straw. The potted history that William gave him was notable more for its gaps than its inclusions. Her maiden name had been Hill, but whether that was her mother's or her father's surname, he didn't know.

"I don't think they were married," he said.

"And Kate never knew him?"

"No. He left when she was a baby."

She and her mother had lived in a council flat in Birmingham, although he had no idea where it was, which school Kate had gone to, where she had trained as a secretary, or even where she had worked before joining Pharmatec UK. Galbraith asked him if she had any friends from that time with whom she had kept in contact, but William shook his head and said he didn't think so. He produced an address book from a drawer in a small bureau in the corner of the room and said Galbraith could check for himself. "But you won't find anyone from Birmingham in there."

"When did she move?"

"When her mother died. She told me once that she wanted to put as much distance between herself and where she grew up as she could, so she moved to Portsmouth and rented a flat over a shop in one of the back streets."

"Did she say why distance was important?"

"I think she felt she'd have less of a chance to get on if she stayed put. She was quite ambitious."

"For a career?" asked Galbraith in surprise, recalling Sumner's assertion the day before that Kate's one ambition had been to have a family of her own. "I thought you said she was happy to give up working when she got pregnant."

There was a short silence. "I suppose you're planning to talk to my mother?"

Galbraith nodded.

He sighed. "She didn't approve of Kate, so she'll tell you she was a gold-digger. Not in so many words, perhaps, but the implication will be clear. She can be pretty vitriolic when she chooses." He stared at the floor.

"Is it true?" prompted Galbraith after a moment.

"Not in my opinion. The only thing Kate wanted was something better for her children than she had herself. I admired her for it."

"And your mother didn't?"

"It's not important," said Sumner. "She never approved of anyone I brought home, which probably explains why it took me so long to get married."

Galbraith glanced at one of the vacuously smiling photographs on the mantelpiece. "Was Kate a strong character?"

"Oh, yes. She was single-minded about what she wanted." He gave a lopsided smile as he made a gesture that encompassed the room. "This was it. The dream. A house of her own. Social acceptance. Respectability. It's why I know she'd never have had an affair. She wouldn't have risked this for anything."

Yet another display of naiveté? Galbraith wondered. "Maybe she didn't realize there was a risk involved," he said dispassionately. "By your own admission, you're hardly ever here, so she could easily have been conducting an affair that you knew nothing about."

Sumner shook his head. "You don't understand," he said. "It wasn't fear of *me* finding out that would have stopped her. She had me wound around her little finger from the first time I met her." A wry smile thinned his lips. "My wife was an old-fashioned puritan. It was fear of other people finding out that ruled her life. Respectability *mattered.*"

It was on the tip of the DI's tongue to ask this man if he had ever loved his wife, but he decided against it. Whatever answer Sumner gave, he wouldn't believe him. He felt the same instinctive dislike of William that Sandy Griffiths felt, but he couldn't decide if it was a chemical antipathy or a natural revulsion that was inspired by his own unshakable hunch that William had killed his wife.

Galbraith's next port of call was The Old Convent, Osborne Crescent in Chichester, where Mrs. Sumner senior lived in sheltered accommodation at number two. It had obviously been a school once but was now converted into a dozen small flats with a resident warden. Before he went in, he stared across the road at the solidly rectangular 1930s semidetached houses on the other side, wondering idly which had been the Sumners' before it was sold to buy Langton Cottage. They were all so similar that it was impossible to say, and he had a sneaking sympathy for Kate's desire to move. Being respectable, he thought, wasn't necessarily synonymous with being boring.

Angela Sumner surprised him, because she wasn't what he was expecting. He had pictured an autocratic old snob with reactionary views, and found instead a tough, gutsy woman, wheelchair-bound by rheumatoid arthritis, but with eyes that brimmed with good humor. She told him to put his warrant card through her letter-slot before she'd allow him entrance, then made him follow her electrically operated chair down the corridor into the sitting room. "I suppose you've given William the third degree," she said, "and now you're expecting me to confirm or deny what he's told you."

"Have you spoken to him?" asked Galbraith with a smile.

She nodded, pointing to a chair. "He phoned me yesterday evening to tell me that Kate was dead."

He took the chair she indicated. "Did he tell you how she died?"

She nodded. "It shocked me, although to be honest I guessed something dreadful must have happened the minute I saw Hannah's picture on the television. Kate would never have abandoned the child. She doted on her."

"Why didn't you phone the police yourself when you recognized Hannah's photograph?" he asked curiously. "Why did you ask William to do it?"

She sighed. "Because I kept telling myself it couldn't possibly be Hannah—I mean, she's such an unlikely child to be wandering around a strange town on her own—and I didn't want to appear to be causing trouble if it wasn't. I phoned Langton Cottage over and over again, and it was only when it became clear yesterday morning that no one was going to answer that I phoned William's secretary and she told me where he was."

"What kind of trouble would you have been causing?"

She didn't answer immediately. "Let's just say Kate wouldn't have believed my motives were pure if I made a genuine error. You see, I haven't seen Hannah since they moved, twelve months ago, so I wasn't one hundred percent sure I was right anyway. Children change so quickly at that age."

It wasn't much of an answer, but Galbraith let it go for

the moment. "So you didn't know William had gone to Liverpool?"

"There's no reason why I should. I don't expect him to tell me where he is all the time. He rings once a week and drops in occasionally on his way back to Lymington, but we don't live in each other's pockets."

"That's quite a change, though, isn't it?" suggested Galbraith. "Didn't you and he share a house before he was married?"

She gave a little laugh. "And you think that means I knew what he was doing? You obviously don't have grown-up children, Inspector. It makes no difference whether they live with you or not, you still can't keep tabs on them."

"I have a seven- and five-year-old who already have a more exciting social life than I've ever had. It gets worse, does it?"

"It depends on whether you approve of them spreading their wings. I think the more space you give them, the more likely they are to appreciate you as they get older. In any case, my husband converted the house into two self-contained flats about fifteen years ago. He and I lived downstairs, and William lived upstairs, and days could go by without our paths crossing. We lived quite separate lives, which didn't change much even after my husband died. I became more disabled, of course, but I hope I was never a burden to William."

Galbraith smiled. "I'm sure you weren't, but it must have been a bit of a worry, knowing he'd get married one day and all the arrangements would have to change."

She shook her head. "Quite the reverse. I was longing for him to settle down, but he never showed any inclination to do it. He adored sailing, of course, and spent most of his free time out on his Contessa. He had girlfriends, but none that he took seriously."

"Were you pleased when he married Kate?"

There was a short silence. "Why wouldn't I be?"

Galbraith shrugged. "No reason. I'm just interested."

Her eyes twinkled suddenly. "I suppose he's told you I thought his wife was a gold-digger?"

"Yes."

"Good," she said. "I hate having to tell lies." She raised the back of a gnarled hand to her cheek to wipe away a stray hair. "In any case there's no point pretending I was happy about it when anyone around here will tell you I wasn't. She *was* a gold-digger, but that wasn't why I thought he was mad to marry her. It was because they had so little in common. She was ten years younger than he was, virtually uneducated, and completely besotted by all the material things in life. She told me once that what she really enjoyed in life was *shopping.*" She shook her head in bewilderment that anything so mundane could produce a height of sensation. "Frankly, I couldn't see what was going to keep them together. She wasn't remotely interested in sailing and refused point-blank to have anything to do with that side of William's life."

"Did he go on sailing after they married?"

"Oh, yes. She didn't have a problem with him doing it, she just wouldn't go herself."

"Did she get to know any of his sailing friends?"

"Not in the way you mean," she said bluntly.

"What way's that, Mrs. Sumner?"

"William said you think she was having an affair."

"We can't ignore the possibility."

"Oh, I think you can, you know." She gave him an old-fashioned look. "Kate knew the price of everything and the value of nothing, and she'd certainly have calculated the cost of adultery in terms of what she'd lose if William found out about it. In any case, she wouldn't have been having an affair with any of William's sailing friends in Chichester. They were all far more shocked by his choice of wife than I was. She made no effort to fit in, you see, plus there was a generation gap between her and most of them. Frankly, they were all completely bemused by her rather inane conversation. She had no opinions on anything except soap operas, pop music, and film stars."

"So what was her attraction for William? He's an intelligent man and certainly doesn't give the impression of someone who likes inane conversation."

A resigned smile. "Sex, of course. He'd had his fill of intelligent women. I remember him saying that the girlfriend before Kate"—she sighed—"her name was Wendy Plater, and she was such a nice girl . . . so suitable . . . that her idea of foreplay was to discuss the effects of sexual activity on the metabolism. I said, how interesting, and William laughed and said, given the choice, he preferred physical stimulation."

Galbraith kept a straight face. "I don't think he's alone, Mrs. Sumner."

"I'm not going to argue the point, Inspector. In any case, Kate was obviously far more experienced than he was, even though she was ten years younger. She knew William wanted a family, and she gave him a baby before you could say Jack Robinson." He heard the reservation in her voice and wondered about it. "Her approach to marriage was to spoil her husband rotten, and William reveled in it. He didn't have to do a damn thing except take himself to work every day. It was the most old-fashioned arrangement you can imagine, with the wife as chief admirer and bottle-washer, and the husband swanking around as breadwinner. I think it's what's known as a passive-aggressive relationship, where the woman controls the man by making him dependent on her while giving the impression she's dependent on him."

"And you didn't approve?"

"Only because it wasn't my idea of a marriage. Marriage should be a meeting of minds as well as bodies, otherwise it becomes a wasteground where nothing grows. All she could talk about with any enthusiasm were her shopping expeditions and who she'd bumped into during the day, and it was quite clear William never listened to a word she said."

He wondered if she realized William had yet to be eliminated as a suspect. "So what are you saying? That he was bored with her?"

She gave his question long consideration. "No, I don't think he was bored," she said then, "I think he just realized he could take her for granted. That's why his working day got progressively longer and why he didn't object to the move to Lymington. She approved of whatever he did, you see, so he didn't have to bother spending time with her. There was no challenge in the relationship." She paused. "I hoped children would be something they could share, but Kate appropriated Hannah at birth as something that was the preserve of women, and if I'm honest the poor little thing created even more distance between them. She used to roar her head off every time William tried to pick her up, and he soon got bored with her. I took Kate to task about it, as a matter of fact, told her she wasn't doing the child any good by swamping her in mother love, but it only made her angry with me." She sighed. "I shouldn't have interfered. It's what drove them away, of course."

"From Chichester?"

"Yes. It was a mistake. They made too many changes in their lives too quickly. William had to pay off the mortgage on my flat when he sold the house across the road, then take out a much larger one to buy Langton Cottage. He sold his boat, gave up sailing. Not to mention flogging himself to death driving to and from work every day. And all for what? A house he didn't even like very much."

Galbraith was careful to keep the interest out of his voice. "Then why did they move?"

"Kate wanted it."

"But if they weren't getting on, why did William agree to it?"

"Regular sex," she said crossly. "In any case, I didn't say they weren't getting on."

"You said he was taking her for granted. Isn't it the same thing?"

"Not at all. From William's point of view she was the

perfect wife. She kept house for him, provided him with children, and never pestered him once to put himself out." Her mouth twisted into a bitter smile. "They got on like a house on fire as long as he paid the mortgage and kept her in the manner to which she was rapidly becoming accustomed. I know you're not supposed to say these things anymore, but she was awfully common. The few friends she made were quite dreadful . . . loud . . . over-made-up. . . ." She shuddered. "Dreadful!"

Galbraith pressed his fingertips together beneath his chin and studied her with open curiosity. "You really didn't like her, did you?"

Again Mrs. Sumner considered the question carefully. "No, I didn't," she said then. "Not because she was overtly unpleasant or unkind, but because she was the most self-centered woman I've ever met. If everything—and I do *mean* everything—in life wasn't revolving around her she maneuvered and manipulated until it did. Look at Hannah if you don't believe me. Why encourage the child to be so dependent on her unless she couldn't bear to compete for her affections?"

Galbraith thought of the photographs in Langton Cottage, and his own conclusion that Kate Sumner was vain. "If it wasn't an affair that went wrong, then what do you think happened? What persuaded her to take Hannah on board someone's boat when she hated sailing so much?"

"What a strange question," the woman said in surprise. *"Nothing* would have persuaded her. She was obviously forced on board. Why should you doubt that? Anyone who was prepared to rape and kill her, then leave her child to wander the streets alone, would obviously have no qualms about using threats to coerce her."

"Except marinas and harbors are busy places, and there have been no reports of anyone seeing a woman and child being put on board a boat against their will." Indeed, as far as the police had been able to establish so far, there had been no sightings of Kate and Hannah Sumner at all at any of the access points to boats along the Lymington

River. They hoped for better luck on Saturday when the weekenders returned, but meanwhile, they were working in the dark.

"I don't suppose there would have been," said Angela Sumner stoutly, "not if the man was carrying Hannah and threatening to hurt her if Kate didn't do what he said. She loved that child to distraction. She'd have done anything to prevent her being harmed."

Galbraith was about to point out that such a scenario would have depended on Hannah's willingness to be carried by a man, which seemed unlikely in view of the psychiatric report and Angela Sumner's own admission that she screamed her head off every time her own father tried to pick her up, but he had second thoughts. The logic was sound even if the method had varied. . . . Hannah had obviously been sedated. . . .

CHAPTER 11

Memo

To: Detective Superintendent Carpenter
From: Detective Inspector Galbraith
Date: 12 August 97—9:15 P.M.
Re: **Kate & William Sumner**

Thought you'd be interested in the enclosed
report/statements. Of the various issues raised,
the most telling seem to be:

1. Kate made few friends, and those she had
   came from her own milieu.
2. She appears to have had little interest in
   her husband's friends/pursuits.
3. There are some unflattering descriptions of
   her—i.e., manipulative, sly, deceitful, malicious.
4. William is under stress over money worries.
5. The "dream house" was clearly Kate's idea,
   but the consensus view is that William made
   a mistake buying it.
6. Finally, what on earth was the attraction?
   Did he marry her because she was pregnant?

Some interesting vibes, don't you think?

John

Witness statement: James Purdy, Managing Director, Pharmatec UK

I've known William Sumner since he joined the company fifteen years ago at the age of twenty-five. I recruited him myself from Southampton University, where he worked as an assistant to Professor Hugh Buglass after gaining his MSc. William led the research into two of our pharmaceutical drugs—Antiac and Counterac—which between them represent 12 percent of the antacid market. He is a valued and valuable member of the team and is well respected in his profession. Until his marriage to Kate Hill in 1994 I would have described William as the eternal bachelor. He had an active social life, but his real interests were work and sailing. I remember him telling me once that a wife would never allow him the sort of freedom his mother did. Various young women set their caps for him over the years, but he was adroit at avoiding entanglement. I was surprised therefore when I heard that he and Kate Hill were planning to get married. She worked at Pharmatec for some twelve months in '93–'94. I was extremely sorry to hear about her death and have authorized extended leave for William while he comes to terms with his loss and sorts out the care of his daughter. As far as I am aware William was in Liverpool during the weekend of 9–10 August, although I had no contact with him after he left on the morning of Thursday, 7 August. I barely knew Kate Hill-Sumner while she was here and have not seen or heard from her since she left.

James Purdy

Witness statement: Michael Sprate, Services Manager, Pharmatec UK

Kate Hill-Sumner worked as part of my team from May '93 to March '94, when she left the company. She had no shorthand, but her typing skills were above average. I had one or two problems with her, principally in relation to her behavior. This could be very disruptive at times. She had a sharp tongue and was not averse to using it against the other secretaries. I would describe her as a bully who had no qualms about spreading malicious gossip in order to undermine someone she had taken a dislike to. She became particularly difficult after her marriage to William Sumner, which she clearly felt gave her an elevated status, and had she not decided to leave voluntarily, I would certainly have sought to have her transferred from my department. I know William only slightly, so cannot comment on their relationship as I have not seen or heard from Kate since she left Pharmatec UK. I know nothing about her death.

Michael Sprate

Witness statement: Simon Trew, Manager, R&D, Pharmatec UK

William Sumner is one of our leading scientists. His most successful research resulted in Antiac and Counterac. We are optimistic that something may come of the project he is working on at the moment, although he has hinted for some time now that he might be leaving us to work for one of our competitors. I believe the pressure to move has been coming from his wife. William took on an expensive mortgage some twelve months ago, which he is having trouble honoring, and the increase in salary we can offer him does not match the offer from elsewhere. All our employee contracts contain indemnity clauses relating to the unauthorized use of research ideas funded by Pharmatec UK, so if he decides to leave, his research will remain with the company. I understand that he is reluctant to abandon the project at what he believes to be a crucial point; however, his financial commitments may force his hand sooner than he would like. I have never met Kate Sumner. I joined the company two years after she left, and my relationship with William has always been strictly professional. I admire his experience and expertise, but I find him difficult to get on with. He carries a permanent chip on his shoulder because he sees himself as undervalued, and this causes friction within the department. I can confirm that William left for Liverpool on the morning of Thursday, 7 August, and that I spoke to him by telephone shortly before he delivered his paper on the afternoon of Friday, 8 August. He appeared to be in good spirits and confirmed a meeting with me for 10:00 A.M. on Tuesday, 12 August. In any event the meeting did not take place. I know nothing about Mrs. Sumner's death.

Simon Trew

Witness statement: Wendy Plater, Research Scientist, Pharmatec UK

I've known William Sumner for five years. We were very close when I first joined the company, and I visited him and his mother in Chichester and also went sailing once or twice on his boat. He was a quiet man with a dry sense of humor, and we spent some pleasant times together. He always told me he wasn't the marrying kind, so I was very surprised when I heard that Kate Hill had hooked him. If I'm honest, I thought he had better taste, although I don't think he stood a chance once she set her sights on him. There is nothing nice I can say about her. She was uneducated, vulgar, manipulative, and deceitful, and she was out for anything and everything she could get. I knew her quite well before she married, and I disliked her intensely. She was a stirrer and a malicious gossiper, and she was never happier than when she was pulling people down to her own level or below. Lying was second nature to her, and she told some appalling lies about me for which I have never forgiven her. The sad part is William changed for the worse after his marriage. He's been a right bitch since he moved to Lymington, constantly complaining about the people he works with, disrupting team spirit, and whinging on about how he's been cheated by the company. He made a mistake selling his boat and taking on a huge mortgage, and he's been venting his spleen on his work colleagues. I believe Kate to have been a terrible influence on him; however, I cannot conceive of a single circumstance that would have caused William to have anything to do with her death. The impression I have always had is that he was genuinely fond of her. I was at a disco on Saturday night, 9 August, with my partner, Michael Sprate. I haven't seen or heard from Kate Sumner since she left Pharmatec UK, and I know nothing about her murder.

Wendy Plater

Witness statement: Polly Garrard, Secretary, Services, Pharmatec UK

I knew Kate Hill very well. She and I shared an office for ten months while she worked in Services. I felt sorry for her. She had a hell of a life before she moved to Portsmouth. She lived on a run-down council estate in Birmingham, and she and her mother used to barricade themselves behind their front door because they were so terrified of the other tenants. I think her mother worked in a shop, and I think Kate learned her typing while she was still at school, but I can't swear to either. I remember she told me once that she had been working in a bank before her mother died and that they'd sacked her because she took time off to care for her ma. On another occasion she said she resigned voluntarily in order to nurse her mother. I don't know which story is true. She didn't talk much about her life in Birmingham except to say it was pretty rough. She was okay. I liked her. Everyone else thought she was a bit sly—you know, out for what she could get—but I just saw her as an incredibly vulnerable person who was looking for security. It's true she took against people and picked up bits of gossip about them and spread them around, but I'm not convinced she did it from malice. I think it made her feel better about herself to know that other people weren't perfect. I visited her a couple of times after she and William got married, and on both occasions her mother-in-law was there. Mrs. Sumner Sr. was very rude. Kate married the son, not the mother, so what business was it of hers if Kate talked with a Brummie accent and held her knife like a pencil? She was always lecturing Kate on how to bring up little Hannah and how to be a good wife, but as far as I could see she was making a success of both without any interference from anyone. The best thing she did was move to

Lymington, and I'm really upset she's dead. I haven't seen her for over a year, and I know nothing about her murder.

Polly Garrard

Addendum to report on Hannah Sumner ("Baby Smith") following conversation with William Sumner (father) and telephone conversation with Dr. Attwater, GP

Physical: As before.

Psychological: Both father and doctor agree that Hannah's mother was overprotective and would not allow her to develop naturally by playing with other children or by being allowed to explore her own environment and make mistakes. She had some contact with a mothers' and toddlers' group, but as Hannah's play tends to be aggressive, her mother chose <u>less</u> exposure to other children rather than <u>more</u> as a means of dealing with it. Hannah's "withdrawal" is manipulative rather than frightened, and her "fear" of men has everything to do with the sympathetic reaction it inspires in women and nothing to do with any real terror. Both father and doctor describe Hannah as being of below-average intellect, and blame both this and her mother's overprotectiveness for her poor verbal skills. Dr. Attwater has not seen Hannah since her mother's death; however, he is confident that my assessment of her does not differ materially from the assessment he made six months ago.

Conclusions: While I am prepared to accept that Hannah's backward development (which I believe to be serious) may not be due to any recent event, I can only reiterate that <u>this child's welfare must be continuously monitored.</u> Without supervision, I consider it probable that Hannah will suffer psychological, emotional, and physical neglect, as William Sumner (father) is immature, lacks parental skills, and appears to have little affection for his daughter.

Dr. Janet Murray

CHAPTER 12

S teven Harding was released without charge shortly before 9:00 A.M. on Wednesday, 13 August 1997, when the review officer declined to authorize his continued detention due to lack of evidence. However, he was informed that both his car and his boat would be retained for "as long as is necessary." No further explanation was offered for their retention. With the cooperation of the Hampshire Constabulary, he was remanded on police bail to Twenty-three Old Street, Lymington, the house of Anthony Bridges, and was ordered to present himself at the Lymington police station daily so that a regular check could be kept on his movements.

On the advice of a solicitor, he had made a detailed statement about his relationship with Kate Sumner and his movements over the weekend of 9–10 August, although it added little to what he had already told the police. He explained the fingerprint evidence and the presence of Hannah's shoes on *Crazy Daze* in the following manner:

> They came on board in March when I had the boat lifted out of the water to clean and repaint the hull.

Crazy Daze was in Berthon's yard, sitting on a wooden cradle, and when Kate realized I couldn't get away from her because I had to finish the painting, she kept coming to the yard and hanging around, making a nuisance of herself and irritating me. In the end, just to get rid of her, I agreed to let her and Hannah climb the ladder and look at the inside while I stayed below. I told them to take their shoes off and leave them in the cockpit. When the time came for them to climb down again, Kate decided Hannah couldn't manage the ladder so lowered her down to me instead. I strapped Hannah into her buggy, but I didn't notice whether or not she was wearing shoes. To be honest I never look at her much. She gives me the creeps. She never says anything, just stares at me as if I'm not there. Some time later I found some shoes in the cockpit with H. SUMNER written on the strap. Even if they were too small to be the ones Hannah was wearing that day, I have no other explanation for their presence there.

Although I knew where the Sumners lived, I did not return Hannah's shoes because I was sure that Kate had left them there deliberately. I did not like Kate Sumner, and I did not want to be alone with her in her house because I knew she had a serious crush on me which I did not reciprocate. She was very peculiar, and her constant pestering worried me. I can only describe her behavior as harassment. She used to hang around by the yacht club waiting for me to come ashore in my dinghy. Most of the time she just stood and watched me, but sometimes she'd deliberately bump into me and rub her breasts against my arm. The mistake I made was to visit Langton Cottage with her husband shortly after she introduced me to him in the street at the end of last year. I believe that was the beginning of her infatuation. At no time was I inclined to respond to her advances.

Some time later, at the end of April, I think, I was moored up to the Berthon fueling pontoon, waiting for the dockie to come and operate the pump, when Kate and Hannah walked down "C" pontoon toward me. Kate said she hadn't seen me for a while but had spotted *Crazy Daze* and felt like a chat. She and Hannah came on board without invitation, which annoyed me. I suggested Kate go into the aft cabin to retrieve Hannah's shoes from the port shelf. I knew there were some clothes belonging to other women in the cabin, and I thought it would be a good thing if Kate saw them. I hoped it would make her realize that I wasn't interested in her. She left soon afterward, and when I went into the cabin, I found she'd taken off Hannah's nappy, which was dirty, and had ground the mess into the bedclothes. She had also left the shoes behind again. I believe both acts were done deliberately to show me that she was angry about the women's underclothes in the cabin.

I became seriously concerned about Kate Sumner's harassment of me when she found out where I parked my car and took to setting off the alarm to get Tony Bridges and his neighbors riled with me. I have no proof it was Kate who was doing it, although I am sure it must have been because I kept finding feces smeared on the driver's-side handle. I did not tell the police about my suspicions because I was afraid of becoming even more involved with the Sumner family. Instead I sought out William Sumner sometime in June and showed him photographs of myself in a gay magazine because I wanted him to tell his wife I was gay. I realize this must seem odd after I had shown Kate evidence that I entertain girlfriends on board *Crazy Daze,* but I was becoming desperate. Some of the photographs were quite explicit, and William was shocked by them. I don't know what he told his wife, but to my relief, she stopped harassing me almost immediately.

I have seen her in the street maybe five times since June but did not speak to her until the morning of Saturday, 9 August, when I realized I couldn't avoid her. She was outside Tesco's, and we said good morning to each other. She told me she was looking for some sandals for Hannah, and I said I was in a hurry to get off because I was sailing to Poole for the weekend. That was the extent of our conversation. I did not see her again. I admit that I was very aggrieved by her persecution of me, and developed a strong dislike for her, but I have no idea how she came to drown in the sea off the Dorset coast.

A long interview with Tony Bridges produced a corroborative statement. As DS Campbell had predicted, Bridges was known to the Lymington police as a cannabis user, but they took a tolerant view of it. "Once in a while his neighbors complain when he has a party in there, but it's alcohol that makes them raucous, not cannabis, and even the blue-rinse brigade are finally beginning to realize that." Rather more surprisingly, he was also a respected chemistry teacher at one of the local schools. "What Tony does in the privacy of his home is his own affair," said his headmaster. "As far as I'm concerned, the policing of my colleagues' morals outside school hours isn't part of my job description. If it were, I would probably lose some of my better staff. Tony's an inspirational teacher who enthuses children in a difficult subject. I have a lot of time for him."

I've known Steven Harding for eighteen years. We attended the same primary and secondary schools and have been friends ever since. He sleeps in my house when his boat's out of commission or during the winter when it's too cold for him to stay on board. I used to know his parents quite well before they moved to Cornwall in 1991, but I have not seen them since. Steve sailed down to Falmouth two summers ago, but I don't believe he's made any other visits to Cornwall. He divides his life between his flat in London and his boat in Lymington.

He told me on more than one occasion this year that he was having problems with a woman called Kate Sumner, who was stalking him. He described her and her child as weird, and said they scared him. His car alarm kept going off, and he told me he thought it was Kate Sumner who was activating it and asked me if he should report it to the police. It was a pretty odd story, so I wasn't sure whether to believe him or not. Then he pointed out the feces on the car-door handle and told me how Kate Sumner had wiped her child's nappy on his sheets. I told him that if he brought the police into it it would get worse rather than better and suggested he find somewhere else to park his car. As far as I know, that sorted the problem.

I have never spoken to Kate or Hannah Sumner. Steve pointed them out to me once in the middle of Lymington then dragged me around a corner so we wouldn't have to speak to them. His reluctance was genuine. I believe he found her seriously intimidating. I met William Sumner once in a pub at the beginning of this year. He was drinking alone and invited Steve and me to join him. He knew Steve already because they'd been introduced to each other by Kate after Steve had helped her with her shopping. I left after about half an hour, but Steve told me later that he went back to William's house to continue a discussion they were having about sailing. He said William used to race a Contessa and was interesting to talk to.

Steve's a good-looking bloke and has an active sex life. He has at least two girls on the go at the same time because he's not interested in settling down. He's obsessed with sailing and told me once that he could never get serious about anyone who didn't sail. He's not the kiss-and-tell type, and as I never listen to names, I've no idea who he's got on the go at the moment. When he's not acting, he can always get regular work as a photographic model. Mostly he models clothes, but he's done a few sessions for pornographic magazines.

He needs money to fund the flat in London and keep *Crazy Daze* afloat, and that kind of work pays well. He's not ashamed of the photographs, but I've never known him to show them around. I've no idea where he stores them.

I saw Steve on the evening of Friday, 8 August. He dropped in to tell me he was off to Poole the next day and wouldn't see me again until the following weekend. He mentioned that he had an audition in London on Monday, 11 August, and said he was planning to catch the last train back on Sunday night. Later, a mutual friend, Bob Winterslow, who lives near the station, told me that Steve had rung from his boat to ask if he could borrow a sofa Sunday night in order to catch the first train on Monday morning. But he stayed on board and missed his audition. This is standard for Steve. He tends to come and go as he pleases. I became aware that Steve had cocked up when his agent, Graham Barlow, phoned me on Monday morning to say there was no sign of Steve in London and he wasn't answering his mobile phone. I phoned friends to see if anyone knew where he was, then borrowed a dinghy to go out to *Crazy Daze*. I discovered that Steve was badly hung over, and that this was the reason for his nonappearance.

I spent the weekend, 9–10 August, with my girlfriend Beatrice "Bibi" Gould, whom I've known for four months. On Saturday night we went to a rave at the Jamaica Club in Southampton, returning home at approximately 4:00 A.M. We slept through till sometime Sunday P.M. I know nothing about Kate Sumner's death, although I am completely sure that Steven Harding had nothing to do with it. He is not an aggressive person.

(Police note: this rave certainly took place, but there is no way of checking whether A. Bridges & B. Gould were present. Rough estimate of numbers at the Jamaica Club on Saturday night: 1,000+.)

Beatrice Gould's statement supported Bridges' and Harding's in all relevant details.

I'm nineteen years old, and I work as a hairdresser in Get Ahead in Lymington High Street. I met Tony Bridges at a pub disco about four months ago, and he introduced me to Steve Harding a week later. They've been friends for a long time, and Steve uses Tony's house as a base in Lymington when he can't stay on his boat for any reason. I've come to know Steve quite well over the time Tony and I have been together. Several of my friends would like to go out with him, but he's not interested in settling down and tends to avoid heavy relationships. He's a good-looking bloke, and because he's an actor as well, girls throw themselves at him. He told me once that he thinks they see him as a stud and that he really hates it. I know he's had a lot of problems in that way with Kate Sumner. He was nice to her once, and afterward she wouldn't leave him alone. He said he thought she was lonely, but that didn't give her the right to make his life a misery. It got to the point that he'd hide behind corners while Tony or I checked to see if she was on the other side. I think she must have been mentally disturbed. The worst thing she did was smear her daughter's dirty nappies on his car. I thought that was completely disgusting and told Steve that he should report her to the police.

I didn't see Steve the weekend of 9–10 August. I went to Tony's house at 4:30 P.M. on Saturday, 9 August, and at about 7:30 P.M. we left for the Jamaica Club in Southampton. We go there a lot because Daniel Agee is a brilliant DJ and we really like his style. I stayed at Tony's until 10:00 P.M. on Sunday night, then went home. My permanent address is Sixty-seven Shorn Street, Lymington, where I live with my parents, but I spend most weekends and some weekday nights with Tony Bridges. I like Steve Harding a lot, and I don't believe he had anything to do with Kate Sumner's death. He and I get on really well together.

Detective Superintendent Carpenter sat in silence while John Galbraith read through all three statements. "What do you think?" he asked when the other had finished. "Does Harding's story ring true? Is that a Kate Sumner you recognize?"

Galbraith shook his head. "I don't know. I haven't got a feel for her yet. She was like Harding, a bit of a chameleon, play-acted different roles to suit different people." He reflected for a moment. "I suppose one thing in Harding's defense is that when she rubbed someone up the wrong way she did it in spades—really got under their skin, in other words. Did you read those statements I sent you? Her mother-in-law didn't like her at all, and neither did Wendy Plater, William's ex-girlfriend, who was cut out of the running by Kate. You could argue it was straightforward jealousy on both counts, but I got the impression there was more to it than that. They used the same word to describe her. 'Manipulative.' Angela Sumner referred to her as the most self-centered and calculating woman she had ever met, and the girlfriend said lying was second nature to her. William said she was single-minded about what she wanted and had him wound around her finger from the first time she met him." He shrugged. "Whether any of that means she was stalking a man she became infatuated with, I don't know. I wouldn't have expected her to be so blatant but"—he spread his hands in perplexity—"she was pretty blatant in her pursuit of a comfortable lifestyle."

"I hate these cases, John," said Carpenter with genuine regret. "The poor little woman's dead, but her character's going to be blackened whichever way you look at it." He pulled Harding's statement across the desk toward him and drummed his fingers on it in irritation. "Shall I tell you what this smells of to me? The classic defense against rape. *She was panting for it, guv. Couldn't keep her hands off me. I just gave her what she wanted, and it's not my fault if she cried foul afterward. She was an aggressive woman, and she liked aggressive sex.*" His frown deepened to a chasm. "All Harding's doing is laying some neat groundwork in case we manage to bring charges against him. Then he'll tell us her death was an accident . . . she fell off the back of the boat and he couldn't save her."

"What did you make of Anthony Bridges?"

"I didn't like him. He's a cocky little bastard, and a damn sight too knowledgeable about police interviews. But his and his blowsy girlfriend's stories tally so closely with Harding's that, unless they're operating some sort of sick conspiracy, I think we have to accept they're telling the truth." A sudden smile banished his frown. "For the moment anyway. It'll be interesting to see if anything changes after he and Harding have had a chance to talk together. You know we've bailed him to Bridges' address."

"Harding's right about one thing," said Galbraith thoughtfully. "Hannah gives *me* the creeps, too." He leaned forward, elbows on knees, a troubled expression on his face. "It's codswallop about her screaming every time she sees a man. I was waiting for her father to bring me some lists he'd made, and she came into the room, sat down on the carpet in front of me, and started to play with herself. She had no knickers on, just pulled up her dress and got going like there was no tomorrow. She was watching me the whole time she was doing it, and I swear to God she knew exactly what she was about." He sighed. "It was bloody unnerving, and I'll eat my hat if she hasn't been introduced to some sort of sexual activity, whatever that doctor said."

"Meaning you've got your money on Sumner?"

Galbraith considered for a moment. "Put it this way, I'd says he's a dead cert if, one: his alibi doesn't check out and, two: I can work out how he managed to have a boat waiting for him off the Isle of Purbeck." His pleasant face broke into a smile. "He gets under my skin something rotten, probably because he thinks he's so damned clever. It's hardly scientific but, yes, I'd put my money on him any day before Steven Harding."

For seventy-two hours, local and national newspapers had been carrying reports of a murder inquiry following the finding of a body on a beach on the Isle of Purbeck. On the theory that the dead woman and her daughter had been traveling by boat, sailors between Southampton and Weymouth were being asked to come forward with any sightings of a small blond woman and/or a three-year-old child on the weekend of 9–10 August. During her lunch break that Wednesday, a shop assistant in one of the big department stores in Bournemouth went into her local police station and suggested diffidently that, while she didn't want to waste anyone's time, she thought that something she'd seen on Sunday evening might be connected to the woman's murder.

She gave her name as Jennifer Hale and said she'd been on a Fairline Squadron called *Gregory's Girl* belonging to a Poole businessman called Gregory Freemantle.

"He's my boyfriend," she explained.

The desk sergeant found the description amusing. She'd never see thirty again, and he wondered how old the boyfriend was. Approaching fifty, he guessed, if he could afford to own a Fairline Squadron.

"I wanted Gregory to come and tell you about it himself," she confided, "because he could have given you a better idea of where it was, but he said it wasn't worth the bother because I didn't have enough experience to know what I was looking at. He believes his daughters, you see. They said it was an oil drum, and woe betide anyone who disagrees with them. He won't argue with them in case they complain to their mother when what he ought to be doing . . ." She heaved the kind of sigh that every potential stepmother has sighed down the ages. "They're a couple of little madams, frankly. I thought we should have stopped at the time to investigate, but"—she shook her head—"it wasn't worth going into battle over. Frankly, I'd had enough for one day."

The desk sergeant, who had stepchildren of his own, gave her a sympathetic smile. "How old are they?"

"Fifteen and thirteen."

"Difficult ages."

"Yes, particularly when their parents . . ." She stopped abruptly, reconsidering how much she wanted to say.

"It'll get better in about five years when they've grown up a bit."

A gleam of humor flashed in her eyes. "Assuming I'm around to find out, which at the moment doesn't look likely. The younger one's not too bad, but I'd need a skin like a rhinoceros to put up with another five years of Marie. She thinks she's Elle MacPherson and Claudia Schiffer rolled into one, and throws a tantrum if she isn't being constantly petted and spoiled. Still . . ." She returned to her reason for being there. "I'm sure it wasn't an oil drum. I was sitting at the back of the flying bridge and had a better view than the others. Whatever it was, it wasn't metal . . . although it *was* black . . . it looked to me like an upturned dinghy . . . a rubber one. I think it may have been partially deflated, because it was pretty low in the water."

The desk sergeant was taking notes. "Why do you think it was connected with the murder?" he asked her.

She gave an embarrassed smile, afraid of making a fool of herself. "Because it was a boat," she said, "and it wasn't far from where the body was found. We were in Chapman's Pool when the woman was lifted off by helicopter, and we passed the dinghy only about ten minutes after we rounded St. Alban's Head on our way home. I've worked out that the time must have been about six fifteen and I know we were traveling at twenty-five knots because my boyfriend commented on the fact as we rounded the Head. He says you'll be looking for a yacht or a cruiser, but I thought—well—you can drown off a dinghy just as easily as off a yacht, can't you? And this one had obviously capsized."

Carpenter received the report from Bournemouth at three o'clock, mulled it over in conjunction with a map, then sent it through to Galbraith with a note attached.

Is this worth following up? If it hasn't beached between St. Alban's Head and Anvil Point, then it'll have gone down in deep water somewhere off Swanage and is irretrievable. However, the timings seem very precise, so assuming it washed up before Anvil Point, your friend Ingram can probably work out where it is. You said he was wasted as a beat copper. Failing him, get on to the coastguards. In fact it might be worth going to them first. You know how they hate having their thunder stolen by landlubbers. It's a long shot—can't see where Hannah fits in or how anyone can rape a woman in a dinghy without turning turtle— but you never know. It could be that boat off the Isle of Purbeck you wanted.

In the event, the coastguards happily passed the buck to Ingram, claiming they had better things to do at the height of the summer season than look for imaginary "dinghies" in unlikely places. Equally skeptical himself, Ingram parked at Durlston Head and set off along the coastal path, following the route Harding claimed to have taken the previous Sunday. He walked slowly, searching the shoreline at the foot of the cliffs every fifty yards through binoculars. He was as conscious as the coastguards of the difficulties of isolating a black dinghy against the glistening rocks that lined the base of the headland, and constantly reexamined stretches he had already decided were clear. He also had little faith in his own estimate that a floating object seen at approximately 6:15 P.M. on Sunday evening, some three hundred yards out from Seacombe

Cliff—his guess at where a Fairline Squadron might have been after ten minutes traveling at twenty-five knots from St. Alban's Head—could have beached approximately six hours later halfway between Blackers Hole and Anvil Point. He knew how unpredictable the sea was, and how very unlikely it was that a partially deflated dinghy would even have come ashore. The more probable scenario was that it was halfway to France by now—always assuming it had ever existed—or twenty fathoms under.

He found it slightly to the east of where he had predicted, nearer to Anvil Point, and he smiled with justifiable satisfaction as the powerful lenses picked it out. It was upside down, held in shape by its wooden floor and seats, and neatly stranded on an inaccessible piece of shore. He dialed through to DI Galbraith on his mobile. "How good a sailor are you?" he asked him. "Because the only way you'll get close to this little mother is by boat. If you meet me in Swanage I can take you out this evening. You'll need waterproofs and waders," he warned. "It'll be a wet trip."

Ingram invited along a couple of friends from the Swanage lifeboat crew to keep *Miss Creant* on station while he took Galbraith in to the shore in his own inflatable. He killed the outboard motor and swung it up out of the water thirty yards from land, using his oars to maneuver them carefully through the crops of jagged granite that lay in wait for unwary sailors. He steadied the little craft against a good-sized rock, nodded to Galbraith to get out and start wading, then followed him into the water and used the painter to guide the lightened dinghy onto what passed for a beach in that desolate spot.

"There she is," he said, jerking his head to the left while he lifted his inflatable clear of the waterline, "but God only knows what she's doing out here. People don't abandon perfectly good dinghies for no reason."

Galbraith shook his head in amazement. "How the hell

did you spot it?" he asked, gazing up at the sheer cliffs above them and thinking it must have been like looking for a needle in a haystack.

"It wasn't easy," Ingram admitted, leading the way toward it. "More to the point, how the hell did it survive the rocks?" He stooped over the upturned hull. "It must have come in like this, or its bottom would have been ripped out, and that means there won't be anything left inside. Still"—he raised an inquiring eyebrow—"shall we turn it over?"

With a nod, Galbraith grasped the stern board while Ingram took a tuck in the rubber at the bow. They set it right-way-up with difficulty because the lack of air meant there was no rigidity in the structure and it collapsed in on itself like a deflated balloon. A tiny crab scuttled out from underneath and slipped into a nearby rock pool. As Ingram had predicted, there was nothing inside except the wooden floorboards and the remains of a wooden seat, which had snapped in the middle, probably on its journey to and fro across the rocks. Nevertheless, it was a substantial dinghy, about ten feet long and four feet wide, with its stern board intact.

Ingram pointed to the indentations where the screw clamps of an outboard motor had bitten into the wood, then squatted on his haunches to examine two metal rings screwed into the transom planking aft and a single ring screwed into the floorboarding at the bow. "It's been hung from davits off the back of a boat at some point. These rings are for attaching the wires before it's winched up tight against the davit arms. That way it doesn't swing about while the host boat's in motion." He searched the outside of the hull for any sign of a name, but there was none. He looked up at Galbraith, squinting against the setting sun. "There's no way this dropped off the back of a cruiser without anyone noticing. Both winching wires would have to snap at the same moment, and the chances of that happening would be minimal, I should think. If only one wire snapped—the stern wire, for example—

you'd have a heavy object swinging like a pendulum behind you, and your steering would go haywire. At which point you'd slow right down and find out what the problem was." He paused. "In any case, if the wires had sheared they'd still be attached to the rings."

"Go on."

"I'd say it's more likely it was launched off a trailer, which means we need to ask questions at Swanage, Kimmeridge Bay, or Lulworth." He stood up and glanced toward the west. "Unless it came out of Chapman's Pool, of course, and then we need to ask how it got there in the first place. There's no public access, so you can't just pull a trailer down and launch a dinghy for the fun of it." He rubbed his jaw. "It's curious, isn't it?"

"Couldn't you carry it down and pump it up *in situ?*"

"It depends how strong you are. They weigh a ton, these things." He stretched his arms like a fisherman sizing a fish. "They come in huge canvas holdalls, but trust me, you need two people to carry them any distance, and it's a good mile from Hill Bottom to the Chapman's Pool slip."

"What about the boat sheds? The SOCOs took photographs of the whole bay and there are plenty of dinghies parked on the hard standing beside the sheds. Could it be one of those?"

"Only if it was nicked. The fishermen who use the boat sheds wouldn't abandon a perfectly good dinghy. I haven't had any reports of one being stolen, but that might be because no one's noticed it's missing. I can run some checks tomorrow."

"Joyriders?" suggested Galbraith.

"I doubt it." Ingram touched his foot to the hull. "Not unless they fancied the hardest paddle of their life to get it out into the open sea. It couldn't have floated out on its own. The entrance channel's too narrow, and the thrust of the waves would have forced it back onto the rocks in the bay." He smiled at Galbraith's lack of comprehension. "You couldn't take it out without an engine," he explained, "and your average joyrider doesn't usually bring his own means of locomotion with him. People don't leave outboards lying around any more than they leave gold ingots. They're expensive items, so you keep them under lock and key. That also rules out your pumping up *in situ* theory. I can't see anyone lugging a dinghy *and* an outboard down to Chapman's Pool."

Galbraith eyed him curiously. "So?"

"I'm thinking on the hoof here, sir."

"Never mind. It sounds good. Keep going."

"If it was stolen out of Chapman's Pool, that makes it a premeditated theft. We're talking someone who was prepared to lug a heavy outboard along a mile-long path in order to nick a boat." He lifted his eyebrows. "Why would anyone want to do that? And, having done it, why abandon ship? It's a bit bloody odd, don't you think? How did they get back to shore?"

"Swam?"

"Maybe." Ingram's eyes narrowed to slits against the brilliant orange sun. He didn't speak for several seconds. "Or maybe they didn't have to," he said then. "Maybe they weren't in it." He lapsed into a thoughtful silence. "There's nothing wrong with the stern board, so the outboard should have pulled it under as soon as the sides started to deflate."

"What does that mean?"

"The outboard wasn't on it when it capsized."

Galbraith waited for him to go on, and when he didn't, he made impatient winding motions with his hand. "Come on, Nick. What are you getting at? I know sweet FA about boats."

The big man laughed. "Sorry. I was just wondering what a dinghy like this was doing in the middle of nowhere without an outboard."

"I thought you said it must have had one."

"I've changed my mind."

Galbraith gave a groan. "Do you want to stop talking in riddles, you bastard? I'm wet, I'm freezing to death here, and I could do with a drink."

Ingram laughed again. "I was only thinking that the most obvious way to take a stolen rib out of Chapman's Pool would be to tow it out, assuming you'd come in by boat in the first place."

"In which case, why would you want to steal one?"

Ingram stared down at the collapsed hull. "Because you'd raped a woman and left her half dead in it?" he suggested. "And you wanted to get rid of the evidence? I think you should get your scene-of-crime people out here to find out why it deflated. If there's a blade puncture, then I'd guess the intention was to have the boat and its contents founder in the open sea when the tow rope was released."

"So we're back to Harding?"

The constable shrugged. "He's your only suspect with a boat in the right place at the right time," he pointed out.

Tony Bridges listened to Steven Harding's interminable tirade against the police with growing irritation. His friend paced the sitting room in a rage, kicking at anything that got in his way and biting Tony's head off every time he tried to offer advice. Meanwhile, Bibi, a silent and frightened observer to their mounting anger, sat cross-legged on the floor at Tony's feet, hiding her feelings behind a curtain of thick blond hair and wondering whether it would make the situation better or worse if she announced her intention of going home.

Finally, Tony's patience snapped. "Get a grip before I bloody *flatten* you," he roared. "You're acting like a two-year-old. Okay, so the police arrested you. Big deal! Just be grateful they didn't find anything."

Steve slammed down into an armchair. "Who says they haven't? They've refused to release *Crazy Daze* . . . my car's in a pound somewhere . . . What the hell am I supposed to do?"

"Get the solicitor onto it. That's what he's paid to do, for Christ's sake. Just don't keep bellyaching to us. It's fucking *boring,* apart from anything else. It's not our fault you went to Poole for the sodding weekend. You should have come to Southampton with us."

Bibi stirred uncomfortably on the floor at his feet. She opened her mouth to say something, then closed it again when caution prevailed. Anger was bubbling in the room like overheated yeast.

Harding slammed his feet onto the floor in a rage. "The solicitor's worse than useless, told me the bastards were entitled to hold evidence for as long as is necessary or some legalized crap like that . . ." His voice tailed off in a sob.

There was a long silence.

This time fondness for Tony's friend got the better of caution, and nervously Bibi raised her head. She scraped a gap in her hair to look at him. "But if you didn't do it," she said in her soft, rather childish way, "then I don't see what you're worrying about."

"Right," agreed Tony. "They can't prosecute you without evidence, and if they've released you then there isn't any evidence. QED."

"I want my phone," said Harding, surging to his feet again with crackling energy. "What did you do with it?"

"Left it with Bob," said Tony. "Like you told me to do."

"Has he put it on charge?"

"I wouldn't know. I haven't spoken to him since Monday. He was pretty stoned when I gave it to him, so the chances are he's forgotten all about it."

"That's all I need." The angry young man launched a kick at one of the walls.

Bridges took a pull at his lager can, eyeing his friend thoughtfully over the top of it. "What's so important about the phone?"

"Nothing."

"Then leave my fucking walls alone!" he bellowed, surging out of his own chair and thrusting his face into Harding's. "Show some respect, you bastard! This is *my* house, not your crappy little boat."

"Stop it!" screamed Bibi, cowering back behind the chair. "What's wrong with you both? One of you's going to get hurt in a minute."

Harding frowned down at her, then held up his hands. "All right, all right. I'm expecting a call. That's why I'm twitched."

"Then use the phone in the hall," said Bridges curtly, flinging himself into the armchair again.

"No." He backed toward the wall and leaned against it. "What did the police ask you?"

"What you'd expect. How well you knew Kate . . . whether I thought the harassment was genuine . . . whether I saw you on Saturday . . . where *I* was . . . what kind of pornography you were into . . ." He shook his head. "I knew that garbage would come back to haunt you."

"Leave it out," said Harding tiredly. "I told you I'd had enough of your bloody lectures on Monday. What did you tell them?"

Tony frowned warningly at Bibi's bent head, then touched a hand to the back of her neck. "Do you want to do me a favor, Beebs? Hop down to the off-license and get an eight-pack. There's some money on the shelf in the hall."

She rose to her feet with obvious relief. "Sure. Why not? I'll leave them in the hall, then go home. Okay?" She held out a reluctant hand. "I'm really tired, Tony, and I could do with a decent night's kip. You don't mind, do you?"

"Of course not." He gripped her fingers for a moment, squeezing them hard. "Just so long as you love me, Beebs."

She tore herself free, cradling her hand under her arm, and made for the hall. "You know I do."

He didn't speak again until he heard the front door close behind her. "You want to be careful what you say around her," he warned Harding. "She had to give a statement, too, and it's not fair to get her any more involved than she is already."

"Okay, okay . . . So what did you tell them?"

"Aren't you more interested in what I *didn't* tell them?"

"If you like."

"Right. Well, I didn't tell them you shagged Kate's brains out."

Harding breathed deeply through his nose. "Why not?"

"I thought about it," Bridges admitted, reaching for a packet of Rizla papers on the floor and setting about rolling himself a joint. "But I know you too well, mate. You're an arrogant son of a bitch with an overinflated opinion of yourself"—he squinted up at his friend with a return of good humor in his eyes—"but I can't see you murdering anyone, particularly not a woman, and never mind she was pissing you off something rotten. So I kept shtoom." He gave an eloquent shrug. "But if I live to regret it, I'll have your stinking hide . . . and you'd better believe that."

"Did they tell you she was raped before she was murdered?"

Bridges gave a low whistle of understanding as if pieces of a jigsaw were finally coming together. "No wonder they were so interested in your porno shoots. Your average rapist's a sad bastard in a dirty raincoat who jerks off over that kind of trash." He pulled a plastic bag out from the recesses of his chair and started to fill the Rizla papers. "They must have had a field day with those photographs."

Harding shook his head. "I got rid of the lot over the side before they came. I didn't want any"—he thought about it—"confusion."

"Jesus, you're an arsehole! Why can't you be honest for once? You got shit-scared that if they had evidence of you performing sex acts with an underage kid, they'd have no trouble pinning a rape on you."

"It wasn't for real."

"Chucking the photos away was. You're an idiot, mate."

"Why?"

"Because you can bet your bottom dollar William will have mentioned photos. *I* sure as hell did. Now the filth will be wondering why they can't find any."

"So?"

"They'll know you were expecting a visit."

"So?" said Harding again.

Bridges cast him another thoughtful glance as he licked the edges of the spliff. "Look at it from their point of view. Why would you be expecting a visit if you didn't know it was Kate's body they'd found?"

CHAPTER 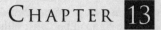 13

W e can go to the pub," said Ingram, locking Miss Creant onto her trailer behind his Jeep, "or I can give you some supper at home." He glanced at his watch. "It's nine thirty, so the pub'll be pretty raucous by now, and it'll be difficult to get anything to eat." He started to peel off his water-proofs, which still streamed water from his immersion in the sea. He had stood at the bottom of the slip as he had guided *Miss Creant* onto the trailer while Galbraith oper-ated the winch. "Home, on the other hand," he said with a grin, "has drying facilities, a spectacular view, and silence."

"Do I get the impression you'd rather go home?" asked Galbraith with a yawn, levering off his inadequate waders and turning them upside down to empty them in a Nia-gara Falls over the slip. He was soaked from the waist-band down.

"There's beer in the fridge, and I can grill you a fresh sea bass if you're interested."

"How fresh?"

"Still alive Monday night," said Ingram, taking some spare trousers from the back of the Jeep and tossing them across. "You can change in the lifeboat station."

"Cheers," said Galbraith, setting off in stockinged feet toward the gray stone building that guarded the ever-ready Swanage lifeboat, "and I'm interested," he called over his shoulder.

Ingram's cottage was a tiny two-up, two-down, backing onto the downs above Seacombe Cliff, although the two downstairs rooms had been knocked into one with an open-plan staircase rising out of the middle and a kitchen extension added to the back. It was clearly a bachelor establishment, and Galbraith surveyed it with approval. Too often, these days, he felt he still had to be persuaded of the joys of fatherhood.

"I envy you," he said, bending down to examine a meticulously detailed replica of the *Cutty Sark* in a bottle on the mantelpiece. "Did you make this yourself?"

Ingram nodded.

"It wouldn't last half an hour in my house. I reckon anything I ever had of value was smashed within hours of my son getting his first football." He chuckled. "He keeps telling me he's going to make a fortune playing for Manchester United, but I can't see it myself."

"How old is he?" asked Ingram, leading the way through to the kitchen.

"Seven. His sister's five."

The tall constable took the sea bass from the fridge, then tossed Galbraith a beer and opened one for himself. "I'd have liked children," he said, splitting the fish down its belly, filleting out the backbone, and splaying it spatchcock fashion on the grillpan. He was neat and quick in his movements, despite his size. "Trouble is I never found a woman who was prepared to hang around long enough to give me any."

Galbraith remembered what Steven Harding had said on Monday night about Ingram fancying the woman with the horse and wondered if it was more a case of the *right* woman not hanging around long enough. "A guy like you'd do well anywhere," he said, watching him take some chives and basil from an array of herbs on his windowsill and chop them finely before sprinkling them over the sea bass. "So what's keeping you here?"

"You mean apart from the great view and the clean air?"

"Yes."

Ingram pushed the fish to one side and started washing the mud off some new potatoes before chucking them into a saucepan. "That's it," he said. "Great view, clean air, a boat, fishing, contentment."

"What about ambition? Don't you get frustrated? Feel you're standing still?"

"Sometimes. Then I remember how much I hated the rat race when I was in it, and the frustrations pass." He glanced at Galbraith with a self-deprecating smile. "I did five years with an insurance company before I became a policeman, and I hated every minute of it. I didn't believe in the product, but the only way to get on was to sell more, and it was driving me nuts. I had a long think over one weekend about what I wanted out of life, and gave in my notice on the Monday." He filled the saucepan with water and put it on the gas.

The DI thought sourly of his various life, endowment, and pension policies. "What's wrong with insurance?"

"Nothing." He tipped his can in the direction of the DI and took a swill. "As long as you need it . . . as long as you understand the terms of the policy . . . as long as you can afford to keep paying the premiums . . . as long as you've read the small print. It's like any other product. Buyer beware."

"Now you're worrying me."

Ingram grinned. "If it's any consolation, I'd have felt exactly the same about selling lottery tickets."

WPC Griffiths had fallen asleep, fully clothed, in the spare room but woke with a start when Hannah started screaming in the next room. She leaped off the bed, heart thudding, and came face to face with William Sumner as he slunk through the child's doorway. "What the hell do you think you're doing?" she demanded angrily, her nerves shot to pieces by her sudden awakening. "You've been told not to go in there."

"I thought she was asleep. I just wanted to look at her."

"We agreed you wouldn't."

"*You* may have done. *I* never did. You've no right to stop me. It's *my* house, and she's *my* daughter."

"I wouldn't bank on that, if I were you," she snapped. She was about to add: Your rights take second place to Hannah's at the moment, but he didn't give her the chance.

He clamped fingers like steel bands around her arms and stared at her with dislike, his face working uncontrollably. "Who have you been talking to?" he muttered.

She didn't say anything, just broke his grip by raising her hands and striking him on both wrists, and with a choking sob he stumbled away down the corridor. But it was a while before she realized what his question had implied.

It would explain a lot, she thought, if Hannah wasn't his child.

Galbraith laid his knife and fork at the side of his plate with a sigh of satisfaction. They were sitting in shirtsleeves on the small patio at the side of the cottage beside a gnarled old plum tree that flavored the air with the scent of fermentation. A storm lantern hissed quietly on the table between them, throwing a circle of yellow light up the wall of the house and across the lawn. On the horizon, moon-silvered clouds floated across the surface of the sea like windblown veils.

"I'm going to have a problem with this," he said. "It's too damn perfect."

Ingram pushed his own plate aside and propped his elbows on the table. "You need to like your own company. If you don't, it's the loneliest place on earth."

"Do you?"

The younger man's face creased into an amiable smile. "I get by," he said, "as long as people like you don't drop in too often. Solitude's a state of mind with me, not an ambition."

Galbraith nodded. "That makes sense." He studied the other's face for a moment. "Tell me about Miss Jenner," he said then. "Harding gave us the impression he and she had quite a chat before you got back. Could he have said more to her than she's told you?"

"It's possible. She seemed pretty relaxed with him."

"How well do you know her?"

But Ingram wasn't so easily drawn about his private life. "As well as I know anyone else around here," he said casually. "What did you make of Harding, as a matter of interest?"

"Difficult to say. He gives a convincing performance of wanting nothing to do with Kate Sumner, but as my boss pointed out, dislike is as good a reason for rape and murder as any other. He claims she was harassing him by smearing crap all over his car because he'd rejected her. It might be true, but none of us really believes it."

"Why not? There was a case down here three years ago when a wife smashed her husband's Jag through the front door of his lover's house. Women can get pretty riled when they're given the elbow."

"Except he says he never slept with her."

"Maybe that was her problem."

"How come you're on his side all of a sudden?"

"I'm not. The rules say keep an open mind, and that's what I'm trying to do."

Galbraith chuckled. "He wants us to believe he's a bit of a stud, presumably on the basis that a man who has access to sex on tap doesn't need to rape anyone, but he can't or won't produce the names of women he's slept with. And neither can anyone else." He shrugged. "Yet no one questions his reputation for laddish behavior. They're all quite confident he entertains ladies on his boat even though the SOCOs couldn't come up with any evidence to support it. His bedlinen's stiff with dried semen, but there were only two hairs on it that weren't his, and neither of them was Kate Sumner's. Conclusion, the guy's a compulsive masturbator." He paused for reflection. "The problem is his damn boat's positively monastic in every other respect."

"I don't get you."

"Not a whisper of anything pornographic," said Galbraith. "Compulsive masturbators, particularly the ones who go on to rape, wank their brains out over hard-core porn videos because sensation begins and ends with their dicks, and they need more and more explicit images to help them jerk off. So how does our friend Harding get himself aroused?"

"Memory?" suggested Ingram wryly.

Galbraith chuckled. "He's done some pornographic photoshoots himself but claims the only copies he ever kept were the ones he showed William Sumner." He gave a brief rundown of both Harding's and Sumner's versions of the story. "He says he threw the magazine in the bin afterward, and as far as he's concerned, porno shoots become history the minute he's paid."

"More likely he got rid of everything over the side when it occurred to him I might put his name forward for further questioning." Ingram thought for a moment. "Did you ask him about what Danny Spender told me? Why he was rubbing himself with the phone?"

"He said it wasn't true, said the kid made it up."

"No way. I'll stake my life on Danny getting that right."

"Why then?"

"Reliving the rape? Getting himself excited because his victim had been found? Miss Jenner?"

"Which?"

"The rape," said Ingram.

"Pure speculation, based on the word of a ten-year-old and a policeman. No jury will believe you, Nick."

"Then talk to Miss Jenner tomorrow. Find out if she

noticed anything before I got there." He started to stack the dirty dishes. "I suggest you use kid gloves, though. She's not too comfortable around policemen."

"Do you mean policemen in general, or just you?"

"Probably just me," said Ingram honestly. "I tipped off her father that the man she'd married had bounced a couple of bad checks, and when the old boy tackled him about it, the bastard did a runner with the small fortune he'd conned out of Miss Jenner and her mother. When his fingerprints were run through the computer, it turned out half the police forces in England were looking for him, not to mention the various wives he'd acquired along the way. Miss Jenner was number four, although as he never divorced number one, the marriage was a sham anyway."

"What was his name?"

"Robert Healey. He was arrested a couple of years ago in Manchester. She knew him as Martin Grant, but he admitted to twenty-two other aliases in court."

"And she blames you because she married a creep?" asked Galbraith in disbelief.

"Not for that. Her father had had a bad heart for years, and the shock of finding out they were on the verge of bankruptcy killed him. I think she feels that if I'd gone to her instead of him, she could somehow have persuaded Healey to give the money back and the old man would still be alive."

"Could she?"

"I wouldn't think so." He placed the dishes in front of him. "Healey had the whole scam down to a fine art, and being open to persuasion wasn't part of his MO."

"How did he work it?"

Ingram pulled a wry face. "Charm. She was besotted with him."

"So she's stupid?"

"No . . . just overly trusting . . ." Ingram marshaled his thoughts. "He was a professional. Created a fictitious company with fictitious accounts and persuaded the two women to invest in it, or more accurately persuaded Miss

Jenner to persuade her mother. It was a very sophisticated operation. I saw the paperwork afterward, and I'm not surprised they fell for it. The house was littered with glossy brochures, audited accounts, salary checks, lists of employees, Inland Revenue statements. You'd have to be very suspicious indeed to assume anyone would go to so much trouble to con you out of a hundred thousand quid. Anyway, on the basis that the company stock was going up by twenty percent a year, Mrs. Jenner cashed in all her bonds and securities and handed her son-in-law a check."

"Which he converted back into cash?"

Ingram nodded. "It passed through at least three bank accounts on the way, and then vanished. In all, he spent twelve months working the scam—nine months softening up Miss Jenner, and three months married to her—and it wasn't just the Jenners who got taken to the cleaners. He used his connection with them to draw in other people, and a lot of their friends got their fingers burned as well. It's sad, but they've become virtual recluses as a result."

"What do they live on?"

"Whatever she can make from the Broxton House livery stables. Which isn't much. The whole place is getting seedier by the day."

"Why don't they sell it?"

Ingram pushed his chair back, preparatory to standing up. "Because it doesn't belong to them. Old man Jenner changed his will before he died and left the house to his son, with the proviso that the two women can go on living there as long as Mrs. Jenner remains alive."

Galbraith frowned. "And then what? The brother throws the sister on the streets?"

"Something like that," said Ingram dryly. "He's a lawyer in London, and he certainly doesn't plan to have a sitting tenant on the premises when he sells out to a developer."

Before he left to interview Maggie Jenner on Thursday morning, Galbraith had a quick word with Carpenter to bring him up to speed on the beached dinghy. "I've organized a couple of SOCOs to go out to it," he told him. "I'll be surprised if they find anything—Ingram and I had a poke around to see what had caused it to deflate, and frankly it's all a bit of a mess—but I think it's worth a try. They're going to make an attempt to reinflate it and float it off the rocks, but the advice is, don't hold your breath. Even if they get it back, it's doubtful we'll learn much from it."

Carpenter handed him a sheaf of papers. "These'll interest you," he said.

"What are they?"

"Statements from the people Sumner said would support his alibi."

Galbraith heard a note of excitement in his boss's voice. "And do they?"

The other shook his head. "Quite the opposite. There are twenty-four hours unaccounted for, between lunchtime on Saturday and lunchtime on Sunday. We're now blitzing everyone, hotel staff, other conference delegates, but those"—he leveled a finger at the documents in Galbraith's hand—"are the names Sumner himself gave us." His eyes gleamed. "And if they're not prepared to alibi him, I can't see anyone else doing it. It looks as if you could be right, John."

Galbraith nodded. "How did he do it, though?"

"He used to sail, must know Chapman's Pool as well as Harding, must know there are dinghies lying around for the taking."

"How did he get Kate there?"

"Phoned her Friday night, said he was bored out of his mind with the conference and was planning to come home early, suggested they do something exciting for a change, like spend the afternoon on Studland beach, and arranged to meet her and Hannah off the train in Bournemouth or Poole."

Galbraith tugged at his earlobe. "It's possible," he agreed.

A child of three travels free by train, and the record of sales from Lymington station had shown that numerous single adult fares to Bournemouth and Poole had been sold on the Saturday, the trip being a quick and easy one through a change onto regular mainline trains at Brockenhurst. However, if Kate Sumner had purchased one of the tickets, she had used cash rather than a check or credit card for the transaction. None of the railway staff remembered a small blond woman with a child, but as they pointed out, the traffic through Lymington station on a Saturday in peak holiday season was so continuous and so heavy because of the ferry link to and from the Isle of Wight that it was unlikely they would.

"The only fly in the ointment is Hannah," Carpenter went on. "If he abandoned her in Lilliput before driving back to Liverpool, why did it take so long for anyone to notice her? He must have dumped her by six A.M., but Mr. and Mrs. Green didn't spot her until ten thirty."

Galbraith thought of the traces of benzodiazepine and paracetamol in her system. "Maybe he fed, watered, and cleaned her at six, then left her asleep in a cardboard box in a shop doorway," he said thoughtfully. "He's a pharmaceutical chemist, don't forget, so he must have a pretty good idea how to put a three-year-old under for several hours. My guess is he's been doing it for years. By the way the child behaves around him she must have been a blight on his sex life from the day she was born."

Meanwhile, Nick Ingram was chasing stolen dinghies. The fishermen who parked their boats at Chapman's Pool couldn't help. "Matter of fact it's the first thing we checked when we heard the woman had drowned," said one. "I'd have let you know if there'd been a problem, but nothing's missing."

It was the same story in Swanage and Kimmeridge Bay.

His last port of call, Lulworth Cove, looked more promising. "Funny you should ask," said the voice on the other end of the line, "because we have had one go missing, black ten-footer."

"Sounds about right. When did it go?"

"A good three months back."

"Where from?"

"Would you believe it, off the beach. Some poor sod from Spain anchors his cruiser in the bay, ferries himself and his family in for a pub lunch, leaves the outboard in place with the starter cord dangling, and then tears strips off yours truly because it was hijacked from under his nose. According to him, *no one* in Spain would dream of stealing another chap's boat—never mind he makes it easy enough for the local moron to nick it—and then gives me a load of grief about the aggression of Cornish fishermen and how they were probably at the bottom of it. I pointed out that Cornwall's a good hundred miles away, and that Spanish fishermen are far more aggressive than the Cornish variety and *never* follow European Union rules, but he still said he was going to report me to the European Court of Human Rights for failing to protect Spanish tourists."

Ingram laughed. "So what happened?"

"Nothing. I took him and his family out to his sodding great bastard of a fifty-foot cruiser and we never heard another word. He probably put in for twice the dinghy's insurance value and blamed the vile English for its disappearance. We made inquiries, of course, but no one had seen anything. I mean, why would they? We get hundreds of people here during bank holiday week, and anyone could have started it up with no trouble. I mean what kind of moron leaves a dinghy with an outboard in place? We reckoned it was taken by joyriders who sank it when they got bored with it."

"Which bank holiday was it?"

"End of May. School half-term. The place was packed."

"Did the Spaniard give you a description of the dinghy?"

"A whole bloody manifest more like. All ready for the

insurance. Half of me suspected he wanted it to be nicked just so he could get something a bit more swanky."

"Can you fax the details through?"

"Sure."

"I'm particularly interested in the outboard."

"Why?"

"Because I don't think it was on the dinghy when it went down. With any luck, it's still in the possession of the thief."

"Is he your murderer?"

"Very likely."

"Then you're in luck, mate. I've got all sorts of serial numbers here, courtesy of our Spanish friend, and one of them's the outboard."

CHAPTER 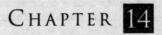 14

Report from Falmouth police, following an interview with Mr. and Mrs. Arthur Harding

---

Subject: Steven Harding

Mr. and Mrs. Harding live at 18 Hall Road, a modest bungalow to the west of Falmouth. They retired to Cornwall in 1991 after running a fish-and-chip shop in Lymington for 20+ years. They used a considerable proportion of their capital to put their only child, Steven, through a private drama college following his failure to gain any A-level passes at school, and feel aggrieved that they now live in somewhat straitened circumstances as a result. This may in part explain why their attitude toward their son is critical and unfriendly.

They describe Steven as a "disappointment" and evince considerable hostility toward him because of his "immoral lifestyle." They blame his wayward behavior—"He is only interested in sex, drugs and rock and roll"—and lack of achievement—"He has never done a day's serious work in his life"—on laziness and a belief that "the world owes him a living." Mr. Harding, who is proud of his working-class roots, says Steven looks down on his parents, which explains why Steven has been to see them only once in six years. The visit—during the summer of 1995— was not a success and Mr. Harding's views on his son's arrogance and lack of gratitude were explosive and earthy. He uses words like "poser," "junky," "parasite," "oversexed," "liar," "irresponsible" to describe his son, although it is clear that his hostility has more to do with his inability to accept Steven's rejection of working-class values than any real knowledge of his son's current lifestyle as they have had no contact with him since July 1995.

Mrs. Harding cites a school friend of Steven's, Anthony Bridges, as a malign influence on his life. According to her, Anthony introduced Steven to shoplifting, drugs, and pornography at the age of twelve, and Steven's lack of achievement stems from a couple of police cautions he and Anthony received during their teenage years for drunk and disorderly behavior, vandalism, and theft of pornographic materials from a newsagent. Steven became rebellious and impossible to control after these episodes. She describes Steven as "too handsome for his own good," and says that girls were throwing themselves at him from an early age. She says Anthony, by contrast, was always overshadowed by his friend and that she believes this is why it amused Anthony to "get Steven into trouble." She feels very bitter that Anthony, despite his previous history, was bright enough to go to university and find himself a job in teaching, while Steven had to rely on the funding his parents provided, for which they have received no thanks.

When Mr. Harding asked Steven how he was able to afford to buy his boat, <u>Crazy Daze,</u> Steven admitted he had received payment for several hard-core pornography sessions. This caused such distress to his parents that they ordered him from their house in July 1995 and have neither seen nor heard from him since. They know nothing about his recent activities, friends, or acquaintances and can shed no light on the events of 9–10 August 1997. However, they insist that, despite all his faults, they do not believe Steven to be a violent or aggressive young man.

CHAPTER 15

Maggie Jenner was raking straw in one of the stables when Nick Ingram and John Galbraith drove into Broxton House yard on Thursday morning. Her immediate reaction, as it was with all visitors, was to retreat into the shadows, unwilling to be seen, unwilling to have her privacy invaded, for it required an effort of will to overcome her natural disinclination to participate in anything that involved people. Broxton House, a square Queen Anne building with pitched roof, red-brick walls, and shuttered upper windows, was visible through a gap in the trees to the right of the stableyard, and she watched the two men admire it as they got out of the car, before turning to walk in her direction.

With a resigned smile, she drew attention to herself by hefting soiled straw through the stable doorway on the end of a pitchfork. The weather hadn't broken for three weeks, and sweat was running freely down her face as she emerged into the fierce sunlight. She was irritated by her own discomfort and wished she'd put on something else that morning or that PC Ingram had had the courtesy to warn her he was coming. Her checkered cheesecloth shirt gripped her damp torso like a stocking, and her jeans chafed against the inside of her thighs. Ingram spotted her almost immediately and was amused to see that, for once, the tables were turned, and it was she who was hot and bothered and not he, but his expression as always was unreadable.

She propped the pitchfork against the stable wall and wiped her palms down her already filthy jeans before smoothing her hair off her sweaty face with the back of one hand. "Good morning, Nick," she said. "What can I do for you?"

"Miss Jenner," he said, with his usual polite nod. "This is Detective Inspector Galbraith from Dorset HQ. If it's convenient, he'd like to ask you a few questions about the events of last Sunday."

She inspected her palms before tucking them into her jeans pockets. "I won't offer to shake hands, Inspector. You wouldn't like where mine have been."

Galbraith smiled, recognizing the excuse for what it was, a dislike of physical contact, and cast an interested glance around the cobbled courtyard. There was a row of stables on each of three sides, beautiful old red-brick buildings with solid oak doors, only half a dozen of which appeared to have occupants. The rest stood empty, doors hooked back, brick floors bare of straw, hay baskets unfilled, and it was a long time, he guessed, since the business had been a thriving one. They had passed a faded sign at the entrance gate, boasting: BROXTON HOUSE RIDING & LIVERY STABLES, but, like the sign, evidence of dilapidation was everywhere, in the crumbling brickwork that had been thrashed by the elements for a couple of hundred years, in the cracked and peeling paintwork and the broken windows in the tack room and office, which no one had bothered—*or could afford?*—to replace.

Maggie watched his appraisal. "You're right," she said, reading his mind. "It has enormous potential as a row of holiday chalets."

"A pity when it happens, though."

"Yes."

He looked toward a distant paddock where a couple of horses grazed halfheartedly on drought-starved grass. "Are they yours as well?"

"No. We just rent out the paddock. The owners are supposed to keep an eye on them, but they're irresponsible, frankly, and I usually find myself doing things for their wretched animals that was never part of the contract." She pulled a rueful smile. "I can't get it into their owners' heads that water evaporates and that the trough needs filling every day. It makes me mad sometimes."

"Quite a chore then?"

"Yes." She gestured toward a door at the end of the row of stables behind her. "Let's go up to my flat. I can make you both a cup of coffee."

"Thank you." She was an attractive woman, he thought, despite the muck and the brusque manner, but he was intrigued by Ingram's stiff formality toward her, which wasn't readily explained by the story of the bigamous husband. The formality, he thought, should be on her side. As he followed them up the wooden stairs, he decided the constable must have tried it on at some point and been comprehensively slapped down for playing outside his own league. Miss Jenner was top-drawer material, even if she did live in something resembling a pigsty.

The flat was the antithesis of Nick's tidy establishment. There was disorder everywhere, bean bags piled in front of the television on the floor, newspapers with finished and half-finished crosswords abandoned on chairs and tables, a filthy rug on the sofa which smelled unmistakably of Bertie, and a pile of dirty washing-up in the kitchen sink. "Sorry about the mess," she said. "I've been up since five, and I haven't had time to clean." To Galbraith's ears, this sounded like a well-worn apology that was trotted out to anyone who might be inclined to criticize her lifestyle. She swiveled the tap to squeeze the kettle between it and the washing-up. "How do you like your coffee?"

"White, two sugars, please," said Galbraith.

"I'll have mine black please, Miss Jenner. No sugar," said Ingram.

"Do you mind Coffeemate?" Maggie asked the inspector, sniffing at a cardboard carton on the side. "The milk's off." Cursorily she rinsed some dirty mugs under the tap. "Why don't you grab a seat? If you chuck Bertie's blanket on the floor, one of you can have the sofa."

"I think she means you, sir," murmured Ingram as they retreated into the sitting room. "Inspector's perks. It's the best seat in the place."

"Who's Bertie?" whispered Galbraith.

"The Hound of the Baskervilles. His favorite occupation is to shove his nose up men's crotches and give them a good slobbering. The stains tend to hang around through at least three washes, I find, so it pays to keep your legs crossed when you're sitting down."

"I hope you're joking!" said Galbraith with a groan. He had already lost one pair of good trousers to the previous night's soaking in the sea. "Where is he?"

"Out on the razzle, I should think. His second-favorite occupation is to service the local bitches."

The DI lowered himself gingerly into the only armchair. "Does he have fleas?"

With a grin, Ingram jerked his head toward the kitchen door. "Do mice leave their droppings in sugar?" he murmured.

"Shit!"

Ingram removed himself to a windowsill and perched precariously on the edge of it. "Just be grateful it wasn't her mother who was out riding on Sunday," he said in an undertone. "This kitchen's sterile by comparison with hers." He had sampled Mrs. Jenner's hospitality once four years ago, the day after Healey had fled, and he'd vowed never to repeat the experience. She had given him coffee in a cracked Spode cup that was black with tannin, and he had gagged continuously while drinking it. He had never understood the peculiar mores of the impoverished landed gentry, who seemed to believe the value of bone china outweighed the value of hygiene.

They waited in silence while Maggie busied herself in the kitchen. The atmosphere was ripe with the stench of horse manure, wafted in from a pile of soiled straw in the yard outside, and the heat baking the interior of the flat through the uninsulated roof was almost unbearable. In no time at all both men were red in the face and mopping at their brows with handkerchieves, and whatever brief advantage Ingram thought he had gained over Maggie was quickly dispelled. A few minutes later she emerged with a tray of coffee mugs, which she handed around before sinking onto Bertie's blanket on the sofa.

"So what can I tell you that I haven't already told Nick?" she asked Galbraith. "I know it's a murder inquiry because I've been reading the newspapers, but as I didn't see the body I can't imagine how I can help you."

Galbraith pulled some notes from his jacket pocket. "In fact it's rather more than a murder inquiry, Miss Jenner. Kate Sumner was raped before she was thrown into the sea, so the man who killed her is extremely dangerous and we need to catch him before he does it again." He paused to let the information sink in. "Believe me, any help you can give us will be greatly appreciated."

"But I don't know anything," she said.

"You spoke to a man called Steven Harding," he reminded her.

"Oh, good God," she said, "you're not suggesting he did it?" She frowned at Ingram. "You've really got it in for that man, haven't you, Nick? He was only trying to help in all conscience. You might as well say any of the men who were in Chapman's Pool that day could have killed her."

Ingram remained blandly indifferent to both her frown and her accusations. "It's a possibility."

"So why pick on Steve?"

"We're not, Miss Jenner. We're trying to eliminate him

from the inquiry. Neither I nor the inspector wants to waste time investigating innocent bystanders."

"You wasted an awful lot of time on Sunday doing it," she said acidly, stung by his dreary insistence on treating her with forelock-tugging formality.

He smiled but didn't say anything.

She turned back to Galbraith. "I'll do my best," she said, "although I doubt I can tell you much. What do you want to know?"

"It would be helpful if you can start by describing your meeting with him. I understand you rode down the track toward the boat sheds and came across him and the boys beside PC Ingram's car. Is that the first time you saw him?"

"Yes, but I wasn't riding Jasper then. I was leading him, because he was frightened by the helicopter."

"Okay. What were Steven Harding and the two boys doing at that point?"

She shrugged. "They were looking at a girl on a boat through the binoculars, at least Steve and the older brother were. I think the younger one was bored by it all. Then Bertie got overexcited—"

Galbraith interrupted. "You said *they* were looking through binoculars. How did that work exactly? Were they taking it in turns?"

"No, well, that's wrong. It was Paul who was looking; Steve was just holding them steady for him." She saw his eyebrows lift in inquiry and anticipated his next question. "Like this." She made an embracing gesture with her arms. "He was standing behind Paul, with his arms around him, and holding the binoculars so Paul could look through the eyepieces. The child thought it was funny and kept giggling. It was rather sweet really. I think he was trying to take his mind off the dead woman." She paused to collect her thoughts. "Actually, I thought he was their father, till I realized he was too young."

"One of the boys said he was playing around with his telephone before you arrived. Did you see him do that?"

She shook her head. "It was clipped to his waistband."

"What happened next?"

"Bertie got overexcited, so Steve grabbed him and then suggested we put the boys at ease by encouraging them to pat Bertie and Sir Jasper. He said he was used to animals because he'd grown up on a farm in Cornwall." She frowned. "Why is any of this important? He was just being friendly."

"In what way, Miss Jenner?"

Her frown deepened, and she stared at him for a moment, clearly wondering where his questions were leading. "He wasn't making a nuisance of himself, if that's what you're getting at."

"Why would I think he was making a nuisance of himself?"

She gave an irritated toss of her head. "Because it would make things easier for you if he was," she suggested.

"How?"

"You want him to be the rapist, don't you? Nick certainly does."

Galbraith's gray eyes appraised her coolly. "There's a little more to rape than making a nuisance of yourself. Kate Sumner had been dosed with a sleeping drug, she had abrasions to her back, strangle marks at her neck, rope burns to her wrists, broken fingers, and a ruptured vagina. She was then thrown . . . *alive* . . . into the sea by someone who undoubtedly knew she was a poor swimmer and wouldn't be able to save herself, even assuming she came around from the effects of the drug. She was also pregnant when she died, which means her baby was murdered with her." He smiled slightly. "I realize that you're a very busy person and that the death of an unknown woman is hardly a priority in your life, but PC Ingram and I take it more seriously, probably because we both saw Kate's body and were distressed by it."

She looked at her hands. "I apologize," she said.

"We don't ask questions for the fun of it," said Galbraith without hostility. "Matter of fact, most of us find this sort of case very stressful, although the public rarely recognizes it."

She raised her head, and there was the glimmer of a smile in her dark eyes. "Point taken," she said. "The problem is, I get the impression you're homing in on Steve Harding just because he was there, and that seems unreasonable."

Galbraith exchanged a glance with Ingram. "There are other reasons why we're interested in him," he said, "but the only one I'm prepared to tell you at the moment is that he'd known the dead woman for quite some time. For that reason alone we'd be investigating him, whether he was at Chapman's Pool on Sunday or not."

She was thoroughly startled. "He didn't say he knew her."

"Would you have expected him to? He told us he never saw the body."

She turned to Ingram. "He can't have done, can he? He said he was walking from St. Alban's Head."

"There's a very good view of Egmont Bight from the coastal path up there," Ingram reminded her. "If he had a pair of binoculars, he could have picked her out quite easily."

"But he didn't," she protested. "All he had was a telephone. You made that point yourself."

Galbraith debated with himself how to put the next question and opted for a straightforward approach. The woman must have a stallion or two in her stables, so she was hardly likely to faint at the mention of a penis. "Nick says Harding had an erection when he first saw him on Sunday. Would you agree?"

"Either that or he's incredibly well endowed."

"Were you the cause of it, do you think?"

She didn't answer.

"Well?"

"I've no idea," she said. "My feeling at the time was

that it was probably the girl on the boat who had got him excited. Walk along Studland beach any sunny day and you'll find a hundred randy eighteen- to twenty-four-year-olds cowering in the water because their dicks react independently of their brains. It's hardly a crime."

Galbraith shook his head. "You're a good-looking woman, Miss Jenner, and he was standing close to you. Did you encourage him in any way?"

"No."

"It *is* important."

"Why? All I know is the poor bloke wasn't in absolute control of himself." She sighed. "Look, I'm really sorry about the woman. But if Steve was involved, then he never gave me any indication of it. As far as I was concerned, he was a young man out for a walk who made a phone call on behalf of a couple of children."

Galbraith laid a forefinger on a page of his notes. "This is a quote from Danny Spender," he said. "Tell me how true it is. 'He was chatting up the lady with the horse, but I don't think she liked him as much as he liked her.' Is that what was happening?"

"No, of course it wasn't," she said with annoyance, as if the idea of being chatted up was pure anathema to her, "though I suppose it might have looked like that to the children. I said he was brave for grabbing Bertie by the collar, so he seemed to think that laughing a lot and slapping Jasper on the rump would impress the boys. In the end I had to move the animals into the shade to get them away from him. Jasper's amenable to most things but not to having his bottom smacked every two minutes, and I didn't want to be prosecuted if he lashed out suddenly."

"So was Danny right about you not liking him?"

"I don't see that it matters," she said uncomfortably. "It's a subjective thing. I'm not a very sociable person, so liking people isn't my strong point."

"What was wrong with him?" he went on imperturbably.

"Oh God, this is ridiculous!" she snapped. "Nothing. He was perfectly pleasant from beginning to end of our conversation." She cast an angry sideways glance toward Ingram. "Almost ridiculously polite, in fact."

"So why didn't you like him?"

She breathed deeply through her nose, clearly at war with herself about whether to answer or not. "He was a toucher," she said with a spurt of anger. "All right? Is that what you wanted? I have a thing against men who can't keep their hands to themselves, Inspector, but it doesn't make them rapists or murderers. It's just the way they are." She took another deep breath. "And while we're on the subject—just to show you how little faith you can put in my judgment of men—I wouldn't trust any of you farther than I could throw you. If you want to know why, ask Nick." She gave a hollow laugh as Galbraith lowered his eyes. "I see he's already told you. Still . . . if you want the juicier details of my relationship with my bigamous husband, apply in writing and I'll see what I can do for you."

The DI, reminded of Sandy Griffiths' similiar *caveat* regarding her judgment of Sumner, ignored the tantrum. "Are you saying Harding touched *you,* Miss Jenner?"

She gave him a withering glance. "Of course not. I never gave him the opportunity."

"But he touched your animals, and that's what put you against him?"

"No," she said crossly. "It was the boys he couldn't keep his hands off. It was all very macho . . . hail-fellow-well-met stuff . . . you know, a lot of punching of shoulders and high-fives . . . to be honest it's why I thought he was their father. The little one didn't like it much—he kept pushing him away—but the older one reveled in it." She smiled rather cynically. "It's the kind of shallow emotion you only ever see in Hollywood movies, so I wasn't in the least bit surprised when he told Nick he was an actor."

Galbraith exchanged a questioning glance with Ingram.

"I'd say that's an accurate description," admitted the constable honestly. "He was very friendly toward Paul."

"How friendly?"

"*Very*," said Ingram. "And Miss Jenner's right. Danny kept pushing him away."

"*Child seducer?*" wrote Galbraith in his notebook. "Did you see Steve abandon a rucksack on the hillside before he took the boys down to Nick's car?" he asked Maggie then.

She was looking at him rather oddly. "The first time I saw him was at the boat sheds," she said.

"Did you see him retrieve it after Nick drove the boys away?"

"I wasn't watching him." Her forehead creased into lines of concern. "Look . . . aren't you jumping to conclusions again? When I said he was touching the boys I didn't mean . . . that is . . . it wasn't inappropriate . . . just, well, *overdone,* if you like."

"Okay."

"What I'm trying to say is I don't think he's a pedophile."

"Have you ever met one, Miss Jenner?"

"No."

"Well, they don't have two heads, you know. Nevertheless, point taken," he assured her in a conscious echo of what she'd said herself. Gallantly he lifted his untouched mug from the floor and drank it down before taking a card from his wallet and passing it across. "That's my number," he said, getting up. "If anything occurs to you that you think's important, you can always reach me there. Thank you for your help."

She nodded, watching as Ingram moved away from the window. "You haven't drunk *your* coffee," she said with a malicious gleam in her eyes. "Perhaps you'd have preferred it with sugar after all. I always find the mouse droppings sink to the bottom."

He smiled down at her. "But dog hairs don't, Miss Jenner." He put on his cap and straightened the peak. "My regards to your mother."

Kate Sumner's papers and private possessions had filled several boxes, which the investigators had been working their way through methodically for three days, trying to build a picture of the woman's life. There was nothing to link her with Steven Harding, or with any other man.

Everyone in her address book was contacted without results. They proved, without exception, to be people she had met since moving to the south coast and matched a neat Christmas card list in the bottom drawer of the bureau in the sitting room. An exercise book was found in one of the kitchen cupboards, inscribed *"Weekly Diary,"* but turned out, disappointingly, to be a precise record of what she spent on food and household bills, and tallied, give or take a pound or two, with the allowance William paid her.

Her correspondence was composed almost entirely of business letters, usually referring to work on the house, although there were a few private letters from friends and acquaintances in Lymington, her mother-in-law, and one, with a date in July, from Polly Garrard at Pharmatec UK.

Dear Kate,

It's ages since we had a chat, and every time I ring, the phone's off the hook or you're not there. Give me a buzz when you can. I'm dying to hear how you and Hannah are getting on in Lymington. It's a waste of time asking William. He just nods and says, "Fine."

I'd really love to see the house since you've had all the decorating done. Maybe I could take a day off and visit you when William's at work? That way he can't complain if all we do is sit and gossip. Do you remember Wendy Plater? She got drunk a couple of weeks ago at lunchtime and called Purdy "a tight-arsed prick" because he was in the hall when she came staggering back late, and he told her he was going to dock her wages. God, it was funny! He would have sacked her on the spot if good old Trew hadn't spoken up for her. She had to apologize, but she doesn't regret any of it. She says she's never seen Purdy go purple before!

I thought of you immediately, of course, which is why I've been ringing. It really is _ages_. <u>Do</u> call. Thinking of you.

Love,
    Polly Garrard

Attached to it by paper clip was the draft of an answer from Kate.

Dear Polly,

Hannah and I are doing well, and of course you must come and visit us. I'm a bit busy at the moment, but will ring as soon as I can. The house looks great. You'll love it.

~~You promised on your honor~~ The story about Wendy Plater was really funny!

Hope all's well with you.

Speak soon.

Love,
    Kate

The Spender brothers' parents looked worried when Ingram asked if he and DI Galbraith could talk to Paul in private. "What's he done?" asked the father.

Ingram removed his cap and smoothed his dark hair with the flat of his hand. "Nothing as far as I know," he said with a smile. "It's just a few routine questions, that's all."

"Then why do you want to talk to him in private?"

Ingram's frank gaze held his. "Because the dead

woman was naked, Mr. Spender, and Paul's embarrassed to talk about it in front of you and your wife."

The man gave a snort of amusement. "He must think we're the most frightful prudes."

Ingram's smile broadened. "Just parents," he said. He gestured toward the lane in front of their rented cottage. "He'll probably feel more comfortable if he talks to us outside."

But Paul was surprisingly open about Steven Harding's "friendliness." "I reckon he fancied Maggie and was trying to impress her by how good he was with kids," he told the policemen. "My uncle's always doing it. If he comes to our house on his own he doesn't bother to talk to us, but if he brings one of his girlfriends he puts his arms around our shoulders and tells us jokes. It's only to make them think he'd be a good father."

Galbraith chuckled. "And that's what Steve was doing?"

"Must have been. He got much more friendly after she turned up."

"Did you notice him playing with his phone at all?"

"You mean the way Danny says?"

Galbraith nodded.

"I didn't watch him because I didn't want to be rude, but Danny's pretty sure about it, and he should know because he was staring at him all the time."

"So why was Steve doing that, do you think?"

"Because he forgot we were there," said the boy.

"In what way exactly?"

Paul showed the first signs of embarrassment. "Well, you know," he said earnestly, "he sort of did it without thinking . . . my dad often does things without thinking, like licking his knife in restaurants. Mum gets really angry about it."

Galbraith gave a nod of agreement. "You're a bright lad. I should have thought of that myself." He stroked the side of his freckled face, considering the problem. "Still, rubbing yourself with a telephone's a bit different from licking your knife. You don't think it's more likely he was showing off?"

"He looked at a girl through the binoculars," Paul offered. "Maybe he was showing off to her?"

"Maybe." Galbraith pretended to ponder some more. "You don't think it's more likely he was showing off to you and Danny?"

"Well . . . he talked a lot about ladies he'd seen in the nude, but I sort of got the feeling most of it wasn't true. . . . I think he was trying to make us feel better."

"Does Danny agree with you?"

The boy shook his head. "No, but that doesn't mean anything. He reckons Steve stole his T-shirt, so he doesn't like him."

"Is it true?"

"I don't think so. It's just an excuse because he's lost it and Mum gave him an earbashing. It's got 'Derby FC' on the front, and it cost a fortune."

"Did Danny have it with him on Sunday?"

"He says it was in the bundle around the binoculars, but I don't remember it."

"Okay." Galbraith nodded again. "So what does Danny think Steve was up to?"

"He reckons he's a pedophile," said Paul matter-of-factly.

WPC Sandra Griffiths whistled tunelessly to herself as she made a cup of tea in the kitchen at Langton Cottage. Hannah was sitting mesmerized in front of the television in the sitting room, while Sandy was blessing the memory of whatever genius had invented the electronic nanny. She turned toward the fridge in search of milk and found William Sumner standing directly behind her. "Did I frighten you?" he asked as she gave a little start of surprise.

You know you did, you stupid bastard . . . ! She forced a smile to her face to disguise the fact that he was beginning to give her the creeps. "Yes," she admitted. "I didn't hear you come in."

"That's what Kate used to say. She'd get quite angry about it sometimes."

Who can blame her . . . ? She was beginning to think of him as a voyeur, a man who got his rocks off by secretly watching a woman go about her business. She had stopped counting the number of times she'd glimpsed him peering around a doorjamb like an unwelcome intruder in his own house. She put distance between herself and him by removing the teapot to the kitchen table and pulling out a chair. There was a lengthy silence during which he sulkily kicked the toe of his shoe against the table leg, shoving the top in little jerks against her belly.

"You're afraid of me, aren't you?" he said suddenly.

"What makes you think that?" she asked as she held the table firm against his kicks.

"You were afraid last night." He looked pleased, as if the idea excited him, and she wondered how important it was to him to feel superior.

"Don't flatter yourself," she declared bluntly, lighting a cigarette and blowing the smoke deliberately in his direction. "Trust me, if I'd been remotely afraid, I'd have taken your fucking balls off. Cripple first and ask questions later, that's my motto."

"I don't like you smoking or swearing in this house," he said with another petulant kick at the table leg.

"Then put in a complaint," she answered. "It just means I'll be reassigned." She held his gaze for a moment. "And that wouldn't suit you one little bit, would it? You're too damn used to having an unpaid skivvy about the place."

Ready tears sprang to his eyes. "You don't understand what it's like. Everything worked so well before. And now . . . well, I don't even know what I'm supposed to be doing."

His performance was amateur at best, diabolical at worst, and it brought out the bully in Griffiths. *Did he think she found male helplessness attractive?* "Then you should be ashamed of yourself," she snapped. "According to the health visitor you didn't even know where the vacuum cleaner was, let alone how to work it. She came here to teach you elementary parenting and housekeeping skills because no one—and I repeat *no one*—is going to allow a three-year-old child to remain in the care of a man who is so patently indifferent to her welfare."

He moved around the kitchen, opening and shutting cupboard doors as if to demonstrate familiarity with their contents. "It's not my fault," he said. "That's how Kate wanted it. I wasn't allowed to interfere in the running of the house."

"Are you sure it wasn't the other way around?" She tapped the ash off her cigarette into her saucer. "I mean you didn't marry a wife, did you? You married a housekeeper who was expected to run this house like clockwork and account for every last penny she spent."

"It wasn't like that."

"What was it like then?"

"Living in a cheap boardinghouse," he said bitterly. "I didn't marry a wife *or* a housekeeper, I married a landlady who allowed me to live here as long as I paid my rent on time."

The French yacht *Mirage* motored up the Dart River early on Thursday afternoon and took a berth in the Dart Haven Marina on the Kingswear side of the estuary, opposite the lovely town of Dartmouth and alongside the steam railway line to Paignton. Shortly after they made fast, there was a blast on a whistle and the three o'clock train set off in a rush of steam, raising in the Beneteau's owner a romantic longing for days he himself couldn't remember.

By contrast his daughter sat sunk in gloom, unable to comprehend why they had moored on the side of the river that boasted nothing except the station when everything that was attractive—shops, restaurants, pubs, people, life, *men!*—was on the other side, in Dartmouth. Scornfully, she watched her father take out the video camera and search through the case for a new tape in order to film steam engines. He was like a small boy, she thought, in his silly enthusiasms for the treasures of rural England when what really mattered was London. She was the only one of her friends who had never been there, and it mortified her. God, but her parents were *sad!*

Her father turned to her in mild frustration, asking where the unused tapes were, and she had to admit there were none. She'd used them all to film irrelevancies in order to pass the time, and with irritating tolerance (he was one of those understanding fathers who refused to indulge in rows) he played the videos back, squinting into the eyepiece, in order to select the least interesting for reuse.

When he came to a tape of a young man scrambling down the slope above Chapman's Pool toward two boys, followed by shots of him sitting alone on the foreshore beyond the boat sheds, he lowered the camera and looked at his daughter with a worried frown. She was fourteen years old, and he realized he had no idea if she was still innocent or whether she knew exactly what she'd been filming. He described the young man and asked her why she had taken so much footage of him. Her cheeks flushed a rosy red under her tan. No particular reason. He was there and he was—she spoke with defiance—handsome. In any case, she knew him. They'd introduced themselves when they'd chatted together in Lymington. *And* he fancied her. She could tell these things.

Her father was appalled.

His daughter flounced her shoulders. What was the big deal? So he was English. He was just a good-looking guy who liked French girls, she said.

Bibi Gould's face fell as she swung lightheartedly out of the hairdressing salon in Lymington where she worked and saw Tony Bridges standing on the pavement, half turned away from her, watching a young mother hoist a toddler onto her hip. Her relationship, such as it was, with Tony had become more of a trial than a pleasure, and for a brief second she thought about retreating through the door again until she realized he had seen her out of the corner of his eye. She forced a sickly smile to her lips. "Hi," she said with unconvincing jauntiness.

He stared at her with his peculiarly brooding expression, taking note of the skimpy shorts and cropped top that barely covered her tanned arms, legs, and midriff. A blood vessel started to throb in his head, and he had trouble keeping the temper out of his voice. "Who are you meeting?"

"No one," she said.

"Then what's the problem? Why did you look so pissed to see me?"

"I didn't." She lowered her head to swing her curtain of hair across her eyes in a way he hated. "I'm just tired, that's all . . . I was going home to watch telly."

He reached out a hand to grip her wrist. "Steve's done a vanishing act. Is he the one you're planning to meet?"

"Don't be stupid."

"Where is he?"

"How would I know?" she said, twisting her arm to try to release herself. "He's your friend."

"Has he gone to the caravan? Did you say you'd meet him there?"

Angrily, she succeeded in tugging herself free. "You've got a real problem with him, you know . . . you should talk to someone about it instead of taking it out on me all the time. And for your information, not everyone runs away to hide in Mummy and Daddy's sodding caravan every time things go wrong. It's a dump, for Christ's sake . . . like your house . . . and who wants to fuck in a dump?" She rubbed her wrist where his fingers had left a Chinese burn on her skin, her immature nineteen-year-old features creasing into a vicious scowl. "It's not Steve's fault you're so spaced-out most nights you can't get it up, so don't keep pretending it is. The trouble with you is you've lost it, but you can't bloody well see it."

He eyed her with dislike. "What about Saturday? It wasn't me who passed out on Saturday. I'm sick to death of being fucked about, Beebs."

She was on the point of giving a petulant toss of her head and saying sex with him had become so boring that she might as well be comatose as not when caution persuaded her against it. He had a way of getting his own back that she didn't much like. "Yeah, well, you can't blame me for that," she muttered lamely. "You shouldn't buy dodgy E off your dodgy mates, should you? A girl could die that way."

CHAPTER 16

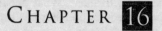

FAX:

From: PC Nicholas Ingram
To: DI John Galbraith
Date: 14 August—7:05 P.M.
Re: **Kate Sumner murder inquiry**

Sir,

I've had some follow-up thoughts on the above,
particularly in relation to the pathologist's report
and the stranded dinghy, and as it's my day off
tomorrow I'm faxing them through to you. Admittedly they are based entirely on the presumption
that the stranded dinghy was involved in Kate's
murder, but they suggest a new angle which may
be worth considering.

I mentioned this a.m. that: 1) there's a possibility the dinghy was stolen from Lulworth Cove
at the end of May, in which case the thief and

Kate's murderer could be one and the same person; 2) that if my "towing" theory was correct, there was a good chance the outboard engine (make: Fastrigger; serial no: 240B 5006678) was removed and remains in the thief's possession; 3) you take another look at Steven Harding's log to see if he was in Lulworth Cove on Thursday, 29 May; 4) if he had a second dinghy stowed on board <u>Crazy Daze</u>—which only required a foot pump to reinflate it—it would solve some of your forensic problems; 5) he probably has a lock-up somewhere which you haven't yet discovered and which may contain the stolen outboard.

***<u>I have since had time to consider the logistics of how the dinghy was actually removed from Lulworth Cove in broad daylight, and I've realized that Harding or indeed any boat owner would have had some difficulty.</u>

It's important to recognize that <u>Crazy Daze</u> must have anchored in the middle of Lulworth Bay, and Harding could only have come ashore in his own dinghy. Joyriders going for a spin would have attracted little attention (the assumption would be that the boat belonged to them) but a man on his own, coping with <u>two</u> dinghies, would have stood out like a sore thumb, particularly as the only way he could have removed them from the Cove (unless he was prepared to waste time deflating them) was to tow them in tandem or parallel behind <u>Crazy Daze.</u> It is <u>highly</u> unusual for a yacht to have two dinghies, and once the theft had been reported, that fact is bound to have registered with the coastguards in the lookout point above Lulworth.

I think now that a more likely scenario for the

theft was removal by foot. Let's say an opportunist thief spotted that the outboard wasn't padlocked, released its clamps, and carried it away
quite openly to his car/house/garage/caravan.
Let's say he wandered back half an hour later to
see if the owners had returned, and finding they
hadn't, he simply hoisted the dinghy above his
head and carried that away too. I'm not suggesting that Kate Sumner's murder was premeditated
at this early stage, but what I am suggesting is
that the opportunist theft of the Spanish dinghy
in May gave rise to an ideal method in August for
the disposal of her body. (NB: thefts of or from
boats represent some of the highest crime statis-
tics along the south coast.) I strongly advise,
therefore, that you try to find out if anyone connected with Kate was staying in or near Lulworth
between 24–31 May. I suspect the sad irony will
be that she, her husband, and her daughter
were—there are several caravan parks and camp-
sites around Lulworth—but I think this will please
you. It strengthens the case against the husband.

For reasons that follow, I am no longer confident that you'll find the outboard. Assuming the
intention was for the stolen dinghy, plus contents
(i.e., Kate) to sink, then the outboard must have
been on board.

You may remember my querying the
"hypothermia" issue in the pathologist's report
when you showed it to me on Monday. The pathologist's view is that Kate was swimming in the
water for some considerable time prior to drowning, which caused her stress and cold. At the time
I wondered why it took her so long to swim a
comparatively short distance, and I suggested

that she was more likely to suffer hypothermia
from being exposed to air temperature at night
rather than sea temperature—the latter being
generally warmer. It would depend of course on
how good a swimmer she was, particularly as the
pathologist refers to her entering the sea a <u>mini-
mum</u> of half a mile WSW of Egmont Bight, and I
assumed she must have swum a great deal farther than his estimate. However, you told Miss
Jenner this morning that Kate was a poor swimmer, and I have been wondering since how a poor
swimmer could have remained afloat long enough
in difficult seas to show evidence of hypothermia
before death. I have also been wondering why her
killer was confident of making it safely back to
shore, since there are no lights on that part of
the coast and the currents are unpredictable.

One explanation which covers the above is that
Kate was raped ashore, her killer presumed her
dead after the strangulation attempt, and the
whole "drowning" exercise was designed to dis-
pose of her body off an isolated stretch of coast.

Can you buy this reasoning? 1) He bundled her
naked and unconscious body into the stolen
dinghy, then took her a considerable distance—
Lulworth Cove to Chapman's Pool = 8 nautical
miles approx.—before he tied her to the outboard
and left the dinghy to sink with its contents
(wind-chill factor would already have caused
hypothermia in a naked woman); 2) once set
adrift, Kate came around from the strangulation
attempt/Rohypnol and realized she had to save
herself; 3) her broken fingers and nails could
have resulted from her struggle to break free of
her bonds then release the clamps holding the

outboard in place in order to eject its weight,
probably capsizing the dinghy in the process; 4)
she used the dinghy as a float and became separated from it only when she lapsed into uncon-
sciousness or became too tired to hold on; 5) in
all events, I am guessing the dinghy traveled
<u>much closer to shore than the pathologist's esti-
mate</u>, otherwise the boat would have become
swamped and the killer himself would have been
in trouble; 6) the killer climbed the cliffs and
returned to Lulworth/Kimmeridge via the coastal
path during the dark hours of the night.

This is as far as my thoughts have taken me,
but if the dinghy <u>was</u> involved in the murder then
it must have come from the west—Kimmeridge
Bay or Lulworth Cove—because the craft was too
fragile to negotiate the race around St. Alban's
Head. I realize none of this explains Hannah,
although I can't help feeling that if you can discover where the stolen dinghy was hidden for two
months, you may also discover where Kate was
raped and where Hannah was left while her
mother was being drowned.

(NB: None of the above rules out Harding—the
rape <u>may</u> have taken place on his deck with the
evidence subsequently washed away, and the
dinghy <u>may</u> have been towed behind <u>Crazy Daze</u>—
but does it make him a less likely suspect?)

Nick Ingram

CHAPTER 17

The sun had been up less than an hour on Friday morning when Maggie Jenner set off along the bridleway behind Broxton House, accompanied by Bertie. She was on a skittish bay gelding called Stinger, whose owner came down from London every weekend to her cottage in Langton Matravers to ride hard around the headlands as an antidote to her high-pressure job as a money broker in the City. Maggie loved the horse but loathed the woman, whose hands were about as sensitive as steam hammers and who viewed Stinger in the same way as she probably viewed a snort of cocaine—as a quick adrenaline fix. If she hadn't agreed to pay well over the odds for the livery service Maggie provided, Maggie would have refused her business without a second's hesitation, but as with most things in the Jenners' lives, compromise had become the better part of staving off bankruptcy.

She turned right at St. Alban's Head Quarry, negotiating her way through the gate and into the deep, wide valley that cleaved a grassy downland passage toward the sea between St. Alban's Head to the south and the high ground above Chapman's Pool to the north. She nudged her mount into a canter and sent him springing across the turf in glorious release. It was still cool, but there was barely a breath of wind in the air, and as always on mornings like this her spirits soared. However bad existence was, and it could be very bad at times, she ceased to worry about it here. If there was any point to anything, then she came closest to finding it, alone and free, in the renewed optimism that a fresh sun generated with each daybreak.

She reined in after half a mile, and walked the gelding toward the fenced coastal path which hugged the slopes of the valley on either side in a series of steep steps cut into the cliffs. It was a hardy rambler who suffered the agony of the downward trek only to be faced with the worse agony of the upward climb, and Maggie, who had never done either, thought how much more sensible it was to ride the gully in order to enjoy the scenery. Ahead, the sea, a sparkling blue, was flat calm without a sail in sight, and she slipped lightly from the saddle while Bertie, panting from the exertion of keeping up, rolled leisurely in the warming grass beside the gelding's hooves. Looping Stinger's reins casually around the top rail of the fence, she climbed the stile and walked the few yards to the cliff edge to stand and glory in the vast expanse of blueness, where the line of demarcation between sky and sea was all but invisible. The only sounds were the gentle swish of breakers on the shore, the sigh of the animals' breaths, and a lark singing in the sky above. . . .

It was difficult to say who was the more startled, therefore, Maggie or Steven Harding, when he rose out of the ground in front of her after hoisting himself over the cliff edge where the downland valley dropped toward the sea. He crouched on all fours for several seconds, his face pale and unshaven, breathing heavily, and looking a great deal less pretty than he had five days before. More like a rapist, less like a Hollywood lead. There was a quality of disturbing violence about him, something calculating in the dark eyes that Maggie hadn't noticed before, but it was his abrupt rearing to full height that

caused her to shriek. Her alarm transmitted itself immediately to Stinger, who pranced backward, tearing his
reins free of the fence, and thence to Bertie, who leaped
to his feet, hackles up.

"You stupid bastard!" Maggie shouted at him, giving
vent to her fear in furious remonstration as she heard
Stinger's snort of alarm and stamping hooves. She turned
away from Harding in a vain attempt to catch the excited
gelding's reins before he bolted.

*Pray God, he didn't . . . he was worth a fortune to Brox-
ton House Livery Stables . . . she couldn't afford it if he
damaged himself . . . pray God, pray God . . .*

But Harding, for reasons best known to himself, darted
across her path in Stinger's direction, and the gelding,
eyes rolling, took off like lightning up the hill.

"Oh, shit!" Maggie stormed, stamping her foot and
raging at the young man, her face red and ugly with
ungovernable fury. "How could you be so bloody infan-
tile, you—you *creep!* What the *hell* did you think you
were doing! I swear to Christ if Nick Ingram knew you
were here he'd *crucify* you! He already thinks you're a
fucking *pervert!*"

She was completely unprepared for his backhand slap
that caught her a glancing blow across the side of her face,
and as she hit the ground with a resounding thud, the only
thought in her head was: What on earth does this idiot
think he's doing . . . ?

Ingram squinted painfully at his alarm clock when his
phone rang at 6:30 A.M. He lifted the receiver and listened
to a series of high-pitched, unintelligible squeaks at the
other end of the line, which he recognized as coming from
Maggie Jenner.

"You'll have to calm down," he said when she finally
took a breath. "I can't understand a word you're saying."

More squeaks.

"Pull yourself together, Maggie," he said firmly. "You're not a wimp, so don't behave like one."

"I'm sorry," she said with a commendable attempt to compose herself. "Steven Harding hit me, so Bertie went for him . . . there's blood everywhere . . . I've rigged up a tourniquet on his arm, but it's not working properly . . . I don't know what else to do . . . I think he's going to die if he doesn't get to a hospital."

He sat up and rubbed his face furiously to eradicate sleep. He could hear the white noise of empty space and the sound of birdsong in the background. "Where are you?"

"At the end of the quarry gully . . . near the steps on the coastal path . . . halfway between Chapman's Pool and St. Alban's Head . . . Stinger's bolted, and I'm afraid he's going to break a leg if he trips on his reins . . . we'll lose everything . . . I think Steve's dying . . ." Her voice faded as she turned away from the signal. "Manslaughter . . . Bertie was out of control . . ."

"I'm losing you, Maggie," he shouted.

"Sorry." Her voice came back in a rush. "He's not responding to anything. I'm worried Bertie's severed an artery, but I can't get the tourniquet tight enough to stop the bleeding. I'm using Bertie's lead, but it's too loose, and the sticks here are all so rotten they just keep breaking."

"Then forget the lead and use something else—something you can get a grip on—a T-shirt maybe. Wind it around his arm as tight as you can above the elbow, then keep twisting the ends to exert some pressure. Failing that, try and locate the artery on the underside of his upper arm with your fingers and press hard against the bone to stop the flow. But you've got to keep the pressure on, Maggie, otherwise he'll start bleeding again, and that means your hands are going to hurt."

"Okay."

"Good girl. I'll get help to you as fast as I can." He cut her off and dialed Broxton House. "Mrs. Jenner?" he said, flicking over to the loudspeaker when the receiver was lifted at the other end. "It's Nick Ingram." He flung him-self out of bed and started to drag on some clothes. "Mag-gie needs help, and you're the closest. She's trying to stop a man from bleeding to death in the quarry gully. They're at the coastal path end. If you take Sir Jasper and get up there PDQ, then the man stands a chance. Otherwise—"

"But I'm not dressed," she interrupted indignantly.

"I couldn't give a shit," he said bluntly. "Get your arse up there and give your daughter some support because, by God, it'll be a first if you do."

"How dare—"

He cut her off and set in motion the series of calls that would result in the Portland Search and Rescue helicopter being scrambled in the direction of St. Alban's Head for the second time in less than a week, when the ambulance service expressed doubt about their ability to reach a man in a remote grassy valley before he bled to death.

By the time Nick Ingram reached the scene, having driven his Jeep at breakneck speed along narrow lanes and up the bridleway, the drama was effectively over. The helicopter was on the ground some fifty yards from the scene of the accident, engine idling; Harding was conscious and sitting up being attended by a paramedic; and another hundred yards to the south of the helicopter and halfway up the hillside, Maggie was busy trying to catch Stinger, who rolled his eyes and backed away from her every time she came too close. She was clearly trying to head him off from the cliff edge, but he was too frightened of the heli-copter to move in its direction, and all she was succeeding in doing was driving him toward the three-foot-high fence and the perilously steep steps that edged the cliff. Celia, clad in a pair of pajama trousers and a tannin-stained bed-jacket, stood arrogantly to one side with one hand grasp-ing Sir Jasper's reins tightly beneath his chin and the other wound into the looped end in case he, too, decided to bolt. She favored Ingram with a frosty glare, designed to freeze him in his tracks, but he ignored her and turned his attention to Harding.

"Are you all right, sir?"

The young man nodded. He was dressed in Levi's and a pale green sweatshirt, both of which were copiously splattered with blood, and his lower right arm was tightly bandaged.

Ingram turned to the paramedic. "What's the damage?"

"He'll live," said the man. "The two ladies managed to stop the bleeding. He'll need stitching, so we'll take him to Poole and get him sorted there." He drew Nick aside. "The young lady could do with some attention. She's shaking like a leaf, but she says it's more important to catch the horse. The trouble is he's torn his reins off, and she can't get close enough to get a grip on his throat strap." He jerked his head toward Celia. "And the older one's not much better. She's got arthritis, and she wrecked her hip riding up here. By rights, we ought to take them with us, but they're adamant they won't leave the animals. There's also a time problem. We need to get moving, but the loose horse is going to bolt in real earnest the minute we take off. It's terrified out of its wits already and damn nearly skidded over the cliff when we landed."

"Where's the dog?"

"Vanished. I gather the young lady had to thrash him with his lead to get him off the lad, and he's fled with his tail between his legs."

Nick rumpled his sleep-tousled hair. "Okay, can you give us another five minutes? If I help Miss Jenner round up the horse, we may be able to persuade her mother to go in for some treatment. How about it?"

The paramedic turned to look at Steven Harding. "Why not? He says he's strong enough to walk, but it'll take me a good five minutes to get him in and settled. I don't fancy your chances much, but good luck."

With a wry smile, Nick put his fingers to his lips and gave a piercing whistle before scanning both hillsides with narrowed eyes. To his relief, he saw Bertie rise out of the grass on the breast of Emmetts Hill about two hundred and fifty yards away. He gave another whistle, and the dog came like a torpedo toward him. He raised his arm and dropped him to the ground when he was still fifty yards away, then went back to Celia. "I need a quick decision," he told her. "We've got five minutes to catch Stinger before the helicopter leaves, and it strikes me Maggie'll have more chance if she's riding Sir Jasper. You're the expert. Do I take him up to her or do I leave him with you, bearing in mind I know nothing about horses and Jasper's likely to be just as frightened of the noise as Stinger is?"

She was a sensible woman and didn't waste time on recriminations. She handed the loop of the reins into his left hand and guided his right into position under Jasper's chin. "Keep clicking your tongue," she said, "and he'll follow. Don't try and run, and don't let go. We can't afford to lose both of them. Remind Maggie they'll both go mad the minute the helicopter takes off, so tell her to ride like the devil for the middle of the headland and give herself some space."

He set off up the slope, whistling Bertie to follow and gathering him in to his left leg so that the dog walked like a shadow beside him.

"I didn't realize it was his dog," said the paramedic to Celia.

"It's not," she said thoughtfully, shading her eyes against the sun to watch what happened.

She saw her daughter come stumbling down toward the tall policeman, who had a quick word with her, then hefted her lightly into Jasper's saddle before, with a gesture of his arm, he sent Bertie out in a sweeping movement toward the cliff edge to circle around behind the excited gelding. He followed in Bertie's wake, placing himself as an immovable obstacle between the horse and the brink, while directing the dog to hamper Stinger's further retreat up the hillside by dashing to and fro above him. Meanwhile, Maggie had turned Sir Jasper toward the quarry site and had kicked him into a canter. Faced with the unpalatable alternatives of a dog on one side, a heli-copter on the other, and a man behind, Stinger chose the sensible option of pursuing the other horse toward safety.

"Impressive," said the paramedic.

"Yes," said Celia even more thoughtfully. "It was, wasn't it?"

Polly Garrard was about to leave for work when DI John Galbraith rang her front doorbell and asked if she was willing to answer a few more questions about her relation-ship with Kate Sumner. "I can't," she told him. "I'll be late. You can come to the office if you like."

"Fine, if that's the way you want it," he assured her. "It might make things difficult for you, though. You probably won't want eavesdroppers to some of the things I'm going to ask you."

"Oh, shit!" she said immediately. "I knew this was going to happen." She opened the door wide. "You'd bet-ter come in," she said, leading the way into a tiny sitting room, "but you can't keep me long. Half an hour max, okay? I've already been late twice this month, and I'm running out of excuses."

She dropped onto one end of a sofa, hooking an arm over its back and inviting him to sit at the other end. She twisted around to face him, one leg curled beneath her so that her skirt rose up to her crotch and her breasts stood out in response to her pulled-back shoulder. The pose was deliberate, thought Galbraith with some amusement, as he lowered himself onto the seat beside her. She was a well-built young woman with a taste for tight T-shirts, heavy makeup, and blue nail polish, and he wondered how Angela Sumner would have coped with Polly as a daughter-in-law in place of Kate. For all her real or imag-ined sins, Kate seemed to have looked the part of William's wife, even if she did lack the necessary social and educational skills that would have satisfied her mother-in-law.

"I want to ask you about a letter you wrote to Kate in July, which concerns some of the people you work with," he told Polly, taking a photocopy of it out of his breast pocket. He spread it on his knee and handed it to her. "Do you remember sending that?"

She read it through quickly, then nodded. "Yup. I'd been phoning on and off for about a week, and I thought, what the hell, she's obviously busy, so I'll drop her a note instead and get her to phone me." She screwed her face into cartoon pique. "Not that she ever did. She just sent a scrotty little note, saying she'd call when she was ready."

"This one?" He handed her a copy of Kate's draft reply.

She glanced at it. "I guess so. That's what it said, more or less. It was on some fancy-headed notepaper, I remember that, but I was pissed that she couldn't be bothered to write a decent letter back. The truth is, I don't think she wanted me to go. I expect she was afraid I'd embarrass her in front of her Lymington friends. Which I probably would have done," she added in fairness.

Galbraith smiled. "Did you visit the house when they first moved?"

"Nope. Never got invited. She kept saying I could go as soon as the decorating was finished, but"—she pulled another face—"it was just an excuse to put me off. I didn't mind. Fact is, I'd probably have done the same in her shoes. She'd moved on—new house, new life, new friends—and you grow out of people when that happens, don't you?"

"She hadn't moved on completely," he pointed out. "You still work with William."

Polly giggled. "I work in the same building as William," she corrected him, "and it gets up his nose something rotten that I tell everyone he married my best friend. I know it's not true—it never was, really—I mean I liked her and all that, but she wasn't the best-friend type, if you know what I mean. Too self-contained by half. No, I just do it to annoy William. He thinks I'm common as muck, and he nearly died when I told him I'd visited Kate in Chichester and met his mother. I'm not surprised. God, she was an old battleaxe! Lecture, lecture, lecture. Do this. Don't do that. Frankly, I'd've wheeled her in front of a bus if she'd been *my* mother-in-law."

"Was there ever a chance of that?"

"Do me a favor! I'd need to be permanently comatose to marry William Sumner. The guy has about as much sex appeal as a turnip!"

"So what did Kate see in him?"

Polly rubbed her thumb and forefinger together. "Money."

"What else?"

"Nothing. A bit of class, maybe, but an unmarried bloke with no children and money was what she was looking for, and an unmarried bloke with no children and money is what she got." She cocked her head on one side, amused by his expression of disbelief. "She told me once that William's tackle, even when he had a stiffy, was so limp it was more like an uncooked sausage than a truncheon. So I said, how does he do the business? And she said, with a pint of baby oil and my finger up his fucking arse." She giggled again at Galbraith's wince of sympathy for another man's problems. "He loved it, for Christ's sake! Why else would he marry her with his mother spitting poison all over the place? Okay, Kate may have wanted money, but poor old Willy just wanted a tart who'd tell him he was bloody brilliant whether he was or not. It worked like a dream. They both got what they wanted."

He studied her for a moment, wondering if she was quite as naive as her words made her sound. "Did they?" he asked her. "Kate's dead, don't forget."

She sobered immediately. "I know. It's a bugger. But there's nothing I can tell you about that. I haven't seen her since she moved."

"All right. Tell me what you do know. Why did your story about Wendy Plater insulting James Purdy remind you of Kate?" he asked her.

"What makes you think it did?"

He quoted from her letter. " 'She'—meaning Wendy—'had to apologize, but she doesn't regret any of it. She says she's never seen Purdy go purple before! I thought of you immediately, of course . . .' " He laid the page on the bench between them. "Why that last bit, Polly? Why should Purdy going purple make you think of Kate Sumner?"

She thought for a moment. "Because she used to work at Pharmatec?" she tried unconvincingly. "Because she thought Purdy was a prick? It's just a figure of speech."

He tapped the copy of Kate's draft reply. "She crossed out, 'You promised on your honor' in this before going on to write 'The story about Wendy Plater was really funny!' " he said. "What did you promise her, Polly?"

She looked uncomfortable. "Hundreds of things, I should think."

"I'm only interested in the one that had something to do with either James Purdy or Wendy Plater."

She removed her arm from the back of the seat and hunched forward despondently. "It's got nothing to do with her being killed. It's just something that happened."

"What?"

She didn't answer.

"If it really does have nothing to do with her murder, then I give you my word, it'll go no further than me," he said reassuringly. "I'm not interested in exposing her secrets, only in finding her killer." Even as he spoke, he knew the statement was untrue. All too often, justice for a rape victim meant that she had to endure the humiliation of her secrets being exposed. He looked at Polly with unexpected sympathy. "But I'm afraid *I'm* the one who has to decide whether it's important."

She sighed. "I could lose my job if Purdy ever finds out I told you."

"There's no reason why he should."

"You reckon?"

Galbraith didn't say anything, having learned from experience that silence often exerted more pressure than words.

"Oh, what the hell!" she said then. "You've probably guessed anyway. Kate had an affair with him. He was crazy about her, wanted to leave his wife and everything, then she blew him away and said she was going to marry William instead. Poor old Purdy couldn't believe it. He's no spring chicken, and he'd been rogering himself stupid to keep her interested. I think he may even have told his wife he wanted a divorce. Anyway, Kate said he went purple and then collapsed on his desk. He was off work for three months afterward, so I reckoned he must have had a heart attack, but Kate said he couldn't face coming back while she was still there." She shrugged. "He started work again the week after she left, so maybe she was right."

"Why did she choose William?" he asked. "She wasn't any more in love with him than she was with Purdy, was she?"

Polly repeated the gesture of rubbing her thumb and fingers together. "Dosh," she said. "Purdy's got a wife and three grown-up children, all of whom would have demanded their cut before Kate got a look in." She pulled a wry face. "Like I said, what she really wanted was an unmarried guy without children. She reckoned if she was going to have to bust a gut to make some plonker happy, she wanted access to everything he owned."

Galbraith shook his head in perplexity. "Then why bother with Purdy at all?"

She hooked her arm over the sofa again and thrust her tits into his face. "She didn't have a father, did she? Any more than I do."

"So?"

"She had a thing about older men." She opened her eyes wide in flirtatious invitation. "Me, too, if you're interested."

Galbraith chuckled. "Do you eat them alive?"

She looked pointedly at his fly. "I swallow them whole," she said with a laugh.

He shook his head in amusement. "You were telling me why Kate bothered with Purdy," he reminded her.

"He was the boss," she said, "the guy with the loot. She thought she'd take him for a few bob, get him to pay for improvements on her flat, while she looked around for something better. The trouble was, she didn't reckon on him getting as smitten as he did, so the only way to get rid of him was to be cruel. She wanted security, not love, you see, and she didn't think she'd get it from Purdy, not after his wife and children had taken their slice. He was thirty years older than she was, remember. Also, he didn't want any more kids, and that was all she really wanted, kids of her own. She was pretty screwed up in some ways, I guess because she'd had a tough time growing up."

"Did William know about her affair with Purdy?"

Polly shook her head. "No one knew except me. That's why she swore me to secrecy. She said William would call the wedding off if he ever found out."

"Would he have done?"

"Oh, for sure. Look, he was thirty-seven years old, and he wasn't the marrying kind. Wendy Plater nearly got him up to scratch once till Kate put a spanner in the works by telling him she was a lush. He dumped her so quick, you wouldn't believe." She smiled reminiscently. "Kate practically had to put a ring through his nose to get him to the registry office. It might have been different if his mother had approved, but old Ma Sumner and Will were like a couple of old folks, and Kate had to work her socks off every night to make sex more attractive to the silly sod than having his laundry done on a regular basis."

"Was it true about Wendy Plater?"

Polly looked uncomfortable again. "She gets drunk sometimes but not on a regular basis. Still, as Kate said, if Will had wanted to marry her, he wouldn't have believed it, would he? He just seized on the first good excuse to get out."

Galbraith looked down at Kate Sumner's childish writing in the draft letter she'd written to Polly and wondered about the nature of ruthlessness. "Did the affair with Purdy continue after she married William?"

"No," said Polly with conviction. "Once Kate made up her mind to something, that was it."

"Would that stop her having an affair with someone else? Let's say she was bored with William and met someone younger—would she have been unfaithful in those circumstances?"

Polly shrugged. "I don't know. I sort of thought she might have something going because she hasn't bothered to phone me for ages, but that doesn't mean she did. It wouldn't have been serious, anyway. She was pleased as punch about moving to Lymington and getting a decent house, and I can't see her giving all that up very easily."

Galbraith nodded. "Have you ever known her to use feces as a means of revenge?"

"What the hell's fee-sees?"

"Crap," Galbraith explained obligingly, "turds, dung, number twos."

"Shit!"

"Exactly. Have you ever known her to smear crap over anyone's belongings?"

Polly giggled. "No. She was much too prissy to do anything like that. A bit of a hygiene freak, actually. When Hannah was a baby she used to swab the kitchen down every day with Dettol in case there were any germs. I told her she was crazy—I mean germs are everywhere, aren't they—but she still went on doing it. I can't see her touching a turd in a million years. She used to hold Hannah's nappies at arm's length after she'd changed her."

Curiouser and curiouser, thought Galbraith. "Okay. Give me a rough idea of the timetable. How soon after she told Purdy she was going to marry William did the wedding actually take place?"

"I can't remember. A month maybe."

He did a quick calculation in his head. "So if Purdy was

off for three months, then it was two months after the wedding that she left work because she was pregnant?"

"Something like that."

"And how pregnant was she, Polly? Two months? Three months? Four months?"

A resigned expression crossed the young woman's face. "She said as long as it looked like her it wouldn't matter, because William was so besotted he'd believe anything she told him." She read Galbraith's expression correctly as one of contempt. "She didn't do it out of malice. Just desperation. She knew what it was like to grow up in poverty."

Celia's adamant refusal to go with Harding in the helicopter and her inability to bend at the hip meant that she was going to either have to walk home in extreme pain or travel flat on her back on the floor of Ingram's Jeep, which was full of oilskins, waders, and fishing tackle. With a wry smile he cleared a space and bent to pick her up. However, she was even more adamant in her refusal to be carried. "I'm not a child," she snapped.

"I don't see how else we can do it, Mrs. Jenner," he pointed out, "not unless you slide in on your front and lie facedown where I usually put my fish."

"I suppose you think that's funny."

"Merely accurate. I'm afraid it's going to be painful whatever we do."

She looked at the uncomfortable, ridged floor and gave in with bad grace. "Just don't make a meal of it," she said crossly. "I hate fuss."

"I know." He scooped her into his arms and leaned into the Jeep to deposit her carefully on the floor. "It's going to be a bumpy ride," he warned, packing the oilskins around her as wadding. "You'd better shout if it gets too much for you, and I'll stop."

It was already too much, but she had no intention of

telling him so. "I'm worried about Maggie," she said through gritted teeth. "She ought to be back by now."

"She'll have led Stinger toward the stables not away from them," he told her.

"Are you ever wrong about anything?" she asked acidly.

"Not where your daughter's knowledge of horses is concerned," he answered. "I have faith in her, and so should you." He shut the door on her and climbed in behind the wheel. "I'll apologize in advance," he called as he started the engine.

"What for?"

"The lousy suspension," he murmured, letting out the clutch and setting off at a snail's pace across the chewed-up turf of the valley. She didn't make a sound the entire way back, and he smiled to himself as he drew into the Broxton House drive. Whatever else she was, Celia Jenner was a gutsy lady, and he admired her for it.

He opened the back door. "Still alive?" he asked, reaching in for her.

She was gray with pain and fatigue, but it took more than a bumpy ride to kill the spark. "You're a very irritating young man," she muttered, as she clamped her arm around his neck again and grunted with pain as he shifted her along the floor. "But you were right about Martin Grant," she admitted grudgingly, "and I've always regretted that I didn't listen to you. Does that please you?"

"No."

"Why not? Maggie would tell you it's the closest I'll ever come to an apology."

He smiled slightly, hefting her against his chest and stepping away from the Jeep. "Is being stubborn something to be proud of?"

"I'm not stubborn, I'm principled."

"Well, if you weren't so"— he grinned at her—"principled, you'd be in the Poole hospital by now getting proper treatment."

"You should always call a spade a spade," she said crossly. "And, frankly, if I was half as stubborn as you seem to think I am, I wouldn't even be in this condition. I object to having my arse mentioned over the telephone."

"Do you want *another* apology?"

She looked up and caught his eye, then looked away again. "For goodness sake, put me down," she said. "This is so undignified in a woman of my age. What would my daughter say if she saw me like this?"

He took no notice of her and strode across the weed-strewn gravel toward her front door, only lowering her to the ground when he heard the sound of running feet. Maggie, flustered and breathless, appeared around the corner of the house, a walking stick in each hand. She handed them to her mother. "She's not allowed to ride," she told Nick, bending over to catch her breath. "Doctor's orders. But thank God she never takes anyone's advice. I couldn't have managed on my own, and I certainly couldn't have got Stinger back without Sir Jasper."

Nick held supporting hands under Celia's elbows while she balanced herself on the sticks. "You should have told me to get stuffed," he said.

She inched forward on her sticks like a large crab. "Don't be ridiculous," she muttered irritably. "That's the mistake I made last time."

CHAPTER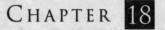

STATEMENT

Witness: James Purdy, Managing Director,
             Pharmatec UK
Interviewer: DI Galbraith

Sometime during the summer of 1993, I was
working late in the office. As far as I was aware,
everyone else had left the premises. On my way
out at approximately 9:00 P.M., I noticed a light
shining in an office at the end of the corridor. The
office belonged to Kate Hill, secretary to the services manager, Michael Sprate, and, because I was
impressed by the fact that she was working late, I
went in to commend her on her commitment. She
had been drawn to my attention when she first
joined the company because of her size. She was
slim and small with blond hair and remarkable
blue eyes. I found her very attractive, but that
was not my reason for going into her office that

night. She had never given any indication that she was interested in me. I was surprised and flattered, therefore, when she got up from her desk and said she had stayed late in the hope that I would come in.

I am not proud of what happened next. I'm fifty-eight years old, and I've been married thirty-three years, and no one has ever done to me what Kate did that night. I know it sounds absurd, but it's the sort of thing most men dream of: that they'll walk into a room one day and a beautiful woman, for no reason at all, will offer them sex. I was extremely worried afterward because I assumed she must have had an ulterior motive for doing it. I spent the next few days in fear. At the very least I expected her to take liberties in her dealings with me; at the worst I expected some sort of blackmail attempt. However, she was extremely discreet, asked nothing in return, and was always polite whenever I saw her. When I realized there was nothing to fear, I became obsessed with her and dreamed about her night after night.

Some two weeks later, she was again in her office when I passed, and the experience was repeated. I asked her why and she said: "Because I want to." From that moment on, there was nothing I could do to control myself. In some ways, she is the most beautiful thing that has ever happened in my life, and I do not regret one moment of our affair. In other ways, I look back on it as a nightmare. I did not believe hearts could be broken, but mine was broken several times by Kate, never more so than when I heard she was dead.

Our affair continued for several months, until

January 1994. For the most part it was conducted in Kate's flat, although once or twice,
under the guise of business trips, I took her to
hotels in London. I was prepared to divorce my
wife in order to marry Kate, even though I have
always loved my wife and would never do anything willingly to hurt her. I can only describe
Kate as a fever in the blood that temporarily
upset my equilibrium, because once exorcized, I
was able to return to normal.

On a Friday at the end of January 1994, Kate
came into my office at about 3:30 P.M. and told me
she was going to marry William Sumner. I was
terribly distressed and remember little of what
happened next. I know I passed out, and when I
came around again I was in the hospital. I was
told I had had a minor heart attack. I have since
confessed to my wife everything that happened.

As far as I am aware, William Sumner knows
nothing about my relations with Kate before their
marriage. I have certainly not told him, nor have
I led him to believe that we were even remotely
friendly. It did occur to me that his daughter
might be mine, but I have never mentioned it to
anyone as I would not lay claim to the child.

I can confirm that I have had no contact with
Kate Hill-Sumner since the day in January 1994
when she told me of her decision to marry
William Sumner.

James Purdy

STATEMENT

Witness:	Vivienne Purdy, The Gables, Drew Street, Fareham
Interviewer:	DI Galbraith

I first learned of my husband's affair with Kate Hill some four weeks after his heart attack in January 1994. I cannot remember the precise date, but it was either the day she married William Sumner or the day after. I found James in tears, and I was worried because he had been making such good progress. He told me he was crying because his heart was breaking, and he went on to explain why.

I was neither hurt nor surprised by his confession. James and I have been married a long time, and I knew perfectly well that he was having a relationship with someone else. He has never been a good liar. My only emotion was relief that he had finally decided to clear the air. I felt no animosity toward Kate Hill-Sumner for the following reasons.

It may sound insensitive, but I would not have regarded it as the worst misfortune that could have happened to me to lose the man I had lived with for thirty-three years. Indeed, in some ways I would have welcomed it as an opportunity to start a new life, free of duty and responsibility. Prior to the events of 1993–94 James was a conscientious father and husband, but his family had always taken second place to his personal ambitions and desires. When I realized that he was having an affair, I made discreet inquiries about the financial position should divorce become inevitable, and satisfied myself that a division of our property would allow me considerable freedom. I renewed my career as a teacher some ten years ago, and my salary is an adequate one. I have also made sensible pension provisions for myself. As a result, I would certainly have agreed to a divorce had James asked for one. My children are grown up, and while they would be unhappy at the thought of their parents separating, I knew that James would continue to be interested in them.

I explained all this to James in the spring of 1994, and showed him the correspondence I had had with my solicitor and my accountant. I believe it concentrated his mind on the choices open to him, and I am confident that he put aside any thought of attempting to rekindle the affair with Kate Hill-Sumner. I hope I don't flatter myself when I say it came as a shock to him to realize that he could no longer take my automatic presence in his life for granted, and that he took this possibility rather more seriously than he took his relationship with Kate Hill-Sumner. I can say honestly that I have no lingering resentment toward James or Kate because it was I who was empowered by the experience. I have a great deal more confidence in myself and my future as a result.

I was aware that William and Kate Hill-Sumner had a child sometime in autumn 1994. By simple calculation, I recognized that the child could have been my husband's. However, I did not discuss the issue with him. Nor indeed with anyone else. I could see no point in causing further unhappiness to the parties involved, particularly the child.

I have never met Kate Hill-Sumner or her husband.

Vivienne Purdy

Inside Broxton House, Nick Ingram abandoned both women in the kitchen to put through a call to the incident room at Winfrith. He spoke to Detective Superintendent Carpenter, and gave him details of Harding's activities that morning. "He's been taken to the Poole hospital, sir. I shall be questioning him later about the assault, but meanwhile you might want to keep an eye on him. He's not likely to go anywhere in the short term because his arm needs stitching, but I'd say he's out of control now or he wouldn't have attacked Miss Jenner."

"What was he trying to do? Rape her?"

"She doesn't know. She says she shouted at him when her horse bolted, so he slapped her and knocked her to the ground."

"Mmm." Carpenter thought for a moment. "I thought you and John Galbraith decided he was interested in little boys."

"I'm ready to be proved wrong, sir."

There was a dry chuckle at the other end. "What's the first rule of policing, son?"

"Always keep an open mind, sir."

"Legwork first, lad. Conclusions second." There was another brief silence. "The DI's gone off in hot pursuit of William Sumner after reading your fax. He won't be at all pleased if Harding's our man after all."

"Sorry, sir. If you can give me a couple of hours to go back to the headland, I'll see if I can find out what he was up to. It'll be quicker than sending any of your chaps down."

But he was delayed by the wretched state of the two Jenner women. Celia was in such pain she was unable to sit down, and so she stood in the middle of the kitchen, legs splayed and leaning forward on her two sticks, looking more like an angry praying mantis than a crab. Meanwhile, Maggie's teeth chattered nonstop from delayed shock. "S-s-sorry," she kept saying, as she took a filthy, evil-smelling horse blanket from the scullery and draped it around her shoulders, "I'm j-just s-s-so c-cold."

Unceremoniously, Ingram shoved her onto a chair beside the Aga and told her to stay put while he dealt with her mother. "Right," he said to Celia, "are you going to be more comfortable lying down in bed or sitting up in a chair?"

"Lying down," she said.

"Then I'll set up a bed on the ground floor. Which room do you want it in?"

"I don't," she said mutinously. "It'll make me look like an invalid."

He crossed his arms and frowned at her. "I haven't got time to argue about this, Mrs. Jenner. There's no way you can get upstairs, so the bed has to come to you." She didn't answer. "All right," he said, heading for the hall. "I'll make the decision myself."

"The drawing room," she called after him. "And take the bed out of the room at the end of the corridor."

Her reluctance, he realized, had more to do with her unwillingness to let him go upstairs than fear of being seen as an invalid. He had had no idea how desperate their plight was until he saw the wasteland of the upper floor. The doors stood open to every room, eight in all, and there wasn't a single piece of furniture in any but Celia's. The smell of long-lying dust and damp permeating through an unsound roof stung his nostrils, and he wasn't surprised that Celia's health had begun to suffer. He was reminded of Jane Fielding's complaints about selling the family heirlooms to look after her parents-in-law, but their situation was princely compared with this.

The room at the end of the corridor was obviously Celia's own, and her bed probably the only one left in the house. It took him less than ten minutes to dismantle and reassemble it in the drawing room, where he set it up close to the French windows, overlooking the garden. The view was hardly inspiring, just another wasteland, untended and uncared for, but the drawing room at least retained some of its former glory, with all its paintings and most of its furniture still intact. He had time to reflect that few, if any, of Celia's acquaintances could have any idea that the hall and the drawing room represented the extent of her remaining worth. But what sort of madness made people live like this? he wondered. Pride? Fear of their failures being known? Embarrassment?

He returned to the kitchen. "How are we going to do this?" he asked her. "The hard way or the easy way?"

Tears of pain squeezed between her lids. "You really are the most provoking creature," she said. "You're determined to take away my dignity, aren't you?"

He grinned as he put one arm under her knees and the other behind her back, and lifted her gently. "Why not?" he murmured. "It may be my only chance to get even. "

I don't want to talk to you," said William Sumner angrily, barring the front door to DI Galbraith. Hectic spots of color burned in his cheeks, and he kept tugging at the fingers of his left hand as he spoke, cracking the joints noisily. "I'm sick of the police treating my house like a damn thoroughfare, and I'm sick of answering questions. Why can't you just leave me alone?"

"Because your wife's been murdered, sir," said Galbraith evenly, "and we're trying to find out who killed her. I'm sorry if you're finding that difficult to cope with but I really do have no option."

"Then talk to me here. What do you want to know?"

The DI glanced toward the road, where an interested group of spectators was gathering. "We'll have the press here before you know it, William," he said dispassionately. "Do you want to discuss your alleged alibi in front of an audience of journalists?"

Sumner's jittery gaze jumped toward the crowd at his gate. "This isn't fair. Everything's so bloody public. Why can't you make them go away?"

"They'll go of their own accord if you let me in. They'll stay if you insist on keeping me on the doorstep. That's human nature, I'm afraid."

With a haunted expression, Sumner seized the policeman's arm and pulled him inside. Pressure was beginning to take its toll, thought Galbraith, and gone was the self-assured, if tired, man of Monday. It meant nothing in itself. Shock took time to absorb, and nerves invariably began to fray when successful closure to a case remained elusive. He followed Sumner into the sitting room and, as before, took a seat on the sofa.

"What do you mean, *alleged* alibi?" the man demanded, preferring to stand. "I was in Liverpool, for God's sake. How could I be in two places at once?"

The DI opened his briefcase and extracted some papers. "We've taken statements from your colleagues, hotel employees at the Regal, and librarians at the university library. None of them supports your claim that you were in Liverpool on Saturday night." He held them out. "I think you should read them."

Witness statement: Harold Marshall, MD Campbell Ltd., Lee Industrial Estate, Lichfield, Staffordshire

I remember seeing William at lunch on Saturday, 9 August 1997. We discussed a paper in last week's Lancet about stomach ulcers. William says he's working on a new drug that will beat the current frontrunner into a cocked hat. I was skeptical, and we had quite a debate. No, I didn't see him at the dinner that evening, but then I wouldn't expect to. He and I have been attending these conferences for years, and it'll be a red-letter day when William decides to let his hair down and join the rest of us for some lighthearted entertainment. He was certainly at lunch on Sunday, because we had another argument on the ulcer issue.

Witness statement: Paul Dimmock, Research Chemist, Wryton's, Holborne Way, Colchester, Essex

I saw William at about 2:00 P.M. Saturday afternoon. He said he was going to the university library to do some research, which is par for the course for him. He never goes to conference dinners. He's only interested in the intellectual side, hates the social side. My room was two doors down from his. I remember seeing the DO NOT DISTURB notice on the door, when I went up to bed about half past midnight, but I've no idea when he got back. I had a drink with him before lunch on Sunday. No, he didn't seem at all tired. Matter of fact he was in better form than usual. Positively cheerful, in fact.

**Witness statement: Anne Smith, Research
Chemist, Bristol University, Bristol**
I didn't see him at all on Saturday, but I had a
drink with him and Paul Dimmock on Sunday
morning. He gave a paper on Friday afternoon,
and I was interested in some of the things he
said. He's researching the drug treatment of stomach ulcers, and it sounds like good stuff.

**Witness statement: Carrie Wilson, Chambermaid,
Regal Hotel, Liverpool**
I remember the gentleman in number two-two-
three-five. He was very tidy, unpacked his suitcase,
and put everything away in the drawers. Some of
them don't bother. I finished about midday on Saturday, but I made up his room when he went down
to breakfast and I didn't see him afterward. Sunday morning, there was a DO NOT DISTURB notice on
his door so I left him to sleep. As I recall, he went
down at about 11:30, and I made up his room
then. Yes, his bed had certainly been slept in.
There were science books scattered all over it, and
I think he must have been doing some studying. I
remember thinking he wasn't so tidy after all.

**Witness statement: David Forward, Concierge,
Regal Hotel, Liverpool**
We have limited parking facilities, and Mr. Sumner reserved a parking space at the same time as
he reserved his room. He was allocated number
thirty-four, which is at the back of the hotel. As
far as I'm aware, the car remained there from
Thursday 7 to Monday 11. We ask guests to leave
a set of keys with us, and Mr. Sumner didn't
retrieve his until Monday. Yes, he could certainly
have driven his car out if he had a spare set.
There are no barriers across the exit.

Witness statement: Jane Riley, Librarian, University Library, Liverpool
(Shown a photograph of William Sumner)

Quite a few of the conference members came into the library on Saturday, but I don't remember seeing this man. That doesn't mean he wasn't here. As long as they have a conference badge and know what they're looking for, they have free access.

Witness statement: Les Allen, Librarian, University Library, Liverpool
(Shown a photograph of William Sumner)

He came in on Friday morning. I spent about half an hour with him. He wanted papers on peptic and duodenal ulcers, and I showed him where to find them. He said he'd be back on Saturday, but I didn't notice him. It's a big place. I only ever notice the people who need help.

"You see our problem?" asked Galbraith when Sumner had read them. "There's a period of twenty-one hours, from two o'clock on Saturday till eleven thirty on Sunday, when no one remembers seeing you. Yet the first three statements were made by people whom you told us would give you a cast-iron alibi."

Sumner looked at him in bewilderment. "But I was there," he insisted. "One of them must have seen me." He stabbed a finger at Paul Dimmock's statement. "I met up with Paul in the foyer. I told him I was going to the library, and he walked part of the way with me. That had to be well after two o'clock. Dammit, at two o'clock I was still arguing the toss with that bloody fool Harold Marshall."

Galbraith shook his head. "Even if it was four o'clock, it makes no difference. You proved on Monday that you can do the drive to Dorset in five hours."

"This is absurd!" snapped Sumner nervously. "You'll just have to talk to more people. Someone must have seen me. There was a man at the same table as me in the library. Ginger-haired fellow with glasses. He can prove I was there."

"What was his name?"

"I don't know."

Galbraith took another sheaf of papers out of his brief-case. "We've questioned thirty people in all, William. These are the rest of the statements. There's no one who's prepared to admit they saw you at any time during the ten hours prior to your wife's murder or the ten hours after. We've also checked your hotel account. You didn't use any hotel service, and that includes your telephone, between lunch on Saturday and prelunch drinks on Sunday." He dropped the papers onto the sofa. "How do you explain that? For example, where did you eat on Saturday night? You weren't at the conference dinner, and you didn't have room service."

Sumner set to cracking his finger joints again. "I didn't have anything to eat, not a proper meal anyway. I hate those blasted conference dinners, so I wasn't going to leave my room in case anyone saw me. They all get drunk and behave stupidly. I used the mini-bar," he said, "drank the beer and ate peanuts and chocolate. Isn't that on the account?"

Galbraith nodded. "Except it doesn't specify a time. You could have had them at ten o'clock on Sunday morning. It may explain why you were in such good spirits when you met your friends in the bar. Why didn't you order room service if you didn't want to go down?"

"Because I wasn't that hungry." Sumner lurched toward the armchair and slumped into it. "I knew this was going to happen," he said bitterly. "I knew you'd go for me if you couldn't find anyone else. I was in the library all afternoon, then I went back to the hotel and read books and journals till I fell asleep." He lapsed into silence, massaging his temples. "How could I have drowned her anyway?" he demanded suddenly. "I don't have a boat."

"No," Galbraith agreed. "Drowning does seem to be the one method that exonerates you."

A complex mixture of emotions—*relief? triumph? pleasure?*—showed briefly in the man's eyes. "There you are then," he said childishly.

Why do you want to get even with my mother?" asked Maggie when Ingram returned to the kitchen after settling Celia and phoning the local GP. Some color had returned to her cheeks, and she had finally stopped shaking.

"Private joke," he said, filling the kettle and putting it on the Aga. "Where does she keep her mugs?"

"Cupboard by the door."

He took out two and transferred them to the sink, then opened the cupboard underneath and found some washing-up liquid, bleach, and pan scourers. "How long has her hip been bad?" he asked, rolling up his sleeves and setting to with the scourers and the bleach to render the sink hygienic before he even began to deal with the stains in the mugs. From the strong whiffs of dirty dog and damp horse blankets that seemed to haunt the kitchen like old ghosts, he had a strong suspicion that the sink was not entirely dedicated to the purpose of washing crockery.

"Six months. She's on the waiting list for a replacement operation, but I can't see it happening before the end of the year." She watched him sluice down the draining board and sink. "You think we're a couple of slobs, don't you?"

" 'Fraid so," he agreed bluntly. "I'd say it's a miracle neither of you has gone down with food poisoning, particularly your mother, when her health's not too brilliant in the first place."

"There are so many other things to do," she said dispiritedly, "and Ma's in too much pain most of the time to clean properly . . . or says she is. Sometimes I think she's just making excuses to get out of it because she thinks it's beneath her to get her hands dirty. Other times . . ." She sighed heavily. "I keep the horses immaculate, but cleaning up after myself and Ma is always at the bottom of the list. I hate coming up here anyway. It's so"—she sought a suitable word—"depressing."

He wondered how she had the nerve to stand in judgment on her mother's lifestyle, but didn't comment on it. Stress, depression, and waspishness went together in his experience. Instead, he scrubbed the mugs, then filled them with diluted bleach and left them to stand. "Is that why you moved down to the stables?" he asked her, turning around.

"Not really. If Ma and I live in each other's pockets we argue. If we live apart we don't. Simple as that. Things are easier this way."

She looked thin and harassed, and her hair hung in limp strands about her face as if she hadn't been near a shower for weeks. It wasn't surprising in view of what she'd been through that morning, particularly as the beginnings of a bruise were ripening on the side of her face, but Ingram remembered her as she used to be, pre–Robert Healey, a gloriously vibrant woman with a mischievous sense of humor and sparkling eyes. He regretted the passing of that personality—it had been a dazzling one—but she was still the most desirable woman he knew.

He glanced idly around the kitchen. "If you think this is depressing, you should try living in a hostel for the homeless for a week."

"Is that supposed to make me feel better?"

"This one room could house an entire family."

"You sound like Ava, my bloody sister-in-law," she said testily. "According to her, we live in the lap of luxury despite the fact that the damn place is falling down about our ears."

"Then why don't you stop whinging about it and do something constructive to change it?" he suggested. "If you gave this room a lick of paint it would brighten it up and you'd have less to feel depressed about and more to be thankful for."

"Oh, my God," she said icily, "you'll be telling me to take up knitting next. I don't need DIY therapy, Nick."

"Then explain to me how sitting around moaning about your environment helps you. You're not helpless, are you? Or maybe it's you, and not your mother, who thinks that getting her hands dirty is demeaning."

"Paint costs money."

"Your flat over the stables costs a damn sight more," he pointed out. "You balk at forking out for some cheap emulsion, yet you'll pay two sets of gas, electricity, and telephone bills just in order to avoid having to get on with your mother. How does that make things easier, Maggie? It's hardly sound economics, is it? And what are you going to do when she falls over and breaks her hip so badly she's confined to a wheelchair? Pop in once in a while to see she hasn't died of hypothermia in the night because she hasn't been able to get into bed on her own? Or will that be so depressing you'll avoid her entirely?"

"I don't need this," she said tiredly. "It's none of your business anyway. We manage fine on our own."

He watched her for a moment, then turned back to the sink, emptying the mugs of bleach and rinsing them under the tap. He jerked his head toward the kettle. "Your mother would like a cup of tea, and I suggest you put several spoonfuls of sugar in it to bring up her energy levels. I also suggest you make one for yourself. The GP said he'd be here by eleven." He dried his hands on a tea towel and rolled down his sleeves.

"Where are you going?" she asked him.

"Up to the headland. I want to try and find out why Harding came back. Does your mother have any freezer bags?"

"No. We can't afford a freezer."

"Cling film?"

"In the drawer by the sink."

"Can I take it?"

"I suppose so." She watched him remove the roll and tuck it under his arm. "What do you want it for?"

"Evidence," he said unhelpfully, making for the door.

She watched him in a kind of despair. "What about me and Ma?"

He turned with a frown. "What about you?"

"God, I don't know," she said crossly. "We're both pretty shaken, you know. That bloody man hit me, in case you've forgotten. Aren't the police supposed to stay around when women get attacked? Take statements or something?"

"Probably," he agreed, "but this is my day off. I turfed out to help you as a friend, not as a policeman, and I'm only following up on Harding because I'm involved in the Kate Sumner case. Don't worry," he said with a comforting smile, "you're in no danger from him, not while he's in Poole, but dial nine-nine-nine if you need someone to hold your hand."

She glared at him. "I want him prosecuted, which means I want you to take a statement now."

"Mmm, well, don't forget I'll be taking one from him, too," Ingram pointed out, "and you may not be so eager to go for his jugular if he opts to counterprosecute on the grounds that he's the one who suffered the injuries because you didn't have your dog under proper control. It's going to be your word against his," he said, making for the door, "which is one of the reasons why I'm going back up there now."

She sighed. "I suppose you're hurt because I told you to mind your own business?"

"Not in the least," he said, disappearing into the scullery. "Try angry or bored."

"Do you want me to say sorry?" she called after him. "Well, okay . . . I'm tired . . . I'm stressed out, and I'm not in the best of moods but"—she gritted her teeth—"I'll say 'sorry' if that's what you want."

But her words fell on stony ground, because all she heard was the sound of the back door closing behind him.

The detective inspector had been silent so long that William Sumner grew visibly nervous. "There you are then," he said again. "I couldn't possibly have drowned her, could I?" Anxiety had set his eyelid fluttering, and he looked absurdly comical every time his lid winked. "I don't understand why you keep hounding me. You said you were looking for someone with a boat, but you know I haven't got one. And I don't understand why you released Steven Harding when WPC Griffiths said he was seen talking to Kate outside Tesco's on Saturday morning."

WPC Griffiths should learn to keep her mouth shut, thought Galbraith in annoyance. Not that he blamed her. Sumner was bright enough to read between the lines of newspaper reports about "a young Lymington actor being taken in for questioning" and then press for answers. "Briefly," he said, "then they went their separate ways. She talked to a couple of market stallholders afterward, but Harding wasn't with her."

"Well, it wasn't me who did it." He winked. "So there must be someone else you haven't found yet."

"That's certainly one way of looking at it." Galbraith lifted a photograph of Kate off the table beside him. "The trouble is looks are so often deceptive. I mean, take Kate here. You see this?" He turned the picture toward the husband. "The first impression she gives is that butter wouldn't melt in her mouth, but the more you learn about her the more you realize that isn't true. Let me tell you what I know of her." He held up his fingers and ticked the points off as he spoke. "She wanted money and she didn't really mind how she got it. She manipulated people in order to achieve her ambitions. She could be cruel. She told lies if necessary. Her goal was to climb the social ladder and become accepted within a milieu she admired, and as long as it brought the goalposts closer, she was prepared to play-act whatever role was required of her, sex being the major weapon in her armory. The one person she couldn't manipulate successfully was your mother, so she dealt with her in the only way possible by moving away from her influence." He dropped his hand to his lap and looked at the other man with genuine sympathy. "How long was it before you realized you'd been suckered, William?"

"I suppose you've been talking to that bloody policewoman?"

"Among other people."

"She made me angry. I said things I didn't mean."

Galbraith shook his head. "Your mother's view of your marriage wasn't so different," he pointed out. "She may not have used the terms 'landlady' or 'cheap boardinghouse,' but she certainly gave the impression of an unfulfilled and unfulfilling relationship. Other people have described it as unhappy, based on sex, cool, boring. Are any of those descriptions accurate? Are they all accurate?"

Sumner pressed his finger and thumb to the bridge of his nose. "You don't kill your wife because you're bored with her," he muttered.

Galbraith wondered again at the man's naiveté. Boredom was precisely why most men killed their wives. They might disguise it by claiming provocation or jealousy, but in the end, a desire for something different was usually the reason—even if the difference was simply escape. "Except I'm told it wasn't so much a question of boredom but more a question of you taking her for granted. And that interests me. You see, I wonder what a man like you would do if the woman you'd been taking for granted suddenly decided she wasn't going to play the game anymore."

Sumner stared back at him with disdain. "I don't know what you're talking about."

"Or if," Galbraith went on relentlessly, "you discovered

that what you'd been taking for granted wasn't true. Such as being a father, for example."

Ingram's assumption was that Harding had come back for his rucksack because, despite the man's claim that the rucksack found on board *Crazy Daze* was the one he'd been carrying, Ingram remained convinced that it wasn't. Paul and Danny Spender had been too insistent that it was big for Ingram to accept that a triangular one fitted the description. Also, he remained suspicious about why Harding had left it behind when he took the boys down to the boat sheds. Nevertheless, the logic of why he had descended to the beach that morning, only to climb up again empty-handed, was far from obvious. Had someone else found the rucksack and removed it? Had Harding weighted it with a rock and thrown it into the sea? Had he even left it there in the first place?

In frustration, he slithered down a gully in the shale precipice to where the grassy slope at the end of the quarry valley undulated softly toward the sea. It was a western-facing cliff out of sight of the sun, and he shivered as the cold and damp penetrated his flimsy T-shirt and sweater. He turned to look back toward the cleft in the cliff, giving himself a rough idea of where Harding must have emerged in front of Maggie. Shale still pattered down the gully Ingram himself had used, and he noticed what was obviously a recent slide farther to the left. He walked over to it, wondering if Harding had dislodged it in his ascent, but the surface was damp with dew and he decided it must have happened a few days previously.

He turned his attention to the shore below, striding down the grass to take a closer look. Pieces of driftwood and old plastic containers had wedged themselves into cracks in the rocks, but there was no sign of a black or green rucksack. He felt exhausted suddenly, and wondered what the hell he was doing there. He'd planned to spend his day in total idleness aboard *Miss Creant,* and he really didn't appreciate giving it up for a wild-goose chase. He raised his eyes to the clouds skudding in on a southwesterly breeze and sighed his frustration to the winds. . . .

Maggie put a cup of tea on the table beside her mother's bed. "I've made it very sweet," she said. "Nick said you needed your energy levels raised." She looked at the dreadful state of the top blanket, worn and covered in stains, then noticed the tannin dribbles on Celia's bed-jacket. She wondered what the sheets looked like—it was ages since Broxton House had boasted a washing machine—and wished angrily that she had never intro-duced the word "slob" into her conversation with Nick.

"I'd rather have a brandy," said Celia with a sigh.

"So would I," said Maggie shortly, "but we haven't got any." She stood by the window, looking at the garden, her own cup cradled between her hands. "Why does he want to get even with you, Ma?"

"Did you ask him?"

"Yes. He said it was a private joke."

Celia chuckled. "Where is he?"

"Gone."

"I hope you thanked him for me."

"I didn't. He started ordering me about, so I sent him away with a flea in his ear."

Her mother eyed her curiously for a moment. "How odd of him," she said, reaching for her tea. "What sort of orders was he giving you?"

"Snide ones."

"Oh, I see."

Maggie shook her head. "I doubt you do," she said, addressing the garden. "He's like Matt and Ava, thinks society would have better value out of this house if we were evicted and it was given to a homeless family."

Celia took a sip of her tea and leaned back against her pillows. "Then I understand why you're so angry," she said evenly. "It's always irritating when someone's right."

"He called you a slob and said it was a miracle you hadn't come down with food poisoning."

Celia pondered for a moment. "I find that hard to believe if he wasn't prepared to tell you why he wanted to get even with me. Also, he's a polite young man and doesn't use words like 'slob.' That's more your style, isn't it, darling?" She watched her daughter's rigid back for a moment but, in the absence of any response, went on: "If he'd *really* wanted to get even with me, he'd have spiked my guns a long time ago. I was extremely rude to him, and I've regretted it ever since."

"What did you do?"

"He came to me two months before your wedding with a warning about your fiancé, and I sent him away"—Celia paused to recall the words Maggie had used—"with a flea in his ear." Neither she nor Maggie could ever think of the man who had wheedled his way into their lives by his real name, Robert Healey, but only by the name they had come to associate with him, Martin Grant. It was harder for Maggie, who had spent three months as Mrs. Martin Grant before being faced with the unenviable task of informing banks and corporations that neither the name nor the title belonged to her. "Admittedly the evidence against Martin was very thin," Celia went on. "Nick accused him of trying to con Jane Fielding's parents-in-law out of several thousand pounds by posing as an antiques dealer—with everything resting on old Mrs. Fielding's insistence that Martin was the man who came to their door—but if I'd listened to Nick instead of castigating him . . ." She broke off. "The trouble was he made me angry. He kept asking me what I knew of Martin's background, and when I told him Martin's father was a coffee-grower in Kenya, Nick laughed and said, how convenient."

"Did you show him the letters they wrote to us?"

"*Supposedly* wrote," Celia corrected her. "And, yes, of course I did. It was the only proof we had that Martin came from a respectable background. But, as Nick so rightly pointed out, the address was a PO box number in Nairobi, which proved nothing. He said anyone could conduct a fake correspondence through an anonymous box number. What he wanted was Martin's previous address in Britain, and all I could give him was the address of the flat Martin was renting in Bournemouth." She sighed. "But as Nick said, you don't have to be the son of a coffee planter to rent a flat, and he told me I'd be wise to make a few inquiries before I allowed my daughter to marry someone I knew nothing about."

Maggie turned to look at her. "Then why didn't you?"

"Oh, I don't know." Her mother sighed. "Perhaps because Nick was so appallingly pompous . . . Perhaps because on the one occasion that I dared to question Martin's suitability as a husband"—she lifted her eyebrows—"you called me a meddling bitch and refused to speak to me for several weeks. I think I asked you if you could really marry a man who was afraid of horses, didn't I?"

"Ye-es," said her daughter slowly, "and I should have listened to you. I'm sorry now that I didn't." She crossed her arms. "What did you say to Nick?"

"More or less what you just said about him," said Celia. "I called him a jumped-up little oik with a Hitler complex and tore strips off him for having the brass nerve to slander my future son-in-law. Then I asked him which day Mrs. Fielding claimed to have seen Martin, and when he told me, I lied and said she couldn't possibly have done because Martin was out riding with you and me."

"Oh my God!" said Maggie. "How could you do that?"

"Because it never occurred to me for one moment that Nick was right," said Celia with an ironic smile. "After all, he was just a common or garden-variety policeman and Martin was such a gent. Oxford graduate. Old Etonian. Heir to a coffee plantation. So who wins the prize for stupidity now, darling? You or me?"

Maggie shook her head. "Couldn't you at least have told me about it? Forewarned might have been forearmed."

"Oh, I don't think so. You were always so cruel about Nick after Martin pointed out that the poor lad blushed like a beetroot every time he saw you. I remember you laughing and saying that even beetroots have more sex appeal than overweight Neanderthals in policemen's uniforms."

Maggie squirmed at the memory. "You could have told me about it afterward."

"Of course I could," said Celia bluntly, "but I didn't see why I should give you an excuse to shuffle the guilt off onto me. You were just as much to blame as I was. You were living with the wretched creature in Bournemouth, and if anyone should have seen the flaws in his story it was you. You weren't a child in all conscience, Maggie. If you'd asked to visit his office just once, the whole edifice of his fraud would have collapsed."

Maggie sighed in exasperation—with herself—with her mother—with Nick Ingram. "Don't you think I know that? Why do you think I don't trust anyone anymore?"

Celia held her gaze for a moment, then looked away. "I've often wondered," she murmured. "Sometimes I think it's bloody-mindedness, other times I think it's immaturity. Usually I put it down to the fact that I spoiled you as a child and made you vain." Her eyes fastened on Maggie's again. "You see it's the height of arrogance to question other people's motives when you consistently refuse to question your own. Yes, Martin was a con man, but why did he pick on us as his victims? Have you ever wondered about that?"

"We had money."

"Lots of people have money, darling. Few of them get defrauded in the way that we did. No," she said with sudden firmness, "I was conned because I was greedy, and you were conned because you took it for granted that men found you attractive. If you hadn't, you'd have questioned Martin's ridiculous habit of telling everyone he met how much he loved you. It was *so* American and *so* insincere, and I can't understand why any of us believed it."

Maggie turned back to the window so that her mother wouldn't see her eyes. "No," she said unevenly. "Neither can I—now."

A gull swooped toward the shore and pecked at something white tumbling at the water's edge. Amused, Ingram watched it for a while, expecting it to take off again with a dead fish in its beak, but when it abandoned the sport and flapped away in disgust, screaming raucously, he walked down the waterline, curious about what the intermittent flash of white was that showed briefly between each wave. *A carrier bag caught in the rocks? A piece of cloth?* It ballooned unpleasantly as each swell invaded it, before rearing abruptly in a welter of spume as a larger wave flooded in.

CHAPTER 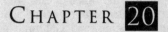 20

Galbraith leaned forward, folding his freckled hands under his chin. He looked completely unalarming, almost mild in fact, like a round-faced schoolboy seeking to make friends. He was quite an actor, like most policemen, and could change his mood as occasion demanded. He tempted Sumner to confide in him. "Do you know Lulworth Cove, William?" he murmured in a conversational tone of voice.

The other man looked startled but whether from guilt or from the DI's abrupt switch of tack it was impossible to say. "Yes."

"Have you been there recently?"

"Not that I recall."

"It's hardly the sort of thing you'd forget, is it?"

Sumner shrugged. "It depends what you mean by recently. I sailed there several times in my boat, but that was years ago."

"What about renting a caravan or a cottage? Maybe you've taken the family there on holiday?"

He shook his head. "Kate and I only ever had one holiday and that was in a hotel in the Lake District. It was a disaster," he said in weary recollection. "Hannah wouldn't go to sleep, so we had to sit in our room, night after night, watching the television to stop her screaming the place down and upsetting the other guests. We thought we'd wait until she was older before we tried again."

It sounded convincing, and Galbraith nodded. "Hannah's a bit of a handful, isn't she?"

"Kate managed all right."

"Perhaps because she dosed her with sleeping drugs?"

Sumner looked wary. "I don't know anything about that. You'd have to ask her doctor."

"We already have. He says he's never prescribed any sedatives or hypnotics for either Kate or Hannah."

"Well then."

"You work in the business, William. You can probably get free samples of every drug on the market. And, let's face it, with all these conferences you go to, there can't be much about pharmaceutical drugs you don't know."

"You're talking rubbish," said Sumner, winking uncontrollably. "I need a prescription like anyone else."

Galbraith nodded again as if to persuade William that he believed him. "Still . . . a difficult, demanding child wasn't what you signed up for when you got married, was it? At the very least it will have put a blight on your sex life."

Sumner didn't answer.

"You must have thought you'd got yourself a good bargain at the beginning. A pretty wife who worshipped the ground you trod on. All right, you didn't have much in common with her, and fatherhood left a lot to be desired, but all in all, life was rosy. The sex was good, you had a mortgage you could afford, the journey to work was a doddle, your mother was keeping tabs on your wife during the day, your supper was on the table when you came home of an evening, and you were free to go sailing whenever you wanted." He paused. "Then you moved to Lymington, and things started to turn sour. I'm guessing Kate grew less and less interested in keeping you happy because she didn't need to pretend anymore. She'd got what she wanted—no more supervision from her mother-in-law . . . a house of her own . . . respectability—all of which gave her the confidence to make a life for herself and Hannah which didn't include you." He eyed the other man curiously. "And suddenly it was your turn to be taken for granted. Is that when you began to suspect Hannah wasn't yours?"

Sumner surprised him by laughing. "I've known since she was a few weeks old that she couldn't possibly be mine. Kate and I are blood group O, and Hannah's blood group A. That means her father has to be either blood group A or AB. I'm not a fool. I married a pregnant woman, and I had no illusions about her, whatever you or my mother may think."

"Did you challenge Kate with it?"

Sumner pressed a finger to his fluttering lid. "It was hardly a challenge. I just showed her an Exclusions of Paternity table on the ABO system and explained how two blood group O parents can only produce a group O child. She was shocked to have been found out so easily, but as my only purpose in doing it was to show her I wasn't as gullible as she seemed to think I was, it never became an issue between us. I had no problem acknowledging Hannah as mine, which is all Kate wanted."

"Did she tell you who the father was?"

He shook his head. "I didn't want to know. I assume it's someone I work with—or have worked with—but as she broke all contact with Pharmatec after she left, except for the odd visit from Polly Garrard, I knew the father didn't figure in her life anymore." He stroked the arm of his chair. "You probably won't believe me, but I couldn't see the point of getting hot under the collar about someone who had become an irrelevance."

He was right. Galbraith didn't believe him. "Presumably the fact that Hannah isn't your child explains your lack of interest in her?"

Once again the man didn't answer, and a silence lengthened between them.

"Tell me what went wrong when you moved to Lymington," Galbraith said then.

"Nothing went wrong."

"So you're saying that from day *one*"—he emphasized the word—"marriage was like living with a landlady? That's a pretty unattractive proposition, isn't it?"

"It depends what you want," said Sumner. "Anyway, how would *you* describe a woman whose idea of an intellectual challenge was to watch a soap opera, who had no taste in anything, was so houseproud that she believed cleanliness was next to godliness, preferred overcooked sausages and baked beans to rare steak, and accounted voluntarily for every damn penny that either of us ever spent?"

There was a rough edge to his voice, which to Galbraith's ears sounded more like guilt at exposing his wife's shortcomings than bitterness that she'd had them, and he had the impression that William couldn't make up his mind if he'd loved his wife or loathed her. But whether that made him guilty of her murder, Galbraith didn't know.

"If you despised her to that extent, why did you marry her?"

Sumner rested his head against the back of his chair and stared at the ceiling. "Because the *quid pro quo* for helping her out of the hole she'd dug for herself was sex whenever I wanted it." He turned to look at Galbraith, and his eyes were bright with unshed tears. "That's all *I* was interested in. That's all any man's interested in. Isn't it? Sex on tap. Kate would have sucked me off twenty times a day if I'd told her to, just so long as I kept acknowledging Hannah as my daughter."

The memory brought him little pleasure, apparently, because tears streamed in murky rivers down his cheeks while his uncontrollable lid winked . . . and winked . . .

It was an hour and a half before Ingram returned to Broxton House, carrying something wrapped in layers of cling film. Maggie saw him pass the kitchen window and went through the scullery to let him in. He was soaked to the skin and supported himself against the doorjamb, head hanging in exhaustion.

"Did you find anything?" she asked him.

He nodded, lifting the bundle. "I need to make a phone call, but I don't want to drip all over your mother's floor. I presume you were carrying your mobile this morning, so can I borrow it?"

"Sorry, I wasn't. So no. I got it free two years ago in return for a year's rental, but it was so bloody expensive I declined to renew my subscription and I haven't used it in twelve months. It's in the flat somewhere." She held the door wide. "You'd better come in. There's an extension in the kitchen, and the quarry tiles won't hurt for getting water on them." Her lips gave a brief twitch. "They might even benefit. I dread to think when they last saw a mop."

He padded after her, his shoes squelching as he walked. "How did you phone me this morning if you didn't have a mobile?"

"I used Steve's," she said, pointing to a Philips GSM on the kitchen table.

He pushed it to one side with the back of his finger and placed the cling film bundle beside it. "What's it doing here?"

"I put it in my pocket and forgot about it," she said. "I only remembered it when it started ringing. It's rung five times since you left."

"Have you answered it?"

"No. I thought you could deal with it when you came back."

He moved across to the wall telephone and lifted it off its bracket. "You're very trusting," he murmured, punching in the number of the Kate Sumner incident room. "Supposing I'd decided to let you and your mother stew in your own juices for a bit?"

"You wouldn't," she said frankly. "You're not the type."

He was still wondering how to take that when he was

put through to Detective Superintendent Carpenter. "I've fished a boy's T-shirt out of the sea, sir . . . almost certainly belonging to one of the Spender boys. It's got a Derby County Football Club logo on the front, and Danny claimed Harding stole it from him." He listened for a moment. "Yes, Danny could have dropped it by accident . . . I agree, it doesn't make Harding a pedophile." He held the phone away from his ear as Carpenter's barking beat against his eardrums. "No, I haven't found the rucksack yet, but as a matter of fact . . . only that I've a pretty good idea where it is." More barking. "Yes, I'm betting it's what he came back for . . ." He grimaced into the receiver. "Oh, yes, sir, I'd say it's definitely in Chapman's Pool." He glanced at his watch. "The boat sheds in an hour. I'll meet you there." He replaced the receiver, saw amusement at his discomfort in Maggie's eyes, and gestured abruptly toward the hall. "Has the doctor been to see your mother?"

She nodded.

"Well?"

"He told her she was a fool not to take the paramedic's offer to have her admitted as an emergency this morning, then patted her on the head and gave her some painkillers." Her lips twitched into another small smile. "He also said she needs a walker and wheelchair, and suggested I drive to the nearest Red Cross depot this afternoon and see what they can do for her."

"Sounds sensible."

"Of course it does, but since when did sense feature in my mother's life? She says if I introduce any such contraptions into her house, she won't use them and she'll never speak to me again. And she means it, too. She says she'd rather crawl on her hands and knees than give anyone the impression she's passed her sell-by date." She gave a tired sigh. "Ideas on a postcard, please, care of Broxton House Lunatic Asylum. What the hell am I supposed to do?"

"Wait," he suggested.

"What for?"

"A miraculous cure or a request for a walker. She's not stupid, Maggie. Logic will prevail once she gets over her irritation with you, me, and the doctor. Meanwhile, be kind to her. She crippled herself for you this morning, and a little gratitude and TLC will probably have her on her feet quicker than anything."

"I've already told her I couldn't have done it without her."

He looked amused. "Like mother like daughter, eh?"

"I don't understand."

"*She* can't say sorry. *You* can't say thank you."

Sudden light dawned. "Oh, I see. So that's why you went off in a huff two hours ago. It was gratitude you wanted. How silly of me. I thought you were angry because I told you to mind your own business." She wrapped her arms about her thin body and gave him a tentative smile. "Well, thank you, Nick, I'm extremely grateful for your assistance."

He tugged at his forelock. "Much obliged I'm sure, Miss Jenner," he said in a rolling burr. "But a lady like you don't need to thank a man for doing his job."

Her puzzled eyes searched his for a moment before it occurred to her he was taking the piss, and her overwrought nerves snapped with a vengeance. "Fuck off!" she said, landing a furious fist on the side of his jaw before marching into the hall and slamming the door behind her.

T wo Dartmouth policemen listened with interest to what the Frenchman told them, while his daughter stood in embarrassed silence beside him, fidgeting constantly with her hair. The man's English was good, if heavily accented, as he explained carefully and precisely where he and his boat had been the previous Sunday. He had come, he said, because he had read in the English newspapers that the woman who had been lifted off the shore had been murdered. He placed a copy of Wednesday's

Telegraph on the counter in case they didn't know which inquiry he was referring to. "Mrs. Kate Sumner," he said. "You are acquainted with this matter?" They agreed they were, so he produced a videocassette from a carrier bag and put it beside the newspaper. "My daughter made a film of a man that day. You understand—I know nothing about this man. He may—how you say—be innocent. But I am anxious." He pushed the video across the desk. "It is not good what he is doing, so you play it. Yes? It is important, perhaps."

Harding's mobile telephone was a sophisticated little item with the capacity to call abroad or be called from abroad. It required an SIM (Subscriber Identification Module) card and a PIN number to use it, but as both had been logged in, presumably by Harding himself, the phone was operational. If it hadn't been, Maggie wouldn't have been able to use it. The card had an extensive memory and, depending on how much the user programmed into it, could store phone numbers and messages, plus the last ten numbers dialed out and the last ten dialed in.

The screen was displaying "5 missed calls" and a "messages waiting" sign. With a wary look toward the door into the hall, Ingram went into the menu, located "voice mail" followed by "mailbox," pressed the "call" button, and held the receiver to his ear. He massaged his cheek tenderly while he listened, wondering if Maggie had any idea how powerful her punch was.

"You have three new messages," said a disembodied female voice at the other end.

"Steve?" A lisping, lightweight—*foreign?*—voice, although Ingram couldn't tell if it was male or female. *"Where are you? I'm frightened. Please phone me. I've tried twenty times since Sunday."*

"Mr Harding?" A man's voice, definitely foreign. *"This is the Hotel Angelique, Concarneau. If you wish us to keep your room, you must confirm your reservation by*

noon today, using a credit card. I regret that without such confirmation the reservation cannot be honored."

"Hi," said an Englishman's voice next. *"Where the fuck are you, you stupid bastard? You're supposed to be kipping here, for Christ's sake. Dammit, this is the address you've been bailed to, and I swear to God I'll take you to the cleaners if you get me into any more trouble. Just don't expect me to keep my mouth shut next time. I warned you I'd have your stinking hide if you were playing me for a patsy. Oh, and in case you're interested, there's a sodding journalist nosing around who wants to know if it's true you've been questioned about Kate's murder. He's really bugging me, so get your arse back PDQ before I drop you in it up to your neck."*

Ingram touched "end" to disconnect, then went through the whole process again, jotting down bullet points on the back of a piece of paper which he took from a notepad under the wall telephone. Next he pressed the arrow button twice to scroll up the numbers of the last ten people who had dialed in. He discounted "voice mail" and made a note of the rest, together with the last ten calls Harding had made, the first of which was Maggie's call to him. For further good measure—*To hell with it! In for a penny, in for a pound!*—he scrolled through the entries under "names" and took them down together with their numbers.

"Are you doing something illegal?" asked Maggie from the doorway.

He had been so engrossed he hadn't heard the door open, and he looked up with a guilty start. "Not if DI Galbraith already has this information." He flattened his palm and made a rocking motion. "Probable infringement of Harding's rights under the Data Protection Act, if he hasn't. It depends whether the phone was on *Crazy Daze* when they searched it."

"Won't Steven Harding know you've been playing his messages when you give it back to him? Our answerphone never replays the ones you've already listened to unless you rewind the tape."

"Voice mail's different. You have to delete the messages if you don't want to keep hearing them." He grinned. "But if he's suspicious, let's just hope he thinks you buggered it up when you made your phone call."

"Why drag me into it?"

"Because he'll know you phoned me. My number's in the memory."

"Oh God," she said in resignation. "Are you expecting me to lie for you?"

"No." He stood up, lacing his hands above his head and stretching his shoulder muscles under his damp clothes. He was so tall he could almost touch the ceiling, and he stood like a Colossus in the middle of the kitchen, easily dominating a room that was big enough to house an entire family.

Watching him, Maggie wondered how she could ever have called him an overweight Neanderthal. It had been Martin's description, she remembered, and it galled her unbearably to think how tamely she had adopted it herself because it had raised a laugh among people she had once regarded as friends but whom she now avoided like the plague. "Well, I will," she said with sudden decision.

He shook his head as he lowered his arms. "It wouldn't do me any good. You couldn't lie to save your life. And that's a compliment, by the way," he said as she started to scowl, "so there's no need to hit me again. I don't admire people who lie."

"I'm sorry," she said abruptly.

"No need to be. It was my fault. I shouldn't have teased you." He started to gather the bits and pieces from the table.

"Where are you going now?"

"Back to my house to change, then down to the boat sheds at Chapman's Pool. But I'll look in again this afternoon before I go to see Harding. As you so rightly pointed out, I need to take a statement from you." He paused. "We'll talk about this in detail later, but did you hear anything before he appeared?"

"Like what?"

"Shale falling?"

She shook her head. "All I remember is how quiet it was. That's why he gave me such a fright. One minute I was on my own, the next he was crouching on the ground in front of me like a rabid dog. It was really peculiar. I don't know what he thought he was doing, but there's a lot of scrub vegetation and bushes around there, so I think he must have heard me coming and ducked down to hide."

He nodded. "What about his clothes? Were they wet?"

"No."

"Dirty?"

"You mean before he bled all over them?"

"Yes."

She shook her head again. "I remember thinking that he hadn't shaved, but I don't remember thinking he was dirty."

He stacked the cling film bundle, notes, and phone into a pile and lifted them off the table. "Okay. That's great. I'll take a statement this afternoon." He held her gaze for a moment. "You'll be all right," he told her. "Harding's not going to come back."

"He wouldn't dare," she said, clenching her fists.

"Not if he has any sense," murmured Ingram, moving out of her range.

"Do you have any brandy in your house?"

The switch was so abrupt that he needed time to consider. "Ye-es," he murmured cautiously, fearing another assault if he dared to question why she was asking. He suspected four years of angry frustration had gone into her punch, and he wished she'd chosen Harding for target practice instead of himself.

"Can you lend me some?"

"Sure. I'll drop it in on my way back to Chapman's Pool."

"If you give me a moment to tell Ma where I'm going, I'll come with you. I can walk back."

"Won't she miss you?"

"Not for an hour or so. The painkillers have made her sleepy."

Bertie was lying on the doorstep in the sunshine as Ingram drew the Jeep to a halt beside his gate. Maggie had never been inside Nick's little house, but she had always resented the neatness of his garden. It was like a reproach to all his less organized neighbors with its beautifully clipped privet hedges and regimented hydrangeas and roses in serried ranks before the yellow-stone walls of the house. She often wondered where he found the time to weed and hoe when he spent most of his free hours on his boat, and in her more critical moments put it down to the fact that he was boring and compartmentalized his life according to some sensible duty roster.

The dog raised his shaggy head and thumped his tail on the mat before rising leisurely to his feet and yawning. "So this is where he comes," she said. "I've often wondered. How long did it take you to train him, as a matter of interest?"

"Not long. He's a bright dog."

"Why did you bother?"

"Because he's a compulsive digger, and I got fed up with having my garden destroyed," he said prosaically.

"Oh God," she said guiltily. "Sorry. The trouble is he never takes any notice of me."

"Does he need to?"

"He's *my* dog," she said.

Ingram opened the Jeep door. "Have you made that clear to him?"

"Of course I have. He comes home every night, doesn't he?"

He reached into the back for the stack of evidence. "I wasn't questioning ownership," he told her. "I was questioning whether or not Bertie knows he's a dog. As far as he's concerned, he's the boss in your establishment. He gets fed first, sleeps on your sofa, licks out your dishes.

I'll bet you even move over in bed in order to make sure he's more comfortable, don't you?"

She colored slightly. "What if I do? I'd rather have him in my bed than the weasel that used to be in it. In any case, he's the closest thing I've got to a hot-water bottle."

Ingram laughed. "Are you coming in or do you want me to bring the brandy out? I guarantee Bertie won't disgrace you. He has beautiful manners since I took him to task for wiping his bottom on my carpet."

Maggie sat in indecision. She had never wanted to go inside, because it would tell her things about him that she didn't want to know. At the very least it would be insufferably clean, she thought, and her bloody dog would shame her by doing exactly what he was told.

"I'm coming in," she said defiantly.

Carpenter took a phone call from a Dartmouth police sergeant just as he was about to leave for Chapman's Pool. He listened to a description of what was on the Frenchman's video then asked: "What does he look like?"

"Five eight, medium build, bit of a paunch, thinning dark hair."

"I thought you said he was a young chap."

"No. Mid-forties, at least. His daughter's fourteen."

Carpenter's frown dug trenches out of his forehead. "Not the bloody Frenchman," he shouted, "the toe-rag on the video!"

"Oh, sorry. Yes, he's young all right. Early twenties, I'd say. Longish dark hair, sleeveless T-shirt, and cycling shorts. Muscles. Tanned. A handsome bugger, in fact. The kid who filmed him said she thought he looked like Jean-Claude Van Damme. Mind you, she's mortified about it now, can't believe she didn't realize what he was up to, considering he's got a rod like a fucking salami. This guy could make a fortune in porno movies."

"All right, all right," said Carpenter testily. "I get the picture. And you say he's wanking into a handkerchief?"

"Looks like it."

"Could it be a child's T-shirt?"

"Maybe. It's difficult to tell. Matter of fact, I'm amazed the French geezer spotted what the bastard was up to. It's pretty discreet. It's only because his knob's so damn big that you can see anything at all. The first time I watched it I thought he was peeling an orange in his lap." There was a belly laugh at the other end of the line. "Still, you know what they say about the French. They're all wankers. So I guess our little geezer's done a spot of it himself and knew what to look for. Am I right or am I right?"

Carpenter, who spent all his holidays in France, cocked a finger and thumb at the telephone and pulled the trigger—bloody racist, he was thinking—but there was no trace of irritation in his voice when he spoke. "You said the young man had a rucksack. Can you describe it for me?"

"Standard camping type. Green. Doesn't look as if it's got much in it."

"Big?"

"Oh, yes. It's a full-size job."

"What did he do with it?"

"Sat on it while he jerked himself off."

"Where? Which part of Chapman's Pool? Eastern side? Western side? Describe the scenery for me."

"Eastern side. The Frenchman showed me on the map. Your wanker was down on the beach below Emmetts Hill, facing out toward the Channel. Green slope behind him."

"What did he do with the rucksack after he sat on it?"

"Can't say. The film ends."

With a request to send the tape on by courier, together with the Frenchman's name, proposed itinerary for the rest of his holiday, and address in France, Carpenter thanked the sergeant and rang off.

Did you make this yourself?" asked Maggie, peering at the *Cutty Sark* in the bottle on the mantelpiece as Ingram came downstairs in uniform, buttoning the sleeves of his shirt.

"Yes."

"I thought you must have done. It's like everything else in this house. So"—she waved her glass in the air—*"well behaved."* She might have said masculine, minimal, or monastic, in an echo of Galbraith's description of Harding's boat, but she didn't want to be rude. It was as she had predicted, insufferably clean, and insufferably boring as well. There was nothing to say this house belonged to an interesting personality, just yards of pallid wall, pallid carpet, pallid curtains, and pallid upholstery, broken occasionally by an ornament on a shelf. It never occurred to her that he was tied to the house through his job, but even if it had, she would still have expected splashes of towering individualism among the uniformity.

He laughed. "Do I get the impression you don't like it?"

"No, I do. It's—er—"

"Twee?" he suggested.

"Yes."

"I made it when I was twelve." He flexed his huge fingers under her nose. "I couldn't do it now." He straightened his tie. "How's the brandy?"

"Very good." She dropped into a chair. "Does exactly what it's supposed to do. Hits the spot."

He took her empty glass. "When did you last drink alcohol?"

"Four years ago."

"Shall I give you a lift home?"

"No." She closed her eyes. "I'm going to sleep."

"I'll look in on your mother on my way back from Chapman's Pool," he promised her, shrugging on his jacket. "Meanwhile, don't encourage your dog to sit on my sofa. It's bad for both your characters."

"What will happen if I do?"

"The same thing that happened to Bertie when he wiped his bottom on my carpet."

* * *

Despite another day of brilliant sunshine, Chapman's Pool was empty. The southwesterly breeze had created an unpleasant swell, and nothing was more guaranteed to discourage visitors than the likelihood of being sick over their lunch. Carpenter and two detective constables followed Ingram away from the boat sheds toward an area marked out on the rocky shore with pieces of driftwood.

"We won't know until we see the video, of course," said Carpenter, taking his bearings from the description the Dartmouth sergeant had given of where Harding had been sitting, "but it looks about right. He was certainly on this side of the bay." They were standing on a slab of rock at the shoreline, and he touched a small pebble cairn with the toe of his shoe. "And this is where you found the T-shirt?"

Ingram nodded as he squatted down and put his hand in the water that lapped against the base of the rock. "But it was well and truly wedged. A gull had a go at getting it out, and failed, and I was saturated doing my retrieval act."

"Is that important?"

"Harding was dry as a bone when I saw him, so it can't have been the T-shirt he came back for. I think that's been here for days."

"Mmm." Carpenter pondered for a moment. "Does fabric easily get wedged between rocks?"

Ingram shrugged. "Anything can get wedged if a crab takes a fancy to it."

"Mmm," said Carpenter again. "All right. Where's this rucksack?"

"It's only a guess, sir, and a bit of a flaky one at that," said Ingram standing up.

"I'm listening."

"Okay, well, I've been puzzling about the ruddy thing for days. He obviously didn't want it anywhere near a policeman, or he'd have brought it down to the boat sheds on Sunday. By the same token it wasn't on his boat when you searched it—or not in my opinion, anyway—and that suggests to me that it's incriminating in some way and he needed to get rid of it."

"I think you're right," said Carpenter. "Harding wants us to believe he was carrying the black one we found on his boat, but the Dartmouth sergeant described the one on the video as green. So what's he done with it, eh? And what's he trying to hide?"

"It depends on whether the contents were valuable to him. If they *weren't,* then he'll have dropped it in the ocean on his way back to Lymington. If they *were,* he'll have left it somewhere accessible but not too obvious." Ingram shielded his eyes from the sun and pointed toward the slope behind them. "There's been a mini-avalanche up there," he said. "I noticed it because it's just to the left of where Miss Jenner said Harding appeared in front of her. Shale's notoriously unstable—which is why these cliffs are covered in warnings—and it looks to me as though that fall's fairly recent."

Carpenter followed his gaze. "You think the rucksack's under it?"

"Put it this way, sir, I can't think of a quicker or more convenient way of burying something than to send an avalanche of shale over the top of it. It wouldn't be hard to do. Kick out a loose rock, and hey presto, you've got a convenient slide of loose cliff pouring over whatever it is you want to hide. No one's going to notice it. Slides like that happen every day. The Spender brothers set one off when they dropped their father's binoculars, and I can't help feeling that might have given Harding the idea."

"Meaning he did it on Sunday?"

Ingram nodded.

"And came back this morning to make sure it hadn't been disturbed?"

"I suspect it's more likely he intended to retrieve it, sir."

Carpenter brought his ferocious scowl to bear on the constable. "Then why wasn't he carrying it when you saw him?"

"Because the shale's dried in the sunshine and become

impacted. I think he was about to go looking for a spade when he ran into Miss Jenner by accident."

"Is that your best suggestion?"

"Yes, sir."

"You're a bit of a suggestion-junky, aren't you, lad?" said Carpenter, his frown deepening. "I've got DI Galbraith chasing over half of Hampshire on the back of the suggestions you faxed through last night."

"It doesn't make them wrong, sir."

"It doesn't make them right either. We had a team scouring this area on Monday, and they didn't find a damn thing."

Ingram jerked his head toward the next bay. "They were searching Egmont Bight, sir, and with respect, no one was interested in Steven Harding's movements at that point."

"Mmm. These search teams cost money, lad, and I like a little more certainty before I commit taxpayers' money to guesses." Carpenter stared out across the sea. "I could understand him revisiting the scene of the crime to relive his excitement—it's the sort of thing a man like him might do—but you're saying he wasn't interested in that."

Ingram had said no such thing, but he wasn't going to argue the point. For all he knew, the superintendent was right anyway. Maybe that's exactly what Harding had come back for. His own avalanche theory looked horribly insignificant beside the magnitude of a psychopath gloating over the scene of murder.

"Well?" demanded Carpenter.

The constable smiled self-consciously. "I brought my own spade, sir," he said. "It's in the back of my Jeep."

CHAPTER  21

Galbraith stood up and walked across to one of the windows which overlooked the road. The crowd of earlier had dispersed, although a couple of elderly women still chatted on the pavement, glancing occasionally toward Langton Cottage. He watched them for several minutes in silence, envying the normality of their lives. How often did they have to listen to the dirty little secrets of murder suspects? Sometimes, when he heard the confessions of men like Sumner, he thought of himself in the role of a priest offering a kind of benediction merely by listening, but he had neither the authority nor the desire to forgive sins and invariably felt diminished by being the recipient of their furtive confidences.

He turned to face the man. "So a more accurate description of your marriage would be to say it was a form of sexual slavery? Kate was so desperate to make sure her daughter grew up in the sort of security she herself never enjoyed that you were able to blackmail her?"

"I said she *would* have done it, not that she did or that I ever asked her to." Triumph crept stealthily into Sumner's eyes as if he had won an important point. "There's no median way with you, is there? Half an hour ago you were treating me like a cretin because you thought Kate had suckered me into marrying her. Now you're accusing me of sexual slavery because I got so tired of her lies about Hannah that I pointed out—very mildly, as a matter of fact—that I knew the truth. Why would I buy her this house if she had no say in the relationship? You said yourself I was better off in Chichester."

"I don't know. Tell me."

"Because I loved her."

Impatiently, Galbraith shook his head. "You describe your marriage as a war zone, then expect me to swallow garbage like that. What was the real reason?"

"That *was* the real reason. I loved my wife, and I'd have given her whatever she wanted."

"At the same time as blackmailing her into giving you blow jobs whenever you fancied it?" The atmosphere in the room was stifling, and he felt himself grow cruel in response to the cruelty of Kate and William's marriage. He couldn't rid himself of memories of the tiny pregnant woman on the pathologist's slab and Dr. Warner's casual raising of her hand in order to shake it to and fro in convincing demonstration that the fingers were broken. The noise of grating bone had lodged in Galbraith's head like a maggot, and his dreams were of charnel houses. "You see, I can't make up my mind whether you loved or hated her. Or maybe it was a bit of both? A love/hate relationship that turned sour?"

Sumner shook his head. He looked defeated suddenly, as if whatever game he was playing was no longer worth the candle. Galbraith wished he understood what William was trying to achieve through his answers, and studied the man in perplexity. William was either extremely frank or extremely skillful at clouding an issue. On the whole he gave the impression of honesty, and it occurred to Galbraith that, in a ham-fisted way, he was trying to demonstrate that his wife was the sort of woman who could easily have driven a man to rape her. He remembered what

James Purdy had said about Kate. *"No one has ever done to me what Kate did that night . . . It's the sort of thing most men dream of . . . I can only describe Kate as a fever in the blood . . ."*

"Did she love you, William?"

"I don't know. I never asked her."

"Because you were afraid she'd say no?"

"The opposite. I knew she'd say yes."

"And you didn't want her to lie to you?"

The man nodded.

"I don't like being lied to," murmured Galbraith, his eyes fixing on Sumner's. "It means the other person assumes you're so stupid you'll believe anything they say. Did she lie to you about having an affair?"

"She wasn't having an affair."

"She certainly visited Steven Harding on board his boat," Galbraith pointed out. "Her fingerprints are all over it. Did you find out about that? Maybe you suspected that the baby she was carrying wasn't yours? Maybe you were afraid she was going to foist another bastard on to you?"

Sumner stared at his hands.

"Did you rape her?" Galbraith went on remorselessly. "Was that part of the *quid pro quo* for acknowledging Hannah as your daughter? The right to take Kate whenever you wanted her?"

"Why would I want to rape her when I didn't need to?" he asked.

"I'm only interested in a yes or a no, William."

His eyes flashed angrily. "Then no, dammit. I never raped my wife."

"Maybe you dosed her with Rohypnol to make her more compliant?"

"No."

"Then tell me why Hannah's so sexually aware?" Galbraith said next. "Did you and Kate perform in front of her?"

More anger. "That's revolting."

"Yes or no, William."

"No." The word came out in a strangled sob.

"You're lying, William. Half an hour ago, you described how you had to sit with her in a hotel bedroom because she wouldn't stop crying. I think that happened at home as well. I think sex with Kate involved Hannah as an audience because you got so fed up with Hannah being given as the excuse for the endless brush-offs that you insisted on doing it in front of her. Am I right?"

He buried his face in his hands and rocked himself to and fro. "You don't know what it's like . . . she wouldn't leave us alone . . . she never sleeps . . . pester, pester all the time . . . Kate used her as a shield . . ."

"Is that a yes?"

The answer was a whisper of sound. "Yes."

"WPC Griffiths said you went into Hannah's room last night. Do you want to tell me why?"

Another whisper. "You won't believe me if I do."

"I might."

Sumner raised a tear-stained face. "I wanted to look at her," he said in despair. "She's all I've got left to remind me of Kate."

Carpenter lit a cigarette as Ingram's careful spadework disclosed the first strap of a rucksack. "Good work, lad," he said approvingly. He dispatched one of the DCs to his car to collect some disposable gloves and plastic sheeting, then watched as Ingram continued to remove the shale from around the crumpled canvas.

It took Ingram another ten minutes to release the object completely and transfer it to the plastic sheet. It was a heavy-duty green camper's rucksack, with a waist strap for extra support and loops underneath for taking a tent. It was old and worn, and the integral backframe had been cut out for some reason, leaving frayed canvas edges between the stitched grooves that had contained it. The frays were old ones, however, and whatever had persuaded the owner to remove the frame was clearly ancient history. It sat on the sheeting, collapsed in on itself under the weight of its straps, and whatever it contained took up less than a third of its bulk.

Carpenter instructed one detective constable to seal each item in a forensic bag as he took it out and the other to note what it was, then he squatted beside the rucksack and carefully undid the buckles with gloved fingertips, flipping back the flap. "Item," he dictated. "One pair of twenty times sixty binoculars, name worn away, possibly Optikon . . . one bottle of mineral water, Volvic . . . three empty crisp packets, Smith's . . . one baseball cap, New York Yankees . . . one blue-and-white checked shirt— men's—made by River Island . . . one pair of cream cotton trousers—men's—also made by River Island . . . one pair of brown safari-style boots, size seven."

He felt inside the pockets and took out some rancid orange peel, more empty crisp packets, an opened packet of Camel cigarettes with a lighter tucked in among them, and a small quantity of what appeared to be cannabis, wrapped in cling film. He squinted up at the three policemen.

"Well? What do you make of this little lot? What's so incriminating about it all that Nick mustn't know he had it?"

"The C," said one. "He didn't want to be caught in possession."

"Maybe."

"God knows," said the other.

The superintendent stood up. "What about you, Nick? What do you think?"

"I'd say the shoes are the most interesting item, sir."

Carpenter nodded. "Too small for Harding, who's a good six foot, and too big for Kate Sumner. So what's he doing carrying a pair of size-seven shoes around with him?"

No one volunteered an answer.

D I Galbraith was on his way out of Lymington when Carpenter phoned through instructions to locate Tony Bridges and put the "little bastard" through the wringer. "He's been holding out on us, John," he declared, detailing the contents of Harding's rucksack, what was on the Frenchman's video, and repeating verbatim the messages that Ingram had taken from the voice mail. "Bridges *must* know more than he's been telling us, so arrest him on conspiracy if necessary. Find out why and when Harding was planning to leave for France, and get a fix on the wanker's sexual orientation if you can. It's all bloody odd, frankly."

"What happens if I can't find Bridges?"

"He was in his house two or three hours ago, because the last message came from his number. He's a teacher, don't forget, so he won't have gone to work, not unless he has a holiday job. Campbell's advice is: Check the pubs."

"Will do."

"How did you get on with Sumner?"

Galbraith thought about it. "He's cracking up," he said. "I felt sorry for him."

"Less of a dead cert then?"

"Or more," said Galbraith dryly. "It depends on your viewpoint. She was obviously having an affair, which he knew about. I think he *wanted* to kill her . . . which is probably why he's cracking up."

F ortunately for Galbraith, Tony Bridges was not only at home but stoned out of his head into the bargain. So much so that he was completely naked when he came to the front door. Galbraith had momentary qualms about putting anyone in his condition through Carpenter's "wringer," but they were only momentary. In the end the only thing that matters to a policeman is that witnesses tell the truth.

"I told the stupid sod you'd check up on him," Bridges said garrulously, leading the way down the corridor into the chaotic sitting room. "I mean you don't play silly buggers with the filth, not unless you're a complete moron. His problem is he won't take advice—never listens to a word I say. He reckons I sold out and says my opinions don't count for shit anymore."

"Sold out to what?" asked Galbraith, picking his way toward a vacant chair and remembering that Harding was said to favor nudity on board *Crazy Daze*. He wondered gloomily if nakedness had suddenly become an essential part of youth culture, and hoped not. He didn't much fancy the idea of police cells full of smackheads with hairless chests and acne on their bottoms.

"The establishment," said Bridges, sinking cross-legged onto the floor and retrieving a half-smoked spliff from an ashtray in front of him. "Regular employment. A salary." He proffered the joint. "Want some?"

Galbraith shook his head. "What sort of employment?" He had read all the reports on Harding and his friends, knew everything there was to know about Bridges, but it didn't suit him at the moment to reveal it.

"Teaching," the young man declared with a shrug. He was too stoned—or *appeared* to be too stoned, as Galbraith was cynical enough to remind himself—to remember that he had already given the police this information before. "Okay, the pay's not brilliant, but, hell, the holidays are good. And it's got to be better than flaunting your arse in front of some two-bit photographer. The trouble with Steve is he doesn't like kids much. He's had to work with some right little bastards and it's put him off." He lapsed into contented silence with his joint.

Galbraith assumed a surprised expression. "You're a teacher?"

"That's right." Bridges squinted through the smoke. "And don't go getting hot under the collar. I'm a recreational cannabis user, and I've no more desire to share my habit with children than my headmaster has to share his whisky."

The excuse was so simplistic and so well tutored by the cannabis lobby that it brought a smile to the DI's face. There were better arguments for legalization, he always thought, but your average user was either too thick or too high to produce them. "Okay, okay," he said, raising his hands in surrender. "This isn't my patch, so I don't need the lecture."

"Sure you do. You lot are all the same."

"I'm more interested in Steve's pornography. I gather you don't approve of it?"

A closed expression tightened the young man's features. "It's cheap filth. I'm a teacher. I don't like that kind of crap."

"What kind of crap is it? Describe it to me."

"What's to describe? He's got a todger the size of the Eiffel Tower, and he likes to display it." He shrugged. "But that's his problem, not mine."

"Are you sure about that?"

Bridges squinted painfully through the smoke from his spliff. "What's that supposed to mean?"

"We've been told you live in his shadow."

"Who by?"

"Steve's parents."

"You don't want to believe anything they say," he said dismissively. "They stood in judgment on me ten years ago, and have never changed their opinion since. They think I'm a bad influence."

Galbraith chuckled. "And are you?"

"Let's put it this way, *my* parents think Steve's a bad influence. We got into a bit of trouble when we were younger, but it's water under the bridge now."

"So what do you teach?" Galbraith asked, looking around the room and wondering how anyone could live in such squalor. More interestingly, how could anyone so rank boast a girlfriend? Was Bibi as squalid?

Campbell's description of the setup after his interview with Bridges on Monday had been pithy. "It's a pit," he said. "The bloke's spaced out, the house stinks, he's shacked up with a tramp who looks as if she's slept with half the men in Lymington, and he's a teacher, for Christ's sake."

"Chemistry." He sneered at Galbraith's expression, misinterpreting it. "And, yes, I do know how to synthesize lysergic acid diethylamide. I also know how to blow up Buckingham Palace. It's a useful subject, chemistry. The trouble is"—he broke off to draw pensively on his spliff— "the people who teach it are so bloody boring they turn the kids off long before they ever get to the interesting bits."

"But not you?"

"No. I'm good."

Galbraith could believe it. Rebels, however flawed, were always charismatic to youth. "Your friend is in the Poole hospital," he told the young man. "He was attacked by a dog on the Isle of Purbeck this morning and had to be shipped out by helicopter to have his arm stitched." He looked at Bridges inquiringly. "Any idea what he was doing there? In view of the fact he was bailed to this address and presumably you have some knowledge of what he gets up to."

"Sorry, mate, that's where you're wrong. Steve's a closed book to me."

"You said you warned him I'd come checking."

"Not you personally. I don't know you from Adam. I told him the filth would come. That's different."

"Still, if you had to warn him, Tony, then you must have known he was about to leg it. So where was he planning to go and what did he plan to do?"

"I told you. The guy's a closed book to me."

"I thought you were at school together."

"We've grown apart."

"Doesn't he doss here when he's not on his boat?"

"Not often."

"What about his relationship with Kate?"

Bridges shook his head. "Everything I know about her is in my statement," he said virtuously. "If I knew anything else, I'd tell you."

Galbraith looked at his watch. "We've got a bit of a problem here, son," he said affably. "I'm on a tight schedule, so I can only give you another thirty seconds."

"To do what, mate?"

"Tell the truth." He unclipped his handcuffs from his belt.

"Pull the other one," scoffed Bridges. "You're not going to arrest me."

"Too right I am. And I'm a hard bastard, Tony. When I arrest a lying little toe-rag like you, I take him out just as he is, never mind he's got a bum like a pizza and his prick's shrunk in the fucking wash."

Bridges gave a throaty chuckle. "The press would crucify you. You can't drag a naked guy through the streets for illegal possession. It's hardly even a crime anymore."

"Try me."

"Go on then."

Galbraith snapped one bracelet onto his own wrist, then leaned forward and snapped the other onto Tony's. "Anthony Bridges, I am arresting you on suspicion of conspiracy in the rape and murder last Saturday night of Mrs. Kate Sumner of Langton Cottage and the grievous bodily assault this morning of Miss Margaret Jenner of Broxton House." He stood up and started walking toward the door, dragging Bridges behind him. "You do not have to say anything, but it may harm your defense—"

"Shit!" said the young man stumbling to his feet. "This is a joke, right?"

"No joke." The DI twitched the spliff out of the young man's fingers and flicked it, still alight, into the corridor. "The reason Steven Harding was attacked by a dog this morning is because he attempted to assault another woman in the same place that Kate Sumner died. Now you can either tell me what you know, or you can accompany me to Winfrith, where you will be formally charged and interviewed on tape." He looked the man up and down, and laughed. "Frankly, I couldn't give a toss either way. It'll save me time if you talk to me now, but"—he shook his head regretfully—"I'd hate your neighbors to miss the fun. It must be hell living next door to you."

"That spliff's going to set my house on fire!"

Galbraith watched the joint smolder gently on the wooden floorboards. "It's too green. You're not curing it properly."

"You'd know, of course."

"Trust me." He yanked Bridges down the corridor. "Where were we? Oh, yes. It may harm your defense if you do not mention, when questioned, something you later rely on in court." He pulled open the door and ushered the man outside. "Anything you do say may be given in evidence." He prodded Bridges onto the pavement in front of a startled old lady with fluffy white hair and eyes as big as golf balls behind pebble spectacles. "Morning, ma'am," he said politely.

Her mouth gaped.

"I've parked behind Tesco's," he told Bridges, "so it'll probably be quicker if we go up the High Street."

"You can't take me up the High Street like this. Tell him, Mrs. Crane."

The elderly woman leaned forward, putting a hand behind her ear. "Tell him what, dear?"

"Oh, Jesus! Never mind! Forget it!"

"I'm not sure I can," she murmured in a confidential tone. "Did you know you were naked?"

"Of course I know!" he shouted into her deaf ear. "The police are denying me my rights, and you're a witness to it."

"That's nice. I've always wanted to be a witness to something." Her eyes brimmed with sudden amusement.

"I'll tell my husband about it. He'll be pleased as punch. He's been saying for years that the only thing that happens when you burn the candle at both ends is the wick gets smaller." She gave a joyful laugh as she moved on. "And, you know, I always thought it was a joke."

Galbraith grinned after her. "What do you want me to do with your front door?" he asked, grabbing the handle. "Slam it shut?"

"Jesus no!" Bridges lurched backward to stop the door from closing. "I haven't got a key, for Christ's sake."

"Losing your nerve already?"

"I could sue you for this."

"No chance. This was your choice, remember. I explained that if I had to arrest you, I would take you out as you were, and your response was: Go on then."

Bridges looked wildly up the road as a man rounded the corner, and Galbraith was rewarded with a scrambling stampede for the safety of the corridor. He shut the door and stood with his back to it, halting further flight by a jerk on the handcuffs. "Right. Shall we start again? Why did Steve go back to Chapman's Pool this morning?"

"I don't know. I didn't even know he was there." His eyes widened as Galbraith reached for the door handle again. "Listen, dickhead, that guy coming up the street's a journalist, and he's been pestering me all morning about Steve. If I'd known where the bastard was I'd have sent the bloke after him, but I can't even get him to answer his mobile." He jerked his head toward the sitting room. "At least let's get out of earshot," he muttered. "He's probably listening at the door, and you don't want the press on your back any more than I do."

Galbraith released the handcuffs on his own wrist and followed Bridges into the sitting room again, treading on the spliff as he went. "Tell me about the relationship between Steve and Kate," he said, resuming his seat. "And make it convincing, Tony," he added, taking his notebook from his pocket with a sigh, "because A: I'm knackered; B: you're getting up my nose; and C: it's completely immaterial to me if your name is plastered across the newspapers tomorrow morning as a probable suspect on a rape and murder charge."

I never did understand the attraction. I only met her once, and as far as I'm concerned, she's the most boring woman I've ever come across. It was in a pub one Friday lunchtime, and all she could do was sit and look at Steve as if he were Leonardo DiCaprio. Mind you, when she started talking, it was even worse. God, she was stupid! Having a conversation with her was like listening to paint dry. I think she must have lived on a diet of soap operas, because whatever I said reminded her of something that had happened in *Neighbours* or *EastEnders,* and it got on my tits after a while. I asked Steve later what the hell he thought he was doing, and he laughed and said he wasn't interested in her for her conversation. He reckoned she had a dream of an arse, and that was all that mattered. To be honest, I don't think he ever intended it to get as serious as it did. She met him in the street one day after the incident with Hannah's buggy and invited him back to her house. He said it was all pretty mind-blowing. One minute he was struggling to find something to talk about over a coffee in the kitchen, and the next she was climbing all over him. He said the only bad part was that the kid sat in a highchair watching them do it because Kate said Hannah would scream her head off if she tried to take her out.

"As far as Steve was concerned, that was it. That's what he told me anyway. Wham, bam, thank you, ma'am, and bye-bye. So I was a bit surprised when he asked if he could bring her here on a couple of occasions in the autumn term. It was during the day, while her husband was at work, so I never saw her. Other times, they did it on his boat or in her house, but mostly they did it in his Volvo. He'd drive her out into the New Forest and they'd dose the kid with paracetamol so she'd sleep on the front seat while they set to in the back. All in all it went on for about two months, until he started to get bored. The trouble was Kate had nothing going for her except her arse. She didn't drink, she didn't smoke, she didn't sail, she had no sense of humor and all she wanted was for Steve to get a part in *EastEnders*. It was pathetic really. I think it was the ultimate dream for her, to get hitched to a soap star and swan around being photographed on his arm.

"In all honesty, I don't think it ever occurred to her that he was only balling her because she was available and didn't cost him a penny. He said she was completely gobsmacked when he told her he'd had enough and didn't want to see her again. That's when she turned nasty. I guess she'd been conning idiots like her husband for so long it really pissed her off to find she'd been taken for a ride by a younger guy. She rubbed crap all over the sheets in his cabin, then she started setting off his car alarm and smearing shit all over his car. Steve got incredibly uptight about it. Everything he touched had crap on it. What really bugged him was his dinghy. He came down one Friday and found the bottom ankle-deep in water and slushy turds. He said she must have been saving them up for weeks. Anyway, that's when he started talking about going to the police.

"I told him it was a crazy idea. If you get the filth involved, I said, you'll never hear the end of it. And it won't be just Kate who's after you, it'll be William, too. You can't go around sleeping with other guys' wives and expect them to turn a blind eye. I told him to cool down and move his car to another parking place. So he said, what about his dinghy? And I said I'd lend him one that she wouldn't recognize. And that was it. Simple. Problem sorted. As far as I know he didn't have any more aggro from her."

It was a while before Galbraith responded. He had been listening attentively and making notes, and he finished writing before he said anything. "Did you lend him a dinghy?" he asked.

"Sure."

"What did it look like?"

Bridges frowned. "The same as any dinghy. Why do you want to know that?"

"Just interested. What color was it?"

"Black."

"Where did you get it from?"

He started to pluck Rizla papers from their packet and make a patchwork quilt of them on the floor. "A mail-order catalogue, I think. It's the one I had before I bought my new rib."

"Has Steve still got it?"

He hesitated before shaking his head. "I wouldn't know, mate. Wasn't it on *Crazy Daze* when you searched it?"

Thoughtfully, the DI tapped his pencil against his teeth. He recalled Carpenter's words of Wednesday: *"I didn't like him. He's a cocky little bastard, and a damn sight too knowledgeable about police interviews."* "Okay," he said next. "Let's go back to Kate. You say the problem was sorted. What happened then?"

"Nothing. That's it. End of story. Unless you count the fact that she ends up dead on a beach in Dorset the weekend Steve just happens to be there."

"I do. I also count the fact that her daughter was found wandering along a main road approximately two hundred yards from where Steve's boat was moored."

"It was a setup," said Bridges. "You should be giving William the third degree. He had far more reason to murder Kate than Steve did. She was two-timing him, wasn't she?"

Galbraith shrugged. "Except that William didn't hate his wife, Tony. He knew what she was like when he married her, and it made no difference to him. Steve, on the other hand, had got himself into a mess and didn't know how to get out of it."

"That doesn't make him a murderer."

"Perhaps he thought he needed an ultimate solution."

Bridges shook his head. "Steve's not like that."

"And William Sumner is?"

"I wouldn't know. I've never met the bloke."

"According to your statement you and Steve had a drink with him one evening."

"Okay. Correction. I don't *know* the bloke. I stayed fifteen minutes tops and exchanged maybe half a dozen words with him."

Galbraith steepled his fingers in front of his mouth and studied the young man. "But you seem to know a lot about him," he said. "Kate, too, despite only meeting each of them once."

Bridges returned his attention to his patchwork quilt, sliding the papers into different positions with the balls of his fingers. "Steve talks a lot."

Galbraith seemed to accept this explanation, because he gave a nod. "Why was Steve planning to go to France this week?"

"I didn't know he was."

"He had a reservation at a hotel in Concarneau, which was canceled this morning when he failed to confirm it."

Bridges' expression became suddenly wary. "He's never mentioned it."

"Would you expect him to?"

"Sure."

"You said you and he had grown apart," Galbraith reminded him.

"Figure of speech, mate."

A look of derision darkened the inspector's eyes. "Okay, last question. Where's Steve's lock-up, Tony?"

"What lock-up?" asked the other guilelessly.

"All right. Let me put it another way. Where does he store the equipment off his boat when he's not using it? His dinghy and his outboard, for example."

"All over the place. Here. The flat in London. The back of his car."

Galbraith shook his head. "No oil spills," he said. "We've searched them all." He smiled amiably. "And don't try and tell me an outboard doesn't leak when it's laid on its side, because I won't believe you."

Bridges scratched the side of his jaw but didn't say anything.

"You're not his keeper, son," murmured Galbraith kindly, "and there's no law that says when your friend digs a hole for himself you have to get into it with him."

The man pulled a wry face. "I did warn him, you know. I said he'd do better to volunteer information rather than have it dragged out of him piecemeal. He wouldn't listen, though. He has this crazy idea he can control everything, when the truth is he's never been able to control a damn thing from the first day I met him. Talk about a loose cannon. Sometimes, I wish I'd never met the stupid bugger, because I'm sick to death of telling lies for him." He shrugged. "But, hey! He *is* my friend."

Galbraith's boyish face creased into a smile. The young man's sincerity was about as credible as a Ku Klux Klan assertion that it wasn't an association of racists, and he was reminded of the expression: with friends like this who needs enemies? He glanced idly about the room. There were too many discrepancies, he thought, particularly in relation to fingerprint evidence, and he felt he was being steered in a direction he didn't want to go. He wondered why Bridges thought that was necessary.

Because he knew Harding was guilty? Or because he knew he wasn't?

CHAPTER 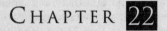 22

A call from the *Dorsetshire Constabulary to the manager of the* Hotel Angelique in Concarneau, a pretty seaside town in southern Brittany, revealed that Mr. Steven Harding had telephoned on 8 August, requesting a double room for three nights from Saturday, 16 August, for himself and Mrs. Harding. He had given his mobile telephone as the contact number, saying he would be traveling the coast of France by boat during the week 11–17 August and could not be sure of his exact arrival date. He had agreed to confirm the reservation not less than twenty-four hours prior to his arrival. In the absence of any such confirmation, and with rooms in demand, the manager had left a message with Mr. Harding's telephone answering service and had canceled the reservation when Mr. Harding failed to return his call. He was not acquainted with Mr. Harding and was unable to say if Mr. or Mrs. Harding had stayed in the hotel before. Where exactly was his hotel in Concarneau? Two streets back from the waterfront, but within easy walking distance of the shops, the sea, and the lovely beaches.

And the marinas, too, of course.

* * *

A complete check of the numbers listed in Harding's mobile telephone, which had been unavailable to the police at the time of his arrest because it had been under a pile of newspapers in Bob Winterslow's house, produced a series of names already known and contacted by the investigators. Only one call remained a mystery, either because the subscriber had deliberately withheld the number or because it had been routed through an exchange— possibly a foreign one—which meant the SIM card had been unable to record it.

"Steve? Where are you? I'm frightened. Please phone me. I've tried twenty times since Sunday."

Before he returned to Winfrith, Detective Superintendent Carpenter took Ingram aside for a briefing. He had spent much of the last hour with his telephone clamped to his ear, while the PC and the two DCs continued to dig into the shale slide and scour the shoreline in a fruitless search for further evidence. He had watched their efforts through thoughtful eyes while jotting the various pieces of information that came through to him into his notebook. He was unsurprised by their failure to find anything else. The sea, as he had learned from the coastguards' descriptions of how bodies vanished without a trace and were never seen again, was a friend to murderers.

"Harding's being discharged from the Poole hospital at five," he told the constable, "but I'm not ready to talk to him yet. I need to see the Frenchman's video and question Tony Bridges before I go anywhere near him." He clapped the tall man on the back. "You were right about the lock-up, by the way. He's been using a garage near the Lymington yacht club. John Galbraith's on his way there now to have a look at it. What I need you to do, lad, is nail our friend Steve for the assault on Miss Jenner and hold him on ice till tomorrow morning. Keep it simple—make sure he thinks he's only being arrested for the assault. Can you do that?"

"Not until I've taken a statement from Miss Jenner, sir."

Carpenter looked at his watch. "You've got two and a half hours. Pin her to her story. I don't want her weaseling out because she doesn't want to get involved."

"I can't force her, sir."

"No one's asking you to," said Carpenter irritably.

"And if she isn't as amenable as you hope?"

"Then use some charm," said the superintendent, thrusting his frown under Ingram's nose. "I find it works wonders."

"The house belongs to my grandfather," said Bridges, directing Galbraith to pass the yacht club and take the road to the right, which was lined with pleasant detached houses set back behind low hedges. It was at the wealthier end of town, not far from where the Sumners lived, in Rope Walk, and Galbraith realized that Kate must have passed Tony's grandfather's house whenever she walked into town. He realized, too, that Tony must come from a "good" family, and he wondered how they viewed their rebellious offspring and if they ever visited his shambolic establishment. "Grandpa lives on his own," Tony went on. "He can't see to drive anymore, so he lends me the garage to store my rib." He indicated an entrance a hundred yards farther on. "In here. Steve's stuff is at the back." He glanced at the DI as they drew to a halt in the small driveway. "Steve and I have the only keys."

"Is that important?"

Bridges nodded. "Grandpa hasn't a clue what's in there."

"It won't help him if it's drugs," said Galbraith unemotionally, opening his door. "You'll all be for the high jump, never mind how blind, deaf, or dumb any of you are."

"No drugs," said Bridges firmly. "We never deal."

Galbraith shook his head in cynical disbelief. "You couldn't afford to smoke the amount you do without dealing," he said in a tone that brooked no disagreement. "It's a fact of life. A teacher's salary couldn't fund a habit like yours." The garage was detached from the house and set back twenty yards from it. Galbraith stood looking at it for a moment before glancing up the road toward the turning in to Rope Walk. "Who comes here more?" he asked idly. "You or Steve?"

"Me," said the young man readily enough. "I take my rib out two or three times a week. Steve just uses it for storage."

Galbraith gestured toward the garage. "Lead the way." As they walked toward it, he caught the twitch of a curtain in one of the downstairs windows, and he wondered if Grandpa Bridges was quite as ignorant about what went into his garage as Tony claimed. The old, he thought, were a great deal more curious than the young. He stood back while the young man unlocked the double doors and pulled them wide. The entire front was taken up with a twelve-foot orange rib on a trailer, but when Tony pulled it out, an array of imported but clearly illicit goods was revealed at the back—neat stacks of cardboard boxes with VIN DE TABLE stenciled prominently on them, cases of Stella Artois lager, wrapped in plastic, and shelves covered in multipack cartons of cigarettes. Well, well, thought Galbraith with mild amusement, did Tony really expect him to believe that good old-fashioned smuggling of "legal" contraband was the worst crime either he or his friend had ever been engaged in? The screed floor interested him more. It was still showing signs of dampness where someone had hosed it down, and he wondered what had been washed away in the process.

"What's he trying to do?" he asked. "Stock an entire off-license? He's going to have a job persuading Customs and Excise this is for his own use."

"It's not that bad," protested Bridges. "Listen, the guys in Dover bring in more than this every day via the ferries.

They're coining it in. It's a stupid law. I mean, if the government can't get its act together to bring down the duty on liquor and cigarettes to the same level as the rest of Europe, then of course guys like Steve are going to do a bit of smuggling. Stands to reason. Everyone does it. You sail to France and you're tempted, simple as that."

"And you end up in jail when you get busted. Simple as that," said the DI sardonically. "Who's funding him? You?"

Bridges shook his head. "He's got a contact in London who buys it off him."

"Is that where he takes it from here?"

"He borrows a mate's van and ships it up about once every two months."

Galbraith traced a line in the dust on top of an opened box lid, then idly flipped it back. The bottoms of all the boxes in contact with the floor showed a tidemark where water had saturated them. "How does he get it ashore from his boat?" he asked, lifting out a bottle of red table wine and reading the label. "Presumably he doesn't bring it in by dinghy, or someone would have noticed."

"As long as it doesn't look like a case of wine there isn't a problem."

"What *does* it look like?"

The young man shrugged. "Something ordinary. Rubbish bags, dirty laundry, duvets. If he sticks a dozen bottles into socks to stop them rattling, then packs them in his rucksack, no one gives him a second glance. They're used to him transporting stuff to and from his boat—he's been working on it long enough. Other times he moors up to a pontoon and uses a marina trolley. People pile all sorts of things into them at the end of a weekend. I mean if you shove a few cases of Stella Artois down a sleeping bag, who's going to notice? More to the point, who's going to care? Everyone stocks up at the hypermarkets in France before they come home."

Galbraith made a rough count of the wine boxes.

"There's six-hundred-odd bottles of wine here. It'd take him hours to move these a dozen at a time, not to mention the lager and the cigarettes. Are you seriously saying no one's ever questioned why he's plying to and fro in a dinghy with a rucksack?"

"That's not how he shifts the bulk of it. I was only pointing out that it's not as difficult to bring stuff off boats as you seem to think it is. He moves most of it at night. There are hundreds of places along the coast you can make a drop as long as there's someone to meet you."

"You, for example?"

"Once in a while," Bridges admitted.

Galbraith turned to look at the rib on its trailer. "Do you go out in the rib?"

"Sometimes."

"So he calls you on his mobile and says I'll be in such-and-such a place at midnight. Bring your rib and the mate's van and help me unload."

"More or less, except he usually comes in about three o'clock in the morning, and two or three of us will be in different places. It makes it easier if he can choose the nearest to where he is."

"Like where?" asked Galbraith dismissively. "I don't swallow that garbage about there being hundreds of drop-off points. This whole coast is built over."

Bridges grinned. "You'd be amazed. I know of at least ten private landing stages on rivers between Chichester and Christchurch where you can bet on the owners being absent twenty-six weekends out of fifty-two, not to mention slips along Southampton Water. Steve's a good sailor, knows this area like the back of his hand, and providing he comes in on a rising tide in order to avoid being stranded, he can tuck himself pretty close in to shore. Okay, we may get a bit wet, wading to and fro, and we may have a trek to the van, but two strong guys can usually clear a load in an hour. It's a doddle."

Galbraith shook his head, remembering his own soaking off the Isle of Purbeck and the difficulties involved in winching boats up and down slips. "It sounds like bloody hard work to me. What does he make on a shipment like this?"

"Anything between five hundred and a thousand quid a trip."

"What do you make out of it?"

"I take payment in kind. Cigarettes, lager, whatever."

"For a drop?"

Bridges nodded.

"What about rent on this garage?"

"Use of *Crazy Daze* whenever I want it. It's a straight swap."

Galbraith eyed him thoughtfully. "Does he let you sail it or just borrow it to shag your girlfriends?"

Bridges grinned. "He doesn't let *anyone* sail it. It's his pride and joy. He'd kill anyone who left a mark on it."

"Mmm." Galbraith lifted a white wine bottle out of another box. "So when was the last time you used it for a shag?"

"A couple of weeks ago."

"Who with?"

"Bibi."

"Just Bibi? Or do you shag other girls behind her back?"

"Jesus, you don't give up, do you? Just Bibi, and if you tell her any different I'll make a formal complaint."

Galbraith tucked the bottle back into its box with a smile and moved on to another one. "How does it work? Do you call Steve in London and tell him you want the boat for the weekend? Or does he offer it to you when he doesn't want it?"

"I get to use it during the week. He gets to use it at weekends. It's a good deal, suits everyone."

"So it's like your house? Anyone and everyone can pile in for a quick shag whenever the mood takes them?" He flicked the young man a look of disgust. "It sounds pretty sordid to me. Do you all use the same sheets?"

"Sure." Bridges grinned. "Different times, different customs, mate. It's all about enjoying life these days, not being tied to conventional views of how to conduct yourself."

Galbraith seemed suddenly bored with the subject. "How often does Steve go to France?"

"It probably works out at an average of once every two months. It's no big deal, just booze and cigarettes. If he clears five thousand quid in a year he reckons he's done well. But it's peanuts, for Christ's sake. That's why I told him he should come clean. The worst that can happen is a few months in jail. It would be different if he was doing drugs but"—he shook his head vigorously—"he wouldn't touch them with a bargepole."

"We found cannabis in one of his lockers."

"Oh, come on," said Bridges with a sigh. "So he smokes the odd joint. That doesn't make him a Colombian drug baron. On that basis, anyone who enjoys a drink is smuggling alcohol by the lorry load. Look, trust me, he doesn't bring in anything more dangerous than red wine."

Galbraith moved a couple of boxes. "What about dogs?" he asked, lifting a plastic kennel out from behind them and holding it up for Bridges to look at.

The young man shrugged. "A few times maybe. Where's the harm? He always makes sure they've got their anti-rabies certificates." He watched a frown gather on Galbraith's forehead. "It's a stupid law," he repeated like a mantra. "Six months of quarantine costs the owner a fortune, the dogs are miserable while it's happening, and not a single one has ever been diagnosed with rabies in all the time this country's been enforcing the rabies regulations."

"Cut the crap, Tony," said the DI impatiently. "Personally, I think it's a crazy law that allows a smackhead like you within a hundred miles of impressionable children, but I'm not going to break your legs to keep you away from them. How much does he charge?"

"Five hundred, and I'm no fucking smackhead," he said

with genuine irritation. "Smack's for idiots. You should bone up on your drug terminology."

Galbraith ignored him. "Five hundred, eh? That's a nice little earner. What does he make per person? Five *thousand?*"

There was a distinct hesitation. "What are you talking about?"

"Twenty-five different sets of fingerprints inside *Crazy Daze,* not counting Steve's or Kate and Hannah Sumner's. You've just accounted for two—yours and Bibi's—that still leaves twenty-three unaccounted for. That's a lot of fingerprints, Tony."

Bridges shrugged. "You said it yourself, he runs a sordid establishment."

"Mmm," murmured Galbraith, "I did say that, didn't I?" His gaze shifted toward the trailer again. "Nice rib. Is it new?"

Bridges followed his gaze. "Not particularly, I've had it nine months."

Galbraith walked over to look at the two Evinrude outboards at the stern. "It looks new," he remarked, running a finger along the rubber. "Immaculate, in fact. When did you last clean it?"

"Monday."

"And you hosed the garage floor for good measure, did you?"

"It got wet in the process."

Galbraith slapped the inflated sides of the rib. "When did you last take it out?"

"I don't know. A week ago maybe."

"So why did it need cleaning on Monday?"

"It didn't," said Bridges, his expression growing wary again. "I just like to look after it."

"Then let's hope Customs and Excise don't rip it apart looking for drugs, my son," said the policeman with poorly feigned sympathy, "because they're not going to buy your story about red wine being Steve's most dangerous import any more than I do." He jerked his head toward the back of the garage. "That's just a blind in case you're sussed for anything more serious. Like illegal immigration. Those boxes have been in there for months. The dust's so thick I can write my name in it."

Ingram stopped at Broxton House on his way home to check on Celia Jenner and was greeted enthusiastically by Bertie, who bounded out of the front door, tail wagging. "How's your mother?" he asked Maggie as he met her in the hall.

"Much better. Brandy and painkillers have put her on cloud nine, and she's talking about getting up." She headed for the kitchen. "We're starving, so I'm making some sandwiches. Do you want some?"

He followed with Bertie in tow, wondering how to tell her politely that he'd rather go home and make his own, but kept his counsel when he saw the state of the kitchen. It was hardly up to hospital standards, but the smell of cleaning rising from the floor, countertops, table, and stove was a huge advance on the ancient, indescribable aroma of dirty dog and damp horse blankets that had shocked his scent and taste buds earlier. "I wouldn't say no," he said. "I haven't had anything to eat since last night."

"What do you think?" she asked, setting to with a loaf of sliced bread, cheese, and tomatoes.

He didn't pretend he didn't know what she was talking about. "All in all, a vast improvement. I prefer the floor this color." He touched the toe of one large boot to a quarry tile. "I hadn't realized it was orange or that my feet weren't supposed to stick to it every time I moved."

She gave a low laugh. "It was damned hard work. I don't think it's had a mop on it for four years, not since Ma told Mrs. Cottrill she couldn't afford her anymore." She glanced critically around the room. "But you're right.

A coat of paint would make a hell of a difference. I thought I'd buy some this afternoon and slap it on over the weekend. It won't take long."

He should have brought the brandy up a long time ago, he realized, marveling at her optimism. He would have done if he'd known she and her mother had been on the wagon for four years. Alcohol, for all its sins, wasn't called a restorative for nothing. He cast an interested eye toward the ceiling, which was festooned with cobwebs. "It'll slap right off again unless you shift that little lot as well. Do you have a stepladder?"

"I don't know."

"I've got one at home," he said. "I'll bring it up this evening when I've finished for the day. In return will you put off your paint-buying trip long enough to give me a statement about Harding's assault on you this morning? I'll be questioning him at five o'clock, and I want your version of the story before I do."

She looked anxiously toward Bertie, who, at Ingram's fingered command, had taken up station beside the Aga. "I don't know. I've been thinking about what you said and now I'm worried he's going to accuse Bertie of being out of control and attacking *him,* in which case I'll be faced with a prosecution under the Dangerous Dogs Act and Bertie will be put down. Don't you think it would be better to let it drop?"

Nick pulled out a chair and sat on it, watching her. "He'll probably try to bring a counterprosecution, anyway, Maggie. It's his best defense against anything you might say." He paused. "But if you let him get in first, then you'll be handing him the advantage. Is that what you want?"

"No, of course it isn't, but Bertie *was* out of control. He sank his teeth into the stupid idiot's arm, and I couldn't get him off for love or money." Angrily, she turned a ferocious glare on her dog, then stabbed her knife into a tomato and splattered seeds all over the chopping board. "I had to thrash him in the end to make him release his hold, and I won't be able to deny it if Steve takes me to court."

"Who attacked first, Bertie or Steve?"

"Me, probably. I was screaming abuse at Steve, so he lashed out at me, then the next thing I knew Bertie was hanging off his arm like a great hairy leech." Unexpectedly, she laughed. "Actually, in retrospect, it's quite funny. I thought they were dancing until red saliva came out of Bertie's mouth. I just couldn't understand what Harding thought he was playing at. First he appears out of nowhere, then he runs at Stinger, then he slaps me and starts dancing with my dog. I felt as if I was in a madhouse."

"Why do you think he slapped you?"

She smiled uncomfortably. "Presumably because I made him angry. I called him a pervert."

"That's no excuse for slapping you. Verbal abuse does not constitute an assault, Maggie."

"Then maybe it should."

"The man hit you," he remarked curiously. "Why are you making excuses for him?"

"Because, thinking back, I was incredibly rude. I certainly called him a creep and a bastard, and I said you'd crucify him if you knew he was there. It's your fault, really. I wouldn't have been so frightened if you hadn't come and questioned me about him yesterday. You planted the idea that he was dangerous."

"Mea culpa," he said mildly.

"You know what I mean."

He acknowledged the point gravely. "What else did you say?"

"Nothing. I just screamed at him like a fishwife because he gave me such a shock. The trouble is, he was shocked, too, so we both sort of lashed out without thinking . . . he in his way . . . me in mine."

"There's no excuse for physical violence."

"Isn't there?" she asked dryly. "You excused mine earlier."

"True," he admitted, rubbing his cheek reminiscently.

"But if I'd retaliated, Maggie, you'd still be unconscious."

"Meaning what? That men are expected to show more responsibility than women?" She glanced at him with a half-smile. "I don't know whether to accuse you of being patronizing or ignorant."

"Ignorant every time," he said. "I know nothing about women except that very few of them could land me a knock-out blow." His eyes smiled at her. "But I know damn well that I could flatten any of them. Which is why—unlike Steve Harding—I wouldn't dream of raising my hand against one."

"Yes, but you're so wise and so middle-aged, Nick," she said crossly, "and he isn't. In any case, I don't even remember the way it happened. It was all over so quickly. I expect that sounds pathetic, but I've realized I'm not much good as a witness."

"It just makes you normal," he said. "Very few people have accurate recall."

"Well, the truth is I think he wanted to try and catch Stinger before he bolted and only hit out when I called him a pervert." Her shoulders sagged despondently as if the brandy-courage in her blood had suddenly evaporated. "I'm sorry to disappoint you. I used to see everything so straightforwardly before I got taken to the cleaners by Martin, but now I can't make up my mind about anything. I'd have insisted on a prosecution like a shot this morning, but now I realize I'd *die* if anything happened to Bertie. I love the stupid animal to distraction, and I absolutely refuse to sacrifice him on a point of principle. He's worth a slap from a toe-rag any day. Goddammit, he's *faithful*. All right, he visits you from time to time, but he always comes home to love me at night."

"Okay."

There was a short silence.

"Is that all you're going to say?"

"Yes."

She eyed him with suspicion. "You're a policeman. Why aren't you arguing with me?"

"Because you're intelligent enough to make your own decisions, and nothing I can say will change your mind."

"That's absolutely right." She slapped some butter on a piece of sliced bread and waited for him to say something else. When he didn't, she grew nervous. "Are you still going to question Steve?" she demanded.

"Of course. That's my job. Helicopter rescues don't come cheap, and someone has to account for why this morning's was necessary. Harding was admitted to hospital with dog bites, so I have a responsibility to establish whether the attack on him was provoked or unprovoked. One of you was assaulted this morning, and I have to try and find out which. If you're lucky, he'll be feeling as guilty as you are and there'll be a stalemate. If you're unlucky, I'll be back this evening requesting a statement from you in answer to his assertion that you had no control over your dog."

"That's blackmail."

He shook his head. "As far as I'm concerned, you and Steven Harding have equal rights under the law. If he says Bertie made an unprovoked attack on him, I will investigate the allegation, and if I think he's right I'll submit my findings to the Crown Prosecution Service and suggest they prosecute you. I may not like him, Maggie, but if I think he's telling the truth I will support him. That's what society pays me for, irrespective of personal feeling and irrespective of how it may affect the people involved."

She turned around, back against the worktop. "I had no idea you were such a cold fucking bastard."

He was unrepentant. "And I had no idea you thought you ranked above anyone else. You'll get no favors from me, not where the law's concerned."

"Will you favor me if I give you a statement?"

"No, I'll be as fair to you as I am to Harding, but my

advice is that you'll gain an advantage by getting your statement in first."

She whipped the knife off the chopping board and waved it under his nose. "Then you'd bloody well better be right," she said fiercely, "or I'll take your testicles off— *personally*—and laugh while I'm doing it. I *love* my dog."

"So do I," Ingram assured her, putting a finger on the hilt of the knife and moving it gently to one side. "The difference is I don't encourage him to slobber all over me in order to prove it."

I've sealed the garage for the moment," Galbraith told Carpenter over the phone, "but you'll have to sort out priorities with Customs and Excise. We need a scene-of-crime team down here pronto, but if you want a hard charge on which to hold Steven Harding, then C and E can probably deliver for you. My guess is he's been ferrying illegal immigrants in wholesale and dropping them off along the south coast . . . Yes, it would certainly explain the fingerprint evidence in the saloon area. No, no sign of the stolen Fastrigger outboard . . ." He felt the young man beside him stir, and he glanced at him with a distracted smile. "Yes, I'm bringing Tony Bridges in now. He's agreed to make a new statement . . . Yes, very cooperative. William? . . . No, it doesn't eliminate him any more than it eliminates Steve . . . Mmm, back to square one, I'm afraid." He tucked the telephone into his breast pocket and wondered why he'd never thought of taking up acting himself.

At the other end, Superintendent Carpenter looked at his receiver in surprise for a moment before cutting the line. He hadn't a clue what John Galbraith had been talking about.

Although he hadn't been aware of it, Steven Harding had been under observation by a woman detective constable from the moment he was admitted to the hospital. She sat out of sight in the Sister's office, making sure he stayed put, but he appeared in no hurry to leave. He flirted constantly with the nurses, and much to the WDC's irritation, the nurses reciprocated. She spent the waiting hours pondering the naiveté of women, and wondered how many of these selfsame nurses would argue vehemently that they hadn't given him any encouragement if and when he decided to rape them. In other words, what constituted encouragement? Something a woman would describe as innocent flirting? Or something a man would call a definite come-on?

It was with some relief that she handed over responsibility to PC Ingram in the corridor outside. "The Sister's discharging him at five, but the way things are going, I'm not sure he'll be leaving at all," she said ruefully. "He's got every nurse wound around his little finger, and he looks set for the duration. Frankly, if they turf him out of this bed, it wouldn't surprise me if he ends up in a nice warm one somewhere else. I can't see the attraction myself, but then I've never been too keen on wankers."

Ingram gave a muted laugh. "Hang around. Watch the fun. If he doesn't walk out of his own accord on the dot of five, I'll clap the irons on him in there."

"I'm game," she agreed cheerfully. "You never know, you might need a hand."

The video film was difficult to watch, not because of its content, which was as discreet as the Dartmouth sergeant had promised, but because the picture rose and fell with the movement of the Frenchman's boat. Nevertheless, his daughter had succeeded in capturing considerable footage of Harding in close detail. Carpenter, sitting behind his desk, played it through once, then used the remote to rewind to where Harding had first sat down on his rucksack. He held the image on pause and addressed the team of detectives crammed into his office. "What do you think he's doing there?"

"Releasing Godzilla?" said one of the men with a snigger.

"Signaling to someone?" said a woman.

Carpenter played back a few frames to follow, in reverse, the panning of the camera lens across the shadowy, out-of-focus glare of the white motor cruiser and the blurry bikini-clad figure lying facedown across the bow. "I agree," he said. "The only question is, who?"

"Nick Ingram listed the boats that were there that day," said another man. "They shouldn't be too difficult to track down."

"There was a Fairline Squadron with two teenage girls on board," said Carpenter, passing across the report from Bournemouth about the abandoned dinghy. *"Gregory's Girl* out of Poole. Start with that one. It's owned by a Poole businessman called Gregory Freemantle."

Ingram detached himself from the wall and blocked the corridor as Steven Harding, arm in sling, came through the door of the ward at 4:45. "Good afternoon, sir," he said politely. "I hope you're feeling better."

"Why would you care?"

Ingram smiled. "I'm always interested in anyone I help to rescue."

"Well, I'm not going to talk to you. You're the bastard who got them interested in my boat."

Ingram showed his warrant card. "I questioned you on Sunday. PC Ingram, Dorsetshire Constabulary."

Harding's eyes narrowed. "They say they can keep *Crazy Daze* for as long as is necessary but won't explain what gives them the right. I haven't done anything, so they can't charge me, but they can sure as hell steal my boat for no reason." His angry gaze raked Ingram. "What does 'as long as is necessary' mean, anyway?"

"There can be any number of reasons why it's deemed necessary to retain seized articles," explained the constable helpfully, if somewhat misleadingly. The rules surrounding retention were woolly in the extreme, and policemen had few qualms about smothering so-called evidence in mountains of paperwork to avoid having to return it. "In the case of *Crazy Daze,* it probably means they haven't finished the forensic examination, but once that's done you should be able to effect its release almost immediately."

"Bollocks to that! They're holding it in case I abscond to France."

Ingram shook his head. "You'd have to go a little farther than France, Steve," he murmured in mild correction. "Everyone's mighty cooperative in Europe these days." He stood aside and gestured down the corridor behind him. "Shall we go?"

Harding backed away from him. "Dream on. I'm not going anywhere with you."

"I'm afraid you must," said Ingram with apparent regret. "Miss Jenner's accused you of assault, which means I have to insist that you answer some questions. I would prefer it if you came voluntarily, but I will arrest you if necessary." He jerked his chin toward the corridor behind Harding. "That doesn't lead anywhere—I've already checked it out." He pointed toward a door at the end where a woman was consulting a notice board. "This is the only exit."

Harding began to ease his arm out of its sling, clearly fancying his chances in a sprint dash against this simple, forelock-tugging, 240-pound yokel in a uniform, but something changed his mind. Perhaps it was the fact that Ingram stood four inches taller than he did. Perhaps the woman by the door signaled that she was a detective. Perhaps he saw something in Ingram's lazy smile that persuaded him he might be making a mistake. . . .

He gave an indifferent shrug. "What the hell! I've nothing else to do. But it's your precious Maggie you should be arresting. She stole my phone."

CHAPTER 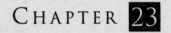 23

*S*ecured in the passenger seat of the police Range Rover, where Ingram could keep an eye on him, Harding sat huddled in moody silence for most of the trip back to Swanage. Ingram made no attempt to talk to him. Once in a while their eyes met when the policeman was checking traffic to his left, but he felt none of the empathy for Harding that Galbraith had experienced on *Crazy Daze*. He saw only immaturity in the young man's face and despised him because of it. He was reminded of every juvenile delinquent he'd arrested down the years, not one of whom had had the experience or the wisdom to understand the inevitability of consequence. They saw it in terms of retribution and justice and whether they would do "time," never in terms of the slow destruction of their lives.

It was as they drove through the little town of Corfe Castle, with its ruined medieval ramparts commanding a gap in the Purbeck chalk ridge, that Harding broke the silence. "If you hadn't jumped to conclusions on Sunday," he said in a reasonable tone of voice, "none of this would have happened."

"None of what?"

"Everything. My arrest. This." He touched a hand to his sling. "I shouldn't be here. I had a part lined up in London. It could have been my breakthrough."

"The only reason you're here is because you attacked Miss Jenner this morning," Ingram pointed out. "What have the events of Sunday got to do with that?"

"She wouldn't know me from Adam but for Kate's murder."

"That's true."

"And you won't believe I didn't have anything to do with that—none of you will—but it's not fair," Harding complained with a sudden surge of bitterness. "It's just a bloody awful coincidence, like the coincidence of bumping into Maggie this morning. Do you think I'd have shown myself to her if I'd known she was there?"

"Why not?" The car sped up as they exited the thirty-mile speed limit.

He turned a morose stare on Ingram's profile. "Have you any idea what it's like to have your movements monitored by the police? You've got my car, my boat. I'm supposed to stay at an address you've chosen for me. It's like being in prison without the walls. I'm being treated like a criminal when I haven't done anything, but if I lose my temper because some stupid woman treats me like Jack the Ripper I get accused of assault."

Ingram kept his eyes on the road ahead. "You hit her. Don't you think she had a right to treat you like Jack the Ripper?"

"Only because she wouldn't stop screaming." He gnawed at his fingernails. "I guess you told her I was a rapist, so of course she believed you. That's what got me riled. She was fine with me on Sunday, then today . . ." He fell silent.

"Did you know she might be there?"

"Of course not. How could I?"

"She rides that gully most mornings. It's one of the few

places she can give her horses a good gallop. Anyone who knows her could have told you that. It's also one of the few places with easy access to the beach from the coastal path."

"I didn't know."

"Then why are you so surprised she was scared of you? She'd have been scared of any man who appeared out of nowhere on a deserted headland when she wasn't expecting it."

"She wouldn't have been scared of you."

"I'm a policeman. She trusts me."

"She trusted *me,*" said Harding, "until you told her I was a rapist."

It was the same point Maggie had made, and Ingram conceded it was a fair one—to himself if not to Harding. It was the grossest injustice to destroy an innocent person's reputation, however it was done, and while neither he nor Galbraith had said that the young man was a rapist, the implication had been clear enough. They continued for a while in silence. The road to Swanage led southeast along the spine of Purbeck, and the distant sea showed intermittently between folds of pastureland. The sun was warm on Ingram's arm and neck, but Harding, sitting in shade on the left-hand side of the car, hunched tighter into himself as if he was cold and stared sightlessly out of the window. He seemed lost in lethargy, and Ingram wondered if he was still trying to concoct some sort of defense or whether the events of the morning had finally taken their toll.

"That dog of hers should be shot," he said suddenly.

Still concocting a defense then, thought Ingram, while wondering why it had taken him so long to get around to it. "Miss Jenner claims he was only trying to protect her," he said mildly.

"It bloody savaged me."

"You shouldn't have hit her."

Harding gave a long sigh. "I didn't mean to," he admitted as if realizing that continued argument would be a waste of time. "I probably wouldn't have done it if she hadn't called me a pervert. The last person who did that was my father, and I flattened him for it."

"Why did he call you a pervert?"

"Because he's old-fashioned, and I told him I'd done a porno shoot to make money." The young man balled his hands into fists. "I wish people would just keep their noses out of my business. It gets on my tits the way everyone keeps lecturing me about the way I live my life."

Ingram shook his head in irritation. "There's no such thing as a free lunch, Steve."

"What's that got to do with anything?"

"Live now, pay later. What goes around, comes around. No one promised you a rose garden."

Harding turned to stare out of the passenger window, offering a cold shoulder to what he clearly felt was a patronizing police attitude. "I don't know what the fuck you're talking about."

Ingram smiled slightly. "I know you don't." He glanced sideways. "What were you doing on Emmetts Hill this morning?"

"Just walking."

There was a moment's silence before Ingram gave a snort of laughter. "Is that the best you can do?"

"It's the truth," he said.

"Like hell it is. You've had all day to work this one out, but by God, if that's the only explanation you've been able to come up with, you must have a very low opinion of policemen."

The young man turned back to him with an engaging smile. "I do."

"Then we'll have to see if we can change your mind." Ingram's smile was almost as engaging. "Won't we?"

Gregory Freemantle was pouring himself a drink in the front room of his flat in Poole when his girlfriend showed in two detectives. The atmosphere was thick enough to cut with a knife, and it was obvious to both policemen that they had walked in on a humdinger of a row. "DS Campbell and DC Langham," she said curtly. "They want to talk to you."

Freemantle was a Peter Stringfellow lookalike, an aging playboy with straggling blond hair and the beginnings of desperation in the sagging lines around his eyes and chin. "Oh God," he groaned, "you're not taking her seriously about that bloody oil drum, are you? She doesn't know the first thing about sailing"—he paused to consider—"or children, for that matter, but it doesn't stop her being lippy." He raised one hand and worked his thumb and forefingers to mimic a mouth working.

He was the kind of man other men take against instinctively, and DS Campbell glanced sympathetically at the girlfriend. "It wasn't an oil drum, sir, it was an upturned dinghy. And, yes, we took Miss Hale's information very seriously."

Freemantle raised his glass in the woman's direction. "Good one, Jenny." His eyes were already showing alcohol levels well above average, but he still downed two fingers of neat whisky without blinking. "What do you want?" he asked Campbell. He didn't invite them to sit down, merely turned back to the whisky bottle and poured himself another drink.

"We're trying to eliminate people from the Kate Sumner murder inquiry," Campbell explained, "and we're interested in everyone who was in Chapman's Pool on Sunday. We understand you were there on a Fairline Squadron."

"You know I was. She's already told you."

"Who was with you?"

"Jenny and my two daughters, Marie and Fliss. And it was a bloody nightmare, if you're interested. You buy a boat to keep everyone happy, and all they can do is snipe at each other. I'm going to sell the damn thing." His drink-sodden eyes filled with self-pity. "It's no fun going out on your own, and it's even less fun taking a menagerie of cats with you."

"Was either of your daughters wearing a bikini and lying facedown on the bow between twelve thirty and one o'clock on Sunday, sir?"

"I don't know."

"Does either of them have a boyfriend called Steven Harding?"

He shrugged indifferently.

"I'd be grateful for an answer, Mr. Freemantle."

"Well, you're not going to get one, because I don't know and I don't care," he said aggressively. "I've had a bucketful of women today, and as far as I'm concerned the sooner they're all genetically engineered to behave like Stepford wives the better." He raised his glass again. "My wife serves me with notice that she intends to bankrupt my company in order to take three-quarters of what I'm worth. My fifteen-year-old daughter tells me she's pregnant and wants to run away to France with some long-haired git who fancies himself as an actor, and my girlfriend"—he lurched his glass in Jenny Hale's direction—"that one over there—tells me it's all my fault because I've waived my responsibilities as a husband and a father. So cheers! To men, eh!"

Campbell turned to the woman. "Can you help us, Miss Hale?"

She looked questioningly toward Gregory, clearly seeking his support, but when he refused to meet her eyes, she gave a small shrug. "Ah, well," she said, "I wasn't planning on hanging around after this evening anyway. Marie, the fifteen-year-old, was wearing a bikini and was sunbathing on the bow before lunch," she told the two policemen. "She lay on her tummy so that her father wouldn't see her bump, and she was signaling to her boyfriend, who was jerking off on the shore for her benefit. The rest of the time she wore a sarong to disguise the fact that she's pregnant. She has since told us that her boyfriend's name is

Steve Harding and that he's an actor in London. I knew she was plotting something because she was hyped up from the moment we left Poole, and I realized it must be to do with the boy on the shore, because she became completely poisonous after he left and has been a nightmare ever since." She sighed. "That's what the row has been about. When she turned up today in one of her tantrums I told her father he should take some interest in what's really going on because it's been obvious to me for a while that she's not just pregnant but has been taking drugs as well. Now open war has broken out."

"Is Marie still here?"

Jenny nodded. "In the spare bedroom."

"Where does she normally live?"

"In Lymington, with her mother and sister."

"Do you know what she and her boyfriend were planning to do on Sunday?"

She glanced at Gregory. "They were going to run away together to France, but when that woman's body was found they had to abandon the plan because there were too many people watching. Steve has a boat apparently, which he'd left at Salterns Marina, and the idea was for Marie to vanish into thin air out of Chapman's Pool after saying she was going for a walk to Worth Matravers. They thought if she changed into some men's clothes that Steve had brought with him, and slogged it back across land to the ferry, they could be on their way to France by the evening and no one would ever know where she'd gone or who she was with." She shook her head. "Now she's threatening to kill herself if her father doesn't let her leave school and go and live with Steve in London."

While the garage in Lymington, and its contents, were being taken apart systematically by scene-of-crime officers in search of evidence, Tony Bridges was being formally interviewed as a witness and under taped conditions by Detective Superintendent Carpenter and DI Galbraith.

He refused to repeat anything he had said to Galbraith about his or Harding's alleged smuggling activities, however, and, as that particular matter was being passed to Customs and Excise, Carpenter was less exercised by the refusal than he might otherwise have been. Instead, he chose to shock Bridges by showing him the videotape of Harding masturbating, then asked him if his friend made a habit of performing indecent acts in public.

Surprisingly, Bridges *was* shocked.

"Jesus!" he exclaimed, wiping his forehead with his sleeve. "How would I know? We lead separate lives. He's never done anything like that around me."

"It's not that bad," murmured Galbraith, who was sitting beside Carpenter. "Just a discreet wank. Why are you sweating over it, Tony?"

The young man eyed him nervously. "I get the impression it's worse than that. You wouldn't be showing it to me otherwise."

"You're a bright lad," said Carpenter, freeze-framing the video at the point where Harding was cleaning himself up. "That's a T-shirt he's using. You can just make out the Derby FC logo on the front. It belongs to a ten-year-old kid called Danny Spender. He thinks Steve stole it off him around midday on Sunday, and half an hour later we see him ejaculating all over it. You know the guy better than anyone. Would you say he has a yen for little boys?"

Bridges looked even more startled. "No," he muttered.

"We have a witness who says Steve couldn't keep his hands off the two lads who found Kate Sumner's body. One of the boys describes him using his mobile telephone to bring on an erection in front of them. We have a policeman who says he maintained the erection while the boys were around him."

"Ah, shit!" Bridges ran his tongue around dry lips. "Listen, I always thought he hated kids. He can't stand working with them, can't stand it when I talk about teaching." He looked toward the frozen image on the television screen. "This has to be wrong. Okay, he's got a thing about sex—talks about it too much—likes blue movies—boasts about three-in-a-bed romps, that kind of thing—but it's always with women. I'd have bet my last cent he was straight."

Carpenter leaned forward to examine the other man closely, then shifted his gaze to look at the television screen. "That really offends you, doesn't it? Why is that, Tony? Did you recognize anyone else in the sequence?"

"No. I just think it's obscene, that's all."

"It can't be worse than the pornography shoots he does."

"I wouldn't know. I've never seen them."

"You must have seen some of his photographs. Describe them for us."

Bridges shook his head.

"Do they include kids? We know he's done some gay poses. Does he pose with children as well?"

"I don't know anything about it. You'll have to talk to his agent."

Carpenter made a note. "Pedophile rings pay double what anyone else pays."

"It's got nothing to do with me."

"You're a teacher, Tony. You have more responsibility than most people toward children. Does your friend pose with children?"

He shook his head.

"For the purposes of the tape," said Carpenter into the microphone, "Anthony Bridges declined to answer." He consulted a piece of paper in front of him. "On Tuesday you told us Steve wasn't the kiss-and-tell type; now you're saying he boasts about three-in-a-bed sex. Which is true?"

"The boasting," he said with more confidence, glancing at Galbraith. "That's how I know about Kate. He was always telling me what they did together."

Galbraith wiped a freckled hand around the back of his neck to massage muscles made sore by too much driving that day. "Except it sounds like all talk and no action,

Tony. Your friend goes in for solitary pursuits. On beaches. On his boat. In his flat. Did you ever wonder if he was lying about his relationships with women?"

"No. Why should I? He's a good-looking bloke. Women like him."

"All right, let me put it another way. How many of these women have you actually met? How often does he bring them to your house?"

"He doesn't need to. He takes them to his boat."

"Then why is there no evidence of that? There were a couple of articles of women's clothing and a pair of Hannah's shoes on board but nothing to suggest that a woman was ever in the bed with him."

"You can't know that."

"Oh, come on," said Galbraith in exasperation, "you're a chemist. His sheets have semen stains all over them but nothing that remotely suggests there was anyone else in the bed with him when he ejaculated."

Bridges looked rather wildly toward the superintendent. "All I can tell you is what Steve told me. It's hardly my fault if the stupid sod was lying."

"True," agreed Carpenter, "but you do keep shoving his prowess down our throats." He produced Bridges' statement from a folder on the table and spread it flat in front of him, holding it down with his palms stretched on either side. "You seem to have a bit of a thing about him being good-looking. This is what you said at the beginning of the week. *'Steve's a good-looking bloke,'*" he read, "*'and has an active sex life. He has at least two girls on the go at the same time . . .'*" He lifted inquiring eyebrows. "Do you want to comment on that?"

It was clear that Tony had no idea where this line of questioning was leading and needed time to think. A fact which interested both policemen. It was as if he were trying to predict moves in a chess game and had begun to panic because checkmate looked inevitable. Every so often his eyes flicked toward the television screen, then dropped away rapidly as if the frozen image was more than he could bear. "I don't know what you want me to say."

"In simple terms, Tony, we're trying to square your portrayal of Steve with the forensic evidence. You want us to believe your friend had a prolonged affair with an older married woman, but we're having difficulty substantiating that any such affair happened. For example, you told my colleague that Steve took Kate to your house on occasion, yet, despite the fact that your house clearly hasn't been cleaned in months, we couldn't find a single fingerprint belonging to Kate Sumner anywhere inside it. There is also nothing to suggest that Kate was ever in Steve's car, although you claim that he drove her to the New Forest on numerous occasions for sex in the back of it."

"He said they needed out-of-the-way places in case they were spotted together. They were scared of William finding out, because according to Steve, he was so jealous he'd go berserk if he knew he was being two-timed." He wilted before Carpenter's unconvinced expression. "It's not my fault if he was lying to me," he protested.

"He described William to us as middle-aged and straight," said Carpenter thoughtfully. "I don't recall him suggesting he was aggressive."

"That's what he told me."

Galbraith stirred on his chair. "So your entire knowledge of Steve's *alleged*"—he put careful stress on the word—"affair with Kate came from a single meeting with her in a pub and whatever Steve chose to tell you about her?"

Bridges nodded but didn't answer.

"For the purposes of the tape, Anthony Bridges gave a nod of agreement. So was he ashamed of the relationship, Tony? Is that why you only got to meet her once? You said yourself, you couldn't understand what the attraction was."

"She was married," he said. "He was hardly going to parade a married woman around the town, was he?"

"Has he *ever* paraded a woman around town, Tony?"

There was a long silence. "Most of his girlfriends are married," he said then.

"Or mythical?" suggested Carpenter. "Like claiming Bibi as a girlfriend?"

Bridges looked baffled, as if he was struggling with half-heard, dimly understood truths that were suddenly making sense. He didn't answer.

Galbraith leveled a finger at the television screen. "What we're beginning to suspect is that the talk was a smokescreen for no action. Maybe he was pretending to like women because he didn't want anyone to know that his tastes lay in an entirely different direction? Maybe the poor bastard doesn't want to recognize it himself and lets off steam quietly in order to keep himself under control?" He turned the finger accusingly on Bridges. "But if that's true, then where does it leave you and Kate Sumner?"

The young man shook his head. "I don't understand."

The DI took his notebook from his pocket and flipped it open. "Let me quote some of the things you said about her: *'I think she must have lived on a diet of soap operas . . .' 'Kate said Hannah would scream her head off . . .' 'I guess she'd been conning idiots like her husband for so long . . .'* I could go on. You talked about her for fifteen minutes, fluently and with no prompting from me." He laid his notebook on the table. "Do you want to tell us how you know so much about a woman you only met once?"

"Everything I know is what Steve told me."

Carpenter nodded toward the recording machine. "This is a formal interview under taped conditions, Tony. Let me rephrase the question for you so there can be no misunderstandings. Bearing in mind that the Sumners are recent newcomers to Lymington, that both Steven Harding and William Sumner have denied there was any relationship between Steven and Kate Sumner, and that you, Anthony Bridges, claim to have met her only once, how do you explain your extensive and accurate knowledge of her?"

* * *

Marie Freemantle was a tall, willowy blond with waist-length wavy hair and huge doe-like eyes, which were awash with tears. Once assured that Steve was alive and well and currently answering questions about why he had been at Chapman's Pool on Sunday, she dried her eyes and favored the policemen with a heavily practiced triangular smile. If they were honest, both men were moved by her prettiness when they first saw her, although their sympathies were soon frayed by the self-centered, petulant nature beneath. They realized she wasn't very bright when it became clear that it hadn't occurred to her they were questioning her because Steven Harding was a suspect in Kate Sumner's murder. She chose to talk to them away from her father and his girlfriend, and her spite was colossal, particularly toward the woman whom she described as an interfering bitch. "I hate her," she finished. "Everything was fine till she stuck her nose in."

"Meaning you've always been allowed to do what you liked?" suggested Campbell.

"I'm old enough."

"How old were you when you first had sex with Steven Harding?"

"Fifteen." She wriggled her shoulders. "But that's nothing these days. Most girls I know had sex at thirteen."

"How long have you known him?"

"Six months."

"How often have you had sex with him?"

"Lots of times."

"Where do you do it?"

"Mostly on his boat."

Campbell frowned. "In the cabin?"

"Not often. The cabin stinks," she said. "He takes a blanket up on deck, and we do it in the sunshine or under the stars. It's great."

"Moored up to the buoy?" asked Campbell, with a rather shocked expression. Like Galbraith earlier, he was wondering about the generation gap that seemed to have opened, unobserved, between himself and today's youth. "In full view of the Isle of Wight ferry?"

"Of course not," she said indignantly, wriggling her shoulders again. "He picks me up somewhere and we go for a sail."

"Where does he pick you up?"

"All sorts of places. Like he says, he'd get strung up if anyone knew he was going with a fifteen-year-old, and he reckons if you don't use the same place too often, no one notices." She shrugged, recognizing that further explanation was necessary. "If you use a marina once in two weeks, who's going to remember? Then there's the salt flats. I walk around the path from the Yacht Haven, and he just shoots in with his dinghy and lifts me off. Sometimes I go to Poole by train and meet him there. Mum thinks I'm with Dad; Dad thinks I'm with Mum. It's simple. I just phone him on his mobile, and he tells me where to go."

"Did you leave a message on his phone this morning?"

She nodded. "He can't phone me in case Mum gets suspicious."

"How did you meet him in the first place?"

"At the Lymington yacht club. There was a dance there on St. Valentine's Day, and Dad got tickets for it because he's still a member even though he lives in Poole now. Mum said Fliss and me could go if Dad watched out for us, but he got shit-faced as usual and left us to get on with it. That's when he was going out with his bitch of a secretary. I really *hated* her. She was always trying to put him against me."

Campbell was tempted to say it wouldn't have been difficult. "Did your father introduce you to Steve? Did he know him?"

"No. One of my teachers did. He and Steve have been friends for years."

"Which teacher?"

"Tony Bridges." Her full lips curved into a malicious smile. "He's fancied me for ages, and he was trying to make this pathetic move on me when Steve cut him out. God, he was pissed about it. He's been needling away at me all term, trying to find out what's going on, but Steve told me not to tell him in case he got us into trouble for underage sex. He reckons Tony's so fucking jealous he'd make life hell for us if he could."

Campbell thought back to his interview with Bridges on Monday night. "Perhaps he feels responsible for you."

"That's not the reason," she said scornfully. "He's a sad little bastard—*that's* the reason. None of his girlfriends stay with him because he's stoned most of the time and can't do the business properly. He's been going out with this hairdresser for about four months now, and Steve says he's been feeding her drugs so she won't complain about his lousy performance. If you want my opinion, there's something wrong with him—he's always trying to touch up girls in class—but our stupid headmaster's too thick to do anything about it."

Campbell exchanged a glance with his colleague. "How does Steve know he's been feeding her drugs?" he asked.

"He's seen him do it. It's like a Mickey Finn. You dissolve a tablet in lager, and the girl passes out."

"Do you know what drug he's using?"

Another shrug. "Some sort of sleeping pill."

I'm not going to explain anything without a solicitor here," said Bridges adamantly. "Look, this was one sick woman. You think that kid of hers is weird? Well, trust me, she's as sane as you and me compared with her mother."

WPC Griffiths heard the sound of smashing glass from the kitchen and lifted her head in immediate concern. She had left Hannah watching television in the sitting room, and as far as she knew, William was still in his study upstairs, where he had retreated, angry and resentful, after his interview with DI Galbraith. With a perplexed frown, she tiptoed along the corridor and pushed open the sitting-room door to find Sumner standing just inside. He turned an ashen face toward her, then gestured helplessly toward the little girl, who stalked purposefully about the room, picking up pictures of her mother and throwing them with high-pitched guttural cries into the unlit fireplace.

Ingram put a cup of tea in front of Steven Harding and took a chair on the other side of the table. He was puzzled by the man's attitude. He had expected a long interview session, punctuated by denials and counteraccusations. Instead Harding had admitted culpability and agreed with everything Maggie had written in her statement. All that awaited him now was to be formally charged and held over till the next morning. His only real concern had been his telephone. When Ingram had handed it to the custody sergeant and formally entered it into the inventory of Harding's possessions, Harding had looked relieved. But whether because it had been returned or because it was switched off, Ingram couldn't tell.

"How about talking to me off the record?" he invited. "Just to satisfy my own curiosity. There's no tape. No witnesses to the conversation. Just you and me."

Harding shrugged. "What do you want to talk about?"

"You. What's going on. Why you were on the coastal path on Sunday. What brought you back to Chapman's Pool this morning."

"I already told you. I fancied a walk"—he made a good attempt at a cocky grin—"both times."

"All right." He splayed his palms on the edge of the table, preparatory to standing up. "It's your funeral. Just don't complain afterward that no one tried to help you. You've always been the obvious suspect. You knew the victim, you own a boat, you were on the spot, you told lies about what you were doing there. Have you any idea how all that is going to look to a jury if the Crown Prosecution Service decides to prosecute you for Kate Sumner's rape and murder?"

"They can't. They haven't got any evidence."

"Oh, for Christ's sake grow up, Steve!" he said in irritation, subsiding onto his chair again. "Don't you read the newspapers? People have spent years in prison on less evidence than Winfrith has against you. All right, it's only circumstantial, but juries don't like coincidence any more than the rest of us, and frankly, your antics of this morning haven't helped any. All they prove is that women make you angry enough to attack them." He paused, inviting a reply that never came. "If you're interested in the report I wrote on Monday, I mentioned that both Miss Jenner and I thought you were having difficulty coping with an erection. Afterward one of the Spender boys described how you were using your telephone as a masturbation aid before Miss Jenner arrived." He shrugged. "It may have had nothing to do with Kate Sumner, but it won't sound good in court."

A dull flush spread up Harding's throat and into his face. "That sucks!"

"True nevertheless."

"I wish to God I'd never helped those kids," he said with a burst of anger. "I wouldn't be in this mess but for them. I should have walked away and left them to cope on their own." He pushed his hair off his face with both hands and rested his forehead in his palms. "Jesus Christ! Why do you have to put something like that in a report?"

"Because it happened."

"Not like that it didn't," he said sullenly, the flush of humiliation lingering in his cheeks.

"Then how?" Ingram watched him for a moment. "Headquarters thinks you came back to gloat over the rape and that's what caused your erection."

"That's bullshit!" said the young man angrily.

"What other explanation is there? If it wasn't the thought of Kate Sumner's body that excited you, then it had to be Miss Jenner or the boys."

Harding raised his head and stared at the policeman, his eyes widening in shocked revulsion. "The boys?" he echoed.

It crossed Ingram's mind that the facial expression was a little too theatrical, and he reminded himself, as Galbraith had done, that he was dealing with an actor. He wondered what Harding's reaction would be when he was told about the videotape. "You couldn't keep your hands off them," he pointed out. "According to Miss Jenner, you were hugging Paul from behind when she rounded the boat sheds."

"I don't believe this," said Harding in desperation. "I was only showing him how to use the binoculars properly."

"Prove it."

"How can I?"

Ingram tilted his chair back and stretched his long legs out in front of him, lacing his hands behind his head. "Tell me why you were at Chapman's Pool. Let's face it, whatever you were doing can't be any worse than the constructions that are being put on your actions at the moment."

"I'm not saying another word."

Ingram stared at a mark on the ceiling. "Then let me tell you what I think you were doing. You went there to meet someone," he murmured. "I think it was a girl and I think she was on one of the boats, but whatever plans you'd made with her were scuppered when the place started jumping with policemen and sightseers." He shifted his attention back to Harding. "But why the secrecy, Steve? What on earth were you intending to do with her that meant you'd rather be arrested on suspicion of rape and murder than give an explanation?"

It was two hours before a solicitor arrived, courtesy of Tony's grandfather, and after a brief discussion with his client, and following police assurances that, because of his alibi, Tony was not under suspicion of involvement in

Kate Sumner's death, he advised him to answer their questions.

"Okay, yes, I got to know Kate pretty well. She lives—lived—about two hundred yards from my grandfather's garage. She used to come in and talk to me whenever I was in there because she knew I was a friend of Steve's. She was a right little tart, always flirting, always opening those baby blue eyes of hers and telling stories about how this and that man fancied her. I thought it was a come-on, particularly when she said William had a problem getting it up. She told me she went through pints of baby oil to help the poor sod out, and it made her laugh like a drain. Her descriptions were about as graphic as you can get, but she didn't seem to care that Hannah was listening or that I might get to be friendly with William." He looked troubled, as if the memory haunted him. "I told you she was sick. Matter of fact, I think she enjoyed being cruel to people. I reckon she made that poor bastard's life hell. It certainly gave her a kick slapping me down when I tried to kiss her. She spat in my face and said she wasn't that desperate." He fell silent.

"When was this?"

"End of February."

"What happened then?"

"Nothing. I told her to fuck off. Then Steve started dropping hints that he was balling her. I think she must have told him I'd made a pass, so he thought he'd swagger a bit to rub it in. He said everyone had had her except me."

Carpenter pulled forward a piece of paper and flicked the plunger on his pen. "Give me a list," he said. "Everyone you know who had anything to do with her."

"Steve Harding."

"Go on."

"I don't know of anyone else."

Carpenter laid his pen on the table again and stared at the young man. "That's not good enough, Tony. You describe her as a tart, then offer me one name. That gives me very little confidence in your assessment of Kate's character. Assuming you're telling the truth, we know of only three men who had a relationship with her—her husband, Steven Harding, and one other from her past." His eyes bored into Bridges'. "By any standards that's a modest number for a thirty-year-old woman. Or would you call any woman who's had three lovers a tart? Your girlfriend, for example? How many partners has Bibi had?"

"Leave Bibi out of this," said Bridges angrily. "She's got nothing to do with it."

Galbraith leaned forward. "She gave you your alibi for Saturday night," he reminded him. "That means she has a great deal to do with it." He folded his hands in front of his mouth and studied Bridges intently. "Did she know you fancied Kate Sumner?"

The solicitor laid a hand on the young man's arm. "You don't need to answer that."

"Well, I'm going to," he said, shaking himself free. "I'm fed up with them trying to drag Bibi into it." He addressed Galbraith. "I didn't fucking well fancy Kate. I loathed the stupid bitch. I just thought she was easy, that's all, so I tried it on once. Listen, she was a cock-teaser. It gave her a buzz to get blokes excited."

"That's not what I asked you, Tony. I asked you if Bibi knew you fancied Kate."

"No," he muttered.

Galbraith nodded. "But she knew about *Steve* and Kate?"

"Yes."

"Who told her? You or Steve?"

Bridges slumped angrily in his chair. "Steve mostly. She got really worked up when Kate started smearing Hannah's crap all over his car, so he told her what had been going on."

Galbraith leaned back, letting his hands drop to the tabletop. "Women don't give a toss about a car unless the guy who drives it matters to her. Are you sure your girl-friend isn't playing away from home?"

Bridges erupted out of his seat in a fury of movement. "You are *so* fucking patronizing. You think you know it all, don't you? She got mad because there was shit all over the handle when she tried to open the door. That's what got her worked up. Not because she cares about Steve or the car, but because her hand was covered in crap. Are you so stupid you can't work that out for yourselves?"

"But doesn't that prove my point?" said Galbraith unemotionally. "If she was driving Steve's car, she must have had more than a nodding acquaintance with him."

"*I* was driving it," said Bridges, ignoring the solicitor's restraining hand to lean across the table and thrust his face into the inspector's. "I checked the driver's-side handle and it was clean, so I released the locks. What never occurred to me was that the bloody bitch might have changed tactics. This time the crap was on the passenger's side. Now, get this, dickhead. It was still soft when Bibi touched it, so that meant Kate must have put it there min-utes before. It also meant that Bibi's hand stank to high bloody heaven. Can you follow all that, or do you want me to repeat it?"

"No," said Galbraith mildly. "The tape recorder's pretty reliable. I think we got it." He nodded toward the chair on the other side of the table. "Sit down, Tony." He waited while Bridges resumed his seat. "Did you see Kate walk away?"

"No."

"You should have done. You said the feces were still soft."

Tony pulled both hands across his peroxided hair and bent forward over the table. "There were plenty of places she could have been hiding. She was probably watching us."

"Did you ever wonder if you were the target and not Steve? You describe her as sick and say she spat at you."

"No."

"She must have known Steve allows you to drive his car."

"Once in a while. Not often."

Galbraith flipped another page of his notebook. "You told me this afternoon that you and Steve had an arrangement regarding your grandfather's garage and *Crazy Daze*. A straight swap, you called it."

"Yes."

"You said you took Bibi there two weeks ago."

"What of it?"

"Bibi doesn't agree with you. I phoned her at her parents' house two hours ago, and she said she's never been on *Crazy Daze*."

"She's forgotten," he said dismissively. "She was drunk as a skunk that night. What does it matter anyway?"

"Let's just say we're interested in discrepancies."

The young man shrugged. "I don't see what difference it makes. It's got nothing to do with anything."

"We like to be accurate." Galbraith consulted his notebook. "According to her, the reason she's never been on *Crazy Daze* is because Steve banned you from using it the week before you met her. *'Tony trashed the boat when he was drunk,'* " he read, " *'and Steve blew his stack. He said Tony could go on using the car but* Crazy Daze *was off limits.'* " He looked up. "Why did you lie about taking Bibi on board?"

"To wipe the stupid smirk off your face, I expect. It pisses me off the way you bastards behave. You're all fascists." He hunched forward, eyes burning angrily. "I haven't forgotten you were planning to drag me through the streets in the buff even if you have."

"What's that got to do with Bibi?"

"You wanted an answer so I gave you one."

"How about this for an answer instead? You knew Bibi had been on board with Steve, so you decided to offer an explanation for why her fingerprints were there. You knew we'd find yours because you went out to *Crazy Daze* on Monday, and you thought you'd be safe pretending you and Bibi had been there together. But the only place we lifted your prints in the cabin, Tony, was on the forward hatch, while Bibi's were all over the headboard behind the bed. She likes being on top, presumably?"

He dropped his head in misery. "Fuck off."

"It must drive you up the wall the way Steve keeps stealing your girlfriends."

CHAPTER 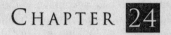 24

Maggie lowered *her aching arms and tapped pointedly on her* watch when Nick shouldered his way through the scullery door, carrying an aluminum stepladder. She was perched precariously on a garden chair on top of the kitchen table, her hair sticky with cobwebs, her rolled-up sleeves saturated with water. "What sort of time do you call this?" she demanded. "It's a quarter to ten, and I have to be up at five o'clock tomorrow morning to see to the horses."

"Good God, woman!" he declared plaintively. "A night without sleep won't kill you. Live dangerously and see how you enjoy it."

"I expected you hours ago."

"Then don't marry a policeman," he said, setting up his ladder under the uncleaned part of the ceiling.

"Chance'd be a fine thing."

He grinned up at her. "You mean you'd contemplate it?"

"Absolutely not," she said, as if offering him a challenge to even try to chat her up. "All I meant was that no policeman has ever asked me."

"He wouldn't dare." He opened the cupboard under the

sink and hunkered down to inspect it for cleaning implements and buckets. She was above him—like the rare
occasions when she met him on horseback—and she felt
an awful temptation to take advantage of the fact by dripping water onto the back of his neck. "Don't even think
about it," he said, without looking up, "or I'll leave you to
do the whole bloody lot on your own."

She chose to ignore him, preferring dignity to humiliation. "How did you get on?" she asked, stepping down
from the chair to dunk her sponge in the bucket on the
table.

"Rather well."

"I thought you must have done. Your tail's wagging."
She climbed back onto the chair. "What did Steve say?"

"You mean apart from agreeing with everything in your
statement?"

"Yes."

"He told me what he was doing at Chapman's Pool on
Sunday." He looked up at her. "He's a complete idiot, but
I don't think he's a rapist or a murderer."

"So you were wrong about him?"

"Probably."

"Good. It's bad for your character to have everything
your own way. What about pedophile?"

"It depends on your definition of pedophilia." He
swung forward a chair and straddled it, resting his elbows
along the back, content to watch her work. "He's besotted
with a fifteen-year-old girl who's so unhappy at home she
keeps threatening to kill herself. She's an absolute stunner
apparently, nearly six feet tall, looks twenty-five, ought to
be a supermodel, and turns heads wherever she goes. Her
parents are separated and fight like cat and dog—her
mother's jealous of her—her father has a string of bimbos—she's four months pregnant by Steve—refuses to
have an abortion—weeps all over his manly bosom every
time she sees him"—he lifted a sardonic eyebrow—
"which is probably why he finds her attractive—and is so
desperate to have the baby and so desperate to be loved

that she's twice tried to slit her wrists. Steve's solution to all this was to whisk her off to France in *Crazy Daze,* where they could live"—another sardonic lift of an eyebrow—"love's young dream without her parents having any idea where she'd gone or who she'd gone with."

Maggie chuckled. "I told you he was a good Samaritan."

"Bluebeard, more like. She's fifteen."

"And looks twenty-five."

"If you believe Steve."

"Don't you?"

"Put it this way," he said dispassionately, "I wouldn't let him within half a mile of a daughter of mine. He's oversexed, deeply enamored with himself, and has the morals of an alleycat."

"A bit like the weasel I married, in other words?" she asked dryly.

"No question about it." He grinned up at her. "But then I'm prejudiced, of course."

There was a glint of amusement in her eyes. "So what happened? He got sidetracked by Paul and Danny and the whole thing was deep-sixed?"

He nodded. "He realized, when he had to identify himself, that there was no point going on with it and signaled to his girlfriend to abandon it. Since then, he's had one tearful conversation with her over his mobile on his way back to Lymington on Sunday night, and hasn't been able to talk to her since because he's either been under arrest or separated from his phone. The rule is, she always calls him, and as he hasn't heard from her he's terrified she's killed herself."

"Is it true?"

"No. One of the messages on his mobile was from her."

"Still . . . poor boy. You've locked him up again, haven't you? He must be worried sick. Couldn't you have let him talk to her?"

He wondered at the vagaries of human nature. He would have bet on her sympathies being with the girl. "Not allowed."

"Oh, come on," she said crossly. "That's just cruel."

"No. Common sense. Personally, I wouldn't trust him farther than I could throw him. He's committed several crimes, don't forget. Assault on you, sex with an underage girl, conspiracy to abduct, not to mention gross indecency and committing lewd acts in public . . ."

"Oh my God! You haven't charged him with having an erection, have you?"

"Not yet."

"You *are* cruel," she said in disgust. "It was obviously his girlfriend he was looking at through the binoculars. On that basis you should have arrested Martin every time he put his hand on my arse."

"I couldn't," he said seriously. "You never objected, so it didn't constitute an assault."

There was a twinkle in her eye. "What happened to indecency?"

"I never caught him with his trousers down," he said with regret. "I did try, but he was too bloody quick every time."

"Are you winding me up?"

"No," he said. "I'm courting you."

Half asleep, Sandy Griffiths squinted at the luminous hands on her clock through gritty eyes, saw that it was three o'clock, and tried to remember if William had gone out earlier. Yet again, something had disturbed her intermittent dozing. She thought it was the front door closing, although she couldn't be sure if the sound had been real or if she'd dreamed it. She listened for footfalls on the stairs but, hearing only silence, stumbled out of bed and dragged on her dressing gown. Babies she thought she could probably cope with—a husband, *never* . . .

She switched on the landing lamp and pushed open Hannah's bedroom door. A wedge of light cut across the crib, and her alarm subsided immediately. The child sat in the concentrated immobility that seemed to be her nature, thumb in mouth, staring wide-eyed with her curiously intense gaze. If she recognized Griffiths, she didn't show it. Instead she looked through her as if her mind saw behind and beyond the woman images that had no basis in reality, and Griffiths realized she was fast asleep. It explained the crib and the locks on all the doors. They were there to protect a sleepwalker, she understood belatedly, not to deprive a conscious child of adventure.

From outside, muffled by closed doors, she heard the sound of a car starting, followed by gears engaging and the scrunch of tires on the drive. What the hell did the bloody man think he was doing now? she wondered. Did he seriously believe that abandoning his daughter in the early hours of the morning would endear him to social services? *Or was that the whole point?* Had he decided to ditch the responsibility once and for all?

Wearily she leaned against the doorjamb and studied Kate's blank-eyed, blond-haired replica with compassion and thought about what the doctor had said when he saw the smashed photographs in the fireplace. *"She's angry with her mother for deserting her . . . it's a perfectly normal expression of grief . . . get her father to cuddle her . . . that's the best way to fill the gap. . . ."*

William Sumner's disappearance raised a few eyebrows in the incident room at Winfrith when Griffiths notified them of it, but little real interest. As so often in his life, he had ceased to matter. Instead, the spotlight turned on Beatrice "Bibi" Gould, who when police knocked on her parents' door at 7:00 A.M. on Saturday morning, inviting her back to Winfrith for further questioning, burst into tears and locked herself in the bathroom, refusing to come out. When threatened with immediate arrest for obstruction, and on the promise that her parents could accompany her, she finally agreed to come out. Her fear seemed out of proportion to the police request and when asked to explain it she said, "Everyone is going to be angry with me."

Following a brief appearance before magistrates on his assault charge, Steven Harding, too, was invited for further questioning. He was chauffeured by a yawning Nick Ingram, who took the opportunity to impart a few facts of life to the immature young man at his side. "Just for the record, Steve, I'd break your legs if it was my fifteen-year-old daughter you'd got pregnant. As a matter of fact, I'd break your legs if you even laid a finger on her."

Harding was unrepentant. "Life's not like that anymore. You can't order girls to behave the way you want them to behave. They decide for themselves."

"Watch my lips, Steve. I said it's *your* legs I'd be breaking, not my daughter's. Trust me, the day I find a twenty-four-year-old man besmirching a beautiful child of mine is the day that bastard will wish he'd kept his zip done up." Out of the corner of his eye he watched words begin to form on Harding's lips. "And don't tell me she wanted it just as much as you did," he snarled, "or I'd be tempted to break your arms as well. Any little jerk can persuade a vulnerable adolescent into bed with him as long as he promises to love her. It takes a man to give her time to learn if the promise is worth anything."

Bibi Gould refused to have her father in the interview room with her, but begged for her mother to sit with her and hold her hand. On the other side of the table, Detective Superintendent Carpenter and DI Galbraith took her through her previous statement. She quailed visibly in front of Carpenter's frown, and he only had to say: "We believe you've been lying to us, young lady," for the floodgates of truth to open.

"Dad doesn't like me spending weekends at Tony's . . . says I'm making myself cheap . . . He'd have gone spare if he'd known I'd passed out. Tony said it was alcohol poisoning because I was vomiting blood, but I think it was the bad E that his friend sold him . . . I was sick for hours after I came around . . . Dad would have killed me if he'd known . . . He hates Tony . . . He thinks he's a bad influence." She laid her head on her mother's shoulder and sobbed heartily.

"When was this?" asked Carpenter.

"Last weekend. We were going to this rave in Southampton so Tony got some E from this bloke he knows . . ." She faltered to a stop.

"Go on."

"Everyone's going to be angry," she wailed. "Tony said why should we get his friend into trouble just because Steve's boat was in the wrong place."

With considerable effort Carpenter managed to smooth his frown into something approaching fatherly kindness. "We're not interested in Tony's friend, Bibi, we're only interested in getting an accurate picture of where everyone was last weekend. You've told us you're fond of Steven Harding," he said disingenuously, "and it will help Steve considerably if we can clear up some of the discrepancies around his story. You and Tony claimed you didn't see him on Saturday because you went to a rave in Southampton. Is that true?"

"It's true we didn't see him." She sniffed. "At least I didn't . . . I suppose Tony might have done . . . but it's not true about the rave. It didn't start till ten, so Tony said we might as well get in the mood earlier. The trouble is I can't remember much about it . . . We'd been drinking since five, and then I took the E . . ." She wept into her mother's shoulder again.

"For the record, Bibi, you're telling us you took an Ecstasy tablet supplied to you by your boyfriend, Tony Bridges?"

She was alarmed by his tone. "Yes," she whispered.

"Have you ever passed out before in Tony's company?"

"Sometimes . . . if I drink too much."

Pensively, Carpenter stroked his jaw. "Do you know what time you took the tablet on Saturday?"

"Seven, maybe. I can't really remember." She blew her nose into a Kleenex. "Tony said he hadn't realized how much I'd been drinking, and that if he had he wouldn't have given it to me. It was awful . . . I'm never going to drink or take Ecstasy ever again . . . I've been feeling ill all week." She raised a wan smile. "I reckon it's true what they say about it. Tony thinks I was lucky not to die."

Galbraith was less inclined to be fatherly. His private opinion of her was that she was a blowsy slut with too much baby fat and too little self-control, and he seriously pondered the mysteries of nature and chemistry that meant a girl like this could cause a previously sane man to behave with insanity. "You were drunk again on Monday," he reminded her, "when DS Campbell visited Tony's house in the evening."

She flicked him a sly up-from-under look that curdled any remnants of sympathy he might have had. "I only had two lagers," she said. "I thought they'd make me feel better—but they didn't."

Carpenter tapped his pen on the table to bring her attention back to him. "What time did you come around on Sunday morning, Bibi?"

She shrugged self-pityingly. "I don't know. Tony said I was sick for about ten hours, and I didn't stop till seven o'clock on Sunday evening. That's why I was late back to my parents'."

"So about nine o'clock on Sunday morning then?"

She nodded. "About that." She turned her wet face to her mother. "I'm ever so sorry, Mum. I'm never going to do it again."

Mrs. Gould squeezed the girl's shoulder and looked pleadingly at the two policemen. "Does this mean she'll be prosecuted?"

"What for, Mrs. Gould?"

"Taking Ecstasy?"

The superintendent shook his head. "I doubt it. As things stand, there isn't any evidence that she took any." *Rohypnol, maybe* . . . "But you're a very stupid young woman, Bibi, and I trust you won't come whining to the police with your troubles the next time you accept unknown and unidentified tablets from a man. Like it or not, you bear responsibility for your own behavior, and the best advice I can offer you is to listen to your father once in a while."

Good one, guv, thought Galbraith.

Carpenter tented his fingers over Bibi's previous statement. "I don't like liars, young woman. None of us does. I think you told another lie last night to my colleague DI Galbraith, didn't you?"

Her eyes stretched in a kind of panic, but she didn't answer.

"You said you've never been on *Crazy Daze* when we think you have."

"I haven't."

"You volunteered a set of your fingerprints at the beginning of the week. They match several sets found in the cabin of Steve's boat. Would you care to explain their presence in light of your denial that you've never been there?" He scowled at her.

"It's . . . Tony doesn't know, you see . . . oh God!" She shook with nerves. "It was just . . . Steve and I got drunk one night when Tony was away. He'd be so *hurt* if he found out . . . he's got this thing about Steve being good-looking, and it'd *kill* him if he found out that we . . . well, you know . . ."

"That you had intercourse with Steven Harding on board *Crazy Daze?*"

"We were drunk. I don't even remember much about it. It didn't *mean* anything," she said desperately, as if disloyalty could be excused when alcohol loosened inhibitions. But perhaps the concept of *in vino veritas* was too obscure for an immature nineteen-year-old to understand.

"Why are you so frightened of Tony finding out?" asked Carpenter curiously.

"I'm not." Her eyes stretched wider in a visible demonstration that she was lying.

"What does he do to you, Bibi?"

"Nothing. It's just . . . he gets really jealous some-times."

"Of Steve?"

She nodded.

"How does he show it?"

She licked her lips. "He's only done it once. He jammed my fingers in the car door after he found me in the pub with Steve. He said it was an accident, but . . . well . . . I don't think it was."

"Was that before or after you slept with Steve?"

"After."

"So he knew what you and Steve had done?"

She pressed her hands to her face. "I don't see how he could have done . . . he wasn't around for the whole week, but he's been—well, *odd*—ever since . . ."

"When did this happen?"

"Last half-term."

Carpenter consulted his diary. "Between twenty-four and thirty-one May?"

"It was a bank holiday, I know that."

"Fine." He smiled encouragingly. "Only one or two more questions, Bibi, and then we're done. Do you remember an occasion when Tony was driving you some-where in Steve's car and Kate Sumner had smeared the passenger door handle with her daughter's feces?"

She pulled an expression of disgust. "It was horrible. I got it all over my hand."

"Can you remember when that was?"

She thought about it. "I think it was the beginning of June. Tony said he'd take me to the flicks in Southampton, but I had to wash my hands so much to get all the filth off that in the end we never went."

"After you'd slept with Steve then?"

"Yes."

"Thank you. Last question. Where did Tony stay while he was away?"

"*Miles* away," she said with emphasis. "His parents

have a caravan at Lulworth Cove, and Tony always goes
there on his own when he needs to recharge his batteries. I
keep telling him he should give up teaching because he
really *hates* children. He says if he has a nervous break-
down it'll be *their* fault, even though everyone else will
say it was because he smoked too much cannabis."

Steven Harding's interview was tougher. He was
informed that Marie Freemantle had given the police a
statement about her relationship with him and that,
because of her age, he could well face charges. Nevertheless, he declined the services of a solicitor, saying he had
nothing to hide. He seemed to assume that Marie had been
questioned as a result of his off-the-record conversation
with Nick Ingram the previous evening, and neither Carpenter nor Galbraith disabused him of the fact.

"You are currently in a relationship with a fifteen-year-
old by the name of Marie Freemantle?" said Carpenter.

"Yes."

"Whom you knew to be underage when you first had
sexual intercourse with her?"

"Yes."

"Where does Marie live?"

"Fifty-four Dancer Road, Lymington."

"Why did your agent tell us you have a girlfriend called
Marie living in London?"

"Because that's where he thinks she lives. He got her
some work, and as she didn't want her parents to know
about it, we gave the address of a shop in London that acts
as a postal drop."

"What sort of work?"

"Nude work."

"Pornography?"

Harding looked uncomfortable. "Only soft porn."

"Video or stills?"

"Stills."

"Were you in the shots with her?"

"Some," he admitted.

"Where are those photographs now?"

"I dropped them over the side of my boat."

"Because they showed you performing indecent acts with an underage girl?"

"She doesn't look underage."

"Answer the question, Steve. Did you put them over the side because they showed you performing indecent acts with an underage girl?"

Harding nodded.

"For the purposes of the tape, Steven Harding nodded agreement. Did Tony Bridges know you were sleeping with Marie Freemantle?"

"What's Tony got to do with it?"

"Answer the question, Steve."

"I don't think so. I never told him."

"Did he see the photographs of her?"

"Yes. He came out to my boat on Monday, and they were on the table."

"Did he see them before Monday?"

"I don't know. He trashed my boat four months ago." He ran his tongue around his dry mouth. "He might have found them then."

Carpenter leaned back, his fingers toying with his pen. "Which would have made him angry," he said, more as a statement than a question. "She's a pupil of his and he had a fondness for her himself, albeit a hands-off one because of his position, which you knew about."

"I—er—guess so."

"We understand you met Marie Freemantle on fourteen February. Was that while you were having a relationship with Kate Sumner?"

"I didn't have a relationship with Kate." He blinked nervously, trying like Tony the night before to pre-guess the direction the questions were going. "I went back to her house one time and she kind of . . . well . . . threw herself at me. It was okay, but I've never been that keen on older women. I made it clear I wasn't interested in anything long term, and I thought she understood. It was just a quick shag in her kitchen—nothing to get excited about."

"So when Tony tells us the relationship went on for three or four months, he's lying?"

"Oh, Jesus!" Harding's nervousness increased. "Listen, I may have given him that impression. I mean I knew Kate . . . you know, as an acquaintance . . . for quite a while before we actually got it together, and I may have . . . well, given Tony the idea there was a bit more to it than there actually was. It was a joke, really. He's a bit of a prude."

Carpenter watched him for a moment before lowering his eyes to a piece of paper on the table in front of him. "Three months after meeting Marie, sometime during the week twenty-four–thirty-one May, you had a one-night stand with Bibi Gould, Tony Bridges' girlfriend. Is that right?"

Harding gave a small groan. "Oh, come on! That really *was* nothing. We got drunk in the pub and I took her back to *Crazy Daze* to sleep it off because Tony was away and his house was locked up. She came on to me a bit strong and . . . well, to be honest, I don't remember much about it. I was rat-arsed and couldn't swear that anything happened worth recording."

"Does Tony know?"

He didn't answer immediately. "I don't— Look, why do you keep going on about Tony?"

"Answer the question, please. Does Tony know that you slept with his girlfriend?"

"I don't know. He's been a bit off recently, so I've been wondering if he saw me ferrying her back to the slip the next morning." With a worried gesture, he pulled at the hair that flopped across his forehead. "He was supposed to be staying the whole week in his folks' caravan, but Bob Winterslow said he saw him that day at his granddad's place, getting ready to tow his rib out."

"Can you remember which day it was?"

"Bank-holiday Monday. Bibi's hairdressing salon

doesn't open on bank holidays, which is why she was able to stay over on Sunday night." He waited for Carpenter to speak, and when he didn't, he gave a small shrug. "Listen, it was no big deal. I planned to square it with Tony if he ever said anything"—another shrug—"but he never did."

"Does he normally say something when you sleep with his girlfriends?"

"I don't make a habit of it, for Christ's sake. The trouble is . . . well, Bibi was like Kate. You try and be nice to a woman, and the next minute they're climbing all over you."

Carpenter frowned. "Are you saying they forced you to have intercourse with them?"

"No, but—"

"Then spare me the excuses." He consulted his notes again. "How did your agent get the idea Bibi was your girlfriend?"

Harding tugged at his hair again and had the grace to look embarrassed. "Because I told him she was a bit of a goer."

"Meaning she'd be amenable to pornographic stills?"

"Yes."

"Would your agent have mentioned that to Tony?"

Harding shook his head. "If he had, Tony would have taken me apart."

"Except he didn't take you apart over Kate Sumner, did he?"

The young man was clearly baffled by the question. "Tony didn't know Kate."

"How well did *you* know her, Steve?"

"That's the crazy thing," he said. "Hardly at all . . . okay, we did it once but . . . well, it doesn't mean you get to know someone, does it? I avoided her afterward because it was embarrassing. Then she started treating me as if I'd wronged her in some way."

Carpenter pulled out Harding's statement. "You claimed she was obsessed with you, Steve. *'I knew she had a serious crush on me . . .'* " he read. " *'She used to hang around by the yacht club waiting for me to come ashore. . . . Most of the time she just stood and watched me, but sometimes she'd deliberately bump into me and rub her breasts against my arm. . . .'* Is any of that true?"

"I may have exaggerated a bit. She did hang around for about a week till she realized I wasn't interested. Then she sort of . . . well, abandoned the idea, I suppose. I didn't see her again till she did the thing with the nappy."

Carpenter sorted Tony Bridges' statement from the pile. "This is what Tony said: *'He told me on more than one occasion this year that he was having problems with a woman called Kate Sumner, who was stalking him. . . .'* Did you decide to exaggerate a bit when you told Tony?"

"Yes."

"Did you refer to Kate as a 'tart'?"

He hunched his shoulders. "It was just an expression."

"Did you tell Tony Kate was easy?"

"Listen, it was a joke. He used to have a real hang-up about sex. Everyone used to tease him, not just me . . . then Bibi came along and he . . . well, lightened up."

Carpenter studied him closely for a moment. "So did you sleep with Bibi for a joke?"

Harding stared at his hands. "I didn't do it for any particular reason. It just happened. I mean she really *was* easy. The only reason she hangs around with Tony is because she's got a thing about me. Look"—he hunched farther into his seat—"you don't want to get the wrong idea about all of this."

"What wrong idea's that, Steve?"

"I don't know, but you seem to have it in for Tony."

"With reason," said Carpenter, easing another piece of paper from the pile in front of him and hiding the contents with cupped fingers. "We've been told you watched him feed Bibi a drug called"—he lowered his eyes to the paper, as if the word were written there—*"Rohypnol* so she wouldn't complain about his performance. Is that true?"

"Oh, shit!" He rested his head in his hands. "I suppose

Marie's been spouting her mouth off?" His fingers caressed his temples in soft, circular movements, and Galbraith was fascinated by the gracefulness of his actions. He was an extraordinarily beautiful young man, and it didn't surprise him that Kate had found him more attractive than William.

"Is it true, Steve?"

"Sort of. He told me he slipped it to her once when she was giving him a load of grief, but I didn't see him do it, and for all I know he was lying through his teeth."

"How did he know about Rohypnol?"

"Everyone knows."

"Did you tell him?"

Harding lifted his head to look at the paper in front of the superintendent, clearly wondering how much information was written there. "His granddad hasn't been sleeping too well since his wife died, so the GP prescribed him Rohypnol. Tony was telling me about it, so I laughed and said it could sort all his problems if he could get hold of some of it. It's not my fault if the stupid fucker used it."

"Have you used it, Steve?"

"Do me a favor! Why would I need to?"

A faint smile crossed Carpenter's face as he changed tack. "How soon after the incident with the nappy did Kate start smearing Hannah's feces on your car and setting the alarm off?"

"I don't know. A few days, maybe."

"How did you know it was her?"

"Because she'd left Hannah's crap on the sheets in my boat."

"Which was sometime toward the end of April?" Harding nodded. "But she didn't start this"—Carpenter sought a suitable phrase—" 'dirty campaign' until after she realized you weren't interested in pursuing a relationship with her?"

"It's not my *fault*," he said despairingly. "She was . . . so . . . fucking . . . boring."

"The question I asked you, Steve," repeated Carpenter

patiently, "was did she start her 'dirty campaign' after she realized you weren't interested in her?"

"Yes." He jabbed the heels of his palms against his eyelids in an effort to recall detail. "She just made my life hell until I couldn't stand it any longer. That's when I thought of persuading William to tell her I was an arse-bandit."

The superintendent ran a finger down Harding's statement. "Which was in June?"

"Yes."

"Any particular reason why you waited a month and a half to put a stop to it?"

"Because it was getting worse not better," the young man said with a sudden rush of anger as if the memory still rankled deeply. "I thought she'd run out of steam if I was patient, but when she started targeting my dinghy, I decided enough was enough. I reckoned she'd start on *Crazy Daze* next, and there was no way I was going to let her do that."

Carpenter nodded as if he thought the explanation a reasonable one. He pulled out Harding's statement again and ran his finger down it. "So you sought out William and showed him photographs of yourself in a gay magazine because you wanted him to tell his wife you were gay?"

"Yes."

"Mmm." Carpenter reached for Tony Bridges' statement. "Tony, on the other hand, says that when you told him you were going to report Kate to the police for harassing you, he advised you to move your car instead. According to him *that's* what sorted the problem. In fact, he thought it was pretty funny when we told him last night that your solution to Kate's harassment was to show William gay pictures of yourself. He said: *'Steve always was as thick as two short planks.'* "

Harding shrugged. "So? It worked. That's all I was interested in."

Slowly, Carpenter squared the papers on the table in front of him. "Why do you think that was?" he asked. "I mean, you're not seriously suggesting that a woman who was so angry at being rejected that she was prepared to harass and intimidate you for weeks would meekly give up when she found out you were gay? Or are you? Admittedly I'm no expert in mental disorders, but I'd guess the intimidation would become markedly worse. No one likes to be made a fool of, Steve."

Harding stared at him in perplexity. "Except she *did* stop."

The superintendent shook his head. "You can't stop something you never started, son. Oh, she certainly wiped Hannah's nappy on your sheets in a moment of irritation, which probably gave Tony the idea, but it wasn't Kate who was getting her own back on you, it was your friend. It was a peculiarly apt revenge after all. You've been crapping on his doorstep for years. It must have given him a hell of a buzz to pay you back in your own coin. The only reason he stopped was because you were threatening to go to the police."

A sickly smile washed across Harding's face like wet watercolor. He looked ill, thought Carpenter with satisfaction.

William Sumner's mother had long since given up trying to induce her son to talk. Her initial surprise at his unheralded appearance in her flat had given way to fear, and like a hostage, she sought to appease and not to confront. Whatever had brought him back to Chichester was not something he wanted to share with her. He seemed to alternate between anger and anguish, rocking himself to and fro in bouts of frenetic movement only to collapse in tear-sodden lethargy when the fit passed. She was unable to help him. He guarded the telephone with the single-mindedness of a madman, and handicapped by immobility and dread, she withdrew into silent observation.

He had become a stranger to her in the last twelve months, and a kind of subdued dislike drove her toward cruelty. She found herself despising him. He had always been spineless, she thought, which was why Kate had gained such an easy ascendancy over him. Her mouth pinched into lines of contempt as she listened to the dry sobs that racked his thin frame, and when he finally broke his silence, she realized with a sense of inevitability that she could have predicted what he was going to say. ". . . I didn't know what to do . . ."

She guessed he had killed his wife. She feared now he had also killed his child.

Tony Bridges rose to his feet as the cell door opened and viewed Galbraith with an uneasy smile. He was diminished by incarceration, a small, insignificant man who had discovered what it meant to have his life controlled by others. Gone was the cocksure attitude of yesterday, in its place a nervous recognition that his ability to persuade had been blunted by the stone wall of police distrust. "How long are you going to keep me here?"

"As long as it takes, Tony."

"I don't know what you want from me."

"The truth."

"All I did was steal a boat."

Galbraith shook his head. He fancied he saw a momentary regret in the frightened gaze that briefly met his before he stood back to let the young man pass. It was remorse of a kind, he supposed.

. . . I didn't mean to do it. I didn't do it—not really. Kate would still be alive if she hadn't tried to push me over the side. It's her fault she's dead. We were getting on fine until she made a lunge at me, then the next thing I knew she was in the water. You can't blame me for that. Don't you think I'd have drowned Hannah too if I'd intended to kill her mother . . . ?

CHAPTER 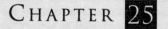 25

Broxton House slumbered peacefully in the afternoon sunshine as Nick Ingram pulled up in front of the porticoed entrance. As always he paused to admire its clean, square lines and, as always, regretted its slow deterioration. To him, perhaps more than to the Jenners, it represented something valuable, a living reminder that beauty existed in everything; but then he, despite his job, was enduringly sentimental, and they were not. The double doors stood wide open, an invitation to any passing thief, and he picked up Celia's handbag from the hall table as he passed on his way to the drawing room. Silence lay across the house like a blanket of dust, and he worried suddenly that he had come too late. Even his own footfalls on the marble floor were just a whisper in the great emptiness that surrounded him.

He eased open the drawing-room door and stepped inside. Celia was propped up in bed, bifocals slipping off the end of her nose, mouth open, snoring quietly, with Bertie's head on the pillow beside her. They looked like a tableau out of *The Godfather,* and Nick was hard-pushed not to laugh out loud. The sentimentalist in him viewed them fondly. Maybe Maggie was right, he thought. Maybe happiness was more to do with bodily contact than with hygiene. Who cared about tannin in teacups when you had a hairy hot-water bottle who was prepared to lie with you and love you when no one else would? He tapped lightly on one of the door panels and watched with amusement as Bertie opened a cautious eye then closed it again in obvious relief when he realized Nick wasn't going to make any demands on his loyalty.

"I'm not asleep, you know," said Celia, raising a hand to adjust her spectacles. "I heard you come in."

"Am I disturbing you?"

"No." She hoisted herself into a more upright position, tugging her bedjacket across her chest in a belated attempt to safeguard her dignity.

"You shouldn't leave your bag on the hall table," he told her, walking across to put it on the bed. "Anyone could steal it."

"They're welcome to it, my dear. There's nothing in it worth taking." She examined him closely. "I prefer you in uniform. Dressed like that, you look like a gardener."

"I said I'd help Maggie with the painting, and I can't paint in my uniform." He pulled forward a chair. "Where is she?"

"Where you told her to be. In the kitchen." She sighed. "I worry about her, Nick. I didn't bring her up to be a manual laborer. She'll have builder's hands before she's finished."

"She already has. You can't muck out stables and scrub horse buckets day after day and keep your hands pretty. The two are mutually exclusive."

She tut-tutted disapprovingly. "A gentleman doesn't notice that kind of thing."

He'd always been fond of her. He didn't know why, except that her forthright approach appealed to him. Perhaps she reminded him of his own mother, a down-to-earth Cockney, who had been dead for ten years. Certainly he found people who spoke their minds easier to get on with than those who cloaked their feelings in hypocritical smiles. "He probably does, you know. He just doesn't mention it."

"But that's the whole point, you silly fellow," she said crossly. "A gentleman is known by his manners."

He grinned. "So you prefer a man who lies to a man who is honest? That's not the impression you gave me four years ago when Robert Healey did his bunk."

"Robert Healey was a criminal."

"But an attractive one."

She frowned at him. "Have you come here to annoy me?"

"No, I came to see if you were all right."

She waved a hand in dismissal. "Well, I am. Go and find Maggie. I'm sure she'll be pleased to see you."

He made no move to go. "Were either of you ever called as a witness in Healey's trial?" he asked her.

"You know we weren't. He was tried only for his last fraud. All the rest of us had to take a backseat in case we confused the issue, and that made me more angry than anything. I wanted my day in court so that I could tell the little beast what I thought of him. I was never going to get my money back, but at least I could have taken my pound of flesh." She folded her arms across her chest like armor plating. "However, it's not a subject I wish to dwell on. It's unhealthy to rake over the past."

"Did you read the reports of the trial?" he went on, ignoring her.

"One or two," she said curtly, "until I gave up in fury."

"What made you furious?"

A small tic started above her lip. "They described his victims as lonely women, desperate for love and attention. I've never been so incensed about anything. It made us look such fools."

"But your case wasn't tried," he pointed out, "and that description applied to his last victims—two elderly unmarried sisters who lived alone in an isolated farmhouse in Cheshire. A perfect target for Healey, in other words. It was only because he tried to speed up the fraud by forging their names on checks that he was discovered. The sisters' bank manager was worried enough to go to the police."

The tic fluttered on. "Except I sometimes think it was true," she said with difficulty. "I never thought of us as lonely, but we did rather blossom when he came into our lives, and I'm humiliated every time I remember it."

Ingram reached into the back pocket of his jeans and pulled out a newspaper clipping. "I brought something I want to read to you. It's what the judge told Healey before he passed sentence." He smoothed the paper on his lap. " 'You're an educated man with a high IQ and an engaging manner,' " he read, " 'and these qualities make you extremely dangerous. You display a ruthless disregard for your victims' feelings while at the same time exercising considerable charm and intelligence to convince them of your sincerity. Too many women have been taken in by you for anyone to believe that their' "—he stressed the word—" 'gullibility was the only reason for your success, and I am persuaded that you represent a real menace to society.' " He laid the clipping on the bed. "What the judge recognized is that Healey was a charming and intelligent man."

"It was pretense," she said, reaching for the comfort of Bertie's ears and tugging at them. "He was an actor."

Ingram thought of Steven Harding's very moderate acting skills, and shook his head. "I don't think so," he said gently. "No one could keep up a pretense like that for a year. The charm was genuine, which is what you and Maggie were attracted by, and it seems to me that the problem you both have is coming to terms with that. It makes his betrayal so much worse if you liked him."

"No." She pulled a tissue from under her pillow and blew her nose. "What upsets me more is that I thought he liked us. We're not so difficult to love, are we?"

"Not at all. I'm sure he adored you both. Everyone else does."

"Oh, don't be absurd!" Celia snapped. "He wouldn't have stolen from us if he had."

"Of course he would." Ingram propped his chin in his hands and stared at her. "The trouble with you, Mrs. J, is that you're a conformist. You assume everyone does and should behave the same way. But Healey was a professional con man. Theft was his business. He'd made a ten-year career out of it, don't forget. That doesn't mean he wasn't fond of you, any more than it would mean I wasn't fond of you if I had to arrest you." His mouth twitched into a crooked smile. "We do what we're good at in this life if we don't want to starve, and we cry all the way to the bank if it upsets us."

"That's nonsense."

"Is it? Do you think I take pleasure arresting a ten-year-old kid for vandalism when I know he comes from a lousy home, is truant because he can't read, and is likely to get a belting from his drunken mother because she's too stupid to deal with him in any other way? I caution the boy because that's what I'm paid to do, but I'm always a damn sight fonder of him than I am of his mother. Criminals are human like everyone else, and there's no law that says they aren't likable."

She peered at him over her bifocals. "Yes, but *you* didn't like Martin, Nick, so don't pretend you did."

"No, I didn't," he admitted, "but it was a personal thing. I thought the guy was a grade-A jerk. If I'm honest, though, I never believed for one moment that Mrs. Fielding was telling the truth when she accused him of trying to steal her antiques. As far as I was concerned he was whiter than white . . . bloody perfect, in fact . . . every young woman's dream." The smile became even more crooked. "I assumed—and still do because it didn't fit Healey's MO—that it was Mrs. Fielding's senility talking, and the only reason I came to you about it was because I couldn't resist the opportunity to take him down a peg or two." He raised his eyes to hers. "It certainly didn't give me any insights into what he was really up to. Even when Simon

Farley told me he'd passed a couple of dud checks in the pub and asked me to get it sorted quietly because he didn't want any fuss, it never occurred to me that Martin was a professional. If it had, I'd have approached it differently, and maybe you wouldn't have lost your money and maybe your husband would still be alive."

"Oh, for God's sake!" she said gruffly, pulling so hard on Bertie's ears that the poor animal furrowed his brow in pain. "Don't you start feeling guilty, too."

"Why not? If I'd been older and wiser I might have done my job better."

With an uncharacteristic display of tenderness, she laid a hand on his shoulder. "I have enough trouble coping with my own guilt without carrying yours and Maggie's as well. According to Maggie, her father dropped dead because she was shouting at him. *My* recollection is that he threw a two-week tantrum then dropped dead after a drinking bout in his study. If my son is to be believed, he died of a broken heart because Maggie and I treated him like a cipher in his own house." She sighed. "The truth is Keith was a chronic alcoholic with a history of heart disease who could have died at any moment, although clearly Martin's shenanigans didn't help. And it wasn't as though it was Keith's money that was stolen. It was mine. My father left me ten thousand in his will twenty years ago, and I managed to work it up to over a hundred thousand by playing the stock market." She frowned in irritation at the memory before giving Ingram's shoulder a sudden sharp rap. "This is ridiculous. When all's said and done, the only person to blame is Robert Healey, and I refuse to let anyone else take responsibility."

"Does that include you and Maggie, or are you going to go on wearing sackcloth and ashes so that the rest of us feel guilty by association?"

She regarded him thoughtfully for a moment. "I was right about you yesterday," she said. "You are a *very* provoking young man." She flapped a hand toward the hall. "Go away and make yourself useful. Help my daughter."

"She's doing a fine job on her own. I'll probably just stand back and watch."

"I wasn't talking about painting the kitchen," Celia retorted.

"Neither was I, but the answer's still the same."

She peered at him blankly for a moment, then gave a throaty chuckle. "On the principle that everything comes to him who waits?"

"It's worked up till now," he said, reaching for one of her hands and holding it lightly. "You're a gutsy lady, Mrs. J. I always wanted to know you better."

"Oh, for goodness sake, get on with you!" she said, smacking him away. "I'm beginning to think Robert Healey was a novice compared with you." She wagged a finger at him. "And don't call me Mrs. J. It's appallingly *infra dig* and makes me sound like a cleaner." She closed her eyes and took a deep breath as if she were about to bestow the crown jewels on him. "You may call me Celia."

". . . I couldn't think properly, that was the trouble . . . if she'd just listened to me instead of shouting all the time . . . I suppose what surprised me was how strong she was . . . I wouldn't have broken her fingers otherwise . . . it was easy . . . they were tiny, like little wishbones, but it's not the kind of thing a man wants to do . . . put it this way, I'm not proud of it . . ."

Nick found Maggie in the kitchen, arms crossed, staring out of the window at the horses in the drought-starved paddock. The ceiling had received a coat of brilliant white emulsion but none of the walls had yet been touched, and the paint roller had been abandoned to harden in the tray. "Look at those poor brutes," she said. "I think I'm going to phone the RSPCA and have their beastly owners prosecuted."

He knew her too well. "What's really bugging you?"

She swung around defiantly. "I heard it all," she said. "I was listening outside the door. I suppose you thought you were being clever?"

"In what way?"

"Martin took the trouble to seduce Mother before he seduced me," she said. "At the time I was impressed by his tactics. Afterward, I decided it was the one thing that should have warned me he was a cheat and a liar."

"Perhaps he found her easier to get on with," Nick suggested mildly. "She's good news, your ma. And, for the record, I have no intention of seducing you. It'd be like fighting my way through half a mile of razor wire— painful, unrewarding, and bloody hard work."

She favored him with a twisted smile. "Well, don't expect *me* to seduce *you*," she said tartly, "because you'll be waiting forever if you do."

He prized the paint roller out of the tray and held it under a running tap in the sink. "Trust me. Nothing is further from my mind. I'm far too frightened of having my jaw broken."

"Martin didn't have a problem."

"No," he said dryly. "But then Martin wouldn't have had a problem with the Elephant Man as long as there was money in it. Does your mother have a scrubbing brush? We need to remove the hardened paint from this tray."

"You'll have to look in the scullery." She watched in an infuriated silence while he scrabbled around among four years' detritus in search of cleaning implements. "You're such a hypocrite," she said then. "You've just spent half an hour boosting Ma's self-esteem by telling her how lovable she is, but I get compared with the Elephant Man."

There was a muffled laugh. "Martin didn't sleep with your mother."

"What difference does that make?"

He emerged with a bucket full of impacted rags. "I'm having trouble with the fact that you sleep with a dog," he said severely. "I'm buggered if I'll turn a blind eye to a weasel as well."

There was a brief silence before Maggie gave a splutter of laughter. "Bertie's in bed with Ma at the moment."

"I know. He's about the worst guard dog I've ever encountered." He took the bundle of cloth out of the bucket and held it up for inspection. "What the hell is this?"

More laughter. "They're my father's Y-fronts, you idiot. Ma uses them instead of J-cloths because they don't cost anything."

"Oh, right." He put the bucket in the sink to fill it with water. "I can see the logic. He was a big fellow, your dad. There's enough material here to cover a three-piece suite." He separated out a pair of striped boxer shorts. "Or a deckchair," he finished thoughtfully.

Her eyes narrowed suspiciously. "Don't even think about using my father's underpants to seduce me, you bastard, or I'll empty that entire bucket over your head."

He grinned at her. "This isn't seduction, Maggie, this is courtship. If I wanted to seduce you I'd have brought several bottles of brandy with me." He wrung out the boxer shorts and held them up for inspection. "However . . . if you think these would be effective . . . ?"

". . . Most of the time it's just me, the boat, and the sea . . . I like that . . . I feel comfortable with space around me . . . people can get on your nerves after a while . . . they always want something from you . . . usually love . . . but it's all pretty shallow . . . Marie? She's okay . . . nothing great . . . sure I feel responsible for her, but not forever . . . nothing's forever . . . except the sea . . . and death . . ."

CHAPTER 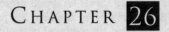 26

John Galbraith paused beside William Sumner's car in the Chichester street and stooped to look in through the window. The weather was still fair, and the heat from the sun-baked roof warmed his face. He walked up the path toward Angela Sumner's flat and rang the doorbell. He waited for the chain to rattle into place. "Good afternoon, Mrs. Sumner," he said when her bright eyes peered anxiously through the gap. "I think you must have William in there." He gestured toward the parked car. "May I talk to him?"

With a sigh, she released the chain and pulled the door wide. "I wanted to phone you, but he pulled the wire out of the wall when I suggested it."

Galbraith nodded. "We've tried your number several times, but there was never any answer. If the phone wasn't plugged in, that explains it. I thought I'd come anyway."

She turned her chair to lead him down the corridor. "He keeps saying he didn't know what to do. Does that mean he killed her?"

Galbraith laid a comforting hand on her shoulder. "No," he said. "Your son isn't a murderer, Mrs. Sumner. He loved Kate. I think he'd have given her the earth if she'd asked him for it."

They paused in the sitting-room doorway. William sat huddled in an armchair, arms wrapped protectively about himself and the telephone in his lap, his jaw dark with stubble and his eyes red-rimmed and puffy from too much weeping and too little sleep. Galbraith studied him with concern, recognizing that he bore some of the responsibility for pushing him toward the brink. He could excuse his prying into William's and Kate's secrets on the grounds of justice, but it was a cold logic. He could have been kinder, he thought—one could always be kinder—but, sadly, kindness rarely elicited truth.

He squeezed Angela Sumner's shoulder. "Perhaps you could make us a cup of tea," he suggested, moving aside for her wheelchair to reverse. "I'd like to have a few words with William alone, if that's possible."

She nodded gratefully. "I'll wait till you call me."

He closed the door behind her and listened to the whine of the battery fading into the kitchen. "We've caught Kate's killer, William," he said, taking the seat opposite the man. "Steven Harding has been formally charged with her abduction, rape, and murder, and will be remanded to prison shortly to await trial. I want to stress that Kate was not a party to what happened to her, but on the contrary fought hard to save herself and Hannah." He paused briefly to search William's face but went on when there was no reaction. "I'm not going to pretend she didn't have sex with Steven Harding prior to the events of last week, because she did. However, it was a brief affair some months ago, and followed a prolonged campaign by Harding to break her down. Nevertheless—and this is important"—he glossed the truth deliberately in Kate's favor—"it's clear she made up her mind very quickly to put an end to the relationship when she recognized that her marriage was more important to her than a mild infatuation with a younger man. Her misfortune was her failure to recognize that Steven Harding is self-fixated and dangerously immature and that she needed to be afraid of him." Another pause. "She was lonely, William."

A strangled sob issued from the other man's mouth. "I've been hating her so much . . . I knew he was more than a casual acquaintance when she said she didn't want him in the house anymore. She used to flirt with him at the beginning, then she turned vicious and started calling him names. . . . I guessed he'd got bored with her. . . ."

"Is that when he showed you the photographs?"

"Yes."

"Why did he do that, William?"

"He said he wanted me to show them to Kate but . . ." He lifted a trembling hand to his mouth.

Galbraith recalled something Tony had said the previous evening. *The only reason Steve does pornography is because he knows it's inadequate guys who're going to look at it. He doesn't have any hang-ups about sex, so it gives him a buzz to think of them squirming over pictures of him. . . .*

"But he really wanted to show them to you?"

Sumner nodded. "He wanted to prove that Kate would sleep with anyone—even a man who preferred other men—rather than sleep with me." Tears streamed down his face. "I think she must have told him I wasn't very good. I said I didn't want to see the pictures, so he put the magazine on the table in front of me and told me to"—he struggled with the words, closing his eyes in pain, as if to blot out the memory—" 'suck on it.' "

"Did he say he'd slept with Kate?"

"He didn't need to. I knew when Hannah let him pick her up in the street that something was going on . . . she's never let me do that." More tears squeezed from his tired eyes.

"What *did* he say, William?"

He plucked at his mouth. "That Kate was making his life hell by smearing Hannah's nappies on his possessions, and that if I didn't make her stop he'd go to the police."

"And you believed him?"

"Kate was—like that," he said with a break in his voice. "She could be spiteful when she didn't get her own way."

"Did you show her the magazine?"

"No."

"What did you do with it?"

"Kept it in my car."

"Why?"

"To look at . . . remember . . ." He rested his head against the back of the chair and stared at the ceiling. "Have something to hate, I suppose."

"Did you tackle Kate about it?"

"There was no point. She'd have lied."

"So what did you do?"

"Nothing," he said simply. "Went on as if nothing had happened. Stayed late at work . . . sat in my study . . . avoided her . . . I couldn't *think,* you see. I kept wondering if the baby was mine." He turned to look at the policeman. "Was it?"

Galbraith leaned forward and clamped his hands between his knees. "The pathologist estimated the fetus at fourteen weeks, making conception early May, but Kate's affair with Harding finished at the end of March. I can ask the pathologist to run a DNA test if you want absolute proof, but I don't think there's any doubt Kate was carrying your son. She didn't sleep around, William." He paused to let the information sink in. "But there's no doubt Steven Harding accused her wrongly of harassment. Yes, she lashed out once in a moment of pique, but probably only because she was annoyed with herself for having given in to him. The real culprit was a friend of Harding's. Kate rejected him, so he used her as a shield for his own revenge without ever considering the sort of danger he might be putting her into."

"I never thought he'd do anything to her . . . Jesus! Do you think I wanted her killed? She was a sad person . . . lonely . . . boring. . . . God, if she had anything going for her she kept it well hidden. . . . Look, I know this sounds

bad—I'm not proud of it now—but I found it funny the way Steve reacted. He was shit-scared of her. That stuff about dodging around corners was all true. He thought she was going to attack him in the middle of the street if she managed to catch him unawares. He kept talking about the movie Fatal Attraction, *and saying Michael Douglas' mistake was not to let the Glenn Close character die when she tried to kill herself."*

"Why didn't you tell us this before?" Carpenter had asked.

"Because you have to believe someone's guilty before you get yourself into trouble. In a million years I wouldn't have thought Steve had anything to do with it. He doesn't go in for violence."

"Try violation instead," Carpenter had said. *"Offhand, can you think of anything or anyone your friend has* not *violated? Hospitality . . . friendship . . . marriage . . . women . . . young girls . . . every bloody law you can think of . . . Did it never occur to you, Tony, that someone so intensely sociopathic as Steven Harding, so careless of other people's sensibilities, might represent a danger to a woman he thought had been terrorizing him?"*

Sumner continued to stare at the ceiling, as if answers lay somewhere within its white surface. "How did he get her onto his boat if she wasn't interested anymore?" he asked flatly. "You said no one had seen her with him after he spoke to her outside Tesco's."

"She smiled at me as if nothing had happened," Harding had told them, *"asked me how I was and how the acting was going. I said she had a bloody nerve even talking to me after what she'd done, and she just laughed and told me to grow up. 'You did me a favor,' she said. 'You taught me to appreciate William, and if I don't hold any grudges, why should you?' I told her she knew fucking well why I held a grudge, so she started to look cross. 'It was payment in kind,' she said. 'You were crap.' Then she walked away. I think that's what made me angry—I hate it when people walk away from me—but I knew the woman in Tesco's was*

watching, so I crossed High Street and went down behind the market stalls on the other side of the road, watching her. All I planned to do was have it out with her, tell her she was lucky I hadn't gone to the police . . ."

"Saturday's market day in Lymington High Street," said Galbraith, "so the place was packed with visitors from outside. People don't notice things in a crowd. He followed her at a distance, waiting for her to turn toward home again."

"She looked pretty angry, so I think I must have upset her. She turned down Captain's Row, so I knew she was probably going home. I gave her a chance, you know. I thought if she took the top road I'd let her go, but if she took the bottom road past the yacht club and Tony's garage I'd teach her a lesson. . . ."

"He has the use of a garage about two hundred yards from your house," Galbraith went on. "He caught up with her as she was passing it and persuaded her and Hannah to go inside. She'd been in several times before with Harding's friend Tony Bridges, so it obviously didn't occur to her there was anything to worry about."

"Women are such stupid bitches. They'll fall for anything as long as a bloke sounds sincere. All I had to do was tell her I was sorry and squeeze a couple of tears out—I'm an actor so I'm good at that—and she was all smiles again and said, no, she was sorry, she hadn't meant to be cruel and couldn't we let bygones be bygones and stay friends? So I said, sure, and why didn't I give her some champagne out of Tony's garage to show there were no hard feelings? You can drink it with William, I said, as long as you don't tell him it came from me. If there'd been anyone in the street or if old Mr. Bridges had been at his curtains, I wouldn't have done it. But it was so bloody easy. Once I'd closed the garage doors, I knew I could do anything I wanted. . . ."

"You need to remember how little she knew about him, William. According to Harding himself, her entire knowledge of him came from two months of constant flattery and attention while he wanted to get her into bed, a brief period of unsatisfactory lovemaking on both sides which resulted in *him* giving her the cold shoulder and *her* taking petty revenge with Hannah's nappy on his cabin sheets, then four months of mutual avoidance. As far as she was concerned, it was ancient history. She didn't know his car was being daubed with feces, didn't know he'd approached you and told you to warn her off, so when she accepted a glass of champagne in the garage, she genuinely thought it was the peace offering he said it was."

"If she hadn't told me William was away for the weekend I wouldn't have gone through with it, but you kind of get the feeling that some things are meant to happen. It was her fault really. She kept on about how she had nothing to go home for, so I offered her a drink. If I'm honest, I'd say she was up for it. You could tell she was pleased as bloody punch to find herself alone with me. Hannah wasn't a problem. She's always liked me. I'm about the only person, other than her mother, who could pick her up without her screaming. . . ."

"He put her to sleep, using a benzodiazepine hypnotic drug called Rohypnol, which he dissolved in the champagne. It's been called the date-rape drug because it's easy to give to a woman without her knowing. It's powerful enough to keep her out for six to ten hours, and in the cases reported so far, women claim intermittent periods of consciousness when they know what's happening to them but an inability to do anything about it. We understand there are moves to change it to a schedule-three controlled drug in 1998, add a blue dye to it, and make it harder to dissolve, but at the moment it's open to abuse."

"Tony keeps his drug supplies in the garage, or did until he heard you'd arrested me, then he went in and cleared the whole lot out. He'd taken the Rohypnol off his granddad when the poor old bugger kept falling asleep during the daytime. He found him in the kitchen once with

the gas going full blast because he'd nodded off before he had time to put a match to it. Tony was going to chuck the Rohypnol out but I told him it could do him some good with Bibi so he kept it. It worked like a treat on Kate. She went out like a light. The only problem was, she let Hannah drink some of the champagne as well, and when Hannah went out she fell over backward with her eyes wide open. I thought she was dead. . . ."

"He's very unclear what he was intending to do to Kate. He talks about teaching her a lesson but whether the intention was always to rape her then kill her, he can't or won't say."

"I wasn't going to hurt Kate, just give her something to think about. She'd been pissing me off with the crap thing, and it had been really bugging me. Still, I had to have a rethink when Hannah keeled over. That was pretty frightening, you know. I mean, killing a kid, even if it was an accident, is heavy stuff. I thought about leaving them both there while I scarpered to France with Marie, but I was afraid Tony might find them before I met up with her, and I'd already told him I was going to Poole for the weekend. I guess it was the fact that Kate was so small that made me think about taking them both with me. . . ."

"He took them on board under everyone's noses," said Galbraith. "Just motored *Crazy Daze* into one of the visitors' pontoons near the yacht club and carried Kate on in the canvas holdall that takes his dinghy when it's not in use. They're substantial items, apparently, big enough to take eight feet of collapsed rubber, plus the seat and the floorboarding, and he says he had no trouble folding Kate into it. He took Hannah on board in his rucksack and carried the buggy quite openly under his arm."

"People never question anything if you're up-front about what you're doing. I guess it has something to do with the British psyche, and the fact we never interfere unless we absolutely have to. But you kind of want them to sometimes. It's almost as if you're being forced to do things you don't really want to do. I kept saying to myself,

ask me what's in the bag, you bastards, ask me why I'm carrying a baby's buggy under my arm. But no one did, of course. . . ."

"Then he left for Poole," said Galbraith. "The time was getting on for midday by then, and he says he hadn't thought what he was going to do beyond smuggling Kate and Hannah aboard. He talks about being stressed out and being unable to think properly"—he raised his eyes to Sumner—"rather like your description of yourself earlier, and it does seem as if he opted to do nothing, left them imprisoned and unconscious inside the bags on the principle of out of sight out of mind."

"I guess I'd realized all along I was going to have to dump them over the side, but I kept putting it off. I'd sailed out into the Channel to get some space around me, and it was around seven o'clock when I hauled them up on deck to get it over with. I couldn't do it, though. I could hear whimpering coming out of the rucksack, so I knew Hannah was still alive. I felt good about that. I never wanted to kill either of them. . . ."

"He claims Kate started to come around at about seven thirty, which is when he released her and let her sit beside him in the cockpit. He also claims it was her idea to take her clothes off. However, in view of the fact that her wedding ring is also missing, we think the truth is he decided to strip her body of anything that could identify her before he threw her overboard."

"I know she was frightened, and I know she probably did it to try to get into my good graces, but I never asked her to strip and I never forced her to have sex with me. I'd already made up my mind to take them back. I wouldn't have altered course otherwise, and she'd never have ended up in Egmont Bight. I gave her something to eat because she said she was hungry. Why would I do that if I was going to kill her . . . ?"

"I know this is distressing for you, William, but we believe he spent hours fantasizing about what he was going to do with her before he killed her, and when he'd stripped her he went ahead and played out those fantasies. However, we don't know how conscious Kate was or how much she knew about what was going on. One of the difficulties we have is that *Crazy Daze* shows no recent signs of Kate and Hannah being on board. What we think happened is that he kept Kate naked on the deck for about five hours between seven thirty and half past midnight which would explain the evidence of hypothermia and the lack of forensic evidence connecting her with the interior. We're still looking for evidence on the topsides but I'm afraid he had hours during the trip back to Lymington on Sunday to scrub the deck clean with buckets of salt water."

"Okay, I was way out of line at the beginning, I'll admit that. Things got out of control for a while—I mean I panicked like hell when I thought Hannah was dead—but by the time it was dark I'd got it all worked out. I told Kate that if she promised to keep her mouth shut I'd take her to Poole and let her and Hannah off there. Otherwise, I'd say she came on board willingly, and as Tony Bridges knew she had the hots for me, no one would believe her word against mine, particularly not William. . . ."

"He says he promised to take Kate to Poole, and she may have believed him, but we don't think he had any intention of doing it. He's a good sailor, yet he steered a course that brought him back to land to the west of St. Alban's Head when he should have been well to the east. He's arguing that he lost track of his position because Kate kept distracting him, but it's too much of a coincidence that he put her into the sea where he did, bearing in mind he was planning to walk there the next morning."

"She should have trusted me. I told her I wasn't going to hurt her. I didn't hurt Hannah, did I . . . ?"

"He says she lunged at him and tried to push him overboard, and in the process went over herself."

"I could hear her shouting and thrashing about in the water, so I brought the helm around to try and locate her. But it was so dark I couldn't see a damn thing. I kept calling to her but it all went silent very quickly and in the

end I had to give up. I don't think she could swim very well. . . ."

"He's claiming he made every attempt to find her but thinks she must have drowned within a few minutes. He refers to it as a terrible accident."

"Of course it was a coincidence we were off Chapman's Pool. It was pitch black, for Christ's sake, and there's no lighthouse at St. Alban's Head. Have you any idea what it's like sailing at night when there's nothing to tell you where you are? I hadn't been concentrating, hadn't taken the tidal drift and wind changes into account. I was pretty sure I'd sailed too far west which is why I altered course to sail due east, but it wasn't until I came within sight of the Anvil Point lighthouse that I had any idea I was within striking distance of Poole. Look, don't you think I'd have killed Hannah as well if I'd meant to kill Kate . . . ?"

When Galbraith fell silent, Sumner finally dragged his gaze away from the ceiling. "Is that what he'll say in court? That she died by accident?"

"Probably."

"Will he win?"

"Not if you stand up for her."

"Maybe he's telling the truth," said the other man listlessly.

Galbraith smiled slightly. Kindness *was* a mug's game. "Don't ever say that in my presence again, William," he said with a rasp in his throat. "Because, so help me God, I'll beat the fucking daylights out of you if you do. I saw your wife, remember. I wept for her before you even knew she was dead."

Sumner blinked in alarm.

Galbraith straightened. "The bastard drugged her, raped her—several times we think—broke her fingers because she attempted to release her daughter from the rucksack, then put his hands around her neck and throttled her. But she wouldn't die. So he tied her to a spare outboard his friend had given him and set her adrift in a partially inflated dinghy." He thumped his fist into his palm. "Not to give her a chance of life, William, but to make sure she died slowly and in fear, tormenting herself about what he was going to do to Hannah and regretting that she'd ever dared to take revenge on him."

"The kid never cried once after I took her out of the rucksack. She wasn't frightened of me. As a matter of fact I think she felt sorry for me because she could see I was upset. I wrapped her in a blanket and laid her on the floor in the cabin, and she went to sleep. I might have panicked if she'd started crying in the marina, but she didn't. She's a funny kid. I mean she's obviously not very bright, but you get the feeling she knows things. . . ."

"I don't know why he didn't kill Hannah, except that he seems to be afraid of her. He says now that the fact she's alive is proof he didn't want Kate to die either, and he may have decided that as she was never going to be a threat to him he could afford to let her live. He says he changed her, fed her, and gave her something to drink from the bag that was on the back of the buggy, then took her off the boat in his rucksack. He left her asleep in the front garden of a block of flats on the Bournemouth-to-Poole road, a good mile from Lilliput, and seems to be more shocked than anyone that she was allowed to walk all the way back to the marina before anyone questioned why she was on her own."

"There was some paracetamol in the buggy bag, so I dosed her up with it to make sure she was asleep when I took her off the boat. Not that I really needed to. I reckon the Rohypnol was still working, because I sat and watched her in the cabin for hours and she only woke up once. There's no way she could have known where Salterns Marina was, so how the hell did she find her way back to it? I kept telling you she was weird. But you wouldn't believe me. . . ."

"On the trip back to Lymington he put everything overboard that could connect him in any way at all with Kate and Hannah—the dinghy holdall, Kate's clothes, her ring, the buggy, Hannah's dirty nappy, the rug he wrapped her in—but he forgot the sandals that Kate left behind in April." Galbraith smiled slightly. "Although the odd thing is he says he did remember them. He took them out of a locker after he left Hannah asleep on the cabin floor and put them in the buggy bag, and he says now that the only person who could have hidden them under the pile of clothes was Hannah."

"I got sidetracked worrying about fingerprints. I couldn't make up my mind whether to clean the inside of Crazy Daze *or not. You see, I knew you'd find Kate and Hannah's fingerprints from when they were on board in April, and I wondered if it would be better to pretend that visit had never happened. In the end I decided to leave it exactly the way it's been for the last three months because I didn't want you lot imagining I'd done something worse than I had. And I was right, wasn't I? You wouldn't have released me on Wednesday if you'd found any evidence that I set out to hurt Kate the way you're saying I did. . . ."*

Sumner's eyes welled again but he didn't say anything.

"Why didn't you tell me Kate and Harding had had an affair?" Galbraith asked him.

It was a moment before William answered and, when he did, he lifted a trembling hand in supplication, like a beggar after charity. "I was ashamed."

"For Kate?"

"No," he whispered, "for myself. I didn't want anyone to know."

To know what? Galbraith wondered. That he couldn't keep his wife interested? That he'd made a mistake marrying her? He reached over and took the telephone from Sumner's lap. "If you're interested, Sandy Griffiths says Hannah's been walking around the house all day, looking for you. I asked Sandy to tell her I'd be bringing you home, and Hannah clapped her hands. Don't make a liar out of me, my friend."

He shook with grief. "I thought she'd be better off without me."

"No chance." He raised the man to his feet with a hand under his arm. "You're her father. How could she possibly be better off without you?"

CHAPTER  27

Maggie lay on the floor stretching her aching back while Nick meticulously poked a loaded paintbrush into all the nooks and crannies that she'd missed. "Do you think Steve would have done it if Tony Bridges hadn't wound him up by smearing crap all over the place?"

"I don't know," said Nick. "The superintendent's convinced he's an out-and-out psychopath, says it was only a matter of time before his obsession with sex spilled over into rape, so maybe he'd have done it anyway, with or without Tony Bridges. I suppose the truth is Kate was in the wrong place at the wrong time." He paused, remembering the tiny hand waving in the spume. "Poor woman."

"Still . . . does Tony walk away scot-free? That's hardly fair, is it? I mean he must have known Steve was guilty."

Nick shrugged. "Claims he didn't, claims he thought it was the husband." He dabbed gently at a spider and watched it scurry away into the shadows. "Galbraith told me he and Carpenter hung Tony up to dry last night for keeping quiet the first time they interviewed him, and Tony's excuse was that Kate was such a bitch he didn't see why he should help the police screw her husband. He reckoned Kate got what she deserved for spouting off about the poor bastard's performance. He has trouble on that front himself, apparently, so his sympathies were with William."

"And this man's a *teacher?*" she said in disgust.

"Not for much longer," Nick reassured her, "unless his fellow inmates have a yen for chemistry. Carpenter's thrown the book at him—perverting the course of justice, supplying drugs, false imprisonment of his girlfriend, rape of said girlfriend under the influence of Rohypnol, incitement to murder . . . even"—he chuckled—"criminal damage to Harding's car . . . and that's not to mention whatever Customs and Excise chooses to throw at him."

"Serves him right," said Maggie unsympathetically.

"Mmm."

"You don't sound convinced."

"Only because I can't see what prison will do for someone like Tony. He's not a bad guy, just a misguided one. Six months' community service in a home for the disabled would do him more good." He watched the spider sink into a pool of wet emulsion. "On a scale of one to ten, spasmodic impotence doesn't even register compared with severe physical or mental handicap."

Maggie sat up and clasped her arms about her knees. "I thought policemen were supposed to be hard bastards. Are you going soft on me, Ingram?"

He looked down at her with a gleam of amusement in his dark eyes. "Courtship's like that, I'm afraid. The hardness comes and goes whether you like it or not. It's nature."

She lowered her face to her knees, refusing to be diverted. "I don't understand why Steve drowned Kate off Chapman's Pool," she said next. "He knew he was going there the next morning and he must have realized there was a chance she'd wash up on the beach. Why would he want to put his meeting with Marie in jeopardy?"

"I'm not sure you can apply logic to the actions of

someone like Harding," he said. "Carpenter's view is that, once he had Kate on board, there would only ever be one place he'd kill her. He says you can tell from the Frenchman's video how hyped up he was by all the excitement." He watched the spider lift his legs from the wet paint and wave them in useless protest. "But I don't think Steve expected her body to be there. He'd broken her fingers and tied her to an outboard, so it must have been a hell of a shock to find she'd managed to free herself. Presumably the intention was to gloat over her grave before absconding with Marie. Carpenter thinks Harding's an embryo serial killer, so in his view Marie's lucky to be alive."

"Do you agree with him?"

"God knows." He mourned the spider's inevitable death as the exhausted creature dipped its abdomen into the paint. "Steve says it was a terrible accident, but I've no idea if he's telling the truth. Carpenter doesn't believe him and neither does DI Galbraith, but I have a real problem accepting that anyone so young can be so evil. Let's just say I'm glad you had Bertie with you yesterday."

"Does Carpenter think he wanted to kill me, too?"

Nick shook his head. "I don't know. He asked Steve what was so important about the rucksack that he'd risked going back for it, and do you know what Steve said? 'My binoculars.' So then Carpenter asked him why he'd left it there at all, and he said: 'Because I'd forgotten the binoculars were in it.' "

"What does that mean?"

Nick gave a low laugh. "That there was nothing in it he wanted, so he decided to dump it. He hadn't had any sleep, he was knackered, and Marie's desert boots kept banging against his back and giving him blisters. All he wanted to do was get rid of it as fast as possible."

"Why is that funny?"

"It's the exact opposite of why I thought he'd left it there."

"No, it's not," she contradicted him. "You told me it

would incriminate him because he used it to carry Hannah off his boat."

"But he didn't kill Hannah, Maggie, he killed Kate."

"So?"

"All I did by finding it was help the defense. Harding will argue it proves he never intended to murder anyone."

He sounded depressed, she thought. "Still," she said brightly, "I suppose they'll be offering you a job at headquarters. They must be awfully impressed with you. You homed in on Steve as soon as you saw him."

"And homed straight out again the minute he spun me a plausible yarn." Another low laugh, this time self-deprecating. "The only reason I took against him was because he got up my nose, and the superintendent knows that. I think Carpenter thinks I'm a bit of a joke. He called me a suggestion-junky." He sighed. "I'm not sure I'm cut out for CID work. You can't take a wild guess then invent arguments to support the theory. That's how miscarriages of justice happen."

She cast him a speculative glance. "Is that something else Carpenter said?"

"More or less. He said the days are long past when policemen could play hunches. It's all about putting data into computers now."

She felt angry on his behalf. "Then I'll phone the bastard and give him a piece of my mind," she said indignantly. "If it hadn't been for you, it would have taken them months to make the connection between Kate and Harding—if ever, frankly—and they'd never have found that stranded dinghy or worked out where it was stolen from. He ought to be congratulating you, not finding fault. *I'm* the one who got it all wrong. There's obviously a flaw in my genes that makes me gravitate toward scumbags. Even Ma thought Harding was the most frightful creep. She said: 'Fancy making such a performance over a dog bite. I've had far worse, and all anyone offered me was antiseptic.'"

"She'll have my guts for garters when she finds out I made her wreck her hip for a murderer."

"No, she won't. She says you remind her of James Stewart in *Destry Rides Again.*"

"Is that good?"

"Oh, yes," said Maggie with a sardonic edge to her voice. "She goes weak at the knees every time she sees it. James Stewart plays a peace-loving sheriff who brings law and order to a violent city by never raising his voice or drawing his gun. It's fantastically sentimental. He falls in love with Marlene Dietrich, who throws herself in front of a bullet to protect him."

"Mmm. Personally, I've always fancied myself as Bruce Willis in *Die Hard.* The heroic, bloodstained cop with his trusty arsenal who saves the world and the woman he loves by blasting hell out of Alan Rickman and his gang of psychopaths."

She giggled. "Is this another attempt at seduction?"

"No. I'm still courting you."

"I was afraid you might be." She shook her head. "You're too nice, that's your trouble. You're certainly too nice to blast hell out of anyone."

"I know," he said despondently. "I don't have the stomach for it." He climbed down the stepladder and squatted on the floor in front of her, rubbing his tired eyes with the back of his hand. "I was beginning to like Harding. I still do in a funny kind of way. I keep thinking what a waste it all is and what a difference it would have made if someone, somewhere, had warned him that everything has a price." He reached up to put the paintbrush in the tray on the table. "To be fair to Carpenter, he *did* congratulate me. He even said he'd support me if I decided to apply for the CID. According to him, I have potential"—he mimicked the superintendent's growl—"and he should know because he hasn't been a super for five years for nothing." He smiled his crooked smile. "But I'm not convinced that's where my talents lie."

"Oh, for God's sake!" she declared, revealing more of her genes than she knew. "You'd make a brilliant detective. I can't think what you're worried about. Don't be so bloody cautious, Nick. You should seize your chances."

"I do . . . when they make sense to me."

"And this one doesn't?"

He smiled and stood up, removing the tray to the sink and running water into it. "I'm not sure I want to move away." He glanced about the transformed room. "I rather like living in a backwater where the odd suggestion makes a difference."

Her eyes fell. "Oh, I see."

He rinsed the emulsion out of the brush in silence, wondering if she did, and if "I see" was going to be her only response. He propped the brush to dry on the draining board and seriously considered whether fighting his way through half a mile of razor wire wouldn't be the more sensible option after all. "Shall I come back tomorrow? It's Sunday. We could make a start on the hall."

"I'll be here," she said.

"Okay." He walked across to the scullery door.

"Nick?"

"Yes?" He turned.

"How long do these courtships of yours usually take?"

An amiable smile creased his eyes. "Before what?"

"Before . . ." She looked suddenly uncomfortable. "Never mind. It was a silly question. I'll see you tomorrow."

"I'll try not to be late."

"It doesn't matter if you are," she said through gritted teeth. "You're doing this out of kindness, not because you have to. I haven't asked you to paint the whole house, you know."

"True," he agreed, "but it's a courtship thing. I thought I'd explained all that."

She clambered to her feet with flashing eyes. "Go *away*," she said, pushing him through the door and bolting it behind him. "And for God's sake bring some brandy with you tomorrow," she yelled. "Courtship stinks. I've decided I'd rather be seduced."

The television was on and Celia, remote control in hand, was chuckling to herself when Maggie tiptoed into the drawing room to see if she was all right. Bertie had abandoned the stifling heat of the bed and was stretched out on his back on the sofa, legs akimbo. "It's late, Ma. You ought to be asleep."

"I know, but this is so funny, darling."

"You said it was wall-to-wall horror movies."

"It is. That's why I'm laughing."

Maggie fixed her mother with a perplexed frown, then seized the remote control and killed the picture. "You were listening," she accused her.

"Well . . ."

"How *could* you?"

"I needed a pee," said Celia apologetically, "and you weren't exactly whispering."

"The doctor said you weren't to walk around on your own."

"I had no option. I called out a couple of times, but you didn't hear me. In any case"—her eyes brimmed with humor—"you were getting on so well that I decided it would be tactless to interrupt you." She appraised her daughter in silence for a moment, then abruptly patted the bed. "Are you too old to take some advice?"

"It depends what it is," said Maggie, sitting down.

"Any man who invites the woman to make the running is worth having."

"Is that what my father did?"

"No. He swept me off my feet, rushed me to the altar, and then gave me thirty-five years to repent at leisure." Celia smiled ruefully. "Which is why the advice is good. I fell for your father's overinflated opinion of himself, mistook obstinacy for masterfulness, alcoholism for wit, and laziness for charisma . . ." She broke off apologetically, realizing that it was her daughter's father she was criticizing. "It wasn't all bad," she said robustly. "Everyone was more stoical in those days—we were taught to put up with things—and look what I got out of it. You . . . Matt . . . the house . . ."

Maggie leaned forward to kiss her mother's cheek. "Ava . . . Martin . . . theft . . . debts . . . heartache . . . a wonky hip . . ."

"Life," countered Celia. "A still-viable livery stable . . . Bertie . . . a new kitchen . . . a future . . ."

"Nick Ingram?"

"Well, why not?" said Celia with renewed chuckles. "If I was forty years younger and he showed the remotest interest in me, I certainly wouldn't need a bottle of brandy to get things moving."